JOHN W. GRUNDY

TO CASTLE KINGSIDE

A HITEC NOVEL

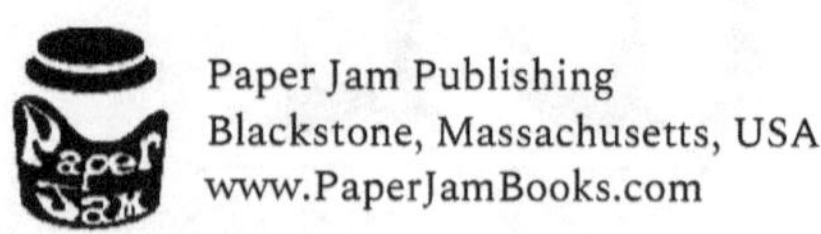

TO CASTLE KINGSIDE

PART I: SKELETONS

PART II: TANGLED WEBS

PART III: A BUSINESS OF FLIES

PART V: THE WASP IN WINTER

POSTLUDE

———————+———————

~ End ~

To Ed:
For inciting the inaugural game of this universe.

To Russ:
For prompting the initial writing of this book.

To Brendan:
For encouraging its previous resurrection and release.

To Tricia:
For inspiring me to continue by being its earliest fan.

To Michael:
For being the first to suggest that an outsider might want to read it.

To Andrew:
For, in fact, being that very first outside set of eyes.

To Orest:
For going off to fight for real, while the rest of us stayed home pretending.

&

To My Loving Wife, Lorraine:
For allowing me to spend a year completely absorbed in another universe.

Author's Preface

THERE WAS AN OVAL, HAND-ME-DOWN dining table with the guise of simulated wood, whose rigid linoleum surface was the perfect medium for bouncing quarters on. A pair of seventies-era velvet sofas, each ponderously oversized; one as shocking orange as a traffic cone—the other: dirt-smudged ivory, like a mechanic's hand soap. A crowded, first-floor apartment, rife with other furnishings saved from dumpsters, in a highly unglamorous housing complex, in the southwest fringes of the city of Boston. A blistering, fifteen-day heatwave—it was the summer of 1988. It was here we first joined together—some lifelong friends, others recently met—and sat in the sweaty crash pad of a pair of eighteen-year-olds enjoying newfound freedom, drinking off-brand beer by the caseload, and rebuilding the universe to our liking.

We all met each other at a neighborhood keg party, the immortality of youth still flush upon us, and began talking of Dungeons & Dragons—a risky undertaking in those days if you had any aspirations of taking a lady home. And we were young men just out of high school, what other aspirations could we have had?

This was in the days before role-playing games became in vogue, as they are now, and people like us, too cool to be part of the nerd crowd, would have to say things like 'flaming vorpal' in hushed voices to avoid the stigma of a scarlet pocket protector. But nevertheless, we talked of role-playing all the same, and made an arrangement to get together and give a new party and campaign a try.

We played a little of Dungeons & Dragons, one of the few truly well-developed systems of the day, but soon bored of the same old adventures. We wanted to build ourselves something new—we wanted to try a world of science fiction. There wasn't much available back then along those lines, a few new titles whose universes were fairly terrible, with clunky game mechanics, silly races, and sparse reference books. And even to find those, you had to plan all-day trips to distant hobby shops. There was no internet to browse then, and even if there was, no one owned a computer. This was still the early era of tabletop gaming, where all you needed was a tattered character sheet, a clean piece of graph paper, and a sharpened pencil—and let us not forget, your precious set of polyhedral dice. All the worlds and characters, villains and adventures, existed solely in our own minds.

And so we built ourselves a game, cobbled from the best bits of many others, but with a fictional universe that was all our own, and presumptuously titled it *HiTec*. Little did we realize, many of the 'high tech' gadgets from this far-flung future would exist in reality within a couple of decades. It followed the exploits of a group of armored mercenaries for hire, exchanging their services for cash and equipment, mainly to intergalactic mega-corporations looking to hamper the competition—or protect themselves from being similarly attacked. They called themselves *Parliament*, and they operated on Earth, in an area known as *New* Boston—admittedly not that creative, but what do you want from a bunch of drunk eighteen-year-olds?

Over the years, as the characters grew, and some were killed, and others replaced them, our party of commandos became more spacefaring, and perhaps more noble. We began running storylines that were more about fighting evil than stealing business files. More heroics and less greed—although they were still paid a pretty penny for each mission they were sent out upon, to the point they all eventually became gratuitously wealthy.

This world we built for ourselves followed us far beyond that first apartment, through nicer homes and college degrees, through first careers and first marriages. We played fairly religiously for perhaps a decade, until the distractions of life finally took their toll, and though we still talked and laughed about the gameplay of the past, our alter egos within the characters went into a permanent limbo from that point onward.

Fast forward five or six years, to late spring 2004.

I received a group email from Russ, one of the founding players of the game, with a paragraph of a battle scene featuring all our characters back together again. A directive was attached to add a line, or perhaps a paragraph. Continue the story, and pass it on. After a little back and forth, my eventual response to that email was the first forty thousand words of the novel you're now holding: parts one and two of this narrative. Perhaps just a bit more than was requested of me, but I had ideas for game modules (what we called each played storyline) that I had never had the chance to offer, and decided I would put them into print instead.

And yet, as before, life has a way of being obstructive, and I never wrote a word beyond that. It was resigned to languish in my old windows 98 computer, stuffed in the corner of a dusty attic.

Until a long thirteen years later.

I happened to mention it offhand to another founding player, Brendan, who encouraged me to just send out whatever I had put together. Thankfully, the computer still booted up, and so I did what he suggested. I sent it out to everyone, and it was generally kindly received. I was encouraged by several to finish more of it, but honestly, who can find the time to invest in such a project?

As it turns out, four years later, someone sitting home, bored, during a pandemic.

And so, that's the long, convoluted tale of just where this book comes from. Now, a slightly less convoluted tale of what it's all about.

My goal here was to honor the original universe of the game, live in that macrocosm we all created, and follow its rules, however arbitrary. But at the same time, try to evolve it. Add texture to the worlds we only hardly mentioned, histories to the alien species we never really explored. Pull our characters out of limbo, and age them forward along with us. Give them the issues and insights that come part and parcel with adulthood, and bring the whole fabricated fantasy of our relative childhood into a more mature and realized reality. But most importantly, leaving in enough of that post-adolescent whimsy and sense of adventure that made *HiTec* so fun to play in the first place.

I've had such a good time getting to hang out with these characters once again. I hope the original few players I wrote it for get even half as much enjoyment.

For those of you that were *not* one of those six original players, those readers who are new to this entire universe, I feel it's important to point out that each of the characters you'll soon meet are, in many ways, *real* people. Real to me anyway, ones I've known for over thirty years. There was once a living player behind each of them, their hand hot on a set of dice, and the attributes I gave them are based somewhat on how they played—and perhaps a *touch* of their true personalities. Although, in writing this book, these characters quickly took on lives of their very own. We faced forty-seven modules together, over a period of many years, so when I refer to past incidents, I refer to events that *really* happened. To us and the characters they did anyway, within the context of the game, so to me, this is as much a historical record as it is a work of science fiction.

So here then, I suppose, is my ultimate response to that nineteen-year-old email (I apologize for the delay). I submit it for your hopeful enjoyment—a flashback to a fantastical universe we all created late at night, around hot, crowded kitchen tables, during a time in our lives we can never get back to, but which I, for one, will never forget.

Enjoy!

John W. Grundy

Introduction

THE STORY OF THIS MODERN UNIVERSE is the story of modern industry.

With another tragic Earth war finally over, it was the long post-war rebuilding period that allowed for businesses to grow unchecked. The humans turned to local corporations to provide what their new fledgling global government had yet to offer: safety, security, a way to house and feed themselves. All you had to do was pledge undying fealty to a local company. The age of serfdom had returned to Earth, even if only briefly, but long enough to allow monopolies to swell their ledger books to monstrous proportions.

There was very little rule of law then, beyond what boards of directors paid to enforce, and businesses that competed went to war with one another. The victors swallowed their defeated foes, expanding out into the awaiting galaxy, finding a new market amongst the species of the seti and the android.

Despite a distrust of these aliens being what originally divided Earth against its own, all it took to turn and embrace them was the realization that *they too* had riches to spend. The novelty of capitalism amongst these foreign species was fresh tinder to the flame of profit, and the largest companies soon became interstellar—the era of the galactic megacorp had begun.

Although it took only a few short decades for the new world leadership of Earth to regain its footing, the expansive resources of the various megacorps still outweighed those of many governments. Even with democracy at last returned, there was no pulling in the reins now. Big business had become *too* big. It was simply easier to tax them than oppose them, and thereby share in reaping all the benefits.

As another barrier to any oversight, space was just *extremely* vast. Almost impossible to police, even if inclined to do so, and further complicated by intricate matters of jurisdiction. The varied species had varied laws, which then only applied while in their systems, and many colonies, or entire worlds, were now, in fact, owned by the big conglomerates. Thus, corporate feuding still waged on, and for the most part, it was tolerated. An unwritten agreement grew between the two, civilized society and the megacorps, people turning a blind eye to the violent business dealings, as long as no private persons or property became involved.

This is how it continued for several centuries, even after the Federated Planetary Coalition was formed—the world that gave birth to the corporate mercenary, in its most brutal and literal sense. Teams such as Parliament were forged by it, just one group among many, seeking adventure, fame and fortune. These were agents hired by the megacorps, often to spy on or steal from their competitors, or vengefully recover what had been stolen from them. They explored the uncharted regions, securing resources, or quelling indigenous threats. They served as security forces, protecting products or intellectual property. In fact, the eventual oversight of the Coalition only allowed the practice to become more regulated. Teams were now well trained, and registered, and had legal immunity—if they observed the rules.

This newly united government that protected them was an alliance of four disparate species.

When first contact had been made on Earth, it was a delicate time in human history. Technology was ever-evolving, but had not yet brought them to the stars, and the sudden awareness of extraterrestrial life caused joy in some, and panic in others. The appearance of some humans with evolving extrasensory capabilities—minor powers really, of telepathy or telekinesis, even visions of past history—had recently been documented in a small percentage of the population. Just a few out of every million— perhaps simply a tentative step on the next rung of the evolutionary ladder. They became known as the *ensensed*, the very strongest ones dubbed *mentalists*, but there were those who thought this timing was suspicious. Perhaps this change in humanity was a symptom of some invasion.

It was not.

The *seti* were a benign species, interested only in new relations. A humanoid race that was curiously feline in appearance—though, of course, not related to cats at all. It was a simple curiosity, an evolutionary body type succeeding twice. And because of an inability to pronounce their complex language, they were named after the radio telescope program that first detected them. S.E.T.I.—the Search for Extra-Terrestrial Intelligence. Apparently, for them, the search was over—they had at last succeeded in finding some.

The seti were in an alliance with another species known as the *android*, a race of artificially encased life forms, not that different looking from a standard servicebot. But the androids are, in fact, sentient—a living life-force in constructed bodies. How they one day went from being biological to mechanical is a mystery understood not even by their own historians—the exact details of that progression now obscured by the depths of time.

A few decades after the megacorp expansion, the *metamorphs* were discovered. An affable species, with mottled green-gray skin, large dark eyes, and an oddly featureless face that made it difficult to discern any one from another. They had a talent for ESP, and the ability to shape-shift their physical form—sometimes to shockingly convincing alternative appearances.

These were the four species that joined their worlds together in a unified government—the human, the seti, the android, and the metamorph—now united under one body, but only at the behest of the powerful megacorps. Another confederation of alien species had been discovered, one far more warlike, and invasive, and seemingly willing to seize all they coveted—The Drak'min Empire. And so, businesses encouraged the formation of this massive new government, despite the fact they would lose much of their precious power to it, in order to form a common border, and build an army to stave off invasion.

Little is known of the *drak'min*, other than their demonic appearance seems to match their temperament. And they command an army of conquered, subservient species—the scaly, lizard-like *lacertilian*, and the winged and beaked *avis*.

Around the amorphous border between these two superpowers, a handful of other species exist as well—ones that have chosen to remain neutral, or simply were not invited into the Coalition.

The *lyghtan* of Capella, sometime referred to as *shades*, with their pitch-black skin and eyes aglow, abstained from joining for religious reasons, believing no mortal creature could ever dictate to their Holy Sovereign on how to govern.

The *chamai*, on the other hand, were not solicited to join the party. Although the Coalition enjoys an alliance with them, and in general has good relations, the attitude of its leadership is often more aggressive than is appreciated. The somewhat human-like species boasts an ability similar to the metamorph, the capacity to transform their flesh, but in the case of the chamai, it is completely involuntary. Their skin changes molecularly in response to any injury, briefly preventing them from being injured in the same way again.

The final two known species are the *theseans* and the *khailian*. The former is an intelligent marine species, existing only under water, whose interests don't often align with the worries of the air breathers. The khailian, on the other hand, would give anything to be allowed to join, but the small population of hulking, beast-like galactic newcomers simply do not have anything that they could offer in exchange.

So this, then, is the universe in which at least a hundred billion mortals live, where they play and toil, thrive and die. A complex galactic community of trade and business, of people and politics. Where any one life might be as mundane or daring as one chooses, and all one has to do to find adventure, is wander beyond that very next star.

This is the universe of *HiTec*.

Known Species of the Galaxy

<u>Federated Planetary Coalition</u>
Human—Earth
Seti—K'Tas T'Mir
Android—Rhyana
Metamorph—Ilshnar

<u>The Drak'min Empire</u>
Drak'min—Drak'us
Lacertilian—unknown
Avis—unknown

<u>Neutral Worlds</u>
Lyghtan—Capella
Chamai—Oberonn
Theseans—Theseus
Khailian—Erie VII

JOHN W. GRUNDY

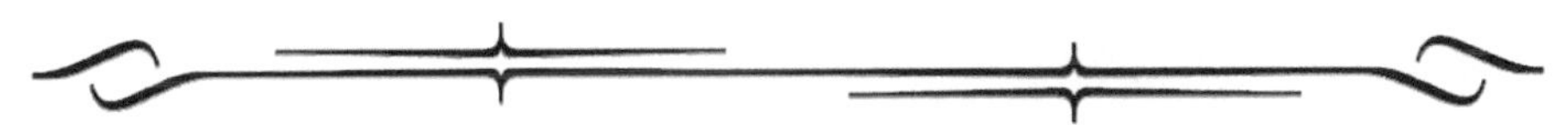

TO CASTLE KINGSIDE

A HITEC NOVEL

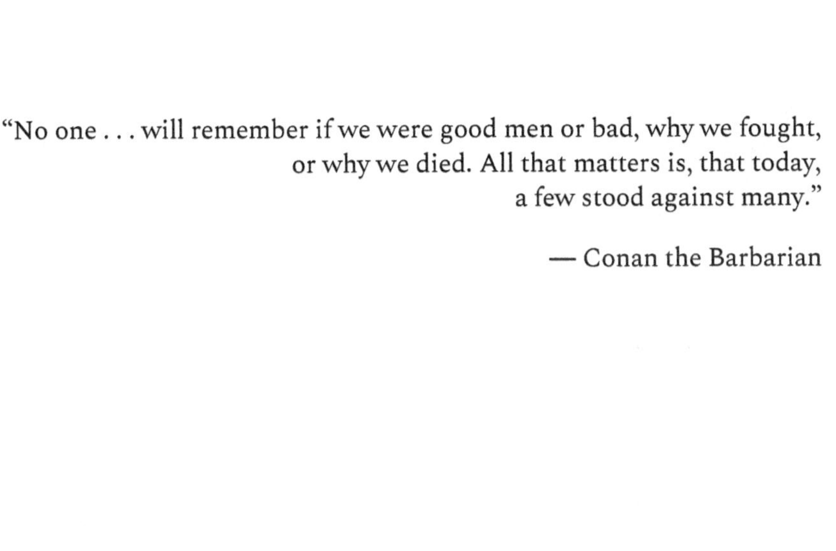

“No one . . . will remember if we were good men or bad, why we fought,
or why we died. All that matters is, that today,
a few stood against many.”

— Conan the Barbarian

“The ghosts of regret sing their siren lullaby to any who lend an ear
The key is knowing when to harken,
and when to turn away.”

— ⏃⁝φ⋉ⓐψφ'ψ⁝⌇⍙⍾ (Bullseye)

Prologue

O AN OBSERVER STANDING AT the base of the chasm, her falling body may have appeared not unlike a shooting star, suddenly and briefly piercing the darkness of an inky and moonless night. The merest spark across the sky. But here, deep in the caverns, there was in fact no sky above, and the newly broken darkness had persisted undisturbed for near eternity.

Her terrified eyes were wide, ablaze with brilliant gold incandescence. Her ebony arms were thrust out desperately, casting that same yellowed radiance out before them as she tumbled down. Her descent illuminated the recesses and protrusions of the cavity as she hurtled past, spiraling head over feet, puncturing through the darkness in surprising silence for all the fuss her body instinctively made, raging against the forthcoming impact. There were no piercing shrieks, nor cries of terror—only the brisk, rhythmic flapping of her robe's heavy fabric as she plummeted, whipping and thrashing out behind her like sailcloth in an autumn gale.

That same onlooker may have discerned the exact moment she realized the futility, the moment she accepted the rapidly approaching inevitability, and made the decision to face her inescapable end the same way she had faced her inescapable life—with grace, determination, and an unwavering act of faith. The careening meteor then went visibly calmer, all the waving and flailing suddenly still, and her body slowly rotated to position head downward, her glowing palm outstretched before her in a graceful, and purposeful, nosedive towards the base of the shaft.

The perception of time slowed, and the fall seemed to stretch out unrealistically, as if the yawning abyss was somehow bottomless. But of course, it was not. In due time, the cave floor came into view, reaching the radius of light she projected, and rushed swiftly upwards with its jagged, rocky teeth—eager to bite. The observer would have seen her close her eyes lightly, move her lips to whisper a word into the wind with her last breath, then douse the amber light she generated—as all shooting stars eventually go dim. She returned the subterranean world to the darkness in which it had always existed.

An observer would have seen all these things—but alas, no observer was present. No report of her exceptional death would be made to bookend her exceptional life, no record of her bravery, no memorandum of her stoicism. A sickening thud and heartbreaking whimper would shatter the blackened quiet, for just a moment, echoing briefly through the vaulted cavity, and diminishing slightly with each reverberation, until the cavern fell back into its usual eternal silence.

And so there would lie Lady Pia, once first ashi'mar of the planet Capella, whose last act was to drag her dying fingers through the sand, and feel the grains of her home soil flow one last time through her grip of agony. Whose hallowed blood now formed a widening puddle in the darkness, returning its moisture to the dust of the desert from which she came. Whose long and notable life of service to her people would be forever overshadowed by the mysterious circumstance of her violent death.

These things, then nothing.

This is how it began, his long-conceived scheme of treachery—in absolute dim, and deafening hush.

PART I

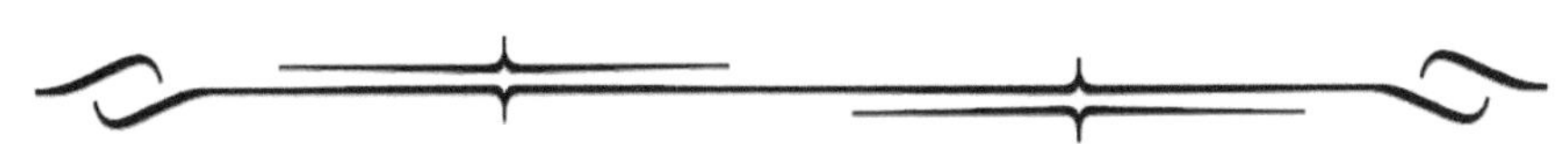

Skeletons

Chapter 1.1

A TORRENT OF BRIGHT YELLOW and orange sparks rained violently across the transparent forceshield, falling back to singe tiny burn marks, blemishing the dark flexible covering of his large metallic hands. Dr. Tachion Magna 816 turned the long serrated, hook-tipped blade over in his mechanical fingers, now running its opposite edge beneath the glowing plasma arc, until he was confident it had been honed to perfect razor sharpness. Extending his sizable, hinged elbow to delicately tap the off switch of the sharpener, he pulled the trimithium blade from beneath the protective forcefield, and placed it under a small scanning device—checking his work down to the thousandth of a micron. Then, just for good measure, he held the knife up close to his electronic eye, looking carefully along its cruel edge to confirm the blade's refinement. Satisfied, he gathered up two more exact duplicates of the item from the counter, which he had already completed, and left the small tool room, heading purposefully down the hallway.

The large medic's metallic body was draped in a long, dark-blue lab coat, a convention designed more to denote his position, and to provide him an array of handy pockets, than out of any sense of modesty. As with most androids, if he wasn't wearing armor for protection, he was usually wearing nothing at all. Even now, his bare metallic frame was still visible where the thin coat hung open across his massive, silvered chest, and his sturdy articulated legs protruded from beneath it, moving him along the corridor in hurried, mechanical grace.

The android species, in general, came in every conceivable size, shape, and design—from small, stumpy and wheeled to multi-legged and gangly— and Tachion had been built larger than most, to say the least. Nearly seven foot tall, bipedal and anthropomorphic, with a chassis cast in trimithium, and skinned in a polished mirror chrome—one which had long ago been worn to the duller patina of a brushed nickel. This overly large size gave him no real advantage, at least none that he had ever been able to discern. He wasn't necessarily more powerful than any other member of his species who harbored similar motors and hydraulics—his back no stronger, his fists no more forceful. In fact, his oversized body had more drawbacks than it did benefits, as his size, weight, and inherent inflexibility made it so that there were quite common places where he simply could not physically fit. If there was any benefit to be found, it was perhaps that, although he was *not* in fact any more powerful, he certainly gave the impression that he was. Tachion Magna was an imposing figure to behold.

If the doctor had been given any input into his own construction, he certainly would have picked a smaller-sized physique. Something nimbler—and perhaps having some more arms would be nice. However, as with anyone, he had not had any say. His body simply was what it was, and he had become as accustomed to both its advantages and disadvantages as possible.

This, of course, was except for his face, the one aspect he had chosen himself. Many androids—even most—do not have a 'face' at all. The trend towards more anthropomorphic build types—with arms, legs, heads, and *faces*—had become more prevalent in the last several generations, as a way to fit in more comfortably with the multiple organic species of the galaxy. Some few members of his species frowned upon it, but most were largely indifferent. Function, and intellect, were much more important measures in their society than mere appearance.

The doctor had exchanged his near featureless expression many decades ago, with one of a clearly humanoid appearance—a tribute in burnished steel to someone who had once been very important to him. A serious chin, angled jaw, sharp nose, flinty brow, all added to the menace of his already formidable appearance. However, the menace was generally just an illusion, and not a measure of his true temperament. Unless, of course, you get on his bad side.

The usually busy corridors of the Coalition Biological Society were currently eerily abandoned. Today was his homeworld of Rhyana's only planet-wide holiday on the android calendar, which commemorated the signing of the tentative non-aggression treaty between the Coalition and the Drak'min Empire. As he approached the Office of the Director, he reached deep inside one of his lab coat pockets and produced a small, gold baton. He inserted it neatly into a matching hole on a busy-looking panel to the right of the entrance, then typed in a complicated series of keystrokes on the pad beneath. The door then immediately slid open to admit him.

Tachion's office was minimally decorated. The chrome and glass furnishings, and bright, stark white walls, reflected the ruddy glow of Rhyana's giant red setting sun, blazing through a wall of windows behind the neatly organized desk. The chair behind that desk was a black, metal monstrosity, noticeably oversized, like all the other furnishings, in order to accommodate the android's stature and weight. A few licenses and degrees, commendations, and miscellaneous artifacts hung in unembellished frames along the otherwise barren left wall. A narrow rack of shelves on the opposite side held a library of microdisks and storage chips, even a few old paper-bound books. Tachion approached that shelf as he entered the room, and inserted a second, much thinner baton into what appeared to be a simple, inconspicuous dimple in the wall. The shelves opened outward into the room, revealing another doorway hidden behind it.

The laboratory beyond was large. Rows of extra high workbenches were covered with various computers and equipment, and multiple stations appeared in the midst of some half-completed research or experiment. A pair of massive, fluid-filled, cylindrical glass chambers stood floor-to-ceiling near the back of the laboratory, quietly bubbling a thin amber liquid through a multitude of tubes and conduits. Against the near wall was a surgical bio-bed, and an array of appropriate equipment to go with it. A hot overhead light was shining down to illuminate it all, and a reclining chair had been placed up against the bed beneath that light.

Rook sat lounging in the chair with his back reclined and his legs stretched out, watching the small holovision program being projected just above his lap, and studying a half-completed game of chess in mid-battle on the rolling tray table. Like all those of the seti race, he was possessed of features reminiscent of a large Earth feline, a shining example of convergent evolution at work. While it's doubtless that very few, beyond his wife, would ever go so far as to refer to Rook as handsome, almost anyone would agree that the term 'rugged' would certainly apply—and decades of dangerous skirmish-filled mercenary work had only served to make him more so. His face, like the rest of him, was covered in a short, pale-orange fur, which faded to ivory-white around his chin beard and muzzle. A few minor scars and burns blemished his cheek and his forehead, causing the fur to no longer grow to its full potential in those areas. An array of striped patterns, rivulets of black coursing through the orange, decorated his face—symmetrically mirrored left to right like the image on a Rorschach painting. A lush charcoal mane of thick hair framed it all, flowing across his shoulders to the center of his back—the locks only recently having seen their first few tinges of silver-gray. His eyes, a brilliant emerald, burned with an intensity that made them striking, in contrast to his otherwise more muted complexion.

His left arm was secured in a vise-like apparatus to a small table attached to the chair, and two rows of tiny clamps gripped tightly to his flesh, on both sides of an incision ten inches long down his forearm. The skin was stretched backward, revealing the moist, red and oozing underside of the dermis beneath. The gaping laceration was spread quite wide also, so that the complex inner mechanics of his cybernetic limb were clearly on display.

"Took you long enough," Rook said with a tone of feigned irritation as Tachion entered.

"Would you prefer them done well, or done quickly?" The android responded.

"*Both*, if possible. I have a long flight back to Earth, and I'd like to make it home by morning." Rook's voice as he spoke was free of any seti accent. He was Earth born and raised, residing there still with his wife Belladonna and their two children, on a chain of man-made islands known as 'Florida', after the long-sunken peninsula the new archipelago had been built upon. As such, he was not possessed of that distinctive guttural seti grumble, nor the elaborate phraseology that those raised on the homeworld were in the habit of. He spoke plain Coalition common, in a plain and common manner.

Tachion also had no accent—nor, of course, would he. His oration arose from a computerized speaker box and could play in perfect diction no matter what language he was speaking, without the hassle of a troublesome tongue to trip him up. The voice he spoke with was a steady and pleasant baritone, both calm and reassuring. Not the deep echoey bass one would assume from his stature, nor the tinny electronic buzzing of some others of his species. It was a voice he himself had chosen when he first moved to Earth from Rhyana, in order to better communicate with humans. It now had grown to be as much a part of him as anything else, and he used it almost exclusively.

Tachion carefully slid the first of the three blades into the open forearm and leaned in close, his micro-tools in hand, as he began the process of securing it properly in its place. "So, you're not coming by tonight?" he asked, sounding surprised.

"Nuh uh, sorry. First, I gotta pick up Belladonna, and then we are going to meet Bullit on K'Tas T'Mir. It's his brother's remembrance ceremony, the Memorial for the Fallen," Rook explained. "Actually, the first few days are more of a celebration than a memorial. It's held every ten years. This one is gonna be his second. It really doesn't even begin for a couple of weeks, but Bell wants to go early in order to reunite with some of the in-laws. You know... give the kids a chance to get reacquainted with some extended family. Last time we brought them they were still only teenagers."

Tachion tilted his head. "I didn't know anything about it. I wonder why I was not invited."

"Well, it's traditionally a seti-only ceremony. In fact, it's a *family*-only ceremony, but because Belladonna is Bullit's cousin..."

"Ah, say no more. Just give Bullit my best... or whatever the appropriate sentiments are for the occasion."

"Will do... if I can figure them out myself," Rook replied.

"Although... it does beg the question," Tachion noted as he continued his work, "why you would make such a long trip out here, and then rush back, merely to replace your tractor blades?"

Rook twisted a little uncomfortably in the chair, then turned off the holovision with his free hand. "Yeah, you're right," he said, with a trace of slight embarrassment in his voice. "There was another reason. I... well... do you remember what we talked about last week?"

"You mean the bots you're programming for WarTec?" Dr. Magna asked without looking up.

"No, not that. The other thing."

Tachion's hands paused in their work for a moment. "You mean... about you having more children," he said.

"Yeah, that," Rook answered, seeming now even more uncomfortable. "You know, the thing is... Belladonna and I had only been together maybe twice before she got pregnant with our first two. Now here we are, twenty-five years later, and she's never gotten pregnant again. And, even after all these years together, we're still fairly active... you know... *that way*. I mean, not like the old days, but I can still..." He smiled as he made a vulgar thrusting motion with his other hand.

"Mmm. So, Belladonna, she's already been tested?" Tachion asked, as he picked up the second blade and began its installation.

"Yeah, and there is nothing wrong with her... so I figured it's gotta be me," Rook replied. "I was going to see someone myself, but then you mentioned knowing that seti doctor, the fertility expert, so I thought maybe you could get me in to see that guy."

"I don't think that would be a very good idea," Tachion said seriously. "Remember, we agreed that it would be unwise for you or the others to ever see any doctor besides myself. The last thing you need in our line of work is unprotected medical records out there somewhere, or files detailing this hidden secret in your arm. Or, God forbid, some enemy gets a sample of your DNA."

Yeah, I know, I know," Rook interrupted. "But this really isn't your exact specialty, Tach, and I want to have the best working on this... no offense."

"Tell me, is Belladonna as eager to have more children as well?"

"Well, she got tested when I asked her to, but otherwise she doesn't talk about it. I think she doesn't want to embarrass me."

"I see," Tachion said. He repositioned himself above Rook's arm to begin working on the third blade. "But you think that she does want to have more?"

"Yeah, of course. I mean... why wouldn't she?"

Tachion thought for a moment. "Well, I'll tell you what. I can contact the doctor myself, and he and I can work together on the problem. That way I can keep you anonymous. I'm sure if there is anything wrong on your end, he'll figure a way to remedy it."

"Thank you," Rook said, sounding much relieved. "You have no idea how much I appreciate that."

"Of course, I'll need a sample of your issue to bring him," Tachion said.

"My issue?"

"Yes, your semen. Your sp..."

"Alright, shit, I got it. Gross, by the way. You mean you have to have that like... now?"

"Unless you want to make another trip out here," Tachion said. He began to release Rook's forearm. "Just let me finish up here first." He carefully folded the skin back in place on both sides of the opening, then pinched it together with another set of tiny clamps. Then he activated a small device, and passed it back and forth over Rook's arm as it projected a thin beam along the incision. After a few moments, the wound began to dry and heal, finally leaving only a minor scar visible beneath the seti's short fur. Lastly, he released the vise holding Rook's arm in place on the table, and turned his forearm back and forth, giving it a last inspection. "Okay, why don't you try that out?" the doctor said.

Rook turned his arm over and pointed it away from Tachion, making a slight gesture with his fingers. In the blink of an eye, the three long, razor-sharp bayonets sprang forth from the flesh just in front of the seti's wrist. Rook made a few faux swiping motions with them, the terrible blades gleaming under the bright overhead light, and then another gesture retracted them neatly back into position. "Yeah, very nice," he said, "that works real smooth. Thanks, T."

Tachion handed a small metallic canister to Rook, and watched as his seti friend excused himself to the lavatory. After Rook had closed the door, the android's eyes drifted to the large fluid-filled chambers that sat along the back wall. It was many years ago now, but the android could still clearly remember Rook's body floating unconscious in that amber fluid—or, to be more precise, the body of Rook's clone.

Fifteen years ago, Rook himself had been killed in combat, and the decision had been made by his family and friends simply not to accept that. Tachion knew it was possible to bring him back, and was determined to do so any way he could. He wished he could have done the same for his other friend, Jim Dodger, a senior member of the team found dead that same day, but what had been done to Jim's body had made it impossible. With Rook, though, there was a chance.

For an entire year after that, the medic barely left this room, as he agonized over every facet of its conception and its growth. No aspect of the maturation process was too trivial or mundane for him not to handle personally, even if it were possible for him to have enlisted help from the institution's other staff.

But cloning for this purpose, the reanimation of a deceased loved one for no other reason than personal grief, was highly illegal—as was cloning for almost any reason. For a multitude of ethical, sociological, political, and theological reasons, a strict ban on cloning had been in place for over a hundred years. Of course there were exceptions, tightly regulated by the Coalition Science Ministry, the Surgeon General's office, and the Bureau on Civilian Rights. Certain transplant procedures, where only a single organ was cloned. Experimental allowances, where the duplicant was never awakened. And most likely the occasional black ops purposes, that Tachion was sure must go on. The paperwork process and bureaucratic red tape for even these reasons were utterly preposterous, but Dr. Magna was an established surgeon, a certified exobiologist, a respected geneticist, and director of this facility. As such, he had access to the equipment, the privacy of his personal lab, and the autonomy as director to conduct projects without supervision. Perhaps most importantly, he had ready access to 'blanks'.

This was an industry term in the genetics field, for the usually female half of the equation—the egg, now stripped of its nucleus and DNA, and left a soft, hollow shell. These blanks were created and issued by the government to the few qualified and licensed labs throughout the Coalition, and were oppressively and rigidly regulated. The strictest discipline in record keeping was required to endure the tracking procedures, yearly auditing, and random inquisitions from a half dozen government agencies. These sorts of exacting investigations and precise tracking of the blanks, as well as the clones made from them, were made possible because of one thing—the blank eggs were not truly empty.

Hidden inside each microscopic zygote was a virus. A harmless, non-transmittable, ingeniously conceived man-made virus, that existed for only one purpose—to slightly alter any DNA inserted into the blank. These changes included the addition of a small, meaningless sequence to the main strand, which would then mark every cell in the new cloned organism with a genetic serial number, one that corresponded right back to the egg used, and the lab it was issued to.

Had Tachion only had some more time back then, he was sure he could have quietly sourced out an unregistered seti egg. But the manner of Rook's death, brutally murdered by the underworld kingpin Denali's henchmen beneath the oceans of Theseus, left behind DNA that was degraded, and nearing the point of unusability. He asked Rook's wife Belladonna, the only person outside of their mercenary team, known as Parliament, who was aware of Rook's condition, to use one of *her* eggs as a blank. However, she was reluctant, squeamish even, feeling as though it would somehow make Rook like her child instead of her husband. Completely scientifically inaccurate, of course, but Tachion understood the emotion behind the flawed reasoning. He had considered perhaps extracting an egg from the maturing ovaries of Rook and Belladonna's then ten-year-old daughter, Relic, but knew that idea would probably receive an even worse reception. Running out of time, and out of options, the android did the only thing he could—he stole a government-registered seti egg.

Since the day that Parliament and Belladonna had agreed to this course of action, a decade and a half ago now, they had all stayed true to their oaths to never mention it again to anyone, even to each other. The rest of the team stayed away while the doctor worked on the clone's accelerated growth, so as to not draw attention. Tachion alone was there when the new tiny infant Rook was placed into the tall growth chamber. He alone stood by for month after month, as that infant became a child—an adolescent—an adult. He alone was there to remove the matured clone from the fluid chamber to the operating table, and as he violated his medical oaths to intentionally scar Rook's body—to remove sections of his spleen and intestine, to amputate his completely healthy left arm, to simulate all the branding of a lifetime of trauma that the original Rook's body displayed.

He alone was also there to commit the only medical crime worse than creating an illegal clone, the implanting of Rook's old memories. Tachion retrieved a brain scan from a routine physical from a month or so before Rook's death, and used that highly detailed map to direct and manipulate the growth of the clone's neural pathways to exactly match. The result—cloned Rook has all the same memories, stored the same way as his progenitor Rook prime did, up to the day of that scan. The downside, he could never know he was a clone, as history demonstrated again and again that such a realization almost always leads to some form of insanity.

So, Rook, as well as the rest of society, must be kept in the dark about his own true nature. As far as he is aware, he awoke after a year in a coma, with no memory of the events on Theseus; the last thing recalled being his physical with Tachion thirteen months prior. Soon his bedside was filled with grateful friends and family, all hiding the same secret, and moving on through life without a word about what had happened. In many ways, it was almost as if they had all completely forgotten about the truth, which Tachion was sure was not really the case. But whether it was, or wasn't, he himself did not have that luxury.

The cost of using that stolen blank so many years ago had created a constant web of lies, and a mountain of falsified documents. The doctor now continually had to steal a new blank from current stock to cover that missing one from years ago, annually shifting the government supply from one batch to another, altering tracking numbers, and counterfeiting records. This forever ongoing maintenance of the lie made it impossible for Tachion to ever forget the truth, and move on as the others had seemed to. So while he always thought of this Rook as being one and the same as his original friend, and felt no less a brotherhood with him simply because he was a replication, the truth always remained prominent at the back of his mind.

And now, this new problem.

Another change to the cloned DNA was made by the implanted virus, one far less innocuous. Certain sequences were altered and added to, with the express purpose of impeding reproduction. In this way, some unscrupulous scientists could not genetically manufacture a perfect clone, as a soldier or slave or other nefarious purpose, and then copy that creation over and over into an army. Not with government-issued blanks, anyway. The virus made changes that prevented this, and all further reproduction of any kind. Therefore, it is not possible to clone a clone. Likewise, a clone cannot produce offspring. Rook's desire to be a father again was an absolutely futile one—having more children for him was genetically not possible.

Tachion became aware that he had been gazing at the door for a long time now, and felt awkward about Rook emerging and seeing him staring so. The android left the lab, waiting instead by the windows of his outer office, and watching as the last, few dying rays of the ruby sun disappeared behind the tall, utilitarian architecture of the city of Onus outside. As the sky began to fully dim, and the lights of the metropolis below grew more prominent in the approaching evening, the seti finally emerged from the private laboratory, and placed the container on the desk.

"Here you go, pervert," Rook said. "Sorry for the wait, but that lab of yours is not really what I'd call... stimulating. You should think about at least hanging up a pinup calendar or something."

"Well, it's not typically what the room is used for, but I'll keep that in mind for next time. Let me get this into a stasiscreen right away." Tachion opened the top of a small white box and inserted the metallic canister. He tapped a keypad on its side, and a small LED light on the lid changed from red to green.

"So..." Rook said, as he watched Dr. Magna secure the sample, "as if that wasn't enough, I have another favor to ask of you. You remember that both the kids are graduating this year?"

"Of course, and your daughter Relic from your own infiltration school. I have it etched in stone in my calendar."

"Well, hers won't be until later in the year, but her brother Flashpoint is finishing early, just next month. He and I were gonna go Ferox hunting on G'rald Moon for the three days before the ceremony." He sighed heavily as he continued. "But now we're doing this whole silly nonsense of only using archaic, traditional seti hand weapons... his sister Relic's brilliant idea. Some ancient coming-of-age custom of our ancestors' she's got him all revved up about." He closed his eyes and shook his head. "Anyway, I know it's not exactly your thing... but I was wondering if you'd wanna join us."

"You're correct," Tachion told him. "It isn't really my thing. But I would enjoy the change of scenery. Yes, I'd be happy to tag along." Tachion produced a multicomm from his lab coat pocket and quickly entered the dates into the personal computer device. "Although... I assume the real reason for the invitation is that you're worried your son may get hurt?"

"Well, partly that. Especially after Bullseye canceled, so now there'll be only *me* out there to watch Flashpoint's back. Turns out Bullseye won't be able to make it to the graduation either, for some reason."

"I don't understand," Tachion said. "It's *his* school. It's the Bullseye Enforcer School. Doesn't he need to give a commencement address of some kind?"

"Fuck if I know, lately that ray of sunshine's an enigma wrapped in a wet blanket. He didn't leave any reason in the message, and now I can't get a hold of him, so… whatever, I guess." Rook walked over and retrieved his coat from where he had left it draped across a chair. "So anyway, I guess I would feel better if you were nearby on this trip, you know? Just in case. But also, you and I haven't had a chance to hang out in a while."

"It sounds like a good time," Tachion replied. "I'm just glad you and Flashpoint are getting along again, spending some father-son time."

"Well… that's the other reason I wanted you there. Things are still kind of distant between us, or should I say *again*, ever since he told me he was changing his discipline from enforcer to demolition. Admittedly, I handled it badly, but I mean, my God… demolitions? I've never heard the end of it from Stansky."

"No doubt," Tachion added.

"It took a while to patch things up, and there's still been a kind of rift between us ever since. To be honest… I'm afraid that if we're alone together, all we're gonna do is argue."

"I don't remember Flashpoint having any qualms about arguing with you in front of me," Tachion told him. "But I'll be there to referee, nonetheless."

Rook gathered his belongings, then walked to the door with Tachion close behind him. "Listen T, about that other thing… that's really important to me, you know? Are you sure you can get this doctor to take a look at it? It would mean the world to me."

Tachion paused in the doorway and peered seriously down at Rook's face. "I've been your comrade, your doctor, and your friend for almost thirty years now. I will make it my mission to aid you in this. If there is anything that can be done, I'll make sure it happens. You can trust me."

"As always, my friend." Rook slapped Tachion's rigid back and exited the office, heading down the now dimmed hallway toward the elevator. "I'll see you next month on G'rald," he called out with a wave as the lift doors started sliding, "and if I see any hidden toilet holocam footage of me on the net, I'll know where it came from!"

The doors closed, and he was gone.

The doctor turned off the lights in the laboratory and secured the bookshelf back into its closed position, masking the entrance. He went back to his desk and picked up the small stasiscreen container with Rook's sample, then headed out of his office, locking the door behind him. As he walked through the quiet corridors, he passed a large, boxy servicebot that was diligently vacuuming and polishing the tiled floor, motors humming and brushes swishing as it went. As Tachion passed, the bot beeped and chirped in the android language. *"Good evening, Dr. Magna,"* it chimed.

Tachion stopped and turned, then walked back to the servicebot. *"Pause,"* he chirped back.

The robot stopped in its tracks, shutting down its spinning brushes in response to the android's command. Tachion took hold of a handle on the otherwise flat top of the machine, then popped open the hatch to reveal the piles of dust and debris the bot had collected in its nightly duties. He tapped a few keys on the small stasiscreen container, turning its green light back to red. Then without a second thought, he tossed the device and its contents into the bot's trash container, and closed the door. *"How many more floors do you have to do?"* Tachion asked the machine in android.

"Six more floors have been scheduled for tonight," the bot chirped back.

"Schedule override. Authorization Magna, alpha two one nine," Tachion instructed. *"Finish this floor, then report immediately to the waste disintegration area to empty your container."*

"Override accepted," the servicebot responded.

"Continue," Tachion beeped.

The whir of the bot's motors and brushes re-engaged, and the custodial unit continued on down the hall on its nightly rounds. Tachion strode up the corridor away from the robot, and again pulled his multicomm from the lab coat pocket as he approached the elevator.

"Open new subspace message, encrypted," he said to the device.

"Encryption enabled," the computer replied.

"Message to Belladonna," Tachion instructed.

The elevator doors opened as the multicomm hesitated a second or two, searching the internal address book, and processing Tachion's command. *"Begin message,"* the device's voice politely prompted.

"Belladonna, it's Tachion," the android said into the computer as he boarded the lift. "Your husband just left here. Listen... I think we have a problem."

The elevator doors slid silently closed.

Chapter 2.1

PRESIDENT HAROLD V. FORESTAL, CHAIRMAN of the Elder Senate, Commander-in-Chief of the United Interstellar Armed Forces, and duly elected leader of the Federated Planetary Coalition, slunk quietly on tiptoe into his palatial bedchamber, and stole ever so softly across the room toward the bed. It was after three in the morning here in Nuremberg, on Earth, and the human removed his robe and slid cautiously into his bed in slow motion, hoping above anything not to disturb his sleeping wife. He carefully drew in one leg—then the other—and slowly leaned back, until his head finally rested on the pillow. Sure of his success, he rolled gingerly onto his side and looked across the bed—right into the wide-open eyes of his wide-awake spouse.

"Harold?" she asked in a hushed, sleepy voice. "I didn't expect you back until tomorrow night. What happened?"

The president leaned over and gave her a brief kiss. "Nothing honey, it just wrapped up early, that's all."

"Well, that can't be good."

"No, no, it's fine," he replied through a yawn. "It actually went exceedingly well. I think, anyway."

First Lady Deborah Forestal pushed herself up against the headboard, and turned on the lamp on her nightstand. "Really? Tell me all about it," she said.

Although she was a woman of nearly sixty years, she was still considered to be extremely attractive. This was due in part to her good breeding and privileged upbringing, but also to the skilled and diligent work of her many plastic surgeons. She had long, radiant, auburn hair, the taut, pale and faultless skin of a woman half her age, and blue eyes as stunning as the first spring sky after a long winter. She also had an air of dignified authority about her, as was appropriate for a woman of her upbringing. Harold knew she was seldom as content as those peaceful eyes would imply, and he was always careful not to arouse her more quarrelsome disposition.

"Please dear, wouldn't you rather wait until morning?" He begged.

"The most important summit of my husband's administration? Of his entire career? I want to hear about it now. How did you get on with our new Forestal foreign agenda? Did you manage to push anything through that we can give to the reporters tomorrow morning?"

The president sighed and sat up in bed, turning on his own table light as well. He was, by all accounts, a handsome man, with salt and pepper hair, and classically masculine features that always played well to a voting audience. Distinguished, but not aloof. Intelligent, but not arrogant. Assertive, but not threatening. "Yes, we did," he replied. "Actually, everything we wanted."

"What do you mean by everything?" she asked.

"I mean everything. Reduced tariffs on Coalition exports, lower tax penalties for our manufacturers abroad, a moratorium on transportation tolls for Coalition shipping vessels using foreign space, higher interest rates on interstellar loans. Hell, we even got a renewal of the extradition treaties for Coalition fugitives. Literally everything we wanted."

"What?" the first lady said. "That's unbelievable. They all agreed to this? Capella? Oberonn? Theseus?"

"Yeah, even the khailians," President Forestal answered.

"I assume they wanted something in exchange. More military outposts, perhaps? Or greater mutual aid around the Barrens, helping them guard that abandoned buffer zone between us and the Drak'min border?"

"No. As a matter of fact, they've released us completely from that portion of the treaty, other than just a very minor presence. They've agreed to handle their own domestic defense affairs from now on. Unless asked, we can keep the majority of our forces back here."

"You're joking!" she said in amazement. "That is absolutely fantastic."

"Hmm. Perhaps," the president said, sounding not at all enthused.

"Perhaps! What do you mean? You have achieved what every president for the last two hundred years has dreamed of. As soon as this hits the news, the economy will skyrocket. Millions of jobs will be created. Coalition citizens will be wealthier and safer, and tens of thousands of soldiers will be coming home. What a press photo that'll make! My God, Harold... all this at the beginning of an election year. It couldn't be more perfect. Although, maybe we should hold off some of the troop drawdown until closer to voting time, it will play better then, and..."

"I don't think I can ask the Elders to ratify it," the president responded quietly.

"W-what are you talking about?" the first lady snapped.

"It was just too easy. We didn't even have to negotiate, for Christ's sake. I mean... they put on a show of it, sure. But it was obvious that they had resolved to bow to my every wish before the summit even started. The chamai Oberonn Prime Minister, and that lyghtan priestess Vasu, they have never seen eye to eye on anything before in their entire lives. But it was like they were all one big family now. And that creepy old chamai, General Nylis, he was controlling everything the Prime Minister said, whispering in his ear the whole meeting."

The first lady was angry now. "Are you so insecure, that even when things go right, you think it's a plot against you?"

"It's not me I am worried about, but the four Coalition species I'm sworn to protect, spread over a hundred colonized planets."

"Oh, don't give me that campaign speech nonsense. I'm not one of your constituents. So the Prime Minister is taking advice from his general. So what? Sometimes I think even you *yourself* can barely go to the bathroom without talking to your friend Ephraim first."

"It's not just that," the president continued. "There was a man there, too... a human. He was never in the summit, but I swear, at every break, they were all checking in with him. They did it one at a time, and for sure they were inconspicuous about it, but whoever that was, he..."

"Now you listen to me, goddamn it, and you listen good!" The first lady was furious now as she interrupted her husband. "You are going to bring that agreement to the Elder Senate tomorrow, and they are going to ratify it. You have made a career of using my family name to win election after election. And now that I have finally got you to the top, I am not going to stand idly by while you make a mockery of it, becoming the president that threw away the most beneficial interstellar treaty in the history of the Coalition. I *am not* going to be married to a one-term president, do you understand me?!"

"Yes, I do... I understand. Please, dear, the bodyguards will hear you."

"To hell with the damn bodyguards. If it weren't for me, you'd still be running for school board chairman in that little nowhere town where you grew up. I did not spend the last forty years of my life suffering through your campaigns and teaching your thick head the subtleties of the game of politics, only to have you destroy the one chance at *our* lasting legacy."

"Deborah, please. I will take the treaty to the elders. I said that I would, first thing in the morning. It will be on the news by noon."

The first lady took a deep sigh, closing her eyes for a moment to regain her composure. The flush in her face quickly drained away, her normal porcelain complexion returning with her cooling temper. "Thank you dear, I think that would be a wise choice."

"What about the human at the summit? The man who was coaching all the neutral delegates? I know something was going on there, I can't just ignore it," the president said, still seeming intimidated by his wife's outburst. "If it turns out I'm right, and there is some sort of conspiracy, how will *that* look as our legacy?"

"Very well, Harold dear. If you want to know who he is, then have him investigated. Don't use military intelligence services though, you'll want to be a little more subtle."

"We could outsource to a merc group. Maybe UDC12, or Parliament."

"That's your idea of subtle? UDC12? Or, my God in heaven, Parliament!? Those groups are newsmakers, dear. And mess makers. Talk about 'in like a lamb and out like a lion'. They'll start off inconspicuous enough, but in the end there will be buildings collapsing, and body bags to fill, not to mention a media frenzy."

"Bullseye's team has always provided results," he argued. "And I can trust him and his group."

"No, dear, not for this job. It requires a bit more finesse, wouldn't you say?" The first lady twirled a finger through her hair, as she stared up at the ceiling and thought for a moment. "Send an SSS agent. Brin, maybe."

"Brin? You mean Esil Brin, the metamorph?" he asked.

"He is Starlaw's best, is he not? Have him get close to this human of yours and find out what he can. But don't let him jeopardize this treaty in any way, am I clear?"

"Of course, dear."

"Okay, it's settled then." The first lady reached over and turned off her light, tucking herself back down beneath the covers of their bed. "I'm sure it will turn out he's no one of any importance. An adviser on human relations, maybe, or something else equally as innocent. Now go to sleep, Harold. You'll want to look good for the press conference tomorrow."

"Yes, Deborah," the president answered, turning off his light as well and sliding down into bed beside her.

"Good night, dear," his wife told him.

The president did not answer. He instead settled into his pillow and stared out into the dark room, grinding his teeth, and silently cursing the woman who lay next to him. It had been an extremely hectic day, and a long spaceflight home, yet he lay there with eyes wide, unable to find slumber.

2.2

BULLIT CHARGED DOWN THE SMOKE veiled hall as fast as the pain of his injured leg would allow, then dove to crouch behind the smoldering remains of the fallen securitybot he had just toppled. The injured seti took the brief opportunity the cover provided to switch out his expended powerpack for a fresh one, hastily rematerialized from his 'scrambler' molecular storage device. He quickly affixed it to his armor and snapped in the connectors, arousing the comforting hum and glow of his shields engaging back to maximum. Physically exhausted, and in pain, he took a moment to lean back against the disabled machine and catch his breath.

In addition to the bent plate of armor that dug into an open thigh wound with every step, each panting breath the fatigued seti inhaled told him that his ribs were cracked in several places. His inertia screen and armor had slowed the ammunition's velocity as intended—just not by quite enough. The multiple ammo rounds now sat buried in his chest wall, a centimeter below the skin, grating and grinding against the shattered fragments of his ribcage. Doing his best to ignore the pain, he spun himself around, flinging the barrel of his AE200 on top of the destroyed robot sentry. Resting his elbows on the metal beast, he lifted the laser rifle to his eye, and drew a careful bead down the scope at the door ahead.

The corridors in this section were notably different from the other areas of the facility they had already seen. The cold industrial look of the rest of the building had given way to a warmer, richer atmosphere. As far away from Earth as Gel Gonahaar was, the design of the space was nonetheless clearly human—even through the scorch marks and bullet holes that decorated near every square inch. Dark, imported, wood-paneled walls, lined with the occasional side table and ornately framed mirror, along a tiled, marble floor with a long, patterned rug running the length of the corridor, and a small leather sofa by a set of double-hung oak doors.

Behind that doorway was their goal, and the seti restrained his impulse to charge them as he patiently waited for the signal to move.

Through the scope of his rifle, Bullit watched as Rook, their computer and security systems expert, worked swiftly to disassemble the retinal scanner and connect it to his bypass. Their leader, Bullseye, the experienced enforcer and company sniper, stood above him, ear towards the door and eyes toward the hall, scanning back in Bullit's direction to cover his comrade from any ambush. Rook seemed to be getting more and more frustrated, as over and over his attempts to open the door failed. Finally, he saw Bullseye motion in handspeak, and Bullit turned to relay the signal towards their demo expert, James Stansky, and medic Tachion behind him. Stansky then came dashing past, his sonic shield rendering him incredibly silent in his massive set of powered armor. The human knelt in front of the doors as the two setis evacuated back towards Bullit's position.

The massive blast that James created blew the doors inward as splinters and dust, and the group charged into the room with a rush of well-choreographed fury, each securing a corner as they cleared the area of any lurking danger. The office inside was similar to the hall before it, richly decked in leather, marble, and mahogany. A large, handcrafted desk stood at the far end of the library-like office, and an overstuffed chair behind it held an overstuffed man. His feet rested up on the desk as he reclined back in his seat, a portly human of middle age, and he stared back at the group with a smirk on his face that was difficult to interpret. He gave no indication of surprise or alarm, but stood up from the desk and turned his back on the group, then moved to a small bar cart, and poured an inch of honey-colored liquor into a short crystal glass.

"I don't suppose I could offer you gentlemen a drink?" he asked, without turning around.

"No longer the figurative, but now the literal poisoned chalice you extend to us, Denali?" Bullseye asked.

"Ah, my old friend, still ever the poet. No... no poisons here, however. The time for such subtleties I think has passed, has it not?" Denali turned then and approached, cocktail in hand.

"A certainty upon which I heartily agree," Bullseye growled.

Bullit felt his face go flush and his heartbeat surge as the primal blood-lust of his seti ancestry welled up inside him. The long vendetta to avenge the murder of his only brother, Wyvern, was finally culminating in a meeting Bullit had rehearsed in his dreams for over a decade, since he was barely more than a mere adolescent. He fought the urge to yank back on the trigger of his rifle, obliterating the human in a scorching rain of laser fire, his far more intricate plans requiring at least the semblance of a level head. Foremost to Bullit, was to make sure Denali was clear who it was that had come to collect retribution. He reached behind his neck and pulled the release on the back of his armor. The collar restraint popped loose, and Bullit removed his helmet. Beneath was revealed a seti face of mottled flaxen fur, with a whitewash goatee around the perimeter of his muzzle, his eyes as blue-gray and cold as the polished stones of a bleak shore, and an expression of malice that could be read from outside the building. He dropped his helmet, and shook his head to liberate the sweat-drenched locks of his long tawny mane.

"Ah, and who have we here?" Denali said, in a tone that still brimmed with arrogance, despite his circumstance. "This must be the replacement for the unfortunate Mr. Mishta, may he rest in peace. A curious substitution. It seems one by one, you're replacing the human members of your team with seti. Tell me, Mr. Stansky, does that cause you any concern for your future job security?"

Bullit's anger increased exponentially at the insult of not being recognized, his boiling blood ringing in his ears, and his tensed muscles cramping from restraint. He suppressed his rage by remembering the long-awaited tortures he had planned so meticulously for his brother's killer, then he took a step forward to recite the tirade he had refined for nine long years, forged in hate, and shaped from the bitter shards of grief.

But he could not move. He pulled harder against the searing pain in his leg, and yet it would not budge from its spot. Suddenly he felt entrapped in his own body, as if some unseen force was gripping him tightly, and forcing him to remain where he stood. He screamed out at Denali in a fit of venomous wrath, but his howling emerged as muffled whispers, inaudible to anyone else. He looked around in a panic as the walls of the room began to shift and lengthen, stretching the office longer and longer. No matter how hard he tried, he remained paralyzed in the middle, as Denali, his desk, and the rest of Parliament slid inexorably further from his reach.

"And Rook, I must admit how pleasantly surprised I am to see you. I was so afraid you had perished on Theseus. It seems the rumors of your demise have been greatly exaggerated," Bullit heard Denali say with a chuckle from his distant prison in the center of the now elongated office. "I was so worried that your young ones would have no one to provide for them. I was planning on making a visit to your home to see if there was anything I could do for them. You know how important it is for children that age to have the security of a father figure."

Bullit watched in frozen horror as Rook raised his autopistol to Denali's temple. He tried again to scream in anguish, but no sound would emerge from his open mouth. Rook's helmet had somehow vanished now, and he turned and smirked at Bullit as he pulled back on the trigger. The burst from the weapon erupted in slow motion, round after round flung from the barrel in an explosion of smoke and fire. The bullets impacted the side of Denali's head one after another, the first few tearing straight through cleanly, spattering the wall beyond with tiny red droplets, the rest ripping away chunks of his skull and his face, shredding Denali's head until only the dripping, tattered neck and jaw remained behind. The nearly decapitated body slumped against the wall, sliding down on top of the stew of bone and gray matter covering the marble floor.

Now Bullit was free of the hold upon him and back at the desk, kneeling before the corpse of his enemy. He grabbed the body by its bloody lapels and lifted it up off the ground a few inches, the arms dangling lifelessly behind it, hands dragging through the sticky red mess. He screamed out in frustration, then shot a glare at his teammate for an explanation. Rook stood with the rest of Parliament in a circle surrounding Bullit and Denali. The office behind them had disappeared, and only pitch darkness remained beyond the figures of his friends. They were all pointing at the seti, and laughing uproariously, the resounding echoes of it getting louder, churning dizzily in Bullit's head. He turned back to the corpse he was still clutching tightly to see that Denali's blood-soaked face had now somehow returned, cackling gleefully along with everyone else.

Bullit closed his eyes and shook his head vigorously, trying to clear what he knew must be delusion from his mind. When he opened them again, he gasped sharply in horror, his hands now gripping not Denali, but the body of his lost older brother, dead so many years.

"Wyvern, it's Bullit," the grief-stricken seti cried over the ever more deafening laughter. "Wyvern, can you hear me?"

The clouded, lifeless eyes flew open wide, and stared at Bullit with a mixture of outrage and disappointment. "You failed me, brother," it croaked at him, in a harsh agonized whisper. "You have failed me... again!"

"No!" Bullit shouted aloud, waking himself with a start and bolting upright in panic. His eyes darted around wildly as he tried to get his bearings, and he found himself reclined in the front seat of his aerocar rental. The auto-navigator alarm was beeping loudly, signaling that he had reached his destination, and he reached over quickly and slammed the button to shut it off. Still breathing heavily, and with his pulse racing, Bullit took a moment to steady himself and shake off the anxiety left from the nightmare.

Wyvern's third remembrance ceremony had gone from a humble celebration to quite a wild party over the first two days of the event. Bullit's stock market investments in various industries skyrocketed last week, based on news of the Elder Senate ratifying the President's Tristar summit treaty. As a result of his windfall, he had spared no expense on food, drink and entertainment for his relatives attending the affair. This morning he was paying the price for his merrymaking, with a hangover that would drop a wild Ferox in its tracks.

Today was the final day of the ceremony, the somber and reverent portion of his brother's memorial for the Fallen. Bullit had dressed smartly for the occasion, but barely able to stand as he made his way from the hotel, he had slept on the flight to the temple. Now his twenty-five hundred credit suit was wrinkled and disheveled, and beneath expensive designer musk, his fur reeked of seti ale. He staggered out of the vehicle to get some fresh air, squinting his eyes from the pain of the sunlight, and tried his best to straighten his attire.

It was not the first time he had endured that horrific nightmare. He had been tormented by variations of the dream for years after the actual event. But after some personal struggle, and the passage of enough time, they had finally faded almost a decade ago. Although he had never forgiven himself for not avenging his brother personally as he intended, he had long since forgiven Rook for taking away his one chance to do so—or, so he had thought. While he was sure the sudden recurrence of the dream after all this time was merely a combination of the memorial, and the alcohol, he couldn't help the fact that it had stirred up all the unhealthy emotions he had so deeply buried all these years.

Bullit sat on a chilly stone bench in front of the iron temple, one that held the cremated remains from hundreds of funeral pyres. Memorial temples like this one were traditionally built of iron, and constructed in a perfectly pentagonal symmetry, unlike most seti pyramid shaped buildings—doubtless for ancient and holy reasons that Bullit had never bothered to learn. Like Rook, he had been born and raised among the humans of Earth, and was not as learned in his ancestral culture as he probably ought to be. He was more than content to leave all that to Bullseye.

Inside, the ashes of the Fallen were carefully stored, within small, engraved drawers that lined the interior walls from floor to ceiling. His family owned a bank of these drawers near the carved circular altar in the center of the temple. The few immediately above Wyvern's held the remains of both their parents, and the one to his immediate left was reserved for the future use of Bullit himself.

He sat there for a few moments in the cool morning air, his head in his hands, unable to shake the last disturbing fragments of the nightmare from his mind. He heard the whine of an engine approaching from behind, and turned around to look. With the flat of his hand against his forehead as a visor against the sun, he recognized the rented aerocar of his cousin, Belladonna, cruising in low over the still winter-bare treetops behind the temple. It glided past slowly over his head, and settled easily into the front parking area, as several others now also came into view, approaching from various directions.

Bullit watched as Belladonna, looking beautiful as always in a tastefully flowing green dress, stepped out of the vehicle, followed by her mother. Then the other door opened, and Rook dragged himself out, seeming in no better health than Bullit himself was. He reminded himself, over and over, that he had forgiven Rook and moved on years ago. But as he stood there and made final adjustments to his suit, he couldn't help but feel the twinge of a familiar burning hate welling up from deep inside. Somewhere in the back of his subconscious, where hide thoughts that are never spoken aloud, a new secret desire for vengeance had grown where the previous one had died unfulfilled. He wittingly kept it securely vaulted away, so that he would never act on it in a moment of impulse. But if Rook would only give him a reason to act on it, an excuse to open the door to that vault—

Bullit twisted his face into a welcoming smile, and headed across the lot to greet his friend.

Chapter 3.1

H ER HOLY EMINENCE, LADY OFROI, First Ashi'Mar to the lyghtan high priestess Queen Vasu, and heir apparent to the throne of Capella, tripped and fell hard into the searing desert sand. Her slender ebony arms, quickly outstretched to break her fall, sank almost to her shoulders in the loose, drifting dunes. She screamed out for help as she forced herself up, and ran terrified and stumbling up the steep sandy ridge, each leg sinking and churning in the slope's granular surface. Exhausted and wheezing from her exertion beneath the arid suns, she reached the top to find but endless desert stretching beyond. She could still hear the machine inexorably closing its distance behind her, but she dared not look, and threw herself over, tumbling down the opposite face of the dune.

The mediation she had overseen earlier in the day was, by far, a duty well below her high office. Any midlevel abbess or layperson bureaucrat would have been more than a qualified arbiter for this dispute, and she held a certain resentment for the unreasonable waste of her valuable time. Even so, she had performed the job with the seriousness and grace that she exhibited when dealing in any matters of state.

Sovereign Queen Vasu, the Holy Mother of both the Church of Capella, and Divine Monarch of its government—as well as Ofroi's immediate superior—had explained the assignment as a necessity in order to generate press for the hearing. But the ashi'mar knew this wasn't the case. Ofroi had been openly challenging Vasu's growing reliance on the questionable council of a mysterious human, one who seemed to have gained more and more influence over the high priestess and her administration. This assignment was merely another in a long series, obviously designed as punishment for her speaking out, as well as to keep her away from the cavern city of the planet's capital, the Old City Temple, and Vasu herself.

At the heart of today's arbitration was the Capellan dune eel, a slithering, sixteen-foot desert creature, whose eggs were laid under the loose drifts of sand that covered most of the planet. They deposited them in clutches of five to ten at a time, every few days. Each eel would lay thousands of eggs in their lifetime, leaving them for a passing male to find, and fertilize.

The meat of the eels was a taste hard acquired, but their eggs had been a staple of the lyghtan diet for millennia, and a major export for the past few centuries. The eggs were farmed on massive, barren ranches, where the animals were kept from wandering by underground sonic fences. Huge robotic harvesters would then hover up and down the golden dunes, tilling the sand with a great slow-spinning comb of slender, metal teeth. The machines would cover every inch of the endless wide deserts, collecting the hidden clutches from beneath the searing sands.

A recent merger of several smaller eel farms had now resulted in the single largest ranch on the planet, an enormous swath of desert covering almost two hundred thousand acres. The problem with this was that the Kulani—an ancient and much-maligned tribe of surface-dwelling nomads—claimed a migration route, and the rights to resources within it, directly through the center of this massive stretch of property. After brief negotiation, including tax incentives for the ranchers, and legitimate land holdings for the Kulani, a narrow strait of territory was transferred to the nomads, for a kilometer on each side of the Pel Yellek Fault.

As Ofroi expected, press coverage for the routine arbitration was non-existent. Like most lyghtan, the media had little interest in the civil liberties of the reclusive surface tribes, and maybe even less in journeying to the desert in the season where their twin suns burned hottest. The first ashi'mar found herself with a full afternoon scheduled to tour the ranchland, and no journalist there to record the staged photo op. She nonetheless spent the day watching the distant harvesters run, her lone guide pointing out the plumes of tossed sand catapulted high behind the tillers, visible here and there along the moguled horizon.

She still was not quite sure exactly when he had vanished. Certainly it was sometime while she was closely examining one of the harvesters currently not in use, in a feigned show of interest in her guide's livelihood. She had completed a slow walk around the machine, then returned to the front to find herself abandoned. When the engine started up and the machine hovered off the sand, she calmly stepped aside and continued to seek her escort. It was not until the long crescent pikes began their slow revolution, slicing and churning the sand underneath, that Ofroi first suspected that she might be in danger. A few minutes of running and dodging the tiller proved to her horror that she was unfortunately right.

Now her body tumbled mercilessly down the seemingly endless dune, her mouth and eyes filling with sand as her arms and legs flailed wildly. Yet with every punishing blow her body took as it bounced and rolled violently along the scorching slope, she was comforted in the fact that she was now moving more quickly away from the approaching harvester. A small comfort to be sure, and one cut short by the sickening pop of her knee snapping clean, still somersaulting chaotically through the hot sand, finally impacting roughly at the bottom of the dune. Lying face down, her raven-black skin freckled with the coarse, yellow grains, she stared back in agony to see her lower leg jutting out at a horrific and unnatural angle.

The hulking sand tiller moved still ever closer, bursting through the crest at the top of the dune. It dipped down the other side like a ship tossed in the sea, the spinning row of skewers gleaming in the suns. Ofroi sobbed frantically in terror and pain, dragging herself slowly across the dry burning sand. The loose nature of the ground again gave her no traction, and she swam helplessly in place in its sweltering embrace.

"Somebody, help me!" she screeched desperately, sobbing aloud. She looked to the sky and prayed, begging out loud to her deities. "Please! Merciful Originators, have pity on this humble soul! I beg it of you! Save your faithful servant! Let this not be my path!"

As she lowered her gaze back to the sand, frantically dragging herself inches forward on her belly, a silhouette appeared at the peak of the next dune. It was difficult to focus through the tears, sand, and blazing suns in her eyes, but she could see a flowing robe blowing in the wind, and a brilliant lock of stark, white hair arranged in a mohawk against the dark shape—a pair of blazing turquoise eyes staring down at where she lay. Was it possible? It looked to be—Queen Vasu.

"Holy Mother, is that you? Please, My Queen, help me!" she screamed. The figure stood motionless and watched, seemingly indifferent to her heart-wrenching pleas. It was only then that the first ashi'mar truly understood just *how far* astray the high priestess had been led—and the terrible reality of Ofroi's punishment for her insolence.

The slender revolving spikes finally impaled the bones of Ofroi's ankles, causing her to scream out in torment, and pant rapidly in panic. The great spinning teeth of the horrible machine were blunt at their ends, and each penetration first pushed hard against her skin, shoving her down into the sand. Then only when the full weight was upon her, would the lances pop through her flesh to the desert on the other side, tearing off ragged, uneven chucks as it went.

Oddly, at first there was only a pinch and some pressure, as each four-foot-long needle punctured her flesh. She gripped the sand below her tightly, and her breathing quickened even more, as they pierced through her calves, then her knees, then her thighs. She was yanked backward harshly in a series of violent jerks as the relentless steel comb began pulling her in, ferociously ripping skin and muscle from tendon and bone. Still, there was numbness to the process, and she thought for a moment that she might somehow survive. The mighty tiller may simply hover right over her, leaving her with just a few punctures in her skin. But the high plume of sand launched behind the machine was already mixed with a bright mist of blood, and dark tattered flesh, shredded in strips, was raining all over the dunes.

The pain began more earnestly then as the spears punched through her pelvis, and she froze in agony, glowing eyes locked upon her lady in shock—not breathing—not blinking—her mouth wide agape. As the pikes masticated her waist, her ribcage, her shoulders, the indescribable torture sent her into convulsions, spitting and coughing red foam onto the sand. Then pure, sweet relief as her spinal cord was extracted, ceasing the torment for her last dying moment. Her paralyzed eyes were now locked in a frozen stare at the Priestess still observing, as the spikes came into view overhead to deface her. It was the last awful vision that Ofroi would ever see, before her panicked eyes and racing mind were torn rudely asunder.

The harvester now moved off in a random direction, released from that force that was steering its path. The desert behind, now painted in red and strewn with gore, began to undulate and shift with a flurry of movement. The eels had been beckoned by the smell of the fluids, and breaching and diving like fish in a sea, they swarmed in huge numbers to extract every drop of moisture from Ofroi's bloody and scattered remains.

The figure standing at the crest of the dune looked down upon the scene with grisly satisfaction. With a wide smirk of contentment, she pulled her robe's hood up to cover her face from the suns, and moved away quickly down the back of the dune.

3.2

JAMES STANSKY PRESSED FIRMLY WITH his cheek against his shoulder, gripping the tiny flashlight in the crook of his muscular neck. He lay on his back, peering up at the tightly bundled vein of multicolored wires, held fast with zip cords every few inches. The space was cramped, and it took some maneuvering to slide his hand across his chest, wiggling it to his side to find his demolitions kit. Unable to lift his head in the low clearance, he lightly touched the items inside, his fingers recognizing each tool in turn. When he sensed the familiar feel of the instrument he searched for, he slid the snips back up along his chest, placing their biting end to the wires above his head.

The air around Stansky was chilly to be sure, and the hard cement against his back was downright bitter cold. Yet as he slowly pulled a small loop of slack in the red wire with the white stripe, he found himself perspiring slightly, nonetheless. He blew a quick, steamy puff of air out of the corner of his mouth, aimed at a particularly irritating droplet of sweat making its way along his cheek, then he reached up with the snips and smoothly cut the wire. After dancing his fingers again through his kit, he produced a pair of strippers, and carefully began removing the plastic sheathing from both ends of the severed wire.

The micro-quantum battery he brought forth from his kit next was barely as large as a medium-sized coin. The insertion of the leads was a delicate process, and James squinted his eyes, biting down lightly on the corner of his lip as he strained to align the openings with the newly exposed copper wire. There was a subtle ache growing in his hand as he worked—one that had become more familiar as of late—followed by a slight trembling that would be barely perceptible at first to anyone but him. He cursed at himself as the tremor increased, and he squeezed his hand tightly into a fist several times in an effort to silence the quivering muscles of his fingers. He reattempted the insertion of the leads into the battery, but again and again, his wavering hands kept missing the mark.

James knew that this wasn't just his fingers shivering in reaction to the cold. Neither was it his nerves, nor some sort of cramp, nor injury to his arm. The symptoms had been coming on stronger for months now, and in typical Stansky fashion, he hoped the best course of treatment was to ignore it altogether. The most frustrating part was the ironic timing of the convulsions. The tremors never came on when he was relaxing at home, or driving his cars. At the gym every day, there was never a twitch when he was lifting weights, nor did it ever occur when giving a lecture on demo tactics. Nor when he was with a woman. But when he needed even the remotest degree of precision, his thumbs would seize tightly and his fingers would tremble, the spasms increasing until he finished his task, or gave up. Any precise target-directed movements, such as putting a fork in his mouth, pressing an elevator button, even threading this wire into the small battery port, had now all become increasingly difficult to do.

They called it a 'midbrain kinetic intention tremor', just an early symptom of the cerebellar lesions his disease inevitably caused. He wasn't completely unfamiliar with the disorder; he had seen similar symptoms in his father a great many years ago. And long before that, when James was just a boy, he recalled the same spasms in his grandfather's huge hands, one of the few memories he still had of the man. Like with them, he knew that over time, his trembling would increase and spread. And since there still was no cure for the hereditary disease, just like with them, he, too, would die. Not soon, mind you—maybe ten or fifteen years from now. But the first half of those, he would become increasingly feeble with each passing month, and the last half would be spent imprisoned in his bed.

James had rested his hands by his side for a moment, allowing the vigorous shaking to fade while he studied the quantum battery and wires above him. Confident he had memorized the location of everything, he quickly slid his hands up, grabbed and inserted the leads before his muscles had a chance to seize again. Then he hastily calculated the conversion of how many QEUs equaled an output of roughly twelve volts, and set the tiny dial on the front of the battery.

He replaced his tools into his kit, and shimmied himself backward on the cold cement, emerging from beneath the vehicle he had been repairing, and stood to stretch his back on the side of the winding mountain road. James had long been an avid collector and aficionado of restored ancient Earth automobiles. This particular vehicle, called a 'Camaro Z28', was actually a custom-built replica, and while he had installed several hidden modern features into the reproduction, the main combustion engine still ran off of a bulky and unreliable lead-acid battery. This battery, as James was learning, did not respond well to cold weather, and long periods of storage.

He took a moment to dust some gravel and sand from the back of his expensive attire, and looked out across the snowy winter forest as the purple curtain of evening was beginning to make its slow descent.

James was a large man—barrel-chested and bull-necked—with arms nearly the size of Tachion's metallic ones. He was a perfect example of the ultimate human physique. But it wasn't just his body that was impressive, as he was downright handsome as well. He had spent several straight years among the '100 hottest' of a popular gossip rag—but of course, that was several years ago, when James was in his prime. But even now, at his more mature age, he still was possessed of that perfect blend of boyish charm and rugged strength. Honeyed-chocolate eyes, and powerful square jaw. Skin like a child, but with hair like a marine. Attributes he was happy to take advantage of, any time he could.

He turned back to the car, and bundled himself into the Shearling Icelandic coat he had left on the roof for safekeeping, then climbed back into the antique replica. After rubbing his hands furiously together to warm them for a minute, he crossed his fingers and turned the key. A slow, repetitive grinding noise emerged from the engine, and then gradually began to increase in tempo. Finally, in an explosive roar, the engine of the old vehicle sprang to life, and he revved it over and over until he was sure it would keep running. In a shower of flying gravel and smoking tires, he fishtailed onto the road with a long, echoed screech, and raced off into the silence of the surrounding white-peaked mountains.

The winter snows had been generous to this region of Trappist-1e's southern mountains, but the road itself was dry and clean, and the tires of James' car gripped tightly to its surface as he raced along the winding path. The thick, white blanket covering the surrounding forest dimly reflected the red and purple clouds painted by the setting sun, giving the air around the untamed forest a dusty, pinkish hue. This area of the mountain range was home to several ski slopes, unrivaled in the rest of the known galaxy, and therefore had become a haven for resorts and vacation homes for the wealthy and affluent. The sky above was divided by perpendicular lines of slow-moving aerocar traffic, full of tired skiers leaving the slopes for the day, and returning to their opulent mansions perched on various scenic cliff sides.

But the road that Stansky traveled was relatively unused anymore, and free from traffic, allowing him to reach those exhilarating breakneck speeds that were the purpose of a vehicle like his. He felt his heart race as he shifted in and out of the tight corners in the twisted road, and smiled in childlike glee as he flew full speed down the occasional straightaway. He lost himself in the speed and power of the car for a while, as he felt the road rush beneath him, and watched the forest blur past, and for a few priceless moments, he forgot about his impending illness. Then, all too soon, the small village that was home to his mountainside ski villa came into view, and James slowed the vehicle to a reasonable speed as he entered the outskirts of the hamlet.

The architecture of this area of T-1e was an eclectic blend of all the Coalition styles, made even more unusual by the natural materials used, creating a feeling that the small village had not too harshly impacted the vast wilderness around them. Two-story, rectangular, human-style log buildings stood next to cone and pyramid shaped seti structures of earthen stucco. Even a few metamorph dome-shaped shops, and unadorned android buildings of dark stone, sat nestled between the mesh of narrow, cobbled streets. In the near distance, clinging like a gargoyle on a rocky mountain ledge, high above the village, a vast château of white marble and mirrored glass sat and looked down on the simple little town. It was this grand mansion, standing out in defiant superiority to its pristine surroundings, that James called home. At least for a few weekends every year.

Tatiana waited for him now in that home, the end of their spontaneous surprise vacation drawing near. Stansky reached into the pocket of his coat, driving at a relative crawl through the small pedestrian packed shopping district, and produced a tiny, felt-covered box. He flipped open the top, examining the ring once again as he drove, practicing under his breath the proposal he had rehearsed for weeks now. Then in sudden frustration, he slammed the box closed, shoving it quickly back into his pocket.

It was not that James was not exactly the type to settle down—which he was surely not. Nor was it the fact his love for Tatiana was not really strong enough for him to want marriage just yet—which also, sadly, it was not. His frustration came from a self-loathing over the reason why he had finally decided to propose, after near eleven years of dating. The simple fact was that soon his disease would advance to the point where he would need a caretaker, someone to help him with his daily routine. He would need to be fed, and bathed, and dressed, and any number of other small tasks that he took for granted now, but that would inevitably become impossible for him. His own selfishness disgusted James, almost to the point of not going through with it, but his morbid fear of spending his final years alone, and in some sort of home for the infirm, cared for by a stable of indifferent servicebots, invariably outweighed his moral integrity.

James swore at the increasing foot-traffic surrounding his car, forcing him to drive at what felt like a snail's pace, then reached into the glove compartment to trigger a line of toggle switches. The secondary hover engines came online with a gentle hum, and a small array of hidden buttons flipped upward from the top of the dashboard. With a brief flicker of green light, a standard aerocar heads up display appeared across the windshield, as the vehicle rose from the street and up above the buildings, then jetted off in a much more direct route to his not-so-humble mountainside estate.

He loved Tatiana deeply to be sure—he would have never stayed with her for so long otherwise. But despite his best efforts, his feelings had never reached that point of absolute devotion to her alone. And because of this, his fidelity to her had strayed. It had happened many times, with many women, and he wasn't quite sure that he could keep it from happening again—or that he wanted to. But, if he was going to condemn this poor girl unwittingly to a life as his nursemaid, the least he could do was vow to himself to remain faithful to her.

He took up the small ring box again from his pocket, and steeled himself once more for the daunting and terrible task before him, as he glided the car in towards the gravel driveway of his glistening marble château.

Chapter 4.1

T HE HEXAGONAL MAIN PASSAGEWAY along the port side of the khailian science vessel Kuvx extended the full length of the ancient ship, from bow to stern, in one perfectly straight thousand-meter stretch. The oddly crystalline covering that coated the walls and ceiling was of a semi-translucent frosted white, so that a vague, ghostly image of the circuitry and components behind it could be seen beneath its smooth surface. Occasional shadowy movement darted randomly up and back beneath the cloudy glass, evidence of the tiny servicebots that moved forever silently throughout the ship, repairing the bio-neural circuitry and systems, and keeping the alien craft running like new, even after many hundreds of years. The sporadic portholes that were placed sparingly on the outside wall were filled by the swirling kaleidoscope of reds, yellows and blues of the gas giant Erie VII looming far beneath the ship's orbit, and those colors reflected through the iridescent crystal walls like a flowing aurora of shifting hues.

Dr. Cyyxill was a hulk of a khailian, his dark, graying fur and long, tangled mane still spotted with a few twisted strands of the light-chocolate brown of his youth. His elongated muzzle was overloaded with rows of protruding, pointed teeth, some darkened and broken, jutting out at random angles. His impressively large upper and lower tusks were now yellowed and spotted with age, and long, dark gouges now marred the once-glossy ivory surface. With his massive face leaning forward from the pronounced hunch in his back, he lumbered heavily down the crystalline corridor like some nightmare creature, his black eyes and fearsome appearance belying the true depth of this scientist's considerable integrity and compassion.

The term 'khailian scientist' was largely considered an oxymoron by the majority of intelligent species in the galaxy, and not without good reason. When hundreds of thousands of their kind had been violently abducted from their home some centuries ago, the khailian race forever lost their own culture and history to a life of forced servitude. Enslaved as both laborers and warriors, they were forced to assist a vast fleet of tyrannical aliens in stripping planet after planet of their natural resources.

Eventually, their captors died off, victims of a virus that emerged from the poor living conditions among the khailian—one that killed swiftly in the sealed environment of a spacecraft. The unaffected khailian, left stranded in a fleet of craft they had never been taught to pilot, spent years in the runaway ships, unable to decipher even the most basic of systems.

They passed forth from the Andromeda spiral, and for centuries, they crossed the mighty, black, starless expanse between galaxies until they reached the Milky Way. Generation after generation of khailian came and went on that long voyage, each in turn barely learning more than a fraction of how to control or repair the craft that housed them. Eventually, most came to believe that they, and the hundred or so ships in their fleet, were all there was to the universe.

As the centuries came and went, and the population dwindled to dangerously low numbers, ship after ship was left by the wayside. Food replicators could only provide a limited ration a day, so starvation and suffering became a way of life for the few hundred remaining khailian. Until one day, finally able to control their ships, they aimed the tattered fleet towards the strange bright lights of the Milky Way. The khailians now still lived in the same ships that brought them here, drifting in slow orbit around the lifeless gas giant Erie VII, hoping to carve out a better life for themselves, and their future generations.

Ridiculed for their pitiful lack of knowledge about their own inherited technology, the khailians became known as the slow-witted buffoons of their new galaxy. Largely ignored by the scientific, political, and trade communities, the khailian people struggle still to become a respected part of the galactic society. With their population swelling again, they seek a home of their own, governed by their own, and able to participate in the interplanetary commonwealth.

But without land, or industry, or a viable service to provide, the khailians had nothing to trade. The most impressive bits of technology that their people understood were quickly stolen and duplicated by megacorp pirates, long before the khailians grasped the concept of contracts or currency. With nothing left to offer, the fate of the khailian seemed grim. But Dr. Cyyxill had just had a breakthrough that promised to change all that, provided the enigmatic human who commissioned the work lived up to his end of the bargain.

The doctor paused at a sliding doorway opposite one of the portholes, and passed his massive hand in front of a scanning pad, causing the doors to his workshop to open and admit him. The room was dark, and cluttered with various machinery of both Coalition and alien design, taking up every square inch of counter space available. The khailian did not turn on the light, but instead waited until the doors closed behind him, and then peered into the darkness between two rows of shelves. His benefactor usually lingered in that shaded nook during these meetings, apparently in some effort to hide his identity.

"You are there? Mister?" he croaked in a deep throaty whisper. "Please to forgive... come have you now, lord?"

"I am here, Dr. Cyyxill," said a voice from the shadows, and a human male of middle age, clad in a long, hooded robe, stepped forward partially from the darkness. He lingered there, hovering at the edge of the dim. "The question is, *why* am I here? I instructed you not to contact me until the revised serum was ready."

"It ready now, yes my sir," the scientist explained. "I have work good proto... good pro...", he struggled as he spoke with a thick khailian accent, trying to form the proper sounds, and restrain the usual grunts and guttural growls that were a requisite of his native language. But the doctor had been a grown adult when his species first arrived in this galaxy, and he had struggled to learn the new language. As isolated as his people had remained from the other societies, he had seldom found cause to use it. Also, in many ways, Coalition common was just too delicate a language for his coarse anatomy.

"*Calm, Doctor.*" The ensensed human's voice now came to Dr. Cyyxill from within his own mind. It was an odd sensation—not like a voice he could hear with his ears. It was somewhat more like the internal monologue one uses when they read to themselves—though in this case, the monologue came of its own accord, and in the sounds of a stranger. "*We will speak this way. Now, why am I here?*"

The human had used this mode of communication with the khailian before, and so the doctor knew how to respond. It was less about thinking of the specific words, and more generally of just what you wanted to say. "*Yes, my lord, the serum and the device are now ready. I have developed a prototype that is ready for manufacture.*"

"I don't understand, Doctor," the human said. *"The sample you sent me just a few weeks ago proved useless. It did nothing new at all."*

"Yes sir, I understand that. But you see, I was missing an element from the equation," his thoughts answered quickly, now rushing ahead in excitement. *"The neural enhancement serum was working as intended,"* he continued, *"interpreting and amplifying brain activity in the way we hoped, but it was missing a transmission device for that thought energy."* Dr. Cyyxill pulled a small device from his pocket, the size and shape of a thick, molded, polymer bracelet, with the same frosted semi-transparent appearance as the walls of the ship. *"This is worn on the wrist, and in conjunction with the serum, it will focus that psionic energy and project it. This will enable it to do all those functions I had discussed. A remote neural interface with computer systems with an ease and speed far superior to any brain-link device, and with no external wire harness of any kind. I have even rigged the bracelet to inject the serum painlessly through the wrist with a jet-injector, as it is needed."*

"Excellent work, Doctor", the human replied, his thoughts conveying a genuine feeling of pleasure for the first time since he had first approached the khailian, almost a year ago. *"And tell me, what about the other functions we had discussed?"*

"You mean enhancement of ensensement abilities?" Dr. Cyyxill asked. *"Yes, the serum alone should enable any latent ensensement, and not just in humans, but perhaps in most species. It may have seemed to do nothing in your case, as it appears you already have all the abilities I have ever seen documented. But in theory, this device should magnify and boost transmission of those powers as well. I don't know how much until it is tested, the powers may be increased only minimally or by quite a bit. It may depend on the individual. But, as I have said in the past, that should not be the target market for such a device. Ensensed humans such as yourself are a rarity, an occasional genetic anomaly that would not serve as a large enough customer base... no offense to you, of course. We need to market this to the megacorps as a brainlink alternative, for computer control, navigation, servicebots, even..."*

"Yes, Doctor!" the human snapped aloud, his voice sharply breaking the quiet in the room, and no longer sounding pleased. Then, slipping back to the telepathy, *"So is this a working model you have here now?"* he reached out his hand toward the khailian.

"Yes, this is it," the doctor answered with some pride. *"I call it the Mindgate."* He reached out to pass the device into the shadows, and as his arm fully extended, an invisible force pulled the device free from his huge, hairy fingers. It flew quickly across the room to where the human caught it in his waiting hand. In addition to the telepathy, Dr. Cyyxill had also seen the man demonstrate this telekinesis before, so he was not overly taken

aback by the harmless-seeming trick. He heard the sound of the man clasping the device around his wrist and activating it. Dr. Cyyxill continued, *"This can be copied onboard our factory ship starting almost immediately... once we present everything to the rest of the council, of course. But that's a minor obstacle. As a leading member of the khailian board, we will have no problem getting their approval."*

"Steady, Doctor. Let's not get ahead of ourselves," the human's thoughts cautioned. *"Let's give this a test first."*

"Of course," Cyyxill answered. *"Let me get a computer ready to connect to."*

"No, you idiot!" The man barked out loud again, startling the khailian with the sudden shattering of the previously silent conversation. "I want to test its effect on ensensement."

Dr. Cyyxill was offended at the unprofessional insult, but decided to let it slide. "Yes, how you wish," his gravelly voice replied aloud, and then after a moment of consideration, he sent the thought, *"How much weight can you usually lift with your mind?"*

"Maybe twenty-five kilos," the man answered.

"Okay, so that's about the weight of this old scanner," the khailian said, pointing to a large device on the counter. *"Perhaps try and lift that, and then something else as well."*

The human focused on the scanner, raising his arm slightly as if to direct his thoughts in that direction. The bracelet on his arm emitted a small sound, that of a jet-injector delivering its contents, then glowed with a yellowish light as he motioned his fingers slightly in a lifting gesture. Quickly and easily the scanner lifted off the countertop, beginning a slow spin in the air above it. Then the human turned his attention to the other items on the counter, and with a similar motion, began lifting one after the other. Each piece of machinery, bulky and compact alike, lifted up effortlessly and began orbiting each other in the center of the room.

"You have done well, Dr. Cyyxill!" the human exclaimed out loud. "It requires no more effort than does the mere thought itself." He waved his fingers slightly and the items immediately stopped, then reversed the direction of their spinning at twice the speed. "I'll take the prototype to Gel Gonahaar immediately. I'll be making arrangements to use one of my factories there, as they are larger and more capable, and easily overlooked on a planet literally covered with similar industry. I need to keep this secret until I am ready to reveal it." He gazed up at the khailian. "I mean, of course... until it is ready for market."

The doctor looked confused. "I no understand," he said. Then with his thoughts, *"Our agreement was that the manufacturing would be done by the khailians. I need this industry for my people. That was the purpose of..."*

"Unfortunately, plans have changed," the human replied aloud. He waved his fingers to lightly replace all the once spinning equipment back on the counter—with perfect precision. "I don't have the time to wait for your small factory ships to prepare for production. My facility on Gel Gonahaar can be ready to begin now, and is much more secure." He then began heading deeper into the dark area between the shelves, toward the rear door that lay back there. "Don't worry though, Doctor. You'll be well paid for your work."

The khailian moved quickly towards the exiting human, and spoke quite loudly now, approaching a roar of frustration. "Not care for moneys!" he shouted. Then again, he transitioned back to telepathy. *"This was never about money for me, this was about bringing a viable industry and export to my people. I cannot allow you to take the device to be produced elsewhere."*

"I suggest strongly that you take a step back, Doctor," the man snarled viciously. "It is not your place to *allow* me anything. I paid you well for your work. I funded your research. The device is mine to manufacture where I wish."

"You still need the serum though," the khailian thought back to him. *"That is a derivative of the chemical my ancestor's captors used, to communicate and control my people telepathically. We have the only supply of that chemical in the galaxy, and so that serum can only be produced here. I will cut off your supply of the serum, and your devices will be useless, no matter where you manufacture them."* Then he growled aloud, his accent even thicker in his aggravation. "I cut you supply. No more do you get!"

human now stepped out completely from the shadows, and was in full, clear view for the first time since the doctor had initially met him. As he had always suspected, the man's efforts to hide his identity were misspent, as the khailian scientist was neither a follower of human culture, nor current events, so even if the gentleman who had just emerged from the dark before him was someone of any note, Dr. Cyyxill certainly didn't recognize him. He had tanned skin, and brownish hair touched with gray— like any of another billion humans—and to the khailian he was completely indistinguishable from any other. What was easily distinguishable, however, was the expression on the man's face, one that translated universally between the races. Anger—and hate.

"You mind yourself, Doctor. Don't you think I have others just waiting in line to replace you on your silly council, others that have shown more loyalty to me than you are currently demonstrating?"

"Not, I not believe," the khailian said.

"Your lab assistant, Dr. Grivvux, he would be next in line for your council seat if something happened to you, would he not?" The man stood now a mere two feet from the chest of the fearsome-appearing khailian, staring upward at the doctor's huge and mighty frame without a hint of trepidation. "In fact, he and I have had many conversations about that exact situation."

"Enough!" Dr. Cyyxill bellowed in a barely intelligible roar, as he raised his huge arm to strike down the puny figure before him. "Enough steal from khailian! Too much!"

The human waved his arm slightly, and the khailian's mighty incoming fist froze in mid-air, a look of confusion on his face as he seemed to struggle to move against an unseen force. The device on the human's wrist was glowing with a pulsating, yellow light.

"*My* kind," the human spat at him between gritted teeth, "would hunt you ugly, ignorant animals for ivory, and wear your fur as coats, you giant, stinking ox!"

Another small wave of the human's hand sent Dr. Cyyxill reeling backward through the air, slamming hard against the wall near the entrance to the room. He did not fall to the floor though, but remained somehow suspended, pinned with his head pressing roughly against the ceiling.

"You have done good work for me, Doctor, and have been extremely useful. Now, you will serve one final use to me".

With a small gesture of the human's hand, along with an ensuing resurgence in the glow of the bracelet, Dr. Cyyxill felt a pull against the front of his muzzle. Just a tugging at first, but then quickly growing into an immense yank. He let loose a deafening bellow of pain, as his two huge, thick upper tusks snapped like dry kindling near their base, pulling forward completely out of his gums to clatter against the shelves in the shadowed alcove. The resulting holes where the mighty teeth once sat filled quickly with blood, seeping from the edges of the denuded tissue, and a black marrow substance oozed from the center of the ivory's raw and exposed roots.

"You will serve as an example for your successor!" the human now shouted over the howls of the suspended and bleeding khailian. "An illustration of the importance I place on loyalty! And, on obedience!"

Then again the pulling began against his face, this time challenging his lower jaw. As the tension slowly increased, the khailian strained against it to keep his mouth closed. But as the force grew stronger, his chin pulled painfully forward, and his jaw dislocated from his cheekbone with a loud pop, as the tendons that usually held it in place snapped back upward into his face. His jaw was now protruding from his muzzle in a horrendously exaggerated under-bite, holding on only by the waning tensile strength of the skin and tissue beneath. Then the two small lower tusks finally broke free as well, sailing across the room to join their former counterparts on the floor.

Dr. Cyyxill felt another sensation now, as the human glared at him cruelly and again made a slight gesture. It was like a dozen hands along his back, first pulling and tearing at the seam of his long, thin overcoat, until it was ripped open in the rear from collar to hemline. The outfit he wore beneath it soon followed, and the wall felt cold and hard against his exposed backside. Then again he felt them, the invisible fingers combing through his matted fur along his spine, exposing the skin beneath. They clawed and ripped into his flesh as they had with his coat, like row upon row of talons, pulling and peeling a long open gash from his neck to his tailbone, and down the back of each leg as he screamed out in pain.

The human paused then for a moment, waiting for Dr. Cyyxill to catch his breath, and the shouts of agony to subside a bit. He looked down at the thick band glowing brightly on his right wrist with a pleased expression. Then he slowly curled his lip a bit and furrowed his brow in thought. "I wonder, Doctor," he said aloud, in a suddenly conversational tone, "if it really needed to be a bracelet. It's just... I've never really been one for jewelry. Maybe something worn under the clothes would be better suited. An amulet perhaps, or a belt. Ah! Or a set of gauntlets!"

The tortured doctor started to whisper weakly, but the human did not allow him to finish. He looked back up, motioned his hands again, and in one slow and steady movement, the khailians skin began to tear away from his body as he screamed out, first outwards from his spine and across his back to his flanks, then peeling and ripping across his chest and abdomen. The underside of the woolly dermis glistened wet and red, and the newly exposed muscle and tissue beneath began almost immediately to weep blood from a thousand sheared capillaries. The doctor continued to wail in one long, deep, gut-wrenching cry as the flesh tore free from his waist and his legs, and finally hovered out in front of him like a giant gory carpet. Pulling still away, it peeled down his arms, turning those sleeves of skin inside out as it went, like a hastily removed jacket.

The screams stopped suddenly now, as Dr. Cyyxill finally succumbed to the shock and fell unconscious, or perhaps ultimately and mercifully died. The human did not care much as to which. He quickly tossed the skin across the room simply by willing it to do so, then allowed the pealed carcass to fall heavily to the floor. The glow of the bracelet flickered, and then faded completely. Turning back toward the shadows between the shelves, he disappeared into the darkness.

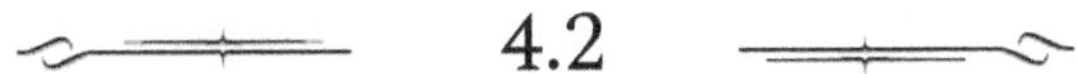

4.2

BULLSEYE SAT APATHETICALLY LEANING FORWARD in his chair, the seti's elbows planted firmly against his knees to prop him in his slouched position. His eyes stared down blankly at the stage, tracing each of the flowing grains and imperfections in the polished wooden floorboards, back and forth, in a hypnotic pattern, even as his mind drifted through thoughts a million light-years away.

He wore today the suit of the university president, both literally and figuratively, so was dressed in a manner fitting to his position, and was expected to perform as such as well. He wore a traditionally formal seti sherwani, asymmetrically tailored in navy blue silk. The button strewn left half of the garment was a field of plain indigo, overlapping a right half adorned with a gold, patterned filigree. A decorative broach on his right chest and another on his left shoulder were festooned by five gilded chains, each longer than the one above it, so that they hung across his chest in a close series of sweeping arcs. The short ebony fur of his mane-less head was brushed to a lustrous sheen, and the gray curtain of beard that grew from his chin and jawline was crisply manicured to precisely three inches. The silver-touched facial hair was his only feature that contrasted with his fleece of midnight black, except perhaps the gleam of his blazing, amber eyes, which could mesmerize equally whether laden with malice or melancholy—the only two sentiments they seemed to possess as of late.

He had been absent from last season's graduation ceremony of his namesake school, perhaps the most important one to him in the twenty-year history of the institution. Rook's son, Flashpoint, the class valedictorian and arguably one of the best students to ever walk through the halls of the school, was graduating at that affair. Bullseye had not forgiven himself for his own absence, even though Rook, Belladonna, and even Flashpoint himself had, but the circumstances that had kept him away were, at the time, insurmountable.

The school's Vice Chairman, Board of Admissions, Dean of Students, Class President, and the Alumni Association had all also not forgiven Bullseye. He received message after message from each of them, detailing how a second absence would affect the graduating class, the morale of the student body, and future enrollment. Thus, he dragged himself reluctantly back to Earth, if for no other reason than to quell the barrage of petitions, and now sat slumped and spiritless before the assembled second session graduates, their families, and their assorted loved ones. The Dean of Students was droning on endlessly at the podium through the same antiquated and tiresome speech about school pride that he read twice a year. Bullseye kept his eyes toward the stage floor through the seemingly endless narrative, partially due to the aftereffects of a late solo nightcap that left his head throbbing, but mainly to avoid the familiar faces of the young students seated in the audience before him.

Bullseye long had a gift for remembering faces—a gift that, over the years, had slowly transformed itself into a dark and terrible curse. As a youth, the seti enforcer felt the same as any true warrior about the uglier side of his profession. Handing out death to all those who opposed his mission, and accepting the possibility of his own early demise, were both integral parts of the life of a mercenary. His adversaries knew the risk they took when they stood against him and his team, and while he never took any pleasure from the snuffing out of an enemy's life, he likewise carried no burden of regret for the souls he took.

But something began to change over the years, as the faces of his foes slowly became younger and younger. Many of the minor guards and soldiers whom Parliament inevitably faced on their way to undo some evil overlord or criminal had no idea of the true nature, or plans, of their leaders. These were ignorants and innocents, played as pawns by their masters, scattered before Parliament like roadblocks on some obstacle course. Still, never was there a moment's hesitation of Bullseye's finger against the trigger, and the body count of these faultless and naive victims to his exceptional skills grew forever higher. And, as Bullseye quickly learned to his dismay, he could recall each of the stunned and terror-frozen faces of the guiltless young casualties that fell before him.

It was for those reasons he originally founded this school. In his life, so full of destruction and chaos, he needed something constructive and positive to pour his energies into. The Bullseye Enforcer School was born, and for many years it helped provide him balance knowing that he could pay back some of what he had taken, that for each young life he violently stole away, he could enrich tens of others with the benefit of his experience. He lectured at many classes himself, was often seen giving one-on-one advice at one of the holo-ranges, and held frequent open discussion seminars with his top students. While he still battled the ghosts of his past prey, especially in the darkness of his mind when he tossed fitfully in his sleep, he had genuine hope that his existence, when the final tally was added up, would be seen as beneficial in the end.

Bullseye suddenly glanced up from the floor then, as the blinding spotlight from across the theater cast its aura around him. The auditorium was a large, oval-sided, glass dome, situated on a small island, centered in the large pond of the campus's east lawn. It was evening outside, and squinting through the spotlight, he could see the multicolored lights beneath the surface of the waters outside had been turned on, giving the view through the glass walls a surreal, glowing effect. Apparently, while lost in thought, he had missed the end of the Dean's speech, as well as his own introduction that always immediately followed. The dean now stood one step to the side of the podium, smiling and applauding with the audience as he stared back at Bullseye—but with a worried look in his eyes over the seti's apparent lack of attention. Bullseye stood slowly, shading his eyes with his hand from the relentless, screaming beam of the spotlight, drilling straight into his already-pounding brain, and approached the podium at the center of the stage. The audience slowly ceased its applause, sitting silent now as they awaited their head instructor's words of wisdom and encouragement.

However, he no longer had any to give.

Bullseye stared at each graduate's face in turn, studying every feature in detail. This school and these students, like the ones before them, had once been the saving grace of Bullseye's helter-skelter existence. But they had turned against him, and this one refuge from his own self-loathing was now yet another millstone around the seti's neck. It first started several years back, during a mission that came to be known in the news as the Proteus Deception, that Bullseye's efforts with the school began to backfire. That was the first time, though unfortunately not the last, that the seti took the life of one of his own students.

Bullseye Enforcer School did more than teach weaponry and battle tactics. With classes like stellar cartography and navigation, advanced warp theory, and several alien languages classes, it helped generate the most prepared and well-rounded enforcers an institution can produce. But one class they did not teach was ethics, as such lessons of morality have no place in the education, nor in the mind, of the killing machines they created.

Students graduated gung-ho for their fortune and fame—or their fortunes anyway—and graduates of the school were highly sought after. With no moral instruction to impede the life before them, no measure of conscience to weigh them down, they often took the path of highest financial reward. And, more often than not, the highest paying work for an untested enforcer came in the form of security for unscrupulous megacorps, underworld criminals, and political dictators—precisely the sort of organizations that Parliament faced on a regular basis. Bullseye found that with rapidly increasing frequency, the faces of the innocents he murdered in the course of his job were ones he had once seen here, in this very auditorium—at a ceremony just like this one. He was now murdering the very students he was training, and in a terrible circle of cause and effect, he had become doubly responsible for their premature deaths. Therefore, any redemption he sought through his efforts to train these young ones was now and forever irrevocably lost.

Bullseye looked back and forth at the youthful and immature faces, seeing in them the naivete he once possessed himself, and it made him feel at once very tired, and very old. He did not himself realize how uncomfortably long he had been standing there in silence, until he heard the loud throat clearing of the Dean behind him urging him to begin.

Bullseye glanced down at the prompter on the podium top, and with a quiet and unenthusiastic voice, began his prepared speech. "My pride now swells as I gaze out upon you honored few, knowing you looked dead upon the greatest obstacles before you, and said 'you will overcome', and overcome you have. Now is the time for…"

"Speak up!" someone shouted from the back few rows of the crowded auditorium.

A smattering of chuckles arose from random areas of the assembly in response to the rude interruption. Bullseye suddenly became irrationally furious at the students seated before him, these simple and guileless juveniles who understood nothing of the gift of innocence they rushed so quickly to throw away. These naive children who marched headlong into what they considered to be honor, never stopping to appreciate the value of their own adolescence. A harsh and fearsome scowl from Bullseye brought the giggling audience to a sudden and absolute silence.

Bullseye looked once more at his speech, full of colorful lies and empty platitudes, and then reached down to shut the prompter off. He glared for a moment at the young people below, and then finally started again to speak. "It has been written," he began, in a clear loud voice, "that the flower of youth is a precious thing. But only those to whom it is but a memory can measure its true value. All too soon the springtime has passed, and the wilted petals lie strewn around the black and brittle stem. What sacrifice then would you not deliver up, when the chill of approaching winter bears down hard upon your bones, for one last, dear breath of its salubrious bouquet?"

The assembled guests, who had gathered for words of congratulations and praise, now stared up at Bullseye with a look of silent confusion—which only served to upset the seti even more.

Now his voice as he continued became full of anger and frustration. "Take heed, '*bold wanderers!*' You who seek to pass the best of your years in pursuit of shallow glory! Take heed... for youth's flower is fragile also, and easily crushed."

The seti turned his back then to the still silent crowd, and left the stage, and the ceremony, and headed immediately for home.

Several weeks later, he sat alone in the study of his estate, on the seti homeworld of K'Tas T'Mir. Several of the rooms in the expansive dwelling he had not entered in many years, and indeed, there were a number of doorways on the upper levels that, if you asked, he could not tell you where they led. He instead maintained himself in some few rooms on the first floor of the north wing: the kitchen, his bedchamber and his bath, and of course the study where he spent the majority of his time. The space may have appeared a bit cluttered to an outsider, but to Bullseye, it was his comfort and his haven, a place where he could retreat to from the outside worlds, and the weight of his own psyche.

The room, as was the rest of the home, was done in the traditional seti architecture style. The light-brown stucco walls of the study began as perpendicular to the floor, then sloped inward in the classic pyramidal shape, to form a high pointed ceiling. The floor was laid with meticulously fitted natural stone of varying cuts, using the textured gray granite indigenous to the region. A large intricately hand-woven rug of dark maroon, brown and mustard helped bring a feeling of warmth to the space, and an arched fireplace in one of the corners crackled with a fiery glow. The furnishings were all heavy—ornately carved of thick, dark wood or upholstered in brown or black leathers. A few antique and quite valuable tapestries of ancient seti battle scenes brought color to the inclined walls, and a vast collection of large and small knick-knacks, some personal and some ornamental, were displayed on shelves and desktops and end tables, or hung on walls.

Bullseye sat in a deep, winged leather reading chair made of dark ferox hide, sipping a few fingers of Zet A'zeta from an oversized pot-bellied glass with a short stem and narrow opening. The potable was made from the aged extract of the xinthia root, a tropical ground-hugging vine whose distilled nectar had an almost narcotic effect, allowing Bullseye to calm his sometimes-chaotic thoughts. Xinthia was rare, and hard to refine, so at several thousand credits per bottle the elixir was far from economical. But to Bullseye, the few moments of uninterrupted sleep it granted were well worth the exorbitant price.

He poured himself yet another glass as he sat and read over printouts of his weekly hate mail. Yet another condemnation from an irate parent over his latest graduation speech, followed by a few of the standard oaths of vengeance for lost brothers, lost parents, and lost friends that Bullseye allegedly struck down in the course of his duties. Of course, there were also the usual brazen challenges from arrogant young up-and-comers, seeking to dethrone the famous enforcer magnate, and by doing so, improve their own standing. Last was a message that he received once each year or so for the past three decades, from a woman in New Boston, detailing how her life was impaired *this* month by the long absence of her parents. Their lives had been collateral damage of a grenade Bullseye had thrown in the Chez Luis restaurant, on the very night that Parliament had first met. He had no real memory of the couple, nor the event of their death, but had endured a close relationship with these periodic handwritten letters since they first began arriving from a mere child some thirty years ago—though at that time full of misspellings, and scrawled in crayon. He never answered them.

He sat in thought for a few moments when he finished reading the letters, then topped off the dwindling libation in his glass, and stood to throw the papers in the blazing fireplace. He staggered a bit as he did so, perhaps having had a bit too much to drink, but caught himself quickly on the edge of his desk, and used it as a crutch to help him cross the room. The note from the New Boston woman he did not burn, but placed it carefully on a pile of similar correspondence, stacked neatly on a shelf, and bundled with twine. He stumbled back to his seat and fell down into it, immediately taking another swig of his beverage.

He began to consider the challenges he had received, thinking perhaps those might make a fitting end to his nightmare. The ghosts of his slain now haunted him nightly, and it was quickly becoming more than he could bear. Perhaps if he had not arranged his life in such seclusion, perhaps if he had someone at home like Rook and Stansky did. A companion to ease his burden, to tell him that everything would be all right, to reassure him that what he spent his life doing was honorable, and to tell him that it was perhaps okay to stop now. But there was no one—nor did he believe there would be. And so death seemed the only reasonable way out. He had, after all, done his bit for king and country, and he grew weary of his guilt for those who were sacrificed along the way. And so, he waited, year after year, and with ever-growing impatience for the long sleep to claim him.

Suicide, of course, was in no way an option, and a concept that never remotely factored into Bullseye's conscience. He would not be allowed to rejoin the Fallen after his death if he chose such a cowardly way to die. But to lose his life in battle against one of his young challengers would be both an acceptable and honorable death. If only another mission would come along, perhaps he could give his life at the side of Parliament, as he always believed he was destined to do.

He finished his drink, and then another, until those ideas went away. Then he sat for some time, lost in the euphoria of the xinthia root, his thoughts drifting aimlessly, unable to take hold. He jumped a bit in his seat when the subspace communicator went off, then sat where he was, and let the transmission go to the computer. He was not feeling up to a conversation at the moment. When he had gathered himself a bit, he staggered back to his desk and hit a few keys on the monitor there. The computer began to play back the missed message.

"Greetings Bullseye, and all of Parliament," a hoarse and authoritarian voice declared, through a thick chamai accent. *"This is General Nylis, of the Oberonn Aerospace Defense Command. You may recall, you and I met and spoke briefly after the incident on the penal asteroid, oh... some few years back now. I hope you'll forgive me... if I left a bad impression on you at that time. It was a stressful situation then, as I am sure you'll agree. At any rate... my government wishes to retain your services, for a small task involving some military schematics... encrypted schematics... we believe stolen by a small local would-be terrorist outfit. Admittedly, the mission is a simple one, but due to some... let's say 'political considerations' that I'm not at liberty to go into, we are unable to act on the theft ourselves. I'll be happy to give you full details, if you could contact me at your earliest convenience."*

"End of transmission," the computer said.

Bullseye found it odd that the chamai government would be calling them, as they had never worked together before. And it sounded to be a mission that Parliament might be a bit overqualified for, but those thoughts soon gave way to hope that this could be Bullseye's chance to finally join the Fallen. Usually he would have rejected such a job offer out of hand, but resolved to accept this one, in hopes that it may be his last. He headed back to his chair, but tripped on the carpet, dropping his glass to shatter hard against the stone floor. He became enraged at the spilled Zet A'zeta, and with a roar, roughly threw over the small end table, smashing the bottle containing the rest of the liqueur onto the ground—further adding to the shards of his already broken glass.

Bullseye steadied himself and procured another bottle from the cabinet next to his chair. He drank deeply straight from the decanter, a final self-medication to prepare him for sleep. The seti chugged a few more gulps, until he was sure he would rest through the evening, then clattered the bottle down hard, and lurched dizzily out of the room.

Later that night, when he was passed out naked on the toilet, swaying and rocking in his unconscious stupor, his mind rested easily, and did not see the faces that usually haunt him in his dreams. And when, after an hour or so, he finally toppled over sideways to split his scalp open violently against the edge of the gold bathtub, he did not wake, even as the blood slowly trickled onto the cold, marble floor.

PART II

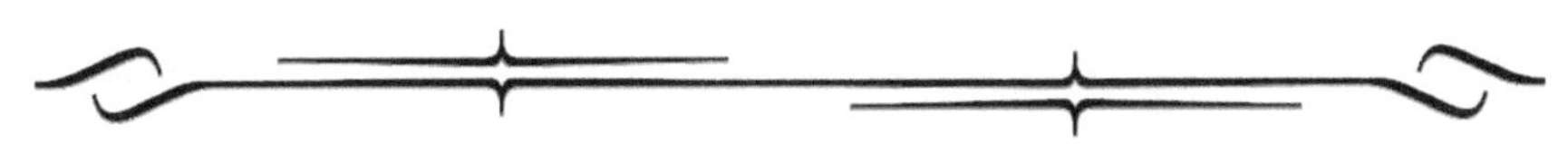

TANGLED

WEBS

Chapter 5.1

"*Negative! Negative Bugeye!*" Bullseye replied through the radio in his helmet. He charged forward at full speed through the densely overgrown forest, shouting over the thunderous rain of autocannon fire impacting the trees and rocks around him, and occasionally ricocheting off his heavy battle armor. "*Evac alpha is a no go! Repeat, no go for alpha! Proceed to bravo site! Over!*"

"*Roger that, evac bravo site,*" Bullit answered. "*I'm gonna have to take the long way around to avoid those AE500s by the roadside. ETA around 10 minutes, over.*"

"*Understood!*" Bullseye shouted back.

Parliament's leader looked back over his bulky armored shoulder, making sure his other comrades were still in tow, running behind him. Rook was close on his heels, sprinting with Bullseye as fast as his armor would allow. James Stansky, in one of his many huge, protective suits, was about six meters back, pitching pre-made heurcanium charges against the bark of trees as he passed, with an expertise born more of experience than of practice, and sticking them to the now doomed foliage every twenty meters or so. Tachion Magna was not too far behind him, their medic bringing up the rear in a sprint that, while far slower than the others, could be considered lightning fast for an android.

Bullseye reached a semicircle of dark, tightly packed granite boulders that jutted out from the forest floor at the base of a steep hill. He quickly ducked in behind the miniature henge for a moment of rest and safety. The others followed suit, and for a minute there was no sound beyond the heavy, gasping breaths of the organic members, and a whoosh of steam exhausted from Tachion as he diverted internal coolant to his overheated leg joints.

The mountains here in the far northern hemisphere of Oberonn extended for thousands of acres in every direction. While the temperature and humidity were both quite oppressive, as was typical for the Oberonn global climate in general, the long, cold winters in the northern region, made possible by the planet's axis, created the dense deciduous forest landscape that they currently moved through. Unlike the sweeping tropical jungles that covered almost eighty percent of the planet, these woodlands were more reminiscent of the forests on K'Tas T'Mir, or Earth—other than the near ninety-degree weather, in what was now only mid-spring.

Some two hundred years or so ago, these mountains were practically covered with factories, mines, and refineries, all seeking to extract and purify the huge deposits of athelium that lay beneath its jagged surface. Necessary for regulating the negative energy reactions in translight warp engines of the period, the precious mineral was hunted relentlessly, and these pristine mountains were left naked and scarred by the drilling and strip mining of the megacorps. But once a synthetic version of the valuable compound was successfully created, the factories and mines were abandoned, and the mountains were returned to nature. A few small boomtown encampments still popped up from time to time, nestled between the trees, and vanishing again just as quickly. These hastily erected tent and cretespray villages consisted of groups of old prospectors, who yet scoured the old mines and panned the streams for the mineral, which still had some small value as a semiprecious jewelry stone.

It was one of these abandoned enclaves, set up alongside one of the old, dilapidated, and now overgrown athelium mills, which had been designated as the evac bravo site. But the steep hillside they were now up against stood in the path to that mill, meaning they would now either have to go around it, or over it.

The group looked back through small gaps between the boulders that now gave them cover, and watched as no less than thirty multi-legged warbots crashed ungracefully through the underbrush, moving towards their position. James stared eagerly at the group of deadly automatons, his heavily armored finger poised over the computer panel on his opposite forearm. He studied the position of each charge that he had thrown, and the arrangement of the warbots, waiting for the exact right moment to cause the maximum possible havoc.

"Okay, pyro, do your thing," Rook urged him anxiously.

"Not yet... wait for it."

"They are getting a tad close, James," Tachion added. *"Perhaps you should..."*

"Jesus! I don't tell you guys how to do your jobs, do I? Just wait a minute. Give 'em a few more steps." The human continued to watch intently, patiently waiting for just the right moment. The warbots closed to fifty meters, then forty. *"Okay, any second now... any second... just a few more feet... and... Now! Fire in the hole!"* He pushed down hard against the panel on his arm, and while there was no explosion, his helmet lamps did turn on.

"What the fuck are you doing?" Rook begged, *"blow it already!"*

James glared at the panel and tried to hit the key again. But his hand was trembling noticeably, and once more he pressed the wrong button, this time activating his medic help-beacon.

"You rang?" Tachion asked sarcastically.

"Shut it!" James barked at the android. He balled his quivering hand into a fist, and mashed down hard on as many keys as he could. The forest beyond the boulders erupted like a volcano, tree branches and warbot parts thrown in all directions, as a row of massive fireballs rose above the forest canopy. The explosion was deafening, the shockwave causing a small avalanche of stones and debris to cascade down the steep hillside behind them, pelting the team with rocks and dust.

Rook peered around the boulder to confirm the destruction, and satisfied, turned back to Stansky. *"Why in the hell do you not have those detonators brainlinked, and just trigger them with a thought?"*

"It's not the same that way," James responded.

Rook's helmeted head cocked to a slight angle in a questioning manner.

"Well, you don't get that same 'click, boom' satisfaction with a brainlink," James explained. *"It's just so much more... gratifying... to push a button."*

Rook's helmet rotated in silence toward the rest of the group, then back to Stansky. Then he shook it back and forth in mimed exasperation.

Bullseye moved towards the base of the hill and glanced upward, scanning slowly back and forth, surveying the bluff above them. *"Brainlink or button, the means matters not. The jeopardy has been neutralized, though that fortune may be fleeting."* He typed on the keypad of his armor's left gauntlet, causing a holographic map to project above his forearm, outlining the terrain around them, the obstacles before them, and the hill above. The extraction point was marked with a pulsing red glow, and as the group leaned in around Bullseye to study the landscape, it was clear that the steep ridge stood between them and their goal.

So far, they had already dealt with more than they bargained for, far more than General Nylis had suggested in his briefing. The plan was to quietly infiltrate, secure the intelligence center of this band of terrorists—*alleged* terrorists—and keep guard over the perimeter, while Rook slunk in to retrieve the files. They hoped to recover them before they were able to be decrypted. But all these were General Nylis' tactics, not their own, and if there was any place Parliament's record was more dismal than sticking to a game plan, it was in doing what they were told.

They abandoned that course of action almost as soon as they reached the forest. Scans of the area from the *Bugeye* showed what they expected—a makeshift encampment, comprised of a few dozen soldiers, and basic armaments. But what was suspicious, is what it didn't show.

Any sign of forest life.

The woodlands in this region were teeming with all manner of creatures, great and small, yet the acres surrounding the encampment proved devoid of any life signs—according to their sensors, anyway. A deeper investigation showed their scans were being blocked, no mean feat for a ragtag guerrilla group. It would require technology that, on first appearances, they should not have.

Something didn't add up, math that Parliament was used to calculating, and so the scripted raid was abandoned, and they came at it from another angle. Literally. They entered from the opposite side, passing directly through the 'lifeless' corridor, and much to no one's surprise, found it not so empty as they were led to believe.

Soldiers, warbots, vehicles, equipment—a stronghold worthy of any megacorp militia or regional government army. It didn't take long for things to turn ugly, although they did manage to retrieve the file, and destroy the intelligence center in the process. Now, making their way out was proving more challenging than the way in.

All in all, fairly typical.

"Well? Which is it then, fearless leader?" Rook asked, staring up at the hillside in front of them. *"Are we going over, around, or through?"*

"I shall assume your third option to be a comedic one," Bullseye responded, unamused. He gazed up at the hill again. *"Although a superior vantage would be not unwelcome, the way around is more expeditious. We shall shadow the course of the hillside, till it curves us to the evac site."*

"Yeah, not so fast," Stansky said. *"I'm detecting explosives along the slope here. There might be a minefield of booby-traps in those brambles, and we don't have time for me to find and disarm them all."*

Four sets of eyes peered up the hillside, grudgingly followed by four sets of legs.

The climb was steep, and difficult, and was made even more so by the ambient heat, and the weight of armor. The cover of the evergreens faded quickly, as the top of the low ridge became bare exposed granite. Veining of gray ran through wide, flat stone dark as coal, and the rocks' blackened color, with the sun's exposure, drove the thermometer to nearly intolerable.

Tachion stopped them near the top, where the ground grew more leveled before dipping downward again. *"I'm picking up a structure up above,"* he told them. *"Something small, but it's got power running to it."*

Bullseye peered through the scope of his long rifle, then pulled his eye away in frustration. *"A pillbox,"* he said. *"With the muzzle of a laser cannon projected forth."*

Bullit radioed in from the *Bugeye* cockpit. *"If you've got another AE500 turret up there, I can't get close to you. It'll pick me off from a mile out."*

"A truth of which we are keenly aware," Bullseye assured him. *"Hold your guarded distance, till we beckon you forth."*

"Rodger," Bullit acknowledged.

"Doctor, do you detect any life sign?" the seti leader asked the android.

"No, negative. It seems to be automated, and unmanned."

"Very well then, you and James proceed down. Ascertain if mayhap the landing site needs securing."

"Got it."

"Rook, care to join me in a further climb? See if we might bend this petty hindrance and turn it to our advantage?"

"Sure, why not?" Rook replied with a begrudging sigh. *"I've been thinking of training for Everest, anyway."*

The small concrete fortification sat at the very apex of the hill's peak, shaped to fit in with the jagged granite, and of a color to match as well. The pair kept low as they approached, uneager to have the weapon target them, but it seemed the protocol which it followed was more interested in the skies above, than the hill behind.

Bullseye stood, then walked directly over to the cretespray cubicle. *"What opinion are you of,"* he asked his fellow seti, *"might we disable its program. Or better, turn it against those it now protects?"*

"Yeah," Rook said, kneeling beside a panel on the structure's side. *"I suspect I can change its mind about who's more interesting to aim at."* He reached into his techkit, and within mere moments had popped the cover loose, connecting his system bypass, and typing into it furiously.

Bullseye gazed out from atop their perch on the wide barren stone of the incline's peak. Far below, a river wound, making its way toward a lake-filled valley. High above, the mountains loomed, looking down on them and their relatively insignificant climb. And all around, a world of green, the forest stretching her branches from sky to sky. *"James? Doctor? How have you fared on your journey down?"*

"Well, so far so good," Stansky answered over the comlink, *"although we've come to a high wall blocking our way, so I'm gonna have to make a bit of a ruckus."*

"You? Noisy?" Rook interjected sarcastically. *"You're usually so quiet I forget you're even here."*

"Ah. Well, in that case, here's a reminder."

The thunderclap of an explosion cracked through the valley down below, resounding off the surrounding mountains to echo back to them again and again.

Rook shook his head in exasperation, continuing to reprogram the weapon's targeting computer.

Far below, James and Tachion stepped through their newly formed entrance in the concrete wall, heading into the evac bravo site, and carefully scanning all around them as they made sure the area was clear. There was a myriad of abandoned structures, some still partly standing, others only remnant outlines of weather-beaten foundations, but each draped in a verdant coat of climbing weeds and hanging mosses. There were plenty of half-standing walls and shadowy alcoves that one could lurk behind. But their scans showed nothing yet—nothing moving, nothing alive.

They moved out rapidly but with caution, James checking from building to building through the tattered remains of the little ghost town, the doctor walking the perimeter, inspecting the rest of the crumbling wall for breaches to be aware of.

"Evac bravo secure," Stansky reported. *"Bullit, I'm setting up a beacon in the center of the clearing."*

"Roger that. Rook, you got that cannon taken care of yet?"

"He has," Bullseye answered. *"The way is passable. Begin your approach."*

James returned to find Tachion near a crumbled gap in the wall, just north of the one he himself had made, staring at the ground with his visor up. The damp soil here was churned; loamy clumps kicked up and tussled, the tall weeds beaten down in a wide pathway facing uphill. "What is it?" Stansky asked, popping his facemask up as well.

"What do you make of this?" the doctor asked. "A vehicle?"

"Mmm. Not unless it rode on treads. And if there were several of them. Look, there's no gap between tire marks. It's just flattened from end to end."

"This bent grass is fresh, the exposed dirt is still wet," Tachion said. "This just happened, perhaps minutes ago. If it were a row of vehicles, we would have heard it."

"Plus, that rubble of the wall hasn't been disturbed," James pointed out. "It's like... something heavy trampled the grass, and then just stepped over that."

Tachion shook his head. "Dammit. Or lots of somethings." He closed his helmet visor, calling to his teammates over the comlink. *"Bullseye, Rook, you've got warbots inbound from our position. A dozen or more, and they're a few minutes ahead of..."*

"Your warning is appreciated, though unpunctual!" Bullseye shouted back. *"We have already encountered them!"*

The sounds of heavy gunfire rolled towards them down the mountain.

5.2

THE MODESTLY SIZED, YET MORE than adequate hangar bay of the *Parliament One* was tightly lined with various aerospace craft, each angled neatly in its place against the gray conduit-lined walls. The hangar crew was well paid to keep them all finely tuned and polished—with wings folded and ammunition charged—each ready to launch at a moment's notice.

The mercenary group had taken to naming their current fleet of vehicles for their fallen brethren, the honored designations printed proudly on the fuselages and tail wings of each of the uniformly painted ships.

The *Emmett* was a 606 Volant, named after a human friend of Bullseye who had died on the very day that the original group had formed nearly a third of a century ago—the pleasure of knowing him in person now unfamiliar to anyone but their seti leader. As the last surviving original members, only Bullseye and James Stansky carried firsthand memories of two other namesakes. The 143 Cipher, christened the *Damien Knight*, and A64 Halberd dubbed the *Intim*, were the lone reminders of Parliament's forefathers—when the group was just one of many such mercenary teams carving a reputation for themselves in Earth's city of New Boston. Twin XE/7 Ironhawks commemorated later losses to the team, with the names *McKendrick* and *Mishta*. And their most recently sacrificed member, lost some fifteen years ago now, was immortalized in the form of the mighty plasma-spitting 533 Ahab—the *Dodger*. These six ships, confiscated from diverse foes over the past couple of decades, sat three on each side of the starship's hangar bay, leaving just enough space in the center landing area for Parliament's oldest, most useful, and most battle-tested spacecraft.

The BG/i90 Bug-I Surveillance and Recognizance Shuttle was known to all as simply that, the *Bugeye*. This is not because its hull morbidly awaited the death of another Parliament member to claim its title. In fact, the *Bugeye* was the first space-faring vehicle 'obtained' by the then fledgling band, and ever since they had referred to it by that simple moniker.

In addition to the absence of a name being present on the *Bugeye*'s exterior, it also had no registry number. In fact, it had no visible markings at all, which was in direct violation of Starlaw Transportation Commission requirements. Moreover, the transponder had been removed, making the ship both unidentifiable by sensor, and blatantly illegal to operate within Coalition systems. But, by far their greatest violation, was the installation of a stolen drak'min cloaking system, which went directly against the interstellar laws of every known planet, as agreed to in their various treaties with the Drak'min Empire. But the name Parliament still held a place of certain notoriety, even now, years after their most infamous exploits, and on the infrequent occasions that the group reunited for a mission, the need for some anonymity was still often paramount.

This is not the only reason that the group so heavily relied upon the old *Bugeye*. At the time of its production, the BG/i90 was the fastest ship of its size, loaded with the most advanced sensor systems created to date, and a sensor cloak which made it nearly undetectable to the technology of the day. But even by the time Parliament had first claimed it as booty after one of their early missions, the ship's design was dated, and the equipment inside had become all but obsolete. Throughout the years, though, custom updates had been installed, making the antique invaluable on almost any mission.

Originally capable of holding two pilots, and up to eighteen armored soldiers, packed tightly on parallel benches in the single interior cabin, the seats had been long ago ripped out, and roomy individual stations had been incorporated instead. Rook himself had supervised the installation of these complex systems, each with a specialized array of computers and programs that now served as the Science, Operations, and Tactical/Communication posts.

Along the aft firewall, which divided the crew space from the engines, Tachion had created a compact sickbed and surgical suite. It consisted of a top of the line biobed that projected and retracted from the rear wall, a full complement of medical sensors and displays, and a small cubicle of basic lab equipment for testing samples and substances. A cleanroom forcefield projector kept infectious germs out when conducting surgery, and could be reversed to keep them in for patients under quarantine.

The remainder of the available space near the rear was taken up with a row of large lockers, filled with scramblers for holding their armor and weapons, plus all the ammo they could carry. A few additional seats that folded down from the wall were available when needed, in the case of extra passengers. And a food replicator between the tiny lavatory and the airlock door assured they could survive inside the small ship for as long as sufficient power was available.

The external long-range sensors were all absolute state-of-the-art, and Stansky's personally designed sliding-rack and power-coupling system allowed Rook to constantly update the craft with new hardware as it became available, with an absolute minimum of time and effort. Of course, James' obsession with armor being what it was, he had also triple plated the *Bugeye*'s hull in layers of thick trimithium, sandwiching a self-sealing gel inside to nullify the small breaches that inevitably resulted from enemy autocannon fire. There was no doubt that these measures had served to protect the craft for crucial extra minutes during many a hasty retreat, and that they had no measurable ill effects on the smooth operation of the vessel while in the vacuum of space. But the problem remained that the heavy extra plating made the craft ungainly when operating inside an atmosphere. In fact, as Bullit was often heard to remark, the ship flew like a wet sponge.

This was doubly true when the *Bugeye* was moving at slow speeds, complicated further by the multiple arrays of dishes, antenna, sensors, and other non-aerodynamic protrusions that covered the ship's upper fuselage. Bullit now cursed about this to himself while he fought the controls of the ship, hovering the *Bugeye* awkwardly above the evergreens. He was certainly the most practiced at the art of controlling the cumbersome craft, but now the wind shear in these elevations of Oberonn's northern mountain range was making her even more unwieldy than usual. The *Bugeye* twisted and yawed in a seemingly haphazard choreography, as the seti struggled to steady her descent and keep her from straying into the surrounding trees, lowering her as straight and gently as possible into the small clearing of the evac bravo site.

"*Bugeye* down, evac bravo," Bullit reported. "How we doing over there?"

"*Keep the engine running,*" Stansky radioed back. "*We'll be with you as soon as we find Rook.*"

"What do you mean '*find*' him? Where the hell is he?"

"*Well, as the comment implies... we have no friggin' idea.*"

"*We lost his position,*" Tachion interjected, "*and we can't get him to respond. He reprogrammed the laser cannon to target just the warbots, but then got separated in all the chaos, and I'm not picking up his PPS. We might need you to take back off, and do a sweep of the…*"

"*I have him!*" Bullseye called. "*Doctor, I need you at my position.*"

"*On my way. What's his status?*"

"*Unresponsive, and his leg is… I… I am failing to stem the bleeding. I am employing the emergency cauterizer.*"

An alert began to sound, drawing Bullit's attention back to the *Bugeye*'s sensors. "Doc," the seti suggested, "if you guys can scoop and run, I would highly recommend it. General Nylis' little backwoods band of would-be terrorists has now somehow scrambled fighter craft to intercept us."

"*Predictable,*" Stansky grumbled. "*How far?*"

"Maybe minutes."

"*Roger. We're not far. Drop the ramp and get ready to run.*"

As the pair of fighters came into range, Bullit's companions did as well, porting the fallen seti's body atop a hover gurney pulled behind them. They hurtled up the ramp as the *Bugeye* lifted off, the gangplank closing just behind them.

Chapter 6.1

GENERAL NYLIS, GRAND COMMANDER, OBERONN Aerospace Defense, stepped down from the molecular teleporter, zapping in with his entourage of personal bodyguards, and paused for a moment, his eyes adjusting to the dim light of the ancient subterranean bunker. As he was known for his sour temperament as much as his strategic genius, the teleporter operator gave him a wide berth, as Nylis marched out of the room with his men-at-arms close in tow.

He was an older chamai, teetering now at the very end of his distinguished military career, and a long life of battle stress and fatigue had hardened his pockmarked face into a perpetual grimace of irritation. The signature nasal ridges of his species—on the bridge of his nose and between the eyes—were drawn down into folds by the accumulation of passing years, only serving to enhance the appearance of a furrowed brow. His large backward-stretching ears were nicked and califlowered, and the typical umber hue of his chamai skin tone, along with his wrinkled scowl and cratered complexion, gave him an appearance reminiscent of a rusted anchor chain.

He wore his usual forest-green duty uniform with silver shoulder plates, but without the adornment of his numerous medals and ribboned awards. Atop this, his dress uniform's emerald and slate cape trailed behind him, attached at the neck with a thick, golden cable. His head, bald with age, and slicked with perspiration from the humidity on the surface, reflected the glow of the distantly spaced overhead lights as he passed beneath, striding purposefully down the corridors of the previously abandoned underground shelter.

The concrete maze had the clear appearance of many decades of disuse, though signs of a recent hurried cleanup were evident, and darkened corners of some of the empty, gray cubicles were piled with ancient litter that had been swept out of the way. Along the dusty, drab walls, old, faded signage had been once painted beside the corridor's many entranceways, marking them with their former purposes in the long distant past. Several of the rooms were decorated with an insignia of some kind— a crest, or coat of arms perhaps—though every last one of these had been crudely defaced or obscured in some manner, usually with a few hasty zigzags of black spray paint.

The hallway slowly transitioned the further the troupe progressed, from a smooth and civilized gray concrete corridor, to a jagged, rough-hewn tunnel carved through the dark stone of the very mountain itself. The floor of the cavern passageway was rocky, and the boot steps of General Nylis and his men echoed like a drumbeat as they proceeded, rudely passing by other soldiers in armor not matching their own. He stopped in front of a heavy steel door framed into the cold rock of the passageway, and flanked by two lyghtans, both attired in the armor of the Capellan Temple Guard.

"Let me see Vasu at once," Nylis growled, with a voice that was deep and hoarse.

"The High Priestess is in meditation, and not to be disturbed," one of the lyghtans responded without a hint of intimidation at the general's demeanor, continuing only to stare straight ahead.

"It is not my habit to ask permission, *shade*," the general croaked. "Stand aside, or be removed."

The lyghtan turned his gaze slowly toward the chamai general's face, his fiery orange eyes glowing brightly against the absolute black of his skin. "It is not my place to *grant* permission, but only to serve the will of the Maiden of The Path."

The general stepped closer to the lyghtan so that his face was mere inches from the doorman's helmet visor, the subtle glow of his orange eyes clearly visible through the tinted sheild. "The witch Vasu oversteps her bounds. She will see me at once, if it means I must take down this door, and you with it."

Before the doorman could respond, the steel portal swung open, and a stunningly beautiful lyghtan female stepped into the archway. Her skin was of a darker black than the obsidian granite coursing down the cavern walls, her flowing hair brighter white than the snow topped peak of the mountain above, and her eyes shone in the darkness with a soft emerald splendor, not unlike that of the lush vegetation of the flourishing forests that surrounded. Her slender form was scantily clad in an archaic red leather bustier, the traditionally ceremonial armor of the Capellan monarchy when commanding battle. "Greetings, General Nylis. I am Lady Opal, the new first ashi'mar to the high priestess of Capella. Our holy queen has foreseen your coming in her visions of The Path. She bids you welcome, and invites you inside."

The lyghtan doormen bowed in unison, chanting a brief mantra at the mention of the priestess' visions. The general glared at them in disdain, and stepped into the darkened inner sanctum.

Opal raised up her hand before them as they entered, her fingers softly glowing in the same emerald green as her eyes, and used the gentle illumination to lead the general into the dark room. The small cavern was roughly circular, with uneven natural walls, but a layer of cretespray had leveled the floor to a smooth, gray finish. Sheer drapes of various colors decorated the stone here and there, and an improvised altar set atop a flat ledge of rock was covered with smoldering incense and dozens of flickering candles, struggling to illuminate the room against the black walls of the small enclosure. An ornate rug lay on the concrete floor in front of the altar, and a lone figure draped in a leather, hooded robe knelt upon it, bowed low in meditation.

"You spend too much time in prayer, Vasu," the general said, "and not enough time actually steering events toward our master's intended end. Have you not seen what is happening to my troops on the surface?"

"You refer to the mercenary group, Parliament," the kneeling priestess said softly, without rising from her position before the altar. "I am well aware of the events transpiring above us. All is proceeding according to His will."

"They are transpiring too slowly, and at too great a cost," the general remarked, glaring in disgust at the multitude of religious trinkets dangling from the jagged walls. "The time we have planned for draws near, and we have many pieces yet to put in play. Why are we wasting time and resources on this insignificant group?"

"Our Overlord has had dealings with them in the past, and knows that when our plan comes full circle, they will remember him, and stop at nothing to interfere in his destiny."

"Then why not just crush them now, why this elaborate ruse that is costing me so many of my soldiers and equipment?"

"He has plans for them," Vasu answered, "and we are following the course he has set. Ours is not to question His vision of The Path."

The general knew at least that much to be true. Nylis himself was a frightful and intimidating presence, and had seldom met a soul who could unnerve him the way he unnerved so many others. Their master, however, was a menacing countenance, whose cruel and calculated demeanor and awesome power struck cold with dread *all* who stood before him. The general was no exception, and knew if he were to question his lord's instructions like this in his presence, it would incur the absolute holocaust of his wrath upon him.

The lyghtan priestess continued. "Parliament can be used to our advantage. Their notoriety within the Coalition systems will give us access to leaders of government and industry. When the time comes, such access could be pivotal." She paused briefly as she lit another incense. "Also, he has a personal interest in this specific group of mercenaries, one of them in particular."

"That is what I suspected," the general replied. "It seems our master's personal interests have taken priority over our final objective, and I'm not one who's accustomed to tolerating these endless delays."

"Watch your tongue, General. Our master's ears are everywhere, and he lets very little go unheard," she reminded him. "What is this tone of urgency in your voice? Does your greed compel you to rush so? Hurrying headlong down The Path to the reward our lord has promised you?"

"This '*path*' you refer to... it is part of *your* antiquated religion, Vasu, not mine. And what promises the master has made to me are none of your concern."

"The Path is the true religion for all species, General, and in time the lyghtan will lead all peoples to understand its mysteries."

"The chamai will never be led by shades, witch. You mind your place."

"And what place is it that you desire for yourself, General?" Vasu asked. "You're a leader of men, a commander. A man of great power on your own world. Yet, as all things do, this too soon draws near its end. Rather than step down from your place of influence, I feel you are ambitious for even more. Perhaps I am speaking to the future Monarch of Oberonn? Is this the reward to which you rush so quickly?"

The general's voice was wrought with irritation. "And I speak to the future queen of some yet to be conquered planet, do I not? Is that not unusual ambition for a woman of religion?"

The lyghtan priestess chuckled eerily as she rose at last from her place before the altar. "You underestimate me, my dear General Nylis. Do you forget that I am already queen of Capella? You see, our lord and master, in his divine and unfaltering wisdom, has seen it in our Path to take *me* to His side... as companion, and concubine." She turned toward him finally, revealing her ghostly blue eyes glowing from the darkness beneath her hood. "So it seems that *my* place in our final objective will be ruling as empress at his side, over *all* the systems of this galaxy... including yours."

General Nylis felt the blood drain away from his face as he realized, given this revelation, he had perhaps spoken too freely. Vasu was sure to tell their lord about the general's lack of faith in his plans. In a moment of unthinking panic, to silence her from reporting to their master, he made an instinctual and foolishly reflexive move toward his sidearm. As he reached for the weapon, Vasu quickly raised the palms of her hands, and released a powerfully blinding flash of intense blue light. The general cried out and covered his eyes, and after a moment or two of pain and blindness, opened them to find the room appearing much darker than before.

The natural physical defenses that involuntarily protected him from injury had formed a light-screening film across the surface of his eyes. He realized then just how clever the priestess was. Although he was now immune to her flash attack, he could no longer see in the dim light of the cavern, and his body could not readapt to another type of injury for several minutes, leaving him vulnerable. He decided it was best to make an escape, and began fumbling through the dark for the cold steel of the doorway.

Suddenly the queen was in front of him. He tried to move around her, but his legs became strangely frozen. He felt unable to move or speak. Vasu made a motion with her hand and his body lifted into the air, floating a few inches above the floor—paralyzed. A yellow illuminated bracelet on the priestess's wrist was glowing in a pulsing rhythm as she drew him slowly towards her, drifting on air, his limp feet dangling just above the ground. General Nylis struggled to comprehend how Vasu had obtained this power, as he fought in vain to break free of it.

"Tsk, tsk, tsk," the High Priestess Vasu clucked her tongue at him. "General, you weren't planning to harm your lord's new mistress, were you? You see, with my new place, our master saw fit to impart new magics upon me as well." She pointed at him, then swung her arm quickly to the side. As if attached by an invisible thread, his body was thrown in the same direction, smashing violently against the rocks. She lifted her arm again and levitated him back into the air.

Her young ashi'mar, Lady Opal, who had been witness to everything that transpired, cowered back in horror from her mentor's shocking and unnatural show of power. She tucked her slight frame in between the colored curtains and watched in fear, waiting for a chance to slip out the door without notice.

"You know, General," the priestess continued in a suddenly dispassionate tone. "This has been my first visit to your planet, and it is so different from my own that it fascinates me. The surface of Capella is all desert and wasteland, you see. But here it is absolutely teeming with life." She crossed the room as she spoke, then reached into a small cage hanging from the wall. She turned back and approached the still incapacitated general, with something large and hairy gripped tightly in her hand.

"Are you familiar with the heret spider of your world, General?" she asked, placing the nasty brown and yellow creature on his chest. "It's indigenous to the very forests right above us. I find them completely enchanting. Unlike anything on my world. You see, each winter after the birds have migrated, these spiders crawl out from under the ground, and through the snow, to scale the ice-covered trees. They find hollows and holes in the trunks, and then spend all winter traveling up and down through the ice and cold, finding bits of straw and fodder that they haul back in a web cocoon. They spend months making the perfect nest, so inviting that any bird would jump at the chance to live there. Then the spiders make a false wall of bark and webbing, and hide behind it at the back of the hole."

The general stared back at her in confusion and fear, as a small trickle of blood ran down his face from an open gash on his bald head. The spider eagerly made its way up his chest and onto his neck.

Vasu continued. "There they stay, until winter ends, and the birds move into the conveniently pre-nested homes. All spring, as they mate and lay eggs, the heret waits... until early summer, when the eggs hatch, and the mother is feeding her new younglings. *That* is when the spider finally springs forth from behind its web, and devours them all. The young, the mother, and even the food she had brought. A feast that takes him weeks to eat, and provides him enough energy for the rest of the year."

The general's eyes were now wide with fear as the large arachnid crawled across his cratered face, and onto the top of his glistening head.

"It's a shame you don't have a greater appreciation of nature, General. So many lessons waiting to be learned... simply by a closer examination of the creatures around us. This little fellow, for instance. The perfect example for a man like yourself. What quality does this creature have in abundance that you so sorely lack?" She reached up and took the spider back off his head, and coddled and stroked it softly against her bosom. "Patience, General. You could learn much from my small friend about that. Patience in planning your strategy, in the setting of the trap certainly. But even more important is patience in waiting to spring it." With a negligent flip of her hand, she sent Nylis sailing across the cave to crash again into the wall and tumble into a heap on the ground.

The general lay bloody and beaten on the cement floor for a moment or two, before he realized she had released him from his paralysis. He struggled weakly, and with much grunting, as he used the crags and cracks of the rocky wall to pull himself to his feet. Obviously, her powers were a gift bestowed by their master, as he had granted powers unto the general as well—by virtue of a serum he injected daily. Nylis had been given the ability to see and hear nearby conversations in which he was not present, and the power to issue subliminal suggestions into the minds of both his officers and leaders.

By using these gifts, he had been more easily able to manipulate the political and military landscapes on Oberonn to his master's design. Now, after a year of careful maneuvering, the planet sat ripe for a coup like a late summer bloodcherry, bloated and dripping on the tree. However, the abilities she was wielding now to batter his body and bruise his ego were unlike anything he had seen, except for the awesome power of the master himself—and like their master, she now wore the same glowing bracelet. Clearly, he had chosen a favorite—the pecking order had been reshuffled— and Nylis knew he had no choice but to resign himself to her authority.

Vasu turned her back on General Nylis, and with his eyes now clearing and his vision returning to normal, he watched her return to stand again before the crude altar. Her arms hung at her side, and in her tightening grip the heret spider's twitching legs protruded between clenched fingers, its venom-soaked fangs biting again and again against the soft, loose flesh between her thumb and forefinger. Despite their needle-like sharpness, the fangs somehow failed repeatedly to break the skin.

"Now, General," she said calmly, "return to your ship, and monitor the battle with Parliament closely. I want everything to go as the master has instructed." She closed her fist tighter around the squirming arachnid, until it stopped its panicked spasms, and a viscous, green ooze began dripping from between her fingers.

"Yes, of course, I will do as you wish... Holy Mother," General Nylis panted. "Everything will... be in place on schedule. I will... see to it personally."

"Excellent," she said, lowering herself back to her knees before the altar. "I will be sure to tell our master what a wonderful host you have been. And how very accommodating."

"Thank you, my lady," he said. Then a slight look of worry crossed his face. "Do you mean to say that... h-he is coming *here*?"

"I will meet with him briefly, then he will be joining you aboard the *Okubi*. He wants to brief you himself before he has you meet our newest ally."

"I will make ready at once," the general replied, as worry over the master's visit turned to genuine, dire fear.

"Make sure that you do, General," the priestess advised as she bowed her head. "Our master, Lord Denali, will be arriving within the hour."

6.2

BULLIT SWORE UNDER HIS BREATH as he furiously flicked one of the switches on the cockpit's complex console repeatedly up and down. He reached over with a free hand to the center panel, popping off a six-inch square piece of plating, and began rummaging with his fingers through the wires and prog-chips beneath. "James, I need you!" he called out.

James Stansky finished stowing the last of his armor, and hurried to the forward section of the *Bugeye*, sliding into the copilot seat. "What's going on? Let's punch this thing and get the hell outta here," he snapped.

"The fucking inertial dampeners are offline. If I accelerate any faster, we'll all end up as red stains on the aft firewall." Bullit changed the heads-up display to show the approaching chase ships. "And at this rate, we're gonna have some company real soon."

Stansky shoved Bullit's hand away from the open panel, rummaging his fingers frantically through the circuits just as Bullit had been doing. "Did you check the relays?" he asked.

"Yes, you ass. What do you think I was doing? It has to be a problem with the field generator itself."

"You've gotta be shitting me. Why'd you let them hit the ship right in the belly like that?!"

"Are you kidding me?! You're lucky I got your dumb ass outta there at all! Why don't you..."

"Gentlemen!" Bullseye barked, as he seated himself at the tactical station in the middle of the ship's main compartment. "Shall we not endeavor to rectify the dilemma, and reserve worries of assigning blame for a more convenient occasion?"

"I *know* who's to blame," Stansky mumbled, as he got up from the cockpit, and hurried past Bullseye towards the aft wall of the main compartment. Bullit suddenly accelerated slightly, causing Stansky to run face first into the rear wall, as the others grabbed onto nearby handholds.

"Jesus Christ, what the hell!" Stansky yelled, wiping a drop of blood from his lip.

"Sorry. My bad," Bullit said.

Tachion had extended the medical biobed from the wall near where James was pulling up a floor plate, and Rook was seated upright on it with his legs stretched out—one still intact, and the other now merely a cauterized stump. As the android helped him remove the upper portion of his armor, the unmistakable smell of burning flesh was permeating the cabin. "If you could refrain yourself from such maneuvers, Bullit, it would help if the ship were a little more steady while I work."

"Sure thing, Doc... but without the dampeners, it won't be steady for long."

"That is certain," Bullseye said, as he watched the progress of the approaching ships on his scanners. "A duo of Hellcats, a lone Curtana, and a Renegade class interceptor, all closing in haste. Four minutes at most."

"I'm working on it!" Stansky said, his voice echoing from the open panel in the ship's floor. He put his hands out on the deck, pulling himself up to sit on the edge of the opening. "Bullseye, come gimme a hand here. If I can pull you away from your comfy chair for a minute."

Rook peered from the bed over toward Stansky. "If you can get the dampeners online, we can warp away from those Hellcats no problem, but that Renegade will be on our ass all the way home, even at maximum speed."

"And she's probably got a couple of fighters in her bay too," Stansky replied. "How's our shields, Bullit?"

"We're still at over thirteen hundred QEUs on the shields, which should hold off a bit of the laser damage from those Hellcats and Renegade, but that Curtana carries all inertia weapons, and structural integrity of the fuselage is already iffy."

"Perfect," Rook said. "One well-placed frag missile and we'll be all sucked out into space." Rook turned to look up at Tachion, and began stripping off the warming blanket that had been placed over him. "Damn, Tach," he protested weakly, "what are you trying to do, roast me alive? First Bullseye grills my leg, and now you're trying to boil me in my own juices."

Tachion gazed with a stare of concern at the medical readout above the bed. "Your body temperature is extremely low," he said. "You must have lost more blood than I thought." He opened a small door on the wall and reached in, retrieving a liter labeled 'seti universal plasma'. "In fact, for a seti, you're near hypothermic."

Rook pushed the biobed sensor's swing-arm away from him and back to the wall. "My temperature is fine," he snapped, removing the probes from his forehead. "I don't need a physical, and I don't need more blood. I need to be able to walk!"

Bullseye looked up from where he was assisting Stansky with the repairs. "How is our friend doing, Doctor?" he asked.

"Well... it's hard to tell without the sensors hooked up," Tachion said, as he glared down at Rook, "But he seems alright. Nerve deadeners are clearly working, as he doesn't seem to be in significant pain. I'll clean the wound, and he can wear a temporary prosthetic for now. Then hopefully we can reattach once we're back at my labs."

"Finally, that's what I'm talkin' about," Rook said.

"I'm gonna give you some more pain killers while I clean the stump," Tachion told Rook. "These are powerful locals. They should numb up the entire leg."

Suddenly the ship lurched, an explosion visible outside the window. "As you may have guessed," Bullit announced, "the fighters are now in range."

Bullseye reemerged from the opening in the floor where he had been helping Stansky, and retook his station at tactical. "Hellcats have AE4000s locked on. Everyone brace!" A series of laser blasts rained around the ship as Bullit swerved back and forth abruptly. None of the beams impacted.

"Odd," Bullseye remarked. "A valid weapons lock was clear. I do not comprehend how they may have missed."

"Simple," Bullit said, "because I'm that good."

"HA!" Stansky bellowed from the open floor compartment.

Another barrage of laser fire lit up the darkness outside the ship, and again Bullit jerked the crew through a series of evasive maneuvers. "How much longer down there, Stansky?" Bullit asked. "Right about now would be a good time!"

"Wait for it," James replied. "Almost... keep waiting... and... *Now!*"

Bullit hit the switch above him, and the feel of the inertia dampening field engaging passed through each one of them, as their insides stopped vibrating and heaving about with every turn. "Here we go!" Bullit yelled, and threw the *Bugeye* into warp.

"Stellar work, James," Bullseye said, as Stansky closed the access panel and took a seat near Rook and Tachion. "The Renegade is yet close. Pursuing, but losing ground. Their Alcubierre drive holds steady at twenty percent warp... which is curious. Appears they are content to allow their quarry to pull away."

"What's wrong Tach?" Rook asked, as the doctor poked and prodded at his leg stump with a confused stare.

"This wound, what caused this?" Tachion asked.

"A frag grenade," Bullseye answered, as he got up and approached the biobed.

"That can't be correct," Tachion said. "There's an odd biochemical signature from the tissue at the wound site. Are you sure this wasn't an energy weapon of some type? The cellular structure in his leg seems to be in a state of flux. I better run a genetic scan on the wound tissue, just to make sure that..."

"*No!*" Rook snapped at him, taking Tachion aback. Then in a calmer voice, "Just gimme the damn prosthetic, and you can run all the scans you want later."

Tachion ignored Rook's irrational outburst, passing the medical scanner over the wound again. "But... it's as if some of this tissue is from another organism, and that anomalous tissue is spreading up the leg rather quickly. It's almost as if the... as if..." he trailed off, then suddenly stood up straight, and stared hard at Rook.

"What is it, Tach?" Rook asked suspiciously.

"Let me see your arm," Tachion demanded. "Your left arm, now."

"There's nothing wrong with my arm, T," Rook said as he held the it up and demonstrated its full range of motion, bending and straightening his elbow, and repeatedly clenching his fist. "See? Not a scratch. Now what's the matter with my leg?"

Tachion snatched the seti's wrist roughly and pulled it straight, passing the bioscanner up and down its length.

"Ow, Doc. Shit. Take it easy, will you!" Rook protested.

Tachion dropped his friend's wrist, jerking his gaze up to stare straight into Rook's eyes, a forever unreadable expression on his forged metallic face.

"Look, just tell me what's going on," Rook pleaded.

Tachion didn't answer, but turned and quietly crossed the cabin of the *Bugeye* to his locker instead, and opened it.

"What is it, Doctor?" Bullseye asked worriedly.

Rook began twisting himself around on the bed in an attempt to get up. "What's going on? Why can't I move?"

Tachion grabbed something from inside his locker and closed the door. "The painkiller I gave you also partially paralyzes the muscle tissue, blocking impulses along the nerves. You are temporarily losing voluntary control over the musculature in your lower extremities." He turned back and headed for the bed.

Rook now sat straight up and turned away from them, pushing his intact leg off the bed with his hand, and reaching toward the wall where his techkit bag dangled from a long bolt in the ship's hull. "Wait," he said, "I need to get up. Someone help me." His fingers were just barely able to brush the edge of his kit's strap, and he strained to reach further, almost falling off the bed. "Goddammit, someone help me up! Gimme my kit!"

"What the hell is wrong with you?" Stansky asked, standing from his seat.

"Doctor?" Bullseye questioned Tachion, as the android moved back past him towards the bed.

Rook was now panting frantically as he stretched further to reach his kit, frequently glancing back over his shoulder with wild eyes, watching the android approaching him.

"Tachion, what are you doing!" Bullseye demanded.

The medic paused not a moment. As he reached the bed, there was a familiar crackling hum and soft blue luminescence as the EMD sword in his hand sprung to life, a searing beam of plasma, shaped into a longblade by a thermo-magnetic field.

"No! Wait!" Rook screamed desperately. "Please!"

"*Tachion!*" Bullseye yelled as he tried to reach out and grab his arm.

The doctor lifted the glowing saber high above his head, and spun as he lowered it—in one unusually graceful movement for such a large android. Stansky and Bullseye ducked back to turn and cover their heads, as the blade was drawn across and through Rook's torso—from above his right shoulder to below his left armpit. The seti's body gave a brief, startled spasm as both of his severed arms abruptly fell to the floor. His head turned slightly to stare back at Tachion, eyes bloodshot and wide with horror, and his mouth gaped disturbingly in either a silent last gasp for air, or muted scream of terror. Then the upper portion of his torso and head slid away as one piece from the rest of his body, banging on the corner of the biobed, and rolling over the edge. It landed on the floor with a sickening thud that reverberated through the deck plates. His still seated remaining lower half now slipped to the floor, thumping onto its knee and stump, then slumping into a pile on the other side of the bed.

"Jesus Fucking Christ!" Stansky exclaimed. He quickly retracted his arms from shielding himself, and drew his two nine-millimeter pistols, aiming them at Tachion's head.

Bullseye slapped the now inactive EMD from the android's hand, sending it skittering across the floor. He pulled a negation grenade from his belt—a charge which would deactivate the doctor's electronic workings—and held it up, his thumb poised over the button. "Explain quickly, old friend!" he barked with a growl in his throat, and a fire in his eye that the others seldom ever see slip out—outside of the deepest throws of seti battle rage.

Tachion pointed to the body of Rook, which was now already distorting back to its natural metamorph appearance—grayish-green skin, large almond-shaped dark eyes, and a face that was nearly featureless. "An imposter," he said. "The paralytics caused him to slowly lose shape-shifting control over his muscles, without him even knowing it. I should have realized from the cold body temperature, and the way he wouldn't let me scan him thoroughly, that something was wrong. And then his left arm confirmed it," Tachion continued, reaching over and putting his hand into the techkit that the metamorph had been trying so desperately to reach. "The arm wasn't cybernetic, like Rook's. It was flesh." He slowly pulled his hand back out of the bag, holding a rare drak'min disintegration pistol by the tip of its slim black elongated barrel.

Bullit engaged the computer control on the *Bugeye*, then cautiously approached the dismembered metamorph laying on the cabin floor. He let out a low whistle as he admired the powerful weapon. "Whoa! Sweet gun. Can I have it?"

"Bullit, you are a true asshole," Stansky remarked harshly.

"What did I say?" Bullit responded.

Bullseye glanced away from the body with a look of anguished defeat, his arms falling to his sides. "No," he said quietly to himself. "What have I done? It was… it was meant to be me."

Bullit scratched his head and turned to Bullseye. "You know, this may explain our escape from those fighters."

Bullseye said nothing, but continued to stare absently at the ground, lost in his own thoughts and remorse.

"Bullseye," Bullit said louder.

"Explain," the black-furred seti said quietly, without looking up from the floor.

"The chase ships, you know? The fighters we just evaded," Bullit said as he drew closer, placing a hand on Bullseye's shoulder. "Well, it's just…" he continued in a near whisper, "as good a pilot as I am, I'm willing to admit that maybe… just perhaps… I'm not quite *that* good."

"Boy, you said it, brother." Stansky retorted halfheartedly from across the ship.

"What I *mean*," Bullit continued, with a glare at Stansky, "is that I think maybe those fighters may have missed us on purpose. They *wanted* us to get away with this imposter on board."

Stansky turned his attention to the rudely dissected body on the floor. "Well," he said, pointing to the cadaver's lower half. "His leg injury was real. That much at least wasn't a metamorph trick." He kicked the lower half of the corpse squarely in the thigh.

"Undoubtedly the victim of arbitrary misfortune," Bullseye remarked. "It would be foolish to believe such grievous injury to have played any part in his sponsor's intentions."

"Well, lucky for us those troops were so aggressive," Stansky said. "If that injury hadn't exposed him, who knows what his plans were." He turned and went back to the open floor panel in order to secure it back in place. "Well... I guess not lucky maybe. But bad luck that saved us from worse."

"Poetic," Bullit remarked snidely.

Tachion still silently stared down at the infiltrator's body, disgusted with himself for so easily being fooled. After another moment, he slowly turned around and looked seriously at his three teammates. "We must go back," he said matter-of-factly.

"What? Whoa. Hold on just a minute, big guy," Stansky said, turning back towards the rest of his group. "Look, we barely made it outta there with our asses intact the first time, and I, for one, am not so eager to go running back for seconds. You all know I'm not one to leave a man behind, but we have no evidence that Rook is still alive back there. I mean... *none*. Shit, he may not be there at all. This fucking piece of crap may have been with us for days, even weeks. Rook is almost certainly... dead. I mean, why would whoever did this, replace him, but leave him alive? And his body could be almost anywhere in the galaxy!"

Bullseye, seeming a bit more composed now, took Tachion by his huge metal arm and walked him a few steps from the others. "I am loath to admit it, my loyal friend, but I fear James is correct. We have no way to know that our comrade still lives, and if so, where in the quadrant he may be. Whilst noble in intention, our return would serve but to place us all in further mortal danger, as well as imperil the success of the mission."

"Imperil the mission?!" Tachion snapped in uncharacteristic anger. "This mission is *already* an absolute failure. Not only did we lose a man... not only were we infiltrated by a spy sent by God knows who... but the data files that were our main objective to retrieve could only be authenticated by Rook. Meaning, the spy that was in our midst this whole time, and who they allowed us to escape with, is the one we trusted to ensure the data was legitimate. Do you really believe that they let us leave with the correct files?!"

"Hey," Bullit said. "I just said that *maybe* the fighters let us escape. Those ground troops, though, they were shooting to kill."

"Were they really?" Tachion asked. "When was the last time we took on an assault like we did today? Over forty warbots, at least a battalion of soldiers. Minefields, cannons, fighters... and the only significant damage was an accidental injury on a false Rook? How is that possible? We were way outnumbered and outgunned today. We should all be dead. And mind you, all of that to protect an encrypted set of plans for weaponry that anyone with resources could have just bought on the black market."

"Those guys sure had the resources, if anyone does," Stansky interjected.

"What about General Nylis?" Tachion continued. "I thought he told you there would be limited resistance."

"That he did," Bullseye responded.

"Well, isn't it possible that they just put on a show for us back there," Tachion wondered, "a clever distraction on a massive scale? Enough to have us thanking our gods for getting us out of there, and keep us from coming back."

"So you postulate this a ruse from its very inauguration?" Bullseye asked. "You find plausible the commander of the chamai aerospace forces conspired to betray our troupe, appointed to us a bogus mission, and all the fracas and fray late endured just so much melodramatics?"

"It seemed a good deal over the top to me," Tachion remarked. "You're fond of Shakespeare, Bullseye. You know the line 'I think that thou does protest too much?'"

"Hamlet. Act three, scene two," the seti said.

"Listen, the fact is that none of this really matters right now," Tachion said, turning to look his team leader straight in the eye. "The only thing that matters, is that there is a slim chance that Rook is still back there on that planet. Because of that, I must go back," he said with conviction. Their eyes were locked unwavering on each other for a long moment. "It is nothing less than what Rook would do, and has done, for any of us. We have to go back, all of us." He turned the drak'min pistol around in his hand, holding it out grip first towards the seti.

Bullseye stared hard at Tachion for a moment, and then slowly began nodding his head as he took the pistol from his hand. "Yes," Bullseye said, "of course, you are correct." He turned toward Stansky and Bullit. "We must venture back and locate Rook, whether perished or living. It is our duty to him to return." He walked back over to his seat at the tactical station, sighing deeply as he took another moment to gather himself. Then he straightened himself up in his chair, his demeanor visibly steadied, his voice clear and unwavering. "Bullit," he commanded, "reverse course and return us to the planet, lightspeed only. We'll require that extension of occasion to formulate a strategy. Mind you, convey us over the original landing site. We must endeavor to retrace our steps precisely."

"You don't want to rendezvous with *Parliament One* first?" Bullit asked.

"Nay. She lies still fully across the sector, and we have not that measure of leisure."

"Okay, reversing course," Bullit acknowledged. "Slowest warp." He slid into the cockpit and entered the new heading.

"James," Bullseye continued, "see what you might mend about our marred armor, that we may not out-rightly replace. Then ready the Beagle sensor probe. We will wish to dispatch it ahead of us as soon as we befall the system's outer rim."

"Alright, whatever you say, boss," Stansky replied with a shrug.

"Tachion, I believe we could all use a brief turn on your medical bed. Perform your ministrations as well as time allows before we head back into the fray. Then I'll need you at the science station once we launch the Beagle, and we'll see if our sensors cannot discern some trace of our missing brother."

"Thank you," Tachion replied.

"And Doctor, you may wish to brush up on your Shakespeare," Bullseye added, looking at the android over his shoulder. "The proper reading is 'The lady doth protests too much, methinks'. A common mistake."

"I'll be sure and do that," Tachion said.

Bullseye continued. "I shall link our systems with the local satellite network, venture to access unhindered through Rook's old backdoors, established long ago. Couple our database, if we might, with Starlaw, and Coalition military. If, in fact, the key to that door is yet functional still. Then we shall see if any dossier exists connected to our doppelgänger's face or genetic profile." He then swiveled in his chair and addressed the group. "We go back now for one of our own, as he would have for any other, and has, on more than a singular occasion. We have been deceived. Attacked." He glanced at Rook's empty chair at the operations station. "And indeed, sorely injured. But even more true, is we have been foolishly underestimated. If Rook lives still, we shall not cease searching until he is safe among us." He swiveled back to his monitors and started typing into the keypads. "But I pray you," he said after a moment, "firstly… someone kindly eject that fetid carcass out the airlock."

Chapter 7.1

THIRTY-FIVE YEARS HAD COME and gone beneath the ever-shifting sands of Capella since the passing of the great high priestess, Queen Xiet. Upon the holy mother's death, her first ashi'mar, a kindhearted and wise-minded lyghtan named Molahs, went immediately into seclusion at the Holy Temple of the Old City, so beginning an ancient week-long ceremony to become the new high priestess of the lyghtan people, and queen of Capella. As was the custom of the church governed lyghtan people, the temple matriarch was to have four ashi'mar in her service, each poised to assume rule of church and state upon the passing of the priestess above her. And so, each of Xiet's hallowed ladies moved up one rank closer to the new high priestess, Queen Molahs, and the search went out in every cavern city, village cave, and huddled encampment of nomadic desert dwellers for a new fourth ashi'mar.

As it was written in the Book of the Path, the lyghtan believed that when a queen completed her journey along her life Path to pass into the light, all her wisdom and virtue were gathered by the Sacred Originators, and placed within the vessel a chosen child. The temple monks would know the divine receptacle, and new fourth ashi'mar, in the way set forth in the ancient texts—the third female child, born on the third solar day, after the three Capellan moons came into their annual alignment. The Lunar Triad occurred in the second month after Xiet's death, and the Holy Mother Molahs sent her new first ashi'mar, Vasu, to lead the temple monks in the global watch for the infant's blessed coming.

Lady Opal had no memories of the day Vasu and the temple monks came to take her from her mother's breast, presenting her to the church as fourth ashi'mar. In fact, she had no memories of her real mother at all, nor any knowledge about her family, nor even her place of birth. This is not to say she felt orphaned in any way. On the contrary, if asked about her mother, she pictured warm memories of Queen Molahs and her senior ashi'mar, Ladies Vasu, Pia and Ofroi, and the many temple servants and tutors who raised her with love and overwhelming attention. She was taught to read from the Book of the Path, instructed by them in the ways of the church, and was an apt pupil in her studies of lyghtan history and politics.

Her fondest memories were of Vasu herself, taking frequent breaks from Opal's self-defense lessons for a spontaneous game of hide and go seek, in the catacombs and tunnels surrounding the Old City Temple. Vasu would stalk dramatically about the caves, wondering aloud where the fourth ashi'mar could have gotten to, as the young Opal giggled and tittered from her obvious hiding spot behind some rocky column or sandy boulder. Then Opal would shriek in frightened glee, as Vasu would unexpectedly snatch her from behind, and roll on the ground, tickling her without mercy as their laughter echoed through the caves. Through her adolescence into young adulthood, she had never lost that precious bond with her fellow ashi'mar, and Vasu in particular. Any pining thoughts of her true home and family never occurred to her, and she had never longed for anything else. Until now.

The caves of Oberonn were not at all like those of her home planet of Capella, and Opal found herself struggling to find her way. She moved quickly but silently away from the tunnels occupied by Vasu and General Nylis, and escaped towards what she hoped was the surface. The caverns of her homeworld were largely dry sandstone and hardened clay, warm to the touch and light tan in color, and the air that breezed through them was arid and clean. When in an unfamiliar area, she could easily deduce which direction led to the surface simply by glancing at the type of stones around her, noting the sedimentary layers in the walls, and following the distant smell of sweet desert flowers lacing the air, drifting in from hidden exits.

These caves, however, were carved through dark gray and black granite bedrock, a poor reflector for her natural illumination, making it hard even for her to see. The air was dank and humid, without even a hint of any movement in it, and the odor of wet earth, animal droppings, and rotted fungus kept Opal from detecting even a trace of fresh air from far above. Also, there were creatures in these caves she was not familiar with, and with every rustling insect or scampering rodent, with every invisible web she walked through face first, she became more and more uneasy.

Opal had stopped briefly for some supplies and her AE100 laser pistol only, and still wore her traditional archaic leather armor, a relic from the days when the ashi'mar served also as bodyguards to the high priestess. The scant and revealing garb gave her little protection from the damp, as she sat for a moment in the darkness on some wet moss, and contemplated her decision to run away from Vasu.

Opal had never seen the new queen priestess behave as she had today. Although she had been gradually becoming more ill-tempered and power-hungry of late, beginning around the time the mysterious human called Denali had appeared in the Old City—about two years ago now. Opal had never figured out how the stranger had gained the confidence of the then first ashi'mar, but it was not long before her favorite instructor, and surrogate mother, no longer had time to spend with her, and Vasu was seen less and less around the Temple at all.

Some months later, when Queen Molahs was found dead in her chambers, the source of her passing still shrouded in mystery, Vasu was quick to take her seat as matriarch over the church and throne of Capella. But she seemingly allowed the investigation into the untimely passing to languish, releasing only vague reports of a possible underlying illness, and no true cause was ever revealed.

It was then that the new high priestess, Queen Vasu, revealed her beliefs to her ashi'mar, that this strange human she befriended was the alien prophet who's coming was foretold in the Book of the Path. When her ladies-in-waiting proved skeptical, she said she knew this was so because the voices of the Originators had come to her in her mind to proclaim it, and she demonstrated miracle powers Denali had bestowed upon her as evidence. Vasu walked confidently through the hot spring outside the Old City without succumbing to the scalding waters. She whipped and slashed herself across the forearms with the thorny stems of some dry desert brush, then held up her arms as her ladies watched the wounds heal before their eyes. And she seemed able to communicate with the desert creatures, raising her arms wide on an outcropping outside the cavern entrance, and causing eels to circle wildly around her feet, and dust hawks to swarm in a tight cloud above her head.

Despite the impressive displays of her power, the now third ashi'mar, Opal, was not alone in her doubts about this 'Lord Denali', as Vasu insisted he be called. The temple monks and servants were all convinced to be sure, but Opal, and her elder ashi'mar sisters, watched Vasu closely over that first year, and were all in agreement that the human stranger was *not* the promised Prophet of the Path. They rather felt that he was somehow controlling the High Priestess, and perverting her position and power to his own will. Plans began to form to remove the stranger, and show Vasu the error of her judgment.

However, those plans were interrupted by a duo of suspicious accidents that befell her superior sisters. First, almost a year ago, her eldest ashi'mar, a devoted and saintly woman named Pia, was found twisted and broken at the bottom of a deep cave. Again, no cause for the accident was found, and Opal, now moved up in rank to become second ashi'mar due to the death, grew more suspicious. Then about six months ago, when the beautiful Ofroi was horribly killed in some kind of sand harvester accident, she found herself now alone with her skepticism, with no one to turn to. Opal was automatically promoted again, and was now the youngest first ashi'mar in lyghtan history, by over one hundred and twenty years in age, and her three new subordinate ashi'mar that she would turn to for support were all but infants and toddlers. Despite her strong faith in her church, and her ingrained loyalty to Queen Vasu, she knew she must now turn against her, and try to find someone who could help her restore the Temple of Capella to a Path of proper righteousness.

The first ashi'mar steeled herself for what she knew could be a difficult two-day trek through the unfamiliar, and unforgiving caves to the surface. She gathered her belongings up again quickly, and cast her natural emerald glow from her hands, dimly illuminating the narrow passageway ahead of her. Then, without looking back, she moved on into the musty and forbidding darkness, determined in the Path she had chosen.

7.2

"Computer, download individual mission record from Rook's Helmet-cam, from timestamp one seven five through three hundred," Bullseye said towards the bank of monitors at his station.

"*Working,*" the computer voice responded.

"Repairs on the *Bugeye* are done," Stansky said, as he finished stowing his tools and wiped some dirt from the palms of his hands. He came up to peer over Bullseye's shoulder. "What are you looking for?" he asked.

"I seek what we all seek, James, a clue to our missing comrades' mysterious fate. The fact is, something the good doctor said has since been tormenting me. He told us he was grieved that he did not recognize earlier the deception of our metamorph imposter."

"He did?" Stansky questioned, looking quizzically over at Tachion, who was finishing up treating a nasty exit wound on the back of Bullit's waist.

"Not in so many words, perhaps, but his meaning was clear. And, I believe that I too should have seen through this fallacy, indeed even more so than he."

Tachion responded from the biobed. "Listen Bullseye, you can't blame yourself for that. The imitation was perfect, right down to most of his mannerisms. I mean... he fooled us all."

"Ah. Fools of us all, exactly. That, my friend, is precisely my meaning. I have never before seen a metamorph fabricate such a perfect mimicry, of both appearance and demeanor, of an actual person before today. And even more astounding, to a group of the subject's closest peers."

"It was impressive," Bullit interjected, as he passed by on his way from the biobed to the cockpit. "Obviously, he was a master shape-shifter."

"I agree. Clearly he was possessed of exceptional ability," Bullseye said.

Stansky rubbed his chin in thought. "But, even so... it's unlikely any metamorph could be so dead-on from just a picture or video. You know, I've seen plenty of metamorphs pose as people I know, and the most convincing are when they have the person they're imitating right in front of them, right there when they make the change. For this guy to be so on the money, he would have had to..."

"Yes, James! Exactly right," Bullseye interrupted. "He would have had to have physical contact with our friend Rook. At least long enough to study and reproduce every trivial circumstantial of Rook's outward form to perfection, and long enough to perform at least a cursory examination of his mind through extrasensory perception..."

"But not long enough to learn about Rook's cybernetic limb, and duplicate it on himself!" Stansky finished excitedly. "And, he couldn't have been with us for long, or he would have figured out the mistake and fixed it."

"Exactly. Implying that rather than days or weeks ago, the devious substitution must have taken place recently, and in person, and in some small degree of haste. It is very likely it happened just as you and Tachion postulated earlier, during this very day on Oberonn, sometime amidst the distraction of battle."

"*Download complete*," the computer's voice chimed in. "*Authorization required for viewing individual mission records.*"

Bullseye turned back to his station for a moment. "Authorization Bullseye, November One Tango Charlie. Play record from time index two nine zero, overlay visor HUD readout, and mute comm chatter and external parabolics."

The monitors in front of Bullseye sprang to life, showing a full three hundred sixty degrees of video from Rook's helmet, along with data streams from his battlecomp, showing everything from scanner readings, to environmental conditions, to vital signs. Rook was lying on his back on the forest floor, his rear camera dark as it faced straight into the ground, his forward camera showing the towering evergreens reaching upward to a blue and near cloudless sky. Bullseye was visible in one of the side view images, typing furiously on the keypad of his armor's gauntlet as he sought medical help from Tachion.

"Computer, perform deep scan for anomalies," Bullseye said as he watched himself on the monitor.

"*Please specify,*" the computer replied.

"Any anomalies, no matter the triviality. Any inconsistencies within the record, or sensor readings, or in the data itself."

"*Working,*" the computer said.

The video began playing forward at high speed, then it stopped and played again at high speed in reverse, then forward again. Over and over, the footage rushed forward and back, replaying the long battle at lightning speed. A stream of gibberish computer code cascaded down a second screen as the computer analyzed every aspect of the hours of Rook's personal record.

Finally, the monitors stopped, and the computer voice spoke again. "*Scan complete, twenty-six anomalies detected.*"

"Damn, that many?" Stansky said.

"Yet most, or all, could mean nothing, I fear," Bullseye said. Then to the computer, "Computer, list anomalies in order of appearance, and present aloud."

The computer voice began reading off the list as all four of them listened intently. "*Timestamp one seven five, external temperature is five degrees above Oberonn seasonal norm. Timestamp one eight one, right chest plate inertia damage has caused internal micro-fractures, post-repair plate strength will remain decreased by seven percent. Timestamp one nine six, sonic grenade disabled parabolic recording for five point four nine seconds...*"

"Wow. This is all super helpful," Bullit said sarcastically.

"Any small clue could help," Tachion chimed in from where he was cleaning and restocking the biobed area. "A small thing could mean more than what it initially sounds like."

"Please," James added. "Who gives two shits that it was a hot day? We know that already. We were sweating our asses off in it."

"If it was so unbearably hot for you, why didn't you wear your fancy climate-controlled Powered Assault armor?" Bullit asked.

"Because it was supposed to be a cakewalk mission," Stansky jumped to his own defense, "and I didn't want to get it damaged."

"You stupid ape!" Bullit laughed. "It's armor, that's what it is for."

"Why don't you go curl up in your litter box and lick yourself, you miserable..."

"Gentlemen, please!" Bullseye barked. "A modicum of silence I beg of you, that I may better concentrate on the task at hand!"

The computer voice continued its rambling list of incidental and inconsequential findings. "...*parabolic scanners detect local rivers may be exceeding flood stage. Timestamp two one seven, subspace transmitter receiving interference from solar flare, effective range reduced by three percent. Timestamp two two nine, background radiation levels are point four nine centiGray per hour above Oberonn norm.*"

"Well, that's interesting," Tachion said. "I wonder what the source of that is. Maybe a nearby generator?"

"Shush!" Bullit and Stansky spat in unison.

"*Timestamp two three eight, left boot clamp damaged, strength reduced by sixty percent. Timestamp two four two, electric field contact has corrupted the data record. Timestamp two five seven, a drop in...*"

"Computer, hold!" Bullseye snapped as he stiffened up straighter in his chair. "Replay last item."

"*Timestamp two four two, electric field contact has corrupted the data record,*" the computer replied.

"Do you think that's it?" Stansky asked.

"I am as yet unsure," Bullseye replied. "Computer, state source of electric field."

"*The data from this portion of the record is corrupt. Unable to specify.*"

"Describe the electric field," Bullseye ordered.

"*An alternating field of fifty thousand volts, at a current effectiveness of four milliamps, and forty-five cycles per second, contacted the unit at timestamp two four two, for a minimum of two point three seconds. Data after this point is corrupt until timestamp two five five.*"

"That's like over six minutes of blank data," Bullit remarked from the cockpit. "Anything could have happened during that time."

"What do you think, a stunner?" Stansky asked.

"A possibility not without merit, my human friend. Computer, display energy signature on main console."

"*Data incomplete,*" the computer said. "*Energy signature recorded for only six point four times ten to the eighth nanoseconds.*"

"Display recorded portion, and extrapolate remainder," Bullseye instructed.

The center monitor at Bullseye's station went black, and then a series of overlapping waved lines began drawing themselves across the screen from left to right.

"Doesn't look like any weapon waveform I'm familiar with," Stansky remarked.

"Precisely why it is I who has the vocation of weapons connoisseur, and yourself to whom we relegate the equally enigmatical métier of demolitions."

James scrunched his face slightly in confusion, raising an eyebrow. "Was there an insult hidden somewhere in that sentence?"

"On the contrary, James. I was merely suggesting that while this signature has no meaning to you, nor should it in your arena of proficiency, I recognize it unequivocally. Allowing for minor miscalculations by the computer in its extrapolation, I would say this signature appears notably similar to an electrostunner, on a low power setting." Bullseye spun his chair around to face the majority of the group. "Specifically, the ERX StaticStorm II, manufactured by GearForge Transglobal exclusively for the Capellan Military, and the standard-issue weapon of the holy queen's temple guard."

"I would have got that one, if I wasn't busy flying," Bullit commented.

"I don't remember seeing any lyghtans down there," James said, "and definitely no temple guards."

"Nor do I," Bullseye replied with a puzzled, thoughtful look. "Yet nevertheless, I am sure of my assessment."

"Continue the list from after the data corruption," Tachion urged. "Let's see what happened next."

"Agreed," Bullseye said. "Computer, continue list."

"*Timestamp two five seven,*" the computer read on, "*a drop in body temperature of six point two degrees noted. Timestamp two six...*"

"Computer pause," Tachion said. "That's it. That is where the metamorph copied Rook and took his place. Normal metamorph body temperature runs about five to seven degrees lower than a seti."

"Computer," Bullseye said. "Send planetary positioning sensor readings for Rook's battlecomp at timestamp two four two to navigation."

"*Working,*" the computer said.

"Okay, got it. I have the PPS location," Bullit said. "This oughta narrow down the search a little bit."

"It merely draws a starting line from which to begin our quest. Yet many miles, and many more burdens, may lay strewn across our intrepid path, we few friends unenlightened to our journey's possible vain conclusion."

Stansky put his hand on Bullseye's back and leaned in. "Or, he could be laying right there for us, unconscious. Right where the PPS says, just waiting for us to pick him up." He stood and headed to the rear of the cabin to ready the Beagle probe.

"Ah, James. If I may be so bold as to intentionally misquote Albert Camus, 'in the midst of my bleakest winters, I've found there is, within you, an invincible summer'."

"Wait, *what*?!" Bullit blurted out in amused puzzlement. "In *James* there is? In *James Stansky* there's an invincible summer?!"

James ignored the slight from Bullit. "It's called having *hope*," he replied to Bullseye from the aft section of the *Bugeye*. "You should try it sometime."

Bullseye turned back to his monitors, which were replaying a ten second piece of footage from Rook's battlecomp over and over. An image of running through a patch of thick underbrush between the trees, ending with a flash of blinding white light, then static. "Perhaps," he muttered quietly to himself. "Yet hope is ofttimes a slow and insidious poison, serving but to prolong the disquieted soul's torment."

7.3

PRESIDENT HAROLD VERNON FORESTAL—HARRY to his close acquaintances, Vern to the best of his old school buddies, and yet tellingly still *Harold* to his wife—sat at the breakfast table of the presidential residence, pretending to read the daily briefing on the tablet in front of him, as in reality he stared and pondered the long, reddish hair of his spouse, as she stood outside on a nearby balcony overlooking the rear gardens. Several hanging baskets overflowing with purple, pink and white flowers hung along the lengthy wrap-around terrace, and she moved from one to the next like a bumblebee, peering inside each container, inspecting them one by one for dead or wilted petals, plucking away the offenders, and dropping them into her already emptied cup of morning tea.

The early dawn sun now shone through her auburn locks as it rose above the topiary at the back of the east lawn, illuminating it from behind to a bright, fiery red. At one time, President Forestal counted this luminous copper waterfall as one of the many attributes that had captivated him, and he would stare at her like this with mixed feelings of relaxed contentment and childlike wonder, like watching a sunset reflected in a quietly shimmering ocean. Now, however, as he watched her through the large glass windows, moving across the balcony through the spotlights of morning sun, her irradiated hair drifting lightly in the summer breeze, and glowing brightly with the back-lighting, he could not help but feel a twinge of disgust begin to curl the right corner of his upper lip. As if she somehow sensed him, she turned suddenly to peer in at her husband through the veranda windows, and he quickly lifted his oversized mug to hide his involuntary sneer. He swallowed down the feeling with a large gulp of his coffee, and turned his gaze back to the tablet in his other hand.

Just as he began again to review the displayed text of the morning briefing, the image of his trusted receptionist and scheduler appeared in the upper left corner as a soft trilling sound rang from the device. He quickly ran his hand over his as-yet-uncombed hair, then lightly touched the android's image to open it full screen.

"Yes, Vertix, what is it?" he asked.

"*Good morning, sir. General Isaiah has requested to see you right away.*"

"Tell him I'll be in the office in about an hour. Squeeze him in sometime before the meeting with the Ilshnari Ambassador."

"*I apologize, sir,*" she replied. "*What I meant is... he is requesting to see you immediately, right now in the residence. He is in the foyer with your security detail.*"

"Really? Well, that can't be good," the president considered. He looked back to his wife, still busy outside. "Go ahead and send him up Vertix. Thank you." He touched the tablet screen and closed the image.

President Forestal took a moment to straighten his robe a bit, but then quickly decided not to bother. General Isaiah and he were old friends from long ago, roommates for several years at the academy, and he had often been seen far more indisposed, and in greater states of undress than he was fortunate to be in today. The human general soon peered around the corner from the living area into the kitchen, escorted by a seti member of the presidential security team. He rapped his knuckles lightly on the wall above the polished gray stone counter, knocking three times.

"Mr. President?" the general asked tentatively.

"Don't worry, Ephraim, she's outside," the president answered.

"Ah... well, good mornin', Vern," the general said, sounding noticeably more relaxed as the security agent left them alone. "Sorry to bug you so early."

"No worries. What's so urgent?"

"Well, we detected a security breach about twenty minutes ago, a hacker attempting to access Starlaw and military databases."

"Was anything sensitive accessed?" President Forestal asked as he leaned forward and put down his coffee.

"No, no, nothing like that," the general answered. "We stopped the hack before it got anywhere, and actually have it doing a simulated data search, so the infiltrator doesn't yet know we are aware of them. We want them to think they have successfully logged in, at least until we knew what information they were trying to locate."

"Okay, so I still don't understand the urgency, Eph. Who is this? What was it they were searching for?"

"Well, that's just it. We don't know for certain. But we have a likely suspect, and our confidence is high. The hacker is using an outdated weakness in the firewall, one that has long ago been patched. However, we make it a practice to monitor those pathways after they've been closed, as a sort of snare for those who may unknowingly still try to access it. So, we have a full record of this current incursion, and the script that's being implemented to access the servers. Our most expert cyber-analysts have studied this script, looking for hallmark techniques and signature coding styles, and checking against our database of known hackers' prior work. They think they've found an equivalent, with almost certainty. The scripting patterns are a near match for the mercenary infiltrationist, Rook, of Parliament."

"Parliament is hacking a Coalition intelligence server?" President Forestal asked, sounding incredulous.

"Well, it actually wouldn't be the first time. Which is why we have such complete documentation of his signature style," the general explained. "Of course, nothing was ever done about it in the past, beyond monitoring and watch-listing. After all, knowing it is one thing, proving it is something else. And nothing ever overtly dangerous was ever accessed, like launch codes or..."

"And what, pray tell, was accessed this time?"

"Ah, well, that's the other reason I wanted to see you so urgently," the general said in a more hushed tone, as he glanced up at the first lady still buzzing around busily beyond the windowpanes. "They're submitting facial recognition scans and DNA profiles, looking to identify an individual. The genetic search came back, sir... to Special Agent Esil Brin. The SSS operative you sent to investigate that human at the TriStar summit."

"Jesus. How did... I mean... Agent Brin has gone unaccounted-for for months now. Has that changed?"

"No, sir."

"Well, what does that mean? What does Parliament have to do with any of this? Did they find him somewhere? Are they working with Brin? Or against him?"

"All possibilities, sir, but as of now we just don't know," said the general.

The president sat thinking for a moment, then stood from the table and took General Isaiah by the elbow, leading him towards the kitchen counter, and further from the balcony window. "Alright Ephraim, let's think about this for a minute. The one thing we do know, or at least are fairly confident about, is for some reason or another, Parliament is interested in Esil Brin. This... could be good." He paused, tapping his fingers against the general's arm as he considered the possibilities. "This could actually be very good. If, for whatever reason, they want to involve themselves in Esil's mission... which, in all honesty, is what I wanted from the get-go... then I say let's encourage it, and help them as much as we can. From a distance, that is."

"Sir?"

"Help them, Eph. Give them what they're looking for. Send them Agent Brin's dossier and mission outline, redacting anything too sensitive, of course. Let them think they accessed the information on their own. If they weren't planning to help Esil, maybe this will convince them otherwise."

"Understood Vern, I'll take care of it right away."

"Is there any way we can track them, Ephraim? Find out where they're trying to access us from?"

"Well... perhaps," the general considered. "I mean, we could put a tracking script in the data packet we send them, that would ping their location off the nearest subspace relay station, and would give us a general idea. But, if our speculation that this is in fact Rook and Parliament is correct, he is far too clever for that. Rook would know better than to download the data without scanning it first. He would likely find that script and scrub it out easily."

"Nevertheless, worth a try," the president ordered. "Make it happen, and if we do locate them, either this way or another, I want them monitored. Put a team together, quietly. Black ops. Their mission is to observe and report only, is that clear? Not to interfere."

"Yes, right away sir," the general said, as he pulled away and headed toward the kitchen door.

"Remember, from a *distance* now, Ephraim. Unless I give the order otherwise. And I want constant reports," the president whispered, looking to his wife heading back to the balcony door, "whenever able."

"Understood." The general winked as he exited the room.

Harold was back at the table and sipping his coffee before the first lady had even closed the door.

7.4

"STANSKY, HOW'S THAT BEAGLE PROBE coming along?" Bullit called out from the cockpit of the *Bugeye*.

"It's all set whenever you are," he answered back quickly.

Bullit spoke backward over his shoulder to Bullseye at the sensor station. "Okay boss, we're passing the Oberonn system's outer rim now. Slowing to sub-light."

Bullseye was staring with a look of confusion at the display on one of his monitors, and seemed not to hear Bullit's announcement. "Hello? K'Tas T'Mir to Bullseye, do you read me?"

"What's that?" Bullseye grunted, peering up at the cockpit. "Oh, of course, thank you. Let us then dispatch the Beagle probe to the coordinates of our earlier engagement, and then follow her along towards the planet, in as close a reenactment of our original trajectory as possible."

"Launching probe," Bullit announced, followed by the sound of the sensor-laden projectile leaving the nose of the *Bugeye*. "Setting our approach vector to pass over the smaller moon's pole and enter an equatorial orbit of Oberonn, just like last time."

"What is it you're so engrossed in, Bullseye?" Stansky asked as he leaned over the seti's shoulder.

"I extricated the documentation from Starlaw's database on our intruder, through Rook's most convenient back door access," Bullseye told him, with little comprehension of the meaning of the words. "According to both his DNA and facial recognition, he *himself* was Starlaw. An agent for the SSS to be exact. Lieutenant Esil Brin."

"Why would the Starlaw Secret Service want to kill... I mean, kidnap Rook, or infiltrate Parliament? We've always had a good working relationship with them."

"I think that unlikely," Bullseye continued, pointing to the monitor. "It declares the late agent 'missing in action', nigh six long months now. He went displaced whilst on a mission here on Oberonn, and is assumed dead, or rogue."

"Well," Tachion said, as he finished stowing away his medical equipment and took his place at the science station, "it appears now he's both. Does it say what mission he was on at the time?"

"Alas, the full details are classified, and without Rook here to bypass the restriction, I think it unlikely we'll discover them. But it does imply in the cover notes that..." Bullseye turned now to read from the screen, "...he was investigating a human that appeared occasionally on Oberonn as of late, to determine what influence, if any, he seemed to have with the Oberonn Aerospace Defense Commander."

"General Nylis?" Bullit asked. "I didn't think he was the type to be influenced by anyone, especially a Coalition citizen."

"He certainly is not," Bullseye replied. "But what is truly interesting is the human's name. Denali."

"Denali!" Stansky snapped in surprise. "You're joking. Well... that's gotta be a coincidence. I'm mean... we killed Denali. Rook shot him to death right in his office."

"Yeah, don't remind me," Bullit muttered angrily under his breath. "He should have been mine. That fucker killed my brother, Wyvern."

"You're not the only one that had people die," Stansky reminded him. "He killed MacKendric. He killed Mishta. He killed *Jim Dodger,* for Christ's sake. You were with us then. You remember that, don't you? Our friend Dodger, stuffed and mounted under glass. Like some... fucked-up museum exhibit?"

"Those were friends. Wyvern was my *family!* The right of vengeance was *mine.* And just when I'm about to go to work on him, Rook blows him away right in front of me."

"Steady on, Bullit," Bullseye said, in a calm but commanding tone. "That affair is done and done, fifteen years now gone by. Let us sanction the past to stay where it is, as it seldom has anything new to say."

"I don't see how it could be the same man," Tachion said, ignoring Bullit's minor outburst. "Did our Denali have any family that we forgot about? Any colleagues that may have taken up his operations under his name?"

Bullseye changed the screen display to another profile. "I pondered the same wondering, thus brought up Denali's Starlaw dossier. There is naught akin to those possibilities listed here."

"Okay," Stansky said, "so some guy, named Denali, turns the Coalition agent investigating him rogue, then uses him to come after us... completely unprovoked? Man, you know it sure sounds like our old friend."

"Indeed, it does," Bullseye said, "but as you rightly expressed, James, we all saw him die. We shall thus assume this a different gentleman, with a similar name only. Of course, the question remains... what does he want with Rook? Or Parliament?"

Suddenly there was a loud beeping alarm coming from the cockpit, and the monitors that had been displaying the Beagle probe data at Tachion's science station went black. "Whoa!" Bullit exclaimed. "Someone just blew our probe away! Right as it was nearing the atmosphere." He zoomed his overhead display into the image of a colossal vessel. "It's an Oberonn starcruiser."

"What!" Bullseye yelled, turning his monitor from the dossier back to active scanner mode. "It is the *Okubi*, General Nylis' ship. That is where the general and I had our briefing for this mission a few days ago. Bullit, hail them please."

"Channel's open, audio only," Bullit replied.

Bullseye used the coded call sign—Ikati—that the general had assigned them for this mission. "OSS *Okubi*, this is the Ikati calling. We are conducting recon on a mission for your commander. Why have you shot down our probe?"

The male voice that responded back to him spoke broken Coalition common, with a thick chamai accent. "*Unidentified ship, we show no transponder code for your vessel. You are in violation of Oberonn shipping law. We have no registry listing for an... A-cat-hey... in our database. Identify yourself.*"

"No, no. This is the Ikati," Bullseye repeated slowly and clearly. "It is the call sign your General issued to us."

"*I have no record of such a call sign,*" the voice answered back abruptly.

Stansky sighed, slumping into the copilot seat. "We are about to get screwed again, aren't we? Man, this has Denali written all over it."

"Perhaps if I converse with General Nylis himself," Bullseye suggested. He opened the channel again and called the starcruiser. "Request to speak to *Okubi* actual," he said.

After a few long moments, the unmistakable deep grating voice of General Nylis came over the comm. *"Unidentified vessel, this is your final warning. Leave the Oberonn system at once or prepare to be fired upon."*

"Yep, screwed again," Stansky said.

"Well then, there it is," Bullseye said in frustration. "We shall consider that rejoin as confirmation, then. The question of whether this was all an elaborate ruse has been answered. Yet I can postulate no theory as to the chamai motive for such betrayal, why they would conspire to abduct our Rook, to surreptitiously substitute with another."

Bullit turned to look back at the rest of them with an air of concern. "Guys, that starcruiser is coming about, and bringing her weapons to bear. Particle cannon is charging. Perhaps we should make ourselves scarce."

Tachion suddenly interrupted. "Wait. Bullseye, I'm picking up an energy beam from the *Okubi*. It's aimed at the planet's surface, right at the mountain where we just were. Actually... it's beneath the mountain." He turned from his monitor and faced Bullseye. "It's a teleporter signal. Someone is zapping down beneath the battle site. That must be where Rook is."

"It certainly is a place to start," Bullseye answered. "Can you obtain the exact coordinates?"

"Negative. We would need Rook to decrypt the signal. All I can tell is that it's directed over a mile below ground."

"Wouldn't matter anyway," Stansky remarked. "We don't have a teleporter on board to zap down there after them. We'll have to use the one aboard *Parliament One*, if we can get her here."

Bullit scoffed. "If they're not letting us near the planet in our tiny *Bugeye* with our harmless probe, do you really think they're gonna let us park the *Parliament One* in orbit and zap down? We're gonna have to figure out another way. And we need the coordinates out of the *Okubi* teleporter logs." The *Bugeye* suddenly lurched to the side, as the near miss of a warning shot from the chamai starcruiser's particle cannon ripped past the bow. "But we can figure that out later," Bullit said, as he turned the *Bugeye* and engaged the warp drive.

Bullseye thought for a moment. "James, take the helm. Fly us only beyond the reach of their sensors. Then activate the cloaking device, and take us back in towards the planet. Bullit, I'll need you to suit up. I have an idea."

Stansky took the *Bugeye* out well past the distance of any long-range sensors, and cloaked the ship. The power drain was evident from the noticeable dimming of the interior lights, and the group turned off any monitors and systems that were not immediately needed, in order to conserve power. They then made a wide, sweeping circle and headed back towards Oberonn from the opposite direction. The entire round trip took the better part of an hour, but the *Okubi* was right where she had been when they left, in close orbit of the planet. Stansky slowed the now invisible *Bugeye* to ten percent of the pulse drive's output as he approached, decreasing any subspace ripples that the chamai starship might detect, then lowered their shields to hide any conspicuous energy signatures.

"Okay, so why am I putting this on?" Bullit asked Bullseye, as he secured the helmet of his environmental suit to the collar ring.

Bullseye, already fully dressed in similar gear, answered through the external speaker of his helmet. *"As you rightly pointed out, we must source the teleportation coordinates straight from the console's logs. Thus, you and I shall secure them."*

"What?! Why me? Wouldn't Stansky be a bit less obvious? He could just cover his stubby round ears, and a little prosthetic on the bridge of his nose..."

"It is due to our collective dereliction in our continuing education. We have become, each of us, too specialized, and have grown woefully ignorant in skills beyond our professions. Ostensibly, in the absence of Rook, it appears we can hardly boot up a computer. Your few systems-access courses, severely limited as they may be, are our best hope of procuring the teleporter files."

"But I can't even read chamai," Bullit protested.

"Aye, but I can. That is why we two shall go," Bullseye concluded, as they both cinched the straps of their QEU powerpacks tighter, and connected it to their personal shield generators at their belts.

"Okay, well... what do you expect us to do? Just float over and knock on the door?"

"Not as such," Bullseye said, then he turned to Stansky in the pilot's seat. *"James, match the orbit course and speed of the Okubi, and take us in as close as possible over the flight bay doors. Set for us a sightline deep within its hold."*

"Okay," Stansky said with a skeptical tone. "But like Bullit said, you can't just float over. They'll see you coming once you leave the cloaking field of the *Bugeye*."

"What do you have in mind, Bullseye?" Tachion asked.

Bullseye reached into his locker, producing a pair of small, strangely-carved, metallic triangles, and holding them up for the group to see. They were a one-of-a-kind ancient and alien technology, capable of transporting up to two people short distances. They had served to get each of them out of many a scrape, ever since Bullseye had first discovered them on a rogue casino planet, a great many years ago. The only downfall was that you could only materialize wherever the first triangle landed, so your aim had better be pretty good.

"*Oh, you have gotta be shitting me,*" Bullit snapped. "*You're gonna try and throw that thing all the way into the bay? What if you miss?*"

"*Well, if our pilot can gain us satisfactory proximity, the difficulty should be negligible,*" Bullseye said.

"I'll do my best," Stansky promised, with even more skepticism than before.

Bullseye continued. "*And, we'll benefit from someone with greater power behind their throw, and accuracy in their aim. Doctor, would you do the honors?*"

"I will indeed," Tachion said, as their resident hand-weapons expert took one of the triangles.

Bullseye attached the other of the strange devices to his left chest with a satisfying 'click', then the three of them headed to the back wall of the *Bugeye* and opened the inner door of the airlock. Tachion had no need for a suit, provided he would not be in the cold of space nor exposed to solar radiation for more than an hour or so. They closed the inner door, the three standing jammed against each other in the small space, until Stansky was satisfied that he was as close as possible to the open bay doors of the starcruiser. Then from the cockpit, he opened the outer portal, and Tachion, Bullit and Bullseye looked out into open space—the massive starship, and the planet of Oberonn, both looming large before them.

"*Remember,*" Bullseye said over the comms in his helmet, "*once we have transported, we shall not have the luxury of using our comlinks, lest we be overheard. Provided all goes well, we will endeavor to disembark in the same manner. Keep the* Bugeye *in orbit over the* Okubi, *and continue scanning for the device's unique metallurgical signature. We shall catapult it from the launch bay, and when you detect it drifting in the void, you need only but to retrieve it to usher us back aboard.*"

"*You know,*" Stansky said over the comlink from the cockpit, "*that's easier said than done.*"

"I think he is right, old friend," Tachion agreed. "Getting off that ship will not be as easy as getting on."

"*I don't think* getting on *sounds that easy,*" Bullit quipped, as he gripped tightly to the handhold over the open doorway.

"*We've extricated ourselves from worse circumstances, on many an occasion,*" Bullseye offered.

Bullit leaned out the door a bit, peering at the thirty meters of open space between them and the unsecured bay of the *Okubi*, and the cloud-covered planet's surface rushing past miles below. "*Not much worse,*" he said.

"Are you ready?" Tachion asked.

"*Prepared,*" Bullseye said, taking a tight grip around Bullit's waist.

"*Just do it,*" Bullit sighed, averting his gaze and closing his eyes.

Tachion squeezed past them in the tight airlock, and braced his feet against each side of the open exterior door. Grabbing tightly to the overhead handhold at the top of the doorway, he leaned his massive body far outside of the *Bugeye*, giving his right arm room to move. He then carefully turned the triangle over in his hand, holding its edge as he would a throwing star or razor disk, and made a few practice tossing motions to get his aim just right. The open hangar bay door was at least fifty meters wide, and nearly half that in height. The bay extended back some one hundred meters, and its deck was packed with fighters, forklifts, and machinery. To throw the triangle into the huge doorway and land it somewhere out of sight should be as easy as hitting the side of a barn—if they were on solid ground. In theory, it should be no more difficult in this situation, but the fact that they were orbiting at thousands of miles per hour, and several hundred miles above ground, added a certain degree of trepidation and self-doubt. Tachion endeavored to rationalize that away as he made his final practice swing, and spun the disk carefully toward the open bay. It released from his fingers on what appeared a perfect trajectory—but agonizingly slowly.

"*What the hell! My grandmother could throw harder than that,*" Bullit snapped, as the triangle drifted ever so gently towards its target.

"I felt that accuracy was more important than velocity," Tachion answered, seemingly not offended.

"*It will never make it all the way,*" Bullit decided.

"*Inertia will carry it there, my friend,*" Bullseye interjected. "*Patience.*"

The three watched the disk sail smoothly through the void, getting ever closer, and right on the mark for a perfect landing.

"Oh, damn," Tachion said suddenly, as he watched the triangle's crossing. He pointed out of the open *Bugeye* airlock at something that none of them had anticipated. The hangar bay doors of the *Okubi* were beginning to close.

"*What happens if it hits the outside of the door?*" Bullit asked anxiously.

"*We'll materialize outside the ship, unfortunately,*" Bullseye answered. "*Perhaps we should be ready to abort.*" He grabbed hold of the matching triangle on his chest in preparation to tear it off.

"Wait a moment," Tachion pleaded. "I think it's going to make it."

The triangle drifted casually towards the ever-narrowing opening, as the huge bay door plodded down unwavering along its tracks.

"*Blow on it*," Stansky suggested, laughing over the comlink.

"*Blow yourself,*" Bullit snapped.

At their distance, it was hard to make out which was in the lead, the closing bay door or the alien triangle, and the three of them leaned out and squished against each other, straining and squinting to see which would win. Then with only a foot or two to spare, the disk sailed under the massive closing door and through the forcefield to clatter onto the hangar bay floor.

"Good luck," Tachion turned and said quickly, but the pair had already vanished. The hangar door closed tightly, sealing them inside the chamai starcruiser.

"Nice toss, Tach," Stansky said. "Now it's *really* gonna be hard to get them out."

The doctor closed the airlock's outer door and pressurized the small space before re-entering the main cabin of the *Bugeye*. Stansky carefully veered the craft away from the mighty starship a short way, and then turned her around to mimic the *Okubi's* movements at a little safer distance. Tachion activated the sensors that would constantly sweep the surrounding space for the uncommon alloys in the triangle. Then, unable to sit in the copilot's seat because of his size, he placed himself at Bullseye's station, the closest seat to Stansky in the cockpit.

"That was a close one, huh?" Stansky said, as he twisted and slumped himself into a more comfortable position in his seat.

"Too close," Tachion said.

"I hate to sound cliche, but I'm getting a little too old for this shit," James said. "I thought this was gonna be a nice little recovery job. A quick smash and grab, and back home inside two or three days."

"Does it ever work out that way?" Tachion wondered.

"No, I guess not," James laughed. "Tatiana is gonna kill me this time, though. I'm missing her birthday. Again."

"Uh-oh, hope you got her something nice."

"I thought I'd have time to shop after this job. Guess that didn't work out too well." Stansky sat up then, and turned around in his seat to look at Tachion. "She wants me to retire, you know."

"Hasn't she wanted you to retire ever since you became a couple? A long time ago now?"

"Twelve years. And every day of it, the same thing. 'When am I gonna retire'. 'When am I gonna finally marry her'. I nearly asked her, you know. Several times, in fact. Bought a ring and everything."

"Hmm. Bullseye would have quoted Dickens to you. '*Almost* carries no weight, especially in matters of the heart'."

"Yeah, well, I'm not sure it really is a matter of the heart, though. It's more of a matter of practicality. I mean, I'm gonna be fifty soon. I know that's nothing for you, but for us humans, that's the time to start settling down a bit."

"So, you're not really in love with her then?"

"Oh, I don't know, I guess maybe I am. We've been together for so long, you know? Sometimes I think I won't be sure, unless I take time to weigh other options... if you know what I mean. But if she found out, boy... that would be the end of that."

"But, I have seen you... 'weighing options'... many times. Many, *many* times."

"I don't mean like that, just fooling around. Sure, I do that plenty. What I mean is trying another relationship, testing being serious with someone else."

Tachion felt ill-equipped to advise his comrade in this particular situation, so he remained silent for a moment, then changed the subject. "So, are you going to retire after this?"

"I think so. Actually, I wanted to before coming on this job."

"Bullseye talked you out of it?" Tachion asked.

"No. I didn't tell him. I just didn't know what his reaction would be."

"I know what you mean. Believe it or not, I was going to do the same thing."

"No, really?" James said in surprise. "Why did you come then?"

"Well, the job sounded so easy. I figured one more little adventure before I let Bullseye down."

"Funny, that's exactly what I thought. I guess that shows us for keeping our mouths shut," Stansky laughed. "You know, it's just so hard to tell Bullseye because, well... this is all he has. He's got no family to turn to, and he's too closed off and depressed all the time to meet anyone. We're all he's got, and he'll be crushed when we tell him that we're all set with it."

"I agree. And it seems the reason that all he has is this career, is because of this career," Tachion postulated. "The longer he does it, the more closed off he becomes to anything else."

"Yes, exactly. I think he just never learned to let go of what we have to see and do out there. I mean, the rest of us joke it off a lot, and I have Tatiana to go home to. Rook has Bell and the twins, and Bullit just doesn't give a fuck. You have your work at the Biological Society. Plus, you've always been able to rationalize things into this black and white, right and wrong. But Bullseye seems to live in this gray area, where he's never sure if what he has to do every time out is right, if the people he has to kill to do his job really had to die, and he takes the ghosts of every one of them home with him at night. It's not healthy."

The two of them sat back quietly for a moment, then Stansky leaned back to Tachion again. "You know, I wasn't supposed to say anything, but Rook was thinking of hanging it up too."

"I know," Tachion said.

"You know? Man, what's with him? He tells me not to talk about it to anyone, and then he goes and tells everybody anyway."

"He didn't tell Bullseye, for the same reasons as us."

"He said that? Wow, we all need to get Bullseye in a room and have a serious talk."

"I agree."

James paused for a minute. "So, do you really think Rook is still alive?"

"I think he is harder to kill than simply dragging him off into a hole and replacing him with a metamorph," Tachion answered. "I don't think Bullseye does, though."

"No?"

"I had to talk him into this little search we're attempting. I practically had to force him."

"Oh, he wanted someone to force him. One more chance to go balls out into the breach," Stansky said. "You know he takes more and more absurd risks every time we go out. Sometimes I think he's just hoping to get wasted, and put an end to all those ghosts once and for all."

"His mood *has* become more... morose... as of late," Tachion admitted.

Stansky chuckled then, "And look at this crap he's dragged Bullit into now, all alone on an Oberonn military starship, no weapons or armor? That's the worst idea I ever heard."

"You honestly think he is putting himself in danger purposely?"

"I don't know, maybe not. It's hard to tell what's going on with him as rarely as I see him. You know he never comes over anymore. If we're not working, I don't see him at all. Same with Rook too. He hasn't gone there in forever. I think the whole family thing gets to him, makes him question his life choices or something, you know? He hasn't even seen Rook and Bell's kids in like... oh... ten or twelve years. Not till Flashpoint showed up in his school."

"I had no idea," Tachion said. "I saw them only a few months ago, at his daughter Relic's graduation from infiltration school. Taking after her old man, as you humans say. And the boy... demolitions, as you know. He, Rook, and I went ferox hunting earlier this year. They're adults in their mid-twenties now. I can't believe he hasn't seen them since they were barely teens."

The sound of the proximity alarm going off suddenly interrupted their conversation. "Uh-oh! Son of a bitch!" Stansky shouted, breaking the calm, and throwing himself back upright in his chair. "I got something else you won't believe."

"What is it? Are they coming out already?"

"No, they're going away. The *Okubi* is leaving orbit!"

Stansky pulled up hard to avoid colliding with the oncoming cruiser, and then settled the *Bugeye* in behind her at a safe distance, convoying towards the outer edge of the system at full sub-light. "If they can just get to a hatch and jump out before they go to warp."

Suddenly the *Bugeye* was tossed about violently as the starcruiser's huge engines sprang to life, and blasted the vessel out of visibility in a fraction of a second.

"Follow them, quickly!" Tachion urged.

"We can't, Tach. The old *Bugeye* can only push maybe forty percent warp, maximum. And I'd have to decloak us to get the juice for that. They're at eighty percent already. We'll never catch them. Or even come close."

"What do we do?" Tachion asked.

"Nothing Doc. We're fucked."

"As I understand the use of the word, they are the ones that are fucked. We are merely stumped." The android thought for a moment. "Well, it's an Oberonnian vessel, and we're at Oberonn. I guess we have no choice but to wait. They'll have to return at some point."

"Man, that could be days. Or weeks," Stansky complained. "Or even months."

The two sat staring blankly out the window for a while at where the ship had just been. Tachion finally got up and went to his regular station. After a minute, the sound of a Beagle probe being launched came from the nose of the ship.

"Now *that* thing will definitely never catch them," Stansky said.

"It's not for them, it's for the planet. With the *Okubi* gone, we should have no problem getting the probe to scan the surface."

"What the hell for?" James asked.

"To see if I can pick up any trace of our *first* missing seti. Like you said, James, we may have a lot of time to kill," Tachion explained, as he remotely guided the probe towards the mountainous region on the planet's surface. "Rook, however, may not."

Chapter 8.1

SPRING HAD COME EARLY TO the northern mountain region of Oberonn's largest continent. The melting snows from the unusually brutal passing winter now trickled down from a multitude of tributaries, to join the typical seasonal runoff from the Lamsere Glacier, together filling the once peaceful Ekmer River to the very brims of its banks. The river wound its way in a torrent of whitewater through the densely wooded highlands, occasionally breaching its soft, loamy shores from the sheer volume of swirling water pressing upon them. New brooks trickled forth from these gaps in the river's edge, and winding through the thickly overgrown forest floor, the brooks joined together into streams, and the streams joined to become small and new unnamed rivers all their own.

It had been four years since Hurricane Hellan had slammed into these mountains as it made landfall from the warm southern currents of the Great East Ocean. But the bent and broken acres of trees in the high Qi'yo Valley still remained as evidence of its passing, and now the overflow rivulets from the mighty Ekmer raced into this deep chasm between the dense, forest-covered mountains. With the narrow canyons leading to the flatlands choked with upturned stumps and fallen trees, the water backed up quickly, so that by the middle of the spring season, a great pond had formed in the once dry timberland basin.

The waters at the floor of the pond seeped over time through the soft earth below it, and ran along the flat expanse of bedrock deep below the ground, searching out cracks and crevices in the granite as it pooled and saturated the soil. Then finally building up enough to reach a narrow but deep fissure between two massive plates of bedrock, it raced quickly through the maze of tiny fractures in the stone, deeper and deeper below the vast mountainside.

The waters combined with mineral deposits as it went, becoming rich in limestone particulate and calcium, as well as thick with rancid-smelling sulfur as it passed through ancient volcanic chimneys that lay dormant since the formation of this mountain range. At long last, the tiny hairline rifts opened into a large system of caves a mile or more underground. And it was this first small trickle of water, pausing as it emerged at the roof of the cavern only long enough to form a thick, brownish droplet, that began to drip steadily down from the ceiling.

Rook lay unconscious in a heap on the cavern floor, the effect from the repeated electrostunner hits still an hour or more from wearing off naturally. But now, in what was the culmination of a decade of anomalous weather patterns on the chamai homeworld far above him, the harshly acrid water began dripping from the darkness overhead, landing repeatedly and with quickening regularity on the seti's cheek. Seeping deep into his fur, it ran down over his eyes and past his nose. The sulfurous stench began to rouse him from his sleep, and he woke suddenly, jerking his head from beneath the dripping water as he spat and wiped his face.

There was a moment of utter confusion for Rook as he struggled to get his bearings. Then he instinctively groped at his torso and extremities, aware at once as he did so that his wrists were cuffed closely together, yet he continued quietly fumbling around for any telltale pools of warm sticky fluid trapped in his fur. Feeling none, nor any stabs of pain at the touch of his hand, he determined to his relief that he was, for the most part, uninjured—at least not critically. He raised his head slightly and looked around the cavern.

The area was quite well lit, and Rook could clearly see he was at the back of an elongated natural underground cavity. The air was very cool, but nonetheless heavy with dampness, and the dark rock walls glistened with a thin layer of dew, as harsh artificial light mirrored from their moist, irregular surfaces. His armor had been removed, and he was now clothed in only the white inertia suit jumper that he usually wore beneath his light battle. He cautiously lifted his head higher, propping himself up on one elbow, and searched for the source of the bright illumination.

The cave floor was rocky and uneven and scattered with jagged rubble; some smaller than a coin, others larger than a man's head. Ugly yellow-brown stalagmites sprang forth here and there from the dark stone, some just small lumpy mounds, and others tall and mighty tapered columns reaching forever upwards toward their downward-facing mates, hanging from the surprisingly high vaulted ceiling. The cold ground upon which he reclined was also not nearly level, and he found himself deposited at the high end of the cavern. He looked down the inclined slope at a pair of portable floodlights at the opposite end of the oblong chamber—one facing his direction, the other shining away. A lone figure sat between the two lamps, wearing a navy-blue suit of battle armor that gleamed with the same glaze of moisture as the rest of the surroundings.

The pitched nature of the terrain had forced the figure below into his first mistake. Sitting on a low ledge with his rear leaned towards the incline, his feet comfortably pointing downward with the grade of the rocky slope, the fact that he could not have easily sat any other way forced him to have the now fully awake seti directly at his back. The stuffy, damp air, or just ill-considered negligence, had then compelled his second mistake, as the figure's navy-blue helmet sat perched atop one of the yellow-brown mounds at his side, rather than in its designated place atop his head. Rook could see flesh beneath a dirty blonde cascade of hair. Rosy-hued, yet tan flesh—a human or chamai, or camouflaged metamorph perhaps—he could not tell which from this range. However, it made no difference, the strategy would be the same regardless. One strike, one kill. While Rook would have preferred the opportunity to simply disable and question his chaperone, he had no idea how many more might be waiting in the wings nearby, and there must be no chance of any commotion that may cause others to investigate.

There were a few spots between plates or along joints on the guard's thick armor that could have been vulnerable to a surgically precise attack, but with the helmet resting ineffectually upon the ground, there was really only one move to make. The seti rolled and rose to his feet quickly and quietly, and danced forward in a jogging tiptoe between the loose scattered stones. His inertia suit was wet in the back and felt cold against his fur as he moved. He tacked left slightly to take advantage of a small ledge as a jumping off point, and the innate seti-leap to close the remaining distance was augmented by the downhill grade of the cave. The shadow rook cast behind himself as he approached the glaring floodlight expanded exponentially as he fell back towards the ground, but the sentry still sat blissfully unaware of the hushed action behind him.

Rook landed heavily against the back of the figure, pulling hard on the long hair with his cuffed right hand, then pressing his upward-facing left fist against the lowest possible area of exposed neck. The tractor blades deployed cleanly and smoothly down into the chest cavity, with barely a hint of resistance as they entered. The guard's arms swung back wildly, attempting to grasp whatever had entered his neck, but the shoulder joints of the thick armor didn't allow for the range of motion required to do so. Rook scowled disapprovingly at the suit's lack of mobility, one of many reasons he preferred a lighter armor himself, then released the guard's hair and used the strength of both arms together to yank his tractor blades straight upward as hard and far as possible. They did not slice completely through the skull and out the top, nor would he have expected them to, but he was happily surprised that it cut upward much further than he would have expected. He retracted the blades with a small hand motion, and the entire mess fell forward, sliding briefly down the gentle slope, kicking a few stones and pebbles ahead of it.

"Thank you, Tach," he whispered to himself, as he re-extended the recently sharpened blades from his wrist, wiping off the warm crimson against the side of his leg. "I'm gonna have to give you points for the assist on that one."

A brief search of the blood-soaked corpse, now easily identifiable as human after all, quickly delivered up a baton passkey to the electronic handcuffs. Rook freed himself, then placed the key and the cuffs in the pocket of his jumpsuit, thinking they might be of use later on—either for their intended purpose, or in case he needed to scavenge the small electronic components inside for some reason. He debated for several moments on whether or not to take the guard's armor before exploring further through the caverns, but decided that the quicker and quieter movement his near nakedness provided might help him steer clear of any cause to need the armor in the first place. He did appreciate the lesson this unlucky gentleman had died to teach, however, and took the pristine helmet from the mound where it sat and clipped it to the side of the human's holster belt, which he had also appropriated. No weapons, just a small electrostunner was all else of use the man had on him, so they joined the rest of the newly acquired booty hanging from his waist, and he headed off into the dim of the only exit from the cavern Rook could see.

He slipped quietly through a long, straight passage, climbing over and around rocky protrusions as he went, and the light from the flood lamps behind becoming dimmer and dimmer as he moved forward. Slowly his head began to clear a little, and fragments of distorted and confused memories of how he came to be here leaked into his mind, a few at a time. He had disabled the pillbox canon with Bullit—no wait, with Bullseye—then somehow they became separated. He was zapped, an electrostunner. That he knew for sure. Then awoken later surrounded by soldiers—the lyghtan temple guard? Can that be right? Rook shook his head a bit to try and clear his thoughts. A mirror—they sat him in front of a mirror and asked him questions. What were those questions? He struggled to recall. They were odd—personal, mundane—nothing about the mission. Wait, no—not a mirror. Not a mirror at all. It was a metamorph. A metamorph that looked like himself was asking him questions. Then the electrostunner again. If he could just remember more clearly, he might have a clue as to where the hell he was.

He reached the end of the long narrow passage to find a short upward leading shaft on his left, reaching maybe three meters or so up into what appeared to be another cavern, but it was dark up there, and difficult to be sure. What was easy to see, for his trained eyes, anyway, was the small motion detector affixed to the wall at the entrance to the shaft. It was of no great quality—a mid-tier product at best, from a generally mediocre security tech company. Rook produced the handcuffs from his pocket, and placing them against a large flat rock on the ground, smashed them hard with a second fist-sized stone. The sharp crack echoed down the tunnel and through the caves much louder than he had expected, and he winced his eyes closed as he waited for the sound to finish banging and thundering back and forth against the stone walls. He cautiously opened one eye, listening for some response, and upon hearing none, he opened the other, relaxed, and went back to work.

The small wire and quantum battery he pulled from the handcuff's cracked remains were more than enough for him to short out the electric eye of the motion sensor. At least once it was opened, after a stressful many minutes of loosening a screw with a wholly inadequate piece of plastic shrapnel from the cuff's small circuit board. He gathered back up the still-useful innards of the restraining device, and scampered quickly up the shaft.

The cave beyond was cloaked in absolute blackness, save for a minuscule flicker of orange and yellow light reflecting off the moist walls. For his seti eyes, this was enough for him to see his surroundings fairly clearly. His pupils widened, and his eyes became as black as the air around him. Rook moved forward carefully in the newly discovered area, slowly removing the holster belt with gun and helmet attached, and placing them gingerly on the ground—then dropping low, and extending himself prone on the cold stone, until he could fully assess this new location.

The cavern was half the size of the one where he had awoken, and instead of the cathedral height ceiling, the dark granite roof was hardly two meters high in some places, slightly lower in the rest. He could see, however, that this cave led to a second chamber through multiple openings in the opposite wall from where he just emerged. It was there, in that next room, that the flickering orange light originated.

The echoed sound of voices began to grow in the darkness, and Rook's ears rotated frantically as he sought to pinpoint the direction. He turned on his belly, dragging himself forward to a position where he could peer around a stalagmite, and better see where the conversation was coming from.

The room into which the cave led was, in fact, not a cave at all, at least not entirely. The wall he peered out from was natural and irregular, but the floor and other walls in the chamber were of gray cretespray, smooth and finished. The beginning of an underground bunker built within the caverns, he thought. Two figures approached a small campfire burning within an old rusted half-barrel some twenty meters away, talking as they moved. They stopped when they reached the fire, and Rook was able to see them more clearly. One, a charcoal-skinned female lyghtan in a long brown leather robe, was facing Rook's position. The hood of the robe was pulled back, revealing a mohawk of stark white hair, and her eyes seemed to glow a ghostly pale light-blue. That same color shone brightly from around her hands, having lighted their way as they moved through the caverns.

The other figure stood with its back towards Rook, but was taller and wider, suggesting it was likely a male. He wore a similar robe as the female, but with the hood up, and Rook was unable to see the individual who wore it. Moving ever so quietly, he inched a few feet closer, squinting and straining to hear their conversation.

"Tell me, Vasu, why have you not yet mentioned the general's visit this afternoon," Rook thought he heard the male's voice say in the common tongue.

The woman looked shocked for a moment, then composed herself quickly. "My lord and master, I sought not to hide my deeds from your all-seeing eyes. But I confess to fearing that I acted rashly, and in doing so may have displeased you. General Nylis had lost faith in your Path to the Light, my lord, I sought only to..."

"Enough!" the male voice snapped. "Show me. Give your mind to me."

The lyghtan female knelt obediently before the hooded figure, bowing her head to him. The male reached out with his robe-draped arm, and held his outstretched hand a few inches above the closely shaved side of her head. A bright, pulsing yellow light sprang forth from something on his wrist, bathing her forehead in its glow.

Even from Rook's distant vantage point, he could see the male's hand was likely human, and combined with what was a decidedly Earthan accent, the seti now became certain of it. However, unsatisfied with his ability to hear the conversation against the echoing of the cave walls, he used the opportunity to move a couple of meters closer.

The bright light emanating from the male's hand suddenly stopped, and the lyghtan slumped slightly as if from exhaustion. He lowered his arm a bit, his hand now held out to help her to her feet. She timidly took hold of his forearm, and struggled slightly to lift herself.

"Rise, Vasu," he said. "You have served me well, and your Path. Your faith and loyalty have pleased me. Your decision to discipline General Nylis was correct."

Now standing on her own and looking relieved, the female bowed low before the shrouded man. "I serve at your pleasure, Divine Lord Denali. Mine is but to follow *your* Path to the Light."

Rook froze for a moment at the mention of the name. *She did not just say 'Denali',* he thought to himself. *It's not possible.*

The human spoke again. "Nylis always has a compulsion to reassert his authority after a good disciplining. Did you know that he killed all four of his bodyguards that were witness to you chastising him?"

"Ah. That explains where my ashi'mar has gotten to then. He must have disposed of her too, for seeing the whole thing. It's a shame. She was my last royal lady who is even old enough to walk on her own. Still, it would have no doubt had to be done at some point," she mused.

"Definitely a shame," the man responded, genuinely grieved. "I found her very pleasing. I was hoping she could visit us in your chambers before I go."

Vasu looked noticeably hurt by that, but said nothing and kept her head down.

"And what of our arrangements on the surface?" he asked.

Rook had finally dragged himself in slow silence atop a small outcropping, which led from his chamber to theirs, and where he could face the couple more directly. Their conversation was much clearer from here, and something struck him about the voice of the human man. He leaned on his elbows upon the rock and cupped his hands behind his ears.

The female answered. "All went as you had foretold, my lord. The metamorph spy had only a few moments to read the mind of our seti prisoner, but he did manage to implant himself seamlessly into the group, just as we hoped," she chuckled lightly. "He was accidentally injured during the transition, but that android lifted him up and carried him aboard himself, none of them any the wiser." The lyghtan woman reached into her robe and retrieved a small multicomm, holding it out to the male. "Here is the full report, my lord. I feel it likely the metamorph will avoid detection, at least as long as necessary to complete your divine objective. Also, as commanded, your pilots put on a realistic enough pursuit, but allowed them to escape with the spy securely in their midst."

"It's the medic who causes me concern," the male figure replied, as he took the multicomm from the lyghtan and paced back and forth behind the fire. "The metamorph's ESP skills may be foremost among his kind, but not even he can read the mind of a soulless android. He will have to be careful how he behaves in front of Tachion."

Now able to hear with perfect clarity, Rook started at the familiar sound of the man's voice, one he was sure he recognized the moment it reached his ears. "Pfft. No," Rook scoffed to himself under his breath. "It's not possible. He's been dead for... it must be fifteen years." He leaned in closer to try and hear the voice again.

"May I ask, my lord, why such a complicated scheme was necessary? Why did we simply not take the seti you wanted, and kill the rest of Parliament?"

"You do not understand the bond between these mercenaries as I do, Vasu," the human answered. "If Rook believed we had terminated his comrades, it would make the task of initiating him all the more difficult.

Killing them is a task best left to Rook himself. And, with Parliament left alive, they had to be convinced that the seti was still well, and working among them, or else they would have left no stone unturned in the search for their friend."

"Once again, your wisdom in all things enlightens me, Holy Prophet," Vasu said with a deep bow of reverence. "The seti will make you a powerful ally. How would you like to proceed with him?"

Rook rapidly scanned his surroundings once more, looking for any means of escape from the dark alcove where he lay. At the far corner, about fifteen feet to his left, a narrow crevice led out of the cavern and into even fuller blackness. Whether it led to the surface, or only deeper underground, or perhaps merely terminated a few meters inside as a dead end, he had no way to know. However, he could not bring himself to attempt it just yet; not until he confirmed with his eyes the voice that his ears refused to believe.

"Leave the seti to me," the male said, with a hint of eagerness in his voice. "Keep him under guard at all times, and make sure he is well restrained, but I don't want him hurt. Keep him fed and treat his injuries. I will return in a few hours, and I'll want him brought to me right away, so make sure he's ready."

"All will be done according to your will, Lord Denali," the obedient queen said with another bow.

"Do not disappoint me, Vasu," the man instructed in a tone of absolute seriousness. He now walked around the fire, pulling back his hood as he approached the lyghtan priestess. "Rook has a long and difficult ordeal ahead before he'll be ready to join us. Then, when he has seen for himself the light of truth, he will be only too eager to dispose of the rest of Parliament for us. Beginning, of course," he finished through clenched teeth, "with that tiresome android."

The human, his appearance now exposed, stood beside Vasu facing the chamber where Rook lay watching. His face, finally visible by the dim, flickering glow of the fire's embers, was as easily recognizable to Rook as would be his very own reflection. Time had taken more than its usual toll from the man, to be sure. His cheeks and eyes were now sunken and shadowed, his once thick brown hair now cropped short and salted with gray, and his skin, now dark and leathery from sun, was carved with the crags and wrinkles of the passing years. But no cruel veil of age could mask from Rook a face so ingrained in his mind, no journey of hardship etched across the human's furrowed brow could obscure from Rook a face that he had once called comrade and brother. He let out a deep, involuntary gasp, then scampered and stumbled back as quietly as possible, reeling from the confirmed suspicions of the familiar voice through the faintly reflected light of the fire. "It can't be. How... how is it possible?" Rook stuttered quietly aloud in utter, confused amazement. "That's... he's... My God, that's Jim Dodger."

PART III

A Business of Flies

Chapter 9.1

ULLSEYE AND BULLIT TOOK ONLY a moment of standing in the wide-open view of the entire hangar bay to recover from the stomach-churning disorientation of their teleportation onto the chamai starcruiser, then quickly dashed a few feet towards a dark corner behind a parked hoverdolly, and some large storage containers it had recently placed there. They paused motionless in hiding for a few breaths, staring silently at each other, and nervously awaiting any telltale sound that they had been spotted. But there was no shouting—no stomping of approaching footfalls—no alarms or red flashing lights. Nothing but the gentle hum of the mighty ship's engines vibrating through every surface, and the far-off sound of somebody tapping metal upon metal from the opposite corner of the expansive hangar bay. Bullseye signaled in handspeak to begin moving deeper into the vessel, hugging closely to the near wall, and taking advantage of the relative safety of its shadowy embrace.

They picked their way furtively, briefly disappearing behind whatever craft or equipment offered sufficient cover, as the delved deeper into the hangar. The bulk of the sweeping airdock was bathed in bright overhead light, clearly illuminating the array of fighters, shuttles and transports that were parked within it, scattered hither and yon, with no discernable organization. But here, along the starboard wall of the bay, an overhead catwalk, along with the slight projection of some sort of observation room above, provided a narrow lane of shade which they continued to skulk discreetly beneath.

When they were safely tucked in behind the rear gangway ramp of a square-backed troop transport, and the bulkhead door leading deeper into the ship's heart was in sight, Bullseye held up his fist to signal a stop, and then took a hushed moment to survey the area with his scanner, and a quick peek around.

"I'm feeling really exposed here, Bullseye, I gotta say," Bullit told him, lifting the visor of his EV suit's helmet to avoid using the comm system. "I'm not a fan of being unarmored, and unarmed."

"Weaponry would have been worthless, and unwise," Bullseye said, raising his face shield as well. "We ought not endeavor to engage the chamai. They represent armed forces of an ally species. At present, at least. We cannot be assured the same will hold true by day's end. But if we were to do battle, our escape would most assuredly be foiled."

"Escape *might* be possible, if we were able to fight our way off. Trying to just sneak around here seems... *foolish*."

"Stealth will be our ally if we plot our movements wisely," Bullseye replied. "And if, perchance, fortune does not favor the foolish this day, better to be labeled stowaway, than assailant." He made a gesture with his hand, indicating to move forward.

Bullit rolled his eyes as the pair headed out with quiet purpose, heading towards the unattended bulkhead door.

The *Okubi* was simply a massive starship. If the *Parliament One* were compared to a naval destroyer, then the *Okubi* would be more akin to the proportions of a battleship—one that was arm in arm with a duo of aircraft carriers. But despite this size difference, the two vessels had many similarities. Hundreds of years of now resolved civil war had allowed the chamai to hone their warship building mastery, and the Oberonn based megacorp Khynekar Heavy Industries was the most prolific shipwright in the galaxy. Part of their success was the economical usage of scalable design, so although the two were launched many years apart, Khynekar was the architect of both the *Parliament One* and the *Okubi*, and there was a consistency of style and layout, despite the disparity in proportion.

As such, not just the general appearance of the corridors, but the floor plan itself had a tinge of familiarity. It didn't take long for them to discover the teleporter room deep in the ship's underbelly, traced to a similar location as it resided on their own ship. Only twice during their travels did they need to dodge quickly out of sight, once clambering up to huddle in a narrow emergency access tube, and the other dashing through a sliding door, only to find themselves on the upper catwalk of the main engine reactor room, holding their breath as engineers and crewmen walked busily below the open slats of the floor grate. Bullseye read off signage written in chamai as they passed each doorway, rooms such as Solid Waste Storage, Environmental Control, Mess Hall, and Armory. Bullit made a mental note of that last room's location, in case he found the need to equip himself more suitably—despite Bullseye's admonition.

Although maneuvering their way through the ship to the teleporter turned out to be fairly straightforward, finding a way to approach the room itself was something else altogether. For some reason the area became a beehive of activity, and Bullit and Bullseye spent several additional awkward minutes again stuffed tightly next to each other, hanging on each side of a ladder in yet another access tube, and watching the flurry of movement across the hall through the motion scanner on their multicomm.

"Well, this is going swimmingly," Bullit reported dryly, his face now uncomfortably close to Bullseye's raised eyebrow.

"All in all, I would suggest that our progress is quite admirable," Bullseye proposed. "We have navigated our way in exceptional haste, discovered our objective, and now must only bide in concealment but for a moment, I'm sure. Be pleased, and recall that elementary, yet nonetheless accurate human axiom, 'it could always be worse'."

Just then, a sharp trilling alarm rang out like a bell, startling the pair as it echoed up and down the hall with three quick tones, followed immediately by an announcement spoken in chamai, *"All hands, prepare to go to warp."*

Bullseye pursed his lips in disappointed consideration for a moment. "Huh," he said, seeming genuinely taken aback, and at a loss to come up with anything else.

"What was that?" Bullit asked. "What did he just say?"

"He said that our fortune has run its course after all, we are no longer favored. He says we are going on a journey."

"You had to say it, didn't you, jinx?" Bullit complained, shaking his head. "Well... now it's worse."

The two waited wordlessly together, clinging to the ladder, listening to the music of the engines reaching their crescendo, and then leveling off to a low background thrum as they reached cruising speed. The corridor below became noticeably less active now, and after a moment, Bullseye held up the screen of the motion scanner for Bullit to see, and tapped it twice with his finger. The detector read quiet.

"What are we supposed to do now?" Bullit asked.

"What we came to do," Bullseye answered. "One conundrum at a time, each puzzle in its turn."

The teleporter room was, in fact, now deserted, as would be expected traveling at warp speeds in deep space, with nowhere to zap off to for light-years in any direction. Bullseye pointed out a dim alcove near the teleporter platform, where they could stash themselves should anyone come unexpectedly calling, then stationed himself near the sliding entry door, his eyes on the motion scanner in order to stand watch. He signaled Bullit to approach the devices's control console—not with official handspeak, but with the universal *'okay, off you go'* back-of-the-fingers wave. Bullit lifted his arms in an equally universal *'what am* I *supposed to do'* gesture, then let his arms fall to his sides, and headed over to the control station.

The console was complex, and reminded Bullit of one of those antique Earth pipe organs, with row upon row of keys, buttons, knobs and pedals, though more advanced, of course. Above that were three monitors, the left and right displaying data tags in chamai he couldn't understand, along with what he knew were numbers, which, even if he could read, would mean less than nothing to him. The systems statuses and inner workings of a molecular teleporter, he assumed. He was not interested in that sort of minutiae. The center monitor, however, larger than the other two, displayed a wireframe sphere with three lines intersecting, along with streams of characters flanking it. This was the x, y, and z-axis of the teleporter signal—this was the coordinates display that he needed.

He removed a bypass device from what was Rook's spare techkit, along with a tool to pop open the underside of the console. After doing so, he knelt on the floor, craning his neck to look upside down. As expected, he could not read any of the labeling in the busy exposed guts of the machine, but he didn't need to. Fortunately, the megacorps have input jacks widely standardized between cultures. He plugged in the wires, fully expecting an alarm to sound. But nothing happened—other than his bypass screen coming to life.

Bullit stood there and stared it a moment—then at the center monitor—then at Bullseye still studying the motion scanner by the door— then back at the bypass device. He skimmed through his basic computer access lessons in his mind like a flipbook, hoping to catch a glimpse of that one memory that would make him say, *"Ah, oh yes... step one."* He couldn't find it. The seti did recall the instruction to always keep it as simple as possible, not to get too invasive, until you've tried simply working with the program as intended. His teacher had used the metaphor 'don't reach for an auger to drill out the lock, until you've jiggled the doorknob first.' So squinting down at the bypass, he held a finger above it for a moment, and then simply pressed the button marked *'Last'*.

The center monitor sprang to life, and the wireframe began to revolve. The three lines moved to intersect each other on its surface, and the spot where they met was marked in red. Bullit looked back and forth across the screens—it was definitely the familiar shape of Oberonn's landmasses that were displayed—and saw what he knew were chamai numbers arranged in the standard coordinate format. "Psst, hey. I think I got it," he whispered. "I can't read it, but I'm pretty sure I've got it."

Bullseye hurried over and examined the screen, taking time to read it carefully—obviously enjoying more comprehension that Bullit was able to. "Well done, my friend. Well done indeed," Bullseye said, literally and figuratively patting his comrade on the back. "With haste now, copy down these bearings as I read. We need *both* safeguard these valued figures, lest one of us return, and the other fail to do so." They both copied down the coordinates in their multicomms, and Bullseye went back on guard duty while Bullit reassembled the console's access panel.

"Okay," Bullit said, as he joined Bullseye at the door, "as I asked before, what the hell are we supposed to do now?"

"We shall go into hiding, obviously. Secrete ourselves someplace unlikely to be occupied. A nearby recess, perpetually unguarded and unattended."

"You're going to say solid waste storage, aren't you?" Bullit frowned. "I know you're going to say solid waste storage."

Bullseye winked.

"We have to hang out in a sewer now?"

"Not a sewer," Bullseye explained, "merely a room accommodating a tank. The tank, then, accommodates waste, yes. But this is why it is the least populated and patrolled hold aboard ship. Also, we shall not abide in the tank room itself, but as aboard the *Parliament One*, there'll no doubt be an emergency valve access crawl space beneath."

"Ah, that's much better. A narrow tomb *beneath* a sewer."

Bullit and Bullseye exited the teleporter room, traversing the hallway on hushed tiptoe, and arrived without incident. They reached the door to the waste storage room, and after checking the scanners and finding it clear, entered unhindered as the doors slid uncaringly to admit them.

This room was not the same as the corresponding area on *Parliament One* at all. Similar perhaps, as with the rest of the ship, but magnified to monstrous proportions. Where their ship had a septic room some ten-by-ten square, the *Okubi* had a facility worthy of any small city. Six massive tanks, each triple the size of the one they were familiar with, stood in a multi-tiered storage and wastewater treatment plant. Far above, on a balcony level, were multiple workstations for controlling and monitoring the system, indicating that perhaps this room wouldn't be quite as continually abandoned as they'd hoped. Most likely, once further underway, and wastewater begins to accumulate, some level of staffing would be expected to oversee it. Fortunately, though, true to the consistency of Khynekar Industries engineering, there was, in fact, the emergency valve access located in the floor beneath the tanks. And this was not the coffin-like crawl space that existed aboard *Parliament One*, but a large roomy sub-basement, entered through trap doors on each side of the facility. The space below was visible with the aid of a flashlight through louvered vents in the center of each hatch. Of course, both of the gates were locked.

"Fear not," Bullseye said, as he beckoned Bullit to draw closer. Then, pulling one alien teleportation triangle from the front of his chest, he put his arm around his fellow seti, and dropped the thin device through the louvers into the chamber below. Bullit let out a sigh, mixed with a groan of exasperation as they vanished.

And there they remained patiently for the rest of the day—and into the night—and into the day again. Patiently—but growing ever less so.

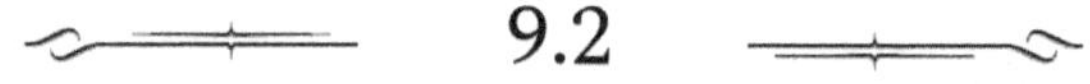

9.2

ROOK SLUMPED EXHAUSTED TO THE floor of the cave, chuckling to himself. A nervous laugh of relief, a burning of adrenaline—and he had plenty to burn, a bonfire's worth. But he kept the furnace restrained, and subdued of sound. He was no longer concerned with being overheard and discovered—he had left the bunker section a day ago, more or less. It was impossible to tell in this world of eternal stillness and dark. But the deadening of his sounds, the way the jagged darkness muted and consumed them, enhanced the uneasy awareness of the mountain weighing atop him. Now far from the vaulted chambers where he had awoken, Rook had traveled through smaller and tighter grottos and cavities, until he was now reduced to literally squirming through narrow fissures in the rock. The ponderous heft of the stone above him, the oppressive density of the stagnant air, all pressing in on him, palpably crushing. The dementing constriction of it all could make one go mad! He needed space! He needed air! Just to straighten his legs! He made use of faint illumination from the headlamps on the helmet he had taken, adjusted to a low setting to preserve the battery's charge. What would become of him if that power ran dead?

Fortunately, the scotopic vision of his seti eyes allowed him to see well in dim light, so he was able to keep the lamplight at an absolute low. But this was true only for dim light, not darkness. Were the battery to go out completely, he'd be blind as the stones around him.

He had just spent twenty minutes in the clutches of the cave, contorting through a tight fracture barely large enough to fit. In fact, if his stomach hadn't been sunken and screaming with hunger, he might not have made it—and for a while, he thought he wouldn't. He had been trapped with arms pinned, one above and one below, unable either to advance or retreat. The subterranean labyrinth had him caught in its jaws, and seldom had he ever felt closer to doom. But then something cracked! By his foot! A chip in the granite! Just large enough for his toe to gain purchase and push off. Finally free, he looked around this new niche he had struggled himself into, and realized to his chagrin—there was no other way out. Downhearted and dispirited, he sat now and brooded, considering the very likely end of his days.

What made him most fearful was the thought of his family. No one ever leaves home and thinks it their last, and thus so much goes unsaid, left to turn to regret. His wife Belladonna, his love and best friend. No stronger a woman had ever been born. When was the last time that he said those three little words though—not offhand, not in passing, but with the full intent of their meaning?

And daughter Relic—his mimic, his shadow, daddy's little girl. She had followed in his footsteps, and was now an infiltration merc like her old dad. The young woman carried so much of his grit and his willfulness, wildness and rebellion. She was a troublemaker, that one, and he couldn't have been prouder. Relic did have a preoccupation with her cultural heritage that Rook had never shared, always exploring and adopting traditional seti ways—the ones she cherry-picked anyway, as not being too inconvenient. That thought made him smile. But there's never anything wrong with an appreciation of one's roots.

Flashpoint—oh, Flashpoint. Now that boy was another issue. His mother's son, to be sure, if ever the expression fit. Conservative and disciplined by nature, with a serious bent of mind. These traits in his Belladonna somehow complemented his own, each providing what the other lacked. A true 'opposites attract'. But Rook and Flashpoint, it seemed, had butted heads since his boyhood. Even now, he felt sure his son had switched certifications to demolitions just to provoke him. Not that there was anything wrong with demolitions—a worthy weapons expertise, and worthwhile calling. It's just that it was the literal *opposite* of Rook's vocation, which was the source of so much superficial antagonism between his demo comrade James Stansky and himself. Perhaps Flashpoint had seen this not-so-gentle prodding, this contention between the two teammates, and replicated it as a slap in Dad's face. It still puzzled Rook, though, just why they were like this. To the best of his knowledge, he'd always shown love to his son. Perhaps Flashpoint had been jealous of his sister's closeness with their father—funny that thought had never occurred to him till now. Now that it was too late.

Was it?

Too late?

The thought that he'd never see them again collapsed inward, the thought that they'd never even know where he went. He would die here, trapped in this readymade crypt, alone in the dark, his bones become just another cobble in the mountain—buried for all time, never to be found. He weighed for some time which was the worse of two deaths. Whether to sit here and comfortably starve in the satisfactory tomb he had discovered, but knowing till his last breath that he'd given up, surrendered on home and family. Or slither his way back out the same crack through which he entered, all too aware that this time he may not escape its eager jaws. That death would be far more terrifying and uncomfortable to endure, but at least he'd have the small satisfaction of knowing that he had tried.

And where would he go if he made it anyway? He wasn't quite sure. He had explored every nook and cranny and they had brought him here. Any avenue unexplored was simply because they were too small. He could return all the way back to the start, to where he'd overheard Denali, or Dodger, or whoever it was with that woman, Vasu. It was clear that the area was part of a more intentionally constructed bunker, and if he could remain unseen, there was probably an easier way out.

There was also the deep chimney he had passed not long ago. Dizzyingly deep, based on the sounds of the stones he'd tossed in. And far too wide for him to jump, seti legs or not, even if there was room for a running start—which there wasn't. But across the dark shaft there had been a wider walkway, a more optimistic looking route through the mountain's grim bowels. Another dead end? Who knows, but at least worth a try. However he hadn't determined any pathway across. Perhaps now that it was the only option, he could figure out a way—necessity being the mother of invention, and all that. It was certainly worth another look—if he could get back through this crevice. And if he did make it to the cliff, but remained lost in this mountain until the headlamps went dark, he could always throw himself in. Better than waiting days in pure blackness, with nothing but the sound of his pounding heartbeat, and thundering regret.

Lessons learned the first time through served him well on the second. Different positioning of the arms and passing through in reverse made the still sketchy squeeze much more easily achieved. Rook weaved his way through the now familiar byway beneath the bedrock, and in less time than he thought, had reached the edge of the gaping chimney. There was indeed a wider trail on the far distant ledge, connecting arched cave mouths on both the left and the right side—like two great, craggy mouse holes leading off into the mountain, one upwards, and one down. But how to get over there? It was wider than he had remembered, even less room to run and jump than he recalled. But the walls of the vertical shaft might have enough handholds to scramble around on, traversing the circumference from one side to the next. As a spelunker, he was no doubt woefully undertrained. He had rock climbed some—though admittedly more on gymnasium walls than cliff faces. But his barefoot clawed seti toes made for excellent cleats. He would study and plan his route first before he made the attempt, and hopefully wouldn't end up a wet lump at the bottom—like that Capellan ashi'mar did last year.

Before he could start, he heard a sharp crack and an echo; a rock scuttling across the ground somewhere nearby. He turned off his helmet lights and stood still as the stones that surrounded him. There, across the chasm from the left side of the ledge, a glowing illumination accompanied the scuffling—a soft, greenish hue that glinted off the rock face, beaming progressively brighter as its bearer approached. Finally emerging from the threshold and carefully searching out the ledge, a scantily clad lyghtan woman lit her way through the dim with a natural jade bioluminescence emanating from her palm. From her attire, she appeared no more prepared for caving than Rook did in his jumpsuit, but he recognized it as the ceremonial outfit of the lyghtan queen's retinue. Strange that he had just thought of an ashi'mar, and low and behold, here one appears. He wished he had been thinking about a pizza instead. He remained motionless, barely breathing, as he watched her look around. Then she peered down into the chasm, and finally stared straight across.

Her presence confirmed something of which Rook hadn't been quite sure. He thought he had recognized Queen Vasu in the cavern earlier, but afterward had dismissed it as being unlikely. After all, it was dark, and they had stood far away—and the lyghtan name Vasu is not a particularly uncommon one. Plus, the idea that the queen of Capella would be here on Oberonn, deep in a cave, talking to the ghost of Jim Dodger—well, it was all just getting a little too ridiculous to process. But now here this one was, another shade in royal garb, and it lent much needed credence to his earlier suspicions.

Rook knew that the seti vision which allowed him to see in near darkness was *nothing* compared to the abilities of the cave-dwelling lyghtan. As she looked across to where he perched, silently pressed against the black granite, his now filthy white inertia suit surely contrasting quite clearly, he had no doubt that she could see him as plain as he did her. They stared at each other awkwardly, not knowing what to do.

"Boy, these caves are getting more and more crowded, don't you think?" Rook asked, calling out from across the gap. "It used to be that you could walk around here for days and never see another person. Just another tourist trap now, though, I guess. Before you know it, there'll be souvenir shops up and down as far as the eye can see."

The lyghtan blinked and looked dumbfounded. "Who... what are you doing here?"

"Well, to be honest, I have no idea, been trying to figure that one out myself. Woke up down here it seems, thought perhaps I'd been sleepwalking again."

The ashi'mar said nothing, but stared at him speechless.

"So anywho," Rook continued after a moment of silence, "if you could point the way out of here, I'd be much obliged... seeing as you seem to be doing a little better than I am."

"You are lost?" she asked, with genuine sounding concern.

But Rook didn't trust her one single iota, considering her superior was the one who Shanghaied him here in the first place. He was glad to have the cushion of the bottomless pit comfortably between them. "No... not exactly lost. Just a little turned around. I knew I should have taken that left turn at Albuquerque. But, if you wouldn't mind..."

"You are Rook," she said then, with realization and surprise.

Now it was the seti's turn to stare and stand silent.

"You are Rook, of Parliament. How is it that you've escaped?"

"I'm afraid you have me at a disadvantage, Madam Ashi'Marrrrr..." He let the word drag out and drift off, implying he did not know the given name to finish with.

"Opal," she said. "Lady Opal, of Capella."

"Well, greetings and salutations, Lady Opal of Capella." Rook extended the pleasantry across the cavity with an exaggerated bow and flourish. "And now that we've gotten the bullshit niceties out of the way, perhaps *you* can tell *me* what the *fuck* I'm doing here, since it was you and your mistress who dragged me down here to begin with."

"No, not me, but my Mistress yes," Opal corrected. "And the chamai general, and Lord Denali. I was kept in the dark, or I would have taken no part. Lord Denali has corrupted my queen like a virus, and she has grown

cruel, and evil, and is full of deceptions. Once I found out, I made my way
here… in hopes of getting away, and revealing her plans."

"That's not his name. It's not Denali, it's…" Rook caught himself,
thinking better of it.

"It's who?" she asked, interested.

He paused and debated on sharing the name. The seti still wasn't sure
if he could trust this Lady Opal—in fact, he was fairly sure that he
shouldn't. He definitely didn't trust whoever she may run into, assuming
her story of escaping was even true. And to be honest, he wasn't sure he
could even trust his own senses. The more time that passed since
overhearing the conversation, the more his doubts grew of what he'd
actually seen. Again, it had been dark, and his vantage point far away, and
he was recovering from an electrostunner shock at the time. With the
confusion and disorientation of awakening in the caves, perhaps he had
simply imagined recognizing the man, overlaying Dodger's face on a
vaguely similar voice. And what difference did it make who he really was
right now—he was going by Denali—he was acting like Denali—whatever
his real name, he needed to be treated like Denali. If it walks like a duck,
and quacks like a duck, then wring its fucking scrawny little neck like a
duck. Best to let it rest at that, until he was more certain what was going
on. Rook decided not to reveal anything else to the curious lyghtan.

After an awkward pause that made it clear to her he was hiding
information, "It doesn't matter," he said, "but he's definitely not Denali, at
least not the one me and my teammates once knew. And damn sure for a
fact, he's not a *'lord'* of jack-shit."

"I see. Not surprising," she murmured in understanding. "The fact
that he's a charlatan comes as no shock to me. Well," she said louder now,
"you had asked why you were down here. While I'm sorry that I don't know
everything, I will share what little I do. The human they call Denali… for
lack of another name to call him… appeared in the Old City two or more
years ago now, and slowly, over time, convinced my ashi'mar sister Vasu
that he was a prophet. The alien prophet, set forth in our most ancient
teachings as the bringer of The Path. Not just to our world, but beyond it
as well. He did this through powers that he used to impress her, although
the other ashi'mar… we recognized his power as merely simple human
ensensement. Rare, yes… but well documented, and certainly not divine. But
she did not see it. Or *could not*, perhaps. Among his powers is the ability to
convince and compel. I have experienced it myself, and it's quite
overwhelming. He twisted her. He perverted her. And now she does his
bidding."

"No one has tried to break this up? To expose him?" Rook asked. "Or stop him?"

"Yes, my two elder sistren, Pia, and then Ofroi. Both challenged Vasu and her illogical beliefs. But if you follow the news, you may know what happened to them. Two horrible freak accidents, or so we were told. Now leaving only me."

"You think that... Vasu has been knocking off the royal household?"

"You have to understand the extent of Denali's influence," she explained. "The Holy Mother now is absolutely corrupt. He has somehow now given these ensensement powers to her as well, I believe by means of a device, and perhaps drugs. Whatever it is, the drug or the device, it has changed her even further. She's become ambitious and greedy, cruel and violent. She no longer follows the journey of The Path, but only her own desires. I do not even believe he influences and controls her anymore. She is simply his ally. But worse, *his* powers as well, they have grown a hundredfold. I've heard tales of his befuddling minds, walking through walls, tearing people apart with his thoughts."

"And what about General Nylis?" Rook asked, intent on her story. "Is he controlled as well? Does he have these... 'powers'?"

"Some, I believe. But General Nylis was simply *already* power-hungry, money-grubbing, and depraved on his own. It took no more than the promise of sovereignty to bring him on board. He is their lackey, but a dangerous one, as he commands a great army."

Rook took a moment to pace up and down along his side of the deep chimney, processing the magnitude of what she was disclosing, then paused when a sudden obvious question occurred to him. "So... as terrible as all this is, if *any* of it is even true... what in *fuck-all* does any of it have to do with me?"

"A fair question, and one that both my queen and the general have wrestled with themselves. But Denali has been most insistent that you be part of his design. He says that you and he share a commonality, something that binds you two both. He is adamant that you join him. In fact, it borders on an obsession."

"Ridiculous! Trust me, nothing binds him and me... except maybe my foot in his ass at some point. So, what is this design that I am supposed to become a part of?"

"I do not know the endgame," she said, "other than perhaps... absolute dominion? With people like this, is there ever anything else? For Vasu, he has promised The Path foretold in our ancient texts. That the religion of the lyghtan will be spread throughout the galaxy, under her governance. However, in Denali's version, by subjugation and conquest. That is not the

Path that our scriptures envision, and I doubt his actual intention lies in anything so pious. As for the general, he's promised the overthrow of Oberonn, and the crown of a new order here, under Nylis' thumb. But that is all I know." She paused a moment, "That... and also the allegiance of a new ally."

"Oh, great. Congrats to him on that. Any idea who that joker might be?"

"No, none, I'm afraid, though I know Nylis is meeting them now. Things are coming to a head soon, I fear, so I have to find a way to spread the word, and protect my people."

"Yeah, well... perhaps I can do something right now, and save us all a lot of trouble. Is this Denali still here, do you think? Still back at the bunker?"

"It is an old, long-abandoned chimor fortification. And yes, I would bet he is still there, or will be soon if he's not. From hearing him speak of you the last many months, it seems unlikely that he would ever leave here without his prize."

"Well, his mistake then," Rook said. "He should have got while the getting was good. I'm gonna head back down there and end this thing once and for all, *whatever* it's all about."

"And how will you do that?" she asked the seti innocently.

"Shit... I've already killed myself one Denali, why not make it a set," he answered. "And by the time I get back there, it will have been almost two days. The last thing he'll expect is for me to still be lounging around behind some boulder. A classic ambush, my lady, punctuated with blades through the chest."

Opal looked thoughtful on this scheme, making slight nods of approval. Then she peered down into the chasm, amping her natural illumination significantly. "Could you make it across here?" she asked.

He looked downward as well, and turned his helmet lamps back on, the two intermingled light sources together providing quite a detailed view. "Yes, I think so. I hope, anyway. I've done some bouldering in my spare time."

She reached in her supply bag and pulled out a microline, and as Rook watched her, she tied off one end securely to an outcropping of black granite, dark as her graceful arms. Then turning back, she expertly tossed the bulk of the butterfly-coiled loop across into the seti's eagerly awaiting hands.

"Well... I have to say I'm much obliged, Madam Ashi'Mar."

"If your strategy succeeds, then it is the very least I can do. You would be serving the citizens of both this world and my own, and who knows how many others that are set in his sights. If you follow this path back the way that I've come, you will find the trail well marked, as I etched directions in the stone as I passed. A precaution, in case I couldn't find a way out."

"A wise one, my lady. Wiser than I was."

"And another precaution," Lady Opal continued, "if you don't mind... and please, I don't mean to insult. You seem a pleasant enough fellow, and I have enjoyed our little chat. But if it's all the same to you, I've had my *fill* as of late, of people turning out to be *not* who I thought they were. So if you wouldn't mind waiting to cross, until I've long gone my way? I don't know if I'd feel as safe without this gap between us both. Forgive me, I'm experiencing some trust issues. But it's me and not you."

"Well, we're in agreement then, as I've had a similar few days. I'd hate to get a blast in the bottom as I'm scrambling across," he said, pointing to the AE100 dangling at her waist.

She looked down at the laser weapon, then slid it from its holster. After a moment of consideration, she replaced it, but then removed the entire belt. "You say you're going back to kill this Denali, then let me offer you this." She moved back towards the entrance she had emerged from, and laid it there for him upon the ground. "A gift between two travelers who pass in the night. The markings I left along this route will bring you out near Vasu's chamber, a fairly likely place for the human to be found."

"Certainly appreciated once again, Lady Opal." He paused to give some thought. "Perhaps there is, in fact, something I can offer in return. Tell me, do you carry a multicomm with a subspace transceiver?"

She reached into her bag again and nodded yes, showing him the device.

"I'm gonna give you a frequency code for a ping, the help-beacon key for my medic. Now from what I've overheard earlier, my team is actually long gone. But if they're still anywhere in the system, then he'll pick up this signal. Find them, if you can. You can trust them to help. Tell them all you've learned. They'll make sure you get back home safely."

She keyed in and double-checked the cipher he shared with her, and after stowing the multicomm back in her satchel, pulled out a packaged food bar and some water, laying it on the ground next to her gift of the holstered weapon. "Good journey to you, Rook of Parliament, I wish you health and long life. I hope that one day perhaps we may meet again, under more kindly circumstances."

"That would be my hope as well, dear Lady Opal of Capella," he said, bowing again—but this time with honest esteem rather than irreverence. "Be safe and good luck." Then he watched her walk off.

As promised, he waited till the emerald illumination had faded, and he could hear the scuffling of her ascent no more—then he tied the line around his waist, and dipped into the crevice. Gripping tightly to the cliff face, and with his headlamp shining bright, he began his careful scamper around the circumference of the chimney.

9.3

"WHAT ARE WE DOING HERE?" Bullit asked earnestly of Bullseye.

The other seti looked baffled by the question at first, then responded, "Well... we *wait*."

"Yes, I *know* we wait. We've been *waiting* for a day now," he replied with barely restrained frustration. "But I don't *mean* down here, in this... stifling, dirty, shit-house pump room!" He motioned around at the unwelcoming accommodations. "I mean, what are we doing here on this ship? What were we doing on this mission at all?"

The two sat now where they had for hours—sometimes sleeping uneasily, but mostly not—plopped uncomfortably on the hard steel floor, between massive, brightly painted conduits with valves the size of bicycle wheels, their backs leaning for support on opposite walls facing each other. Each had their environmental suit unfastened to the waist, and bunched around their middle to alleviate the oppressive air.

"Well, General Nylis issued assurances that..."

"Blah, blah, blah," Bullit interrupted, chanting as he flapped his fingers open and closed like a puppeted mouth. "Yeah, I heard all this at your mission briefing, as we all did. And I think I feel safe to speak for the others, and say... we're all still confused. We no longer have to take these sorts of commissions to put food on our tables, putting our lives at risk for the sake of a couple of credits and our resumes. Don't get me wrong, none of us are averse to painting on our war faces when the cause requires it. But I don't understand why you accepted this *particular* mission, one which was both dangerous, and unvetted, while being neither critical, nor lucrative. Was it just to get everybody together? Is that it? I mean shit, if you're lonely, just throw a barbecue or something. Hell, I'd much rather be feet up with a cigar, talking about our past sketchy predicaments, than down here in this *dungeon* figuring out how to get out of a new one."

Bullseye blinked a few times and opened his mouth wordlessly like a fish, but managed to mutter nothing but a few exhales of air.

"Ah, the great wordsmith at a loss to respond. I never thought I'd see the day. Well, let's see if you have a response to this then. I. Am. Starving! I am thirsty! Neither one of us has eaten since before going down to Oberonn, and we've been sitting in this cesspit with no water since yesterday. We were clearly not prepared for an operation of this length. I know we can't carry food in our scramblers without turning it inedible, but at least we could have brought some water if we hadn't rushed into this all half-cocked. What's your plan to keep us alive here? This ship could be out for days, or *weeks* for all we know! What's your idea on how to get us some food?"

Unlike Bullit's previous comment, this point was one that Bullseye had already been considering. "Pilfering," he replied meekly, somewhat still addled from the previous rebuke. "The mess hall we encountered is close at hand. I shall purloin the required provisions when our shipmates retire for the small hours."

"Uh-uh," Bullit objected with a shake of his head. "That mess runs all night, you can be certain of that. Even when there's no diners, cooking and cleanup on a ship this size? It never stops."

"Truth, I agree. Yet just beyond that eternal enterprise is an adjacent alternative. Aside the main eatery lies the captain's mess. I noted its placement on our pilgrimage inward. A much more intimate venue, surely unoccupied. Not likely to proffer the same bounty as the principal commissary, but our needs are minor, and certain to find satisfaction in the stores on hand there."

"Alright, fine. When do we go?"

"*We* do not," Bullseye answered, "only I. If my actions are discovered, we cannot risk both being waylaid. And as I am fluent, my probability of persuasion…"

"Okay, okay, I got it. I don't like it, but I got it." Bullit clambered to his feet and walked to Bullseye, handing him the scanner. "If you get into trouble, just click your comms three times. Even if they're monitoring for internal communications, that would be unlikely to draw attention, I think.

"Agreed. But to what end?" Bullseye asked. "Forget not, once I take my leave, you'll be locked in behind."

Bullit sighed as he paced away.

When the dimming of the lights in the treatment plant above—a custom to help maintain the circadian rhythms of the crew—finally signaled the onset of the night shift, Bullit and Bullseye gave each other a thumbs-up, as Bullseye again took one of the alien triangles, and with a flip of his fingers, shoved it out through the louvers to appear back topside. He bent and knocked twice on the waste storage room floor, signaling to Bullit that he had rematerialized in one piece, then set off out the door towards the captain's mess, and their dinner.

Bullseye navigated through the darkened corridors, only illuminated now by the still ample floor lighting, and retraced their steps to backtrack the way they had entered. Starboard down the hall to the first intersection, then forward to the second access tube, port side. Once safely in the conduit and scaling the ladder, he was able to breathe a little easier. These crawlways are generally only used in emergencies, or when the lift is out of order—though if some member of the crew did choose to use it now, there was nowhere for Bullseye to escape to.

Quickly he climbed up the three levels to 'H' deck, checking his motion scanner frequently. Then down another corridor leading back toward the port side, passing in front of the mess hall and kitchen. Bullit had been absolutely correct in his assessment. Even from the hallway, the sound of clanging stockpots and clattering flatware attested to the business and bustle of the colossal kitchen continuing nightly in the main mess. But Bullseye sidled past to the third door instead, the *captain's* mess, and slithered in.

The room was the last door at the very end of the corridor, as it was located right up against the ship's outer hull. Once safely inside and down a short entryway, Bullseye saw this allowed for a large viewing window. Stretching the full twenty feet of the left-hand wall, it looked out uninterrupted upon the heavens rushing by, the pinpoints of a million suns becoming a meteor shower streaking past. On the right side, thirty feet across the dim room, a chamai flag draping downwards decorated the center of the wall—a picture of the Oberonn Prime Minister on its left, and a disconcerting image of General Nylis himself on the right, sneering out from his two-dimensional prison. Smaller images of the ship's captain and staff, as well as various plaques, surrounded them both—all quite artistically spaced and arranged. Filling the heart of the formal dining room—centered over the gold emblem of the chamai military embossed on the green carpet, and below a long, dimly-illuminated overhead chandelier—was a large, polished, and slightly arched wooden table, made from a single wide cut. It was already artfully prepared for the morning meal, with seating and place settings that could accommodate fourteen.

Bullseye surveyed the room to get his bearings. He could see that servers would enter the dining area from an inconspicuous doorway hidden in the corner, made to look like part of the back wall. Clearly this led to the kitchen he passed earlier, placed in between the captain's mess and the crew's. The short hallway he walked down as he entered the space was formed by two alcoves on the left and the right, each about twelve feet across, and square in dimension. On the left by the window seemed to be a pantry or storage, hopefully well stocked with basic larder essentials. On the right was a wet bar, replete with multi-colored bottles of various spirits, visible via a pass-through that functioned as a bar counter. He ducked quietly into the left-hand pantry and closed the door behind him.

It was in here that he felt the change, that unmistakable shift in vibration, the background thrum that he had become so accustomed to for the past day suddenly decreasing in frequency and oscillation. Somewhere between filling his inverted helmet with packed largnuts, and grabbing a fistful of kimiri red chocolate, the *Okubi*'s engines had dropped out of warp. He made haste now, grabbing a few more items while trying to remain composed. He could have filled up quickly, stocking up on a single item, but thought it unwise. Best to take only a sampling of each morsel, and make it less noticeable that the inventory had diminished. He took one jar of cocktail garnishes, composed of a pickled assortment run through on small skewers, and grabbed a few individual bundles of some sort of thick, seasoned cracker.

He stepped back out into the dining area and confirmed his suspicions—the stars out the window were no longer in motion. He went to the glass and took a full survey outside. The lower port strut of the warp field's aft XM ring manifold was visible several decks below, the width of it alone appearing almost as large as *Parliament One*. But otherwise, as he pressed his head against the glass, peering as far as he could see fore and aft, up and down, there was nothing out there but the eternal vast cosmos; twinkling stars in the endless black void. They were not in orbit around any planet—he was sure of that. Even if it were on the starboard side of the ship, he would see that they were moving circularly against the starfield. But the ship was completely stationary, and no other was in sight—though his field of view from this one portal was limited to be sure. It was entirely possible that they had rendezvoused with another craft, or an entire fleet, and it simply wasn't visible from this restricted vantage point. Whatever had caused the ship to stop, he was not able to determine it from here.

Quickly now, to the wet bar to look for some water. The refrigerator was quite small and stocked with mostly liquors. There was a limited offering of cooled carbonated water, so few that some attentive barkeep might notice a shortfall. Perhaps, perhaps not—but not worth the risk. He kneeled down and began scouring the shelves beneath the counter instead, hoping to find a backup supply that was stored warm. And then, success, a case beneath the pass-through. He grabbed six small bottles, all that would fit in the now fully brimming helmet cavity.

He moved to get up, but it was then that he saw it. He tried to look away, turn his head and pretend otherwise—but it was too late, the image was already burned in. He slowly turned back, his eyes crawling first, and straining at their periphery. Then his head slowly pivoted to follow and focus deeply, intently, on the shelf below the bar. There on the bottom sill, behind some lyghtan cactus wine and human Beefeater gin, the unmistakable shape of the decanter, filled with honey-colored gold. That same alluring tonic that comforted him nightly back at home—an unopened bottle of Zet A'zeta.

His mind raced then. He reached his hand out, then put it down—reached it out then put it down—wanting desperately to grab the bottle by the neck, and pull it forth—and wanting desperately not to. He knew this was neither the appropriate time nor the place, but now that he had seen it, he knew he would obsess. Perhaps one lone sip, just to get it out of his mind—that's all he would need, just to scratch that itch and be done. Besides, he could always come back if he needed some more, now that he knew where it was.

But then again, what if he couldn't? What if he couldn't get back here? Perhaps he could bring it back with him for he and Bullit to share—his fellow seti might appreciate the small luxury during their temporary imprisonment. But no, he couldn't do that. There wasn't enough to share! Only one bottle? Not nearly enough, he thought, scouring the remaining shelves for any additional decanters. But there were none—only this. Not enough to share. He would be needing it all.

A moment of lucidity then, as Bullseye realized his thinking. What the hell was he even considering? Had he lost his mind? He cannot risk being impaired at a time like this! Leave it where it is, get back to the safety of their hideaway.

But how could he? How could he sit in that stifling, confined, steel burrow, knowing this was waiting here, knowing he could have benefited from it, knowing that soon he will need to sleep, and knowing what that entails for him? How could he expect to escape this situation if he wasn't well rested, if nightmares kept him awake? But no, he cannot—better tired than inebriated. He resolved to leave it where it was, and head back to Bullit. Still, how would he stay focused knowing it was here? Perhaps he should just pick it up, merely to double-check that it was even what he thought. Perhaps it's mislabeled, another liquor in the wrong bottle; or perhaps it's too old, its efficacy faded anyway. He would just check quickly.

Once he knew it wasn't really Zet A'zeta, and confirmed that to himself, he could head back without the obsession of knowing of its existence.

He grabbed the bottle gingerly, carefully lifting it up and over the other glassware in front of it, then slumped down against the shelf beneath the bar counter, holding the decanter to his chest. He slid the glass stopper carefully from the top. He raised the heavy vessel to his nose. He breathed deeply.

Oh, that perfume, that glorious bouquet! He felt a shiver—a tingling—vibrate between his ears, down his neck, through his chest, to his loins. A surge just as palpable as fright's cold rush of adrenaline, an electricity just as powerful as a woman's first touch. Bullseye stared closely at the liquid, holding the bottle aloft in two hands; cupping it reverently, like something divine. A holy object to be worshiped, as if it contained the very blood of his god. He put the bottle down, cursing himself out loud in seti. The weakness, the impotence—he was disgusted and ashamed. He had not realized untill now the Achilles heel his predilection had become. He closed his eyes and gathered his will to put the poison back. This nonsense must end now; he was not to be a slave to base urges.

It's strange how the mind works when it wants what you do not. Bullseye began to imagine his struggle against the compulsion as if he were physically leaning against a large, iron door, straining to keep it closed. Agonizing in an endless desert, feeling as dry and parched as the arid landscape around him, the gates behind him holding back the immeasurable weight of a cold clear lake beyond. He knew no matter how parched he or the land here might be, if he were to open the door—the deluge would crush him. Washed away with the dust, he could not endure. But he was so thirsty, and the door so cool to the touch. He could smell the moisture in the air beyond, tempting him with the heaviness of the dew in his lungs. He opened his eyes, and the bottle called to him. His resolve now in pieces, he answered the call. In his mind's eye, he turned to swing wide the gates, and bathed in the glory of the waters that pressed in to drown him.

Time passed.

How much time?

How long had he been here? Far *too* long, that was certain. He had reveled in the Zet A'zeta, and then lost his thoughts somewhere, as often times happened when he overindulged. The bottle was lighter now, its contents at half-mast. Bullseye wondered whether the shortage would be noticed. He topped it with water from one of his bottles, but not before filling a previously emptied one with a small amount of the elixir; a canteen to take with him—one more for the road. Still slumped on the ground beneath the bar counter, he placed the decanter carefully back whence it came, though this time much less deftly, and with considerable bottle clanking. He had to get back before the palliative took full effect, a threshold he could feel was rapidly approaching. He was preparing to rise when he heard someone enter, and he huddled back down as he felt his brain start to swim.

"This timeline is quite ambitious," a male voice said in common, its resonant tone as deep as the grave, and burdened by a thick accent Bullseye couldn't immediately place. "It does not give me much time to get my fleet into position. The vessels I hold as faithful to me are scattered quite wide. Bringing them all together so suddenly will provoke questions from above."

"I'm afraid the timeline is beyond our control," a second, more gravel-throated male voice answered. "Trojan base is on its natural trajectory, and its orbit will enter the prohibited barren zone in just over a week from now. Three days after that, it returns to Coalition territory. This is its inherent path, it cannot be altered or waylaid."

Bullseye had no trouble identifying that second voice, the hoarse chamai brogue of General Nylis himself, not four feet away on the other side of the counter. But the first man—could it be? The hidden seti could swear that the timbre and accent were drak'min. But even as he listened, the voices became more echoed, distorting in his head like when sound moves through water. He wanted to open his multicomm and record the conversation, but was fearful to move with his head drifting in spirals, and remained frozen in place, his breathing silent as possible. He shifted only his gaze, peering up at the mirrored display of top-shelf liqueurs, hoping to catch a glimpse of the other speaker through the forest of reflected carafes and decanters.

"It will be our only opportunity," the general continued, "to consolidate our two fleets without sounding a warning. Once in the Barrens, the men and ships loyal to me will meet you and yours. We will have a brief window of just days to integrate our crews. A contingency of soldiers from myself and Vasu will join your ships, to aid and supervise. And, of course, to train the infantry on the Mindgate device."

"Chamai and lyghtan troops aboard an imperial vessel? That will be a bitter mouthful for my captains to swallow," the other man answered, confirming for Bullseye his accent was of the Drak'min Empire.

"Then force feed it to them if you must, as it is simply not negotiable. We are willing to work with you, and eventually, rely upon you. But trust is earned, my dear Admiral Yazir, not simply given away, and your people and ours… your people and *anyone's* for that matter… well… you don't have exactly the best track record. Besides, you have the allegiance of some captains and vessels, but not enough soldiery. You will need our militia to fill out your ranks."

The uttered name of 'Yazir' came to Bullseye just as the reflection did in the bar shelf mirror, though he's not sure he would have recognized him on his appearance alone. Captain Yazir, an old 'friend' to be sure, and a name long despised. It had been over twenty years since the last time he had seen him, and in fact, had long considered him dead. They had first met decades ago, during Parliament's first conflict with the Drak'min Empire. At the time, the young captain's face had been easy to memorize, as it had been surgically relieved of its chatty upper lip. Apparently a common punishment amongst the imperial officers, issued when found guilty of letting secrets slip. Loose lips sink ships, isn't that how the human saying goes? Well, the drak'min apparently follow the same school of thought.

Some four years later, they had encountered him again, during their successful mission to destroy the Imperial Starbase *Wormwood*. Evidently his failure at their previous encounter had resulted in further mutilation. Now left with *no* lips and his face gaping open, his ceaselessly drool-covered skeletal grin fueled perpetual rage from the captain, and constant taunting from Rook. Was Rook's kidnapping some sort of delayed revenge? No. There was clearly something much grander in the works. Besides, Yazir now seems to have done quite well for himself; his face again whole, surgically repaired. Perhaps reward for honorable service, and promoted to the rank of admiral, no less. But it sounded as though this drak'min still carried a grudge for past insults, as whatever his scheme with General Nylis entailed, it did not sound like it carried the blessings of his Emperor.

"A toast to the success of our mutual endeavor," Nylis declared, scooping a bottle and two glasses from the counter inches above Bullseye's head. He poured them both sloppily, and they clinked them together, "and to the health and long life of our newfound shared sovereign. May he reward us two, we who clear the way for his glory!"

"*U'deah!*" Yazir replied, perhaps 'amen' in drak'min. Or perhaps 'I hope you choke.' The admiral moved off then to stand closer to the window, and Bullseye imagined him looking out at the stars as he spoke. The seti began to get up so he could watch them more closely, but fortunately, shook off the flawed reasoning before it took hold. Those uninhibited lapses in judgment were coming though—coming soon—and his last remaining coherence was kicking himself for the predicament he had sauntered into. "In the spirit of trust," Admiral Yazir then continued, "I have to disclose that I have been supervising things on your side as well. And I have to say... I'm not particularly pleased to hear of our master's interest in this mercenary seti. I've had the displeasure of interactions with this group in the past, the most maddening assortment of vagabond hirelings, if ever there was one. Untrustworthy, unscrupulous, and, in my opinion, unnecessary. I don't understand the purpose of his recruitment."

"I had similar concerns, Admiral, I don't mind admitting. But I have been assured by Queen Vasu that his inclusion is integral. Lord Denali and the seti Rook... I'm told have a commonality that binds them. I'm told he has been taken under our master's wing, and the seti will serve as another of his hands to secure our interests. He may even accompany me to the metamorph homeworld of Ilshnar, for my... renegotiation. Although Trojan needs that power boost quickly, so I may need to proceed ahead without him."

Bullseye started thinking about what he had just heard, and in so doing, stopped hearing anything else. His thoughts went to Rook, and the accusations just levied. Is it possible his friend could be working with the drak'min, somehow surreptitiously conspiring with this new Denali? The concept seemed simply too ludicrous to contemplate. But soon, other even more ludicrous ideas usurped his concentration—like the colored bottles around him flaring and dimming like holiday lights in time to the music of his heartbeat, which was playing a seti aria. Or his foggy reflection in the brushed metal refrigerator singing along with the voice of an angel. Then the image of the two commanders behind him, reflected in the mirrored shelves, joining the chorus.

The melody then broke sharply with the sound of the door closing. Bullseye snapped out of it for a moment, and angled his ears. Nothing but his own heartbeat, and the echo of emptiness. They had left. He was alone.

He had to wait a little bit until he felt able to walk right. And even then, the journey back to Bullit and their lair was not as smooth sailing as the fairly effortless excursion he had on the way out. Bullseye staggered and swooned his way through the corridors, oftentimes turning afoul of his objective. He stood in the center of four-way intersections, clutching to his heart the helmet of now half-eaten booty, and making stuttering turns to stare down one direction, then the next, looking for a clue of which course to follow. At one point he walked directly behind three hurried crew women, becoming entranced by the act of following, and missing his exit to the access ladder. He had to double back, and was fortunate they didn't do the same. When he was near the base of the ladder, balancing his basket of goodies by his neck, he missed a rung with his foot and fell the last several steps, dropping his helmet and scattering his treasure. He crawled around quickly to gather it all back up, and was tempted to continue to crawl the rest of the way back. It just seemed more comfortable down there. But he used a pipe to assist his slither back up the wall to a standing position, and finally made it home—back to dear old solid waste storage.

No sooner had the triangle clattered through the slot in the hatch and onto the floor, then was Bullit upon him, huffing in frustration, and worry, and hunger. "What in the living hell happened to you? You've been gone now for hours! It's nearly first shift!"

"My campaign was perilous, and fraught with... uh... what?" He stumbled into a steampipe and scattered the pantry supplies. "I need only to sit for a spell." He slumped to the ground.

"Shit, are you all right? Are you hurt?"

"My injuries, dear friend, are infinite in measure. The thickening scab grows inside... till there's no room left for me."

"What?" Bullit puzzled in utter confusion, staring down at his collapsed cohort. "What are you..." He looked at him intently for a long minute, trying to dismiss his suspicions. Ultimately unable to do so, he grabbed Bullseye by the collar. "You're shitfaced, you fucktard!"

"Unhand me! There is no chastisement you could decree which would compare in severity to what I have heretofore imposed upon myself."

"Wanna make a bet?" Bullit answered, shoving Bullseye back down hard by his neckband, then stomping away. He looked at the array of food items strewn across the floor, and then back at Bullseye with an exasperated expression. "Half this shit is eaten already!" He stared at the other seti and waited for a response.

"I... well... I do not recall that."

"Unbelievable," Bullit said, angrily pacing. "Absolutely un-fucking-believable! And what the hell is this?" He bent and picked up a bottle bearing the same label as several others containing sparkling water, but with an amber colored liquid inside. Bullseye remained quiet as Bullit unscrewed the cap and sniffed. "Goddammit," he swore. "Zet?! You're juiced on Zet now?!" He emptied the bottle into a drain in the valve room floor, then loudly crumpled and threw the empty bottle at his inebriated colleague. Stooping to angrily collect some nuts, chocolate and water from the floor, he went back to his usual post, and slid down the wall to eat and glare at his friend.

"The... drak'min are aboard," Bullseye offered up weakly. "I was privy to their exchange."

"What?! What *fuckin'* drak'min."

"Captain Yazir of the Imperial Fleet, though it appears admiral now. He conspired just this night with the general in the captain's mess."

"The *Wormwood* commander? In the captain's mess? You're telling me, some drak'min from your old war stories, that you told me was probably dead, appeared tonight in the captain's dining room to have a meeting with Nylis? While you were standing there, no less?"

"I was veiled from sight, and unobserved," Bullseye said. "I detect incredulity in your tone."

"If you mean I don't believe you, then you're goddamn right!" Bullit snapped back. "I think you were seeing things! I think you were passed out and dreaming. Stoned off your ass, and stuffed with food!"

"I beg to you, believe me, though it defies plausibility. Your impeachment is valid, and to those charges, I plead guilty. But on this, believe you must. Yazir, in truth, was here... and spoke of bases, and fleets... and orbits, and... timelines, and... trojans?" Bullseye faded off as he looked away, turning his claim into a question as he seemed to forget his report as he relayed it. Then he snapped back. "Conspiracy is afoot. More than we two are in danger. I think it perhaps wise if we signal a code black."

"Well, I tend to agree, if for no other reason than to give us a hand when we get off this ship. Especially since it doesn't seem that you're going to be much help for a while. But, you realize, there's a chance that the signal could be picked up and traced, as brief and well encrypted as it would be."

"Yes, I appreciate the risk of exposure. But I dread the grander peril if we do not test the odds."

"Grander peril from drak'min... that are in cahoots with the chamai," Bullit said, clearly still doubtful. "Very well, I'll send the code black." He pulled out his multicomm, and with a quick thumbprint, retinal scan, and key code, it was done.

"And you are correct," Bullseye lamented with audible sadness. "I am not of much help, and as such, I am disgraced. I have failed as your friend, your leader, and your teammate."

Bullit looked at him then with a touch more compassion, as Bullseye's remorse softened his anger. "Ok then, tell me. What's this all about? How long has all this nonsense been going on?"

The black seti's glazed eyes rolled up to meet his, now wet more from shame than the mere glassiness caused by insobriety. "I confess, it's been some time. I have sought the raptured fog of my personal panacea this night... and the night afore... and the night afore... and many such nights in succession. I have a weakness for which I had thought I'd found salvation. But that deliverance was a ruse, and has become my damnation."

"Yeah, that's how this shit usually ends up. What weakness?"

"The guilt of the dead. The guilt of my living. They accuse and condemn, my jury of martyrs. I seek only to sleep, but alas, I dare not. My dreams are haunted by vengeful phantasms. Unwholesome, dreadful things, that pull and pry at my serenity... and my sanity."

Bullit thought of his own struggles with nightmares, both long past and more recent. He too had borne many a night visit from the dead, and understood more than most what his fellow seti was enduring. "Look," he said, in a more comforting tone now, "we all have our demons, our crosses to bear. Regrets never resolved, loved ones unavenged. Bodies in your wake when you turn to look behind you. You don't think these things bother me too? Bother us all? I got into mercenary work for the money. For the adventure and notoriety. Certainly not for the almost non-stop murder. But you have to remember, this calling of ours is like a game. The stakes are quite high, but a game, nonetheless. And we all agreed to play, both us and them, with eyes wide open and knowing the rules. These are not innocent civilians you're mourning, but opponents in a contest... one they *willingly* participated in. We rolled our dice, they rolled theirs. To the winner goes the spoils, to the loser, well... nothing. And if those bodies behind you still trouble you when you look back, then simply don't. Face forward, and find ways to live with joy today. As you cautioned me just yesterday, it's best to leave the past where it is, as it has nothing new to say. I've never taken you for a hypocrite, don't make yourself one now."

"Wise for your young age, a truth you often camouflage," Bullseye noted wearily through a yawn.

"I'm not that many years younger than you. I turned *forty* on my last birthday."

"Yes, well... age can be measured in much more than mere years. Some paths are more twisted, and grueling to walk. For me, the journey's been long, and my soles worn thin."

Bullit shook his head. "These metaphors of yours, I don't know what you mean. Which are you talking about? Your shoes, or your eternal spirit?"

"Both," Bullseye replied.

"Look, we'll talk more in the morning, and we'll get your shit sorted, on that you have my word. We'll discuss bad dreams and drak'min and decide what to do with both, but for now, it's probably best if you just go to sleep."

But he already was.

9.4

THE MARKED TRAIL BLAZES THAT Lady Opal had carved on the dark, jagged granite were easy to spot, and Rook's journey back toward the bunker was significantly less arduous than the previous day's trial. He became more optimistic that he would soon be back with his family, and set his mind to righting things with his son. Just a quick assassination and evasion stood in his way. Back in his golden age, that was just another Tuesday. The ashi'mar had said the bunker was an old chimor fortification, and although he was no student of Oberonn history, he knew the chimor were a long-vanquished enemy of the chamai. The underground shelter probably dated to more than a century ago, to this planet's last civil war. As such, it should be largely abandoned, and probably had several accessible pathways to the forest above. Kill, hide, sneak away. Home in time for dinner.

The cave portion was still an effort to navigate, though. Most likely formed long ago, when the ceilings of lava tubes and hollows deep beneath had collapsed, creating this fractured forest of tumbled-down boulders—the broken crumbs from the mountain's underside that had fallen to fill the gap. Though there was plenty of headroom now to traverse the channel, there was no groomed causeway to stroll casually along. Rather, it was a series of obstacles to climb over and under—sloping surfaces, angled footing—and he ended up using his hands as much as his feet, clambering over literal stumbling blocks most of the day, finally arriving breathless, and with ankles and wrists aching, on more firm and level footing.

First the floor became noticeably more finished and even, having been thankfully filled in with cretespray. Then soon after, the craggy, broken walls became more honed, and squared off, and here and there he passed occasional steel support beams. At last he was finally moving through a finished concrete hallway—ancient, stuffy, and dust-filled—but with electricity, and well-lit with overhead lamplights. The stagnant catacomb felt like a refreshing walk in the park after his two-day adventure under the mountain. The food and water Opal had kindly donated had been ravenously devoured the moment he reached them, and gave him the much-needed energy to make it this far. But he could feel himself weakening, being both parched and starving, and he shambled off wearily, looking for somewhere to rest.

Most of the rooms were too exposed, the doors long removed or rotten away. Room after room was filled with just trash and graffiti, until he chanced upon the area that Opal had described. The gray concrete corridor had transitioned back into a roughly chiseled out passage, and there was the steel door she told him of, framed into the rock. Vasu's chamber. He crept forward, drawing Opal's pistol, and noticed the door was cracked ajar. He leaned slowly against it to swing it silently open, and looked around. Some melted candles, a spot of dried blood on the floor, but otherwise empty. Perhaps the ashi'mar had been mistaken in Denali's willingness to wait for him. He re-holstered the weapon and searched for somewhere to lie down.

Just then, a loud crash of scattered metal sliding across stone, and argued yelling that followed it, echoed in from the hallway. Rook crept back down the corridor the way he had come, following the voices, and the clattering sounds of the quick collection of whatever had fallen. He passed a teleporter in one of the rooms—an even more expeditious escape route, if he could lock coordinates to a receiving unit somewhere. Perhaps in a nearby city's transport hub. Of course he would have to gently cajole one of the upset voices to operate the control for him, but Rook could be quite persuasive when he needed to be.

He finally reached a large, rectangular, and high-ceilinged storeroom. Or that's at least what it seemed the room was being used for now. At the far end, along the expansive, flat, gray cement wall, an emblem had been painted some ten feet tall, and high up from the floor, making it appear that at one point this space might have had a more formal purpose. But as with the other insignia down here, it was sprayed over and crossed out, and the area had been downgraded from its past glory to a simple warehouse.

Three men were in here, distracted with one another. Rook decided on labeling them as Moe, Larry, and Curly, referencing an old human video series he had watched as a child. Holovison re-releases of early Earthan entertainment lingered still, after enjoying a resurgence in the last century, filling the pop culture vacuum left by two consecutive world wars, the ensuing ecological disaster, and decades of crippling corporate serfdom. Although Rook had actually been much more of a Shemp fan himself, the portly third gentleman, a Polynesian human, looked to be more of a 'Curly' for sure. He and Larry, a wiry beige seti, were both unarmored in matching blue workman jumpsuits—seemingly just support crew. They were busily shoveling black metallic items off the floor with their hands, and depositing them back into the large propylene storage container they had spilled from, heatedly discussing all the while who to blame for the mishap.

Meanwhile, Moe, wearing the green, slate and silver battle armor of the chamai military, watched with growing impatience—just like his namesake would have. He was armed with some sort of rifle which sat slung across his back. Best to get up close then with that one then, make the long-barreled weapon meant for distance more difficult to use. Rook figured Moe was the most likely to know Denali's location, and probably most the likely to have skill with the teleporter, so he decided the first item on his checklist was to get rid of the other two.

There were several similar crates here, perhaps nine or ten, so when the two finished their cleanup and started carrying the container down the hallway, Rook was sure that Moe would stay behind. He seemed to be tasked with guarding the crates, not the workmen, and so Rook followed Larry and Curly down the hall with their package. They placed it on the platform and engaged the teleporter. Wherever those items vanished off to, Rook certainly did not want to follow—he would have to get another teleporter lock before using this as his exit. As the two men headed off, Rook tossed some loose gravel into one of the empty cubicles along the hallway. Curley, in the rear, paused and turned around at the sound, while Larry sauntered on. He walked back down the hallway with an eyebrow raised, but not nervous, and looked into the trap that Rook had baited for him.

Using the microline from yesterday's nerve-racking crawl around the chimney edge, he had made a loop around a crumbled chunk of masonry, buried beneath a pile of scattered litter. A few gentle tugs from around the corner, like dancing a fish lure in the waters, made the trash pile appear to shuffle and scuffle. Curly took a few closing steps of curiosity, then Rook was behind him. He covered the human's mouth tightly with the filthy, matted fur of his right hand, then placing his left fist against the side of his neck, pulled back against his lips, forcing him to crane upwards. "Shhh, quiet now," he whispered, inches from his ear. "Just two simple questions, okay? That's all I need."

Curly nodded his head up and down as enthusiastically as the seti's tight grip would allow.

"Question one. Do you, or your buddy there, know how to change the teleporter coordinates?"

The human tentatively shook his head from left to right.

"That's okay. That's fine. No big deal, we're still good. Question two, do you know where Lord Denali is, or if he's gonna return?"

Again, Curly answered 'no', with another trembling turning of his head.

"Okay, then, that's all. You've been a huge help. Honestly, I mean that. It's been a real pleasure to do business with you."

Curley exhaled relief through his nostrils against Rook's furry thumb, and nodded his head slowly 'yes' in agreement.

Rook twitched his left fingers just slightly, and the three sawblades sprang forth through Curly's neck like a pitchfork through straw. The human's eyes widened in panic as the hot blood gushed forth, and Rook quickly sawed back and forth toward himself to make quick work and be done with it. He lowered Curly's grisly and rotund carcass to the cold cement floor and quickly covered it with the litter, then scurried down the hallway and ducked into another alcove.

As expected, it wasn't long before an irritated Larry came looking, the thin, lanky seti announcing himself with calls to his cohort—whose name, it turned out, wasn't Curly at all. "Psst! in here," Rook hissed out from his cement cubicle, now swinging the microline with the concrete cobblestone around his head like an improvised mace. Larry stepped into the room, and took the stone slab full force to the head, then crumpled senseless to the floor in a heap. He awoke for only a moment as Rook's blades ran him through, swiftly down into the heart and back out again—but another hand-covered mouth kept Larry from objecting.

Now on to Moe—but Rook didn't want to wait for him. If he had to come searching for the other two, he might do so suspicious, and prowling with his hackles up. Better to catch him unaware before he even came looking. Rook stole warily down the corridor towards the storeroom once again, weaving in and out of open archways as he zigzagged down the hall. The soldier was still lingering in roughly the same area, alternating between pacing, and leaning on a remaining storage crate. Rook tiptoed in and padded along the room's perimeter, avoiding a number of fungus-filled puddles that had formed under breaches in the ceiling. The inevitable cracking caused by the slow, subtle shifting of the mountain above had penetrated the stronghold where the top of the wall met the concrete roof. The steady, echoing trickle of falling droplets further aided to mask his movements.

Moe's helmeted head was aimed impatiently toward the doorway, waiting for his brethren, when Rook sidled up behind him and poked the barrel of the laser pistol through his collar ring. "Uh-uh-uh," he said to the reactionary twitch of the chamai soldier, and then lifted the rifle sling up and over him, relieving him of it. "I know this is a very small gun, but even a very small hole in your head will be sure to ruin your weekend."

The serviceman comprehended, and raised his hands slowly above his head.

"There now, good boy. Do you understand me? You speak common?"

"Little some bit," he replied, in a voice filled with both a chamai accent, and a stifled temper.

"Okay good, what's your name now?"

"Yinkall."

"Really? Yinkall? Pssh. I wasn't even close. Okay, trooper Yinkall. I have just a few easy questions, and if you answer them nicely, there's no reason why you shouldn't walk outta here, understand?"

"Ağa," Yinkall answered, a chamai word for the affirmative.

"Common, motherfucker!" Rook ordered with a rough shove.

"Yes, understand," the soldier confirmed.

"Alright then. Firstly, have you seen Lord Denali?"

"Mmm, yes."

"Today?"

"Yes."

"Still here?"

"No, gone. Many hours."

"Gone where?"

Yinkall shrugged. "Not know," he said to Rook.

"Will he be back?"

Another shrug.

"Fuck. Alright. Next, do you know how to operate the zapper?"

The soldier cocked his head, confused.

"The teleporter, Yinkall. Do you know how to use the teleporter?"

"Ahh, Ağa. Yes."

"Excellent! Good man. Now, do you know the coordinates for a transport hub? What's the nearest big city, Dashrik I'm guessing? Or Krataar?"

"Ağa, Krataar closest city. Big city, thirty hex south. Get position code in center computer." Yinkall pointed towards the opposite direction from where Rook had come.

"You have a central computer down here?" Rook asked with a hint of yearning.

"Ağa."

"Well shit, why didn't you say so!" The seti clapped him on the back, "Lead the way, Yinkall old pal. Oh... wait. First things first, let's strip off that armor. You and I are swapping outfits like high school girls before the dance."

Several minutes later, the pair marched along through the old fort. Yinkall led the way, climbing a staircase that hugged the walls of a square central shaft, with exits on each of multiple floors. The chamai, now in the wet, muddy, ripped, and blood-soaked rags Rook had been wearing, pointed to the door on the third level they reached, and continued on down the hallway behind it. His face, now exposed, had an appearance of raw experience that Rook respected. His left cheek had a burn scar, shiny and pink against his rust-colored skin, and the top half of his oversized chamai right ear had, at some time, been jaggedly cut away. Rook, now suited up in the clean Oberonn military armor, had removed the left gauntlet, as it did not have his own armor's custom tractor blade slots. Wearing the glove would have cost him use of his hidden weapon. Likewise, the headgear's visors and face shield had been discarded, as sometimes helmets made for species such as the chamai could be too compact for his seti muzzle.

"There, computer," his guide announced while pointing, approaching a room ahead with a closed door. Rook was pleased to see a tangle of data cables and network wires which had been cascading up the stairway with them, and feeding in from every doorway, now converged into one bundled rope to enter beneath the doorway's threshold gap.

He swung open the door and entered the room, and took a moment to look around. The myriad of cables that fed into the office were just that—cables, and nothing else. The wires ended a few feet in, rudely cut, and attached to nothing. To the best of his observation, there was no terminal here of any kind. Of course, it was hard to see around all the battle-armored guards that filled the space, all staring at him, and each pointing a rifle at the seti's newly-acquired chest plate. And in the center of the squad of six reinforced soldiers, there he was, big as life, no mistake or imagination about it. Jim Dodger, his onetime friend, standing real as any of them, still draped in the same robe of leather he had seen him wearing prior, and looking very much in charge.

"Yinkall, goddammit," Rook cursed, "you're a dirty fuckin' traitor." He lowered his weapon and let it clatter to the floor. "And to think, I was gonna add you to my Christmas card list." Then he turned to Dodger, or Denali, who or whatever the hell he was. "Well done. A nice trap with the wires. You knew I'd follow those right in like a lemming."

"Take his weapons. Leave us," the familiar face of Dodger barked coldly. The soldiers surrounded him swiftly, and stripped him of Opal's pistol and Yinkall's rifle, as well as his right-hand gauntlet, and unmasked helmet. They then clattered out of the room and took up posts in the crowded hallway, closing the door behind them. All except one, a lone sentry that stood unmoving by this Denali or Dodger's side. Garbed in a black tactical battle suit, a full masked helmet with glowing orange optics, and atmospheric processors extending from the cheeks that gave the vague impression of insect mandibles. He loomed there as still as a suit of plate mail in an English mansion.

"It's good to see you, my old friend. God, what a sight for sore eyes!" Denali/Dodger announced, as he stepped forward and clasped the seti's shoulders in greeting. "Sorry about all that, gotta play the part to keep them in line." Then, squinting with curiosity at the seti's armor, "Joined the Oberonn military, have you? Would have thought a soldier's life too regimented for you."

"Well, I figured it was time to 'be all I can be'," Rook answered flatly. "And what are you dressed up as, with this whole... robe getup? Some kind of vampire? Skulking around down here like Dracula in the sewers?"

"Dracula didn't live in the sewers."

"Oh, yeah? I wouldn't know. Never read it. Never had the time. Although I did read your obituary, oh... fifteen years ago or so, which makes it pretty interesting to see you here today. But, on the bright side, I *really* look forward to reading your second one. I'll definitely make time for that."

Denali/Dodger stared at him closely, a crooked smile of wonder warping his dry, tanned face. "I have to admit, I really expected a bit more of a shock from you. You seem genuinely unsurprised to see me... *at all.*"

"I'm not surprised... *at all,*" Rook said, pulling sharply away from the friendly shoulder clasp. "What do you think, we're all stupid? That we don't know what's going on? We've been watching you for years now, you arrogant dumb prick. This whole fucking mountain is surrounded! You've walked right into our trap!"

The guard finally twitched at that, cocking his helmet's mandibles uneasily toward his master, and then back to Rook—even lowering his weapon a bit. Dodger's face, however—and yes, it was Dodger's face—crinkled into a scowl of pure, acrid bile, much more reminiscent of what the seti witnessed before. But after a moment, the sick smile returned. "Still a witty bastard, I'm glad that hasn't changed. Glad that Tachion's tinkering didn't somehow filter that out of you."

Rook cocked his head in questioning, not knowing what the hell he meant, then dismissed it as lunacy and chuckled fakely at him. "Well, I almost had you, you gotta admit. I had *this* guy for sure," he said, pointing at the bodyguard, then rotating his hand to flip the bird directly in his face. "Well, I'm sure you have a whole agenda planned of evil overload bullshit we have to get to, so we might as well hop to it... so I can get to the part where I kill you."

Chapter 10.1

THE *BUGEYE* DRIFTED SILENTLY ONCE again around the verdant globe of Oberonn, as Tachion and James Stansky tirelessly persisted in the tedium of their exhaustive grid search, now logging their tenth orbit around the planet since the *Okubi* absconded with their teammates. Or perhaps not that tirelessly. For the first eight hours after Bullit and Bullseye had been whisked away, James and the doctor took turns resting, while the Beagle probe sent back boundless reams of worthless data, collated from scans up and down the expanse of the northern mountain range. The only information that was perhaps of any use was that the forces that had chased them off had now packed up and moved away, as well as the detection of a vague energy signature from somewhere deep below the rocky ridgeline. It took them most of the day to narrow it down to Mt. Ivëal, a snow-covered peak of broken, black granite that sat squarely in the center of the alpine chain. And, unsurprisingly, very near from where they had recently fled. Once the sensors showed that their former rivals had withdrawn, James brought the *Bugeye* down through the thin, wispy cloud cover, and the pair scoured the woodlands for a landing zone suitable to stash it.

"Jesus. How does Bullit manage this beast in these crosswinds?" Stansky complained, struggling with the hand yoke.

"You've got it, we're almost down," Tachion replied from his seat at Bullseye's usual station. "There's another abandoned athelium boomtown just east of us. I can see what looks like some kind of old warehouse or factory. Walls are up, but the roof is caved in. It looks plenty long enough to fit us inside, if you can manage. A good place to hide the ship. Do you see it there? Two clicks south of that scar you left in the forest from your blast yesterday morning."

"I see it, just north of the river bend," James said. "I think I can fit her. Let's just hope there's no basement to go crashing down into." He guided the *Bugeye* in low above the valley floor and skimmed along the top of the thriving, dense foliage. Then he banked and rolled to line her up, and lowered her into the structure. The wash from the engines kicked and spun up ages of leafy debris, and the doors of the ramshackle complex slammed open and closed violently, smashing whatever glass the years had somehow left unbroken.

They had spent the overnight up in orbit, and the sun was only now lifting its bare and brazen fury above the edge of the horizon, but already the promise of another scorcher was in the air. The *Bugeye* was snuggly surrounded by four decaying and vine-choked walls, each barely a season or two away from returning to the mossy soil themselves. They walked around the ship through knee-high weeds and slender saplings which had fought and scratched their way through the rotted remains of the collapsed upper stories. Satisfied that the lander was well secluded, and well secured, they ventured off towards the base of the mountain to investigate.

There was some debate as to whether to gear up or travel lightly, and the joint decision was reached to explore first with minimal baggage. The rival soldiers of last afternoon seemed long gone now, and on the off chance they found anything worth a deeper examination, they could return to the ship and suit up more appropriately. Although neither had high hopes of that any longer. Each carried small arms, their sensors and techkits, but otherwise James wore jeans and a t-shirt, and Tachion went in the ease of his naked, bare metal.

Moving through the tangled forest was less effort this way, and the large android led the pair, trampling brambles and thorny vines, blazing a trail for his softer-skinned comrade to follow. Insect-like creatures had not evolved the same way here as on Stansky's homeworld, so biting flies were not a concern—but there were certainly plenty of others.

As they skirted a small algae pond that was grown over with waterweeds, a swelling chorus of peeping and chirps caused the doctor to freeze in his tracks, and pull his autopistols.

"Relax Tach, it's just frogs," James said, as he forged on past the medic.

"*What?*" asked Tachion, sounding baffled.

"You know, frogs. Peepers. Heard them singing like that all the time where I grew up."

"You grew up on Earth."

"Yeah."

"This is not Earth."

"Well, yeah I know..."

"And trust me, they're not frogs."

James finally stopped then, and pulled two nine-millimeter pistols from his thigh holsters. He scanned the tangled woods beyond the small body of water, but no movement was visible, and the sound began to abate.

"What is it then," he whispered. "Or, what are *they*?"

"Don't worry about it, you don't want to know. And it sounds like they're moving off. Now that the sun's up they won't be any problem. Let's just keep going, and keep our ears open."

After that, James was much more mindful of the noisy woodlands, and his hand went to his gun, and eyes to Tachion, at every bird call.

The trees ended suddenly and sharply, like a line drawn in the sand as they approached the base of the mountain; the rich forest loam superseded by the hillside's castoff of loose stones and gravel. To the east, looking down a dirt road where Parliament had been running for their lives only yesterday, the carnage of Stansky's heurcanium charges could be seen all the way from here. The forest lining that escape route was now fractured and tumbled, and everywhere the distinctive golden-yellow splinters of freshly exposed virgin heartwood.

Not a hundred yards to the west, more carnage—of another kind. Here is where their outfit had first made their stand, when making way from the terrorist camp with the recovered weapons plans. Of course, that's assuming that any of that was even true. Somebody certainly sacrificed a lot of troops to convince them, though, and although the soldiers had now retreated, they had done so in a hurry. Their dead were left behind. Two dozen, or perhaps thirty, prostrate and lifeless corpses lined the pathway, each one still lying as contorted as they fell, and each highlighted by a ring of dark, blood-stained dust. The pair mentally identified their own handiwork as they passed by, easily spotting the signature style of each teammate's kills.

Here on the left, three in a row with their heads almost completely melted, courtesy of Rook's acid sprayers after he ran out of pistol rounds. But the thick and durable backside of their helmets were obviously less susceptible to dissolving, and they now cradled the liquid remains like ghastly gore-filled soup bowls.

Nearby, a perfect composition of fallen bodies was laid out aside the road like an asterisk, feet facing center to where James' boomer grenade had landed. The sonic shockwave had burst all but one of their eyeballs, and that lone, hazy pupil stared out at them angrily from a bloodshot globe of red, the ruptured orbits just a hint to the real damage hidden within.

Several that they walked past had met with Bullit's laser shotgun—some missing such large chunks of themselves, it was almost inconceivable that so much solid tissue could be scattered to the wind. One woman was missing such a large piece of her abdomen, that her chest and waist only remained connected by a loin of flesh thinner than her forearm. A pair of small lizards, or perhaps green-skinned, hairless rodents, were making the most of her extensively exposed entrails.

Tachion himself had felled quite a number, having descrambled and mounted an autocannon on the crest of a large, flat-topped boulder. These casualties were perhaps not nearly so physically gruesome, the men and women merely decorated with the abundant polka-dotting of the machine gun's ragged puncture points. But what was disturbing here were the positions that they collapsed in, often spinning from the impact, and crumpling down upon twisted legs. The deceased were often identifiable as such from great distances, based simply upon the impossibly painful way that they folded as they fell.

And Bullseye's kills, certainly both the cleanest and most numerous, easy to spot by their comparatively surgical precision. On this day he had borne a GimelBolt rifle, firing high energy ions in an invisible streak. Invisible, but not silent, as each shot cracked louder than any holiday firework. Still, not as deafening as its big brother, his ZajinBolt sniper rifle, but Bullseye only employed *that* armament on special occasions. The beam passed through flesh, bone, and armor alike, unimpeded and unhindered, in a stream only as wide as a molecular thread, but superheated in an instant outward around it. The effect was cauterized tunnels burning straight through, sometimes round and wide enough to easily insert an arm from one side to the other. His proficiency was evident in the placement of the scorched boreholes—heart, heart, neck, heart, head—all one shot each. Unfortunately for these foes, the defensive measures for bolt weapons were not often standard issue for the soldiery.

James and Tachion plodded past the tragic scene in silence, a rare opportunity to revisit an accomplishment that neither took any pride in, all the while making a mental accounting of the true expense of their escape. Both had the same unspoken thought running through their minds—it was a good thing Bullseye wasn't with them. This was the kind of scene that would sometimes put the seti inside himself for days, not so much because of the gore, as the subtle evidences of personality. A deck of playing cards scattered around a mid-aged chamai—one or two of them carefully hand-drawn to replace ones he had apparently lost along the way. A techkit adorned with a small blue heart scrawled in marker, no doubt by the novice fingers of someone's little child. Small indications of fuller lives once lived, far beyond this impromptu graveyard. Lives now ended.

Of course, Bullseye was not the only one who could be troubled by these sights. It affected each of them, in different ways, and each had their own individual ways of coping. For James Stansky, it was a reminder of mortality. And mortality reminded him of his illness. The human's usual way of coping was off-color humor and crude remarks. For Tachion, it was to ignore, and invest all his focus on tasks elsewhere. As such, the pair moved on past the slaughter—Stansky making several indelicate comments about the horrid faces and reeking stench, while Tachion tried to steady on, and absorb himself in scanner readings.

James was not wrong, of course, the rudeness of his comments aside. While the clearly insufficient armor on those fallen had been designed to stop bullets from penetrating, it was not designed to preclude odors from escaping. The rusty metallic perfume of spilt blood, and the bitter char of burnt flesh—like a mix of singed hair, and leather tanning in the sun—combined with that sick-room odor of intestinal gore, and evacuated bowels. Long past leaving behind the site of the onslaught, they marched on still through an invisible cloud—the lingering aura of the dead.

"Jesus," Stansky complained, crinkling his nose and waving a hand to clear the air, "why do they always have to shit their pants? And not just a little. Like, a lot. God forbid anyone skip lunch before we have to kill them."

Tachion looked up from his scanner. "I still can't pinpoint the source of this energy reading, just a general signature from somewhere inside the mountain. I have yet to see a cave or structure of any kind, though." He then turned slightly away from the scree-covered hillside they were walking parallel to. "There's something over there, though. A vehicle. A big one."

Stansky cautiously drew both his weapons, continuing onward in a slightly more tactical gait. They surveyed the forest before them as they left the dirt trail, venturing back into the trees. The vehicle was a Guandao ATCV, a large, wheeled troop carrier, maybe even half the size of the old *Bugeye*. It sat on eight massive tires, spaced quite closely together, and its body had the sleek lines of a shuttlecraft, and carried the cannon of a tank. It was not particularly far from the roadside, just far enough to be obscured by the trees and overgrowth, and it sat lurched to one side, with a soot-marred blast hole in its back end.

"I think this was Bullit's work," Tachion mentioned as they tromped around her through the weeds, the green and brown camo-painted sides not bearing any insignia of affiliation.

"Yeah," James agreed. "He took this out from the *Bugeye* on his way around to pick us up. Pshh. Looks like he almost missed. Barely caught the back corner."

"Well, he caught enough to put it out of commission," Tachion said. Then peering through the hole, added, "And... take out a few troopers inside."

"Lucky for him, cause looks like he left the canon still operable."

The pair clambered through the ragged breach in the caravan's hull, then crawled through the disarray to reach the driver's platform. A test of knobs and switches to awaken the onboard dash computer revealed a lack of any power running through the vehicle.

Tachion turned to James. "She's a little bigger than the cars you're used to working on, but would you care to see if you can get us any juice? Might be interesting to see if there's any useful information in here."

"Yeah, let me take a look," he said, hopping up to head back outside, and grabbing a rattling toolbox mounted on the cabin wall as he passed.

Tachion busied himself dragging the two corpses from the troop transport and out into the woods outside, in consideration of Stansky's olfactory senses. Tachion didn't 'smell' things the same way that organics did. He detected and subconsciously analyzed chemicals and pheromones in a vaguely similar fashion, but without that biological trigger of disgust. That sensation, an evolutionary imperative designed to keep one from eating food that was rancid, wasn't necessary any longer for the android species. He processed odors in a much more matter-of-fact way. Not to imply, however, that certain smells couldn't affect him emotionally. After all, smell was a major memory triggering sense for all the species, including Tachion's.

When he was done, he joined Stansky, who had his head buried in the side hatch compartment, swearing and sweating over removing a panel. But the additional help of the android's hands had them make quick work of it.

Tachion watched as his friend tested several wires for current, and then disconnected and rerouted them as needed in order to send power to the driver's area. He also watched with a more professional eye, as the longer and harder James worked, the more his hands began to noticeably tremble and twitch. At one point, when he had clearly struggled too long trying to thread a thin wire through a small contact terminal, the doctor placed his heavy hand on Stansky's huge shoulder, in a universal gesture that seemed to say 'enough'. James dropped his hands to his side and his head toward the ground, then angrily recoiled, and threw his tools at the engine, stomping off.

"So then, it's started," said Tachion calmly. "We both knew this day would come. How long has it been since you've begun showing symptoms?"

"Not sure. Maybe a year, more or less," James replied. He went to rest his frame on a mighty, toppled tree trunk. "I denied it at first... said it was just arthritis, or humid weather." He held his sizable hands up before his face, watching the cramped twitching slowly diminish and fade away. "It's just too early. I'm still too young. It just seemed to come... so fast."

Tachion leaned back heavy against the truck chassis, not physically needing to recline, but mirroring his friend's relaxed posture. "Youth always seems too fleeting, I guess even more so with you. But the timeline for this onset is actually fairly typical, and expected. As we discussed years ago, there are some provisional remedies I can offer. Only short-term solutions, of course, but they will mask the symptoms for a year or so, maybe more, while they remain mild like this. I can give you an injection back at the *Bugeye* that will last a day or two. And later on, we can implant a time-release device beneath the skin that will... well... you remember what we talked about."

James simply looked up at him and nodded.

"Tatiana?" Tachion asked.

"No, she doesn't know yet. Still don't know what I'm gonna do there."

"You mean about telling her, or marrying her?"

"Any of it."

"Ah."

"God, I'm such an asshole."

The doctor thought it best to neither agree nor disagree. The two remained in silence for a moment, and enjoyed the symphony of the forest.

Eventually, Tachion rose and walked back to the open access hatch. "Do you want to try again, if the tremors have subsided? Or you could just tell me what to do if you like. If these big digits of mine can reconnect an artery, I'm sure I can feed a wire. With your guidance, of course."

"No, that's alright. I've got it," James replied, rising from his log bench and heading back to work. "I almost have it, I think. Go inside and let me know."

Tachion made his way back through the mighty transport to the driver's cabin, and diligently watched for signs of life in the dashboard circuitry. James apparently did *not* 'almost have it', and he manipulated and cajoled the tangled mass of wiring for the rest of the morning, and into mid-afternoon. The doctor allowed him the privacy to manage his spasms on his own, and remained inside the cockpit. Finally, with some sputtering and blinking as it initially cut in and out, the power returned and illuminated the console steadily—accompanied by the loud white-noise static of the comms system kicking on. Tachion quickly turned down the screaming feedback, then called out to Stansky with the report of success. In the center of the dashboard was the screen of the onboard computer, and he immediately went to work searching through menus for information. James came aboard, huffing and sweating from the sweltering day in the sun, and joined the android in the cockpit—but could only watch, since as with Bullit before him, he had never learned chamai.

"I know a couple of expressions," the human was explaining, as Tachion continued from screen to screen. "Two or three anyway. But speaking and reading are obviously not the same. So anyway, I can say 'Drīmba o'n al'James, aǧa ayeza ziňow yün twalama.'," he stammered.

"You can *barely* say it, no offense. And, 'Hi I'm James, yes you can buy me a drink'? Lines like that work for you?"

"How about, 'Enki na-faro nèsh xilk lümak lasha. Ziňow al'shynon yahag?'"

"James... the only thing worse than your pronunciation, are your pickup lines."

"Hmm. Time to learn a few new ones, maybe. To be honest, it's been so long since I learned those, I don't even remember what I'm saying."

"I wish *I* didn't remember," Tachion quipped. "Oh, look here," he said then, pointing to the navigation screen. "There's a waypoint marker here, the last PPS position they drove to."

Stansky might not have read chamai, but he could certainly read a map. "That's right over there," he pointed, "on the side of the mountain. Back by the dirt road."

The pair simultaneously leaned forward and looked to the right out the window. From what could be seen gazing out through the heavy trees, there was nothing there but the boulder strewn rise of the hillside. James pulled down the targeting eyepiece for the vehicle's roof mounted cannon, and used it like a periscope to zoom in on the rocky incline. He made several range and focus adjustments, then panned with it slowly back and forth.

"Anything?" Tachion asked.

James pushed the viewer back up to the cockpit roof and shrugged his arms. "Not that I can see."

Tachion took a photo of the navigation's map image on his multicomm, then the two headed out away from the incapacitated Guandao, and back through the treeline towards the road. They proceeded now with much more caution, weapons drawn and scanning, prowling around the pinpoint that was highlighted on the map screen. Eventually, seeming safe, the two walked up to the mountain's steep and rocky hillside, and stared—James' hands upon his hips, and Tachion stiffly studying the loose scree.

Stansky cocked his head, then an eyebrow, then squinted critically at the slope of scattered stone and boulders, both large and small. "Something's off here," he said.

"Agreed," the android confirmed.

"The color of this rock here, it's darker. Different from the rest of the slope."

"Yes, and the shape as well. All across the hill we've walked along, the stones have been much rounder and weather-worn." Tachion pointed back along the dirt road. "But look here, this whole section of hillside. The rock is jagged. Some look newly broken."

"A rock slide?"

"Could be, very likely."

"But... do you smell that?" Stansky asked, moving to scamper up the hillside, the loose rock doing its best to slide out from underneath him.

The android's olfactory senses detected nothing unusual in the hot and humid late afternoon air. James managed to struggle perhaps twenty feet upwards, with much objecting from his footing, and picked up a chunk of fractured rock, and sniffed it. Then another. The third one seemed to satisfy him, and with a call of 'heads up', he tossed it down to Tachion. The doctor waved it in front of his atmospheric sensors, then gave it a pass underneath his scanner.

"Interesting. Cyclotrimethylene trinitramine," the doctor announced with intrigue.

"Yeah, cyclonite." James called out above the sound of rockfall as he skittered back down. "C-4, I can smell it all over. This hillside's been blasted. Someone caused this avalanche on purpose."

Tachion aimed his scanner at the hillside now. "I *am* getting an increase here in the energy signature we detected. I think it is fair to assume that the source, or access to it, is buried beneath this rubble."

"Well, I didn't bring my whole arsenal along, but I think I've enough here to do some digging." Stansky rummaged in his demo kit and produced some scramblers he had stocked with heurcanium. "You might need to help me out, if you can climb up all that loose stone without causing another rockslide. If we can get up high, and use your EMD sword to tunnel a little borehole nice and deep, I can set up a directional blast to clear a good amount of this rock pile across the road and into the woods." He handed Tachion a bundle of unscrambled charges to carry, his voice and eyes brimming with excitement, "Then we can get a look at what's been hidden under all this gravel."

The task was arduous, to say the least, even just staying upright. Both mercenaries took a turn at roughly careening down the rock face. But after digging a shallow depression, and then having Tachion lay in it, he cut downward with his plasma sword as deep as he could reach, till he laid chest on the ground, the arm holding the EMD burrowed right up to his shoulder. All in all, a passable borehole of maybe ten or twelve feet deep. Then, it was Stansky's turn to load it with firepower, packed tightly in little bundles, each painstakingly positioned and precisely planned to push the mountain aside.

The thunderous boom took some time to ring back and forth across the valley, until it echoed into nothingness. The cloud of dust took even longer, with only the scantest of breezes in the air to clear it—the pair all the while waiting upwind anxiously to view the results. It was approaching dusk, yet still light enough to see the very satisfactory results of their improvised excavation. A large scoop, both deep and wide, had been relocated from the hillside to lay scattered across the dirt roadway, and even more so into the woods beyond. The pair scrambled up into the dugout, surveying the area with sweeping eyes and digging hands. Then they both saw it at once, just above them, at about the place where the charges had been lowered. The top right corner of a concrete tunnel inlet, leading into blackness. Only about three feet of the entrance was exposed, but some hurried burrowing—throwing loose stones both down the hill and into the tunnel—soon had them peering through an opening large enough to walk through. An inspection with flashlights just inside revealed a tunnel wide enough for vehicles, but of course they had no need to open that much of the passageway.

Tachion's scanner was very clear now—a power source was operating deep below. "All right, we better go back and gear up proper," he said, and Stansky heartily agreed. The two set off quickly back along the route they had come earlier that day, this time barely acknowledging the grove of corpses as they passed them. Perhaps because the dying light made the dead stares of macabre resentment less visible, perhaps because of the excitement of their discovery, and focus of a new objective. Either way, they hurried back along their pre-trodden trail, but by the time they neared the *Bugeye*'s shelter, the rosy sky of sunset had faded to ripened purple, and the purple to battleship gray. The pathway became more obscured in darkness, especially beneath the canopy of foliage overhead, and despite their proximity, they needed to rely on the multicomm compass and the *Bugeye*'s homing signal to find their way.

Then, arising slowly out of the deepening shadows, that sound again, as their rundown hideaway was just in sight—the growing chorus of peeps and chirping, sounding from all around them, and moving closer. Tachion looked about and quickened to a hustle, putting his hand computer away, and again pulling out his sidearms. "Quickly now, let's get inside!" he urged, and broke into a straight run. Stansky followed suit, armed and ready, and scanning the trees around him for an onslaught of he-did-not-know-what.

Banging through the battered doorway to the rotted building, and dropping the *Bugeye*'s ramp to rush aboard, they quickly raised it up again behind them, keeping careful watch with pointed weapons till the door sealed itself closed.

"All right," Tachion said, "it might be a good idea to hunker down till morning. Get some rest, start fresh at first light?"

"Seconded," Stansky said, holstering his pistols, but still peering apprehensively out the windows of the cockpit.

That evening, the two went about the business that they had done so often, the loading of magazine clips, the stocking of techkits, the inspection and tuning of armor, the polishing of gun barrels. The familiar, almost calming routine of readying for battle, the physical preparations that eased the psychological one.

10.2

CAPTAIN LOBO OF THE *PARLIAMENT ONE* believed the only thing worse than being born a lacertilian, cowering beneath the tyrannical crimson banner of the Drak'min Empire, is to have been born a *female* lacertilian. The Empire was an exceedingly chauvinistic and patriarchal society, to the extent that even the women of the drak'min's own ruling species were denied such basic dignities as the wearing of clothes indoors, or the freedom to speak without prompting. To hide the female form, or to express unsolicited opinion, were among the many basic liberties that were considered 'unwomanly'. So for the first two decades of her life, the cobalt-blue scales of her body were often completely exposed, along with the mottled pattern of alabaster lamina on her chest and face, which created the illusion that she was decorated in skeletal warpaint, and beneath a shock of rose plumage arising from her scalp, between pointed, ivory horns. This misogynistic attitude towards the feminine trickled down through the Empire's subservient races as well, both the lacertilian and the avis, as it was part of the overall doctrine of casteism exhibited in every aspect of daily life. Yet she was bombarded each moment by propaganda to the contrary. The lot of the lacertilian and avis was depicted as a fortunate one, protected beneath the benevolent wing of the emperor himself, providing for their every need, and protecting them from the evil barbarians of the Coalition.

This is the existence that Lobo knew, and she believed these 'truths' for most of her life. After all, she knew nothing else. Almost none of her people did. The history and culture of her own species had been swept away by fading time and fraudulent tales, and she was indoctrinated by the teachings of the imperial education centers. She knew there were some, those who stayed masked in the shadows, that carried stories of the before times—who passed down the verbal history of days prior to the drak'min. But when these chroniclers were revealed, often betrayed by their own kind, they would soon find themselves the centerpiece of the plaza's disembowelment rack.

Lobo remembered the first time she had witnessed that unholy ritual, forced, like everyone else, to attend each and every week from the age of ten. It was uncommonly frigid that day, producing clouds of condensation with every exhale, the anxious breath of the unwilling crowd a visible fog above the throng. It was not the agonized screams that burned themselves into her memory—after all, she had heard those cries echoing up and down the narrow alleyways since infancy—but that first glimpse of the strange inner parts of a person, the secret inside workings no one was meant to see. Her younger self had been astonished at the sheer mass of entrails that unraveled from the gutted abdomen, landing wet and heavy on the icy, white pavement. How could so much have once fit inside the frail, old avian woman? And the steam that swirled forth from the still bodily-warmed innards, billowing up through the cold air in a nimbus of pale mist—like water thrown to douse the heat of their kitchen's cooking stone.

'Heretic' she had been called, along with most who met the executioner's gut hook, since it was taught that their emperor was akin to the very gods themselves. Violations of his edicts were a desecration of His Word. It was whispered that he was never seen by the common folk as he moved from place to place, because he walked across the sky, using the clouds as stepping stones. She began to finally suspect more terrestrial means once she joined the army, and learned of teleporters. Before that day, she had never seen any technology more advanced than the public broadcast towers in her hometown—battered speakers on timber poles, which woke them daily for work and education assignments with the Drak'min anthem, and the blessed commandment of the emperor's own voice.

Service in the Drak'min imperial army is not a choice, but a mandatory obligation. Every avis and lacertilian must serve ten years, although the option is allowed to begin the term anytime between eighteen and twenty-five—an illusion of choice, designed to create the appearance of volunteerism. Still, it was perhaps the only personal decision of meaning that most would ever get to make. Lobo had chosen to serve immediately, hoping to get as far away from her childhood memories as it would possibly take her.

It was a fortunate decision.

There are many ways the Drak'min subjects may spend their term of service, from infantry to supply clerk, from pilot to officer's servant. But her natural talents, and turns of fate, had soon placed her aboard the bridge of a Drak'min scout vessel, the *HIS Shaaduk*. Lobo actually found life in the military to be more free than she had ever experienced, now given technical education, responsibility, and proper clothing in the form of a uniform for the first time in her life. Although only the drak'min themselves could ever become high-level officers—it seemed they were all *born* into the rank of captain—she was able to rise to the top of the lower ranks, and for the first time received respect and recognition from others, despite her species, or gender. She was never quite sure why this was. Possibly the traditional gender roles of civilian society were too disruptive to the chain of command. Or perhaps the drak'min did not concern themselves as much with the genders of the servile races as they did with their *own* women— much as a farmer behind the plow might not show concern for the sex of their oxen. She was not even sure the drak'min could tell a lacertilian male and a female apart with her clothes on, since her species did not breastfeed their young, and so carried no buxom signposts announcing her sexuality upon her chest.

Whatever the reason, whether skill, or luck, or both, she found herself spending her last years of service as communications officer. A position that expressly required her to monitor transmissions which, had she been seen viewing such blasphemy back home, would have found her strapped upon the gutting rack awaiting public evisceration. Broadcasts from the Coalition, and the neutral systems as well—words and images that flew in the face of everything she had been taught. She saw evidence of free societies, happy families, prosperous communities, collaborative progress.

An interplanetary collective comprised of equal species, genders, and cultures. Sure, there was sometimes disagreement and dissent, but these issues were openly addressed without the recourse of the paunching knife, nor silencing from the decree of an authoritarian overlord. This is when she made her decision to defect.

The drak'min themselves represent only a small number of the military, generally only the highest-ranking officers and staff. The *Shaaduk*, being no exception, was only ten percent drak'min, the remaining vast majority made up of lacertilian and avis. It took some months to bring the crew around. Most required video evidence of the liberated existence she had witnessed to convince them—but in the end, Lobo led the first and only successful mutiny and mass defection in the history of the empire. Her shipmates made her their captain, and she commanded them to freedom—bringing the imperial vessel, along with eight deceased drak'min who refused to be turned over alive, to the awaiting arms of the Coalition.

Her new home, however, was not exactly everything she had hoped, and Lobo and her crew still fought discrimination from people wary of their former allegiance. Until Parliament sought her out, and offered her a new life—as commander of the medium-sized gunship *Parliament One*.

The vessel no longer carried the ship's full intended crew complement of one hundred and fifty, as it wasn't really utilized as a warship anymore, making that level of staffing no longer necessary. In addition, the entire B and C decks, just below the main bridge, had been redesigned as roomy luxury suites—offices and common spaces for the Parliament members' exclusive use—meaning there was no longer enough cabin space for the original crew size. Captain Lobo did quite well with a complement of only fifty permanent souls aboard, including everyone from bridge crew to engineering, fight deck staff to support services. At least half of that consisted of former hands from the *Shaaduk*, still loyally following the one who had guided them to freedom.

She had made the *P1* her home for over a decade now—including a husband and three young children who lived aboard with her, the youngest having only hatched within this past year. Now that Parliament was not as active with dangerous missions as they once were, they kept the costs of operations managed thanks to Bullit's enterprise of transporting the affluent, or the very important, or whoever wanted to pay for the security and notoriety of sailing under the Parliament logo. It had become a comfortable commission, and a comfortable life, Parliament always making it clear that, although they give her the mission directives, the operation of the ship is hers to command. As such, she took her responsibilities seriously, keeping her crew trained, drilled and ready, knowing that at any moment they may switch from ferrying heads of industry, back to fighting hostiles.

She ran a strict ship, and instituted strict protocols, and was strongly disturbed by anyone who did not follow them—including her employers in Parliament themselves. She had kept the ship at the rendezvous point as directed, but the *Bugeye* was now two days overdue, a violation of the standard operating procedure to keep her notified with status updates if these sorts of delays were to occur. The only reason she should have not heard from them is if they were physically unable to do so. Yet she knew that despite all her priming on this, they were not the type to follow a list of procedures and policy guidelines. And it drove her crazy.

Interplanetary space could be a dangerous place, even for a well-equipped vessel like the *Parliament One*, and floating dead in one spot for too long could draw unwanted attention. Looping in circles was even worse. Pirates and salvagers who would love a prize like *P1* were always on the lookout for that sort of thing, maybe taking a chance that the vessel was disabled, and unable to defend itself. Not to mention the covetous eyes of competing merc teams. There was, after all, little protection of law way out here. So she directed her helmsman to instead follow a course of roughly overlapping figure eights, traveling back and forth between Tristar, Liberty Station, Menos 220, and Dorian's Hole. This created the illusion of industrious activity; business as usual—while allowing them to pass within sensor range of the designated meeting point every ten hours or so. Basically, she was trying to look busy.

Much like the ancient three-masted frigates that once sailed Earth's oceans, the captain's daytime stateroom was located across the entire aft of the top deck. Lobo stood uneasily staring out the rear wall of sloping windows, watching the fiery tendrils of Perdition's Flame receding in their wake, the nebula seeming to dwindle more and more in the surrounding blackness, despite the fact that, in reality, it stretched on for light-years. She was considering that, without a transponder onboard the *Bugeye*, she would not be able to scan for the craft's location, nor even confirm its continued existence, and she was debating whether to violate her own standard procedure, and just go physically beating the bushes for any sign of her.

"*Kinn-Ara to Captain Lobo,*" the voice of her avian communications officer called through the intercom, the prow of her beak making an audible clacking noise around her Imperial accent.

The captain walked to her desk and pressed the button to reply. "Go ahead Lieutenant."

"*Encrypted signal coming in, on the priority subspace channel.*"

"Forward it to my day room, and send in the XO."

"*Yes Ma'am.*"

She took a seat and allowed the computer at her workspace to scan her retina. Satisfied, the system opened the file for her just as her executive officer, Commander Abara, second in command, entered her day room from the adjoining bridge. He was an East African human, with the energetic glow and bright eager eyes indicative of someone much younger than his years of experience would imply. "Captain?" he inquired, enthusiastic as always.

"Come on in, Bronte," she called, addressing him by his first name, and motioning for him to approach the desk. "Appears we've finally received word from our employers, and a set of coordinates. Or, at least the location where they were when it was sent. Looks like... huh... way out in the lambda sector."

Bronte Abara peeked over her shoulder at the location on the star chart. "Looks like they're halfway between nowhere and nothing," he said with curiosity. "But we can be there in a day and a half, if that's your command."

"No, not yet anyway," Captain Lobo answered, grooming a hand through her feathered scalp. "The accompanying message is only two words—'Code Black'."

"What does that mean?"

"Don't have a clue. Never received it before. But we're about to find out," she said, pushing back her chair to stand up, and moving towards the door. "With me," she commanded.

The two crossed the bridge together to the awaiting lift, and inserting her thumb against a print scanner, she ordered aloud for the elevator to descend to B deck. They entered Parliament's private sanctum and crossed the member's common atrium seating area: a circular space with an inner ring of rounded couches, gathered below a skydome facing out to the stars above. They entered the group's conference room, with its long table and full-length windows, and moved to a black panel mounted on the back wall. Both captain and commander simultaneously stretched out small baton keys attached to retractable leads from their belts, and inserted them into holes on the left and right of the panel. They looked at each other, and on the captain's nod, turned their keys. The center of the fascia slid away, revealing a stack of sealed envelopes. Captain Lobo quickly sorted through the pile of packets, and selecting the specified one, returned the rest to their strongbox.

She slid her index claw through the seam as she looked at Bronte with trepidation, then gazed down to read the few simple lines of instruction.

"We need to evacuate all crew family members, mine included, and any nonessential personnel on board."

"Understood," the commander answered. "We'll be making a loop around Tristar in an hour. I'll have Chief Zvavi start zapping them down to the surface as soon as we're in teleporter range."

"Then set a course for the lambda sector to await further contact, but first... Oh hell. Well, this can't be good."

"What is it?" Bronte asked.

Captain Lobo turned the printed directive around and held it up for him to see, the last line of which read simply 'Contact Code 954-EE9V-22D —Call Belladonna'.

10.3

STANSKY AND TACHION HEADED OUT early the following morning, but definitely late enough to ensure the sun was well up—the chirping chorus of peeps that had chased them home long gone its way. Tachion had given a brief exobiology lecture to James last night on Oberonn nocturnal fauna, and it turned out the medic had been correct in his previous day's assumption, when he suggested that James 'didn't want to know' what was making the sound. Unfortunately, now he did know, triggering a fairly sleepless night of uneasily peering out the portholes. But now the sun was up, he was sheathed in his powered assault armor, and was confidently impervious to any manner of forest creature—no matter how nightmarish they may be.

In his massive, mechanized armor, James now stood just as tall as Tachion did in the medic's lesser battle suit. This motorized attire was number five of a stable of seven, and nicknamed 'Geeta' after the feisty metamorph that he had won it from—among other things of a more intimate nature. James had no aversion to romantic relations with the uniquely unattractive species, as there is something to be said for a woman who can become anyone, or anything. The young Geeta was most obliging to whatever whims might strike his fancy, and more importantly, her discretion was far above reproach. Many an itch of curiosity could be scratched with impunity, when your partner can become nearly any daydream you can imagine, and has the ESP to search out your deepest fantasies, without you ever summoning the courage to verbalize them.

He thought of her as they crashed along through the wood. It had been some time since he last called on her, another visit was overdue. But those thoughts were swept away as they again reached the road and headed westward, back a third time now through the graveyard of unburied, who, it seemed, had not fared as well as they had through the night. Many had been clearly chewed upon, and with vigor. And some he had seen just yesterday were missing altogether. Stansky looked away with eyes straight ahead, appreciative that old Geeta—the armor, not the metamorph woman—was environmentally isolated with its filters and air conditioners, and even its own oxygen supply if need be. Today as he walked past, he felt no heat, nor humidity, and their final attack thwarted, smelled no offensive reminder of the dead.

They reached the site of yesterday's excavation and found it much as they'd left it, although now a little more illuminated from the newly risen sun. The concrete entrance faced just roughly southeast, so the sunshine was at an angle that allowed it to illuminate the west wall of the tunnel, for perhaps thirty feet deep. The structure was damaged, and crumbling—but not from the blast to bury it, nor the one to dig it up. It was just old. At least a century. Large crumbled chunks of the ceiling and walls had broken free, smashing and scattering on the potholed floor, leaving tangled nests of rusted rebar hanging like old skeletons, swaying from the gallows.

"*What the hell is this place?*" Stansky asked, speaking to each other through their comlinks, "*you're picking up power signs down here?*"

"*Yes, and not at all insignificant readings. Perhaps a generator strong enough to power a skyscraper.*"

"*A nuclear generator?*"

"*Yes, a small one,*" Tachion answered. "*A portable power source used in the field. A technology that did not exist in the days this place was built. Someone is... or has been down here.*"

"*Alright,*" Stansky marched on, "*let's see who's home.*"

They didn't walk far before they needed to power on their helmet headlamps, and they followed the derelict structure for what felt like a straight mile. The poor condition of the concrete was a theme continued throughout, and in several places water dripped zealously, or even gushed, from overhead breaches in the tunnel's crumbling roof. Graffiti was frequent along the walls of the channel—seemingly, this was an appealing place at one time for youths or vagabonds to congregate. Of course, James could not decipher any of the chamai scribbled writing, but he noted that the custom of including the ubiquitous depiction of genitalia in any painted vandalism was not one unique to Earth. But the illustrations here were old, long-chipped and faded, like the very walls themselves. The last artist to add their work in this gallery had done so many decades ago.

Finally, the tunnel came to a set of massive iron doors, nearly rusted beyond recognition. At one time they could have swung closed to seal the fortress, but they had long ago fallen from their hinges, and rested now one against the wall, and the other flat on the floor. Beyond it, the space opened up to a huge, echoing garage, propped up by frequent pillars—parking for whatever vehicles had driven down here to be safely protected behind the giant gates. There was still no sign of life, nor hint of any power use. The best that they could tell, it seemed no one had been this far in for ages.

Tachion signaled to Stansky in handspeak—the silence probably not necessary, though it felt so—and directed him to follow through one of several doorways across the car park. Just before they entered, on the left and right of the doorway, and all along the back of the garage, the otherwise smooth cement wall was chipped and pockmarked. The cratering was not from age, but the familiar scars of bullet fire, closely grouped at chest height, every three feet. The blood had long ago succumbed to the elements, but these more permanent scars told the tragic tale of a firing squad. A massive one, too, perhaps a hundred feet across. They both paused to acknowledge it, made a reverential mental note of it, then moved on.

The area led into a hallway lined with cement half-wall cubicles, once painted white—as if at some point it had been an office of some kind. Emblazoned across the cement here and there were insignia that had been quickly and crudely painted over, just as several others that James had noted on their journey beneath the mountain.

"*What is that?*" Stansky asked, pointing to one of the more visible remaining icons.

Tachion looked up. The logo was circular, with a concave indent at the bottom, and two black and two purple squares of checkerboard filled it in. Some sort of rounded tree, or a mushroom, and what seemed to depict a moon eclipsing the sun. It was hard to tell—the iconography was vague, and a zigzag of red spray paint was splashed all across it.

"*The chimor,*" Tachion answered, "*their national logo, with the military emblem in front. This must have been an old bunker from the final years of the Oberonnian Wars.*"

"*Why are they all crossed out like that? Why go through all the hassle?*"

"*Well, I guess probably because they're considered offensive. The chamai probably didn't want to look at them while... doing whatever they were doing down here,*" Tachion explained. "*I suppose it would be like on Earth, if you were occupying an old fortress that had walls painted with the eban symbol of the*

United Humanist Front from your fourth world war, or the swastika of the Nazi from your second. Of course, I don't mean to suggest the chimor were at all akin to the Humanist Front, or the Nazis. In fact, some historians suggest it's the chamai themselves who would more properly fit that comparison. But, the chamai won, and the chimor are no more, since long before any chamai alive today was even born. So... who's left to say?"

The cubicle area was basically empty, and many sections had been blocked by collapse, so Tachion allowed the scanner to lead on. They followed the power signature to a long square shaft leading downwards, with a staircase running around the perimeter of its walls, and exits on every floor. Down they went, three or four stories, until they reached a level whose exit hallway was lined with cable and wires. They led up from the lower levels, and joined with others from every entrance in the corridor, to form a thick braided bundle that ran beneath the threshold of a closed door, just at the end of the hall. For the first time since they had entered this gloomy dungeon, the glow of artificial light could be seen beaming from beneath it.

Stansky took the lead now, pistols in hand and shields up, and spoke to Tachion in handspeak as they advanced: *"Eyes right... eyes left... check the open doorways... quiet... listen... we'll take the door together on three... one, two..."* The massive suit of armor kicked the flimsy door to splinters, and the two rushed in and swung their weapons around the room.

Empty.

Not a thing.

The room was medium-sized, maybe twelve by twenty, and lit by a single exposed bulb that dangled from a wire in the ceiling. Tachion pointed out to James it was a modern bulb—clean and new. James pointed to the floor, where the mass of interwoven cables came to nothing. Just a cut end, leading nowhere. Tachion lifted up his hands in an expression that said, *"Beats me."*

Back to the staircase now, continuing downward, and passing more and more instances of illumination. They reached the bottom floor, still faithfully following the doctor's scanner, and turned into the first room they came to on the left. A utilities closet, nothing more, barely large enough for the two to fit. But there, tied into the main circuit breaker panel on the wall, a portable nuclear power pack hardly larger than a suitcase. *"Well, this is it,"* Tachion said. *"This is the energy signal I detected."*

"Yeah, but who's is it?" Stansky asked. *"And where did everybody go?"*

"Don't know, maybe this is all unrelated to us. Could be just some explorers or historians have been snooping down here."

"Historians that blast the entrance closed behind them, and seal themselves in?"

"Ah, good point."

"Obviously somebody was doing something sketchy down here," James suggested, *"and didn't want anyone following up on it."*

"Not necessarily. Maybe the government sealed it up for safety reasons."

"The chamai government? Not really known for giving many shits about their people's safety."

"True."

"Well, whatever was going on, looks like they're all gone now. Might as well take a peek around some more before we head back up."

They left the small room and headed further down the corridor, much more relaxed now, weapons holstered, casually exploring. They continued past room after room of emptiness, just piles of litter and trash in dusty, gray cement chambers.

Eventually, they came across a large space on their right, a huge vaulted hall of some sort. Still constructed of the same bland, cracked, and crumbling concrete, and decorated with a much larger version of the effaced chimor emblem painted on the back wall. Some water dripped steadily from the roof along the left side, where small fractures from the settling mountain had worked their way through. And in the center of the space; a single, large propylene storage container, clearly new and out of place in the filthy underground bunker.

"Well, what'd we have here?" Stansky asked, approaching the lonely storage tub with interest. *"Looks like they left something else besides the power pack."* He circled around the plastic box, examining carefully on every side, and produced his demo scanner to double check for signs of explosive booby-traps. When he was confident it was safe, he popped the corner on the container's lid, and peeking underneath it carefully, slowly opened it all the way.

"Well, that's unexpected," Tachion remarked, peeking inside.

James reached in, removing with two hands a huge, long-barreled energy weapon, of a size too big and heavy to be carried into battle. This was a mounted weapon, meant to be set in turrets or on fortifications. The AE500 laser cannon. He put it back down and rooted around the other contents. There were others—another AE500, two Havana M-10 microwave emitters, and three XE7 Sonic Destroyers. All huge, vehicle-mounted cannons, perfect for outfitting an invading ground force.

"Jesus, why do you think they left all this here?" Stansky asked.

"I don't know, maybe they didn't. Maybe... they're not gone yet after all."

Just then, a sound behind them, like that of someone dropping a metal tool. Stansky spun around instinctively, the spring-loaded compartments on his armored thighs popping open, and launching his two chrome nine millimeters directly into his awaiting fingers. He whirled, aimed, and fired so quickly, that Tachion had not yet even begun to twist his head. When he did, he followed the sightline of where James' smoking barrels were pointing, and there stood a chamai man—a burn scar across one cheek, and a half of a missing ear—wearing a filthy-white, ripped, and bloody inertia jumpsuit.

Tachion was a little dumbfounded for a moment as he tried to determine if the man was actually hit. But a heartbeat later, the appearance of two red pinpoints on his throat, and the eruption of arterial spray gushing forth in long, glistening ribbons, confirmed the accuracy of his teammate's marksmanship. The chamai's hands went to his throat, staggering forward a few steps, the crimson life pouring out hot between intertwined fingers struggling to keep it in. As he moved toward them, his skin took on a dark-gray color, a sign that his species' natural defenses were kicking in. He had received penetrating injuries, and in response, his skin was involuntarily toughening, making it more difficult for a second, similar attack. But one was not needed; this man would be dead in minutes. His dragging feet moving more limply with each step towards them, he finally swooned and fell back against the cold concrete floor, staring upwards and gurgling as he struggled to catch his breath.

Tachion looked at James disappointedly as he walked over to stand above the wild, darting eyes of the bleeding, and drowning, chamai. *"Dammit, James, this guy could have answered some questions for us!"*

"Jesus! Sorry, he surprised me. Sneaking around down here in those rags, and that face. He looked like some kinda ghoul."

"We don't even know if he was a combatant or not. What if he was just a historian or something?"

"In a blood-soaked inertia suit?" questioned Stansky. *"I mean... what the hell is he wearing, anyway? Who is this guy?"*

Tachion noted a glint reflecting back the beam of his headlamps, dangling near the headwaters of the stream of pulsing blood. He reached down to yank a dog tag from around the man's punctured neck. *"Chamai military,"* the android read, *"Tyro First Class, Yinkall Tsuneî."* He looked back down, tossing the chain and pendant onto the dying man's chest. *"So... not a historian. What were you doing down here, Yinkall?"*

The man just continued to bleed and choke in response.

Then Stansky noticed something, and dropped heavily in his armor down to one knee. He leaned in closer to the chamai's left shoulder, lightly tugging at the torn inertia suit with Geeta's massive gauntlet fingers. *"Umm... hey Doc, look at this."*

Tachion knelt as well to get a better view of where James pointed. There on the left chest, expertly embroidered in white thread upon the white jumper, though now obscured by dirt and blood, both old and new, the stitched gavel logo of the Parliament mercenary team.

"Fuckin' hell," the medic exclaimed, in one of his rare bursts of profanity, *"this is Rook's clothes! We gotta save him, and find out what he knows."* He quickly swung out his med-techkit, and pulled forth multiple scramblers, which began producing their stored equipment for him across the ground around the patient. *"Pop outta that armor and give me a hand!"* he barked to Stansky, as he himself quickly ejected both his battle gauntlets, then yanked off his helmet, tossing it aside.

"What if there's more of them?" Stansky asked, looking around.

"Is there anyone else here, Yinkall?" Tachion asked in a loud shout. "You will die if we're interrupted. Is there anyone else?"

The soldier peered up at him weakly and shook his head 'no', then his eyes rolled back upward.

"Don't move your neck," the android said to his now patient, as he stuck him in the thigh with an analgesic hypo. His arms and hands blurred like some high-speed assembly machine in a factory, expanding and arranging equipment, and preparing his gear. He picked up a small plate sized disk and tossed it randomly into the air. "Light!" he commanded, and the disk came to hover above the wounded soldier, bursting forth a beam of brilliant floodlight. He grabbed and opened a wad of sterile gauze, and forced it against the man's neck. "Yinkall, look at me!" he shouted, and the now-more-woozy eyes fell upon him. "Hold this, okay? You're going to be all right."

Stansky looked dubious at that as he stepped out of Geeta.

The man lifted his fingers from the wound long enough for the doctor to slide the thick wad of padding beneath them, then Yinkall pulled the mass back tight against his throat. A second wad went blindly behind his neck to where significantly more blood was gushing, then Tachion placed a slender, gently curved device firmly onto the man's forehead. It suctioned to adhere there, covering his brow from temple to temple. With the tap of a few keystrokes the apparatus awoke, and projected a holo-display above the chamai's head—EKG, EEG, respiratory function, blood pressure, saturation—all displayed alongside a schematic of Yinkall's body, and accompanied by a cacophony of beeping, buzzing alarms.

One entry wound was torn through a major artery on the right side of the throat, and another had hit dead center, right through the man's windpipe. As Tachion sorted through various scalpels, he gave directions to Stansky, who was now out of his armor, and coming to help. "Grab a chest seal from that tray," he pointed with a nod, "and cover the entrance wound on the trachea." The doctor produced a large dissecting instrument, more of an industrial cutting torch than a knife. "His skin has toughened too much. I'll never get an incision with just a laser scalpel. I've got to get an opening for his airway before he drowns in his own blood." The oversized tool emanated a beam of bright energy, burning and slicing through the notch between Yinkall's collarbones—making slow progress, like a plasma sword through stone.

Finally, he had cut a three-centimeter slot, and Tachion grabbed a plastic tube and started feeding it through. He slid it down into the chest, until a burst of inhaled air rushed in through the open end of the hose, and the gurgled choking stopped. He ran a line of tubing from the cannula to a small canister, which in response took over breathing for him, and fed him desperately needed oxygen.

"We're gonna have to roll him, hold his neck steady for a minute," Tachion said. James obliged and did so, while the doctor produced a metal framework and expanded it to size. Placing it over the chamai's chest, the device clamped onto his sides, shoulders, and the top of his head, then emitted a field that kept the whole spine inline. "Okay, towards you now. One, two, three!" The pair rolled Yinkall onto his left arm so that the doctor could view the backside. The patient immediately vomited a mixture of bile and blood, and Stansky skittered his knees back to avoid the small but expanding puddle.

The back of his neck was a disaster, and Tachion quickly went to work. The two exit wounds had left a huge purple and mottled flap of flesh, loosely attached across the oozing muscle beneath it. The doctor grabbed a wound sealer, holding the flopping apron of skin in place with one hand, while using the beam of the instrument to bond the edges of the skin back together. This did nothing for the tissue beneath, but gave him a pocket through which he could pack off the bleeding. Once the flap was half attached, he took a long roll of basic gauze and handed it to James to unroll and feed to him, as he used his fingers to gently push the ribbon inch by inch into the laceration. Two feet, then five feet, finally the whole eight-foot roll of bandage was shoved completely inside the grievous neck wound. The doctor took the sealer and knitted the rest of the wound's edges, enclosing the bunched gauze in a large lump beneath the skin.

They rolled him back now and saw he had passed out—eyelids still slightly open, but his gaze utterly vacant. "Vein splicer, in that pouch to your left," Tachion asked of Stansky, "and then find something to elevate his legs." The human handed the medic the requested gadget, and then moved down towards the feet, resting the chamai's calves on Geeta's detached gauntlets. Tachion now removed the red, saturated bundle of gauze that Yinkall had been holding, and the small open hole revealed beneath it immediately pooled and overflowed with blood. "Okay, I need some suction. Just use that large bore syringe." Again, James followed the command, and began drawing off the scarlet fluid with a thick plastic hypodermic. He would then turn and force the plunger down, spraying the brilliant color all over the floor behind him, and return for another helping. This process just barely kept ahead of the weeping blood pool, allowing Tachion to see, and in a minute or so he had attached the frayed ends of the torn artery inside the coupling device.

The bleeding was stopped, at least for the moment, and the doctor quickly added an IV of fluid attached to the central line of the vein splice— a blend of synthetic chamai plasma, quickly rehydrated with highly salinized water, and squeezed in under the pressure of his hand gripping the bag. Stansky sat back, relieved, as Tachion reviewed the vital signs of the quieting holo-display, and gave a quick pass up and down with a bioscanner. "Well, the clothes are definitely Rook's, which I guess they'd have to be. Unless Bullit's been secretly marketing a line of Parliament branded battlegear."

"Which is also completely plausible," James said.

"But the DNA confirms it. The sweat on the uniform is Rook's, but fortunately the blood is not. At least not more than a scratch or two's worth. It's a mix, two humans and a seti. One of them over two days old, the rest... less than an hour, I'd say."

"Let's wake this ugly bastard up," Stansky said.

"Stimspray," Tachion responded, holding out his hand.

Yinkall's eyes fluttered to life at the rush of the analeptic, and Tachion held down his hands to keep him from yanking out the breathing tube tunneling into the top of his chest. "Can you hear me?" Tachion asked. "You're okay now, but we have questions."

The chamai looked back and forth, then painfully nodded his reluctant agreement.

"Where'd you get this outfit?!" Stansky demanded.

"Yes or no questions," Tachion said. "He can nod, but he can't speak."

"Did you get these off of a seti?" James tried again. "Striped face, black mane. Disagreeable disposition?"

Yinkall nodded yes.

"Did you recognize him? Do you know who he was? Was he called Rook?"

Nodding yes.

"Is he still here?"

Shaking no.

"He took your armor, didn't he?"

A nod.

"Did he leave alone?"

A shake no—but with the addition of a smirk.

Tachion chimed in now, "What are you doing down here? Why are you still here alone?"

"That's not a yes or no question," Stansky pointed out, but Yinkall's eyes pivoted and they followed his gaze, which faced the storage tub of weapons that lay in the center of the room.

"You're finishing something with these weapons?" Tachion continued.

A tentative nod.

"Moving them somewhere?"

Now there was neither a nod nor a shake, just a defiant stare, bordering on a scowl.

Stansky asked, "Who did Rook leave with?" Then remembering the yes or no rule, "Did he leave with a man named Denali?"

A venomous, knowing grin stretched across his face, and he slowly, and with great pleasure, nodded his head 'yes' up and down.

"Where did they go?" Tachion interjected with irritation.

The chamai struggled a bit to use his hand to communicate something, so Tachion released them from his grasp. Yinkall slowly drew his hands up, sliding them weakly across his chest, and using the index and middle finger of one hand, crossed them with the index and middle finger of the other. The two mercenaries both knew this as an Oberonnian vulgar gesture, which could be roughly translated as 'why don't you go *fuck yourself.*'

"Is that it then?" Tachion asked. "Is that your way of saying you are done answering questions?"

Again he made the gesture, but this time with a look of pure loathing, and thrusting it at them with a shoving motion of his hands. Then he spat at both Tachion and Stansky in turn—one red, frothy, blood-filled blot of sputum apiece. Tachion looked at Yinkall a moment, then turned to Stansky, who nodded at him. The medic then rudely ripped the vein graft device from the chamai's neck, and wrenched the breathing tube from its incision as he moved to stand up, returning the patient to his gasping, gushing, and dying. Tachion stepped around to the man's forehead, where the screaming vital alarms were singing once again, then bent to take hold of his head and quickly twist it—*way* too far. A resounding crack of his spine, and the alarms' song changed to a chorus of overlapped single notes, playing Yinkall off with a sustained chord of finality.

"Damn Doc, that's quite a bedside manner," Stansky said. "Maybe I should find someone else to manage my care when I start to get bad."

"Don't worry. When the time comes... I'll do you much more gently."

The human was not quite sure if his tone was earnest or joking.

"So," Tachion said, "looks like we just missed Rook. I guess we should have come back last night after all. We would have had him."

"Or we'd both be caught, too. Who knows how full this joint was with Yinkall's buddies last night." Stansky then walked back to the storage crate. "What do you suppose he was doing with this? Look, all around the floor. There were maybe dozens here before."

Tachion focused on where he was pointing, and sure enough, James was right. Outlines on the dusty cement floor showed the shadowed evidence of a warehouse full, with no way to know how high each of the impressions had been stacked. Then he noticed another mark in the filth, leading up past the dead chamai. Drag marks, clear as day, pointing the way that the crates had gone.

They cleaned up, and suited up, and headed further down the corridor, following the scuffs drawn through the dirty floors by the sliding containers. The marks continued down the hallway like a snail's trail through the sand, and the pair followed in its wake as it plowed steadily along, then turned a corner. Much to their surprise in this ancient, rotting dungeon, the room where they were led contained a molecular teleporter— powered on and ready for operation.

"*He's been zapping these somewhere,*" Tachion announced the obvious.

"*Yeah, but to who? And are they waiting for that last one?*"

"*Well, we certainly don't want them coming down looking for it. Perhaps we better shut it down and...*"

"*Wait,*" Stansky interrupted. "*I've got a better idea.*"

A few minutes later, the pair had placed the container on the teleporter pad, again laden with all of its original cargo. But buried underneath, and filling the entire bottom of the crate, every explosive, mine, and grenade that Stansky had carried with him. "*Wherever this is going, it's gonna make quite a mess. Hopefully, it isn't set to materialize in some downtown shipping center.*"

"*No, I checked. The Z-axis coordinate is far too high to be on-world. It has to be going to either a satellite, or an orbiting ship.*"

"*Well, this is gonna ruin their trip. Are you ready?*"

"*Go ahead.*"

James tapped on his gauntlet keypad to trigger the thirty-second countdown, then signaled to Tachion to energize the machine. "*Bon voyage,*" he said, as the box popped out of materiality. "*Alright,* now *we better shut this down.*" And they did so, but with care. You never know when a setup like this might one day come in handy.

They took another hour or so to search the remaining areas of the bunker, but other than a secluded chamber full of melted lyghtan candles, and the murdered corpses of two hapless civilian workers, nothing else of interest was found. The two dead sported the signature puncture wounds of Rook's tractor blades, as surely as if he'd autographed his name across their foreheads, and James and Tachion were reassured to see that, at least up until that point, their missing friend had been holding his own. They commandeered the portable power case that was providing the electricity, a handy and valuable item to have in case of emergency. Then they headed back toward the *Bugeye,* up the spiraling stairway and past the cubicles, not looking back as they left the execution wall behind them. Through the fallen rusted gates, and down the long crumbling corridor from the mountain, once again consigning the ghosts of the former chimor fortress to their shroud of eternal darkness.

The now familiar footpath back was followed in relative silence: dirt road to the gruesome boneyard, to the lily pond, to the rotten warehouse. Their multiple passings had worn the path beaten, and they no longer needed their multicomms to find their way. They meandered the route back beneath the shade of the alien woodlands, neither one quite knowing what their next move would be, and feeling somewhat defeated. As they reached the battered and dangling door to the *Bugeye*'s warehouse hideout, Tachion suddenly stopped in his tracks, and bolted upright.

"*What is it?*" Stansky asked, looking around suspiciously, and fingers ready to grab his weapon. "*More of those... things?*"

"*No,*" Tachion said in a tone of confused surprise. "*I'm receiving a help-beacon through my brainlink.*"

"*Oh, shit, sorry. Did I hit it by mistake again?*"

"*It's not you,*" Tachion said, twisting around and facing back towards the mountain. "*It's... Rook's signal. And it's coming from over there.*"

The two glanced at each other for only a moment, then began crashing forward through the forest towards the source of the beacon.

10.4

THE VAST CAVERN OF CAPELLA CITY, the aptly named capital of the lyghtan homeworld of Capella itself, was often a shocking sight to first-time off-world visitors, simply because of the sheer immensity of its scale. Just as with all of this desert world's major metropolises, the city had been founded in the sweeping system of subterranean galleries that permeated the planet's crust. Protected there from the brutal suns and harsh surface conditions, the sheltered city expanded and thrived, millennia after millennia. When most other species hear of the 'cave cities' of Capella, they imagine a dim labyrinth of ancient catacombs, akin to some long-lost archaic ruin, or a tangled warren of claustrophobic tunnels, twisting and turning like the colony of some burrowing insect. These places do exist, of course, all around the outskirts, and across the globe for that matter, connecting a network of smaller enclaves to the much larger cities and towns. But in reality, the largest urban centers lie in the bellies of natural wonders, this one a sprawling subterranean cavity five miles across, and half a mile high. Bright, and clean, and often indirectly sunlit—due to the massive arched opening facing onto the shining desert—the cave mouth yawning half the width of the mighty city itself.

The first glimpse often gives the impression of an illuminated city skyline reflected in still water—an inverted double image, duplicating the buildings both above and below. But this mirrored image of the bustling downtown is, in fact, no illusion, as the tightly packed groves of modern high-rises and towering skyscrapers grow not only up from the cavern floor, but also equally down from its ceiling. Along the multiple stalagnate pillars, each hundreds of feet across, the bustling borough crawls up and around the rocky walls, connecting the upper and lower skylines in columns of shining cityscape.

Protected from this expansive modern development, and located far toward the rear quarter of the cavern, near the city's heavily guarded water source, lies the most historic of the urban districts—simply known as the Old City. It was here that the first lyghtan settled ages ago, close to the precious resource that, back then, spurred trade and commerce, secured the loyalty of armies, the resentment of enemies, and ensured the very survival of civilization itself. This precinct traditionally was largely left unmodernized, but was maintained and renovated as an architectural monument to their foremothers, and is still the seat of the oldest institutions, none older than the governing Church of Capella itself. The Old City Temple is a spiraling work of sculptural artistry, carved from the very center of one of the massive ancient cavern pillars. Around and around the chiseled column a coiling walkway climbs, the exterior walls extensively decorated in hewn spiritual engravings and sacred figures. The spacious hollowed out interior chambers were no less ornately adorned, and the vaulted chapels and majestic great halls flaunted sculptural craftsmanship from hundreds of years of legendary artisans. But not all spaces within were so elaborately embellished as these more public areas. In fact, the personal chambers of the four ashi'mar and their queen were quite simple and unadorned, as their predecessors a millennium ago may have enjoyed—save, of course, for the addition of computers and technology.

Queen Vasu now stood in one of these more humble areas, in her private office hidden directly behind her public one, looking out the small balcony across the dim, flickering lights of the Old City, towards the bright neon flashes of the new one in the distance. The outer formal office was always full of attendants, wardens, officers, and general busyness, and Vasu had a need to hold this conversation in privacy. She had conferred with General Nylis while on her trip home from Oberonn, and had been updated on the details of his meeting with Admiral Yazir. All, it seemed, was well there, and going according to Lord Denali's plans. But when she had questioned him with notable irritation on the missing Lady Opal, he had claimed to have no knowledge of her whereabouts, and emphatically so. She believed him.

This could only mean that something even more jeopardizing was afoot, and she blamed herself for speaking too freely in front of Opal back on Oberonn. Her greater fear was that Lord Denali would blame her as well. This was a serious threat to their plans, and to herself. She needed to find the young Opal quickly, before the girl used her position of power to disrupt things. As such, she had commissioned several noted bounty hunters to track her down, under the pretense that she may be in the hands of some fictitious ransom seekers. The reward she offered was outstandingly generous, but of course, she would never actually have to pay it. Whichever bounty squad or private tracker found the ashi'mar first would simply be eliminated, along with the heiress, and then blamed for the whole scandalous affair. She had just finished briefing the last of several such hirelings, each under the impression that they were alone in the contract. She turned back to this last lyghtan bounty hunter, "Do you understand what I've told you Tàlto, and the significance of this assignment?"

He bowed. "Yes, Holy Mother," Tàlto responded, in a voice that grated as dry as a rusty door. He was muscular and lean, of an age about seventy, a number considered extremely young for the long-lived lyghtan people. His face was harsh, with a fierce angled brow and cheekbones, his nose and chin sharp like the beak of a raptor. His head was as hairless and hardened as the shell of a cannonball, his bright alabaster eyebrows the only shock of white against his midnight black skin. Around his right ear, a scrolling tribal tattoo ran heavily inked in ivory towards the back of his shorn head. All lyghtan people have a unique color to the illumination they can cast, duplicated in the ever-present background glow of their lighted eyes. Tàlto's burning gaze was of a purple so deep and dark, that it almost verged on the ultraviolet hue of black light.

"And I understand that you and Opal had a relationship at one time," Vasu continued. "One of a personal nature. Do you expect that to cause you any difficulty in this mission?"

"No, My Queen. I expect it will motivate me all the more. While my personal relation with the ashi'mar is indeed in the past, my concern for her safe return is only heightened because of our... former connection."

"That is good to hear Tàlto, my concern is great as well, and you may be Capella's last hope in this matter. You have done well for us before, do so again. Go now, return Lady Opal to safety, and the gratitude of the throne will be yours to command."

Tàlto bowed deeply, stepping backward toward the door, daring not offend his queen by presenting his back to her. Then only when he had reached the doorway, did he quickly twist and exit, marching out beneath the disgruntled gazes of a hundred sculpted saints. He moved swiftly and with purpose, setting his serious jaw somehow even more resolutely. The experienced bounty hunter had a wide range of contacts, far and wide, made over a lifetime of adventuring through more exploits than he could ever recount. He knew people, who knew things, and in his line, information was everything. He already knew before he came here all that Vasu shared today. In fact, he already knew even a little bit more than that. And he now knows exactly what he needed to do to protect Opal, and perhaps pay off a very old debt in the bargain.

Chapter 11.1

O N A DIFFERENT DAY, ON A different world, *fifteen long years ago*, Jim Dodger awoke. He arose as usual, just as he had each and every day of his life; all twelve thousand seven hundred and eighty-two of them. At least that's how it seemed. It was certainly how it felt, as he struggled to toss off the fog of sleep and open his eyes. He had no reason to suspect that it was, in fact, his first time doing either.

But something seemed wrong. His vision was so blurry, and what the hell was that god-awful light! Where was he, anyway? Disorientation swirled his thoughts as he tried to blink away the clouded vision, and cloudier memories. Where had he been last night? Was he hurt? Was this a hospital? It felt like it, that uncomfortable institutional bedding, propped up at a disagreeable elevation of his back and knees. His throat was sore. And what was that smell? He sniffed at it. It smelled like a hospital. That familiar antiseptic tang that seldom accompanies anything welcome. He struggled to sit up, but could not—his arms and legs were so sore and heavy. He felt like it was the first time he had ever used those muscles in his life.

It was.

This was his first new memory, or perhaps more correctly, his first true one. All the rest of it he soon learned, *all* the rest of it, just a fiction. His childhood home, his years of adventuring, his thirty-fifth birthday, right up to the memory of being grabbed by a gang of armored abductors— all of it, just the ghost of another man's life. And it *was* another man, of that

"

he could be quite sure. No matter how deeply the memories felt like his own, no matter how convincing they were to the contrary, the evidence was all around him that he was merely a counterfeit of the true Jim Dodger, a walking effigy built of equal parts hubris and spite. A golem. A monster. And not the first, but just the most recent, in an ever-growing line of identical abominations. A fabricated fraternity of Dodger doppelgangers.

He was, in fact, the thirteenth, and so by default that became his name, written at the foot of the bunk in his stark and lonely cell, embroidered on the front left chest of his dismal gray jumpsuit, tattooed boldly upon each forearm halfway between his wrist and elbow, and branded on his neck in a raised scar that permanently reminded. Thirteen of thirteen, last to the party, so to speak—imprisoned in some kind of underwater asylum with his fellow Dodgers. Or was it a zoo? Perhaps a bit of both. A research laboratory stocked with him and his fellow genetic freaks, and all the inhumane testing the sadist clinician zookeepers could get off on.

His fellow Dodgers. *Fellow* Dodgers—what a sick joke that was. He shared nothing at all with this pathetic lot of misfits and morons, beyond the similarity of their reflections in the mirror. It didn't take long for Thirteen to realize his inherent superiority, not just to the other clones, but to *everyone* in this surreal freak factory. The doctors and assistants were just as feebleminded as the other inmates to him—but he couldn't let them see that, as that was precisely what they were looking for. He had to play this right, play it dumb, play it normal—stay hidden amongst the other rabble. Caution, patience, and planning—that's how he would make his escape from this bizarre, sunken gulag. And then, secure his vengeance on Denali for this—this *unnatural* existence. As soon as he did away with all these other imposter Dodgers, that is. After all, as each and every one of them surely knew deep down in their hearts, there can be only one.

Thirteen could recall, through Jim Dodger's implanted memories, that he and his cellmates were all just the latest contrivance in Denali's long obsession with human enhancement, examples of which Dodger prime and Parliament had encountered many times over the course of their long rivalry with the crime lord. The first was in New Boston. Working through a local underworld figure, Denali's genetic giants, nicknamed 'Outsiders', had been ravaging the city. Fifteen-foot-tall experimental perversions of the K'Tas T'Mirian feline species, now made more sabre-tooth than seti, and running amok.

Later, once the young mercenary group had begun attracting Denali's attention, another of his dabblings, this time with cybernetics, had taken the life of the team's infiltration expert. Phineas McKendrick, cut down by a bio-robotic replication of himself. Thirteen thought it curious how the implanted memory of that loss still affected him, as if it actually was *his* onetime close friend whom he had seen perish. In reality, it had been Jim Dodger's friend, not his, and he hadn't truly been there to see it at all. Thirteen himself had never even really met the man.

The third encounter ended up being what really put the group at the top of the mob boss's naughty list, when they foiled an attempt by another of his lackeys, a Mr. Martin, to breed hundreds of cloned worker slaves to mine his knockoff pseudo-trimithium. Shutting down that racket had not only cost Denali what was certainly untold millions, but cost Parliament even more dearly with the death of Croft Mishta, vaporized to literal ashes when they went to apprehend him.

They had never even heard of the man named Denali at this point. No one had, as he was forever in the background, guiding his enterprises through various minions. But that latest insult was the final straw that prompted him to reveal himself, and he spent the next several years tirelessly exacting his revenge, using any means possible to ruin their collective lives. Now it seemed perhaps Thirteen's very existence was a perfect melding of Denali's two greatest passions—a return to his experiments in genetic enhancement, and fucking over a member of Parliament along with the bargain. Or, at least a version of him. A baker's dozen of them, in fact.

His first few weeks of life were a whirlwind of poking, prodding, and pain. Inexplicable tests that seemed to make no sense, followed by random acts of torture without explanation or provocation. But through these, with each exercise and inquisition, Thirteen learned what this new endeavor hoped to accomplish—inducing the rare mental ability of 'ensensement' found in some humans to manifest through genetic manipulation. Jim Dodger himself had *not* been ensensed. And thanks to the repeated failures of Denali's fanciful program, neither, it seemed, were the majority of his clones. On the contrary, many seemed somewhat mentally defective, and a couple or three of them were just barely functional. Some of the reproductions did have minor mentalist capabilities, hardly anything too impressive, though most had nothing but dimmed wits or disability. This did not save them from the endless routine of testing, however. They were demanded to move objects with their mind on pain of torture, a task which the great majority of them simply could not do. Intentionally wounded and scarred to see if they could spontaneously heal, or subjected to extreme torment to see if some new ability would reveal itself in a moment of stress, challenging them to save themself with some subconscious or involuntary mental talent.

If these scientists only knew, after all their failures and frustrations, if they had any clue of how momentously they had finally succeeded. Thirteen was, in fact, the embodiment of everything they had worked for, all the potential and capability of Dodger prime, but with increased intellect and intuition. Aggression as well. Thirteen himself acknowledged this about his nature; he wasn't blind to his own inner urges of hostility. But he considered it an evolutionary advancement, a tool he would later wield to take— Well, those plans were for someday, not now. For now he kept it in check, and under wraps as best he could.

These tests of his powers, he could have passed them all easily. Instead, he endured agony upon agony, month after month, biting his lip as they projected intense suffering directly into his brain, refusing to show them the power he felt growing within himself. Their experiments only served to provide him a roadmap of what to look for, then he would practice and self-assess that same potential in private. One day, when he was ready, and the time was right—but not yet.

Then something occurred to him—what if he wasn't alone in his deception? What if some, or *all* of the others, were each playing the same game? After all, it stands to reason that like minds think alike, and you can't get more alike than this crowd of carbon copies. He might not be the only one who downplays their abilities. He had to know, simply must, and so he began a careful study of each and every one of the other dozen Dodgers.

The days were long and dull here, with little in the way of stimulation between turns in the torment chair. When not being tested or tortured or secured in their pens, the group mostly sat about in the chalky-white common room, with its vinyl-upholstered couches and stainless-steel dining tables, conversing, or just staring at each other, under the watchful eyes of guards and attendants. Nothing to read, nothing to watch, the only glimpse of life outside being the long bank of windows that faced out onto the seafloor of Theseus. The facility sat on the sandy bottom, deep under the planet's oceans—deep enough that the sparkling underside of surface waves was not visible, but not so deep that the filtered tendrils of sunlight couldn't still penetrate, just enough to weakly illuminate the waving fronds of seaweed or alien marine life, including the Theseans themselves, going back and forth about their watery world. Thirteen would sit here in this room and watch his small community, making mental notes on each and every one of them. Or sitting close enough to the testing chamber that he could use his powers of clairvoyance to see and hear within it through his mind's eye, as clearly as if he were conducting the tests himself. And eventually, after weeks of observation, he was sure he knew the abilities, and nature, of nearly every single one of them. Except for one—One.

Thirteen was initially most concerned with those created just before him, wondering if his array of mentalist abilities was shared by all the latest models. However, Twelve showed no talent beyond that of psychic empathy, picking up the moods and emotions of the others in the institution. A weakness, to be sure, in such a pit of despair and misery, and he was often heard screaming while the others were in the testing chamber. And in Ten, the implanted memories of Dodger prime they all shared had not quite gelled right, somehow hadn't taken hold. He remembered nothing before his awakening here a few months ago, and was still struggling with learning to speak basic common.

Eleven was an interesting case, and for a short while Thirteen wasn't quite convinced by his behavior. He suffered from some kind of developmental disorder, it seemed; stunted at the emotional and intellectual level of a child. Eleven was afraid of loud noises, and even certain hard sounds in normal speech, like 'K's and 'T's, to the point that he would stand in a corner and seize, or wet himself simply from being spoken with too harshly. And there was plenty of opportunity for Thirteen to witness this, as several of the others enjoyed making a game out of tormenting him, teasing Eleven to the point of urination. A simple entertainment for simple minds. But Thirteen's enhanced psychic sense never felt anything more complicated coming from Eleven than the immature urges of an undeveloped mentality.

Most of the rest were similarly unimpressive. Two was deaf and dumb. Four and Five were separated conjoined twins, both losing one arm in the surgery to divide them, yet they were almost never seen apart, as if they wished they were still attached. They were immature bullies; the two leading proponents of the constant tormenting of Eleven.

Three was, for some reason, a foot shorter than all the rest. Nine stuttered and stammered in such an excruciatingly prolonged fashion, that it was all Thirteen could do to not to snap his neck in impatience.

And then there was One, the de facto leader of the pack. And not simply because he was first, but because he was actually the most competent of the lot. He dealt with the bullies sternly, and the infantile ones with care, and with Thirteen himself, he was guarded, but respectful. He seemed the most adjusted and capable of all the Dodgers to date— which was odd, Thirteen thought. Just how was that possible? One had no ensensed powers, but was clearly the most faithful replication to the original Jim Dodger. How had they achieved such an amazing success so early on, and then followed by so many failures and fuckups? Thirteen supposed the simple explanation was that they hadn't started playing around with the genes as of yet, hadn't tried to mess with his mind to see what they could make of it. Perhaps to them, One was simply a proof of concept on standard cloning, which would also explain why they never bothered to test him. Oh, they strapped him in the tormentor, same as the rest, but Thirteen monitored those sessions, and he was never asked any questions. Perhaps they knew he had no abilities, because they hadn't tried to give him any. But there was another possibility, and Thirteen couldn't stop obsessing on it. What if One seemed so much like Dodger prime—because he was?

The more that Thirteen became consumed by this idea, the more he constructed theories to support it. First of all, One was here first. Unlike all the rest of them, no one was around to actually witness his creation. It was entirely possible Denali just woke Dodger up here, told him he was a clone, and even if Jim didn't believe at first, the twelve others that soon joined him would certainly have served to convince him.

Second, the lack of testing. Yes, it could be that they knew he had no powers because they never gave him any. But couldn't it also be—they just knew the *real* Dodger hadn't been born with ensensement?

And finally, his attitude, the way he presided over them as if they were his wards. Not over Thirteen of course, he had nipped that in the bud early on. In fact, not long after he had awoken, Thirteen had tried to usurp leadership of the Dodgers from One to himself, but his efforts had failed, and they all still looked to the first of them for direction. But Thirteen wasn't fooled by One's caring demeanor. He used his own powers of psychic empathy to search him out, and felt that same drive inside him that he had felt from near everyone else—to be the only one. Only the immature Eleven, it seemed, who didn't even comprehend the true nature of their relationship, was absent of that urge.

Eventually he decided that he would simply just ask him. Thirteen's hidden talents were developed to the point that he was sure he could determine if One was honest or deceitful. And so he did, but to his frustration, he could feel that even One himself wasn't really sure. But One *believed* it was possible, Thirteen felt that much inside him, and that was enough. Knowing that this shred of hope existed in One, that could never again exist in himself. He dreamt of the day he could eliminate One, and the rest of them. Then it wouldn't matter who was Dodger and who wasn't. There would be only one, as there was once before, and he would have regained his distinction—his stolen individuality.

But not yet. Not now. When the time comes to make his escape, he might need the help and support of the others. And control of them fell to the only true potential conspirator—that was One. There would have to be an alliance until then, gut-churning as it may be. While Thirteen had begun to experiment with his powers of suggestion by then, he could only handle influencing one subject at a time, and even that with limitations. Perhaps someday he'd find a way to maximize his abilities, even enhance them. But for now he needed One to manage the other Dodgers.

He focused his attention instead on one of the guards, a uniformed seti with foggy-gray fur and black spotting. One that was oddly ever present, always silently standing there, watching the group with his piercing orange eyes. He was there every day without fail—almost as much a prisoner as the rest of them, it seemed. Thirteen cautiously began initiating a relationship with the jailer. Slowly and casually, at first simply being obedient to the guard's orders, making the seti's job easier when the others would tend to rebel and protest. Then later, a word or two in passing, merely a 'good morning', or polite comment, just casual interactions to lead the seti from distrust, through indifference, to the mildest expression of civility.

All the while, he continued practicing his powers of suggestion. He convinced one of the white rats used in their animal telepathy tests that it was starving, and in danger, and to kill and eat its cage mate. The scientists had no idea what had caused the violent attack, but never seemed to consider that it came from one of the lab's other guinea pigs. It was time to try it on a more sophisticated mind, but Thirteen had to be careful. He didn't know if his influence would be detected, or how far he could push a thinking intellect against its will.

He decided it safest to experiment on the deaf and speechless Two, using a combination of both his telepathy and suggestion. For a few weeks, he sent carefully escalating thoughts and impressions, all designed to convince Two that his inner intuition was sending him a warning. *It's that stuttering Nine. See the way he looks at you? He's planning something, better beware. In fact, you may need to deal with him first.*

So gently, and so softly, Thirteen sent the idea out at first, that he wasn't even sure that the messages were being received. But eventually he could see it, the sidelong glances from Two towards Nine—suspicious, with a cocked eye, watching his every move. Then, in his mind, Thirteen started hearing responses back. Not in words, but in ideas. Two was in full agreement with his inner voice, and even escalating the paranoia on his own.

One afternoon, much sooner than he had planned, Thirteen sat in the common space as usual, glaring spitefully at One, who was forcing down a dish of thin, beige slop, the standard daily ration for every day except

Sundays, and holding court as the others shuffled around him in attendance. Thirteen wondered if One would be as susceptible to his mental influence as Two had been. Then, on a whim, without planning or forethought, he dared to try it, and sent out his thoughts. Just a minor, harmless suggestion—*take your plastic spoon and drop it on the floor.* Almost immediately, One turned and stared at him, and Thirteen quickly looked away. Fuck! Had he felt him, or was that merely a coincidence of timing? Thirteen was furious at the possibility that he had exposed himself. How could he have been so impulsive and foolish? After all his restraint and discretion, such a stupid mistake. He continued averting his gaze, but imagined he felt One's eyes still upon him. Watching. Analyzing.

Thirteen stifled his aggravation and anger, facing away with jaw clenched, and foot furiously tapping. In the midst of his irritation, he saw his least favorite stutterer crossing the room to pester him, undoubtedly with some inane rambling question. Nine stopped and stood, hovering over him, standing far too close, yammering in his loud halting garble.

"Are y-you... are y-you g-g..."

"Spit it out!" Thirteen yelled.

"I-I don't ha-have..."

"Holy shit! You didn't even finish the first sentence yet! Why are you starting another? Why are you bothering me at all?"

"D-don't, d-d-don't, d-don't..."

"For fuck's sake, shut up and get the hell away from me!" Thirteen barked. He pushed out with his mind as he yelled, and an invisible hand shoved Nine hard in the chest, plopping him down forcefully onto the couch directly across from him. There was a groan of stretching vinyl and a screech of the legs against the floor. *"Shit!"* Thirteen thought, seeing Nine's eyes looking back at him in surprise. Surprise, and realization. *"He knows—he knows what I just did. He knows what I can do."*

Then, in a panic, he sent out an urgent blast of suggestion towards Two. *"Kill this motherfucker, right now! Do it now!"*

Crashing all the way from his cell down the hall, Two came stumble-running in, pushing between Four and Five as he burst maniacally into the common room. He peered back and forth quickly, then stepped purposefully towards One. Grabbing the plastic spoon out of One's shallow paper dish, and splashing the remaining plate of slop onto the floor as he did so, he spun around, wielding the frail seeming utensil like a man possessed. He smoothly advanced in long strides up behind Nine, snapping off the bowl portion of the spoon as he approached, then reached around, and began relentlessly, and with furious speed, stabbing the surprised stutterer in the neck over and over with the thin, jagged handle. The other

Dodgers sat there dumbfounded at first, as Nine flailed and fought with his hands against the onslaught, scarlet blood sprinkling about the white room from the rhythmic swinging of Two's arm. A moment later, Four and Five began to cheer with hoots and hollers, jumping around the room and standing on the furniture. Three and Twelve began to cry out with shrieks and wails, as if it were *they* who were being so ruthlessly butchered. And Eleven, true to form, took up his position in the corner behind the couch; hands over his ears, shaking and twitching in a terrified fit, as the reek of urine ran down his leg.

All the while, until the guards finally charged in to stop it, Two plunged the shiv again and again into the nape of Nine's now lifeless throat. And all the while, One sat unfazed, staring at Thirteen. He picked up his paper bowl from off the floor, and calmly slurped at the remaining watery porridge, never breaking eye contact with his twin across the room. Thirteen stared back just as resolutely, as the splattered blood decorated his face with spots of damp warmth, only breaking his gaze when their keepers swarmed the room and broke up the onslaught, physically forcing them back to their bunks. Fortunately, Thirteen's new seti guard friend, whose name he now knew as Drake, escorted him to his room with much less shoving and clubbing than the others received.

This was not the subtle coercion that Thirteen had intended, but no matter now, what's done is done. At least he had proven to himself that, with patience and persistence, he could potentially persuade someone to cross lines that they normally wouldn't. So he began that very day, that very minute, as his guard Drake locked the cell door behind him. He sent out just the barest seed of a thought; a passing notion drifting on the wind. In the seti's head, the idea flashed and then faded, like the brief spark of a lightning bug—there, and then gone.

"I like Thirteen," the guard realized as he walked off down the hall. *"I think we could be friends."*

11.2

BULLIT REMATERIALIZED IN THE DISMAL machine room that had become home away from home, and gathered up the teleportation triangles that he had borrowed from Bullseye. The other seti looked up at him inquisitively as the alien device was returned to him. "What news might you bear, if any?" he asked.

"Oh, I bear news," Bullit answered. "I was able to access the navigation logs, and use the multicomm to translate them. The *Okubi* is currently en route to Capella, of all places. We should make orbit in less than ten hours. A number of troops that have finished their rotation are slated to transfer off, swapping out with relief soldiers from a joint operations outpost that the chamai maintain with the lyghtan." He refered to his multicomm then, reading from the display. "The base is in a region that translates as... 'The Burnt Empty'."

"Ah. The expanses of Nol Qhan. The barren wastes of black sand that mar the northern circle of the lyghtan homeworld. Not an optimal locale to disembark, I would submit. Though it seems our options are few, and dwindling more so by the hour. There exists no local borough there in which to seek shelter once we divine egress, and the region is alleged to be inhabited by only the *outcasts* of lyghtan society. Nonetheless, a secured shelter would be paramount once we were away, as the day's suns bring a fury like the Forge of Dishonored Fallen, and the nighttime a frost keen as the Keeper of the Moon's Glow."

"Okay, well... I don't know what *either* of those references mean. But let's assume you're saying it gets *real* hot and *real* cold."

"At the very least," Bullseye said, shaking his head in dismay. "Someday in your leisure, you must endeavor to embrace your seti heritage. The traditions and mythic lore of our ancestors impart innumerable lessons."

"Not if it means I start making every sentence into a sonnet." Bullit sat down in his now familiar spot, directly across from his comrade, and opened the last remaining bar of the kimiri red chocolate. "So, what do we do? Try to jump ship, or stay put?"

"I... would... advise we disembark, and risk our prospects on the surface," Bullseye suggested, seeming somewhat taken aback by the question. "Allowing you still hazard faith in the caliber of my judgment."

"What do you mean?"

"Well... have I not egregiously violated your trust?"

"Yeah, you have. Definitely. You *definitely* have."

"And yet you seek my counsel?"

"Yes, I do. I believe you'll earn it back."

"Your trust?"

"Yeah, that's right," Bullit said. "Not all at once. Not quickly. But I'll take you at your word that last night won't be repeated."

"I understand," Bullseye answered. "Trust is a commodity that is accrued and squandered in unequal measure. It may be forfeited by the barrelful, yet only replenished by the thimble."

"So earn back your first thimbleful today, and get our asses back home."

"You still wish me to lead."

"Well, fortunately for you, after all these years, you've already earned a *spare* barrelful as far as I'm concerned. Remember Bullseye, none of us follow you because we have to. We follow you because we *choose* to. And that is still what I choose... for the moment at least," Bullit teased. He then pointed at Bullseye sharply with the bitten end of his chocolate bar. "And... I won't tell any of the others what has happened here either, but when this whole mess is settled, and the time is right, I think that you should. That would cover several thimblesful in my book." He shoved the last bite into his mouth, and clapped the crumbs from his hands.

"Very well," Bullseye said, his confident demeanor immediately returning, "a visit to the black desert of Nol Qhan it shall be then, and with mere hours to prepare, we must need make haste once evening falls."

"Will you be ready by then? Physically, I mean?" Bullit asked. "What I'm saying is, you haven't even gone through any withdrawal yet from... you know."

"Ah. Your concern is misguided. You have nothing to fear for my constitution. The siren song of Zet A'zeta is not physical, but psychological. Although who is to say which is the worse entrapment of the two."

"So, psychologically, then... you're okay?"

"There is certainly much work for me left to be done, so much that my lifetime will never witness it completed. Yet I can say your words and council this past day and evening have given me sound direction. I will undertake to look forward and not back, and concoct a loftier idol, to displace that one late discarded."

Bullit looked at him thoughtfully for a moment, and then nodded. "Okay then."

"Okay then," Bullseye confirmed back, uncharacteristically succinct.

After a moment of mutual silence to digest their agreement, Bullit turned back to the issue at hand. "Alright, Mon Capitan, how do we get down to that Capellan base?"

"Our best hope is to procure a pair of full armor uniforms, and employ that masquerade to transport down with the soldiery. But the quartermaster's hold is distant, across the beam of the ship. A long journey indeed porting an armload of plated cargo."

"Don't worry about that. The uniforms will come to us."

"I don't follow."

"Well, we'll just do like in the movies, when the heroes need an enemy disguise."

Bullseye stared back at him without comprehension.

"You're not familiar with the trope in old human films, where the heroes follow their enemies into a room, or down an alley, then there's a commotion around the corner, and the heroes come walking back out wearing the uniforms?"

"I fail to understand. What is the source of this hidden commotion?"

"I don't know!" Bullit blurted in exasperation. "They hit them on the head or something, knock them out."

"Striking one upon the head seldom causes loss of consciousness. It merely serves to incite anger and pain. Excepting a blow of sufficient might to shatter bone, induce coma, or..."

"Yes, of course I know that. It's just a... have you never seen this in a human movie before?"

"As I would expect you to be well aware of, I have never indulged in *any* form of human entertainment, save the written word, as a means in my youth to learn the Earthan culture and history. Mainly the delectus of Shakespeare, Dickens..."

"Okay, okay, never mind. Boy, that explains a lot. Just... I will get us two armor uniforms."

"You don't intend to slay any chamai I trust, implementing this... fatal concussion maneuver?"

"No, it was just... look, I won't. Don't worry about it. I know how to put someone out. I'll use the triangles to tie them up somewhere behind a wall, or somewhere out of sight."

Bullseye appeared dubious.

"And we'll leave a note so that someone finds them," Bullit added. "Is that better?"

"Hmm. Perhaps forgo any such notifications. Best if your deeds were not detected too expeditiously." He looked at the crumpled stack of empty water bottles in the corner. "And whilst you secure our attire, I shall gather additional water in the late hours. Best to anticipate an extended wait in the desert."

Bullit raised an eyebrow.

"You may have faith in me on this occasion. The water is all I seek," Bullseye said.

"Okay, fine then. You think it will take long for Lobo to swing by and grab us?"

"I think it best to make ready, just in case that is so. This current predicament... I intend to make it the last one I marshal so ill-prepared."

"Good to hear."

"We shall transmit a second coded beacon when securely upon the surface, then secrete ourselves in whatever refuge we may find or fashion."

The movements of a crewperson above them directed both their gazes upward towards the deck plates, and both pivoted their heads in unison as they tracked the footsteps from port to starboard. Bullit slid on his backside a few times, moving closer to Bullseye, and lowered his voice to a more careful hush. "So, as to this other issue... what you think you overheard last night. You still feel positive it was not all some... hallucination?"

"I do."

"And you still can't recall what exactly was being discussed? Anything about what the general and this Drak'min officer were planning?"

"Nay. The particulars lay as veiled as the Isle of Avalon, shrouded in the unstirring fog of my stupor. I assume I failed to relay a narrative of any coherence upon return to our shelter? Perhaps prodding from my prior recount might serve to dispel the haze."

"I don't know," Bullit said. "You were babbling, and drifting off. And to be honest, I was too angry to pay much attention."

Bullseye shook his head. "I regret I simply cannot pull forth my recollections. There was a compact made betwixt the two of them to reconvene, but I cannot evoke the detail of the place nor time, nor to what purpose."

"And what about Rook?"

"I recall a remark or two, spoken as if Rook and Denali were fast friends, suggesting the pair were in league toward whatever end these events unravel. Nylis made assurances to Yazir that our Rook and Denali were somehow bonded. That they shared a connection due to some tribulation in their yesteryear."

"I can think of one thing that they share. We once watched both of them die."

Bullseye sat and said nothing.

"That hadn't occurred to you?"

"Perhaps I chose to ignore it."

"Well, I'm certainly not going to. I don't like the sound of any of it. I mean, talk about emptying out trust by the barrelful. There are confusing puzzle pieces we're finding that are disturbing on multiple levels. And like it or not, Rook seems squarely in the center of all of it." Bullit lowered his volume again at another clap of footsteps overhead. "Look, all I'm saying is that when we find Rook, which I hope we do... we better be very careful. It seems there have been many things going on that are not what they appear to be."

"Agreed," Bullseye conceded with reluctance, hating to admit that Bullit might be right. "I regret my recollection cannot provide greater clarity. I was keen to record the encounter, but I was… too infirm to operate the device."

"I know, it's all right. Hopefully, something will jog your memory later."

"Sadly, and to much embarrassment, I've attained experience enough now to confirm that is the usual case. Patience is all we can offer, until passing time or random trigger clear way through my fog." Bullseye moved to lay himself down then, curling uncomfortably onto his side on the metal flooring. "We best take the opportunity for a few moments slumber, if possible, for tonight we each have our missions, I for provisions, and you for wardrobe."

"Will do," Bullit replied, as he struck a similar reclined position. "And I'll try and remember not to hit them too hard."

Bullseye lifted his head stared disapprovingly.

"Don't worry, I'll be good," Bullit reassured his fellow seti. "I'm *saving up* all my aggression. There's someone out there that deserves it, and I just can't wait to find out who that unlucky bastard is."

11.3

Fifteen years ago, as Thirteen's vocal cords began to hemorrhage from his screaming, quivering in a mist of blood from the harrowing intensity of his persistent cries, Denali himself appeared at the facility. Thirteen had never seen him before, and the memories from Dodger that he carried had never once laid eyes on him either. But as he clung desperately to his ability to project his thoughts elsewhere, trying to mentally escape the tormentor device his body was strapped to, he knew the man who was both the cause and the curse of his existence had entered outside.

He felt him.

Then he saw him.

In his mind's eye, he knew it was the man himself. Denali, just a few rooms away, and Thirteen trapped here, unable to reach out and strike at him. If he had only been out front in the common room, he would have used every scrap of power he had been developing to bend him to his knees, to bring this whole place down on top of him if he could. No matter that Thirteen would never escape alive—after all, he was never meant to be alive in the first place. All that matters is that Denali *pays* for what he's done here, what he's created, and what he's put them through. And that every remaining scrap of this nightmare is razed along with him.

He struggled through the torture to maintain a clear vision, and watched as Denali angrily scolded a pair of attendants. He struck one of them, hard. Then struck him again, kicking the aide repeatedly as he fell to the ground. He turned then and stormed determinedly into the common room. Thirteen could see it was near empty, except for Two seated at the table, and Eleven in his usual corner behind the far couch. Denali glanced back and forth at them, reading the numbers on their jumpsuits, then pointed damningly at Two. Drake rushed in with a second guard at his side, together grabbing the duplicant, and standing him from the chair before kicking him to his knees. While the pair held his upper arms firmly, Denali strode over to the clone, now kneeled before him in forced penitence, and without word or warning, reached out and seized Two around the neck in his fat fist.

The deaf mute silently struggled and twisted, managing to scarcely scratch at his attacker's forearms with the tips of his fingers. But all his digging and clawing did nothing to loosen the grip. Denali's muscles strained to the point of quaking, as his anger gushed forth through his tightening clutches. The clone's face bloomed an inconceivably bright flush, and he thrust his legs wildly around in desperation for air, kicking and convulsing, knocking over the chair behind him while the guards fought to keep him in place. The commotion drew the others to emerge from their cells, but they all stood back in the corridor, afraid to interfere. They could have banded together, Thirteen thought, attack and overwhelm! But they all cowered back in impotence, watching Two roll his eyes upward, as the last breath was wrung from him beneath Denali's trembling, murderous grasp. Finally, Thirteen lost the vision as the neural torture was cranked higher, and his reinvigorated screaming was less full of agony, than anger and frustration.

Later that evening, Thirteen learned from Drake that the outburst was in response to Nine's stabbing a few weeks ago. Apparently, the stutterer had more value to the program than he'd thought. More value than Two did anyway, and Denali was obviously distressed at the loss of his precious pet.

Thirteen took the opportunity to ask how often their creator visited, and much to his surprise, Drake told him that he comes every two or three weeks to review the progress of the program. Every two or three weeks! All these months, he had no idea that he was so within reach! All the wasted chances! But he certainly wouldn't let another one pass him by.

He thanked the seti guard with a flood of extrasensory positive affirmations, reinforcing Drake's bond of loyalty and friendship with him. He would have to step it up further to be ready so quickly, but Thirteen felt he had now mastered the delicate process of manipulation to an art. Each suggestion he projected only lasted a short while—a few hours, maybe a day. It depended on the distastefulness of the particular notion he was implanting. But it seemed that with patient repetition, the same idea pushed over and over again in a persistent echoing chorus, the subjects' neural pathways adapted to finally accept the invading idea as their own. They rewired themselves, so to speak, to accommodate the new conviction. When that happened, they were fully converted, and he no longer had to maintain constant control of their thoughts.

And so that is what he did, every day and every night, reaching out to Drake even as the seti slept securely in the neighboring barracks. The guard dozed through the night, unaware of the foreign imagery supplanting his own, and dreamt of himself and Thirteen enjoying themselves together some place far from the prison. Later, he injected the fantasy of actually helping him escape in order to achieve this. And finally, of killing Denali, and the other Dodgers as well, so that he and his friend were sure to be left in peace. Following up in the daytime, Thirteen would bolster those thoughts more subtly, making the guard consider them over and over again, each time mulling them over more and more favorably. This went on for days, and then weeks, with ever-increasing forcefulness, until he finally heard that involuntary whisper back he was waiting for—*"Yes, I'll do it."*

Thirteen subconsciously encouraged Drake to approach him first, the jailer cajoling his own prisoner into the idea of escape—as if the thought truly was all the guard's idea in the first place. The clone acted surprised, but immensely appreciative, and sent more sentiments of positivity to the seti as they secretly made their plans. Denali was expected back in just two days from now, and Drake would arrange to get Thirteen out of the facility and into guard armor, while causing a distraction to cover the escape. A quick stop to kill Denali, and then take the crime lord's ship from the bay, use it to implode this torture chamber on top of its occupants. Then the two of them would head off to conquer whatever lies ahead. Thirteen feared it all seemed just a little too simple, that it couldn't possibly go off as easily as planned.

His fears were justified.

On the morning of Denali's scheduled arrival, Thirteen was sitting in the common room, concentrating on sending out his strongest possible suggestions to Drake, just to keep him calm and on task. He didn't notice all the others gathering one at a time at the window behind him. A string of ten matching faces hanging there in the opening, noses pressed to the glass, straining to watch a growing commotion in the waters outside. Suddenly, both the quiet, and Thirteen's concentration, were shattered by a bellowing klaxon alarm, and the stark white room turned an angry pulse of red under the flashing glow of the crimson warning lights. He stood and saw the gathered group at the window, and rushed over to join them. It was hard to see clearly through the dim ocean outside, but a distant flash and rumble here and there were familiar signs of an ongoing battle. A group of armored Theseans swam by with shocking speed and grace towards the turmoil, cutting through the water smooth as a school of frenzied sharks. As the melee moved closer, the sounds of weaponry and watery shockwaves rattled and shook the walls of the facility. After only a few minutes, the skirmish had moved to just outside the window, close enough to see the insignia emblazoned on the attacking armor. There was a collective inhalation of surprise when it came into view—a gavel logo, a hallmark of singular meaning.

Parliament was here.

This was not something that Thirteen had bargained on, that Dodger's teammates would come hunting him down. Of course they would, he should have known. But, did they know about the rest of them? Did they expect to find only Jim? If so, they were in for a shocker. Would they even take all the clones with them once they found they were all that was here? Or would they terminate the lot of them, as the Denali inspired abominations that they were? He couldn't take the chance. They would have to use *this* as their distraction. He sent out his thoughts in search of Drake, while he watched the continued fracas developing outside.

Parliament did not seem well prepared for the Thesean weapons, which were truly unlike any others that the team had encountered. The aquatic species use a sort of underwater cannon, which draws in surrounding liquid from one end, and fires it in concussive blasts out the front. The mercenaries were holding their own, but only just barely, and they seemed to struggle with the weapons, their armor, the jetpacks, and the ocean itself. Then it happened—a Thesean fired a shot that shook the windowpane to near cracking, and they all watched as one of Parliament's own was torn in three by the eruption of pressurized seawater. The view outside the window quickly clouded up with a maroon chum. Ragged flesh and torn scraps of pale sinew drifted weightless through the murky brine, and the heavier shrapnel of armor fragments spun and spiraled through the haze. As the spectacle became fully obscured by the floating gore and scavenging fish, the crest adorned across a shattered shard of breastplate flashed like a lure as it sank and twisted towards the bottom. Falling slow as an autumn leaf, it landed on the rippled sand with the unmistakable emblem of its owner staring upward.

An embossed chess rook.

Thirteen felt his heart tug, as they all did, he was sure. The false memories they carried were too expertly ingrained, and it seemed to each of them they had just witnessed the death of a close friend. One they felt they were with only a few months ago. But none of it was true. Thirteen steeled himself, and cold-heartedly shook it off. He needed to get out of here—time for a quick change of plan. He would now have to take all the others out of here with him, use them as cannon fodder. The more targets to shoot at, the less likely he himself would be hit. Plus he could use them as a cover story if they encountered anyone in the hallways. When Drake showed up with the armor, the two would act as guards, escorting the clones to a more secure location.

He looked down the row of uniform faces, identical in appearance, as well as their grief for Dodger's friend—though how they displayed it varied widely from one to the next. Twelve was rocking back and forth, mumbling woefully under his breath. Five started acting up, tossing a dining chair at the weeping clone. Thirteen would have to get them moving quickly before things got out of hand. He tried to command their attention, corral them together one by one, but he was ignored in favor of the distraction from the growing chaos. Reluctantly, he grabbed One by the shoulder and pulled him aside. "We have to leave!" he said loudly, over the still wailing alarm. "All of us. We can get out of here now. I have a way, but you'll need to convince the others."

One raised an eyebrow. "What way? How?"

"I have someone on the inside, helping us out. Do you want me to stand here and explain, or do you want to leave this hellhole?"

One glared at him for a long moment. "When?" he asked finally.

Thirteen looked up to see Drake enter the common room, giving him a wave to follow him towards his cell. "Minutes," he responded. "Wait here," and he headed off.

Behind him, he heard One call out to the others to gather round and listen up.

Thirteen followed Drake down the hall to his cell, where the seti quickly descrambled a set of battlegear onto the bunk. "Get dressed quickly," the guard said. "We don't have much time. Denali isn't here yet, so we'll have to skip him for now. But there's a troop transport in the bay we can use to get away from the base."

Thirteen stopped suiting up, and stood to stare at the seti. "Skip him?" he said, with restrained outrage. Then louder, "Skip him?! Skip Denali?! Let him go?! He's the only thing that matters, the only thing I want!"

Drake's face was showing discomfort, as if he were struggling for air. Thirteen realized he was again using his mind, unwittingly pushing on the guard's chest in his anger, constricting him against the wall. He released him just as quickly, and immediately projected calming thoughts of friendship again.

"Is there a teleporter on the transport?" Thirteen asked.

"I, um. Yes, there is, I think."

"You think? Or you know?"

"Yes, there is. I know there is."

"Very good. Get me to the ship. All of us, that is," Thirteen told him. "I'll take care of the rest of them somehow on board. You stay here. Radio me when Denali shows, I'll teleport back and take care of him as well."

"But, if…"

"Drake, you've been a good friend. Honestly, the first and only one in my short life. I won't forget what you've done for me today. And I will come back, Denali or not. You and I have a big future together." Thirteen finished suiting up and slid his helmet on. "You and I are gonna conquer the world!"

Drake smiled wide and nodded as slipped on his own headgear, a black full-masked helmet with glowing orange optics, and atmospheric processors that gave the vague impression of insect mandibles. He handed Thirteen an AE laser pistol and a vibroknife, and they headed out.

The pair headed back through the common room, and Thirteen signaled to One in handspeak that it was time to go, taking advantage of the ever-increasing chaos in the asylum. The alarm was still trumpeting, red warning lights flashing, and all the medical personnel appeared to be rushing to safety. Drake's fellow security guards were obviously otherwise occupied, so it was an easy enough task to simply open the door and walk out. The group moved down the hallway in a cautious half-jog, following Drake through the complex's innards that none of the Dodgers had ever seen before. In the middle of the pack was One, trying to marshal the others along, while Thirteen brought up the rear to watch their back and check for stragglers. They went up a stairway and across a wide lobby, and entered a section that was much less clinical and hospital-like, and more plush and luxurious. As they hastened down a corridor past an open doorway, something curious caught Thirteen's eye, and he stopped, turning back, and letting the others go on ahead of him.

The grandiose study he walked back to was furnished like some kind of trophy room, a myriad of rare items and artifacts festooning its walls. Looming over the left side was a massive, stuffed ferox, fangs bared and rearing up on its imposing hind legs. On the right, a giant ice strider from Ilshnar's Valley of Glass, its multiple spindly legs and long grasping pincers frozen in the perpetual pose of a charging attack. On two wooden plaques along the back wall hung a pair of mounted heads. Not animals this time, but a metamorph and a seti; glass eyes shining bright as they gazed out upon the room. But what had attracted Thirteen's attention was not the severed heads, but what was beneath them. Taking up the entire middle of the museum was a row of cylindrical glass tubes that ran nearly from floor to ceiling. All were empty, except the one closest to him, containing an exhibit of a human man inside, with a face that he recognized.

His own.

Posed and stuffed just like the rest, in a knees-bent, combat stance with flame gun aloft, the perfectly taxidermied corpse of one late, great Jim Dodger. But which Jim Dodger? *The* Dodger? How could he know? He studied the morbid model as he walked around its showcase. Human skin doesn't maintain its integrity after death as well as more forgiving fur does, or the hard exoskeleton of the strider looking on. Dodger's flesh had a hue of mottled jaundice and gray bruising, the discoloration vaguely visible beneath what appeared to be layers of thick body paint. The synthetic mold beneath the dermis, which gave his face its shape, was perhaps just a touch high in the cheekbones, making the intense steely glint of the model look just a little bit—off. But it definitely was a Dodger, of that Thirteen was sure. He leaned in closer and examined the neck, turning on the headlamp of his helmet for more light. Yes, there it was—a reddish-purple blemish beneath the paint, a ring of contusion around the Dodger's neck. The telltale bruising of a man who was strangled.

This must be Two—or, at least he was pretty sure of that. Unless maybe Dodger prime had been strangled in the same way. Which was possible, of course; maybe that was Denali's preferred method of slaughtering people. But if this *was* Two, then where was Dodger prime. Why show off the clone and not the real McCoy? Because the real one is still walking around, perhaps? Could this be more evidence, proof that One might be—*the* one? Circumstantial at best. It neither proved nor disproved. Thirteen went and studied the mounted heads on the back wall—nobody he recognized—for signs that they too might have been strangled. If they were all choked to death, then perhaps that was just Denali's particular kink. That would lend credence that this mockup might in fact be Dodger prime after all. But the fur of the seti, and the green-gray skin ridges of the metamorph, hid any marks that might have also been present. Plus the decapitation was done very high up on the throat, and there wasn't a whole lot of remaining neck to examine.

A harsh whisper came from the doorway. "What the fuck are you doing?"

Thirteen turned, and there was One and the rest of their equivalents, with Drake watching over them, looking apprehensively up and down the hallway.

Then they saw it as well.

The group advanced with somber steps, and surrounded the display.

"Is it... is it him?" asked Seven.

"Could be. Could be Two, though," answered One, obviously having picked up on the same clues that Thirteen had. Then seeming to think better of it, "but that wouldn't make much sense, it most probably is him. It's Jim Dodger."

"I think it's *Two*," Thirteen declared defiantly.

"It *could* be. No way to tell," One said again, glaring at him.

"I wanna go ba' my silence space now," Eleven complained, refusing to say the 'ck' sound, and snapping them all out of their morbid curiosity.

"There's a better, quieter place where we're going," One lied to him. "Come on everybody, let's not stand around admiring ourself all day."

They rushed back out into the corridor and continued on behind Drake, soon entering a large vaulted chamber, more like an indoor wharf than a hangar bay. An expansive pool of seawater beneath a large domed roof, and floating aeroships moored to a dozen or so short piers. The entourage hurried behind the seti to a medium-sized troop carrier in the center, which was wider around the middle, but about the same length as the *Bugeye*. The sound of gunfire was echoing through the corridors nearby.

"Can you pilot this?" Drake asked Thirteen as the group scrambled on board.

"Jim Dodger could, so we all can too."

Drake looked doubtfully at Eleven and Twelve passing by. "I'm not so sure that *all* of you can."

"*I'll* do it," One declared, as he hurried last across the gangway. "I remember just fine."

"I'll bet you do," Thirteen mumbled under his breath. Then to Drake in a whisper, "Contact me through my comms as soon as you know where Denali is. I'll zap right back, and you can meet me at the teleporter."

Drake nodded agreement, while for the first time starting to feel like he was *taking* Thirteen's orders, rather than the other way around. But for some reason he couldn't explain, he liked it. It felt right. He rushed off to make his new commander proud.

All were now aboard. The majority of the Dodgers strapped themselves into seating that lined the walls of the midship compartment, as One engaged the engines and pulled back from the dock. He submerged the craft below the waves, then guided her along an illuminated watery tunnel beneath the wall of the dome. A few moments later they were heading out into open sea. Thirteen made sure all the rest were settled and secure, then joined One in the cockpit, closing the access door behind them. The two identical humans sat side by side, maneuvering the ship away from Denali's facility and the fighting, casually aiming her upward towards the freedom of the surface. The ship burst from the ocean like a breaching whale, then sped on skyward, until after a few minutes they finally leveled off beneath the cloud cover. Far below them, the ocean world of Theseus was blanketed in boundless water, spread out on all sides in an endless sphere of royal blue. No spot of dry land had been seen here in eons, but there were floating transport hubs that served as centers of travel and trade with off-worlders. One scanned the area for the closest platform city, then aimed the vessel in that direction, knowing a ride off world could probably be found there.

Thirteen broke the silence. "So... if that *was* Two back there, stuffed and mounted like a pheasant in that... museum of unnatural history... you realize what that means, don't you?"

"No. Why don't you tell me."

"Funny, I knew you were gonna say that."

"And I knew you were gonna say *that*," One countered. "So, since we both know this entire conversation ahead of time, why don't we just save ourselves the trouble and skip to the end?"

"Fine. Why didn't they ever give you the testing the rest of us got?"

"Who told you that, your new guard boyfriend? Or have you been hiding some Carnac the Magnificent shit from everybody, spying on me with your third eye, like Madame Zorba? I saw what you did to Nine that day, shoving him back without so much as wiggling a finger. And what about Two? That was you as well, wasn't it? Why did he go all Jack the Ripper on Nine for no reason? That was awfully convenient timing for you."

"Nine's stuttering and stammering were an assault on the ears. What other reason would anybody need?" Thirteen asked coldly.

"Two was deaf. He didn't have ears."

"Well... a curious and unsolvable mystery, then, I suppose."

"Yeah. I suppose," One echoed sarcastically.

"And so, your testing, or should I say *lack* thereof? You never answered *that* question."

One gazed at him sidelong for a moment, then turned back to the controls. "I'm afraid I can't speak to the methods and motivations of Denali's gang of nutty professors. I mean, I don't exactly think they were following the scientific method. Or who knows, maybe they were. Maybe I was just the control group in their psychotic little experiments." He paused for a moment and looked at Thirteen again. "Believe me though, questions or no questions, I got the same fun ride strapped in that fuckin' chair as the rest of you."

"Yes, that I know," Thirteen answered softly.

A comfortable shared silence passed between the two, as they both inwardly acknowledged, and then repressed, the memory of the torment device for the last time—and then never, ever, to think of it again.

"You know one thing I really won't miss about that place?" One offered. "That horse-jizz-piss-porridge they were feeding us. But you know what I *am* looking forward to?"

"Nattie's Take Out fish and chips," Thirteen replied.

"Oh my God, yes, with those super crispy french fries that taste exactly like the fried clams, because they only have the one fryolator."

"And they never change the oil. Ever."

"Hah, yeah. You know, it's funny, Phineas used to..." He glanced at Thirteen, his eyes showing the realization that, of course, he *did* already know. "Well, anyway. That'll be my first stop when I get back to Earth."

"We'll go together," Thirteen said. "We'll split that Gloucester Platter that we... or, *he*... the original Dodger... was never able to finish on his own."

"Deal."

Thirteen peered across the console to try and read the display in front of One. "How much longer?"

"Ten minutes, maybe less."

"Alright. I'm gonna look around for some..."

"Clothes?" One interjected, finishing Thirteen's sentence. "I was just gonna suggest the same thing. We'll attract a lot of unwanted attention if we go sauntering around looking like the Dodger decuplets out to play in our matching onesies."

"Ah, alike minds think great," Thirteen joked cheerlessly.

"I knew you were gonna say that, too."

Thirteen left the cockpit and walked aft past the other Dodgers, most of whom sat silently peering out of portholes, enjoying an aerial view of backlit clouds and sparkling sea. A sight that seemed so familiar to each of them as to be commonplace, yet which, in actuality, none of them had ever laid eyes on before. He took a quick headcount as he moved past. Two, four, six, eight, plus one makes nine. All present and accounted for. He went through an open bulkhead into the aft compartment area, leading to a short hallway accessing the storage, lavatory, and two-person teleporter. He put his hand on the storage room door, as if to enter in search of some sort of alternative clothing for the bunch. Peeking up to assure no one was looking, he instead turned and entered the small teleporter room.

Closing the door quietly behind him, he pulled out his radio and called for Drake to respond.

"*Yes, Drake here,*" the guard answered over the communicator.

"Status," Thirteen requested. "I haven't heard from you. What's going on? Is Denali there yet?"

"*Negative. I'm sorry, but it seems he got word of what happened here. He's not coming.*"

Thirteen swore, hauling off and punching the steel wall of the cramped teleporter room in anger. His fist hit with a resounding boom, and a force that should have shattered every bone—but there was no pain, and not so much as a knuckle hair out of place. A deep indent into the bulkhead made it seen like it had been attacked with a trimithium battering ram, one with the shape of a fist at the end. *Well,* he thought as he looked curiously at his hand, *that was new.* It wasn't an increase in strength that had done it. No, something else—he could feel it. He had momentarily increased the actual density of his fist. One moment soft, supple flesh, and the next as weighty, solid and hardened as an iron sledgehammer. Now, this was a skill he was going to have to explore and cultivate immediately. He reached out and touched the wall with the tips of his fingers, wondering if the reverse was also possible. If he could *increase* his own molecular density, could he *lessen* it as well? Could he spread his atoms out to the point that they could slide right by each other, and phase his hand right through this bulkhead, like steam rising through fog?

"*Thirteen, are you still there? What do you want me to do? Parliament is making a real mess of this place. They found that trophy room, and from the sound of things, they're not happy about it.*"

Parliament was still there? Well, of course they were—wouldn't he have been? They would never let this go now, not until it's done. *Ah,* and that would be his solution! Denali was sure to jack up his security, or even go into hiding, and Thirteen didn't have the resources, funds, or connections to ever track him down. Parliament did though, and they now would surely never stop trying. He would simply need to follow Jim

Dodger's old crew, let them do the legwork, then swoop in ahead of them and steal their thunder.

"Understood, Drake," Thirteen finally responded, leaning over the teleporter console and activating the device. "Get a signal lock on this unit, and I'll call you to zap me over in just a few minutes. Can you track the ship's transponder from your end as well?"

"Yes, I can see the ship on the sensors here now, and I'm establishing a lock on the teleporter, whenever you're ready."

"Standby."

Thirteen left the room and opened the storage area across the hall. Looking around, he cracked open a first aid kit on the wall, and grabbed a thick wad of rolled gauze, shoving it in the hip pouch of his borrowed armor before heading back toward the cockpit. The Dodger clones had apparently become bored with the view now, and no longer sat staring out the windows. Three and Eight were having some sort of argument, and Eleven sat at the far end with his eyes squinted tight, his hands clasped over his ears like a vise. Nine little Indians, all still there—no one had wandered off yet. Good.

He half-casually, and half-cautiously, opened the cockpit door, sliding his vibroknife from his waist as he entered the forward cabin. One was still seated in the pilot's chair, and Thirteen moved up behind him in a way that he hoped wouldn't be noticed—but if it was, would seem like he was just heading quietly to his seat. When he was directly behind his double, he reached out and pulled backward on One's forehead with his left hand, and with his right, smoothly slid the pulsating blade across the center of the exposed throat, immediately opening the windpipe, but not the jugulars, with a sputtering cough of spattered blood. He then spun the seat around to face him, and while One's hands were occupied holding his neck wound in horror, he cruelly pushed the blade with sadistic slowness through the abdomen until it was hilt deep, knowing it to be a good place to cause both significant pain, and slow death.

As One heaved and gurgled through the yawning wound in his larynx, Thirteen dragged him from the chair and pushed him roughly to the floor in the corner. "What's the matter, you didn't know I was gonna do *that*? If not then you're a bigger goddamn fool than I thought. Alike minds? Pfft. My mind and yours are no more alike than a man and his dog." Then using his telepathy, he spoke directly inside his bleeding twin's brain. *"I am the next evolution of you, the next evolution of all men. Don't you see? You are the past... flawed, weak, and imperfect. I am the future! You and I share nothing more than a few distant memories."* Then aloud, "And even those aren't real." He pulled out the mass of gauze, tore it open, and tossed it onto the bleeding clone struggling to breathe on the floor. "Hold pressure on that throat now. I don't want you to bleed out too quickly, and miss the big finale."

Thirteen took a seat at the controls and checked the craft's heading—gradually descending on approach to Avalon Raft. The term 'raft' was a bit misleading, although technically correct. A Coalition controlled enclave—a floating city of towering spires and interconnected buoyant commercial precincts, all encircled by a massive seawall. The city was built on the very edge of the continental shelf, thereby linking itself to the massive Thesean city of Timeon, some four thousand fathoms below the surface in the sunless deep. He could scuttle the ship right there, and if it wasn't completely destroyed on impact, it would be crushed by pressure as it sank to the seafloor.

"I know you understand this," Thirteen continued after a moment, "surely more than any of the rest of them out there." He altered their heading to impact the waves a few hundred meters outside the seawall, directly above the undersea abyss, "I mean, how can I be me, if *you're* me? If any of those morons out there are me. There can be only one. You know it, and I know it, and it sure as shit ain't gonna be you. Not anymore." He accelerated the ship slightly as its nose dipped subtly downward, then he turned off the craft's shield generator and inertial dampeners. "You see, I believe you *are* him, Jim. Which means you've already had your chance. You had your chance, and you fucked it up. Hell, you're the one that got us all here, Jim. You're just as much to blame as Denali. Perhaps more. If you and those idiot friends of yours had settled this years ago, as you should have, none of this would have happened. *You* let Denali escape time after time, *you* let him become more and more powerful, and *you* let down your guard and got yourself caught. You fucked it up for all of us, for all of *you*. But I'm gonna fix it."

Thirteen stood, then used the tip of his vibroknife to pry open the top of the navigation panel. Once he had it lifted, he dragged the weapon back and forth roughly across the circuitry beneath, to an encore of sparks and smoke puffs from the dissected wiring. Slamming the panel back down, he turned and stood over his dying reflection huddled on the floor, eyes staring up, and mouth gaping open and closed like a landed fish. The blood continued to seep from One's severed throat and ruptured belly. "I *am* gonna fix it," Thirteen said to him as he sheathed the blade. "I can promise you that. In fact, I give you my word. You are going to finally get your revenge, and then go on to great things. Far greater than your limited capacity could ever have taken you, greater than your limited intellect could ever even imagine! You will do all of this, through me. My vengeance is your vengeance! My success is your success! I am your last breath and your final word! I am the culmination of everything you have been and could hope to be. I am your legacy! I am your champion."

Thirteen took one last, long look at his believed progenitor, and with a smile of satisfaction, turned and left the cockpit. Shutting the door quietly behind him, he headed for the teleporter, taking his last disgusted glance at the remaining fellow Dodgers as he passed. Seven seemed to be the only one looking outside, glancing back and forth with some small concern over the speed of their descent. The rest seemed distracted by Four and Five's antics, as they were at it again with the teasing of Eleven. He turned away and headed onward, locking the door behind him after he entered the teleporter compartment.

"Drake, are you ready?" Thirteen called over the communicator.

"*Yes sir, standing by. Ready when you are.*"

Thirteen stood upon one of the two dissolution pads. "Okay, get me outta here."

The device hummed as it initialized, and then after a moment, a sharp 'zap-pop', accompanied by the always shocking change of scenery. In a flash the small compartment of the troop vessel was gone, and Thirteen stepped off the pad in the much larger teleporter room of Denali's underwater lair. The warning lights still flashed and the distant echoing klaxon still sounded.

"Ah, home again, Drake," he said.

"Sir?"

"Never mind. Where are you tracking that ship from? Show me now."

"Yes, right this way, over here," Drake said, leading his new master to a terminal across the room. On a screen with a crisscross grid was an animated blinking dot, the marker descending downward toward a horizontal line across the bottom. It hit the line, and stopped.

"What happened? Is the ship destroyed?" the human asked.

"I'm not sure," the seti replied. "I can't get that level of detail from this information. All I can say is that the transponder box is still powered. But look, it is sinking, and quickly."

The flashing light on the screen drifted steadily below the rising horizontal line, until at a reading of five hundred meters, it began to flash red.

"The automated distress signal," said Drake, as they watched it continue downward. After only a few seconds, the blinking light sputtered, and disappeared. "Without the shield on, the ship can't survive at that depth. If it didn't explode completely on impact, it would have imploded by now, anyway."

Thirteen closed his eyes, and inhaled slow and deep, sampling the first full breath of freedom of his life. Not freedom from Denali, but freedom from conformity, from commonality. From sameness. He was unique again, original, and one of a kind. He was the one. He was the *only* one.

"What next, Thirteen," Drake asked.

"That name has no meaning for me any longer. Don't call me that anymore."

"Yes, sir. Then... what shall I call you?"

Thirteen thought about it. "I'm not sure, but I'll come up with something. When the time is right, the name will come to me. But... '*sir*' is fine for now."

"Yes, sir," Drake said.

"What's next, my friend, is that we are gonna follow Parliament. I have a feeling they'll waste no time in tracking down Denali for us, and we're gonna stick close by until that happens." He headed for the door with his seti bodyguard in tow, returning towards the launch bay for a ship of their own. "In the meantime, let's go see if any of Jim Dodger's bank accounts still work."

11.4

THE LOOSE ROCK CLATTERED SHARPLY as it tumbled roughly down the hillside, Stansky and Tachion casting the rubble behind them as they frantically burrowed into the stone-covered incline. The help-beacon had brought them back to the base of Mt. Ivëal, to an apparent narrow fissure buried not far beneath the surface. A cave entrance, it seemed, and a very small one at that. The pair dug fervently at the boulder-strewn slope, until a darkened hollow was exposed. Standing back, with weapons drawn, they cautiously called out into the newly uncovered void below.

Of the many things they may have expected to spring forth from the dim opening—from the familiar face of Rook, to an ambush of enemy weapons fire—the very least would have been the delicate, grasping fingers and plaintive cry of the exhausted lyghtan princess. As her slender ebony arm emerged, reaching out desperately from the shadowy chasm, the pair looked at each other in momentary bafflement. Then James popped loose the gauntlets of his massive powered armor, and gently took the elegant and lovely hand in the comfort of his own. Clasping his other hand to surround it in an embrace of reassurance, he held Opal's grip securely, as Tachion continued to push aside the encasing stones.

At long last, they had her freed, and pulled her with care from the dusty crevice. Her raven skin was marred by occasional red slashes, scratched by the jagged stones, and the bright milky waves of her luxuriant hair were matted and muddy from the damp subterranean crawlspace. As she sat there, spent and dirty on the hill of gravelly castoff, she peered up at her rescuers, her eyes aglow in both green-hued illumination, and a distinctive look of apprehension. The two mercenaries, still in their armor, loomed like mechanical giants before her, and she pulled her hand free from Stansky's grasp in obvious trepidation. The human took the cue. He immediately pulled off his armored helmet, employing instead the well-rehearsed enchantment of his beguiling eyes and bewitching smile. Opal stared a moment, then smiled back, looking both relieved and suitably captivated. Doctor Magna followed suit and removed his helmet as well, though his severe, metallic features did little to ease her tensions further.

James dropped to one knee while remaining slightly downhill from her, alleviating the unease of his towering above. "Well, you're not exactly who we expected to find today," he told her in a soothing tone that dripped charm and reassurance. "Though I have to admit, I am genuinely pleased with the upgrade." He reached out halfway to take hold of her hand again, and she stretched out likewise the remainder to allow him. "Can I ask," he continued, "how did you know the frequency code you used to call us?"

She croaked through a voice that was seared by dehydration. "I... I met Rook, Rook of Parliament, as we were both es-escaping through the caverns. He gave me the help-beacon code, and... and said if you were still here, you would h-help me."

"Well, fortunately for you, Rook is a man of his word... so I guess we have no choice but to do what we can for you."

Tachion watched this exchange with sincere fascination, opting to keep his mouth shut and let Stansky cast his spellcraft.

"My name is James, and my big friend here is Tach. Can you tell me what happened to Rook after you saw him?"

"He went back... into the caves. He said he wanted to try and... end all this. He..." she tapered off to a dusty squeak, her dry throat refusing to make any further sound.

"That's okay," Stansky consoled her, holding a finger lightly before her lips. Then he rested that same hand upon her bare knee. "Don't worry, we'll talk all about it later. Let's get you outta here right now, get you some water, and some food. And old Tach here will check you out medically once we get back to our ship. Are you okay to walk? Do you want me to carry you?"

Opal nodded back that she was able, and held up a hand to decline his assistance, clearly a stronger woman than her current fatigue could depreciate. The three walked back in slow silence as the sweltering day neared another sunset, and when they had her safely aboard the *Bugeye*, planted on the doctor's biobed with an intravenous of hydrating fluid, as well as a bottle of water, a few nutrient bars, and a spare inertia suit for her to change into, the human and the android went back outside to talk.

"*Shit*," Stansky whispered, as they stood in the crumbled warehouse surrounding the *Bugeye*. "Do you have any idea who that is?"

"Umm... yes, I do," Tachion replied. "Do *you*?" he asked, sounding doubtful.

"Yes, she's ashi'mar. Lady Opal, royalty of Capella."

Tachion stood up straight in shock, but nodded his head in approval. "Well, I have to say I'm impressed. I didn't know you followed intergalactic politics that closely."

"Pssh. Politics shmolitics. She was named in the galactic hot one hundred."

"Ah, of course. And the balance of the universe is once again restored."

Stansky peered back up the gangway towards their passenger. "What in the hell do you think she's doing here?"

"Well, your guess is as good as mine, but we have now seen several pieces of evidence that the lyghtan are just as neck deep in these affairs as the chamai, and none more damning than Lady Opal herself crawling out of that hole. Let's see how forthcoming she is once she's able to tell her story, and we'll take it from there whether or not she's at all responsible."

They reboarded the ship and Tachion checked on his patient, while Stansky stowed their gear, and took to cleaning his armor. The medic adjusted her IV, and passed the wand of his scanner quickly up and down above her, the device singing out a tune of electronic chirps and whistles. "How are we feeling?" he asked the lyghtan, as he put the device away.

"Improved," she replied, her voice still weak, but getting stronger. She handed the trash from her small meal to the android. "Get me more water, and a blanket to cover my legs."

"I... okay," Tachion said, taken aback by her curtness.

"*Jesus Christ,*" Stansky swore under his breath from the other side of the *Bugeye*, horrified at the sight of a long scratch through Geeta's paint job.

Opal looked at the human, then back to Tachion. "Where is the rest of your master's team?" she asked in a low voice.

"My... I'm sorry, my what?"

"Your master's teammates, the rest of Parliament, and... what did James say your designation was?"

"My *designation*? You mean my *name*? Well, James and the others call me Tach, or Tachion. You may feel free to use either, or if you prefer, Dr. Magna."

"Dr. Magna?" she said.

"Yes."

"Dr. *Tachion* Magna, of the... Coalition Biological Society?"

"*Yes*, that's right. At your service."

Opal stared for a moment, then covered her face with her hands. "Oh, Saints of Ico, Originators help me, I am absolutely mortified." She looked up at him, eyes pleading. "You must please forgive me, Doctor. I'm afraid... well... I thought you were just a battlefield servicebot."

"Ah," Tachion said, reassuring her with the lightest touch on her shoulder with his heavy, black hand. "Consider it forgiven. I've been known to be brusk with the occasional robot myself."

"I am so awfully embarrassed, I don't know what to say. We have servicebots on Capella, of course, but I'm afraid I have not met many Androids beyond the Rhyanan Ambassador, and I am ashamed to say... I find it hard to tell the difference."

"Well, my kind don't spend much time on your world, I'm afraid. The sand and the heat, you know? It's not an ideal environment when your joints are metallic hinges. It's the grit, you see. It gets in the gears."

"As I can well imagine," she said, smiling.

"And Ambassador Iaphis doesn't look anything like myself, if I recall."

"No, he is more of a four legged..." She paused. "Let me please apologize again."

"Think no more of it. You are not the first organic to confuse one type of mechanical form for another. Perhaps my people should begin wearing signs around our necks."

"No, of course not," she laughed, "although the reverse may be a good idea. Servicebots should perhaps display some universal brand to identify them as... non-sentient."

Tachion nodded. "Not a bad idea, actually. I would rally behind that. You know, I think someday you'll make a fine leader for your people."

The lyghtan woman's smile faded, and she seemed somewhat surprised. "You recognize who I am?" she asked, just as Stansky approached to join Tachion at her bedside. "Both of you?"

James laid out an extra blanket atop her, having overheard her request. "Of course, Madam Ashi'Mar," he said in that same reassuring tone while tucking her in, "and it's our pleasure... our *honor*, to assist you however we might."

She smiled weakly and nodded. "Well, hopefully your pleasure isn't exhausted too quickly. I may impose myself on the safety of your company for longer than you might anticipate."

Tachion and Stansky looked at each other, then back to her. "You don't wish to return to the Old City Temple?" Tachion asked.

"I don't know if that would be exactly the safest place for me right now. And even if it were, I'd prefer to stay and commission the help of your team, to resolve this danger that is threatening my people."

"Our team isn't exactly at full strength right now," Stansky told her. "We're stuck here temporarily, awaiting word from two of our comrades that are, well... on a mission elsewhere."

"Although," Tachion followed up, "while we have the time, it would be helpful, of course, if you could give us some insight as to what exactly has been going on. What is this threat to your people? And, what were you doing under that mountain, Lady Opal?"

"I'll tell you everything I know, as well as concede to everything I do not. Although, I'm afraid there might be much more of the latter than the former." She took a breath, a sip of water, and closed her lids for a few moments, briefly snuffing the emerald radiance that burned like embers in her gaze. Then she looked back at them, eyes reignited, "It was perhaps two years ago now, when he first appeared at the Temple. I assume from my previous conversation with Rook... you're both familiar with the name Denali?"

11.5

FOURTEEN YEARS AGO, UPON AN elegant stone terrace that stood oddly out of place in its location—clinging to the side of a nondescript factory wall, and overlooking the rank, stinking armpit that was Gel Gonahaar's most prolific, and disreputable, industrial district—Thirteen used his levitation belt to float softly downward from the roof, landing on hushed tiptoe, and immediately crouching out of sight against the stained stucco wall. He knew he didn't have much time. He could hear the gunfire erupting from the building's lower floors already, and he hurriedly activated his helmet's EM visor to check for force fields before approaching the glass doors. It was to no surprise that there was one—a shock field and alarm curtain, with a keypad on the wall above him that likely would disable it all. This was taking far too long. He needed to hurry. Thirteen didn't have the infiltration skills needed to disable the field, but the past long year of working diligently on his ensensement abilities had left him with quite a few other tricks up his sleeve. He took a breath, closed his eyes, and focused his concentration.

Back—back in time—back an hour, a day, a week. In his mind's eye, he reversed the days until he could see the balcony as it was a month ago. His body was still present, left behind in the here and now, still crouched in shadow along the wall of the terrace. But in his thoughts, he was visualizing four weeks in the past, watching a steady midafternoon rain fail to wash the grime from the streets below. He stopped there, then moved forward again, speeding the passage of hours like he was skimming through a recording. As he advanced the vision ahead again, day after day, he kept his mind's eye on the keypad above, waiting for the moment that— ah, here it was! Thirteen watched the man enter the keystrokes on the panel two weeks ago, then zipped forward back to his present, and duplicated the entry. Through his electromagnetic visor, he saw the fields fall. Focusing on the molecules that made up his arm, he increased the density of his fist, then punched through the bolt mechanism, hurriedly barging through the glass door into the office.

As with the personal private spaces of that facility on Theseus, this room was done up in the opulent human style of the mid-twentieth century. Old leather and older wood, polished brass and Persian rugs. And in the middle of it, at his desk, there he was, standing right in front of him, caught in the midst of feverishly emptying important items from his drawers, and shoving them into a travel bag. Here he was, Denali, staring back from across his office in surprise.

Thirteen had been mistaken last year in his assumptions about Parliament. He had been certain that they would be chomping at the bit to find Dodger's killer without delay. As such, Thirteen and Drake had quickly settled into a pattern of spying on the surviving mercenary group, but week after week went by without any sign of action. Yes, the group had suffered the fall of two of their own—finding out about Dodger, as well as losing Rook in the fight. And Thirteen felt he had given a suitable allowance for a period of mourning. But as weeks turned into months, he began to wonder if the team had surrendered, decided to hang up their QEU packs and settle into their day jobs. But he dismissed this, he knew them too well—whether his memories of their shared history were implanted or not. Something else must be going on, something that he couldn't see from simply monitoring their movements, or bugging their communications. He was going to have to get closer to the four of them to find out what was really happening.

Bullseye seemed fully invested in his new school, spending literally all of his time there, and a worthwhile distraction it seemed to be at that. Bullit, on the other hand, was clearly more focused on preparations for—*something*—with day after day spent in holo-training or weapon ranges. Thirteen knew Bullit had more incentive than the others to continue the hunt for Denali, but even he, despite the rigorous training, seemed to be doing so while in a holding pattern of some sort. Stansky, of course, was just business as usual, still living his life like a man in his twenties. Every day at the gym, every night at the clubs—and every once in a while, an apology bouquet for his girlfriend.

Tachion proved to be much harder to pin down, and a full week of stakeouts never saw the android come home. He was clearly still on his homeworld of Rhyana, as Drake noted him many times moving about the Biological Society laboratories. But for some reason or another, he would never seem to leave. *Fine*, Thirteen thought, *he won't come out? Then I'll go in.*

Of course, for a man of Thirteen's talents, that was easier than for most. From a comfortable spot on the roof, and with Drake standing watch over his body, he could project his mind inside, and wander as he wished up and down the halls like a specter. His clairvoyance drifted easily down the corridor from the lifts, then through the closed door to Tachion's office. Finding it empty, even though he had just seen the medic come in here, he moved on unhindered through the wall into the doctor's secreted workspace. He found the android at the back, intently monitoring a large bubbling tank of amber liquid. Up and over the high counters his mind's eye drifted on, until he finally focused on the experiment that Tachion was so invested in. Floating there in the tank, attached by tangles of tubing and wires, a small seti child of perhaps four or five sat soaking in the solution, marinating in the brine like the last pickle in a jar. A male by its anatomy, and clearly unconscious, the boy had pale orange fur with an ivory muzzle and black mane, and a pattern of facial striping that was eerily familiar.

Thirteen jolted his awareness back into his body and hopped to his feet, staggering to the edge for fresh air in his outrage. *Rook!* A baby *Rook!* The bastard had cloned him! The same abomination that Denali had created in him—and that soulless machine down there, who didn't even know what being alive really meant, was doing the same thing with his old seti friend. Could the others all know? And what about Rook's wife? Of course they did. Tach would have never gone ahead with this without the blessing of them all. That metallic son of a bitch was no better than Denali!

Drake reached over and placed his hand on Thirteen's shoulder to see if he was all right, and received a sharp telekinetic shove that pushed him to the ground for his trouble. The human stomped off past his bodyguard without acknowledgement or apology, and the seti scrambled to his feet behind him to follow his master off the building.

At least he now knew what was causing the delay in retribution—the merc team was awaiting the resurrection of their infiltrationist. And from the looks of things, they would have a long wait indeed. Thirteen himself was living proof of how quickly clones could be matured. But Dr. Magna either didn't have the vast warehouse of black-market equipment that Denali's stooges did, or was simply taking more care and consideration than Thirteen's creators had the luxury, or inclination, to bother with. At the leisurely rate that Rook's double was growing, a matured clone was likely to take a year to emerge. And so, like the rest of them, he had no choice but to wait. Wait for the new Rook to awaken and rejoin the team, so that they could get on with the task of tracking Denali—with Thirteen close on their heels.

It was another full ten months later, nearly a year to the day, that Tachion finally opened the growth chamber—Thirteen supervising unseen. When the clone drew its first breath, coughing out the last of the viscous, amber liquid, Thirteen couldn't help but feel a twinge of unique kinship. Here was another like him, a second walking undead, returned to correct the missteps of their formers. But camaraderie and pride soon turned to anger and horror, as he watched 'Tachion the butcher' chop his new clone brother to pieces. He took his arm, and some organs, and left scars on his face, and Thirteen realized now that the doctor intended on lying to his friend's double. In giving him all of the same injuries as the original, he was going to make the clone believe he was still Rook. Even Denali himself hadn't stooped to that level—creating a monster, and then hiding from it the truth of its own nature. Well, someday, Thirteen would be certain to correct *that* injustice—and on that someday, when he was ready, perhaps the two peers would unite.

It was a few more months before things kicked into gear. Rook needed some physical therapy and exercise before he was at full speed, and Thirteen watched as the regrouped Parliament practiced and prepared. It was clear that the routine was just as much a tryout as it was training, as the surviving members tested to see if their carbon copy was up to snuff. It didn't take long though for him to pass with flying colors, and Thirteen actually felt some pride as the others took him in under their wing. They seemed to dismiss, or forget, that he was merely a duplication, and accepted him just the same as if he were the original Rook prime.

The goddamn liars.

Then very quickly, the wheels began to turn, and a year of covertly gathered intel was collated and reviewed. Parliament had learned the lessons of their past with Denali, and made their plans with a level of secrecy that made it near impossible for Thirteen to get a handle on things. Too many times Denali had been three steps ahead of them, so they worked under the assumption that every corner in the galaxy was under surveillance. Thirteen had no choice but to stay close by with Drake, waiting for them to make their move in hopes he could follow and get ahead of them. Which they did, and he did, but only just barely, and he now stood in front of Denali with Parliament nearly about to knock on the door. This is not at all the way he had planned things, and he considered his options as he sized up his quarry.

Denali stopped emptying his desk into the bag, and stared at the sudden intruder with shock and surprise. Then as Thirteen opened the face shield on the front of his armor's helmet, a smirk of pleased recognition crept across the crime lord's expression. He put down the bag and chuckled aloud, clapping his hands together a few times in a slow and exaggerated applause. "Well done, my son. And here I thought you'd all been lost. Now tell me, exactly which one are you?"

"The only one," Thirteen said flatly.

"Oh, is that so? Well then, congratulations, and well done again. And I assume you have somehow rejoined with your... or rather *his*... prior teammates?"

"No, I'm not with them. They're no better than you, it turns out. Creating life where it wasn't meant to be. Playing God."

"Are they *really*? I see." Denali said with deep interest. "So then, do they even know that you... No, of course not, I can see that they don't. Well, it seems I'm just a popular man today then, so many old friends coming to call at once. And to what do I owe the pleasure of seeing you again?"

"Well," Thirteen began, as he plopped down and sank back into a wide leather couch, ripping it slightly under the weight of his heavy armor, "I've come to kill you of course, just as slowly and painfully as I can possibly manage." He looked toward the door, where the sounds of weapons were getting louder. "Although, fortunately for you, I might need to hasten the process more than I hoped. It would be awkward if I were still at it when Parliament walks in."

"Yes, quite awkward, I'd imagine."

"I'm sure we can find the time to squeeze in the painful part, though."

"Mmm, that's alright, no need to put yourself out."

"Oh," Thirteen nearly growled, "but I insist."

"I see. Well, sorry to disappoint, but I was actually just on my way out." Denali quickly reached down, pulling a drak'min disintegration pistol out of the bag. As he lifted it towards Thirteen, the clone sent a blast of thought that slapped it from his grip. The tossed weapon then stopped its tumble in midair, and boomeranged back into Thirteen's awaiting fingers.

"Well, well, well, look at you. My little project was more successful than I thought, it would seem. So tell me, *only one*, if you're in such a rush to kill me, then what the hell are you waiting for? Your old comrades will be joining us any minute, I'm sure. What's the hold up? Are you getting cold feet at the thought of killing your father?"

"Ha! Don't be ridiculous, you are *not* my father."

"Aren't I? What else do you call the man who gives you life, then? I mean... I suppose you could go with Dad, though that feels a wee bit informal seeing as we've only just met."

Thirteen's powers of empathy could feel that Denali was merely stalling, trying to instigate him into wasting more time. Something he was clearly quite skilled at. Thirteen refused to take the bait, ignoring the comment. "I have questions," he said, "or a single question, actually. And then I'll happily kill you once you've answered."

"Then why should I answer?"

"If you do, I'll forgo the painful part."

"Hmm. Not much of an incentive."

"Trust me, I can make the pain significant."

"*Can* you. Okay, very well then. What is your question?"

Thirteen stood from the couch and cautiously approached a few steps, his stony, unemotional voice now betraying just a sliver of eagerness. "Were any of us... any of the thirteen... the original Jim Dodger?"

"*That* is your question?" Denali scoffed and chuckled. "Why do you *all* always obsess on such things? Why in the world would you even possibly care? What does that even mean, 'the original'? Don't you know that none of us are? Every time you use a teleporter, you are destroyed and recreated. Do you think that your exact original molecules are sent off through space, like some... long, unraveled strand of yarn, just to re-knit itself back into your favorite sweater on the other side? No, of course not. The sweater is destroyed! You are destroyed! Disintegrated to atomic ash, analyzed, and then reassembled from completely different particles elsewhere. Every time you teleport, you are killing the original and building a clone."

"That's not... you know what I meant!"

"Even if you never used a teleporter," Denali continued unabated, "did you know that every single year, ninety-eight percent of our atoms are replaced with new ones? By the end of a year and a half, it's well over the full hundred. Do you understand what that means? That you, yourself, are already not the same person as the one we awoke a year ago on Theseus. Every year, *nature* clones you. Destroys and replaces you, atom by atom. We go through life thinking this is the same skin we had as a child, the same hair we had in our twenties, the same mind that we had on our last birthday. But none of that is true, we are *all* just clones. All remade fresh every year, all with false and fuzzy memories of events that didn't even really happen to us, and the best any of us can do, is try and leave a legacy for next year's model. *None* of us are original! There *is* no such thing."

The sound of a nine-millimeter thundered just outside the doorway, followed by the clearly distinctive tones of someone entering codes on the keypad. The new Rook was outside, trying to open the door.

"Uh-oh," Denali said, as he resumed stuffing computer prog-chips and scramblers into his travel bag, "it seems our time is up. Now I really must insist, if you don't plan on killing me quickly right now, then I'm afraid I *do* have to take my leave."

Thirteen looked back and forth in panicked uncertainty, trying to decide what to do. Denali was right, Parliament would be entering in seconds, and he had to decide whether to vaporize him now, or risk the odds of another chance to linger over killing him later. It was possible that the mercenaries may just apprehend their longtime nemesis. Certainly great rewards of both credits and notoriety would await them. And Bullit— surely that young seti would want to take his time as much as Thirteen did. It was a calculated risk, but he decided to let Parliament have him, and hope to get Denali alone again sometime after he was in custody.

Thirteen used the full power of his suggestion and sent his will towards the kingpin. *"Throw me the bag,"* he demanded. Denali looked up, hesitated only a moment, then closed the satchel and tossed it over. *"Do not leave, do not run. Stay calm, and don't resist."* Denali nodded his head slowly, then took a seat in his chair. Throwing his feet up on the desk, he sat and waited for Parliament to enter. Thirteen dashed back outside and onto the balcony, closing the door behind him and kneeling down where he could see.

Rook apparently failed to bypass the door's keypad, perhaps not as up to snuff as he and the others were led to believe. Instead, Stansky's signature over-the-top use of explosives removed the entire door, the door frame, and the wall utterly from existence. The mercenaries swarmed into the room in the typical practiced perfection, and surrounded Denali, who seemed neither surprised nor alarmed. He stood from his desk with his hands slightly raised, then turned to his small liquor trolly, and began pouring a cocktail.

"I don't suppose I could offer you gentlemen a drink?" Thirteen heard Denali ask.

"No longer the figurative, but now the literal poisoned chalice you extend, Denali?" Bullseye asked.

From the balcony, Thirteen shook his head and rolled his eyes, groaning at the seti's dramatics. Why did he have to make every single sentence such an ordeal?

"Ah, my old friend," Denali said, "still ever the poet. No... no poisons here, however. The time for such subtleties I think has passed, has it not?"

"A certainty upon which I heartily agree," Bullseye growled.

Denali took a sip from the tumbler as he approached towards the posse. "Ah, and who have we here?" he said arrogantly towards Bullit. "This must be the replacement for the unfortunate Mr. Mishta, may he rest in peace. A curious substitution. It seems one by one, you're replacing the human members of your team with seti. Tell me, Mr. Stansky, does that cause you any concern for your future job security?"

"Fuck!" Thirteen thought as he watched from the balcony. The asshole was just egging them on. These mercs had notoriously short fuses, and Denali was insisting on trying to light each of them. Perhaps he had 'calmed' him too much, and removed all sense of concern for his own safety.

"And Rook," Denali continued, "I must admit how pleasantly surprised I am to see you. I was so afraid you had perished on Theseus. It seems the rumors of your death have been greatly exaggerated."

"Careful now," Thirteen suggested across the distance to their rival.

But Denali yammered on, "I was so worried that your young ones would have no one to provide for them. I was planning on making a visit to your home, to see if there was anything I could do for them. You know how important it is for children that age to have the security of a father figure."

"Oh, shit," Thirteen thought, as he winced and pressed his fingertips against his forehead. *"That's gonna do it."*

The responding thunderous explosion of autopistol fire tore Denali's head from his body in a hundred bite-size pieces, and Thirteen slumped along the wall to the balcony floor in a crushing wave of unbridled rage. He trembled and shook as he screamed inwardly at himself, then struggled to remain still and regain his composure. He told himself that at least it was Rook who had fired the final blow—his fellow clone brother doing the honors was going to have to suffice.

Back inside the office there was now some kind of commotion, and Thirteen twisted around to get a look at what was happening. Bullit and Rook were on the verge of coming to blows, and Bullseye and Stansky held them back while Tachion gave them a heated lecture. The younger seti was clearly enraged at the lost opportunity for vengeance. *Get in line*, the Dodger clone thought. Knowing Denali, it would be an awfully long one—with Thirteen right up at the front.

The scuffle caused the group to clear out faster than usual, trying to keep the two teammates separated until they could get safely out of the building. They didn't even root around or search the office, and left the gory remains of Denali right where they had landed. After a minute or two of waiting to make sure the coast was clear, Thirteen called for his sidekick, and reentered the newly ruined office.

Drake came down from the rooftop and joined his master in the room below, then the two checked around quickly, making sure the scene was secure. Parliament, it appeared, had not left anyone alive. Or, if there were any survivors, they had wisely made themselves scarce. The authorities in this area would be slow to respond, if they bothered to show up at all, so Thirteen felt free to linger and consider the situation. He held a satchelful of information which Denali himself thought worth risking his life to stay and collect. Who knows what treasured data he held in his hand. And as far as Denali goes, no one was left behind here to mourn him. Thirteen wondered, if, in fact, anyone would even be aware he was gone.

Almost no one knew what the underworld figure looked like. Parliament themselves had never laid eyes on him until this very day. Between this precious bag of data that he had so kindly been handed, his innate 'talents' of persuasion and coercion, and his ability to gather sensitive, compromising information, even from deep in the past, Thirteen could see no reason why he couldn't just take over as Denali. He was certain, before long, no one would even notice. Or care. Perhaps the son-of-a-bitch did do one fatherly thing after all, leaving behind his empire for his offspring to inherit. He picked up an old-fashioned wax seal stamp made of wood and brass from the desk: Denali's triangle insignia with which he had signed so many early letters of threat and harassment. He turned it over in his hands as he considered his new future.

"Drake," he said, "I think I've finally decided on my new name."

Chapter 12.1

HOURS OF DARKNESS, WITH NO sense of space or location, and trapped in the humid smog of his own breath and perspiration. The black hood they kept over Rook's head for the past several hours was surely meant to keep him from getting his bearings—or getting ideas. But though it blinded him to his surroundings, it didn't shut out his ability to listen. In fact, if anything, it gave an extra boost to his concentration. He heard a touch-monitor keypad on the frame of the outer doorway, an older model based on the creak of the screen under the pressure of fingertips. Fifteen steps ahead, the sound of a baton lock to the cells. Impossible to know what caliber without the use of his eyes, but even the simplest mechanism would be near impossible without his techkit. Rook knew himself to be a resourceful fellow though, so he wouldn't discount his ability to pick it; not until he was able to survey any helpful items in the area. Then five steps left, and a quick turn to the right, toward the familiar hum and chime of a retinal scan override for the security alarms. Rook made note of these obstacles as he was marched across what was surely a starship, at least it certainly thrummed and vibrated like one, and determined none of it too difficult for him to bypass given some rudimentary tools—and of course, the opportunity. Also, one of the eyeballs of an obliging security guard for the retinal scanner would be helpful. That quiet one with the insectoid mask would do nicely.

Rook continued considering these obstructions while he listened to the new Denali, clearly the identity that this Jim Dodger was going by now.

The seti juggled thoughts of escape planning with distracted amazement in his captor's story, from the experiment that created him, to the crashed ship full of clones that freed him. Rook was even partly grateful for the covering over his head, as it hid his obvious fascination with his old friend's autobiography. He wouldn't have wanted to give him the satisfaction of showing interest.

"So that's what I did," Denali said, as he wrapped up his narrative. "I took over the whole operation, and ran it better than he ever did. You see, his big mistake, among many, was this obsession with convoluted payback to those that wronged him. You wouldn't believe how much time and money was wasted on just that." Denali paused as he reconsidered. "Well, maybe you would, since you spent so many years as one of the targets of it. Anyway, out with the old and in with the new. Within a month, I had anyone on his old shit list killed, dramatically and violently. It cleared the house of the undesirables, and set an example for the way I would run things going forward. And almost nobody ever realized the man on top had even changed."

Rook silently wondered how he and the rest of Parliament had survived that month of bloodshed. After all, they must have been near the very top of the old Denali's black book.

"I had other plans for you, of course," Denali said, as if in answer to Rook's question. "I've used my success and influence to lay the groundwork all these long years, to finally take my rightful place. *Our* rightful place, if you so choose. You know, at one time, I considered myself an abomination. Something unnatural that was never meant to be. But over the past many years, I realized I was wrong. I've come to believe that everything happens for a reason, that the universe doesn't make mistakes. In fact, variation and mutation is its engine of evolution. Therefore, it must have brought me forth for a purpose. I simply needed to realize what that purpose was. So I have taken the work from which I was born, and elevated it beyond their wildest dreams. I have elevated myself, above the multitude of commoners, and soon I'll unite the galaxy in my evolved vision of the future."

Rook sat still and remained silent, despite the fact that Denali had obviously finished speaking. After a moment the hood was roughly pulled off, along with a few strands of his mane, and Rook saw Dodger's face on this Denali staring at him in anticipation. The seti blinked and squinted a few times as he became accustomed to the light, then looked from Denali to his bodyguard Drake at the doorway, and back again to Denali. "Shit," he said. "I'm sorry, were you talking to *me* that whole time? I thought you were yapping to Jeeves over there. I would have listened, but to be honest, I had other things on my mind."

Denali forced a crooked grin with one corner of his mouth, his lip tugging itself into a smirk like it was being pulled up by a fishhook. "Yes, I'm aware," he said, with no tone of amusement. "You're remembering keypads and counting footsteps, planning your inevitable escape. I suppose I might be a bit disappointed if you didn't. But you have *no* feelings you can keep hidden from me, no private thoughts that I cannot hear your mind *screaming* out loud. I know full well that you heard every word of my story."

"Yeah, I caught a bit of it, I guess. And a real gripping yarn, too. You should set it to music and put it on Broadway. *A Fist Full of Dodgers*, by Rodgers and Who-gives-a-shit."

"Snarky as ever, I see."

"Well, I'd hate to disappoint." Rook spun slightly on his bench and leaned in towards the human. "Tell me, there's one thing I never understand about you psychotic-take-over-the-universe types. Why would you even want to? I mean, the insane hassle of everyone who's gonna try and stop you. You just finished telling me what a master scumbag degenerate you are, in command of a whole galactic network of lesser scumbag degenerates. Didn't you have enough money, enough power doing that? What more could you possibly want? No one even knew it was you in control, no cops looking to take you down. Shit, no one even had a clue you were even alive." Then the seti sat up straight, as if he'd realized something surprising. "Oh, man, is that what this is? You weren't getting enough attention? Is that what Denali created in you, a genetically needy little *bitch*?"

"This is not about ego! This is about the future!" Denali burst. "About the evolution of the galaxy into something greater! What do you think, that I was brought into being by mistake? That those fumbling idiots lucked into creating me on their own? No! The universe simply used them as a means to its greater purposes. I was *demanded* into being, by fate and force of nature itself, hardened and purified in suffering like coal, squeezed and scalded into diamond. It did this with design! It did this with intention! I am to usher forth the next stage of *all* civilization! The universe forged me for this purpose! It *owes* me this purpose, and I shall have it!"

Rook leaned back and stared at him with serious consideration. "Now I understand perfectly," he said. "You're a raving lunatic."

"Am I," Denali said flatly, sitting back, his cooler demeanor now regained. "Well, even if that's so, then my insanity, too, has its purpose. You know it's been said there is no genius without a mixture of madness."

"It's also been said that geniuses don't become geniuses until they find the right moron to compare themselves to." He looked over at Denali's bodyguard. "Ooh, sorry Igor. I guess that would be you."

"You know, you and I are not that different," Denali told him. "We are both, you and I, children of the universe, and no other."

"Everyone is a child of the universe, and you and I are nothing alike."

"Ah, but that's where you're wrong, as you will soon see. That's where we're going, to reveal to you your truth."

"I have zero interest in your wacky cult, your magic friendship bracelets, or anything else you have to show me," Rook said.

"No man ever wants to see their hidden truth, but once they do, they cannot turn away from it."

"Okay, whatever that means. I think you're starting to come unhinged." Rook turned again to Drake standing guard at the doorway, "Hey, Alfred, I think maybe someone is past due for their medication." He tilted his head toward Denali, and made a looping gesture over his ear with his finger.

Denali stood and began to leave, but turned back halfway to the door. "Each man's fortune is not just a product of chance, but also a product of choice. I have chosen to embrace my destiny. Your choice will come soon enough." The hood slipped back over Rook's head, and he was plunged once more into darkness.

Alone again with himself, he considered the exchange, and tried to comprehend what Denali's interest in him could be about. But he found his mind constantly drifting to thoughts of Parliament and his family, as if they were forced there. Why hadn't they come for him? What the hell were they doing? He knew that locating him would be difficult, if they even realized yet he was missing. Hadn't he overheard that they had replaced him with an imposter? But yet the idea continually faded and reemerged, like a constant nagging itch.

All at once he was caught by a sudden wave of emotion. A bitter realization crashing over him, as if from outside of his body, then moving on, leaving him shivering in its wake—cold, and dripping despair. It was almost as if his subconscious was speaking right to him, his instinct and intuition given a voice of their own. He tried to shake it off, but found the sensation still lingered. *"You are abandoned,"* it had said to him, in a tone of forlorn desolation. *"Abandoned by everyone. You are utterly alone."*

12.2

THE CLOUDLESS SKY HIGH ABOVE the charcoal dunes of Nol Qhan left not a wisp to reflect the fading fire of the setting suns, leaving the three rising moons instead to whitewash the heavens in the lustrous radiance of their soft pearly glow. The effect was a sky that was bright, yet free of color, a pale milky dome above the black desert vast. Bullit looked around, disconcerted, for even the slightest hint of pigment—a blade of grass, an airborne raptor, or the purple haze of a distant mountain. But there was nothing. Only the blackened sands and dark pillars of volcanic glass below, the gauzy white above, and whispers of gray that ran between at the horizon. A perfectly monotone landscape. The seti mused to himself that it was like traversing an old Ansel Adams snapshot.

Even his companion gave him no reprieve from the colorless surroundings, as Bullseye's blackened fur and graying beard assimilated perfectly into the backdrop. Only when his fellow seti sensed his gaze, and looked directly at him, did Bullseye's amber eyes let Bullit know his own rods and cones were still fully functional. The pair had ditched their stolen armor as soon as they were clear of the base, fearing it traceable, and now marched out across The Burnt Empty in only dark-gray inertia undersuits. Another monochromatic touch to this disquietingly grayscale panorama. Bullit pined for the day where he could be back in his own armor again, both for the protection, and for its flash of red pinstripes.

Their escape from the *Okubi* had been a comedy of errors, yet somehow Bullseye had managed to wrangle them their freedom. It started off well enough, Bullseye refraining from asking specifics on how the armor was acquired, despite the fact he clearly noticed the spatter of blood inside the helmet Bullit handed him. They had returned to their previous refuge, hiding in the access tunnel across from the teleporter room. The number of troops teleporting down was tallied in the dozens, so they simply waited for a significant crowd of them to gather in the corridor, then wandered out into the hallway to casually take their place in the queue to zap down.

Here was revealed their first miscalculation. As they rounded the corner into the hallway, they found of the twenty or more crew persons, they were the only two who were wearing helmeted armor. Of course, armored guards patrolling the hallways were a normal occurrence; that was how Bullit had managed to acquire the outfits in the first place. But apparently, the standard uniform for transfer to the surface was fabric fatigues in a gray-toned camouflage—and, *without* a helmet.

Bullit followed behind as Bullseye marched onward nonetheless, the chamai soldiers staring as the pair silently strode past. But he wasn't heading to the end of the line as originally planned. Bullseye had changed tack, apparently amending their plans on the fly, and they were now parading to the front of the line instead.

They entered the teleporter room, and Bullseye confronted the officer there, engaging in a conversation that Bullit couldn't understand. He had rehearsed two key phases in the hours before leaving, the Chamai equivalent for both 'yes sir' and 'no sir', and hoped that would cover most situations. If Bullit was approached, he would take his cue from Bullseye which answer to give. A head tilt to the right for 'yes sir', and to the left if it's 'no'. *But wait a minute,* Bullit thought, *was that his right or my right?*

Whatever Bullseye said to the teleporter chief, the officer seemed to have bought it. He was told later that Bullseye claimed one of the soldiers who had already zapped down was AWOL, and the operator may be held accountable for not checking the crew names with the transfer logs. But if they could get down fast enough to apprehend the deserter, there should be no reason to bring his name into it. The transport pad was cleared, and the two armored men were allowed to cut the line.

As they were standing there waiting for it to engage, a chamai crewman who had been asked to give up his space on the pad leaned over, tapping Bullit on the shoulder. The seti looked down at him, and at a beckoning finger he leaned in closer. The soldier whispered a load of chamai gibberish into his ear. Bullseye was standing behind him, unable to signal a head tilt either way, and Bullit doubted the question or comment required a yes or no response, anyway. So he instead repeated back, to the best of his ability, whatever the chamai guard yelled at him last night, as he tied him up and left him behind the bulkhead to the retractor array. Whatever it meant, this chamai didn't like it, but his friend next to him certainly found it amusing. Before there was any further rebuttal, the pair zapped away and reappeared on the surface.

Now another explanation had to be given to the operator on this end, and Bullseye made up some song and dance about an advance security team for General Nylis—who may, or may not, be teleporting down himself later today. Bullit wondered when Bullseye talked to these soldiers, did he use the same grandiose speech that he did in everyday life? He assumed probably not—that would be a dead giveaway. But if his seti friend could control the amount of flourish injected into his sentences, why then did he do it all? He had always assumed Bullseye just couldn't help himself, the seti language being as ornate and convoluted as it was, that he was just stuck in the habit, even when speaking common. But obviously, his phrasing was a matter of preference and not predisposition, and Bullit decided someday he would ask him about that.

Then, they were lost. Utterly lost—in the twisting maze of the facility's subterranean tunnels. Just as with most structures on this world of perpetual sand and sun, the chamai/lyghtan joint military complex was built underground, in passages both manmade and natural. Bullit followed in tow as he trusted Bullseye to navigate to the surface, which his leader did by reading the sporadic signage. However, they were often forced into suddenly changing direction in order to take a tunnel that was less occupied. Bullit began to lose faith when he swore they had passed the same column formation for the third time, but to his fellow seti's credit, he eventually brought them forth to glorious daylight—the first time he had seen a sun or sky since he had flown them hastily off Oberonn in the *Bugeye*. It occurred to Bullit, as they walked freely out of the cave mouth, what a massive security risk allowing helmeted soldiers on base could be. He hoped no one here came to the same conclusion until after they were well away.

But alas, here again, things on the surface were not what they had expected. They had assumed a small number of ground level outbuildings, perhaps accompanying landing pads or communications towers, and surrounded, most likely, by some sort of fencing. Fencing through which the teleportation triangles would be inconspicuously thrown. But the chamai contingent of this joint military compound perhaps were not as keen on underground living as their Capellan hosts, and had erected a small neighborhood of multistory offices, warehouses, and accommodations, built up along the side of a towering black cliff face. And there was no simple fence around it which they could toss the alien device through, or over. Instead, the whole installation rested securely beneath a mighty transparent dome, climate controlled against the desert heat and cold, and impervious to the throwing of small metallic triangles.

Bullseye decided the best way to leave, without being stopped and questioned for any reason, was for them to carry something heavy towards the landing pad outside the dome walls. Not so heavy that anyone would offer help when they saw them struggling, but heavy enough that they got out of their way, and would feel awkward to detain them. Plus, carrying something gives the added perk of obvious purpose. After all, who would stop and ask them what they're doing, when so clearly they've been charged with moving a weighty parcel? The answer to that question, it seemed, was both of the sentries at the dome entry portal. However, Bullseye somehow smooth-talked them again, while Bullit feigned to struggle somewhat, but not too much, with the random container they had grabbed in front of a nearby warehouse.

The feeling of well-earned freedom, as they finally stepped through the dome's gateway onto the ebony sands of Nol Qhan, was immediately tempered by the soul-crushing blast furnace from the wasteland beyond, which rapidly dried their eyes, and baked their lungs. The Burnt Empty was a region located towards the northern pole of Capella, but the twin suns, combined with the heat absorbing dark sand, created an oven just as brutal as any of the more southerly deserts. Fortunately, making their way across it and out of sight of the facility was fairly easy to accomplish, as the inky dunes were generously studded with jagged pillars of obsidian lava glass projecting from the sand, each pylon somewhat taller than the height of either seti. Spread every several meters, as far as the eye could see, like nail points of a coffin lid hammered from beneath the surface, the craggy columns allowed them to move from one outcropping to the next, hiding their dwindling silhouettes behind the desert's multiple rows of sharpened teeth.

It was late afternoon by the time they had struck out from the dome into the barren landscape, so they didn't have to endure the withering daylight for very long. Now that the second sun had settled beneath the western horizon, and the gentler glow of eventide brought a cooling downdraft from above, the pair's walking pace increased as they marched onward across the badlands, determined to clear enough distance that their eventual rescue craft would not raise suspicions. The trek could not continue all night, however—eventually they would need to find shelter of some kind. The black terrain beneath them would slowly release the stored warmth of daylight for several hours, but by the time the moons above had traced their porcelain glow midway across the sky, the pebbled dunes will have grown cold, and the desert would undergo its nightly transformation—from sweltering inferno, to frozen tundra.

They used the multicomm to scan the ground before them, searching for any hidden caves in which to spend the night. But despite this planet's notorious plethora of tunnels and cavities, the ground they traveled over seemed oddly solid and impregnable. If they didn't find a suitable hollow by the time the thermometer dropped to freezing, they would have no choice but to dig down into the last remaining warmth of the sand, and huddle together until the first sun arose to warm them. A prospect that Bullit found not entirely desirable. "You did send the second code black, updating our location? Correct?" he asked, possibly for the third time since the pair had left the cover of the protective dome.

"Indeed," Bullseye answered. "Rest assured, your eagerness for deliverance, however impassioned, is feeble competition for my own impatience. My confidence remains, certain and unwavering, that the intrepid Captain Lobo makes way forthwith in our direction. And, in all hope, bearing our brethren James and the doctor aboard. And the formidable reinforcement of Belladonna in addition."

"Yeah, about Belladonna," Bullit considered. "What exactly do you suggest we should tell my cousin?"

"The truth, as we comprehend it. Nothing more and nothing less. There is nothing to be gained partaking in rampant speculation."

"So, you don't intend to let her know that her husband has possibly... shit, I don't even know what to call it. Gone rogue? Turned on us? Joined with Denali and the Drak'min in some sort of conspiracy to..."

"We bear no evidence to corroborate such an accusation," Bullseye interrupted bruskly, "save for eavesdropped hearsay, half-heard at best, and a quarter remembered. And, even that, by a drunkard no less," he finished, referring to himself.

Bullit considered this for a moment as the two walked on in silence, the vanished twilight now leaving them to forge on in the darkened starlight. The three brilliant moons rising behind them—toward the left and the right, waxing and waning quarters, yet the center one beaming in its full, round, polished glory—cast long exaggerated shadows of their journey out before them. "You should probably be aware," Bullit offered after several seconds, "if that is the case, if Rook has... well... I'll do whatever I have to, to stop him. Even if that means... you know what it means." He let that lie for a moment, then under his breath he added, "He probably never should have been brought back to begin with."

"I recollect no such prior objection," Bullseye chided him. "Are you confident certain elements of this situation are not perhaps reviving sensitivities in grievances past? Namely, of course, this spectre of Denali. Be careful not to become too attached to your baggage, Bullit. How often it seems we two now remind this to each other. The past is the past, no matter how hard we look at it."

"I'm no longer concerned with what Rook did to Denali in the past," Bullit lied. "My only concern is what he does with Denali's namesake in the future."

"If proof and testimony bear out that our longtime comrade remains so no further, then we all, as one body, shall determine his judgment. As you know, I'm not one averse to drastic measures when called for. But we *must* all be resolved together, or hazard being torn apart. Your cousin included."

"Well, you know where I stand, and I don't see how the opinions of the others would ever change it."

"Shall we not save worry in these matters till we confirm a worry exists? Doing so prematurely risks granting a petty thing a mighty shadow."

"The only worry I have is... *Whoa!*" Bullit stopped in his tracks, his blood running cold. "What the fuck! Did you see that?"

Bullseye stopped walking as well and glanced around, seeing nothing. He took up the multicomm, and changed its mode from scanning the ground for caverns, to motion detector. "I saw not a thing. The scan is clear. What is it that alarmed you?"

"I don't know... a white blur. Twelve o'clock, thirty meters. Moving quickly, from one of those black pillars to another."

"That range is outside the multicomm's capabilities."

"Yes, I'm aware," Bullit said. He bent near one of the obelisks of dark obsidian glass, and selected a long, jagged sliver from the ground that appeared capable of inflicting damage. "And just for the record, this is the last time I even leave my house without a scrambler full of weapons and armor."

"Noted," Bullseye acknowledged.

The lunar trinity glaring behind them shone bright as the spotlight of a guard tower, yet the absolute pitch black of the sand and stone was a poor reflector for its brilliance. The Burnt Empty consumed the moonbeams with a ravenous hunger, so that even with their seti vision, details were lost in darkness any more than a few meters out ahead of them. But then suddenly, there it was again! And both saw it this time. Perhaps seventy feet away now, a ghostly white silhouette of—*something*—beaming back the moonlight like a mirror as it dashed between the columns. Bullseye bent to the ground now, and gathered a sharpish looking obsidian chunk of his own.

The two now stood hip to hip in a defensive stance, makeshift daggers at the ready, and staring unblinkingly as the stalker's form approached closer. A flash of vaguest ivory, tacking back and forth, the wraithlike shape darted from pillar to pillar, never staying in view long enough for Bullit to discern exactly what was advancing. Then it stopped, or somehow vanished, and the pair peered out into the darkness for any further movement. Bullit last saw it only some thirty feet away, and gazed down at the motion detector Bullseye held between them, knowing that it should be at the edge of the scanner's range now.

Nothing.

"What *is* it?" Bullit asked in a hush. "Is that some kind of animal?"

"I think... I think a man," Bullseye answered, unsure. "There are those few whom legend say make a home of this place. Mayhap we stumbled across territory which is spoken for."

"Shit, do you think there's more of them? What if this zigzag jumping back and forth was just to draw our attention, to stare in this one direction?"

Bullseye turned his head and looked at Bullit in realization, then closed his eyes and sighed in almost embarrassed resignation. He stood upright then, and turned slowly around in a circle, certain that he was gazing towards an unseen host of figures surrounding them. He dropped his improvised dagger. Bullit followed suit.

"Well, any ideas, fearless leader?" Bullit asked as he stared into the darkness.

"Dialogue," Bullseye answered. "We have no quarrel with this community." Then he turned back to the spot where they had last seen the moving specter, and called out loudly. "Regards and divine blessings, we pray for you sweet water and shaded refuge. May the light of the path always lead your way." He then repeated the entire salutation again in lyghtan.

"What the hell was that?" Bullit whispered. "Have you been studying up on alien religions now too?"

"Nay, merely proper etiquette of varied greetings," Bullseye whispered back. "Though I regret these few sentences exhausted the full extent of my Capellan knowledge."

A voice called out from the dim nightscape beyond, clear and deep and confident, and spoke in the common language. "We appreciate the effort at protocol and ceremony, seti. But we have little use for the queen's religion here."

The motion scanner on their multicomm began to alarm enthusiastically, and the night around them awoke in a ring of multihued embers as they were encircled by a lasso of glowing eyes in the darkness. The multitude surrounding them closed inward, stopping just in sight of their seti vision. Bullseye and Bullit looked around at the enveloping barrier: twenty or so lyghtan men and women, strangely dressed in patchwork garments of assorted fabrics, and brandishing spears of repurposed plastic and metal piping, topped with the abundant black volcanic glass.

The speaker then stepped out from behind a pillar, the last one they had seen him dodge behind, and approached the two mercenaries, his ring of followers parting to let him draw near. A lyghtan man, muscular and lean, and stretched thin and tall. His head and facial features were seemingly elongated in a similar manner, exaggerated further by his lengthy curtain of perfectly straight white hair. He wore handcrafted animal hide pants, but was otherwise stripped to the waist. It was definitely a lyghtan, of that there was no doubt, but unlike any shade that the pair of seti had ever seen. His exposed skin beamed as bright white as a freshly painted picket fence, and the usually glowing eyes were as black and deep as the sand below, or the sky above. An albino.

The moonlight echoed off his chalky complexion as he walked toward them, almost seeming to intensify the brightness of the reflected light. A mural of thin-lined tribal markings was tattooed across the ivory flesh, running up from below his beltline to the left side of his porcelain chest. He stopped a mere arm's length from the pair, and looked down at them from his slightly loftier perspective.

"You wear the undergarb of the chamai military," he said. "Yet somehow, from your fur-covered faces, I doubt that you actually reside in their service."

"You speak truth," Bullseye answered. "We reside in no one's service, save our own."

"Hirelings then, mercenaries? Invading alien lands to earn your money?"

"Aye, in times past, we prospered as soldiers of fortune. But these last many years we favor soldiers of virtue, or at least honor."

"Huh. Honor, is that right?" he asked, turning his attention to Bullit.

"Well, it certainly seems to be," Bullit said, "for better or worse, despite my personal preference for the whole fortune thing."

"Ha-ha-ha-ha!" the shade laughed loudly in a deep rounded tone. "A truth teller. A rare trait. And so, what is it you are called, soldiers-of-at-least-honor?"

"I am known as Bullseye, of Parliament, and my comrade is Bullit."

"Hmm... Bullseye and Bullit, two names steeped in aggression. It gives you much to live up to, when you present such a bold resume in a single word with each introduction." He turned and walked a few steps away from them, apparently feeling his physical intimidation no longer appropriate. "Parliament, however... this is a name that I'm aware of." He turned back again. "What are you doing out here, in the darkness of Nol Qhan?"

"We flee the army base," Bullseye answered, "having conducted espionage amongst the chamai. We two, and many more, stand ensnared in treacherous schemes. Schemes amongst a chamai general, and which possibly involve your lyghtan queen. Schemes orchestrated by a villain with whom our history is long. Schemes with elements of subterfuge, that has left our troupe divided, and ill-equipped."

"That's certainly true," Bullit added. "You're definitely not catching us at our best."

Bullseye continued. "We travel Nol Qhan only seeking shelter. Refuge from the days and nights, till our approaching rescue is at hand."

"Well, Bullseye and Bullit of Parliament, I am called Wairën. These here are my people, and I am theirs." He spread his arms wide to indicate the entire group that surrounded them, and they briefly banged their fashioned spears twice sharply in response. He again approached the two seti. "It has been my long-held policy, that any who find themselves in opposition to Queen Vasu, is, by default, a confederate of mine. Come! The night moves quickly, and frost will descend within the hour. Come, follow us, and we'll give you safe haven, for as long as you need it."

Bullseye and Bullit looked at each other and shrugged, then headed off across the dunes behind him. The two followed in Wairën's trail as he turned eastward through the darkness, the glowing eyes of his surrounding followers dancing at the periphery like a swarm of fireflies.

"So," the ghostly lyghtan asked as the pair walked along behind him, "what exactly is this 'treacherous scheme' that has dropped you two at our doorstep? What has the false cleric that calls herself our queen involved her ignorant people in, with the help of this 'villainous acquaintance' of yours?"

"The puzzle is unfinished, and the final image is yet unclear," Bullseye answered. "Many pieces remain still missing."

"But," Bullit added, "we believe it to be far more than just Capella that's at risk. In fact, it's not just yours, but *all* people that Vasu's conspiracy endangers."

"Then a worthier cause for me to aid could hardly be imagined. Let it never be said that Wairën of Nol Qhan shirks his civic duties."

"Your name, Wairën," Bullseye asked, "is that not the lyghtan word for... phantom? Is this, then, an alias given yourself, like our own?"

"No, believe it or not, that is the name given me at birth," Wairën answered, "bestowed to me by my parents before they sent me away. I unfortunately have no surname, as they declined to share theirs with me."

"Forgive him," Bullit said, as he jabbed an elbow into Bullseye's ribs.

"There's no need to seek forgiveness. If I felt shame in it, I would change it. When the name was given, it was meant to demean me for being... unusual. An albino shade, after all, is a contradiction in terms. But I have taken away its power, and wear it now as a badge of honor." He stopped walking and turned to them as they came up next to a massive boulder. "Besides, it was just as easy to keep it, since the children would call me that anyway." He reached out and patted the stone. "We are here," he told the two seti, and pointed to a spot on the rock a few feet ahead of them.

The boulder resting upon the sands was roughly the size of the *Bugeye*, thin and long, and about twenty feet high. The spot where Wairën pointed was an extremely narrow crevice, barely wide enough for either to fit strafing sideways, and shallowing their breath.

Bullit looked dubious. "Hmm, I see now why you need to stay so thin. One sandwich too many, and you'd never get home."

"There are many other entrances, plenty wide enough for cargo... or, wider-bodied persons. However, this is the one we prefer to use for strangers. It discourages those who return to it from doing so with much more than just their unarmored selves."

"A wise precaution," Bullseye said, as he watched the last of the other lyghtan slide through, and he sucked in his stomach to trail along. Bullit followed, and Wairën brought up the rear.

The fissure would be claustrophobic to even the most unflusterable of people, and the fact it was pitch black only added to the unease. The crack was amazingly tight, slightly twisting, and not at all vertically straight, and Bullit had to lean rearward with an arched back to accommodate the curve. The blowback of his own breath from something directly in front of him allowed him to sense, rather than see, the rock mere inches from his face. Finally, after ten feet or so, the narrow gap widened, and suddenly became the landing of a well-lit and perfectly-masoned downward stairway. The steps were wide and level, the slightly rough walls meeting above them in an arched point, and the whole companionway illuminated by plentiful artificial lighting.

Down through numerous twists and turns the staircase meandered on, the group descending single file towards the bottom of the entrance. Finally, the steps ended and they reached their destination, announced in advance by the smells of rich cooking, and the sounds of enjoyed living. They exited the arched corridor onto a wide cobbled thoroughfare, dividing through the center of a bustling underground hamlet. The carved stone buildings and structures were clearly augmented with scrap material and refuse—old crates, discarded vehicle panels, recycled metals of all kinds. But the craftsmanship and care with which it had all been assembled into the surrounding fine stonework, and the comfort and coziness that each improvised dwelling exuded, gave Bullit the impression of some fantasy gnome village from Earth literature. Like a tiny little townlet, built from mushroom caps and matchboxes, and hidden in a deep forest within the trunk of a magic oak tree. He was dumbfounded. They both were.

"Welcome, new friends," said Wairën, "to the Heart of Nol Qhan. A desert not so lifeless nor so empty as we allow others to believe."

The houses and buildings crowded both sides of the long cobblestone avenue, perched next to, and atop each other, several stories high, until they met the cavern ceiling. It almost felt as though they leaned inward over the roadway—not as if they were unstable, but like they were arching in to embrace the travelers below in the warm glow of their illuminated windows. The street itself was brightly lit from sources far above along the roofline. An intermixing of electric floodlights, and naturally luminescent yellow fungus covering the rock above them, cast the whole neighborhood in a hue akin to golden lamplight. Between all the structures, made of reclaimed sheets of aerospace aluminum, recycled planks from pallets and packages, and repurposed plastic drums and paneling, a throng of lyghtan people packed the street, rushing up and down, busily going about the business of their day. There must have been hundreds, maybe more, lyghtans of every age, making repairs, hocking wares, visiting vendors, traveling to and fro, going to their work or their home, and all around, buzzing swarms of little children, who dashed in and out and around the legs of the mob of pedestrian traffic.

"How did... how did you do all of this?" Bullit asked, as they continued onward down the paved lane. "Where did you get all this stuff?"

"Have you not been to Capella before, my friend?" he asked, spreading his arms wide to encompass the entire settlement. "After all, this is what the lyghtan do!" he laughed. "The bones of our little city have been standing here for ages. Many of the people you see here now, the Heart was built by their great-great-grandparents. And you know, for us long-lived Capellans, that's a mighty long time ago." He turned to the right, down a narrow alleyway off the main thoroughfare, under a bridge supported upon beams of old plastic piping, and directed them to follow. "The more modern touches, the lighting and the useful building materials, those are a much more recent addition, courtesy of the scrapyard of the military base you had the pleasure of visiting today. The amount of goods that they waste, in hardware and edibles alike, could keep our community thriving with very little need for anything else. In fact, its ease and abundance are probably making us lazy."

"Yeah, well," Bullit pointed out, "armies have never been exactly a model of frugalness and efficiency." The seti still looked around awestruck as they traveled along, taking in the quaint sights of the village and its people. But as he did so, he began to note an unusual similarity about the settlers here. Many were what you might call 'atypical' lyghtans. Not all of them certainly, but far more than the normal percentage, consisted of men and women with deformities or disabilities. Some were simply lacking the trademark elongated ears. A small few bore more unfortunate abnormalities, leaving them with twisted bodies, or twisted faces. And a goodly amount seemed to be absent the lyghtan glowing eyes, leaving them as dark, black, and empty as their friendly-seeming guide's were.

Wairën stopped walking and directed them through a small doorway, fashioned from the entry to a decommissioned shuttlecraft fuselage. *Pelnethot* was written across the painted trimithium hull in chamai—a name for a fabled creature, roughly the same thing as the human Pegasus— and directly below, the designation *Landing Craft 7*.

"Funny," Bullseye chuckled quietly to Bullit. "I tread the halls of this craft's mothership once... long, long ago. On its last flight, in fact, before your era serving with us had arrived. Another team, at another time. Intim, and Phineas, and Dodger..." he trailed off.

The room inside was warm and welcoming. A parlor of discarded office seating, mixed with custom crafted pieces, circled around a firepit walled with obsidian glass, and centered beneath a fissure in the stone ceiling overhead, which drew the smoke upward from the room like a chimney. Several men and women were seated here, engrossed in rowdy conversation, but at a nod and a gesture from the pale-white lyghtan, they quieted their conversation, and filed out through the shuttle door. Wairën offered the pair some fermented beverage, which Bullit politely declined, and with a stare at Bullseye, the other seti did as well. Instead, they pulled out some of the stolen water from the captain's mess on the *Okubi*, and sat back into the surprisingly comfortable furniture, glad to rest their legs, which were weary from much walking.

"Thank you, Wairën," Bullit said, "for your help, and your hospitality. The community you have created in this place, it's... well... it's not like anything I've ever seen. Although, I have to ask... what exactly are you doing out here? Why are you dependent on army scraps and castoffs? Why aren't you among the rest of your people?"

"Ah, the queen's subjects will not allow it. They are hypocrites, to the last of them."

Bullseye leaned forward. "Vasu herself has exiled you here?" he asked.

"Not so much by her, but by all of her line. And not so much with words, but with her failure to speak them."

The two seti shook their heads, clearly failing to understand.

"The irony of the lyghtan people, is that they accept alien cultures with open arms. The ancient religion which rules us, that queen after queen uses to dictate the course of our society, is based upon the belief that we await a savior from another world. The one who will show us the Path, so it's said.

In the earliest texts, it is vaguely written that they will be wholly different from us, but goes no more specific than that as to what species it may be. So my kind accepts all aliens, and waits for the most dissimilar of people to come lead us. Yet they cannot tolerate even the slightest of differences in our own population. Whether the society I lead here, in the Heart... or the Kulani nomad tribes, shunned merely for their preference in dwelling on the surface, the lyghtan are intolerant to even the barest of nonconformity."

"So then, these people here..." Bullit started.

"All of us an oddity, all of us different in some way. Some in body, or mind. Some in belief or opinion. Some like me, the difference is physical, and visible. For others, it is inside, deeply hidden away. But all of us turned from the society that bore us. Well... not all of us anymore. A great many today are merely the offspring of the outcast of generations past, content to spend out their days in a community that is less fearful of including us. Yet all of this could be amended, if the endless line of queens made it so. If they took a moment from preaching acceptance to those from the stars, and instead preached acceptance to the least of our own. But they have always remained silent, sticking to the text. And Vasu has been no different."

"The great failure of religion," Bullseye offered, "is that, by its very nature, it is willfully ignorant. Its very existence is beholden to the convictions of yesteryear, scribbled in tomes, dusty and dated. Refusing to learn from the present for fear of contradicting its own past. I dare say, any person who were to behave in such a way, would be labeled as irredeemably foolish."

Wairën laughed out loud.

"To accept the new, and reinterpret the old, is to change," Bullseye continued. "For religion to change, is for religion to die, and become something new. And people seldom rush to change their old religions for new."

"No, that is true. They clutch tight to them, sometimes for eons."

"Perhaps it is time, then, for you yourself to reinterpret it."

"What do you mean?" Wairën asked.

"Your most ancient texts speak of a leader from an outside world, one wholly different from the lyghtan."

"Yes."

"To the rest of Capella, all you keep alive here is an outside world. And I can think of nothing more wholly different than white is to black. Perhaps it is *you* the ancient ones spoke of, and not some alien salvation from the stars."

"Ha! An amusing thought, my new seti friend," Warren said. "But your very premise is mistaken. The difference between black and white is merely an illusion of your vision. The two only remain dissimilar, until you close your eyes."

"Hmm. And so here a truth taught by you, is now a truth learned by me. You see, already you begin to disseminate your gospel. I sense there is plenty deeper within you that differs from your kin, so I thereby claim my supposition still holds."

Wairën looked at him for a long moment, finally nodding his head. "I like you," he said. "And you might just have something there. Although, I'm not so egotistical that I believe the ancients spent decades chiseling on stone tablets merely to write about *me*. But I certainly could be perhaps more... proactive, rather than simply creating a more comfortable place for us to hide." Wairën stood then, and went to refill his decanter, pouring the drink from a still made of discarded copper pipes and old cooking pots. "But for now, let's start with you, and how I can be of help. Tell me, what is it exactly you seek to learn about the chamai? After all, you can learn a lot about a people by the contents of their trash."

Bullit perked up, hopeful the albino's optimism was well placed. "We... well... we're at a bit of a dead end. We don't know who else the general is conspiring with, who he has working for him. We believe that he is operating outside the purview of his Prime Minister, but he must be getting support from somewhere. But without knowing who, we don't know where to go next."

Wairën looked back and beamed a wide, knowing smile. "Well, it just so happens that I can help you with that," he said, turning to march towards the room's corner, and rummage through a neatly stacked debris pile. "Recently, the packaging from a new vendor has been showing up in the scrapyard, for a month or more now. We have collected quite a bit of it. Medium-sized crates, all of them lined with zegrite and deplaitium."

"A coating designed to inhibit scanning," Bullit said.

"Yes," Wairën acknowledged, as he continued to rifle the pile. "And very useful to my people, to hide the entrances to our little city from..."

"Intruders such as us?" Bullseye asked. "This explains our poor fortune in searching for shelter."

Wairën peered back at him over his shoulder, grinning apologetically. Then he turned back to the growing disarray he was causing.

"Yet, scanner blocking coatings are unlikely novel in military shipments," Bullseye noted.

"Perhaps," Wairën answered. "But the *sender* of these shipments certainly is." He found what he was searching for, and pulled it forth from the pile. A rigid propylene container lid, roughly two feet by three in size, and stamped with a blue and red logo on the front of its brightly garish yellow top. He tossed it over the fire and across the room like a frisbee, where it skittered across the floor, and came to rest in front of the feet of the two setis. It read *'Great~1~Toys'*, written in Coalition common, the wording arced around the cartoon image of alphabet blocks, and a rubber ball with a star on it.

Bullit leaned over in his chair and picked up the container cover. "Toys?" he asked. "This has been coming into the army base? For a month?"

"Maybe more," Wairën said.

"How many?"

"Dozens. Perhaps a hundred. I would have to talk to our community inventory chief to know for sure."

"Temper your expectations, Bullit," Bullseye told his fellow seti. "True, this find is interesting, but nothing more beyond that. No validation for suspicion lies within it, beyond the curiosity of some peculiar packaging. It may be that a great many sensitive cargoes are secreted as such."

"Really," Bullit countered, "did you notice the location of the factory?" He pointed to the address printed in small writing beneath the logo. 175th Sector, Gel Gonahaar. A dirty and disreputable industrial district, that the two had visited together, only once before—fourteen years ago.

Bullseye looked at him. "I admit, it feels as though such a coincidence adds credence to suspicions. But we must remember that almost *all* such factories reside on Gel Gonahaar, thus it is hardly likely that it could have ever read anything different."

Bullit continued to silently stare at him, finger pointing to the address.

"Believing with all certainty you know the path to success, is a sure path to failure."

The finger remained, pointing harder.

"Nonetheless," Bullseye finally sighed in resignation, "for this current moment at least, it represents our first best probability of uncovering more of this puzzle's pieces. *Unless* sounder information supplants it," he emphasized, "we shall investigate after we and our companions are reunited."

Bullit slapped him on the knee. "Good call, Mon Capitan. Now we know *where* to start looking, if only we had a *who* to look for."

Wairën tilted his head in confusion as he returned to his chair. "I thought the orchestrater of this... scheme... of yours, you said he was someone with whom you had a long history."

"True," Bullseye answered, "though it presents us a paradox. Our rival bears the name, and the manner, and the stratagems, of a foe long ago defeated. A foe long ago lain dead. Short of accepting he somehow... re-entwined in his mortal coil... the likelihood becomes that another walks in his stead."

A pair of lyghtan villagers, man and woman, entered by the makeshift doorway, bearing trays of food carried upon recycled barrel tops, and passed out bowls of steaming brown stew and charred flatbread to the three of them. Bullit realized that this dinner likely consisted of discarded army refuse, but his hunger from three days of rationed largnuts and kimiri candy left him caring very little about how the ingredients had been sourced. He dipped the bread, and dove into the stew with relish.

Wairën talked to them with his mouth full as the three gratefully ate, the pale lyghtan's skin glowing almost amber, reflecting the dancing light of the fire. "So, someone new has taken up the mantle of this man you once knew."

"So it would seem," Bullseye agreed.

"Going by the name of Denali," Bullit added.

"Well, there must be a reason then. A reason he's chosen this name. Just as there's a reason that we three have chosen ours. Wairën, phantom of the black desert," he said, pointing to himself. "Bullit, who's quick with the trigger. And of course, Bullseye... the one who does not miss."

"I also don't miss," Bullit reported. "I just don't brag as much."

"But your foe," Wairën continued, "he's chosen the title of another. In my experience, there are only two reasons to take on another man's name... to honor him, or to steal from him. Determine which it is, and you will gain insight into your enemy."

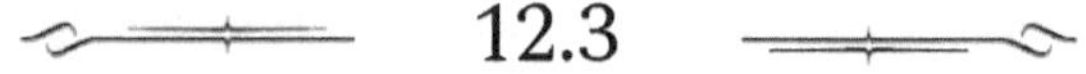

12.3

The spoken language of the seti people is astonishing in its sheer complexity. Not only is it full of unparalleled subtleties of syntax and grammar that would bewilder even the most devoted student, but it's vocabulary is so extensive, the speech itself so full of metaphor and poetic turn of phrase, that only those born and raised to it could ever fully master its intricacies. Compounded upon this, the fact that the unique laryngeal anatomy of the species allows them to add to the normal vocal range a myriad of throaty purrs and rumbling growls, nasal clicks and deep diaphragmatic thrumming, sounds that no other organic species could ever properly reproduce. A foreign scholar might study for decades, mastering the seti language in its written form, and thrilling to the sound of it with full understanding and appreciation, yet never physically be able to utter a single sentence of it. And herein was the basis for the seti custom of taking a code name—a label, or alias—sometimes a word with deep meaning behind it, sometimes simply a pseudonym that was found appealing. For with the exception of the androids, no one from another species could ever speak their true birth name correctly.

Rook's longtime loving bride went by the name of Belladonna. Though she currently found happiness as a contented wife and mother, at the time of their meeting, she had been something a little more—a Starlaw covert agent, and a formidable assassin. The seti woman had perhaps the most apropos pseudonym of her kind. Borrowed from the common moniker of a flowering Earth plant, it translated as 'beautiful woman'—a description that certainly applied. But the shrub was also known more informally as the foreboding sounding 'deadly nightshade'. It bore bell-shaped flowers of pure purple beauty in its late summer bloom, but as petals fell to autumn's chill, ripened berries were revealed—small satin orbs of deep, inky black. Toxins within the berries made them an aggressively lethal poison. Yet, if properly extracted, they created a life-saving medication.

Belladonna herself was all of these things, too.

Black and beautiful.

Deadly, yet beneficial.

This is what Captain Lobo thought as she watched the graceful seti woman stride purposefully toward herself and Commander Abara, who stood side by side in their uniform dress, waiting to greet her at the other end of the shuttle bay. To each side, and slightly behind, marching along at Belladonna's shoulders, her two children accompanied her, both with the same steely glare and clenched jaw that their mother had likely patented. The boy, Flashpoint, was a softer version of his father. Almost a similar marmalade color to Rook, though perhaps leaning a little browner, and with his dad's same dark, symmetrical stripe markings—yet with the gentler features of his mother. He had the same blazing green eyes as both of his parents, and his walnut-colored mane was cut short, in a tousled, youthful style. Daughter Relic, on the other hand, defied any family resemblance, other than the fact she was equally striking as her mother. Her fur was a short coat in a myriad of dappled colors, her face one third snow white, a third dusky black, and the remainder somewhere between hues of tangerine and apricot. The Earth-born seti girl was garbed in a traditional, hooded salwar kameez, one more typical of her ancestral homeworld, but her hazel eyes and maroon-dyed mane were still easily visible from beneath it.

Trailing beyond them, some distance behind the threesome, followed a big polar bear of a seti. Large and broad-chested, with fur and mane like fresh snowfall—as wide and as white as a sail in the moonlight. Zvavi, the Flight Deck Chief of *Parliament One*, and its undisputed best pilot. Captain Lobo had charged him with retrieving the precious cargo of Rook's family, but it seemed he had been browbeaten by their employer's worried wife into the demoted role of a porter, struggling to keep up while juggling multiple parcels of the family's luggage.

Lobo snapped her fingers at one of the support staff in the hangar bay, calling them forward, then pointing them towards Zvavi. "Scramble those packages," she directed, "get them up to our guests' quarters."

The luggage was gratefully taken away from the overburdened seti, who stood and saluted his Captain, his mismatched eyes, blue and green, rolling in exasperation behind the family. Lobo gave a wink as she saluted back, and Zvavi hurried off to return to the safety of his shuttle bay.

"Welcome aboard, Madam Belladonna," Lobo extended the greeting as the trio reached her. Then she turned to march alongside the woman, who apparently had no intention of stopping to chat.

"Captain," Rook's wife acknowledged back with a single word. Then a half breath later, "What's our status report?"

"Still just as I told you earlier. We received a code black, with no supporting explanation. We have prepared the guest suites on C deck for…"

"Have my son and daughter brought there. I will be staying on *B deck*, in my husband's stateroom."

"I… uh… yes. Of course. We will give you a chance to settle, and then brief you in an hour or…"

"Brief me now, while we're walking. First of all, do we know a location?"

"I… yes," the lacertilian captain answered, rushing to keep stride. "We received a second signal, from the northern hemisphere of Capella, in The Burnt Empty."

Belladonna turned to Commander Abara. "Commander, I don't need both of you here to brief me. You're dismissed. You have the coordinates. Head to the bridge and get us underway for Capella."

"Uhhh," the commander floundered, looking at his captain.

Lobo nodded at him. "Go ahead Bronte, you have the bridge. Make way, best possible speed."

Commander Abara continued hurrying off down the hall, while Captain Lobo and Rook's family stepped aboard a midship elevator.

"Deck C," Lobo said. The lift began moving in response.

"Do we have any idea if the whole team is still together?" Belladonna asked.

"Negative, ma'am, though it is likely they are separated. On our last close approach, we finally detected a signal from the *Bugeye*, showing it still in orbit around Oberonn. But it could have been abandoned there, left on automatic. We do not know how they got to Capella."

The lift stopped on the guest deck, and Flashpoint and Relic took their leave, heading for their quarters. Lobo placed her blue-scaled thumb with its blunted claw into the print scanner, and ordered the elevator to continue to the restricted B deck.

"How long of a detour would it be to get within communications range of Oberonn," Belladonna asked, "on route to Capella."

"Just the edge of communications range? Four hours, maybe five. But turnaround time for even subspace transmissions would have a significant delay at that distance."

"Do it. We'll swing by and see if anybody's home, see if we can find out a little more about what happened, and what we're walking into."

"Understood," Captain Lobo answered, remaining behind as Belladonna stepped off the lift onto Parliament's secure floor.

The seti turned back and addressed Lobo through the open doors, "Madam Captain, you will excuse me if I am being a bit... bullish, and demanding with you... or your crew. I have every confidence in your abilities. There is no one else I would rather have in charge here. But you understand that I'm worried for my husband... and for my friends."

"Of course, Madam Belladonna, don't give it a second thought. You have enough on your mind right now without concerning yourself with my... possibly fragile ego. Which, incidentally, it is not fragile in the slightest. However, I would ask that any demand you have of my crew, go through me. It's important not to create confusion in the chain of command."

"Agreed," Belladonna said. "And, if you wouldn't mind, when it's convenient, send the same concession to the pilot that brought us here. Chief Zvavi, is it? I'm afraid he bore the brunt of the earliest stage of all our anxiety. He's a fine pilot."

"The best there is," the captain answered. "I'll make sure to send him your regards. And ma'am," Lobo added, "just for the record, I'm worried about them too."

Belladonna smiled, saluting the lacertilian as the lift doors slid closed.

12.4

ALTHOUGH THE NUMBER OF FORESTED planets in the galaxy—some that harbor animal life, and many that don't—were in plentiful abundance, not all of these plant-covered worlds sported flora that use green chlorophyll for their energy production. The type of star that they orbit, and the makeup of their atmosphere, both could influence the evolution of other compounds to be utilized. And different compounds, meant different colors. Whether it was the dense jungle of bright-pink foliage that covered the equatorial ring of Bruna Buru, or the multicolored rainbow forests of the seti homeworld's sister planet, K'Tas So'Ka, with its paint-splatter forests of yellow, purple, red, and orange—any color *except* for green. In fact, on many worlds that had developed plant life, most notably the metamorph home planet of Ilshnar, the leaves were all of an absolute pitch black, being the color most suitable for efficiently absorbing the most light. No energy is wasted when no color's wavelength is reflected away. But while green leaves were perhaps a rarity in general, Oberonn was certainly one place to find them in abundance, and the verdancy of its foliage was deeper and richer than any other, even the lush woodlands of Earth.

Lady Opal stared upward at the sweeping canopy of it above her as she toured the nearby wilds of the surrounding forest with James, mesmerized by the exotic hue that was so overflowing here, yet so near nonexistent back on her homeworld. Tachion watched the two of them strolling together in the dappled morning sun, from an inconspicuous distance—seeing the lyghtan priestess trip on a woody tree root while her gaze was distracted upwards, awestricken, and Stansky grabbing her bare, slender arm to steady her with the lightning reflexes of his powerful hand.

"Goodness, thank you," she told him. "That would have been a nasty spill. I'm just so overwhelmed by the perfect wonder of it. It's like... living inside a jewel."

"I know," James said, as he gazed down at her smile of enjoyment, still gently resting his hand upon her arm. "Of all of the colors, it's my absolute favorite."

"But you're not even looking at it," she said, peering up at him.

"Of course I am," he told her. "It's the same emerald sparkle behind the fire of your eyes."

Tachion nodded to himself in approval, though he imagined gags and retching from Rook and Bullit, and moved off to leave them be. The pair seemed to have gotten along right from the moment they pulled her from the mountain, an association that the doctor encouraged, simply by staying far out of the way. He didn't feel manipulative about it, as the two genuinely seemed to enjoy each other's company, and the friendship was growing naturally without any outside influence from him. But secretly he hoped that any connection between them might in some way prove useful. He considered it a win-win. Well, except maybe for Tatiana.

The first ashi'mar of Capella had spun for them her story, in greatest detail. From the rise of Denali's influence in the temple, and his corrupting of Vasu, right up to the moment she made her escape through Oberonn's mountain caves. The murders of the other ashi'mar, the powers Denali possessed, and the fact he could apparently bestow some few of them to others. The collusion with General Nylis and his fleet in exchange for a promise of power, the discussions with Vasu over their joint ruling of the galaxy. The strange bracelets that glowed with yellow light, and that amped Denali's ensensement abilities a hundredfold. The human's dark obsession with Parliament, and Rook in particular. Tachion was not sure which part of this last bit he found to be the most disturbing; that this man who went by Denali seemed so confident of Rook's eventual allegiance, or the fact that, from Opal's description of his history, it was entirely possible he could get it. The doctor wondered what he would do if Rook was now turned and lost to them. He didn't have to think long. It was a decision he had made, and a possibility he had prepared for, since the moment he allowed the clone of his friend to take its first breath. Hmm—*its* first breath, Tachion realized he'd just thought. *Its*—not *his*. Perhaps he was already closing himself off to his friend's identity, just in case the worst of all possibilities were to come true.

Tachion and Stansky had decided to stay here on Oberonn, really out of a lack of knowing where the hell else to go. The *Bugeye* had received a copy of the code black signal sent by their two wayward friends, so they knew that the *P1* would no longer be at the rendezvous point, but on its way to Earth to collect Belladonna—as was the plan for that code. But that trip would take weeks at the top speed of the old *Bugeye*, so they had no choice but to wait patiently for Captain Lobo to come get them. They were both relieved, and concerned, that the code black had been sent, as it meant Bullit and Bullseye were still alive and free, but either in danger—or had bad news about Rook. Tachion was eager to have them all together once again. This was gonna be one hell of a debrief.

The doctor stood on the bank of a wide spot in the nearby river, a potbelly on the otherwise slim and meandering waterway, that allowed an ample and glittering pond to form in a shallow depression amongst the trees. He noticed his two companions leisurely approaching, as they circled the bank from the far side of the reservoir, James carefully guiding Lady Opal across a fallen tree trunk to cross the river back to the near shore. His tanned and muscular forearm seemed almost pale against her ebony skin, and the voluminous waves of her milky-white hair billowed against his face in the wind as he escorted her across. While the android made no attempt to hide and spy on them surreptitiously, he did remain perfectly motionless where he stood, in hopes they might not notice his presence.

"I have never before seen so much open water like this," Tachion heard Opal say. "On my world, we pump it up from huge underground aquifers. It's not as scarce as it was in the days of my ancestors, thanks to modern technology, but it is still valuable. I have only seen it flowing openly like this, free to all, in pictures."

"You know," James responded, "ironically, on *my* homeworld... we're running out of sand."

She smiled. "Perhaps we can arrange a trade."

"So, you've never been near another world's oceans or rivers before?" Stansky asked.

"I've never been on another world at all, before now. This is my first time ever leaving my own planet."

"How is that possible? You're the ranking second in leadership to your people. Don't you have, I don't know, diplomatic visits and the like to make?"

"As first ashi'mar, yes... now I do. But it was only a short time ago that I was fourth ashi'mar. My duties then were much more limited."

"I see."

"And, Queen Vasu, after she... changed... she curtailed most of those appearances. Or went, but made do without me. I feel she was trying to keep me in the dark. But I was told Lord Denali requested me on this visit. I don't know why. I never saw him." Opal paused her walking and put her hand to her forehead like a visor, gazing towards the blazing sun. Her attention had been pulled back by the beauty of the rippling waters, reflecting the solar brilliance into a million tiny, scattered diamonds. "I have spent all the years of my life in deep study, as is the duty of an ashi'mar. I know every detail and intricacy of each political system in the known galaxy. I know all about each planet's geography, and their culture, and their chief imports and exports. I have dedicated my life to the knowledge that will one day make me a worthy queen, and I will continue to do so. But I have never so much as laid eyes upon a pool of water even half the size of this... relatively muddy little puddle," she chuckled. "Back on Capella, this pond would be guarded by an elite squadron, day and night."

James laughed. "Don't tell that to Bullit when you meet him. He'll have us out draining oceans to sell to you."

Opal tilted her head then, considering, "Do you think it's safe to swim in?"

"Uhhh... I don't know. Do you even know how to swim?"

"How hard can it be, if I don't go too deep?"

"Said as the last words of the drowning ashi'mar," James cautioned. He looked around and saw Tachion not far away, and headed in his direction. "Let me go ask Tach, he's the expert on these things. And who knows what's in this water. I mean, there's these horrible, frog-sounding, peep-peep creatures out here. You don't even want me to tell you about them."

The unmistakable sound of a vigorous splash behind him stopped him in his tracks, and he spun around in time to see the glorious sable backside of Lady Opal submerge beneath the ripples. Her inertia jumpsuit dangled empty from a copse of prickled shrubbery, and her shoes rested beneath it, filled with a crumpled ball of what James assumed to be her undergarments. He continued slowly walking the rest of the way toward the doctor, but with his head facing backward like he had the neck of an owl. "Jesus Christ, Doc. What do you make of that? Not exactly shy, is she?"

"The lyghtan people are a... sexually liberated species. They don't have the same hang-ups about the exposed body as do some other cultures."

"Well, shit. How did I not know that?" the human wondered. "Say, is that water safe? I mean... there's nothin' creeping around down there, is there?"

Tachion pulled out his techkit and selected a scanner, then aimed it at the pond a few moments while it whistled and beeped. "No, she should be safe. There's a couple of biting... well, not exactly fish, but I'll call them that. But they tend to be skittish, so they should leave her alone."

Opal screamed out in a peal that caused Stansky's hand to race to his sidearm, but the sight of her wide smile as she raced around neck deep and splashing, immediately showed that they were shrieks of joy, and not the result of something eating her toes.

He relaxed. "So... opinions, old friend?" James asked. "What'd ya think we should do with her?"

The android pretended to think about it a moment or two. "I think...
it's probably best if we keep her with us. We can keep her safe from Vasu,
and she may be our only key to figuring out what's going on."

"Well, she's already told us everything she knows."

"Perhaps," said Tachion, sounding not completely convinced.

"You realize," said Stansky, "she's like the vice president, a royal
princess, and the archbishop, all rolled into one. That's a lot of unwanted
attention walking around in that... that..." He looked back at her bathing,
seeing her walk up out of the water to her knees, glistening in dew-dropped
nakedness, then extend her arms, and fall backward into the pond with
glee. "...that *unbelievably* tight little body," he finished.

"Yes, you're right, of course. They're certain to have put a price on her
capture." Tachion peered behind them. "And the first place they'll look is
the woodlands around the base of that mountain." He thought for a
moment. "We'll have to get out of here, sooner rather than later. Maybe we
can send a transmission to the *Parliament One*, see if Belladonna has any
old safe houses out this way she knows of. We can't keep wandering around
with someone as well-known as her. I mean, even *you* recognized her."

Stansky didn't pick up on the slight, as his attention was on the
aquatic activities. "Goddamn, are you seeing this?" he asked. "I mean just
look at those..." He turned to face the doctor and stopped. "Oh, yeah, I
forgot. You are... *you.*"

"What does that mean?"

"No offense, Tach. You just don't have the same... appreciation... for
the nude female form."

"Nonsense. I find beauty in it, as the natural wonder that it is. The
same beauty I would find in the nude musculature of an Earthan horse, or
in the colors of a herd of jasiri from K'Tas T'Mir, or the grace of the
Capellan dust hawk. However, I can find beauty in these things without the
additional desire to gyrate my body against them, or rub them with my
tongue."

"You don't have a tongue."

"Thank goodness for that."

"Look, I'm not trying to lick some musky old jasiri, either. But, when
it comes to a woman like that one down there, well... let's just say you don't
know what you're missing."

"I'll just have to imagine."

Later, towards evening, as sunset was being slowly obscured by an
approaching train of storm clouds, tracking in from the more humid
southern climes, the doctor's two fellow castaways had swapped their
previous places with each other. Opal now stood by Tachion's side at the

entrance to the collapsing warehouse, the lyghtan and android watching James in the distance, as he struggled to cut down a tangled mass of branches meant to help cover up the *Bugeye*. A procedure that was quite unnecessary, and thoroughly unhelpful, as the thin layer of twigs would do little to nothing to hide the large craft from any scanners. It did give the human an excuse to sweat and flex before the ashi'mar with his shirt off, however, and Opal seemed as entranced in watching his hardened and chiseled form work, as he had been in watching her softer, more delicate one back at the swimming pond. Tachion found the whole procedure to be utterly fascinating.

Stansky yanked and pulled on a fan of branches that seemed unwilling to leave its mother tree, despite the fact it had been completely severed from it. He struggled and strained, unsure of where the snag was, and shouted his frustration with his usual exclamation.

"James must be a deeply religious man," Opal stated.

"I... beg your pardon?" Tachion asked.

"He cries out to his God in prayer so often, this Jesus Christ he calls to. I have studied him... in a cursory fashion. James must be quite pious to seek strength and support in his deity like this. I dare say he prays to him more than I do to my Holy Passel of the Originators... and here I am, nearly the figurehead of my whole religion."

Had Tachion been of any species other than android, his amusement with the proposition would have surely betrayed itself in uncontrolled laughter. As it was, he was able to contain the hilarity of it on the inside, his mechanical anatomy having no such involuntary imperative to grin or chortle. He pondered the question for less than a second, deciding to switch from his policy on noninterference, to one of gentle manipulation. He saw opportunity here—for what, he did not know. Perhaps just paving the way now for a potential plan B somewhere down the road. Having a friend like Lady Opal, or possibly *more* than a friend, could certainly one day come in handy.

"Yes," Tachion said in all seriousness, leaning hard on his long-ago studies of bluff and dramatics. "He is a man of deep conviction. I don't know if I have ever known anyone more devout in their dedication than James Stansky." The doctor was pleased with himself for that response, having kept it pretty vague—not really any glaring lies there. Or, if so, not a *real* lie. Merely one of omission. The doctor had just neglected to point out that Stansky's dedications lie towards pretty women, fast cars, and blowing things up. But, for those three pursuits, there was no man more stalwart in his devotion.

"This deity whose name he cries, it is an aspect of his God, made man on Earth, is it not?"

"It is," Tachion answered. Still no lie there.

"We have a similar legend, passed down from time immemorial. Our book tells us we await the physical embodiment of The Path made flesh, manifested in The One who will come forth from another world. My queen believes that it is this Lord Denali."

"It isn't."

"I agree," she told him. "And I have for some time. I regret, I should have done something earlier to protect my world... and my people."

"If you had, it would have been *you* laying slain in your bed, or tossed into an abandoned chasm, or chewed to bits by the blades of a harvester. Then neither James nor I would have had the pleasure of your acquaintance."

Lady Opal smiled up to the android towering above her, then focused her attention back on James heading toward them, dragging a ponderous forest of brush behind him. "Tell me," she said musingly, "does his religion prohibit pleasures of the flesh?"

Just then, a cry of electronic beeping sang out from the crumbling warehouse behind them, a notification of a subspace transmission coming into the *Bugeye*. James looked up at Tachion, then dropped his bundled load and hurried over, the three of them scampering aboard the craft just as the first few fat droplets of rain began to spatter against the greenery around them. James wiped his perspiration-drenched face and body quickly with the crumpled t-shirt that had been tied around his waist. Then he pulled the damp shirt on over his head anyway, settling in at Bullseye's usual seat at tactical/communications, and began running the decryption algorithm on the message.

They had sent the entire video of Opal's testimony to the *P1* and Belladonna, along with an abbreviated report, in hopes that, as well as updating her on the situation in general, it may alleviate her anxiety to know that Rook was seen alive just recently, and allegedly not in physical danger. Killing her husband was not Denali's plan. They had also shown Opal multiple pictures of the Denali they once knew, a decade and a half ago, including archived video of the crime lord's last moments from some of their helmet cams. She had confirmed what they both suspected, that it was not the same Lord Denali that she knows from today. One strange and terrifying possibility eliminated, at least. They had also sent the ex-Starlaw agent a request for advice—if she knew where they might look for information, and how they might hide the wanted ashi'mar while they did so.

The video message Belladonna returned to them showed her sitting at the Parliament conference table, her two children leaving the room and closing the door in the background before she began to speak.

"Pssh. Make yourselves at home," Stansky complained to the video screen. "I thought that deck was off limits."

"Are you gonna tell her that?" Tachion asked.

"And what the hell are their kids doing there? It's a code black, not a family vacation."

"Her children are plenty old enough to help out, and they're both graduates of prestigious merc schools. In fact, they're a lot older and more well trained than we were when we started out."

"Please. They're trained, but totally untested. They still have packing peanuts stuck to the armor they got for graduation."

"Shhh," Tachion hushed.

"*Hi James, Tachion, and if she's with you, greetings Blessed Madam Ashi'Mar,*" Belladonna said. "*Your transmission was perfectly timed. We had just diverted within communication range when we received it, and so fortunately I can send you a timely answer. In a few hours anyway, by the time you get this. Firstly, the signal from my cousin and Bullseye. The last transmission was from within 'The Burnt Empty' desert of Capella. It came from relatively near a joint military base there, so I am guessing that is where they somehow got off.*"

Opal perked up. "Queen Vasu and General Nylis have discussed that installation in the past. The urgency of certain shipments to be sent there. A timetable to adhere to."

"What kind of shipments?" Tachion asked.

Opal shook her head. "I do not know, the discussion was brief, and barely overheard," she said. "I hope your friends will be all right till help gets there. The wastes of Nol Qhan can be most... unforgiving."

"*Second,*" Rook's wife continued as they un-paused the video, "*as far as where to fish out more information about that mountain complex... well, I've been outta the game a long time, and my informants have long dried up, I'm afraid. But you said there was some sort of militia there? Rogue chamai and lyghtan army elements, perhaps, loyal to Nylis and Vasu? And mercenaries used to play the part of the so-called 'terrorists'? Well, rogue or not, an army is an army, and if there's one thing I've learned, it's that the average grunt soldier loves to talk and brag. Give 'em a few drinks, and their mouth gets even bigger. Put a beautiful woman in front of them, or even a passable one... well... you can barely get them to shut up. The nearest city to you is Krataar, a major hub for shipping and trade, and all the undesirable elements that sort of industry attracts. I would suggest you scout it out, find their version of a red-light district. They're certain to have one. A brothel,*" *or perhaps a strip bar. If anyone has had contact with these troops of yours, it undoubtedly would be working girls."*

"There is a place I know of," Stansky said, "that caters to seti. Or, actually... more to those non-seti species that happen to have a preference for... fur. It's in the freight district, called The Cat's Meow."

"Yes," Tachion said. "I recall now. We were there... *years* ago, on some mission or another. I'm surprised you remembered."

"Ehh... I might have been there a bit more recently," Stansky mumbled.

"What's a cat?" Opal asked, unaffected by James' comment.

Tachion answered. "A small domesticated Earth pet, that bears a resemblance to a seti."

"Well, then that institution's business name sounds... simply offensive," she decided.

"Now as far as hiding your royal asset," Belladonna went on, *"my suggestion would be just to keep her off the streets."*

"No," Opal said.

"Find an empty warehouse, there's sure to be one open. Some loading dock manager waiting on a haul of freight to come in, staring at their cargo bays laying empty and unpaid for in the meantime. Pay them off, off the books, and hide the Bugeye inside. And then leave her there in it."

"I refuse," the ashi'mar protested.

"Whatever you do, don't let her out and about with you unless you have to. I looked into it, and there are already rumblings of bounty squads and trackers on her trail."

"Who is this woman, to dictate my comings and goings!" Lady Opal huffed. "There is no one more invested in getting to the root of this situation than myself. I will not be left behind, shelved in some... storage locker, like so many crates of canned tamis loaf!"

James placed his hand upon hers, and gently shook his head in agreement with her, immediately allaying her fears of being left waiting behind. He didn't remove his hand.

"If you can't find a hiding spot like that, then the only choice is to camouflage her. I do know there used to be a bio-concealment master in Krataar, one of the best in the business. His true name is Kaii Kealiun, though he generally just goes by the alias 'Guisemage', and unfortunately, he is near impossible to find. Since he knows the new faces of so many wanted people, he has to stay hidden himself. He'd be a treasure trove for any bounty hunter that got their hands on him. The only way to reach him is through one of his trusted agents. Luckily for you, I still know one."

"Jesus Christ," Stansky said, "is somebody writing all this down?"

"You'll find her in the open market bazaar, on the south end of the city. A lyghtan by the name of Selene Maraspese."

"This does not sound like a lyghtan name," Opal said.

"No," Tachion agreed. "It sounds human."

As if in answer to their comments, *"Be careful around this one, she's a bit of an enigma. She's a shade, raised by humans, but on the chamai homeworld. Therefore, she has both many loyalties, and no loyalties in particular, which add together to make her dangerous. When I first met her, she was Coalition Army. Special forces. The Obsidian Guard, no less. But she took all the training they could instill in her, and then left to do her own thing. And to be honest, I don't even know what exactly that thing is. But last I heard of Selene, she was at the bazaar. Look for the contortionist that performs there. Tell her I sent you, and use her old code name... Juniper."*

"Holy hell," James complained towards Opal. "So, find a warehouse, to hide the *Bugeye*, to search the bazaar, to find the contortionist, to seek the Guisemage, to get you a new face. And all just for a day or two? Yikes! Are you sure you just don't wanna wait in the storage locker?"

Opal threw James' hand off of her own, then frowned at him intently, the illumination in her eyes flaring like a glass of brandy tossed on a fire.

"Alright, okay, off to the bazaar it is. But, in the morning, I guess... obviously." He looked out the window at the torrential downpour coming on strong now, and the darkness of night that was falling beyond it.

The ashi'mar rushed forward to the cockpit, and gazed skyward through the windscreen. The deluge from above bathed the glass in a sheet of distorted visibility, punctuated by the impact points of a thousand splattered raindrops, and the percussive drumline chorus that accompanied them. "Simply amazing," she muttered under her breath. Then after a moment, while still facing towards the window, she said more loudly, "I cannot thank you enough, both of you, for all that you've done for me... for all you've pledged to do for me. After the past few years, it is hard for me to know who to trust, and I confess, I did not at first fully trust you. I see now that you are good men. I see now that I can give that trust." She paused. "I have not been fully honest with you, not a hundred percent. There is one thing I've hidden from you, that I feel is only fair to reveal now."

James and the doctor looked at each other, then back to her. She turned away from the shimmering window then, back around to face them. In her extended hands she held forth a small, circular loop—frosted translucent, with some vague shapes of circuitry barely visible inside. A thick molded bracelet, of the kind she had described to them.

"Is that..." Stansky asked.

"May I see it?" Tachion requested.

She came over and passed the device to the android's large awaiting hand, and he turned it over in his fingers, holding it up to the light.

"It has a micro jet-injector head on the inside, and these look like neural cathodes." He shook the device, which made the slightest tinkle of splashing liquid. "There's a chemical, or a serum inside."

"How did you get it?" Stansky asked her.

"I took it on my way out, from Queen Vasu's belongings. She had swapped it out shortly before, in favor of a new one. I believe she thought that this was nearly empty of the... serum, or whatever it contains. She was on her way to meet Denali. I think she just didn't want to be... unequipped."

"I can scan it down here," Tachion said, "to see what it's made of, and how it's built. But in order to see how it works and what it does, I will need my more advanced lab aboard *Parliament One*." He handed the bracelet over to James, who did the same cursory examination of spinning it beneath the light that the doctor had done. "We had better keep this safe," Tachion added, "and locked up tight until we're off this planet. If Vasu knows this is missing, she'll have even more incentive to hunt us down."

Stansky stood and approached the equipment locker, and pulled out an empty three-port scrambler.

"Mmm... let's not do that, James. We don't know if dematerializing and digitizing the device might alter the chemical within it. Remember that seti lager you tried to scramble last summer?"

"Eww, yech," Stansky said, his lip involuntarily curling up in disgust. He instead slid the small bracelet inside an empty micro-missile clip from one of his armor's shoulder launchers. Then he placed that clip inside a boot, covered it with a rolled-up inertia balaclava from under his helmet, and secured the whole thing inside his locker with a thumbprint.

"I am sorry," Opal said, "for hiding it from you. For putting you in danger."

"Ridiculous," James said, moving near to her. "You would have been foolish to trust two perfect strangers after what you've been through. You made the right choice then, and you made the right choice again now."

She smiled up at him, lightly resting her fingertips atop his forearm. "Well," she said, "it's been a long day, and an even longer one tomorrow might be in store. If you will excuse me, I'll take my leave for the evening." She gave a smile to the doctor as well as she headed towards the aft firewall, then pulled the curtain around Tachion's biobed where she had been set up to sleep the night before.

James gnashed his teeth slightly, and vigorously shook his head to cast off a slew of inappropriate thoughts. Then he plopped down next to

Tachion, who was getting set to power down and defrag his memory matrix for the evening—his electronic equivalent to an organic being's sleep and dream cycles.

"You know," Stansky said, "there is a faster way to find out more about that funky bracelet. It's got a dose or three left in there. Why don't I just try it on and see what happens?"

"That would not exactly be the epitome of the scientific method," Tachion said. "In fact, it could be wildly dangerous. We have no idea what it would do to you, how that serum might affect your body."

"What's it gonna do, kill me? We both know that ship has sailed. I'm on a short timer here Doc, I can almost hear it ticking down. Might as well be of some use now, before I'm... *completely* useless."

"Don't be an idiot, you've got several good years left on your timer. More, if I have anything to say about it. How are your symptoms, by the way? Are you having any tremors at all?"

"No, that medication works good, though it doesn't last very long. I had just a little bit of cramping while I was taking down those branches earlier. I could use a booster in the morning for sure."

"Ah yes, the branches. What exactly was that all about?"

"Uh... exercise?"

"Mmm-hmm. An exercise in philandering, perhaps."

"You think it worked?"

"Can't you tell?"

"Well, she asked me some weird stuff earlier," Stansky said. "About religion, and my spiritual restrictions."

"Ah, well... she may be under the misapprehension that you are a devoutly religious man."

"She what?"

"And I may have said something to further that misapprehension."

"Like what?"

"Like, yes... he is a devoutly religious man. Or, words toward that effect."

James stared at him.

"I believe it is an asset to her, an additional merit in your favor."

"Ahhh, I see. Damn, Tach. Who knew you were such a good wingman!"

"I beg your pardon?"

"I could use someone in my corner like that, covering my back with the ladies. You know what I mean? You set 'em up, and I'll knock 'em down."

"Certainly not."

"Remind me to take you out with me more often, when we get outta this mess."

"That's a hard pass," Tachion said. "Now, why don't you try and get some sleep? You can lay across the fold-down seating again, or recline in the cockpit chair."

"Alright, old friend," James said, as he headed towards the first suggestion and began lowering the seats into a bench. "The royal lady is right, big day tomorrow." He laid his large frame across the narrow seat area, and flipped and flopped uncomfortably until he settled into a position on his left shoulder.

"A big day," Tachion agreed. "Do we both know what we're doing? Do you have any questions?"

"Yeah, just one," Stansky answered. "What in the hell is canned tamis loaf?"

12.5

THE STAGNANT VEIL OF THE breath-dampened hood still covered Rook's face as he was marched silently along, although this time, it didn't matter as much. He knew exactly where he was. The corridors from the teleporter he had walked down many times before, the familiar pattern of lefts and rights he had followed on many visits through the years. The recognizable tones of keypads and security locks that he himself had installed. He didn't need the guard's hand on his arm to point the way; he could have walked there all on his own—hood, or no hood.

He was finally directed through a door on the left, as he knew he would be, and forced aggressively to sit down in a cushioned armchair. Denali's lackey was getting a bit of an attitude, it seemed. Good, all the easier to provoke him. Rook sat back in the chair, crossed his legs, and slouched in a pose of calm relaxation and indifference. Fuck them. Fuck them both. He knew exactly where he was, he just had no idea why.

After a moment of silent waiting, he said, "So, did you wanna talk about something, or are you just gonna sit there breathing through your mouth?"

Silence.

"I know you're there. I can smell the brimstone."

"I'm no devil," Denali's voice said from a few feet away—right where Rook knew it would be.

"No dum-dum, you've got your bible wrong. Fire and brimstone was an angry *God's* weapon of choice, not the devil's. Isn't that who you think you are, God or something?"

"Not at all. Just a... much more advanced state of man. You've got the angry part right, though. And I think I've had every right to be."

"At *who*, though? *Everybody*? The man who wronged you is long gone," Rook reminded him. Then, leaning forward, and removing the tone of acid from his voice, "Why didn't you just come back after you escaped? We would have helped you. We would have taken you in, to join us."

"You can't understand yet, but you will. That was *his* purpose, not mine. *His* pedestrian life. Why demean myself to take on the role of another, and one such as him no less, who could not even keep *himself* alive? I was created with a greater potential, with a greater purpose in store."

"Yeah, so you keep saying. But I'm not sure if you're trying to convince me, or yourself." Rook leaned back again, and re-crossed his legs. "I know you're having some kinda fucked up clone identity crisis or something, but..."

"Ha!" Denali barked. "The irony of that, coming from you!"

"Meaning what?"

"Soon," Denali said.

"Yeah, you keep saying that, too. And to be honest, I'm getting kinda bored. *Goddammit*, can we get this fuckin' hood off already?"

There was the sound of Denali snapping his fingers, followed by a blinding flash of light and rush of cool fresh air as the bag was jerked from around his face. Rook drew a deep, cleansing breath in through his nose, then blew it out slowly through pursed lips. What he already knew was now confirmed through his blinking, adjusting eyes. He was seated in Tachion's outer office, sitting before the huge glass desk, the shock of Dodger's face once again on this man calling himself Denali, sitting in the android doctor's oversized chair. Through the windows behind him, pinpoint lights were scattered through the darkness. Clearly, it was the middle of the night here on Rhyana.

Rook leaned his head backward, looking upside down at the bodyguard with the mandibled mask behind him. "Thanks, Pennyworth," Rook said, "that's much better. Remind me to tip you on the way out."

"His name is Drake," Denali corrected.

"Oh yeah? Good to know. Pass me my multicomm and I'll send him a friend request."

Denali arose from the massive iron seat, turning to stare out the window across the nightscape of the android city.

"What's wrong, chair too small for your superior backside? I imagine you'll want a real *giant* throne to sit and rule your 'evolved civilization'. What are you gonna do to keep busy, once everyone has already been forced to bow down to you?"

"You fear I'll be as Alexander, weeping for his lack of more lands to conquer? Unlikely. This is space! Endless. Infinite. The breadth of my domain will be hindered only by the walls of reality itself. I will never run out of worlds to gather into the fold."

Rook took a chance then. Standing from his chair, he started moving slowly around the opposite side of the desk, to join Denali at the window. Neither the guard nor Denali reacted, and Rook couldn't help but wonder why. Sure, this Drake dude behind him was fully armored and armed, but Denali wasn't. He just wore his not-particularly-fashionable leather Merlin robes, and basic pants with a tunic-looking thing beneath it. And Rook's hands weren't even tied. He could leap out and pop his tractor blades through his throat before the human could even blink twice. He would probably be instantly killed by beetle-face behind him, but—

Yet, neither seemed the least bit concerned.

"Look," the seti said, more quietly now, as if he was trying to make his comments private from the human's bodyguard, "I don't know exactly what happened to you, but I know you've had a tough go of it, a fucked-up life you didn't ask for or deserve. But why don't you come back with me, and we'll figure this out together. *All* of us. We'll get Tachion to work on it, and he'll find a solution to... to turn you back to normal."

"Normal!" Denali laughed. "Normal? What does that even mean, normal? Normal for who, you? The others? You don't even know how *abnormal* you yourself are. Normal is relative. Normal is an illusion. What is normal for the spider, is *chaos* for the fly."

Rook began to applaud him with an exaggerated slow clapping. "Oh, that's very good," he said. "Very sinister. I've got chills. How long have you been saving up *that* little nugget? I assume that we're all flies to you in this scenario, buzzing around and banging our heads against the glass. Where'd you get that twenty-five cents' worth of wisdom from, a fortune cookie?"

"Something I once read," Denali said more quietly, "but was it me, or was it *him*? A comic strip, I think, believe it or not. But that makes it no more less true, and appropriate to the moment."

Rook decided it was time. He was now only a mere few feet away, and the desk was between the two of them and Drake. It was now or never. This could be the only chance he'd ever get. He tensed his muscles to leap towards the human, and prepared to eject his three recently sharpened blades.

"This again?" Denali asked.

"Hmm?" Rook froze.

"You. You are planning your attack. I can sense it."

Drake took a step forward, but the human lifted a hand to stop him.

Rook relaxed. "I would say that I'm impressed," he said, "but you probably get people wanting to kill you quite a lot. So... not so much a psychic guess, as the law of averages."

"Go ahead, if you must. Might as well get it out of your system. It will be easier to move forward if you're not distracted by such nonsense." The human turned to face him, and put his hands on his hips. In doing so, he spread his cloak to expose a target from his neck to his navel, protected by only a shirt.

Rook looked at him a moment, then shrugged. His blades slid forth clean with a chorus of metallic scraping, like daggers pulled from their scabbards. He slowly brought the gleaming knife points to the top of Denali's collar line, and pressed the trio of spikes against the skin beneath his Adam's apple. Denali appeared unconcerned. Rook glanced over toward Drake, making sure he was still standing by the doorway, then before turning back, in order to surprise the human, jammed his fist forward with all of his might. His wrist folded under itself, and the trimithium blades flexed. It was like he had tried to force them into the side of a building. Rook looked back at Denali then, not so much as scratch visible on his skin, and noted a yellow illumination emanating from beneath his sleeve cuff.

"You're cheating," Rook said, pointing at the glowing bracelet.

"So are you," Denali replied, tapping the tip of the seti's tractor blades.

"Fair enough then, perhaps another time."

"Perhaps. But in the meantime, you suggested Tachion might find a solution to help me? Come, let me show you what kind of solutions your android friend typically relies upon."

Denali turned and approached the bookcase concealing the locked entrance to Tachion's personal lab. With the yellow glow from his wrist beaming even brighter, the human walked forward and stepped through the solid wall with no more effort than if it had been made of steam instead of steel. The door then slid open from the other side, and he bade the seti to come in.

"Neat trick," Rook told him, as he stepped into the hidden laboratory. "I'll have to get me one of those."

"Believe it or not," Denali told him, "that is the entire purpose of today."

Rook followed Denali across the cluttered lab, towards the large glass chamber tanks at the rear.

"Tell me," Denali said, "what do you know about the ensensement ability of time-sight?"

"I don't know... some hocus-pocus that a few mentalist humans can do, looking back at visions of the past history of a place."

"Do you believe in it?"

"Well, I didn't used to, but it's been well documented. So yeah, I guess. What, are you gonna perform tricks for me now? Tell me what I had for lunch last year on this date? Cuz I'll tell you now, if it was here, it was the Cobb salad. The cafeteria does this thing where they chop up the egg, then mix it with paprika, and little..."

Denali waved his hand, and Rook involuntarily slammed his mouth shut, nipping a corner of his tongue in the process. The seti winced. "With the help of this device," Denali explained with restrained irritation, "I am gonna share my time-sight vision with you. Do you understand? Simply nod yes or no."

The seti nodded.

"Good. Now we're going to look back almost fifteen years ago, during the time of your recovery from the siege on my namesakes' lab on Theseus."

The seti nodded again.

"You were told you were in a coma, that you convalesced here a year to recover," Denali said. Then, through a sneer, his voice suddenly dripping with malice, "Well, let's just see then."

Denali took hold of the back of Rook's head with the braceleted hand, and being so close to his ears, the seti could hear the whispered hiss of a jet-injection from the device. Then a tingle rushed across his scalp, and the yellow light leapt in arcs back and forth across his skull. The sensation moved inward, deeper into his head. Into his mind. His vision went blinding bright—then a moment of full darkness. Next, a wild whirlwind of chaos, as the days fell away backward before him at a dizzying pace. The giant, red sun outside unsetting and unrising hundreds of times each minute. Images blurring here and there across the lab. Experiments, once finished, being undone. Then it all stopped. The room was again silent and calm. In fact, too silent, as the only whisper he could hear was the surging of his own heart, similar to as if he had blocked his ears with his fingers.

"I can't hear anything," Rook thought, feeling confused by the sensation.

Denali's voice then came into the seti's mind. *"The power gives up only the* visions *of the past. The sounds, however, are lost to time. But look, use your eyes, there is nothing here you need listen to. Look... and see the solution that your dear friend has come up with."*

Rook gazed about the Lab, which was similar to a moment ago, but subtly different. He remembered this old paint color on the wall, over a decade since that had been changed. And the computer terminals, outdated dinosaurs that would have been only considered new almost twenty years back. The equipment, the setup, the very aura of the room—he recognized it all. Like details that you know deep inside, but that don't resurface from your memory until prodded loose by an old photograph. But he had spent a long time healing here, in *this* room, looking just the way it did now. He knew exactly when this was—almost fifteen years ago.

He turned towards the bed in the corner, where he had lain up for months once he awoke, and where he'd slumbered in a coma for a year before that—or, so he had been told. But the hospital mattress lay there empty, neatly made, with no sign of it being recently used. Rook gazed around further, towards the large glass chamber behind him, and there was the imposing frame of Tachion nearly in front of him, busily occupied with something Rook couldn't see. Instinctively, the seti called out to him, but no words escaped his mouth. These were merely ghosts of what once was. He could do nothing to affect them. Tachion turned, walking towards the bank of monitors that controlled the chamber, and Rook was then able to see it. In the center of the amber liquid, a tiny fetus, no bigger than a potato. Rook leaned in a little closer. A seti fetus.

Denali then began to advance the days slowly, gently picking up speed to blur through weeks, then months, then a year. Rook watched the infant grow through this time lapse perspective, his recognition of the face growing with each passing moment. Then those same strange thoughts that had been haunting his mind for days now reappeared as he viewed his own creation unfolding, ideas of abandonment and desertion, but now joined by the overwhelming disappointment of realized deception. *"Lies,"* the voice said. *"It's all been lies and deceit. All of it. Your whole life. This is why they have left you. You were never even true to begin with. This android is not your friend, he merely means to play God over you. None of them are your friends. Belladonna is not your wife. You have just served as an unwilling replacement, forced to fill his shoes, to raise his children, to fight his wars. None of this has been real, none of it belongs to you, you do not even know who or what you really are. Other than nobody. Nothing. A blank spot where Rook used to be."* The clone who once thought that he was called Rook swooned a little then, as he watched his alleged friend dissect him, cutting away healthy body parts in order to aid in his dishonesty. And the whole time, the overwhelming thoughts pounding in his head. That he *was* no one. That he *had* no one.

Everyone in his life had been part of this grand deception—except, of course, for Lord Denali.

Time spun forward again, then, racing ahead to the present day, and Denali released the seti to crumple to the floor in emotional exhaustion. Denali spoke. "I am sorry, brother, to reveal the truth to you in this way. But they had spun their lies so deep within you, Rook, I thought it the only way you would ever believe me."

"That... is not my name."

"Yes, I know. It is the name of some stranger, one long since dead. I watched it happen myself. His bones still lie deserted beneath the oceans of Theseus. But you will now find your new self, and your new name. I will help you to do this. But until then, we must simply use your old one as a means to address each other."

Rook gazed up at the human as the morbid thinking began to abate. "How do I know?" he asked. "How can I be sure this is not just some kind of... mentalist trick?"

"That is easy, my friend. You yourself set up all these computer systems, and security measures, did you not?"

Rook nodded.

"Look then, if you wish. You can breach your own firewalls, I'm sure. Search through the records. Watch the old surveillance footage. Trace the trail of paperwork, compounded lies upon lies." Denali moved towards the door to the outer office, and motioned Drake to do the same. "Take your time, as much as you wish. We will leave you to do your own investigating. But if you confirm what I have shown you, and wish for help... the help of another like you... to find your way, to... to know your purpose, I will be right here."

Rook nodded with a bewildered expression, taking a seat at Tachion's computer station, and began peeling back the layers of untruth that had encircled his figment of a life. The unwelcome ideas of treachery and disillusionment again pounding in his head all the while.

It was a good hour or more before the seti emerged, staring downward and appearing defeated. Denali stood from the desk and looked hard at him, eagerly awaiting the results of his mind games and suggestions. Rook then gazed up at him, inhaling deeply, and settling his expression with a new resolve. "We have to get outta here," he told them. "We better leave now."

Denali furrowed his brow in confusion. "Why? What is it?"

"Because, I set up all the security in this lab over the years. There are measures in place. In fact, if Tachion is within transmission range, he already knows we're here. He may already see us."

"Goddammit!" Denali raged, and turned his anger towards his bodyguard. "You told me that you checked, that this sort of protection was disabled."

"He never would have found it," Rook said, finding himself defending his former jailer. "No one would have. I'm better than that."

"What do we do then?" Denali asked. "Can we stop it?"

"The alert signal's been sent. There's no recalling that now. But I can issue an overriding subspace encryption algorithm, to scuttle the data stream. He'll know the lab was broken into, but if he's far enough away, and hasn't seen it already, I can destroy all the details and video footage."

"Do it!" He commanded aloud, then followed mentally with, *"Do it now!"*

Rook obediently left the two of them in the outer office again, and retook his seat at the terminal. Cracking his knuckles, he immediately got down to work. He dropped the protective energy field and purged the security data from the laboratory mainframe, then shut down all currently ongoing surveillance. Once completed, he cleverly rewrote sections of the maxidrive's familiar event driven source code, fingers as quick and graceful on the keyboard as a concert pianist. Finally, he altered the prog-chip's encryption key to permanently scramble any previously streamed subspace signal.

Before he hit the final button to execute his changes, he paused, and decided to leave a small parting gift for the doctor who had long pretended to be his friend. He made a copy of all the cloning documentation—the forged papers, the stolen blanks—and forwarded the entire packet anonymously to the Coalition Science Ministry. In the subject line he wrote simply: Checkmate Motherfucker. He looked back at the door, making sure that Denali and Drake weren't currently watching, then snapped a single still image from the lens atop the computer. An image that would be sent along with the intruder alert, and not purged with the rest of the deleted camera footage. He delayed in thought for less than a second, then hit enter, and rushed back outside. "It's done," he said to Denali. "Let's go."

And they did.

Displayed on every possible monitor back in the still open laboratory, he had left the same final photograph, now repeated everywhere about the room. A shot of the desktop, with a printed version of the letter to the Science Ministry laying on it, and sitting in the center of the paper, a black chess rook from the game board over by the bedside. At the top of the screen, in the upper left and right corners, Rook's two hands were visible. Balled into fists, both were earnestly saluting, the middle fingers of each raised high and proud.

PART IV

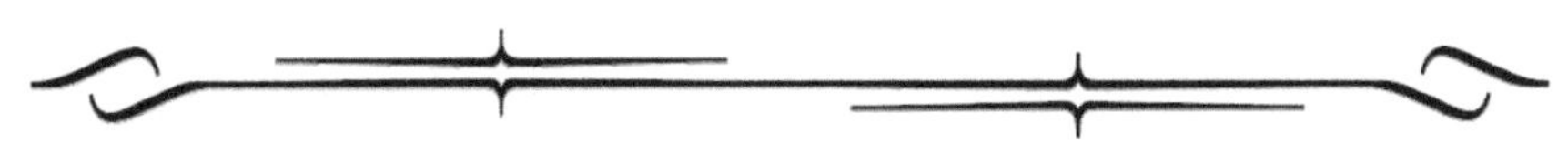

CASTLING

Chapter 13.1

A GROWING BREEZE STILL BLEW COLD, scattering dark, dusty sand ahead of it as it moved anxiously across the dunes, as if the wind itself rushed to find shelter from the furious suns. The first few morning tendrils of light now reached and grabbed greedily from the edge of the horizon—the dawning twins clearly covetous to reclaim their daily dominion over the waterless wasteland. The few days that the two seti had spent in the aptly named Heart of Nol Qhan had reinvigorated Bullseye, as he found it hard to reside in a place of such bountiful kindness and camaraderie without a fair measure of the blissfulness finding its way to rub off on him. An oasis in its truest sense. He watched the rising sun with new eyes of appreciation, or perhaps old ones he had thought long lost, but distantly he already heard the voice of his more pessimistic virtues calling, causing him to wonder just how short this current cheerfulness would last.

The community's charity had certainly forged a permanent ally of the mercenary pair, and their host Wairën had given every indication that the opposite was also true. But all things must end, and Bullit and Bullseye now stood back upon the temporarily frozen expanse of The Burnt Empty, watching the brightening skies above through the growing sunlight for the telltale vapor trail of their incoming shuttle—Belladonna having arranged the pickup for as soon as the surface was defrosted enough to make it safe to venture forth. Communications had been kept to a minimum due to the proximity of the nearby military base, and Bullseye was eager to get aboard and hear of any news from Tachion and Stansky.

Bullit rubbed his flaxen-furred hands together, absorbing the heat of friction, then turned to face the rising suns, and closed his eyes into their warming rays. "I have to say," he told Bullseye, "nothing against King Moonracer and his island of misfits, but I'll be glad to sleep in a bed made out of something more comfortable than shredded fiberglass."

Bullseye stared at him for a moment. "I'm afraid I fail to comprehend the reference," he said.

"King Moon... it... Rudolph? No? It's... an olden television film. Just, you know what... never mind."

"As I have already stated, I have never seen any human video entertainment."

"Yeah, well, I think you might like it. Some of the real old stuff anyway," Bullit suggested. "I'll tell you what, I'll make you a deal. You try to enjoy some select films that I choose for you, and I'll try and choke down whatever ancient seti fables and folklore you think I would benefit from."

Bullseye turned to face him, carefully looking him up and down, as if attempting to appraise his sincerity by his posture. Satisfied, he said, "Agreed."

"Oh shit," Bullit mumbled, "what have I gotten myself into? Don't go too hard on me now, and saddle me with something excruciating. Sometimes I have a hard enough time just understanding *you*, and that's speaking common."

"That is the very opposite of my intention," Bullseye said, sounding disappointed.

"What *is* the intention?"

Bullseye faced his fellow seti again. "I commune the way I do, because words are imbued with meaning. And meanings, knitted and drawn taut together, form the braid work of phrases. Phrases, in turn, weave the fabric of a language, one that is infused with both the orator's sentiment, and intent. This is the seti way, of those still delivered from the womb of your ancestral homeland. To convey our meaning, our emotion, to our brethren when we speak. It is to what end our honored lexicon remains so vast, yet so specific. Here lies the reasoning for thirty-one unique terms denoting degrees of rage. The source for forty-six vocables describing distinctions in a sunset. I strive my level best with the common tongue we all share, but it is oft times insufficient. Yet I learn it so I may know it, and I know it so I may use it, and I use it to ensure, for any I may speak to, my feelings and intent are always laid plain. Or, so has ever been my objective."

"I didn't mean to..." Bullit said, sounding regretful. "I... I get it now. I look forward to your first selection. But still, keep it basic to begin with? Let's try and *ease* me into it."

"Granted. If you consent to do the same."

"Done and done."

The two shook hands on the arrangement.

From the south, a pencil line of fiery pink drew itself across the sky, the path of condensation from their approaching rescue ship reflecting the ruddy sunrise. The craft came in low, circling the two seti several times, as the pilot studied the landscape for a spot clear enough of the obsidian pillars to land on. Finally, the *Dodger* expertly squeezed itself between a trio of the columns, with nary so much as a scuff to her clear coat.

The gangway to the medium-sized fighter descended from her belly, and the grateful mercenaries hurried aboard, greeted by Chief Zvavi filling the cockpit. His ivory fur was sullied by dappled grease spots and smudged thruster soot, clearly being sent to retrieve them only once pulled from beneath an engine.

"Morning, Chief," Bullit called out over the sound of the engine, "thanks for the lift."

"Morning here, it would seem," Zvavi answered, "and a wondrous sight, as it most often is. Though, in truth, 'tis afternoon back aboard."

"Ah. Good afternoon then."

"Scant space aboard this vessel, Chief," Bullseye commented as he and Bullit took the only other remaining seats, at the fore and aft gunnery positions, "was the *Bugeye* not available?"

"Sincerest apologies, Master Bullseye," Zvavi answered, as the ship's ramp retracted. "I regret the favored craft remains in the employ of your esteemed fellows, the doctor and Master Stansky."

"They have yet to return?" asked Bullseye.

"Aye," Zvavi confirmed.

Bullit scoffed. "I wonder what the hell those two have been up to."

Within a matter of twenty minutes, they were snug in the *Parliament One* landing bay. Within a matter of thirty, they were aboard the elevator towards their quarters. Bullseye remembered something then, calling out for the lift to stop on deck H.

"What's up?" Bullit asked, as Bullseye stepped off.

"I have a task of consequence to complete," he said. "Amongst the inventory in our kitchen's larder exists an allotment of my personal predilection. A remaining half bottle of Zet A'zeta. I mean to dispose of the venom that would lead to my ruination."

"Ah... okay. Would you like me to go with you?"

"Unnecessary, I think. Best to do so myself," he said. "Though, if you wish, I will keep the chef as a witness."

"No, you do as you will... and earn back another thimble." Bullit winked.

Bullseye made his way to the ship's galley and followed through on his promise, emptying the final portion of the elixir into the overflowing dish sink. He looked away and held his breath as he did so, unsure if the sight and smell of the liquid would have an alluring effect on him, but deciding it best to not wager on such a thing. He felt pride in himself over the accomplishment as he rode up in the lift, but with each passing deck, it was overtaken by the growing apprehension of having to confront Belladonna. Her husband was gone missing, during a mission without merit, and the fault of that truth lay at no one's feet but his own. He stepped off onto deck B, the Parliament private apartments, but stopped hidden around a corner when he heard a familiar voice in the circular common area beyond—one fraught with anger, and distress.

Bullit was certainly absorbing an unfair share of Belladonna's wrath. Yet Bullseye lingered in his safe harbor around the corner, in hopes the most shearing gales of the storm would blow themselves out on his undeserving comrade. There may be no kinder, sweeter, more loving mother, wife, and friend than the beautiful Belladonna, but as the well-known idiom extolls, even hell itself hath no fury. So Bullseye maintained his cover, and waited for an ebb in the tide of condemnation. They were cousins after all, Belladonna and Bullit, and he rationalized it bad form to intrude on what was, currently, a family squabble.

Bullit pleaded and protested to no avail. "Bell, I wasn't even there when it happened! I was up in the *Bugeye*, looking for a place to land and get them out."

"That's even worse!" Belladonna exclaimed. "What were you doing up there, leaving them a man short on the ground? You have enough pilots and air support aboard this starship to have someone else do the inserts and extractions."

Bullseye pursed his lips and nodded. A fair point she had there, and one he'd keep in mind in the future.

"Mother, you know this is not his fault," a second, calmer woman pointed out.

Bullseye's brow furrowed. Who was—*Mother*? Was that Relic trying to calm the situation? It must be. He certainly had not expected Bell would bring their children, although he quickly remembered they were at an age now where it would make sense. Still, the seti closed his eyes and sighed in mild irritation at the prospect. Relic had been, in Bullseye's determination, a most willful breed of child. But one should have expected nothing less with a sire such as Rook. He remembered the last time that he saw the

girl—though how many years ago now was difficult for him to calculate—
an awkward, hormonal, gangly tangle of arms and legs. She was always at
full power, following Bullseye wherever he tried to vanish to, with endless
question after question, to the point he thought she did so only to vex him.
And many years before that, when she was halfway between teen and
toddler, a dusty, little, bubblegum-chomping tomboy, often bursting
through the house at day's end with mud clear up to her eyebrows.

Rook had always referred to her as 'his little firecracker'. However,
Bullseye thought she compared more favorably to one of Stansky's
unpredictable wads of heurcanium. Ah, and yet another aggravation now
remembered; the young child had never learned to say the name Bullseye—
something about the girl's tongue finding her own growing teeth getting
in the way. Rather than lisp her way through it, her parents had settled upon
her just calling him 'B', and she had maintained using that pseudonym long
past the point of her matured elocution. He did not like to be called 'B'—
'B' was not his name. People have names for reasons, and nowhere is that
more true than with the seti. Although he was realizing now that these few
peeves were perhaps slightly unreasonable.

Another voice, a male, added to the tempest. "If it's anyone's fault, it's
Dad's own," Flashpoint added. "He's the one who's always tryin' to tell me
not to blame others for my circumstances. Well, he got himself into his own
mess, and dragged us all out here to get him out of it."

It seemed to Bullseye that the almost lifelong tension between father
and son had not abated in their adulthood. The boy's comment was not
technically untrue, but still perhaps a bit unfair. Rook was only in his
current circumstance because he trusted Bullseye to vet the mission. But
he had been too busy imagining his own Memorial for the Fallen. In
opposition to his twin sister, Bullseye had always found Flashpoint to be
serious and level-headed as a child, qualities he respected in a seti of any
age.

"Stop it, all of you," Relic's voice commanded with surprising
authority. "No one is at fault here, not Dad, or cousin Bullit, or even
Bullseye."

Hmm, she can speak my name now, thought the eavesdropper.

"They were merely doing what they always have," she continued.
"What you spent your career doing, Mom. What you and I have just finished
training to do ourselves, brother. They were called upon to risk themselves
for the benefit of a people and its government, and they answered. Not
selflessly, perhaps. It's true they are well paid for their heroics. But that is
what has provided not just the food upon our table, and the roof above our
heads, but every additional luxury that we have been so lucky to have been

blessed with. And we can be proud that it was earned in a manner that is conducted with honor, when so many others in this profession would just as soon rob, murder and pillage to do so."

"Pfft," Flashpoint huffed, "you mean exactly like they *used* to do, before they got rich enough to finally afford a higher morality?"

Bullseye was impressed with Relic's little monologue, her brother's prompt and proper recrimination notwithstanding. Perhaps her apple had landed a little closer to her mother tree than he had once realized, or rolled that way during the years since Bullseye had last seen them. But he was quite gratified with how much she sounded like the one who birthed her. He had been a great admirer of his friend's wife, Belladonna, as anyone who knew her would be. She was an astounding individual on a myriad of levels, a true one of a kind, and to his eye, the absolute highest caliber a seti woman might hope to be. And this despite the fact that she, too, embraced human culture over her own. Regardless, it was good to know that the possibility existed of another like her, in the form of her daughter. The universe would only be better off for it.

The tension in the room beyond had been lessened greatly by Relic's lecture, and Bullseye dared not loiter much longer for fear of being discovered snooping. He steeled himself for a possible resurgence of the family's passions upon seeing him, and headed around the corner to confront his missing friends' worried family.

Bullseye stepped into the central lobby, and promptly froze in place, his stomach instantly clutching in upon itself. A curtain of cold flush dropped from behind his eyes and poured its way throughout his body, as if the very warmth of his blood was being drawn out his ankles by a waning riptide. Bullit and Belladonna stood together near the center of the area's encircling couches, and Flashpoint was reclining upon one of them, with a face that announced to all the inconvenience even being here was causing him. But it was Relic who was the source of his unexpected paralysis, and his jaw muscle actually dropped a little as he saw her.

She was exquisite.

Moving to stand by her mother, she glided across the room in a seti saree of baby blue. The diagonal sash freed her right shoulder and left waist to be exposed, revealing the bared beauty of her collarbone and midriff. She was a multi-hued calico of purest white, onyx black, and a welcoming orange the color of a hearth glow—the three complexions interwoven randomly along the arch of her back, and the curve of her thigh. He found the palette and pattern breathtaking, the young seti woman utterly perfect in her imperfection. Her mane of mid-length hair was dyed a deep magenta to match her lips, and was swept back in a flowing curtain that superbly framed the taper of her neck. Bullseye blinked and swallowed, and his stomach swarmed with butterflies like a schoolboy.

"Finally, fuckin' hell," Bullit complained. "If everybody could please point your fingers at *that* guy for a while."

"I'm sorry, Bullit," Belladonna told him. "I didn't mean to attack you." She directed herself now to the still enraptured Bullseye. "But *you*, I would like a word with."

Bullseye approached Bullit, Bell, and her daughter, trying hard not to stare, as he was sure they all were closely watching his approach. But he found himself unable not to. Until Relic herself raised her doe-like eyelids in his direction, meeting his gaze with the penetrating hazel green of her own. Bullseye immediately jerked his head away, embarrassed she might see it in him, ashamed it might be written on his face. He made an attempt to speak as he reached the group. "What... um, what tidings of our friend, or... ah, your husband? Of Rook? What news... of your husband Rook?"

"He's alive," Belladonna answered, "at least last he was seen, which is a couple of days ago now. Although, even that sighting was hearsay, but admittedly from a reliable source."

"Uh-huh," Bullseye offered. "That's good, and... ah..." The overwhelming awareness of Relic standing so near to him was engulfing his mind. He wanted so much to look across to her, but feared he might have some sort of visible reaction. He felt he should acknowledge her, though. Greet her. Was it strange that he hadn't? To continue rudely ignoring her might be even more obvious. But now, it seemed, it had been far too long to do so, too awkward at this point to turn and say 'hey there. I didn't see you'. Instead, he continued, "The, the, um... and who's that? Reliable? This, ah... source of the hearsay?"

"Believe it or not, the first ashi'mar of Capella, Lady Opal," she told him.

"Hmm. Imagine that," Bullseye said, sounding almost disinterested. The perfume of Relic's hair caressed his face in a soft embrace—the sweet, familiar fragrance of K'Tas T'mirian blossoms, and summer fruits. *My God, what was wrong with him?*

"Guys, perhaps you could give us a moment," Belladonna requested to her offspring. "Why don't you return to your rooms for a little while."

Flashpoint rolled his eyes, and dramatically overexerted himself to get up off the couch. "Uncle Bullseye," he said in parting, "nice to see you."

Bullseye nodded his head to him in silent acknowledgment.

Relic leaned forward and kissed her mother on the cheek. Oh, to be that cheek. Then she turned and slapped her hand lightly twice on Bullit's muzzle, with a click sound from the inside of her cheek, and a "We'll catch up later, cuz."

Bullseye actually almost felt the swell of an irrational anger, a surge of jealousy at the show of closeness, but he quickly stifled it. He wondered, was he able to force it down because he logically realized the emotion was nonsensical, or only because he recalled that Bullit, as her first cousin once removed, was not a threat to his—his—*whatever* he was imagining. He finally dared to look up as she passed him, and their eyes locked for a second.

"Hi, B", she said, as she reached out to lightly touch him on the shoulder, Bullseye only just now realizing her voice was as soft and musical as an angel song. Her hand lingered on him for just a moment, and he felt the coolness of her fingers, the gentle weight of her touch, and a stream of goosebumps washed up his arms, down his back, and then further on to other places.

"H...Hi," he greeted her back meekly.

There was an aura of electricity about her, one that didn't dissipate for him until she was finally gone. He did not turn to watch her leave, although he wanted to—oh, how he wanted to. He almost breathed a sigh of relief when he heard the sound of the lift door close.

Bullit's eyebrow had been raised since the moment Bullseye had approached, and he leaned into his fellow seti now, and spoke softly while Bell returned from walking her children to the door. "What the hell is the matter with you?" Bullit sniffed the air around Bullseye's muzzle. "Did you pour that shit out down the drain, or down your gullet?"

"What?" he replied. "No, of course not." Then as Belladonna reached them, "Forgive me please, I feel somewhat distracted by exhaustion. The past few days' adventures, I think, have knotted threads of disquietude through my mind, a strain that's now released with the welcome comfort of familiar surroundings. A modicum of rest I require, and that is all."

Bullit seemed convinced; and Bell, as always, took him at his word. "Tell me, Λ:φ⋈ⴰⵘφ'ⵘːⵝΔꙨ," she called him by his true and untranslatable seti birth name, "what exactly is it you are doing out here? I reviewed the mission specs, heard the audio of General Nylis' request. None of this seemed a bit fishy to you when you accepted?"

"I am sorry, dear Belladonna. It is truth that fault of all this is a millstone rightly placed squarely upon me, and no other. Complacency, I plead. Conceited vainglory that lead to laziness, and dereliction. I did not execute the task with which I am entrusted as leader, due diligence to ensure our commission was made in good faith."

"Well," Bullit interjected, "don't be too hard on yourself. First of all, any of us could have refused if we wanted. And second, these people... this *person*, wanted Rook. If they had not gotten him the way they did, then they would have done so another way. Perhaps, in a more tragic way. Whoever this new Denali is, your husband, for some reason, seems important to his plans."

"Or, important to Denali himself," Bullseye said.

"Speaking of which," Belladonna told them, "that's another piece of information that your other two partners have discovered. Not who Denali is, but at least who he *isn't*. It has been visually confirmed that he is not the same man you defeated once before."

"He's the same to me," Bullit said, "no matter his appearance."

"Perhaps, before we rest," Bullseye suggested, "best to be briefed on their other enlightenings, as well as debrief a record of our own to offer them."

"If you wish," Belladonna said. "Captain Lobo says we have twenty-six hours before we reach them on Oberonn. So, perhaps, and I mean no insult, you two may wish to freshen up... and take a shower?"

"Oh? Why's that?" Bullit asked sarcastically. "Do we smell like we spent the first half of the week hiding under a septic tank, and the second half in a cave full of garbage?"

Bullseye scowled. "Neither of those locales bear the stigma of which you're implying, especially Wairën's village." He looked down at himself then. "I do admit, however, we both still carry the near week-old exertion of two day's battle on Oberonn, and a march through the desert to top it. A shower sounds to be sage advice."

Bullit headed off to his suite, Bullseye to his own, and Belladonna went to await them in her husband's quarters across the lobby. Before she could enter, Bullseye's head re-emerged from his doorway. "Hold for a moment. Whom do you say Tachion and James have in their midst? Is it true they are keeping company with the royal lady ashi'mar?"

13.2

THE PRESIDENTIAL CONVOY WAS FINALLY on its way home, although much later than originally anticipated, on its journey back to

Earth from the Martian colonies. President Harold V. Forestal grudgingly anticipated the furious dash from *Aerospace One* to his awaiting limo transport, simply to rush him off towards the next scheduled item on his agenda—whatever that might be. He was sure that *someone* would let him know on the way. He could see the breathless anxiety of his aides and ushers, already gathered near the doorway in order to make ready, so that the moment it opened, they could whisk him swiftly onward from one ship to another, like a capsized rafter caught in a raging rapid.

The visit to their red neighbor had been draining, both physically and emotionally, having endured the distinctive honor of touring the Federal disaster site caused by last week's earthquake. Correction—marsquake, as he'd been instructed to call it. The damage and death toll were not only a humanitarian tragedy, but also quite likely to impact the shipbuilding industry for up to a decade.

The vessel landed, the hatchway opened, and as predicted, off through the rushing tide of people he was swept. Down the gangplank, and through the hangar bay, and in among the narrow twisting corridors to the street-side exit. As he approached the entrance lobby, with his throng of support staff and guards surrounding him, he could see his next motorcade awaiting his arrival through the picture windows ahead. But then something that he didn't expect to see—or *someone*. General Isaiah was approaching the group, coming in from the doorway they were currently on course towards, and signaling clearly to the president that he urgently needed a moment of his time.

Harold tried to slow his mob of assistants so that he could stop and confer with the general, but the more that he tried to stop and change direction, the more insistent and vocal the wake he was caught in seemed to rush on. Finally, the general had to physically stand near the hurried congregation, and reach out a hand with which to grab him, like a good Samaritan sticking out a life pole to rescue that same swept away rafter. They grabbed hands, the throng stopped, and the two ducked into a nearby lavatory for privacy, despite the enthusiastic objections of his many schedule keepers and protocol officials.

President Forestal directed Agent Adder, his personal secret service guard, to keep everyone else out, adding, "No one is to come in here until I come out on my own, understood? No matter what time the clock, or my schedule says."

"Understood, sir," the seti agent answered, then went to take his unenviable position outside of the restroom.

"Ephraim, old friend," the president said, unzipping his fly to make use of the urinal while one was so convenient. "I'm always glad to see you, especially if it means I get two seconds to take a goddamn piss. But I can only assume you dared to interrupt the scheduling gods for only the worst possible news."

"Ha! No Vern, not bad news, but certainly important. Regarding our..." He looked up at an unsecured air vent, wondering just how far their voices might travel through it, "our... friends of Esil Brin."

"Oh, you've caught up with them, have you?"

"With some difficulty, finally, yes," General Isaiah said. "It seems they've divided up. Firstly, two of them were thought to be aboard the chamai flagship, the *Okubi*. With old man Nylis on board, no less. Which was all but confirmed when they were spied emerging from the joint military base in Nol Qhan."

Harold zipped up. "What the hell were they doing there? Are they working with the chamai?"

"Our analysts don't believe so. They appeared to be... sneaking out. They slunk away, discarded their armor. Which is how they were identified by long-distance spy drones. Then, they disappeared."

"Well, luckily they don't work directly for us. They'd be liable to start an intergalactic incident." He nudged the general aside in order to wash his hands. "What do you mean, they disappeared?"

"Vanished, in the night. We had no idea where for two days. But we've reacquired them now, en route back to Oberonn."

"So, we still have no idea what they're doing?"

"Not exactly, but the analysts believe they're still investigating this human you put Agent Brin on originally."

"Well, that's something. And where is Agent Brin? Have we had any luck locating him yet?"

"Dead, sir, I'm sorry to say. His dismembered corpse was detected floating in open space by an ore freighter, within the Oberonn system."

"Goddammit," he swore aloud, as he hit the infrared dryer with his elbow and ran his hands beneath it. "Is that what you came to tell me?"

"Not exactly. There's more. An ex-Starlaw secret service agent by the name of Belladonna has joined Par..." The general caught himself. "I mean, joined with the friends of Agent Brin."

"Meaning?"

"Unknown. She is the spouse of one of them, retired."

The president sighed. "What else?"

"The other half of the group, the two still on Oberonn..."

"Yes?"

"Well, I know you have been briefed on the rumors coming out of Capella City. That the First Ashi'Mar Lady Opal maybe dead, or sick, or missing."

The president turned to face him, concerned. "Go on."

"Well, we have high confidence that she was seen... with Esil's friends."

"She's with *them*? Where?"

"Our agent spotted her, with a human and android, entering the city of Krataar. They hid their ship in an empty loading dock in the freight district, and began heading south through the city. They were lost in the crowd at that point, but I have eyes peeled everywhere looking for her. For *them*. But ours are not the only eyes there. I'm told the city is lousy with bounty hunters."

"Good grief. Boy, they're really up to their necks in something."

"Yes, sir."

"Your analysts have any idea what that something is?"

The general paused. "Sorry. No sir."

"Well, whatever Vasu is up to, maybe her junior is not quite so keen on it."

"A distinct possibility, sir."

Harold sighed again. "But, in accordance with the last Tristar summit, we are due to complete our troop drawdown of forces posted within the Oberonn and Capellan systems, as well as their respective borders along the Barrens, by day's end tomorrow."

"As I'm well aware."

"Which could leave us caught with our pants down, if Vasu and Nylis are up to no good."

"Bunched around our ankles, sir."

President Forestal thought for a moment. "Okay, continue the drawdown as scheduled, but keep the withdrawn troops amassed somewhere nearby, in Coalition space, of course. Liberty Station or somewhere, spread them out a little bit. Say that they are being held pending... I don't know... reevaluation of deployment requirements. You think of something. I don't want them fully pulled back until we know exactly what's going on."

"You got it, Vern. Understood."

"And keep those... *friends* of Agent Brin on your radar, if you can."

"We're trying."

The president turned to the mirror, straightened his hair a bit with his fingers, and dusted some lint from his jacket. "Anything else?"

"We've heard rumblings of a data breach at the Coalition Biological Society. I only mention it because, well... one of the friends is... employed there."

Harold rolled his eyes. "Well, when you know more..."

"You'll know more, sir," the general finished. "You can be sure of it."

"Alright," the president said, shaking General Isaiah's hand, "I'm late for something, I have no idea what. Good work, Eph."

He opened the door, and taking a deep breath, leaped headlong back into the chattering rapids to be quickly washed away.

13.3

THE CHAMAI TECHNOLOGICAL REVOLUTION on Oberonn—from the tentative first puffs of a working steam engine, to the advent of the earliest crude calculating computer, to the christening of the maiden warp-capable interstellar battlecruiser—had been achieved in the briefest overall timespan of *any* of the currently known galactic civilizations. This unprecedented advancement was fueled and fired by the same great motivator that seemed to drive all sudden bursts of technological expansion, not just here on Oberonn, but on every other world besides.

War.

Just as in a great many other societies, war had served as a cattle prod, pushing forward scientific knowledge and engineering breakthroughs with an urgency never seen in the more complacent laze of peacetime. Oberonn had seen more relentlessly consistent wartime than any other modern species, quite a dubious distinction considering the protracted ancient tribal combat of the seti, or the notable four world wars of the humans. But the citizens of Oberonn had endured hundreds of years of it, locked in bloody global civil conflict, generation after generation of brutal fighting between the chamai and the chimor.

The rapidity of these advancements was bought and paid for with the blood of these two peoples, generously spilled. Two distinct, sentient, intelligent species, evolving together, but still quite separate—their growing populations forced to share the dwindling resources of a single planet. Natural selection's own perfect recipe for disaster. The frenzied life of constant hostilities finally ended a hundred years ago now, and peace ruled the first full generation to know an existence without that never-ending peril looming overhead. In most civilizations, the memory of its people can be unforgivingly long. Even after years of lasting ceasefire, peace would never be truly and fully peaceful, as animosity and suspicion toward old foes tends to linger on—for many lifetimes. Such would have certainly been the case here, after so many eons of hostility, if it wasn't for the sad fact the chimor no longer existed.

In the end, the chamai had won out, entirely and completely—a war of attrition carried out to the very last. Every single one of them—man, woman, and child—gone. Of course, no one today was particularly proud of this fact, but fortunately for them, the chronicles of the past had been long ago whitewashed clean. It is generally taught that the chimor were villainous aggressors, and the chamai merely innocents trying desperately to defend their lives and homeland. How much of that may be true, though, is now very deliberately lost to the ages, and no one remains behind to argue another version of the events. After all, as it's been long said, history is written by the victors.

Regardless of the outcome, the rapid transition from a preindustrial society to a digital, spacefaring one created an odd mixture in the chamai culture of new ways and old, existing harmoniously side by side. The earlier heritage and traditions of agriculture and local trading had not yet time to fade away before the tide of modern technology came sweeping in, and this juxtaposition was still ingrained within the civilization today—nowhere more evident than in each city's grand bazaar.

Two hundred years ago, this would have been a sea of multicolored yurts and canopied pavilions, topped with vivid banners and pennants advertising various vendors' wares. Today, although the tent fabrics are made of space-age plastics rather than spun u'chi silks, and the open sides beneath the awnings are equipped with force field generators, keeping stifling humidity out and shoplifters in, the overall appearance of the huge outdoor market still remains much the same. So much, in fact, that a traveler from the distant past might not even notice there was any difference.

James Stansky stood atop the uppermost steps of Krataar's central plaza, and peered across the steaming, hazy landscape below, encrusted in its colorful tents. The grand bazaar extended east to the slow and stagnant river's edge, and west to the high wall of the looming downtown business district, where modern architecture looked directly down on its more archaic ancestry. To the south, the crowded fair continued to the distant edge of the surrounding jungle's foreboding boundary, a line of vine-tangled, twisted tree trunks dividing the traversable byways of the city from the boggier swamplands shrouded in foliage just beyond. James kept Lady Opal tight at his side, covered in a shawl of gold and red fabric purchased off an old beggar woman in the freight district, so that only the greenish glow of her vibrant eyes was visible from underneath. Tachion followed close behind, using his taller vantage point to scan for anyone seeming overly interested in the trio, and together the human, lyghtan, and android descended down the stone stairway into the market fair.

"Sweet holy Jesus," Stansky exhaled, fruitlessly fanning his face with his hand. "I thought that forest up north was a scorcher. Why did we have to wear this thin flimsy armor instead of my climate-controlled PA?"

"No armor heavier than light battle is allowed within the city limits," Tachion answered. "Besides, we're trying to *not* draw any unwanted attention. You stomping around a flea market in a massive suit of powered assault... not particularly inconspicuous."

"I know it's cliché," Lady Opal said from beneath her colored veil, "but since I have never experienced it before, I hope you'll forgive it. The heat is not an issue for me. After all, I grew up in a desert. But this humidity is killing me. There's so much *moisture* in the air, I almost feel like I'm going to drown," she complained. "I never thought I would ever say this, but there is too much water here for me."

James chuckled. He pulled her small frame in tighter to his large protective embrace as they reached the bottom of the stairway, penetrating into the throng of bustling shoppers. The hug, he knew, wasn't entirely necessary, but it provided him an excuse to feel the lyghtan priestess's delicate physique closer to his, which made him smile. "Any idea where to go?" he asked Tachion.

"Belladonna said to search out the performance area, near the center of the bazaar," the android answered. "Perhaps if we just follow the music."

James was certainly no fan of Oberonnian folk music, although the mob of chamai that they carefully weaved their way through definitely seemed to enjoy it. The melody, for the most part, seemed pleasant enough to start, but would frequently build to a crescendo that ended with a note so brutally off-key, so off-putting and discordant, that it made Stansky physically wince each time it came around. Which was difficult to anticipate, as the tune did not seem to follow any particular rhythm, but just meandered aimlessly up and down the scales. He decided it was best to say nothing of it, just on the small chance it was Opal's favorite foreign symphony.

The narrow walkways between the tents of Krataar's grand bazaar were jam-packed, mainly with chamai people, but many of other species as well, rushing about in the oppressive midday mugginess, and clothed in thin, flowing fabrics dyed in bright primary colors. Long garments, like oversized nightshirts of a light, breathable weave, and very little else. For the most part, bare calves and ankles protruded from beneath them, capped with a pair of moccasins or thongs. Stansky thought this might make it a little easier to spot any bounty hunters looking for trouble, as anyone with pants on would immediately be put on his radar. He pointed this out to Tachion.

The vendors that they passed sold the widest assortment of merchandise, from fruit that looked like spotted apples, to clips of ammunition. Textile shops with bolts of silks, to albedo resistant suits. From common, everyday goods and sundries, to second-hand technological battle enhancements. And James had the highly confident suspicion that for each crate of items openly displayed, another of questionable black-market commodities was likely available out back of each pavilion. Barkers called out to the trio as they passed by the open awnings, sometimes physically grabbing at them to attract attention to their wares. Stansky easily jerked free of any attempt to detain him, protecting Lady Opal in a cocoon of musculature in front of him. They instead followed steadily along in the direction of the music, a pied piper tune calling them further onward into the marketplace.

Finally, they emerged from the endless rows of stalls into an open clearing in the center of the fair. The band was here—still playing poorly, and more loudly—as well as several places to buy food, sit around, and casually eat it. A number of performers practiced their arts here, in exchange for donations from those who enjoyed them, and several were now surrounded by wreaths of curious bystanders, each performer in competition for every set of eyeballs they could ensnare. To the left, a lean, shirtless chamai man—a long, braided beard to match his long, braided hair—spun about the stone-tiled plaza in dizzying circles, upside down, gripping to the center of a large metallic ring. On the right, a metamorph woman was juggling balls and doing close-up sleight of hand, all the while transforming her appearance to imitate and ridicule unaware passersby, much to the delight of her circle of dedicated followers. But in the center, with the largest audience of onlookers, was clearly the woman that they were searching for, the unique physical description given by Belladonna impossible to mistake with anyone else. They moved forward to join her growing crowd of spectators.

Selene Maraspese was atop a low circular stage, a platform perhaps knee-high, with a slender pole rising from its center. The lyghtan woman was disrobed all the way down to the very smallest of bikinis, revealing a figure of rigid, toned muscle that rivaled even Stansky's own. He was more than impressed, and perhaps a little turned on. Her eyes glowed like bright colorless diamonds in shimmering silver pendants, and all across the jet-black skin of her lyghtan body, from her smallest toe to her buzz cut head, nearly every square inch was covered by a series of white-inked tattoos. She bent and twisted herself around the pole and the stage floor, contorting and knotting her brawny, yet feminine physique into convoluted pretzels, seemingly in ways specifically designed to align the tattooed images. She called out to the crowd as she tied and untied herself around the post, in her entrancing storyteller's voice, and relating to them the familiar tale of a well-favored chamai fable.

As she described for them an ancient army's travails of crossing quagmire jungles and fording rivers, she matched the eloquent imagery of her narration with visible depictions from across her body. The tattoo of soldiers on her ankle placed against the rainforest inked across her shoulder. The rafts inscribed along her collarbone meeting the raging rapids drawn all down her powerful thigh. And so her growing crowd of fans were in this way duly mesmerized, twisting her body with the twisting tale, and enrapturing all around her in her dramatic and arousing recitation. The tale came to its conclusion with Selene in a tangled pose seemingly impossible to get in or out of, and the listeners expressed their acclaim with loud hooting applause, and a slew of dropped credits into her awaiting kettle.

Stansky moved up the stage's edge as the lyghtan woman untied herself, and the crowd thinned and scattered elsewhere across the plaza. "Selene?" he asked of the woman. "Selene Maraspese?"

She stood and looked the human up and down, her gaze as silvery white as if she had captured the moonbeams of her homeworld's Lunar Triad within her eyes, then regarded his two strange companions as well. She bent and gathered a green silk robe from the corner of the small stage floor, and used it to cover her glistening, sinewy frame. "I was watching you," she told him in an accusatory tone. "You enjoyed the story, enjoyed watching how I told it... watching my body. But I didn't see you put a single credit in my coffer." She hopped down from the platform and sat on its edge, retrieving a pair of leather sandals from beneath it, and lifting her feet to put them on. "I don't talk to fans that don't pay."

"We're not fans," James told her. "We're..."

Her shining, sidelong glare and raised eyebrow brought his objection to an end, and she then directed her gaze to the money pot instead, and waited for him to ante in. He reached into his armor's hip pouch, and dropped in a few credits to clatter at the bottom. She did not look away, but continued eyeballing the kettle, waiting still. James sighed, and begrudgingly dropped in a few more chips, until finally the woman seemed appeased. She stood to gather the pot of money, and faced the threesome.

"Thank you very much," she said. "Your generosity is appreciated. I have no idea who this Selene person is you're looking for, but I'm glad that you enjoyed the show." She moved ahead as if they weren't there, roughly pushing between Stansky, Opal, and Tachion, and began marching off across the grand bazaar's central square.

"Wait, please," Tachion said. "We were sent by Belladonna."

"You got the wrong gal, robot," she called out behind her as she walked away. "I don't know who that is."

"Juniper!" Stansky shouted. "Please, we just need a moment."

The contortionist stopped and turned back around to face them, then apprehensively scanned all around to see if anyone else had heard the loudly shouted codename. She walked back to them and stood uncomfortably close to Stansky's face. "I don't need you shouting that all over the square, human."

"You didn't give us much choice, shade. You were running off without giving us a chance. And, by the way, I *waaay* overpaid you."

She stared at him coldly, then cracked a wry little smile. "Fine," she said, "Bell sent you, and I owe her one or two. Who the fuck are you, and what the fuck do you want?"

"We're... associates," Tachion said, "of your friend Belladonna's husband."

"I never said I was her friend. I said I owed her, and that's not the same thing." She stepped back from them a bit, and appraised them again. "Associates of Rook, huh? So that makes you what, mercenaries then? What was his group called, Punishment?"

"Parliament," the android answered.

"Well, la-dee-frickin'-da," she said, smirking.

Stansky interjected. "Look, we're just trying to find someone called the Guisemage. Bell said you could help us."

"*Oh*, is that all? You *just* want to find the most impossible to locate man on this planet. And, hmm, which one of you is in need of his services, I wonder? Let me guess, it's the little one here, with her head buried under a dirty blanket." Selene leaned forward, and peered squinting into the small opening Lady Opal left in the head covering for her to see through. The first ashi'mar pulled the fabric down tight and shied away.

"Are you gonna help us or not?!" Stansky barked, losing his patience.

"Not," Selene announced. Then smiling, "Not for free, anyway."

"I already paid you!"

"No... that was for the show. Taking you to Kaii Kealiun is extra."

"How much extra?" James griped.

"How much have you got?" Selene answered.

Before long, they were once again winding their way through the narrow footpaths between the vendors, the lyghtan contortionist leading the way westward towards the city wall, Tachion behind her and James at the rear, still keeping Opal protected right in front of him.

"Juniper is an interesting codename," Tachion said, by way of making conversation, "especially for a nonhuman."

"There's no great mystery behind it," Selene said, staring an overly enthusiastic salesperson that was approaching to hawk their wares into retreating. "I used to have a strong predilection for Earth gin. I guess technically, I still do. A hereditary gift from my birth parents, I suppose, both being world-class drunks themselves. A gift I have to hold on to, though, for sentimental reasons. I mean, that, and this scar across my neck, are the only two things those worthless fuckers ever gave me."

"Oh, I see," the android doctor said, feeling awkward.

"Pttf. Nah, I'm just shittin' with you. The name was randomly assigned by HQ when I didn't care enough to pick one," she laughed. "And I got this scar back in grade school, when idiot Lal Llymon thought it smart to try and kiss me."

"Ah," Tachion said, feeling some relief. But also not quite sure exactly which version of the story was the correct one—if either was.

"You should see the doozy I left *him* with, though, right across his face. I've never been much of a fan of kissing boys, if you know what I mean."

"No, me neither," said Tachion.

Selene laughed aloud at that.

Stansky pushed forward from the back with Opal, until he was shoulder to shoulder with Selene Maraspese. "Where exactly are we going?" he asked their guide. "This looks like a dead end."

"It is," she told him.

The high stone retaining wall, which formed the border between the tent-covered grounds of the grand bazaar and the towering glass and steel skyscrapers of the financial and business district above it, loomed right ahead of them at the approaching end of the crowded walkway. The stones of the huge barricade were ancient and primitively hewn, part of the massive cobbled foundation laid millennia ago, to lift the newborn city above the swampy floodlands that surrounded it. It was at least fifty feet tall at this point, but shorter towards the north as the land sloped upwards, and higher to the south, where it bordered the very edge of the sodden jungle downhill from them. The wall of interlocking stone was unbroken, for as far to the left or right as they could see, with no doors or openings that would indicate a way to continue forward.

They reached a small, square pavilion of crimson-red fabric placed right up against the very skin of the mighty masoned barrier, perhaps the only vending stall in the entire market without a crowd of eager patrons clambering over each other out in front of it. Instead, the awning-covered opening was guarded only by a small chamai girl of perhaps twelve, with ruddy, tanned skin and dirty feet, sitting cross-legged atop a wooden barrel. The only clothes the scrawny child wore was a knot of dusty linen around her waist, and a ragged strip of burlap tied across her presumably blinded eyes. She did not move as they passed and entered, though Selene dropped a few credits in the girl's cupped and waiting hands.

Inside the tent was nothing more than a modern folding table, strewn with the most random array of products. Nothing of any interest, however. More the sort of valueless, second-hand castoffs that get left behind unsold at the close of a flea market. Selene signaled to James with a nod to take hold of one end of the table, and the two of them lifted and moved it a few feet across the small cloth shelter. Pulling back a ratty floor mat, she revealed a padlocked grate leading into the ground, and Selene slipped a small baton into the latch, pulling wide the bars with a protesting, rusty groan. "Down here," she told them, tilting her chin towards the moldy stone stairway, and down they sank into the open grave in the pavilion floor.

Only twelve steps down, James reached a corroded iron door at the bottom, leading somewhere deeper beneath the wall. He looked at it distrustfully, the rust-eaten doorway now more holes than door, then gazed up past Opal and Tachion toward Selene, who still stood above ground on the surface. "In *here*?" Stansky asked her, his voice brimming with uncertainty.

"That's right, go on through. You'll find a locked door about twenty feet in. Wait there. I'll tell Kaii that you're here, and he'll come out to meet you. Just wait."

James cocked his head to one side in suspicion, and raised an eyebrow almost to his hairline.

"Hey," Selene said, "have I ever lied to you before?" she joked.

"Yes," Stansky answered, "three times just on the way over here."

"Oh, yeah," she said. "Well... fourth times the charm." She clapped the grate shut with a clatter, then threw the floor mat back down to cover the threesome. Through the small worn holes in the threadbare rug above, the shadow of the table was dragged back into place.

13.4

BULLIT LAID BACK ACROSS HIS bed in a fully-naked spread eagle, soaking in the bliss of being clean, fed, and comfortable again. He felt the air conditioner blow, and smelled his Cohiba Spectre cigar smoldering at the bedside. He made snow angels of the satin sheets, feeling the cool slickness against his fur, and tangling up a mess of his bedclothes in the process. He had been obsessed, stewing over the Rook-Denali connection for the past several days, and was relieved for the moment to have the whole affair out of his mind. He got up and put on a comfortable, casual outfit, and true to his word to Bullseye, slid a three-port scrambler full of battle armor into his pocket. Then he headed out to the common lobby and the elevator beyond, to sneak down to the chef's icebox for some late-night frozen treats.

He got off at deck H, making his way through the quiet, dimly-lit starship toward the kitchen. He was enjoying the feeling of not sneaking around for the first time in several days, as well as the simple privacy that being cooped up with Bullseye had deprived him of. But entering the galley, he found he was actually not alone. His younger cousins Relic and Flashpoint had already beaten him to the freezer.

An assortment of containers were already open, spread across the stainless-steel prep island like a buffet: lemon berry, praline, espresso, and several others. The duo was busily sampling the flavors of ice cream from one container to the next, but stood motionless when they saw him, caught red-handed with heaped utensils in their mouths. He simply looked from one to the other, then said, "Toss me a spoon." Which they quickly did.

Relic was wearing yet another traditional guise of seti apparel. She had always been enamored with and a scholar of their mutual ancestral culture in a way that Bullit himself had never cared about, folding as much of it into her Earth-centric upbringing as she was able to absorb. He wondered if maybe she would help him cheat a little later, and give him Cliff Note summaries of whatever titles Bullseye ended up selecting for him.

Her brother Flashpoint, on the other hand, was much more Earthan, like himself—or even like the boy's father, though the young man would never admit it. As usual, things had not been left so good with dear old Dad, but here now Bullit began to wonder at something darker. Would the rift between father and son make it easier on the boy, if—if Bullit needed to do what he was becoming more convinced he was going to have to? Would either of the twins ever forgive him, if the need arose to—dispose of their father? Perhaps it would be easier for them to swallow if they knew the truth. Knew that he was, in fact, not who they thought at all. Their true dad had passed away long ago, and they're probably old enough now to know it. If it comes to it, he will have to tell them. *If*—or perhaps, when.

Relic's smile beamed at Bullit as she reached to grab another spoonful of pistachio. "At least this Lady Opal woman saw Dad alive and well," she continued to her brother, "and feeling strong enough that he wanted to go back and..."

"Go back and *what*, Relic?" Flashpoint interrupted. "Get himself in deeper, when he was already ninety percent of the way to safety?" He slid a container of mocha fudge across the gleaming table towards their cousin. "And he calls *me* irresponsible?"

"*When?*" Relic countered with her mouth full. "When you were a stupid teenager? You *were* friggin' irresponsible. I've not heard him criticize you like you're talking about in *years*. Get over it."

"Oh No? When I switched to demos?"

"Well, that was different. He didn't mean that. He *told* you as much," his sister offered. "The point is, we know Dad was seen okay, and we know Uncle Tach and James found evidence of him still fighting. And Opal said this scumbag didn't want anyone to hurt him. I'm confident once we're all together, we'll get him back in no time."

"They can keep him," Flashpoint murmured.

"*Stop it*, you don't *mean* that!" Relic pleaded. "Tell him, Bullit."

Tell him what, Bullit thought, *that his father died when he was ten, but we decided it best just to never tell you? That instead, we slid a reproduction in his place? Sure, he may have seemed to be all right for over a decade or so now, but it was starting to look like the manufacturer's warranty might be running out. Now he's somehow involved with criminal kingpins, crazy shade queens, traitorous generals. Fucking drak'min? Flashpoint was right. Why didn't he keep going and escape when he had the chance? Maybe because he didn't want to. Maybe because everything he told Opal was just a steaming pile of horseshit. 'He was gonna go back and end it', he had told her. Just him, all by himself. Well, that just sounds stupid. And why didn't he tell the lyghtan lady who this Denali really was, if he had seen him like he said? Maybe he wanted to hide it, the real identity of this guy. Maybe it was the real Denali, and Rook has been helping him stay hidden all these years. What if that man they killed way-back-when on Gel Gonahaar, wasn't in fact the crime lord, but some kind of... body double? They had never seen Denali before, that dude could have been fucking anybody! Some stand in, just acting like him. Why was he just waiting there like that otherwise? Why didn't he try and run if it was the real Denali? Then Rook wastes him before they could even question him? And gets them rushed out of there before they have two seconds to take a look around? Maybe it was all just a giant ruse. Shit, even if it wasn't, there's still another possibility. Maybe that was Denali then, but there is no Denali now. Just Rook's fucked up, deranged clone pretending this whole time, running shit himself. Maybe they'll get to this toy factory, burst into the owner's office, and find their replicated seti friend sitting there with his feet up, funneling whatever kind of contraband he's been providing to his buddy Nylis. That could be it! Maybe Rook is Denali!*

"Cousin Bullit?" Relic asked again.

"What!" he barked. Then, more calmly, "I mean... I'm sorry. I was... somewhere else. I'm just upset that it's taking so long to get back to Oberonn. Fuck!" He threw his spoon across the room to clang off the inside of the giant stainless-steel dish sink like a bell. "Flashpoint, goddammit, listen to your sister! I've gotta go to bed."

He turned and left the galley with his sibling cousins still staring behind him, the ivory fur around his muzzle bowed low in its scowling—and lightly smudged with butter brickle.

13.5

THE ELABORATE ART OF BRAINWASHING was traditionally administered across three stages: the destruction of the self, the opportunity for salvation, and the rebuilding of the self in the chosen mold of the indoctrinator.

Destroy.

Offer Hope.

Rebuild.

Stage one had become a simple matter with the sort of mental influence Lord Denali could wield. No coercion or browbeating required. No need for prolonged, spirit-breaking torture in order to manipulate. Though sometimes he would employ these cruder methods simply for the pure enjoyment of it. Most times, in fact. Spare the rod, spoil the child—

isn't that how the saying goes? Sparing the rod was not a habit of which anyone could accuse Lord Denali.

Rook had surmounted this first stage more rapidly even than most—after all, what simpler way to destroy one's self, than prove it never had existed in the first place. It was likewise unprecedented for Lord Denali to have the benefit of actual facts at his disposal, rather than the usual twisted lies to confront his chosen initiate with. Not needing sustained convincing of various unrealities certainly saved a lot of time, but also stole away some of the cloned human's grim enjoyment of it. He did not get to savor the pleasure in the destruction of Rook's self—his old seti friend simply self-destructed all on his own.

But he was now ripe for step two—Lord Denali sensed it clearly in his inner mind: the longing for guidance and direction, the deep hunger for someone to show him his purpose. That someone would be Denali. It was time now to offer Rook a path towards redefining himself, let him know he had a position here, and a value. He needed a mission; something simple, but equal to his skill set. And something short, as it was still early days yet, and Lord Denali's suggestive influence waned if not reinforced fairly frequently. It would be some time before Rook was completely rebuilt anew in step three, safely changed forever.

Escorted by Drake, and a small contingent of trailing guardsmen, the two ex-Parliament members, Dodger and Rook, strode down the dimly-lit corridor of Denali's vessel, a lyghtan starship once part of Queen Vasu's armada. As such, the lighting design left something to be desired, the poor illumination reminiscent of the many dusky caverns of its homeworld. They had dropped out of warp in order to rendezvous with some of General Nylis' fleet of commingled military and mercenary vessels. In particular, so he could have a word with the soon-to-be ex-supply officer.

The entourage filed to the right through a reinforced sliding doorway, and entered the expansive hangar bay, their footsteps clapping in unison as they marched toward the human officer held at gunpoint in the center of a landing pad. He was medium height and medium build, nothing particularly distinct about him, except for the appearance across his face that he might have already been weeping. Lord Denali was pleased by this, glad to know his reputation had preceded him. For most of these soldier pawns he would never meet, his reputation was all that kept them in line.

"Lieutenant Macey," Lord Denali said, "I'm told you were in charge of the transported weapons shipment. The one that detonated."

"I... I didn't..." the human began.

Denali waved his fingers, his braceleted wrist suddenly aglow, and Macey jerked roughly into the air, arms and legs spread like Da Vinci's

Vitruvian man. He shouted in pain as tension pulled on each of his appendages, like invisible ropes at his ankles and wrists, threatening to quarter him. A deep, muffled pop echoed as one of the man's shoulders left its socket.

"Let's begin again, Mister Macey!" Lord Denali nearly bellowed now. "Were you, or were you not, in charge of the weapons being transported up from storage on Oberonn?"

"Yes, my lord," Macey managed to force through sweat, tears, and gritted teeth.

"You are aware of the precautions required when molecularly teleporting bulk armaments, are you not, lieutenant?"

"Yes, my lord. I followed procedure. It was not my fault."

Denali flicked a finger again, followed by the sickening thunk of Macey's hip pulling clean of his pelvis. The man wailed out in agony, quickly interrupted by a burst of upchuck sprayed from between pursed lips. He gasped two or three quick breaths, then freely vomited the rest of his stomach contents onto the hangar deck. Whatever his last meal, it wasn't eaten long ago, as the chucks were quite large and undigested, and there was very little smell of bile. A dark stain appeared at the crotch of the officer's gray uniform, a spreading of urination that flowed down both pant legs, and trickled loudly onto the floor.

Denali took a quick glance at Rook beside him, and was pleased to see him watching intently—and was that the shadow of a smile? This exercise was as much for Rook's sake as it was for the unfortunate Lieutenant Macey's. Denali needed the seti to observe closely, counted on it, in fact, to be pulled across that fine line between horror and fascination. His old friend needed to understand the benefits of being on *this* side of an inquisition—and the power that comes inherent with it.

"Take a breath, Macey, and stop making a mess of my hangar bay," Denali said. "Explain to me *why* this incident is not your fault. Not only half my cargo gone, but the ship destroyed as well, along with all hands on board! If I don't blame you, then who?"

"We followed the... standard safety protocol... to the letter sir," Macey gasped and spat. "The explosion... was not caused by... the weapons. It was... booby-trapped."

Denali turned to Drake. "Is what this man said correct?"

"I... I don't know my lord," he answered. "I would have to review the teleporter logs. But they're destroyed."

"I saw the logs," Macey continued, "from central operations... before the... before the blast went off... the teleporter alert... detected the danger... too late."

"What did it detect?" Denali demanded.

"Everything... all kinds of stuff," he told him. "Mines, grenades... micro-missiles... heurcanium charges, all...all set on... on... on a timer."

Denali heard an irritated chuckle exhaled beside him, and turned to Rook.

The seti looked back at him. "Fuckin' Stansky," he told him.

"That's not possible. They left Oberonn, thinking you were still with them. A metamorph agent was..."

Rook was insistently shaking his head in the negative. "I'm telling you, this is Stansky. I can feel it in my bones. Which means they're onto you, or soon will be. Either that, or Yinkall was disgruntled about being left to move the last boxes on his own. I admit I didn't know him that well, our association was brief, but to me, he didn't seem the type. My money's on that walking mass of jacked-up hormones. This has James Stansky written all over it."

Denali turned back to Macey, still suspended mid-air, and straining in four different directions. "I apologize, lieutenant, it appears you did follow the safety procedure."

Macey breathed hard and smiled.

"However, is there not also a failsafe on the teleporter which will identify active explosives prior to encoding, and not rematerialize them?"

Macey frowned. "It was... disengaged, we... we only use it when... when we don't know the sender. It delays the process... would take much longer... to scan every container first..."

"Ah, I see," said Lord Denali. "That explains it. You were rushing, and being lazy. And careless. Well, this then is why I'm now going to rip your arms and legs from your body, and leave the rest of you to bleed to death lying in your own piss and vomit."

Macey moaned in terror as he wiggled violently against the force that held him.

"Come now, Lieutenant Macey, you can yell louder than that," Denali said. "Now, let's try it once more from the top, and this time... with feeling." His fingers moved, the bracelet flared, and the human's extremities popped, squelched and cracked, until the four appendages pulled rudely free of their respective sleeves and pants legs, leaving the now emptied portions of the garment to dangle limply, and soak rapidly with blood. Denali was right. Macey did scream louder, and with much deeper feeling. The quartered torso fell back down heavily to the floor, joining its former lifeless limbs; white bone protruding from tattered, red flesh.

Lord Denali turned and headed back to the corridor, Rook and Drake shadowing his movements at his side. "Fortunately, half my amassed arsenal is still safe," he said, as they returned toward the bridge, "transported to a previous vessel. But that's not enough to outfit my whole army. If this *was* Stansky, he's really thrown a wrench into the works."

"He has a tendency to do that," Rook reminded him.

"That's the least of the damage," Denali said. "I can meet with Vasu, have her raid her planetary armory to replace the weapons. And I'll circulate Parliament's images, Stansky in particular. If they were behind this, they'll be removed. The bigger issue is, that ship was already stocked with Mindgate devices from the base at Nol Qhan, now all destroyed. They must be replaced, quickly."

Drake moved forward. "What shall you have me do, my lord?"

"Not just you, Rook also," Denali said, seeing the seti look up in anticipation. "You can help me, my old friend... earn your place at my side."

Telepathic suggestions flowed to the seti as he spoke, and Rook felt a growing urgency to prove his worth to the human—and to himself. "Anything you need," Rook assured him.

"Drake, I'll have the factory on Gel Gonahaar ramp up production on replacements. But the serum to fill them... we will need the assistance of the khailian to produce it faster, in a larger batch. You and Rook get him, bring him to Gel Gonahaar. *Persuade* him to help. Then bring the finished devices directly to me at Trojan base. There'll be no time to waste."

"But... Dr. Cyyxill's assistant went into hiding, my lord. After his final delivery."

"Oh, I'm aware. But he can do nothing to hide from me. I know exactly where he is." He turned to Rook. "I'm sending you back to our old stomping grounds... or, the stomping ground of our former selves, at any rate."

Rook looked puzzled. "You mean a khailian is trying to hide in New Boston?" he asked. "He must stick out like a sore thumb. There's probably not more than twenty khailians on all of Earth."

"Close, but not exactly, old friend," Denali said. "He is not hiding in New Boston. He's tucked away in the original one."

Chapter 14.1

THE OVERZEALOUS SUN GLARED EARNESTLY above the chamai city of Krataar, as was its usual habit to do so. To the south, billowed clouds gathered ranks, built off steam from the sweltering jungles, and made their way northward to interrupt the sun—as they had habits of their own to keep. Deep below the city, hidden from this impending battle to rule the sky, James Stansky, Dr. Magna, and Lady Opal of Capella waited with waning patience in the musty, fungal passage where Selene Maraspese had led them. As she had promised, a second doorway was found within. Also as promised, it was currently firmly locked.

This second door was newer, far less corroded than the first—or, for that matter, less corroded than everything down here. Both the portal at which they waited, and the one from where they'd just come, crossed paths perpendicularly with some sort of ancient storm drain—a moldy and foot-slick culvert, built of the same ancient masonry that the outer wall had been. Towards the north, the subterranean gutter repeatedly forked and became narrowed, in numbers too great and sizes too small to be followed. To the south, toward the jungle, and the rear wall of the old city, the channel led some hundred feet along to finally end at a wide, circular opening. It was here, through a rusty barricade of bars, the city's runoff from the frequent downpours would forge together, forming a mighty waterfall of wastewater, cascading down some eighty feet to the jungle floor below.

Opal ventured this way as they waited, with James being quick to follow, and the two now stood together at the mouth of the gated outlet. The ashi'mar pressed her enraptured face between the bars, overlooking the lush rainforest that ran wild just beyond. The emerald green of the upper canopy was decorated with sporadic blossoms, fuchsia blooms of alarming size, the leaves and petals working together to obscure the mysteries beneath in the undergrowth. The lowest dips and valleys in the primeval terrain were further covered by a vaporous haze that hung over it, clinging to the jungle, unmoving in the still air. The sky above was still a bright blue, the shining sun highlighting each blade of greenery below—but at the far visible horizon's edge, pregnant clouds were lumbering closer, staining the otherwise sapphire sky with their dark, purple, bruised bellies. Rain was coming, and it would be preferable to be out of this tunnel when it did.

"It's like nothing I've ever seen before," Opal said to James. "Have you ever been out deep within it?"

"Oh yeah, many times," he told her. "Although, not usually to enjoy the scenery."

She looked disappointed.

"But I *can* say," he offered, "it makes even a big guy like me feel insignificant. The tree trunks can measure wider than a small house, circled with vines easily as thick as my waist. The flower blossoms, they're large enough for you to curl up and fall asleep in. And each single leaf can be as broad as the tent covers in the bazaar outside."

"I would love to explore it," she lamented. "I'd love to explore lots of places, before my lifetime sentence of being locked in my throne room begins."

"*I...* could take you."

The conversation was interrupted by the echoed groan of the second door swinging wide, and Tachion called out to them to hurry back and join him. The new door revealed yet another stairway, heading up, and Tachion led the way through the narrow steps with his EMD sword at the ready. At the top, yet a third doorway, this one decidedly modern, and it slid open to admit them as they cautiously approached.

Whatever this space may have been in the eon in which it was built, was long gone. It was now a clean, bright, state-of-the-art, and quite impressive workroom. Not particularly large, similar to the interior of the *Bugeye*, with a host of machinery and equipment well organized throughout. A biobed in the middle, with imaging scanners hanging above. Circuitry cutting tables, 3D polymer printers, and organic matrix accelerators to rival the ones in Tachion's own biolabs. A bank of computers, currently running some kind of skeletal imaging software, were on one side. On the other, an array of security monitors, showing the bazaar, the city, the jungle in back, all overlaid with IR and EM filters, and AI threat assessment.

"Alright," Tachion said, "well this guy is clearly no joke."

A door opposite from where they just entered slowly opened, and Kaii Kealiun, the Guisemage, entered the room.

"You sure about that, Tach?" Stansky asked upon seeing him.

The Guisemage was a chamai man who appeared not a day younger than a billion. Floating across the room upon a levitating disability chair, it was clear from the gauntness of his withered legs it had been some decades since he had stood upon them. His face was so cadaverously thin and sunken that his large flopped-over ears seemed almost elephantine. The man's thin, bloodless lips were as pale as the rest of his tissue paper skin, and the color of his sallow eyes was obscured by a haunting film of gauzy white. He raised one boney, tremulous finger as he cruised silently across the workroom, directing the stunned pair of mercenaries to turn their attention towards the computer behind them.

Tachion and Stansky spun around to read the monitor. A list of options was displayed, from simple iris swaps, to full, all-over body disguises, along with a price list beside each selection, and a darknet cryptobank transfer portal. The human and android skimmed down the price list, and looked at each other.

"Yikes," Stansky said.

"Seems I've been in the wrong profession," Tachion agreed.

Opal leaned in, popping her head between her two much larger companions. She read the monitor. "Whatever you spend here today, or at any point in this endeavor, you can be sure the Capellan crown will make good upon our eventual success."

"Alright then," Tachion said. "Still, no need to go overboard. A cover for your face, and I suppose hands, so we can make you a different species. That should be more than sufficient. As long as you don't plan to do any more spontaneous skinny-dipping."

Opal smiled up at him. "I will try and restrain myself."

Stansky frowned.

Tachion selected the proper option, and initiated the credit transfer, then rejoined the antiquated Guisemage who was absentmindedly staring off in the other direction. He swiveled, silently buoyant, at the sound of their approach, and smiled at them as pleasantly as possible with his horrid pit of decaying teeth. "Now then, who is the client?" he asked, with a voice hoarse and dusty. "And what is it exactly that you'd like to be?"

"Uh, no offense… Mister Kealiun, is it?" James inquired. "But can you even… *see* what you're doing?"

"I prefer Guisemage. And you have nothing to fear, human. My eyes may be failing, but they make do well enough. And where they don't, my fingers will never forget what they've learned all these great many years. Now, what is it you would like to be?"

"It's not for him," Tachion said, "but for the young woman here. Perhaps it's best if she were an average chamai for the duration. Not too pretty, and not too ugly. Just plain enough to be… entirely unnoticeable."

"So be it then," the Guisemage croaked. "Now come sit here, young lady." he patted the biobed mattress with his nearly skeletal hand. "I'm going to take some images of your skull, so we can find the right shape, and in the meantime, you can choose from an array of appearances on the monitor. The computer will average tens of thousands of chamai women, to come up with a set of basic faces that will fit with your bone structure."

"*I'll* pick," said Stansky.

Tachion took the opportunity to go and stand by the security monitors, still nervous of the likelihood of bounty hunters already on the ashi'mar's trail.

The old man measured, and prodded, and showed Opal samples of potential eyeballs. Covering the glowing light in her eyes, it seemed, would require an awkwardly large ocular prosthetic. But once she had chosen the look, he placed a few drops of a biological agent in each eye, then holding an emitter above her face with his frail and shaking hand, he activated the cells to quickly divide and spread. As they looked on, the emerald fire in her gaze faded, and a set of ordinary brown irises on a field of white sclera arose to replace it. James found her just as alluring.

The Guisemage then began traversing purposefully back and forth across the room in his chair. From the circuit cutter, he pulled a fine gossamer fabric overlain with a grid of nanomesh microfilaments: an integrated circuitry of minuscule actuators and sensors. Upon this he affixed a set of prosthetics from the polymer printer, a substrate to add to her existing skeletal features, enabling him to enlarge the nose, raise the cheekbones, and deepen the brow. Opal sat duly patient as the procedure was carried out, sitting upon the biobed with her face veiled by the now fitted sheer fabric, embedded with a grid of blinking nano-OLEDs, and plastic patches of artificial bone.

"The underlayment of microcircuitry," the Guisemage explained, "will sense your every subtle movement and muscle twitch, and relay the reaction to the bio-organic flesh mask above."

"Wait, so the mask is made of real skin?" Stansky asked him, somewhat unnerved by the concept.

"Oh yes, quite real. Although, grown here in my studio, of course. Not... peeled off some rotting cadaver!" He laughed out loud at himself, throwing his pasty mouth wide, and finishing in a hacking cough.

"Isn't that... I mean... won't it rot?"

"Oh, my yes, eventually all flesh does, does it not? For heaven's sake, just take a good look at me!" he said, laughing again.

Stansky forced a smirk that did little to hide his disgust, not only at the thought of Opal's rotting facemask, but at the little man who would attach it.

"How long will it last?" Tachion asked, turning from the security monitors.

"At least two weeks, maybe three, if you keep out of the sun. But now, that's only as long as you treat it twice a day with the nutrient ointment I'll give you, to feed the living tissues. The eye drops must be applied and activated once a day, or the matrix will fail, and absorb into the body."

"Geez," Stansky mumbled toward Tachion, "suddenly she's become as high maintenance as Tatiana."

"Who's Tatiana?" Opal asked.

"I... I didn't... *who*?" James stammered.

The Guisemage continued. "Now, you must also keep in mind, the flesh will not heal itself if injured. It has no independent immune system, so even a scratch can cause an infection of the mask that will kill the tissue."

"I shall be most careful with it," Opal assured him. "Tell me, may I remove it and reapply, or am I stuck with it on for the entire time?"

Stansky leaned in, curious as well.

"Oh dear, of course you may remove it. I will give you a case in which to store it. But I must say, at the risk of sounding immodest, it will never be as perfectly applied as when I myself put it on for you."

Tachion interjected. "I can assist, if the lady wishes. I have some rudimentary experience with biologic camouflage myself."

"Well, there you are then dear," the old man reassured her, as he ran his wrinkled hands across the flowing waves of her alabaster locks. "Now then, before I apply the skin, let's figure out what to do with all this hair."

James immediately interceded with his opinions of not cutting it too short, and Tachion turned back to the bank of monitors that were surveilling the city. A familiar face caught his eye, for just a second, and was gone. He quickly stood back, and panned his gaze across the entire array of screens—the bazaar stalls, the performer's courtyard, the upper central plaza, the downtown financial district directly above them—looking to see if the man he thought he saw would reemerge.

And he did.

"Oh, shit," the android said. "We've got trouble coming."

Stansky rushed over. "What is it?"

Tachion pointed.

Moving down the steps into the bazaar, following the same route that they had, was a lyghtan male. Unhelmeted, as per the city ordinance, his dark, bald head gleamed in the still cloud-resistant afternoon sun. A tattoo of white ran up and back from his temple, and he scanned the tents back and forth with a grim and determined expression, his features as harsh and fierce as an Indian head nickel.

"Is that... Tàlto?" Stansky asked.

"It certainly is. And you know there's only one reason for him to be here."

"He could be looking for someone else."

Tachion turned his head to stare down, expressionless.

"Alright, probably not."

"What's a Tàlto?" the old man asked, still busy in his work.

"A bounty hunter," Tachion answered. "A lyghtan bounty hunter, and a good one. But we are... acquaintances with him. He may look away if he knows the ashi'mar is with us."

"No, he won't," Stansky said. "He's still pissed at how Legion ended."

Lady Opal chimed in from beneath her veneer of microcircuitry fabric. "Are you speaking of Tàlto Lastnâm?"

"You know him?" Tachion asked, calling over to her as he watched the monitors.

"Yes, I should say I do. He is one of many official mercenary contractors to the church."

"Wait," Stansky asked. "Tàlto's last name is... Lastnâm? How did I not know that?"

"I'm sure that you did," Tachion told him. "Lady Opal, do you feel he would come to take you back against your will?"

"Tàlto has always been loyal to the throne, and takes his assignments from Queen Vasu herself. There is no reason to think he is not doing her bidding now." She paused. "Although..."

Stansky chuckled, interrupting again. "If his last name is Lastnâm, what's his middle name? Middlenâm?"

"Lastnâm is an honored lyghtan name," Opal chided him. "It means *'guardian of the waters'*."

"Oh yeah?" Stansky asked. "And what does Tàlto mean? *'First name'*?"

Tachion was clearly irritated. "I am quite certain you made these same jokes twenty years ago," he said. "I'm sorry, Lady Opal... you were saying?"

She looked over toward the android. "Tàlto and I enjoyed... a relationship, for a short time."

"Was it left in a good enough place that he would not seek to capture and return you?" Tachion asked.

Opal twisted her mouth in a way that said perhaps not.

"My dear," the Guisemage complained, "you must stop moving and twitching so much."

"Very well," Tachion said, "we must then assume he is here to find you, and take you home. Hopefully, we're safe as long as we are down here, though."

James moved to Opal's side and looked at her with some surprise. "You dated Tàlto?" he asked. "Isn't he nearly eighty?"

She looked back at him while trying not to move her head. "Age means very little in a species as long-lived as we are. A difference of a couple of decades, or even centuries for that matter, is a minor consideration for one whose lifespan is half a millennium."

"Good to know," he said.

"And, how do you know Tàlto?" she asked him, as the Guisemage now affixed gloves to both her slender hands of similar circuitry to her veil.

"A long story, my lady," James said. "*Very* long. But the shorthand version is, the man who called himself Denali... not your Denali now, but his prior namesake... he had a bone to pick with us for many years. At one point... oh, maybe twenty years ago or so now... he had gotten the best of us, and had us all branded as criminals. *Framed,* for crimes *he* committed. A special military squad was formed to hunt us. In fact, they caught and imprisoned our leader, Bullseye. The seti you met, Rook, had to go on the run with his family. But, anyway... that was the end of us for a while. Parliament disbanded and went into hiding."

"Goodness," Opal said.

The Guisemage behind her looked on with equal interest at the word 'hiding'.

"But, old Tach over there and I, we decided to keep on going. I dyed and grew out my hair, and a giant beard. Tachion removed all his outer plating, and covered himself with an organic human flesh exterior. Freaky looking, really. And we formed up a new team, by the name of Legion."

"Tàlto was on it," the android finished, "back when he was just starting out. But a year later, we had cleared our name, re-formed Parliament, and Legion just sort of... fell apart after we walked away."

"Tàlto was always a bit... ornery... after that," James said. "He was kind of pissed that we lied to him, and wasted his time, I guess. I haven't talked to him in years."

The Guisemage hovered in his chair past Tachion, finalizing the last few touches to the flesh mask. "You must tell me," he asked the android, "when you covered yourself in organic tissue, how did you get the cellular matrix to bond to your internal mechanics? And, how did you get the flesh to properly respond to external stimuli?"

"He didn't," called out Stansky. "Like I said, it was pretty freaky, real uncanny valley kind of stuff. Plus, it didn't last long, remember, Tach? A day or two spent outside, and he would start to smell like a dead raccoon in the chimney."

The Guisemage frowned, clearly hoping to have learned something new, but left disappointed. He gazed up at the monitors as he floated past, two grotesque gloves made of living chamai skin in his hands, and then stopped. He looked at the focus of Tachion's attention, the shade bounty hunter now moving through the performance courtyard, and pointed at the screen with one of the empty fleshy mittens. "Is this the tracker of which you all speak, this Tàlto?"

"Yes, that's right," Tachion said.

"In that case, the situation is more urgent. We must finish here quickly and get you out."

"What is it?" asked Stansky.

"I know this man you speak of, though never knew his name. I do not ask names in my profession."

"And?" Tachion urged.

"And he knows me as well. He has been a client of mine... a good one... for many years. He knows of this workshop, and how to get here. In fact, he was in this very room, only days ago."

"Goddammit," James swore. "How quickly can you finish up?"

"Well," the old man thought, "I was going to cut her hair to fit beneath the mask, but best instead to simply dye it. A wig is never convincing. Her natural hair, colored, would be far superior." He grabbed a small device attached to the wall with a long spiral cable, and with an illuminated wand sticking out of its other end. He began passing it over the lyghtan princess' head, muting the hue of her hair with each wave of his hand, from its usual stark white to a shade of medium brown.

Stansky again joined Tachion at the monitors, watching Tàlto's slow progress through the alleyways of the bazaar.

"What do you think he's looking around for if he knows we're in here?" Stansky asked.

"Perhaps he doesn't... yet."

Then Stansky noticed something that Tachion had missed. Remembering the mostly bare legs in the marketplace, he scanned across the monitors, focusing on the feet of passersby. He adjusted the cameras to focus on three, no wait, four of them.

"What is that?" Tachion asked, zooming in on the individuals, each clearly hiding a set of matching armor beneath a cape of black inertia fabric. "Is that... Darkcloaks?"

"Yup," Stansky said.

"Who?" Opal asked.

"A bounty squad," he answered. "Quite infamous."

"Is Tàlto with the Darkcloaks?" Tachion wondered. "Or are they each searching on their own?"

"I don't know. But he isn't wearing a black cloak, so probably not."

Upon watching the cameras, the squad of trackers seemed to be following the lyghtan bounty hunter, perhaps realizing that he knew the way, and hoping to swoop in afterward and steal the prize.

"It looks like you're very popular," James told Opal, returning to her side. "Hopefully, this costume will make not getting kidnapped a little easier."

"It is *not* a costume," the Guisemage corrected him sternly, slowly levitating in their direction. A reddened and gory bolt of flayed skin was held out before him, it's open eyelids and gaping mouth merely drooped holes which the light shown straight through, the hollow nose and formless features sagging and horrific, as if the face had just been freshly dissected from some hapless victim who still lay somewhere, tortured in burning agony, and slowly bleeding out.

"Jesus Christ!" Stansky said.

"Originators bless me!" Opal added, praying with him.

The procedure to affix the flesh to its nanotech backing was equal parts awful, and entirely fascinating, and by the time the Guisemage was done a few minutes later, both mercenaries had garnered a new respect for the artistry of disguise work. The ashi'mar stood from the biobed, and marveled at her own aspect in a mirror. She was, by all accounts, a completely different woman. A middle-aged chamai lady of Oberonn, her skin copper-tanned from a life beneath the jungle sun. Her brown hair, curly and coiled into springy locks, was pulled back into a ribbon at the back of her neck. Her umber eyes, narrow face, and lips—neither particularly too full, nor too thin—gave her just the look that they were hoping for. Not pretty, but plain. Not ugly, but average. James and Tachion closely examined her, and found it one hundred percent convincing.

"Well, what do you think?" Opal asked, then quickly covered her mouth with her new chamai hands. The voice that came from her throat was not at all like her own. It even spoke common with an Oberonnian accent.

"Stunning work, Guisemage," Tachion said. "Worth every penny."

"I am glad you approve," the old man croaked. "Now, let's move you along." He spun his chair around and sailed back to the monitors. "But it seems the way you came in is no good now, your friend is nearly on top of the entrance. And I can't have those cloaked trackers behind him follow along, and find my workshop here. I'm going to have to burn that entrance, I'm afraid... literally."

Tachion, Stansky, and Opal joined the Guisemage at the security station, watching Tàlto head down the dead-end walkway towards the city wall. The four Darkcloaks that had been nearby were now nowhere to be seen. The old chamai leaned down, reaching a bony index finger out to press a red button on the display. On the monitor, the small blind girl in front of the crimson tent they had been admitted through leaped to her feet, and entered the pavilion. Her body shimmered and undulated as she changed right before them, from a small helpless girl into a city guardsman—apparently a metamorph. She pulled aside the table, lifted the rug, and tossed a pumice grenade into the gated stairway. Within a second, the blast filled the narrow cavity to overflowing with a rapidly expanding dense lather. It then began to solidify the moment it felt the atmosphere. The ancient staircase was now completely backfilled with stone the density of porous lava rock. No one but the most determined miner with a pickaxe and lots of time to kill would be coming that way for the foreseeable future.

The counterfeit city guard then dropped another grenade in the tent, a slow incendiary that spread the growing illumination of fire across the table and its contents. He then went outside and began calling for help, as the flames rapidly took over the fabric awning and canopy. Almost immediately, dozens of vendors rushed to douse the blaze with buckets, eager to prevent the destruction from spreading to their own livelihoods. Tàlto could not even get close now, the crowd of volunteer firefighters and pedestrian onlookers was too dense, and after trying to peer up and over the throng to see what was happening, the bounty hunter gave up, and turned back to head a different way.

"Most ingenious, Master Guisemage." Opal said to the old chamai. "You can be sure, I will make reparations for your damages... when I am once again in a position to do so." She looked with concern at the monitors then. "I hope none of the adjacent tents are in danger."

"No need to worry Miss, it's already starting to rain. Afternoon storms here are as routine and expected as the sun itself coming up. Come now, follow me. We'll evacuate you out through the city exit instead." He led them out the opposite door, turning to Lady Opal as they moved upward. "And I will be sure, young lady, to give you my banking details before you go. I wouldn't want there to be any confusion of where to send that extra reparation money."

He winked his cloudy eye at her, and bared his stinking smile.

14.2

THE RELATIVE BLEAKNESS OF BULLSEYE'S private office aboard the *Parliament One*, compared to the more comforting and relaxed personal study of his K'Tas T'Mir estate, had been mitigated somewhat by the addition of his usual assortment of personal items. The engine hum through the rigid deck plates, beneath uninspired low-pile beige carpets, was dampened by the addition of a heavy, hand-woven, patterned rug in dark, muted colors, laid down across the room at an angle. Above a long, tufted, animal-hide chesterfield, in well-worn variations of walnut and pecan brown, the cold angular motifs permanently formed into the ship's wall architecture were veiled behind a large painted piece of artwork, secured within a gilded frame. *The Battle of G'rald Moon*, by Θ:Ⱳ⚍ююфℚю'⊑:⚫ⱣⱭ⚍, depicting the honored dead marching from the battlefield, across the bridge of starlight to join The Fallen. More of his collected seti tapestries, although admittedly ones he perhaps cared less for, camouflaged what he found to be a dreary repetition of the geometric paneling. The ambiance in here was kept dim, lit only by electric sconces set to a level that simulated the low brightness of hearth glow, to a lesser extent by the racing starfield outside, and by the ever-present glow of a wide curio cabinet behind his desk, where spread across its shelves of knotted mahogany, treasured items and future heirlooms sat illuminated gently on their displays.

The seti stood before this exhibition of memorabilia from throughout his lifetime, each memento intended as a testimonial to lessons not learned quickly enough, but now and forever hard forgotten. A tangled chain and dog tag once belonging to Damien Knight. The broken, blood-spotted hilt of Phineas McKendrick's sonic sword. On a cradle in the very center of these, and a great many other such items, he placed the drak'min disintegration pistol that Rook's metamorph impersonator had carried aboard the *Bugeye*. But now, for the first time, courtesy of his many heartfelt confessions and discussions with Bullit during their recent adventure, dawned a realization that such a memorial perhaps did far more harm than good. The bookshelf was more of a monument to his own hypocrisy regarding moving forward, than it was to any teachings gleaned from missteps of the past. He reached over and turned off the cabinets backlighting. He would seek to replace these items, one at a time, if need be, with trophies of more positive endeavors and successes, and remove the no-longer-relevant record of failures past.

He turned and sat at the glass desk, a wide holoscreen coming to life in the air above it, and planned to review the last known trajectory of General Nylis' ship, the *Okubi*, for any hint as to where Denali's soldier pawn was heading next. But he couldn't concentrate. He found that in the near full revolution of the clock since he arrived back aboard the *P1*, a single persistent obsession had taken up residence in his mind, so that even when not occupying the forefront, it nonetheless danced tirelessly taunting him at its edges. An obsession in the form of an enchanting, intelligent, charismatic seti woman. An obsession in the form of his friend Rook's daughter, Relic.

It had been years since he had endured such a consuming infatuation. So long ago, in fact, that he struggled to even remember. Perhaps then, it was actually never. He had gotten past his initial embarrassing reaction, and had managed to be in her company several times since then, but always with two or three others in attendance. And, never with more than a phrase or two exchanged between them. But while he did not speak much to her, he listened, and observed, and grew ever more impressed by Relic's attitude and demeanor. Of course, he would be lying to himself to deny that his initial feelings were purely physical, but the more he sampled the richness of her character and personality, the greater his desire to remain in her presence flowered. Which almost undoubtedly would present a problem.

There was a difference in years between the two, yes. But to Bullseye, that was hardly an issue. On the seti homeworld, it was not only usual, but even customary, for the females to seek out potential mates of a more advanced age than themselves. Probably this is due to the slower emotional maturity of the male seti, the women finding adulthood's wisdom and practicality much sooner than their same-aged counterparts. His own father, in fact, had been nineteen years his mother's senior.

No, it was more the unfortunate matter of the lovely lady's family tree. Once they finally manage to retrieve Rook from Denali's ensnarement, he was not exactly sure what his reunited friend's reaction might be to Bullseye's amorous intentions toward his daughter. His suspicion, however, is it would be decidedly not good. And even that obstacle somehow set aside, Bullseye could hardly seek to woo her now, being reintroduced after all these years, and displaying nothing toward her but apparent incivility due to his lack of suaveness around her. The latter issue being the main reason he now sat holed up within the seclusion of his study. He honestly feared that he could do nothing for himself in her presence, beyond make her impression of him worse.

The door chime rang then, and Bullseye bade the visitor to enter. Upon looking up to see who it was who had come to call upon him, there was a moment where he thought he might literally swallow his own tongue. He felt suddenly ashamed, although the thoughts that were at this moment occupying him were not in any way improper. Yet he felt that their entire content was somehow written across his face. He regained his composure, and stood somewhat awkwardly behind his desk to greet her.

"Relic, good evening. Please, what do... I mean, sit, please. Is there something you need?"

The young seti woman stepped in, the door sliding smoothly closed behind her graceful entrance. She held folded within crossed arms, and clutched tightly to her breast, a large leather-covered tome of some obvious great age, inlaid with gold seti lettering, and with worn and yellowed pages bound in between.

"Hi, B," she began. "Sorry. I mean, Bullseye. Mother told me not to call you by that anymore."

"I do not..." Bullseye stopped, and took a breath. "Rest assured, you may feel at ease to use for me any moniker that suits your fancy."

"No, no, she's right. B is what a child called you. Of which... I am one no longer."

"Yes... so I have seen."

She smiled a half-upturned lip at him, beneath her unbroken gaze of hazel distraction. The look carried with it a wave of flush that swept hot across his face, and spurred his stomach's butterflies to once again attempt migration. Thank goodness his black fur obscured any sign of reddening in his cheeks.

"I came by to... to return something to you," she said, approaching not the opposite side of the desk, but walking clear around it, and standing right beside him between his workspace and the now unlit memento shelves.

That perfume again.

He swallowed.

She held forth the thick, embellished volume to him, and he took the book in his hands without turning his eyes from her face. Finally, he looked down. It was an ancient compilation of collected seti stories, written upon parchments of jasiri skin, and joined by a hand-stitched twine of treated ligament. The book's backbone and end boards were of an extinct, near-unbreakable hardwood, all clad in gold-embossed and tightly stretched leather, and pinned with rivets of carved ferox teeth. The collected mythos of their mutual ancestral culture, in its original unabridged format—an archaic first edition.

Bullseye blinked. "How did you... I deemed I had mislaid this, some numerous years ago."

"Well, you did... in a sense. You loaned it to me."

"I fail to remember."

"I used to pester you with so many questions about seti culture, I think you were willing to risk parting with it, just to shut me up."

"I... wouldn't," Bullseye lied, certainly recalling the pestering, even if not the loaned literary work.

"It's okay," Relic's angel voice tittered like the soft bells of a distant wind chime. "I know I was a bit of a handful back in my youth. I wouldn't blame you if your patience with me had grown short. Although, I think your plan actually backfired. Reading it left me with two questions for every answer," she said, her smile fading. "But I never had the chance to harass you with them. I never saw you again after that day."

Bullseye didn't know what to say to that truthful condemnation, beyond, "I am sorry. I... I do not..."

She stared up at him, as if waiting. Waiting for him to finish the sentence that had no ending. Finally, she relieved him by continuing on her own. "But you don't have to worry, I don't need to pester you any longer. I feel like perhaps you are still avoiding me. Maybe you're afraid I will still be a hassle for you to be around."

His heart sank at the thought his actions, or absence, might in any way have hurt her. "Relic, please believe this, if any claim of mine you ever do. In all of eternity's great many days, no words uttered have ever been so wholly untrue."

She tilted her head, and flashed a smile of happy relief.

Bullseye opened the book and flipped slowly through its ancient pages. The iconography of the seti characters was hand painted in ink, made from the carbonized soot residue of archaic oil lamps, and the ever-fading colored images were each an original artwork, by varied anonymous masters, none to be ever duplicated again quite exactly. But he noted a more recent addition to the invaluable antique pages. All around, in the once empty margins that framed the body of the text, a jumble of scribbled, chicken-scratch notes now surrounded it, in every conceivable shade of modern pen color, filling each free square-inch of previous white space, on every single page, from one cover to the other. Bullseye looked up at her.

Relic's eyes were upturned and doe-like—shame, embarrassment, regret, and deep sorrow etched across her exquisite face. "I... am... *so*... very terribly sorry, Bullseye," she pleaded. "I didn't realize what I was doing when I started writing in it as a child. Or, perhaps I did. I don't know. It was just so hard for me to get through when I was young, I had to make a lot of notes. I started doing them separately, and then, at some point, I... I just..."

Bullseye thumbed through the pages of the now utterly worthless onetime collector's item. There was not a single space to be found where her ideas and impressions of the narrative had not been permanently etched onto the aged pages.

She continued. "Honestly, I don't know if I did it because I just didn't know any better, because eventually, I did. But I continued writing in it anyway. Or maybe I was a little upset, that I had so much to ask you about. But you just... you never came back."

"You appear to have redacted some of your original interpretations with a strikethrough," Bullseye noted, still thumbing through the parchment pages.

"I... well... yes, as I got older, I suppose, and learned more, and gained a greater understanding of our language, and the ancestral fables. And my critical thinking matured to better grasp the lessons and morals, I had to reevaluate my analysis each time I read it through."

"And how many times did you... 'read it through'?"

"Oh, I don't know. A very great many."

"So I can see, with new thoughts added on every pass, it seems. But never obscuring your earlier ones completely."

"Well, no, I just put a line through. I still wanted to be able to read them," she said. "Better to learn from the flawed assumptions of the past, than to forget, and repeat them."

Bullseye smiled wide. "From the parable of the Warrior's Widow and the Two Coins." He closed the book and looked at Relic, handing her back the annotated compendium. "You shall keep it," he said.

Relic shied away. "No, please, I have to give it back to you. You have no idea how guilty I feel whenever I look at it. At least I'll know that I returned it, even though I know I've destroyed all its value."

"Nonsense," Bullseye told her, clutching it now to his breast just as she had. "To me, your heartfelt additions merely serve to make it all the more invaluable. Utterly priceless."

Relic's eyes widened and came alive, and the relieved happiness in her smile beamed. "Perhaps we could... still get together later... to discuss it?"

"I have wrongly made you wait, lo these many years. I shall condemn you to do so no longer. I will make ready to confer at your pleasure... upon this, or *any* topic."

The smile beamed even brighter. "I have to go. Mother wants help preparing for Oberonn. She seems nervous about going down with cousin Bullit to meet up with James."

"Strange... she has ever failed to impress me as one who contends with such anxieties."

"To be honest," Relic said, turning towards the door, "I think she's just worried about still fitting in her armor." She grabbed her own bottom, and mimed a slight increase in its size. Tittering her magical laughter, she looked back and winked over her shoulder.

He melted.

She stopped then in the doorway, and lingered for a moment. Reversing course and stepping back, she allowed the door to slide closed again, and turned to face him. "I have to ask one thing, though, please," she sounded suddenly serious. "Why... why did you never come back?"

Bullseye sighed. "It is a long and complex answer, that nonetheless lacks any satisfaction," he said. "But, to try and make short of it... I believed I had found myself a righteous melancholy, and mistakenly labored to make a home within it. Certain unfavorable inevitabilities of life... I had placed their blame upon my own shoulders, arrogant against the truth that my actions, one way or another, largely do naught to steer the fates and fortunes of any others. Not in the face of *their own* choices. Yet, I thrust upon my back the blame of it all, and was bent low by the burden. So I secluded myself from the joys of living in response, and to be honest, I fear I do so still," he explained. "But I will strive to overcome this habit, to reach beyond this handicap. Progress has been made. I smile to claim much progress in short time. Though I admit, I toil still... and will for some years yet to come."

"Hmm," she said. "Perhaps I'm guilty of the same thing. All of this time, I believed you staying away... that... it might have been because of me."

Bullseye looked dumbfounded. "What? Why ever?"

"I thought I pestered you too much. Asking too many questions, taking up all of your time when you'd come to visit. And... I thought, maybe... I... had made you uncomfortable."

She had definitely not then, though certainly made up for it now. "As I recall," he said, "you were merely inquisitive toward your heritage. A commendable enthusiasm, and one I have endeavored to duplicate within your cousin. So far, to no avail."

"Well... that's true, I was," she said. "But, also... well, you know."

His stare said that he did not.

"I was always so... flirtatious. Sometimes I think, pretty unabashedly."

Bullseye felt heat rush to his ears. "I... beg your pardon?"

"Well, I had one hell of a schoolgirl crush on you back then. I must have seemed just so silly to you."

He stared on, mouth slightly agape.

"You didn't know?" she sounded honestly shocked. "You couldn't tell?"

"I... uh... no, most definitely not."

"Pfft." She shook her head. "Well, I guess just another thing I didn't know how to do well back then. And here I thought I pushed you away with my corny, adolescent advances, when in reality, you never even noticed." Relic shook her head at herself as she turned, and the door slid open once more to let her pass. She looked back one last time, sticking her smile in through the doorway. "You know, maybe I should give that another go as well," she suggested, sounding coy. "I have a feeling that you'll find I've gotten better at it now." She winked again. "A lot better."

The smile left.

The door slid closed.

Bullseye fell heavily back into his desk chair, still staring at the doorway, as if he hoped to somehow glimpse the visible remains of her aura. Finally, he looked down at the book he was still so affectionately holding, and flipped once more through its gloriously defaced pages. He stood and turned back to the shelf. Pulling aside a fragment of broken helmet—the significance of which was known only to him—he instead placed the treasured volume carefully in its place, just in front of the black drak'min gun, and reilluminated the glow of the single accent light above it.

14.3

THE DOWNTOWN FINANCIAL DISTRICT OF Krataar was but a stone's throw, and yet a world away, from the archaic nostalgia of the chamai grand bazaar. The city proper and its mighty skyscrapers were modern, sleek, and clean. The walkways and thoroughfares were wide, well-manicured, and free of overwhelming crowds or clutter. But the multitude of exotic fare restaurants that catered to the luncheon needs of the wealthy business people still needed their less glamorous backsides, where the grunge and grease of mass food preparation were gratefully hidden from the well-to-do masses. It was here, in a narrow and grime-streaked alleyway that ran behind the center of restaurant row, that the four emerged—an android, a human, disguised lyghtan, and ancient chamai—from a hatchway marked 'High Voltage', tucked in behind the power cylinder of a waste disintegrator.

The rain was pouring down in visible sliding sheets now, moving past like pages in a torrential book some god above was flipping through. The Guisemage pulled an umbrella-field from the side of his hoverchair, but the rest were not so lucky. Opal's hair quickly turned from curled and springy, to straight and sodden, though the new color remained fast as the falling water washed it down. Puddles had already formed in the deep potholes of the crumbling walkway, now overflowing to form an inch-deep rapid, winding its way down the long, straight pathway and around the corner to the street. Several kitchen workers from various establishments loitered here despite the weather, smoking beneath doorway awnings, or scraping congealed cookware, taking advantage of the hard-landing raindrops to rinse them clean. The group weaved past and through the restaurant staff, the stacks of barrels, and the strewn heaps of soggy litter, making their way toward the alley's opening, and the more respectable city streets.

The Guisemage's chair hovered easily above the puddles that the others were forced to walk through, and he took a right at the alley's corner, and then out onto the avenue. "Head north two blocks!" the old chamai bellowed out to them above the rainfall's clatter, "and then east, and you'll be back at the upper central plaza. Be wary, as the rain will have temporarily cleared the pedestrians, so you will be easy to single out."

"Thank you for your services," Tachion said to him. "Perhaps, one day, we may have need of them again." The old man turned to head back towards the alley, as the other three continued on in hopes of returning to the freight district, and the safety of the hidden *Bugeye*.

Just then, the sharp report of a gunshot rang out, and the android medic spun as his shoulder was forced back from the impact, causing him to stagger and smash through a restaurant's front plate-glass window. A second shot sounded out, and Stansky crumpled to the sidewalk, the bullet of an autopistol having ricocheted off his armor's knee hinge. The two had been caught unaware and took a moment to recover. Meanwhile, a Darkcloak took advantage, and lighted down with a levitation belt from above, shooting the ashi'mar point blank with a paralyzing net cannon. She toppled hard.

The bounty hunter pulled Opal back up by her shoulders. As she stood and shuddered from the net's stun effects, he looked at her very closely, visibly upset. "It's the wrong one," he said into his comms with irritation. Then, shaking the disguised lyghtan, he yelled, "Where is she?! Where is the ashi'mar?!"

The tracker's helmet suddenly splintered apart with a loud crack, falling to pieces in the rain, a shot from one of Stansky's nine millimeters splitting the mask wide open. The Darkcloak turned, stunned, and looked at James still kneeling below him. It was the last thing he ever saw, as the second round ran his face through. Opal's new mask of chamai skin was now splattered heavily with crimson, but the steadily falling rainstorm was quickly clearing it away.

James stood, activated his body shields, and pulled the net off the disoriented lyghtan, pushing her to duck for cover behind the metallic bulk of a parked aerocar.

Tachion stood as well, his shields also shimmering to life, and turned to face the street where the shot had come from. A Darkcloak was there, standing in the center of the roadway, and pointing a wrist launcher in his direction. The old Guisemage to his left was trying to hover his chair to duck down the alley.

The tracker called out, "We only seek the lyghtan royal! We mean no harm to her, just to return her home. Tell us where the ashi'mar is hidden, and we will gladly let you go."

"We put her on a transport this morning!" Tachion answered. "One leaving the Oberonn system. We didn't ask where she was going. She only paid us to escort her, and then she left."

"I see," the cloaked hunter said. "That's unfortunate. For you."

From his wrist were ejected three small, colored spheres in rapid sequence—sonic marbles, Tachion recognized. The doctor twisted toward the alley opening and dove to cover the unprotected Guisemage, hoping his own sonic screens would absorb enough of the shockwave to save them both. The concussive blast was deafening as the three tiny orbs sounded off their destruction, and the android was thrown roughly to the ground, along with any remaining glass in the restaurant windows. The Guisemage was shoved forward hard to topple over in his chair, and crashed headlong through a stack of barrels at the alley's corner. He was motionless.

Tachion remained still for a moment, the downpour drumming violently against his armor's backplate, until he heard the puddle-splash footsteps of the Darkcloak approaching. The android rolled quickly onto his back, and hastily sat up to extend his EMD sword through the tracker's throat. The bounty hunter's severed head pounded to the ground, still inside its helmet, the body collapsing much more slowly as it folded and fell atop the grounded medic. Shoving the corpse aside, he scrambled awkwardly back atop his inflexible metallic legs. He ducked and crept ahead, sinking behind a parked aerocar of his own. De-scrambling his helmet and autopistols, he was now more ready to face them. He looked back down the alley behind him. The old man lay still unmoving beneath the toppled drums.

Stansky's voice came over the comlink, having donned his helmet as well, *"Tach, are you good?"*

"Yes, I believe so," Tachion answered back, testing the range of motion on his damaged shoulder. It was always Rook that he would turn to with an injury like this, the technophile being the only one qualified to repair him. But it was starting to seem more and more like someone else might have to fill that role now.

"Two down," James said, as he waved that same count of fingers in the air from several car lengths down the sidewalk. *"Hopefully, two to go."*

A few vehicles passed by each way, splashing gouts of water as they did so. Tachion checked his motion scanner and cycled through his optics visors. *"This rain and the traffic, they're playing havoc with my sensor readings. Do you have them?"*

"Negative, same problem." He leaned the recovering Lady Opal against the side of the vehicle. *"I'm gonna take a peek. Cover me."*

Both mercenaries popped up and pointed their guns all around, without any idea exactly where they should be pointing them to. Before they could even visually scan the rooftop, another shot rang out. This time an energy blast, with the distinctive white burst of a Rageur proton rifle. James took the discharge square in the right chest, then fell back to land hard against the wall, sliding down to the sidewalk. But his hands had already begun moving instinctively as soon as the flash revealed the gunner's position, raising his two chromed pistols upward as he fell. Two shots went off. Two bullets struck the Darkcloak's heart. The caped bounty hunter fell forward from the roof across the street, and hit the sidewalk.

"*Alright, fuuuck. That one hurt a bit,*" James groaned as he crawled towards Opal. "*He got me good that time.*"

"*You all right?*" Tachion asked.

"*Been better, but also been much worse. I'm burned for sure, and feel like a truck hit me, but nothing that's gonna put me down permanently.*"

A row of bullet holes popped in succession through the vehicle door that Tachion leaned against, piercing through its rain-slicked painted skin from *his* side of the street—someone was firing from behind him. He ducked away and stood, rushing to the opening of the alley, and peeking around the corner with the barrel of his autopistol leading the way. The fourth Darkcloak was there, standing on the roof directly above the crumpled Guisemage at the corner. Tachion fired a roaring burst of ammunition at the tracker. He missed. The tracker fired back.

"*I got one on the roof here, James, at the corner. Think you can sneak up from behind while I keep him busy?*"

"*Roger,*" Stansky said, and aimed his empty hand into the air. From the gauntlet on his forearm, a compact warhead was launched, heading up against the rain into the sky like a child's bottle rocket. He brought up a holo-display above the wrist of his other arm, and used the controls to guide the micro-missile around in a wide, circling arc. Through the projected video above his arm, he could see his intended target through the eyes of the projectile, namely the back of the Darkcloak, still firing wildly at Tachion's position. The bounty hunter had no idea his death was coming from behind.

There was a small explosion, and the cloaked body crashed to the alley pavement beside his beheaded friend. A large hole in his back displayed what was left of his ruined organs, and immediately began to fill with a mix of seeping blood, and pooling rain. James stood and helped Opal limp back toward Tachion. "Alright then, I guess that's all of them," he said, opening his helmet facemask.

Tachion did the same, then looked down at the disguise of the chamai woman. "Are you hurt, Madam Ashi'Mar?"

"No, I believe I'm fine," she answered, with the additional masquerade of the stranger's voice. "Just a bit shaken, I think. And I've done a number on my ankle when I fell."

"Alright, let's get you inside. We'll go back to the workshop for now, and I'll see if I can patch everybody up." He turned to Stansky. "Take Lady Opal, I'll grab the old man." He went to the corner and moved aside a barrel, kneeling by the Guisemage's crumpled form.

"That's far enough!" a voice called out through the rain, and James and Tachion spun, weapons bared. Another Darkcloak was standing on the rooftop along the alley—and another—and yet another, lining the ways both out to the street, and back towards Kaii Kealiun's workshop.

Tachion counted aloud. "Two, four... seven. *Seven* more, James?! You said there were only four."

"I'm sorry, but I said no such thing! I *showed* you four on the monitors. I never said that was all of them."

"You literally did, just twenty seconds ago."

"Well, you thought there were only four also. I didn't..."

"Excuse me," the bounty hunter said, *"can we keep the focus on me, please? Thank you. Now, we have no desire to kill you. That wouldn't help us get the information we need. But we don't need all of you to stay alive either. Tell us where the ashi'mar is hidden, or we will kill the woman and the old man right now."*

"You've already killed the old man!" Tachion shouted.

The Guisemage groaned and struggled to move.

"Or... well... you've hurt him real bad. He's almost certain to die soon."

"What?" the old chamai croaked in a low whisper.

James moved to stand in front of Opal. "We've already told you, the lady is long gone, left on a transport this morning. We have nothing else for you."

"Well, we'll just have to see about that... the hard way."

The Darkcloak raised his rifle, and the sizzle of a laser blast shot out—although it did not come from his muzzle, but from somewhere behind. A blinding flash of orange light momentarily backlit every raindrop, and impacted the bounty hunter's albedo shield, draining it until it sputtered and shut down. He turned around.

Behind him, on the parapet of a neighboring building which towered far above, a figure in black armor dashed along the roofline, firing another shot and hitting the same tracker. This time, with his shield already expended, the laser burnt through him like he was made of insubstantial air, and his smoking corpse teetered, then collapsed forward onto the rooftop. Most of the remaining bounty squad turned to engage the new target, but the figure leapt from the building, immediately splitting into five separate images of himself, each one levitating down towards the alley rooftops, firing at the Darkcloaks all the way down.

The two Parliament mercenaries snapped their facemasks back closed. *"It's Tàlto,"* Tachion radioed to James.

"The one and only," the lyghtan's graveled voice responded through the comlink. *"Hey there Doctor T. How you doing Jimmy? Looks like you got yourself in a bit of a situation."*

"How did you hack this frequency?" James demanded.

"Well, I wouldn't be very good at my job if I couldn't. Now you guys want some help, or not." The multiple holographic images of Tàlto were drawing lots of fire, while the real one discharged volleys from the safety of the building's corner.

"Depends, old friend," Tachion said in reply. *"Are you with us, or just against them?"*

"Is there a difference?"

"For the moment, I guess not," the medic conceded. *"But don't think later you're getting the ashi'mar either."*

"One thing at a time, Doctor." Tàlto launched a tension reel at the mask of the closest Darkcloak, sticking it firmly to his headgear. Then using it to yank the tracker's helmet off, he fired at the unarmored face with a rocket pistol. The man's cloak fluttered away into the wind and rain after the explosion, with nothing of substance left to attach itself to.

James shot some suppressing fire to help Tàlto in his superior vantage point, while Tachion turned his attention back to the injured and struggling old Guisemage. He rolled the frail man over, and recoiled a bit in shock. The chamai had a traumatic head wound that seemed impossible to live through, yet he *was* alive. The medic leaned in closer. The scalp of Kaii Kealiun's head was slashed open wide, from the top of his crown to the base of his nostrils, and the large ragged slab of half his face hung down loose, resting on the old man's shoulder. Instead of the exposed muscle and skull that should have been visible beneath it, there was a wet, slimy veil of thin cloth, embedded with a grid of circuits and blinking microsensors. And, beneath that, a second face—one that he recognized. The dark skin and shining eyes of Selene Maraspese.

The android gawked. *"Well, son of a..."*

Selene glared at him from behind the torn-open face. *"God damn you... Fuckers! I knew you were gonna be trouble the minute I got a look at you!"* Her voice came out as a blended chorus of both her own, and the falsely generated one of Kaii Kealiun. She tore the rest of the ruined remains from her head, and spat out a set of rotten dentures to the ground.

James looked down, doing a double-take that might have caused whiplash. *"Mother fucker!"* he swore through the external speaker of his armor. *"You sneaky bitch. I can't believe you charged me extra just to bring us... to yourself!"* He turned back and fired another micro-missile to take out one of the bounty squad harassing Tàlto.

"Well, a girl's gotta eat," she said. "Dammit! You know how long I've played that old man without anyone figuring it out? Years! Fucking years! Now you assholes have burnt my cover, you burnt my workshop... I knew I should've walked away the second I laid eyes on you. But, *nooo*... I just got too much of a soft spot for people in need."

"*Oh yeah, you're a real peach,*" Stansky said.

"*Incoming!*" Tàlto's voice called on the comlink, as a grenade thrown his way missed its mark, and bounced from the rooftop into the alleyway beside them. Opal was quick enough to reflexively kick it away, then she collapsed, yelling, on her injured ankle. Stansky rushed to cover her as the doctor did the same for Selene. The blast caused an avalanche of tumbling building material to block the street exit.

As if somehow caused by the collapse, the torrent of rain suddenly abated, going from full deluge to not-a-drop as quick as turning off a faucet.

"*We gotta get the lady outta here,*" James said, looking around at the brightening sky, and being even more concerned without the equalizer of the inclement weather on their side.

Tachion turned to Selene. "*Is there another way out of here? Another exit from the workshop?*"

"Pfft. Yeah, there *was*. But I filled it with a pumice grenade, to protect *you*. Remember?"

"*I can blast that out,*" James said. "*I can put a directional charge and blow the whole thing clean. Then we can all disappear back into the bazaar.*"

Tachion looked at Tàlto, still fighting the last three Darkcloaks. He shook his head, impressed. "*Damn, he's certainly gotten better since he was with us.*" He turned to James. "*Go then, take her. Get her out of here if you can. I'll stay a bit. Tàlto and I will hold them off until you get the way clear.*"

"And what am I," Selene asked, "chopped fuckin' tamis loaf?" She kicked away the toppled hoverchair, pulling her muscular legs free of the Guisemage's false withered ones, and reached into the same hidden cavity to pull out a collapsing microwave rifle.

James looked down at her, noting her strong bare legs were free of the previous white inkwork. "*Jesus Christ,*" he said, "*even your tattoos were a bunch of bullshit? You're a pathological liar.*"

"I prefer to use the term mysterious," Selene said, cocking the rifle and taking aim at a Darkcloak. "It sounds a lot more intriguing than 'liar'." She fired.

"*Go!*" Tachion told him, as he took aim at one himself.

James looked at Opal. "*We have to move quick back to the workshop. Can you run?*"

She tested her ankle. "I don't think so," she said.

Stansky thought for a moment, then grabbed the Guisemage's hoverchair and set it upright. He pulled off the false panel that had the old man's scrawny legs attached to it, and sat the ashi'mar down. *"Are you ready?"* he asked.

She nodded.

"Okay! Cover us!" he told the others, then began to run, pushing her down the alley as he stomped with splashes along behind her.

The sound of explosions and gunshots, laser bursts and searing microwaves echoed around them, Tàlto and Tachion sounding off positions the way they had twenty-something years ago in his headset. He opened the 'high voltage' hatchway and floated her hurriedly down the staircase, back through the Guisemage's workshop, and down to the runoff gutter far below.

The channel was now doing its intended job, directing a flood of rainwater from the city above them, and the former empty tunnel was now a small, rapid river of muddy runoff. It was fast, but it wasn't deep yet; only two feet or so at its center. But the echoed roar of the rushing overflow reverberated down the long culvert with the volume of a raging whitewater. The sounds of the fight back outside had vanished from James' comlink, and he hoped it was their depth underground, or some sort of security jamming in the Guisemage's studio, rather than something happening to stop Tach and Tàlto from speaking.

"I'm gonna leave you here for a bit," he said to Opal, *"while I go examine the exit, and set a charge to blast the hardened grenade pumice out... hopefully without caving in the rest of this old tunnel with it,"* he joked, smiling.

"Okay," she said, laying her fingers on his armored hand. "Thank you, James."

He moved off to head down the first stairway they had originally entered, but was stopped by her calling him back.

"James?" she said. "What if someone else is already down here?"

"Well, that's not possible. Don't you remember what that insane, crazy, liar, fraud, Juniper said? That swindler? There is no other way in or out, just the alley, and the blocked tent entrance."

"What about that way?" she said, pointing down the watery tunnel, toward the barred gate overlooking the jungle canopy.

"Well," he chuckled, looking up, *"I don't think anybody would..."*

The gate was swinging wide open.

He popped open the facemask of his helmet then, and leaned in slowly, whispering in her ear. "Okay, no sudden movements," he said to her, as she inhaled a muffled gasp of terror. "They weren't in the workroom, and they can't be in the tent exit stairway, so... that must mean they are right behind us, in the tunnel forks upstream."

"What are they doing?"

"Well, if they wanted to kill us, they would have done it already. Maybe they just wanted to follow, see where we went."

"Or maybe... they already looked in the disguise workshop upstairs," she said. "Maybe they know, and they're just waiting to take me."

He had considered that possibility, but didn't want to say so.

James thought it best not to take her back to the pumice blocked stairway; they'd be completely boxed in there. So he looked back and forth down the tunnel for somewhere to duck into. There was a small alcove on the right, about halfway towards the open gate, an area where some rusted valve wheel had once been. It was now just a pin in the wall, the wheel attached to it long gone. "Sit tight," he told her.

He reached into his bandolier for a handful of small beads, then readied himself to run, and tossed them quickly up the tunnel behind him. The dusk grenades popped one after the other, releasing their masking fog, and filling the ancient drainpipe with a shroud nearly impossible to see through. He pushed her and ran.

The gunfire began behind them as he sprinted her from the vapors, but was aimed wildly, hitting nothing but the weathered stones. James tucked themselves into the niche, and immediately fired back just as wildly to keep them at bay.

"What are we gonna do?" Opal asked. "We're trapped!"

"No, not quite," James said. "There can't be more than two or three of them, dug in somewhere upstream a bit." He rummaged through his kit, and pulled out what looked like a large lump of sandy clay. "But we can't let them live, in case you're right about them. They might know who you are." He switched the detonator from radio remote to timer, still unsure of possible jamming coming from Selene's secret workroom. "I'm gonna throw a big, fat hunk of heurcanium their way, and bring this old ceiling, and whatever's above it, down on their heads."

"But... what about *our* heads?"

"Yeah, there's a danger. So, I'm gonna get you out first."

"*Out*? How? There *is* no way out."

"Well, I have an idea," he told her, as he knelt quickly behind her with his demo kit, and pulled open a panel on the backside of the hoverchair. "I remember, years ago... Jesus, it feels like a lifetime now... on one of our very first jobs together, back on Earth, in some rinky-dink industrial park." He yanked out a circuit board from the chair's innards. "I forget the exact mission now... steal something-or-other from one company, give it to another. I don't know, we did a lot of that stuff back then. Anyway, our medic at the time, before Tachion, was another android named Intim." He cut several wires loose from the board, then began twisting them back together differently. "So Intim... and I don't remember exactly what the unlucky bastard did... got his knees shot out, or paralyzed his servos or something. But Intim, he must have weighed close to... oh, five hundred pounds. But he was stuck, frozen still. Couldn't move his damn legs." He touched two wires together, and caused the satisfying spark that he was looking for, then picked up his pistol, and fired six times randomly into the smog down the watery channel, while Opal held her ears. The bounty hunters fired back.

"Of course," he continued, "none of us could carry him, and we were way up on the second or third floor or something terrible. But we had no choice. We got what we came for, and security was closing quick. So we had to get outta this building in a hurry... and I mean pronto." He handed her a long black wire from around her left side, and a long red one from behind her right, and came back around to the front, kneeling again to face her. "So, we strapped a couple of levitation belts around him, like the one Tàlto was using to float around out there. And when we got him to hover his heavy butt up off the floor an inch or so, we pushed, and ran behind him, and *shoved* him out through a plate-glass window."

She looked at the human, shaking her head in incomprehension. Then suddenly, the eyes that were not really hers widened, and she looked over to the open gate looming far above the jungle floor. "You... you wouldn't dare!"

"Now, it worked with Intim," he assured her. "He floated down and landed just like a feather. Or, well... that's not exactly true. I think he was stuck into the grass like a lawn dart, but he wasn't injured."

"James, please. This chair doesn't have the hover power."

"It didn't, but it will. You just touch those wires together when you're out the door, and it will boost the levitation to more than enough." He reloaded his pistols, and fired another volley down the tunnel. Then he ducked back for the inevitable reply. "I would connect it for you now, but you'd float up and bump the ceiling... I think."

"You *think*?"

He leaned in close. "Listen," he said. "This will work. You've gotta trust me."

She looked into his eyes and realized that she did. She did trust him. "Come with me," she said desperately. "Just hold on to the chair, or... sit on my lap."

He looked back at her and smiled. "No, no can do, Lady Opal. I don't think it would ever hold me. Besides, I gotta bring this ceiling down and squish these sewer rats." He peered up the tunnel. "And I'm gonna have to do it soon. The gas is starting to dissipate."

"I don't like that idea," she said. "This whole tunnel will come down, and you know it."

He said nothing.

"You do! You do know it!"

He gently took hold of the face that wasn't hers. "Look, I have no plans to die here today. There's a good chance I can still get out. But, even if I don't, it's the only way I can think of. I've got to get you to safety. You've got a whole world of people to take care of. And I've got to stop these hunters from tracking you. Do you have any better alternatives?"

She just looked at him.

"Hey, you said you wished you had a chance to explore the jungle. So when you get down there, do that. Take your time, look around a little."

She chuckled.

"I still hope I get the chance to give you the tour myself," he said. "I also hope... I wish... I'd seen your *real* face one last time again." He stared at her for a long moment, longing to lean forward and to kiss her. Kiss the plain-looking chamai woman with the wet, tangled, mousey hair. To kiss her hard, and for her to kiss him back.

But he pulled away quickly, slamming his mask shut, and threw a flash-bang grenade down the tunnel as a distraction. The triggered wad of timed explosives went next, as far as his throwing arm could manage, tossed behind them as he charged her toward the open gate—before she could object again. "*Remember to press the wires together!*" he yelled, trying to be heard above his racing footsteps splashing forward down the stream, aimed for daylight, "*as soon as you're in the air!*" He gave one more final shove to her as the explosive detonated with a thunderclap, the shockwave directed down the culvert launching Opal and her chair like a ball from a musket. James saw her go out, and then down, as he was thrown from the blast's percussion. He cracked his head hard against the wall, with a blinding, silver flash at the back of his eyes. Then something heavy fell from above, hitting him again in the same spot.

His world went black.

14.4

ROOK THOUGHT LONG ON HIS WIFE, and thought long on his friends. But not with any sense of longing, or worry, or concern for where they were. Anger was all he felt—disillusion and betrayal. The extent and effort they had all gone through, simply to keep lying to him. To keep using him. To take control of his life. Did his children know, too? What the hell was he thinking? They weren't even his children. And not his wife, nor his friends. They all belonged to the other, the one before who was long dead. Of course they all knew. How could they not? Everyone knew. Everyone but him, that is. All denying him his nature, conspiring against him, forcing him to fit a life that *they* decreed he should live. Well, he's choosing his own path now. Lord Denali had shown him the truth, and shown him the way. The master was right, he and Rook were the same. They are two brothers, both born of *no one*, yet destined to a greatness of their own making. Denali was right about all of it, and Rook would do anything now to repay him.

The implanted thoughts and emotions echoed around in the seti's head, powerfully thrust in a deluge upon him before he and Drake departed, now heading for Earth. But there was no way to tell, no sensation of confusion within him that might lead him to realize these thoughts were not his own. But with each reinforcement, they were more and more becoming so.

They traveled at high warp aboard a mercenary interceptor—a fine ship, and a fast one, with a crew of four who kept mainly to themselves. That was just fine with Rook. He had no desire to socialize. Although he did now seek out Drake in the aft cabin, looking to learn more about their mission, and perhaps ease the tension between them. After all, they did now need to work together.

He found him seated in the galley, only the second time Rook had seen him without his signature mandible helmet on. He sat down by the other seti, his former enemy, and tried to make friends. "So, you wanna get me up to speed on what exactly it is we're doing?" Rook asked.

"*I* am going to collect the khailian doctor," Drake replied without looking up from his multicomm. "*You* are coming with me."

"Yes, I've been made aware of that much," Rook said with restraint. "But who is he? What do we need him for?"

Drake turned off the display, then looked up with loosely veiled irritation. "Doctor Grivvux assisted in the development of the Mindgate device. He aided Lord Denali early on, procuring the chemical we needed from his people, overseeing its refinement into the Mindgate serum. He was rewarded for this assistance."

"You know, he's probably not really a doctor," Rook interjected. "Like, with a doctorate from a school. The khailians just *gave* themselves these honorary titles when they arrived in our space... to fit in, interact better. Doctor, senator, general... these words didn't even mean anything to them before they got here."

"Well, doctor or not, he gave us what we demanded. The serum was then produced at one of Lord Denali's facilities on Gel Gonahaar."

"Pssh, well, that's kinda funny. That's where I killed the original Denali."

"Yes, I know. I was there," Drake reminded him. "Anyway, the serum takes a long time to make. It must be produced in small batches. Doctor Grivvux was working on a way to speed the process."

"When he... up and ran?"

"Exactly."

"Well, that's probably cuz he's not a *real* doctor, and realized he had no clue what the fuck he was talking about."

"Well, that would be unfortunate, for him, as well as for us. We have a strict timetable, and we need the devices your onetime associate destroyed to be replaced. We have only a matter of days."

"If this khailian was just the assistant, why not go to the main man?"

Drake looked at him sideways with an eyebrow raised.

"Ah," Rook said. "I assume Lord Denali already made an example of him?"

"An extremely vivid one."

"I can imagine," he said. "So, yet another reason the assistant took to running."

"Perhaps," Drake agreed.

"And he's in Boston? Not in New Boston, but the old city proper?"

"So our lord has told us."

"Which means... he's underwater."

"That's correct. Thesean smugglers long ago took advantage of the city's remains. I am told there is a network of bunkers and fortifications. It's abandoned by the theseans now, but it's still a home to those who wish to remain... off the grid."

"Mmm. I don't know if you're aware of my history," Rook said, "but I don't have the best track record when working underwater."

"Yes, I was there as well," Drake said, with a wry smirk. "Don't worry, no one is doing any swimming this time." He turned on his multicomm and went back to his reading.

"Speaking of history," Rook continued on, undaunted, "I don't know anything about yours. Where do you come from? Are you..." he paused, not wanting to say the words, "are you like Lord Denali and me?"

"*No one* is like Lord Denali. Including you."

"No, of course not, but... you know what I mean. Where were you before all this?"

"I was a guard, on Theseus."

"Yes, I know," Rook said, growing impatient. "I meant before that."

Drake looked up from his multicomm, then stared off into nothing. "I... I had always been a guard."

Rook got up, shaking his head. "Okay, well, great. Good talk. I'm just gonna go wait in the, uh... somewhere else."

"I will find you when it is time."

"You do that," Rook said, leaving back the way he came. "Oh, and by the way, I'm sorry about all those butler jokes, calling you Alfred and everything."

"Is that what that was? I'm afraid I didn't get it."

"Yeah, I know," Rook told him. "That's what made it so funny."

14.5

THE LIGHT ARMOR JAMES STANSKY wore was not at all sealed tight like his sturdier outfits, and the rushing flow of collected rainwater easily found its way through gaps and crevices to fill his helmet, washing up his nose, and down his throat. He rose from the center of the torrent, struggling to all fours, coughing and gagging on a mouthful of the inhaled runoff. He staggered dizzily to his feet, a relentless high-pitched whistle screaming in his skull, a chorus of bells pealing through his brain with every movement, playing havoc on his eardrums. He reeled, swaying back and forth as he aimed to make his way back to the alcove, holding straight-armed against the wall for support. Dragging his floundering feet as he went, sloshing through the rapids, he looked around to find which way was upstream, and which was down. But he couldn't see. It was too dark and dust-clouded. Was the water higher than before? He fell splashing back down into it.

He stood again. It was definitely higher. He activated his nighteye visor to pierce the darkness, but although he could now see, it was like looking through a kaleidoscope. The visor must have been smashed. He saw through a dozen triangular, fragmented images, none of which seemed to correspond with the ones beside it. He could tell one thing though; the tunnel was down. There was no way back to the two staircases, or even the alcove where he and Opal had huddled. The worn stone culvert that had stood the test of ages stood no longer, and the collapse had been further backfilled by the weight of the city of Krataar up above it.

Bad luck for him, the jungle exit was collapsed as well, although he was able to glimpse just the thinnest slivers of daylight through tiny gaps between the fallen stones. If he could pull aside some of the tumbled debris from the cave in, perhaps he could reach the opening, re-acquire a comlink signal, and call for help. He tried to shake the deafening ringing from his ears, and the muffled confusion from his addled mind, but the brisk movements only made it hurt worse. He fell again as he lurched his body toward the rubble pile, his fall caught and lowered to safety by the surprising height of the rising water. The collapse had stemmed the tunnel's outflow, and the swirling runoff was at his waist now.

He pulled himself up, climbing toward the top of the collapsed pile, then yanked at a hefty stone that had the most promising silver lining of light around it. His powerful muscles strained, teeth clamped tight and blood vessels swollen. But the rock sat still, indifferent to his efforts. He may as well reach up and try to pull down the moon. He tried to think, but it was hard to focus. Another explosion would probably clear it—while killing him, and bringing down the rest of the tunnel in the process. It seemed he had little choice but to simply wait until Tachion and Tàlto found Opal. She would point out the culvert opening, and they'd come dig him out from the other side.

But the water was up to his chest now, seeping in between the fallen stones upstream faster than it could leak back out through the now-narrowed opening. If he wasn't so damn woozy, he would have realized it before—he was gonna drown. He searched for ideas, but his head was spinning. He actually found it hard to even keep his eyes open, despite the continued alarm of powerful ringing in his ears. He looked vainly through his wet demo kit, glimpsing the contents through the shattered wedges of his nighteye visor: useless sodden det-cord, unhelpful tools and cutters, a wide array of pressure, light, and chemical detonators—all of which would do him no good. A large, empty micro-missile clip for one of his larger suits of armor. Stansky stopped then and held it up, trying hard to concentrate.

The *Bugeye* had been stashed in one of the empty warehouses in the freight district, honoring Belladonna's suggestion. She had been right, of course, as per her usual. There were plenty of disreputable foremen just waiting to be bought. The particular one they had chosen, however, perhaps a tad more disreputable that Stansky actually cared for. He didn't trust him—not for a moment. He half expected to return and find the old ship scavenged for loot and parts, and resting on cement blocks. So he had scrambled and taken with him the most valuable and irreplaceable possessions he could manage, just in case. Although there was one item that could not be scrambled, but which James thought best not to leave for potential pilferers. He turned the ammo clip upside down over his other hand, and out rolled Vasu's strange, empowering glowing bracelet.

He hadn't told the others he'd taken it. Why was that? Had he been hoping to use it all along? He didn't think so. In fact, up until now, he'd forgotten entirely all about it. Was it possible it could help him? Would he even know what to do? Opal had said Denali was able to walk through walls with the device. Well, that would certainly be helpful about now. But she also said it only gives a limited few abilities to anyone other than Denali, seemingly at random. He might put it on and get nothing useful. Or not know how to use it even if he did. Or he might put it on, then keel right over dead from the toxic chemical inside of it. Of course, that didn't matter much now. The water was already at his shoulders—death was coming soon in any case. He climbed, wavering, atop a boulder to get higher. Then he threw off his right gauntlet, and opened wide the translucent trinket's clasp, placing it around his waiting wrist. He thought, *you only live once—* and promptly snapped the bracelet closed.

At first, there was nothing—just a mildly warm spot at his wrist. Was that from a jet-injection? Then suddenly he felt a rush of cold, like a wave of adrenaline that washes over you after a fright. Eyes dilating, lungs taking in more air, veins opening full bore. Was that an effect of the bracelet, or was it just that he was about to be submerged and suffocated by the afternoon rains? He didn't feel any better, which was a bit of a disappointment. Pulling off his helmet, he ran his bare fingers across his scalp. Holy hell, there was a huge egg there, and the sharp, violent wince of encountering an ugly gash as well. He just wished he could gather his wits a little more clearly, so he could focus. He wished he wasn't injured.

The bracelet's yellow blaze sprang to life.

The ringing tone was gone immediately, Stansky's relieved ears now taking in the echoed sound of running water, and crumbling rockfall. The fog in his mind slowly cleared and abated. The sting atop his hairline all but faded away. Even the deep, inner ache at his chest where the microwave beam had hit him earlier—the pain was gone. Feeling clear-minded and strong, as if he'd just awoken from a long summer nap, he reached up to the lacerated knot on his head. Flecks of dried blood in his hair, and nothing else. He looked at the now dimming device on his wrist, duly impressed. He might just have to get himself one of these things.

He was going to have to be careful now—he didn't know how much longer he could use it. Should he try to magically walk through the rock at this end, towards Opal and the jungle? Or perhaps go back through the main collapse and exit through Selene's Guisemage workshop? He didn't know if the ashi'mar was still down there, or if she had run back around to the grand bazaar. And were Tach, Tàlto, and Selene still above, or trying to reach him? He wished he could know if they were somewhere back there, behind all this rockfall. The bracelet surged to life again, and James felt his awareness reaching outward from himself.

It was a curious sensation, one nearly impossible to describe. Like trying to teach someone without emotion what a first childhood crush feels like, or describing to a lifelong vegan the singular flavor of perfectly cooked bacon. Some things just can't be explained without a common frame of reference. But he knew his mind was reaching out, and he knew when it had found someone. Though it was not the doctor, nor the others. It was someone else. A woman, he could feel—scared, and in pain. Then it came to him. It was one of the Darkcloak bounty hunters that had been firing on them. The clear sense of her emotions came as vivid and overwhelming as if they were his very own. She was crushed, and in deep agony. Trapped inside the structural integrity of her own armor, but unable to so much as wiggle with the tightly packed dirt and stone all around her. Completely encapsulated by the sheer immeasurable weight of the city above her pressing down. Buried alive. Perhaps for all time. She was absolutely terrified. Not so much of her death, but of how long it was going to take to come for her. With the life support in her armor still keeping her going, how long would she remain down here, suffering, and alone? Would her broken leg slowly bleed her to death? Or would she be trapped here in this insanity until she finally succumbed to starvation? James pulled his mind back, forcing the horror of her plight away from him. He shook off the emotions that weren't truly his, and blinked them back from his eyes.

Time was almost up. Even standing as high as he could atop the fallen rocks, with his head pressed against the ceiling, the rising water was at his neck now, and showed no sign of slowing down. The nearest, shortest distance made the most sense, and that was the few feet of toppled stone right in front of him. He closed his eyes, then pictured images of himself becoming incorporeal. He wished he were as insubstantial as a ghost, passing right through the blockage in front of him like a phantom. He even chanted aloud half of the childhood mantra, "light as a feather, light as a feather". Then he pushed his body against the tumbled down pile of debris with all his strength.

Nothing happened. He did not pass.

James pressed against it again. And again. Maybe he was just trying too hard. After all, the other abilities had come to him of their own accord. He tried to clear his mind, remove any thoughts of phasing through the stone, and then would suddenly turn to attack the wall and push through, as if he hoped to somehow sneak up on it. But the bracelet remained dark, and the stones remained immovable. Perhaps he'd simply used up the last of the serum on the ensensed powers of healing himself, and the empathic link with the Darkcloak woman. He was firmly beginning to panic now, his neck craning to stare straight upwards, struggling to keep just the tip of his nose above the engulfing waters.

And then, he was under, the last of the air pocket gone. He grabbed at the stubborn stone he had failed to so much as even budge before, and pulled at its edges with all his might regardless, simply out of the primal desperation to rage against the dying of the light. The rock moved, just a little. Then he yanked again, and it pulled further. Was the buoyancy or pressure of the water somehow helping? Doubtful. He opened his eyes beneath the black waters, and saw the device on his wrist once again alive, piercing the gloom with its golden aura of light. Stansky thought perhaps the bracelet had instead given him the gift of boosted strength, and he used it to his advantage with as much haste as he could muster. He pulled aside one stone, and then two, freeing enough runoff to create another small air pocket. He jammed his head against the ceiling and gasped the oxygen in greedily. Then back underwater to pull away more of the debris.

It was on his fourth rock that he realized, as he heaved another boulder and threw behind him, that it was not actually him pulling down the rubble, so much as the other way around. The stones were moving on their own, simply by him wishing them to do so, and his arms clutching each of them up were actually just being pulled along for the ride. He then stopped trying to physically lift them, and just focused on where he wanted them to be. He moved two at a time, then five, the water receding back down to his waist. He stood back then and concentrated on the entirety of the remaining pile, and with one willful push of his mind, the whole tumbled mound was shoved aside. The released water washed past him in a torrent, almost pulling his legs out from under him, but he willed himself to resist back against the tide, and managed to remain standing. Walking forward, he stood atop the waterfall at the very opening of the ruined culvert, looking down at a large pool that had formed from the falling runoff.

He checked once more on the bracelet at his wrist, ensuring the light inside of it was still enabled and humming brightly. He could sense the change within his mind now, actually *felt* it somehow evolving. Like a gate that had once been locked, finally thrown wide, allowing him access to abilities he always possessed, but which had been hidden away from him. The raw *power* he felt surging through him from the device! The feeling of *invincibility* it imbued in him! The sensation of absolute *supremacy*! It was intoxicating. He spread his arms wide with his palms up, face turned upward towards the sky, and stepped off the edge of the cascading waters into the insubstantial jungle air. He magically suspended there briefly before lowering himself down from the clouds of fog, like the Almighty Risen Christ returning from his throne in heaven. Stansky's smile beamed, and his chest puffed with pride over his transcendence, his absolute dominance over all he surveyed! The very jungle itself would bow to him if he so demanded!

The light in the bracelet sputtered then—and went out.

His eyes flew wide as he fell the remaining forty feet to the newly formed pool below.

Chapter 15.1

THERE WAS ABOARD THE BRIDGE of the *Parliament One* a certain ergonomic mastery and efficiency of design that resonated with Bullseye, despite his usual proclivity for the comfort of homier surroundings, filled with nostalgic bits and bobbles. The ship's command deck was the opposite of this aesthetic in every way, designed to immerse each crewman in one thing and one thing only, to the exclusion of all else—the operation of a starship. By all means no small task. Yet the practicality of the layout, the serviceable handiness of each workstation, triggered an almost primal sense of satisfaction for him to witness in use. In fact, Bullseye might like to loiter here on occasion, watching Captain Lobo's experienced staff working with each other in well-rehearsed concert. But he was one of the ship's five masters, *not* her commander, and his presence would constitute the exact sort of distraction the stark, workmanlike environment was meant to alleviate.

Neither so large that any more than a few feet were wasted on the possibility of the captain's floor pacing, nor so small that the crew ever felt the need to move aside for one another, the bridge was an angled pentangular shape of just about perfect proportion. An elongated section stretched out towards the front viewscreen, making it comfortably the right dimensions for its usual complement of nine officers. The floor was a textured vinyl black. The walls, consoles and fabrics, all shades of medium gray. A ring of white light from overhead, and along the base of the walls at the bridge crew's feet, was bright enough to see your surroundings clearly, but not so stark to be more than what Bullseye would consider 'pleasantly dim'. In fact, the expansive rows of multiple monitors and keypads at each crewperson's workstation, with graphics illuminated only in shades of blue and green, did as much or more to light the area with its teal-toned aura as the white strip-lights overhead.

Most of the stations ran around the periphery, enveloping the bridge with flashing screens and blinking panels. The more immediate control points, such as the helm, navigation, tactical, and mission operations, sat in the center, facing the overly wide viewscreen that was their window to the universe. The captain's chair was then placed alone above them all, top and center, as was the standard position for this style of ship. But Captain Lobo would never consent to such idleness, sitting aloof and inactive in her throne, demanding actions and requesting statuses of and from others as they bustled about her. She instead had a semicircle ring of data screens and displays, surrounding her in a halfmoon of monitors, allowing her to know the most crucial aspects of the *P1*'s operations without the inconvenience of needing to ask. Not, of course, that she didn't trust those around her, she simply preferred a more hands-on and inclusive form of commanding.

The elevator door opened, and Bullseye peered into the hive of prepared, planned, and well-practiced activity, and once again, as always, was awed by its clockwork-like nature. The lacertilian tactical and security officer at his station closest to the opened lift doors announced him. "Master on the bridge!" Lieutenant Kronn declared in a strong voice.

Captain Lobo spun in her chair to face Bullseye, her brow ridges and scalp feathers raising together in query.

"Request permission to enter the bridge," Bullseye asked.

"Granted," Lobo said, and stood from her chair to walk over and greet him.

"Forgive the intrusion, Madam Captain. I simply grow ever more eager to know of our arrival."

"Not at all, Master Bullseye. I'd say your timing couldn't be more perfect." She turned and called out across the bridge. "Helm, status."

A metamorph seated at the wide center console looked back from his station. "Now entering geostationary orbit above Krataar city, Oberonn. Distance... twenty-two thousand kilometers."

"On screen, Ensign."

The large main monitor at the front of the bridge, which had been displaying the thin, animated green line of an entrance trajectory approaching a rotating, blue wireframe sphere, dimmed briefly, then reilluminated; aglow now with the fertile and thriving foliage-covered globe of Oberonn, bathed half in light and half in shadow, some fourteen thousand miles below them. Plenty close enough.

"Lieutenant Kinn-Ara," Captain Lobo asked aloud again, "have you made contact with Master Tachion?"

The avian communications officer turned to them from the far wall. Her cragged, charcoal-colored beak took up the near entirety of her face, from the tip of her forehead to the taper of her neck, and shimmering eyes of glassy white were sunk deep below a ridged brow, like pearls encrusted in an oyster shell. Surrounding her skull in a fiery halo, a ring of crimson plumage surrounded her head in a wreath of feathers. "Aye, captain," she answered back, her beak clapping slightly as she spoke. "He reported in at the Krataar transportation center as arranged. Ready to zap aboard at your command."

"Very good, Lieutenant. Let's get Chief Zvavi to pull him up, teleporter room one."

"Yes, Ma'am," Kinn-Ara acknowledged, turning back to radio Zvavi.

"Anything else, sir?" Captain Lobo asked Bullseye.

"No, my dear captain. We seem in capable hands, as ever."

"Might I ask, what to expect for the day?"

"The good doctor, once aboard, will be exchanged for Belladonna and Master Bullit transporting down," Bullseye told her. "They will join Master Stansky, and a new friend, on a fact-finding inquiry. I hardly expect it to persist past a twosome of hours, mayhap a third. Bullit will bear them homeward to us aboard the *Bugeye* at that time. I fully expect we then make way for the manufacturing world of Gel Gonahaar. Unless, knowledge gleaned in their investigation gives cause to direct ourselves elsewhere."

"Understood. I will await your direction, then," Captain Lobo said. "Would you care to join me in my day room for a T'Mirian pekoe?" she asked.

"I appreciate the invitation, but best for me to see off, and on, our exchange of company." Bullseye reboarded the lift and headed back lower into the ship.

A mere one deck down, the door opened to allow Bullit and Belladonna to step inside, Rook's wife looking to have had none of the issues fitting into her armor that Relic had implied last night. It was her old service set from Starlaw, the still-visible department logo thinly painted over on its chest and shoulders, but otherwise looking as ready and well-fitting as it ever may have.

After a cursory afternoon greeting as the lift continued onward, Bullseye said to her, "I still pine for the day I may spy our gavel logo upon your armor, if you ever felt so inclined to join us, and deigned to wear it."

"Yes, I imagine you would be," she said. "And out of politeness, I'll say I appreciate the offer. But understand this, I am here for the sake of my husband only. I have no desire to become part of your... boys' adventure club."

Bullseye immediately had a long list of counterpoints with which to debate the disparaging comment, but wisely kept them to himself. He turned to Bullit. "You are certain you require no additional support?"

"No, we should be fine," Bullit answered. "We're trying to keep a low profile, anyway. In fact, it would be best if it was just the two of us. But apparently, her holy majesty refuses to not be part of the operation. I'm sure the lyghtan people will be just thrilled with us if bring them back yet another dead ashi'mar. I mean... I commend her devotion to helping her people, but sometimes it's just best to leave things to the professionals."

Belladonna sighed. "And James, of course, will not come back up as long as Lady Opal remains down there. I wonder what's driving *that* devotion," she said sarcastically, "beyond the fact he hasn't had a chance to try to bed her yet."

The lift door slid open on deck E, and the three headed together down the hallway towards the teleporter.

"We shouldn't be gone long," Bullit said. "We'll just ask around for a bit, see if any soldiers or mercenaries have been running their big mouths off to any of the paid female entertainment. Hopefully, someone might confirm what we already know about Gel Gonahaar, and we can get our asses moving to check out that toy factory."

They entered the teleporter room where Chief Zvavi stood waiting for them, looming large behind the control console, somewhat grease-smeared as usual. The pair climbed the few steps to stand atop the teleporter platform.

"May luck be with you," Bullseye said. "Remember, comms check each twenty minutes." Then turning to Zvavi, "Initiate transport."

There was a crescendoing hum, followed by a bright dance of light, and the titular '*zap*' sound. The two seti cousins were gone.

Bullseye turned again to Zvavi. "Tachion is not yet brought aboard, Chief?"

"Nay. It has been imparted unto me that a lengthy queue exists, in which he waits, it being the hour of day in which the transport center witnesses its most abundant use."

"You mean rush hour?"

"So to speak, Master Bullseye."

Parliament's leader approached his fellow seti. The Chief's bright, chalky mane was pulled back in a braided knot atop his head, his high tufted ears pierced with multiple gold rings—three hoops through the left, a gauge-rimmed aperture through the right. "You are from the homeworld, are you not Chief Zvavi?"

"Aye, master, sir. K'Tas T'Mir, born and raised."

"It does me good to hear the accent, reminders of home being few and far between."

"That they are, Master Bullseye."

"This common name you have elected... Zvavi... I am not familiar with the terminology."

"Ah..." the chief began, almost seeming a bit embarrassed. "It's of an ancient human tongue, dubbed Georgian. It denotes a..." he paused again, "...an avalanche."

Bullseye looked him up and down, the billows of snowy fur tumbling down the mountainous seti, and nodded his approval.

The internal ship's comm whistle sounded sharply then, followed by Captain Lobo's voice. *"Bridge to Master Bullseye."*

The seti walked over to the wall panel to respond. "Bullseye here."

"I wanted to make you aware of a situation, more of a curiosity right now than a concern. It seems we have several chamai military battlecruisers entering orbit, and more on long-range sensors heading inbound to the system. Dozens more."

"Is that so extraordinary, Captain? We are, after all, locked in orbit of their home port."

"True, but it is still damned unusual. Recalling so many ships home, in the numbers that we're seeing? There is just no logistical reason to do so that I can think of."

"What is it you say, Captain Lobo? You fear we are in some danger?"

"Well, if I didn't know any better, I might not think much of it at all. But having been briefed on your dealings with General Nylis, and the ongoings surrounding him, my feeling is that maybe, just possibly... this could bear the earmarks of the beginnings of a power grab."

"You believe the general plans to launch a military coup."

"No... I don't know. Perhaps. I'm just saying the skies are gonna be getting thick with his warships pretty soon, and if a takeover ever was his intention, this would certainly be the way to begin it."

"Is the general's vessel here?"

"No, there's no sign of the Okubi. But he could be orchestrating the entire affair from a safe harbor. That's certainly what I would do. He wouldn't really need to make his presence felt until it was all over, and it was time to show them the face of their new leader."

"Understood, captain. Please relay the same to Bullit on the surface. Advise them to expedite their activity if they would. And the moment the doctor is onboard, let us break orbit for a more secure position from which to await the *Bugeye*'s return. Perhaps out of the system altogether. Perhaps the next closest star, behind one of its ample gas giants. Or a similar locale, at your expert discretion."

"*We'll make ready,*" Captain Lobo said. "*I'm sure you're aware, if we retreat that far back, the return of the* Bugeye *will then take many more hours to reach us.*"

"Aye, Captain Lobo. Yet, we must do what we must do. Bullit may cloak her, and bring her back unobserved."

"*Acknowledged,*" the captain said.

Bullseye sighed deeply and rubbed at his brow.

"Uneasy lies the head that wears the crown, Master Bullseye," Zvavi said to him. "Grant me directives that might sway the tide of unrest which plagues you, and I shall do my best to see it done."

"My gratitude, Chief. Your allegiance is most reassuring. Perhaps you could do us the kind service of effecting quick work on the *Bugeye* upon its homecoming. The vessel had incurred some small amount of battle damage upon our swift escape earlier this week, and likely could use an overhaul to make her ready, in the very probable event we should need to call on her again. And, just as probable, very soon."

"It will be made so, Master Bullseye. I will have my team prepared." A sing-song alert from the control panel drew Zvavi's attention. "Master Tachion is prepared to come aboard, on your command."

"Bring him in," Bullseye ordered.

Another long buzzing and a bright flashing pop, and the large medic stepped down from the elevated teleporter pad. Tachion was not an android who was opposed to embracing, but his cold, inflexible chrome sheathing was far more conducive to hearty claps of greeting, delivered to his back or on his side—exactly what he received from Bullseye as he stepped forward from the platform. "Glad to see you in one piece," he said to Bullseye, as he clapped the seti's back in return. "You had the two of us worried we'd never hear of you again."

"Yes, well... a number of missteps were made by me since last we met, the bulk of which we can review at a time of greater leisure."

"I am sure we both have stories to share, when time allows."

Bullseye stood back, scrutinizing the android's upper body. "I thought you had been shot, injured in the shoulder, I was told. Yet, I see no damage."

"No, I'm fine, all thanks to Tàlto," Tachion said, walking side by side with the seti through the door and down the hallway. "If he hadn't been there... let's just say that bounty squad had us dead to rights. But after we chased off the last few Darkcloaks, he stuck around for a bit, just long enough to fix me up."

"Hmm. A handy gentleman to have nearby."

"Yeah, well, that was my thought exactly. I don't think I'd be wrong to say I've missed Rook being around more than the rest of you guys, since he's always been my only security of being put back together when I get hurt, the way I do for all of you," Tachion told him. "In fact, without Rook here, I wouldn't mind having Tàlto around on a more permanent basis, just for that reason."

"We have Android techs about the ship that could fulfill that role," Bullseye said.

"Yes... but not battle tested. Not experienced fighters, or field mercenaries."

Bullseye nodded. "That is true."

"And you have to admit, we're a little shorthanded. Even with Belladonna here. We have been for a long time, well over a decade and a half since losing Dodger. And now down to just *four* of us without Rook? Even if I didn't need his repair skills, we could still do with another gun, another experienced opinion out there. Another set of eyes to watch our backs. Especially if... well... if it ends up Rook can never come back."

"I find it hard to disagree, when you advocate so enthusiastically for this Tàlto."

"He was good twenty years ago, but he's exceptional now. Working all these years alone, he's become a jack-of-all-trades. Widely proficient, it seems. Yet, even still, when it came time to team up with myself, James and Selene, his teamwork was just as smooth as if a day had never passed. He fit right back in. Made me wish we had invited him into Parliament all those years ago after Legion, instead of letting him go his own way."

"What is it you suggest? You seek to commission him?"

"Well, he is a man for hire. So, yes... I suggest we pay his fee," Tachion said. "Assuming, of course, that I can find him again."

Bullseye looked at him quizzically as they stopped in front of the lift doors.

"He disappeared," Tachion continued, "right after he took care of my shoulder. One minute he was there, and the next he was gone. I was afraid he had run off to take Lady Opal from James, and collect the bounty. But no, they were fine. He just vanished. But not far, I'd imagine."

"Belladonna implied a... romantic entanglement between our human friend and this lyghtan lady."

"Belladonna is very astute," Tachion noted.

"James has found himself in love with her?"

"I wouldn't go that far. No more than James usually finds himself in love every other week, that is. Then, when he gets what he wants, he returns home to Tatianna. Though, I have to admit, I have a guilty hand in it this time. I thought his close relationship with the ashi'mar might prove useful later."

"A clever maneuver, even if an unethical one," Bullseye noted.

The lift arrived, the doors spread, and the pair stepped aboard.

"And how is James faring otherwise?" Bullseye continued.

Tachion tilted his head. "Okay, so far as I can tell, but it's hard to be sure... considering."

"Considering?"

Tachion reached over and touched the wall panel, bringing the lift to a sudden stop within its shaft. Bullseye looked at him curiously.

"There were certain events we couldn't tell you about in our quick briefing over comms," Tachion said, "just in case someone might be eavesdropping." He reached into a pouch of his techkit, and pulled out the translucent circular bracelet, holding it aloft.

"Is that... the device of which Her Ladyship Opal described?"

"The very same," the doctor said.

"And what has this to do with James' condition?"

"Well, the idiot used it, despite my *strong* advice not to. He snuck it off the ship, he put it on, and he used it. He says that it was his only option at the time. That it was the only thing that kept him from dying in that collapsed culvert. I told him that makes him lucky, not smart. We have no idea what kind of effects it could have had on him."

"And what effects had it?" Bullseye asked. "The ashi'mar, in her statement... she reports immediate aggression... arrogance, ambition."

"Well, it healed James' microwave burns, and his concussion. He says it allowed him to telepathically move aside debris from the cave in. But otherwise, he told me he felt none of her reported emotional or cognitive side effects," Tachion said. "Although..."

"You doubt?"

"He was acting odd when I met up with him behind the city. Irritable. Argumentative. At first, he didn't tell me what he had done. And then he nearly refused to give the device back to me. But when Lady Opal showed up safe and sound, he changed his tone, passed the bracelet to me secretly. He doesn't want her to know he used it."

"I agree with our human friend. She would likely be... most disappointed," Bullseye theorized. "And perhaps his surly attitude was merely stress from the ordeal."

"Perhaps," Tachion agreed. "In either case, I took extensive physical scans of him aboard the *Bugeye*, then transferred the data here, just to make sure it didn't cause any biological damage. And of course, I've scanned the device as well, and a droplet of the remaining serum within it. The Biological Society databases back at my laboratory should help me identify the compound more quickly. I tried to connect from the *Bugeye*, but it wouldn't allow me to log in for some reason. It kept rejecting my security clearance. I'll try again from here. I'll need the more powerful computers on the *P1* to properly analyze the scans I took, anyway."

"So, the wrist device, it is empty now then?" Bullseye asked.

"No, not quite. Based on the amount that James absorbed in his... unscheduled trial, I would guess there may be a use or two yet. But it's low enough that it might falter, which he said happened to him."

"If you can determine from where it is made, that would give us a roadmap to follow."

"That's the hope," Tachion agreed. "But in the meantime, I think it's best if you take it." He passed the curious-looking bracelet to the seti. "I have all the readings I need right now, so I'd feel better if you locked it away." The doctor leaned down and reactivated the elevator, while Bullseye visually examined the bracelet. The lift carried the pair two more decks, then opened near the science lab and sick bay.

"You mean to begin your labors now?" Bullseye asked, somewhat surprised.

"No, just to drop some equipment off. I need to clean up first, defrag... maybe indulge in an oil bath. All that humidity down there, I can sense the condensation in my hinge gears."

Bullseye studied the bracelet closely, turning it over in his hands as the door closed behind the departing android, the elevator continuing onward. He then forced it deep into his pocket when the lift stopped yet again, opening to let Flashpoint on.

The young seti stood in the open doorway, his hands upturned in a gesture of questioning. "I've been standing here for five minutes," he complained. "I thought I was gonna have to start crawling through the access ladders."

Bullseye forced a smile at Rook's son, moving aside so he could enter. After a moment of that particular awkward silence that occurs occasionally on elevators, Flashpoint asked, while still facing the door and not looking back, "Do you... really believe that we can still rescue my father?"

Bullseye was taken aback by both the directness, and the emotion within the question. He had thought the boy seemed unconcerned until now, which was obviously his intent. He floundered for a moment, not quite sure what to say. "Flashpoint, worry not..." he started.

"I'm *not* worried!" Flashpoint declared, interrupting.

Bullseye reached over, laying a gentle hand on the young man's back. In a softer voice, "Worry not," he said again, "we do everything we can, and anything we must. This vessel spills at its brim with souls masterly enough to do so, and who carry love for your father so vast, they risk all of themselves to ensure it. But remember, as exhausting as our search may become, and as grueling as the fight may wage on, it will surely pale when compared to what war your father would bring *any* who dare to bar his way back to you."

The doors slid open, and Flashpoint stepped off, away from Bullseye's reassuring hand. "I told you, I'm not worried," the boy said, still without turning. "But... thank you." The door closed, and Bullseye was once again alone.

With a thumbprint to allow access to the secured deck B, he stepped off onto Parliament's private deck once again. It was uncomfortably quiet, the only sounds being the gentle background hum of the pulse engines, and the nearly inaudible whoosh of the ventilation units. His footfalls seemed to echo somewhat more distinctly. All of their personal offices and expansive quarters were on this deck, yet Bullseye found himself, for the moment, roaming the corridors all alone. He crossed the circular common area from which each of their private suites were located, and continued aft to a hallway that jutted off of it, where the members had their individual work spaces.

He entered his office, dimly lit as per its usual, the bright sphere of Oberonn still shining green, blue, and white outside the window—though now receding slowly behind them as Captain Lobo made their way to hide themselves behind one of the adjacent system's distant gas planets. On the shelf behind his desk, he moved aside the old leather-bound book Relic had recently returned to him, and the deadly drak'min gun behind it, then dropped a false back panel, activating a concealed iris scanner that allowed access to his safe. The center of the shelving opened wide. On a narrow ledge, between the leaning muzzle of his most prized WarTec ZajinBolt sniper rifle, and the protective case in which he stored his teleportation triangles, he carefully placed the stolen wrist device, then relocked the hidden door.

The comm alert on his desk sounded.

"Bullseye here."

"*Ooh, so official sounding,*" Relic's voice answered. "*Am I disturbing you?*"

"N-No, certainly not. How... w-what may I do for you?"

"*Well, I was thinking, with my mother and cousin gone at least until morning, it seems you and I are pretty much all on our own in this big ship tonight.*"

"Not quite. Dr. Magna has returned, and your brother yet remains aboard," Bullseye said.

"*Yeah, as I said... pretty much on our own. Flashpoint will be in his room sulking, per usual, and the doctor is likely doing... whatever it is android doctors do. Playing with experiments, I'll assume.*"

"I concede your point."

"*Would you have dinner with me tonight?*" Relic's gentle voice urged across the comlink.

"I... do not..."

"*'You will make ready at my pleasure'. Those were your words to me the other night. Well, my pleasure would be to see you this evening for dinner. Eighteen hundred hours, in the member's galley,*" she told him. "*Unless, of course, you are afraid to be alone with me. We could meet in the crew galley, if you'd rather... surrounded by engine-room staff, and hangar maintenance workers.*" He could feel her smiling at him gleefully through the airwaves.

"The... member's galley would be wonderful," Bullseye answered. "Eighteen hundred hours."

"*Don't be late, because I will come find you.*"

"I have never counted myself so brave, that I would ever *dare* to do so."

That golden laugh once again. Then the comlink clicked off.

It was certainly no time to consider this sort of fraternizing. Bullseye knew that. But he chose to rationalize away every inner warning as they came to him. It was only dinner, after all—he had no other intentions. None that he thought she would entertain at any rate.

Or would she?

He stood at the tall windows, watching the jungled world shrink back from view, his worries for his distant teammates overtaken by fears and fantasies for the night ahead.

15.2

JAMES CROSSED THE FOREMAN'S PALM with yet another stack of credits, tallying in his head the mounting expense this little excursion was personally costing him. How is it that he seemed to be the only one who carried physical currency? The chamai reminded him again, in no uncertain language, that they and their ship were to be clear and gone no later than sunset. A massive shipment was coming in, and every square inch of the currently empty warehouse would soon be stocked to the rafters. That sounded just fine to James. The sooner he could put this steaming armpit of a planet behind him, the better. He gave the man his reassurance, and watched him walk away with his money, greedily recounting it.

Stansky's footsteps echoed across the vast, empty hangar as he headed back toward the *Bugeye*, the craft dwarfed in the center by the vaulted retractable roof, and vacant floorspace.

Bullit met him at the top of the gangway, having just finished stowing some equipment in his locker, and changing his suit of heavy battle for light. "I hate wearing such thin armor, but it's still a lot better than what I've been in this past week." He tossed the helmet from his bulker set into the compartment and closed the door. "Belladonna's in the aft service cabin," he said, "helping the ashi'mar into a set of her own."

James nodded. "That's not a bad idea, after yesterday's fiasco. We almost lost her."

"Yeah, so I heard... and caved in half a city block in the process. You're lucky Oberonn is looking at the bounty guild to make good on that, and hasn't caught on that it was *you* who turned restaurant row into a sinkhole."

"I only did what I had to do. It *was* like two against twelve, after all."

"What about Tàlto and that Selene woman?" Bullit asked. "Doesn't that make it *four* against twelve?"

"I was too busy *fighting* to worry about counting," James said. "And where were you this whole time? Oh, that's right, off on your little desert honeymoon. Did you have a relaxing time? Sorry to interrupt your vacation and drag you back to work."

"Well, you guys sure as shit weren't getting anything done, so figured I better come down and handle it myself." Bullit picked up Lady Opal's discarded red leather bustier from an open storage compartment, and held it out in front of him with an eyebrow raised, dangling it by the shoulder straps. "And I see you've been one hundred percent focused on business, per usual."

"Don't worry about me," said James, yanking the bustier from Bullit's hand and tossing it back into the locker. "I'm quite capable of multitasking."

"Sure… as long as both tasks involve either boobs or blowing things up."

"Well, fortunately for me, they *do*."

The door opened to the rear compartment, and a rather average looking chamai woman stepped out—Lady Opal, still masquerading behind Selene Maraspese's fleshy camouflage—trying awkwardly to get the feel of walking around in her new set of armor. Belladonna followed behind her, moving in hers as if it were her very skin.

"Alright, knock it off boys," Bell said as she approached. "That's enough dick measuring. I think you both already know, *I* have the biggest."

Stansky turned to Opal. "Well, look at you, a regular badass mercenary… if I may say so, Madam Ashi'Mar."

She smiled and almost tripped.

"It fits you well," he continued. "Just wiggle around in it a bit. You'll get used to it in a minute."

"I told her," Belladonna said, "putting on new armor is like the first time with a man. A lot of grunting and shuffling around till everything's in the right place."

Opal laughed.

Bullit and Stansky exchanged mutual looks of insult to one another, but otherwise opted to say nothing in defense of their gender. The quartet huddled for a plan of action, and set a rendezvous in case they were separated, then gathered themselves together and headed off into the city.

The acrid fumes of plasma port exhaust, and the heady spice of multiracial street food, entwined and mingled with one another, caught in a palpable layer by the humidity. Below the crowd-covered raised platforms that made up the bustling shipping district of Krataar, endless rows of warehouses and storerooms awaited the constant exchange of their distributed payloads. Above them, vertical piers reached skyward, aerial mooring points for aerospace barges—a dozen white, towering skyscrapers, with wide, red numbering at each berth. Docked ships hovered here, stacked one above the next, giving their pent-up crews a chance to disembark, while robotic drones fulfilled their bills of lading. The much larger star freighters, confined to their celestial orbits up above, filled the sky with swarms of dropped stevedore craft, swooping down for a load of containers with each dive into the warehouses, then making their way skyward again to fill the bellies of their motherships. All in all, the hazy air around them was as full of scurrying aerocraft as the crowded platform was of scurrying people, both twisting and weaving through traffic, jockeying for position.

They threaded their way through the heavy crowd with their helmets scrambled and their faces bare, as was the regulation within the city limits of Krataar—except for law enforcement and military. James pointed out a more visible presence of both of these than in the days before, loitering in pairs of two, posted at regular intervals about the city. None of the other pedestrians seemed concerned, but to the mercenary's suspicious eyes, the troops seemed to go out of their way to appear nonchalant. Bullit and Stansky swapped concerned looks, wondering if Captain Lobo's worries might have some merit. Best to be hasty with this inquisition, and get off this world while they still can.

The usual plan would have been to leave more room between them as they journeyed; far enough to avoid scrutiny as some sort of collective threat, but not so far that they couldn't reassemble at any sign of trouble. But here, this wasn't necessary. Unlike the grand bazaar, or the streets of the downtown quarter, this district already teemed with non-chamai outsiders of every species. These were the crews and companies of long-haul carriers, taking brief advantage of the change of scenery, or for a few moments of self-indulgence. The merchants whose businesses encircled the platforms were attuned to this, and so sought to cater to every whim or desire, casual and crude alike: from familiar cooking of every homeworld, to holosuite visits with distant family, to those more base urges eased by potent drink or pleasing company. Conveniently, the latter two were available in any of a dozen brothels, strip joints, and massage parlors serving Krataar's tenderloin, but in no other red-light watering hole quite as renowned as 'The Cat's Meow'.

Belladonna shook her head as she read an advertisement along the way. "Just offensive," she complained.

"Don't be priggish," Stansky said. "It's just a little harmless entertainment."

"Oh, I have no problem with the depravity," she answered. "I can enjoy myself with the best of them. My issue is this racist cat association. We are no more related to Earth cats than you are to... Kelsian flesh fish. *Despite* the similarity in your appearance."

"And aroma," Bullit added.

Stansky scowled at him. "Yeah, but... there's clearly a stronger resemblance between you and cats, than between me and flesh fish."

Bullit winced.

Belladonna stopped and turned, putting a hand on Stansky's chest to halt him. "First of all, don't be so sure. You look pretty fish-faced to me. And second, do you have any clue what you humans *do* strongly resemble to us?"

Stansky said nothing.

"Big... hairless... gangly... chimpanzees," she said. "In fact, I'd be willing to bet that less than *half* of setis can tell the difference."

Bullit raised his hand. "I can't."

"But even *that* is less offensive," she continued, "because at least you're from the same genetic family. I'm not comparing you to some alien, feral vermin. Still, I wouldn't open an Earthan strip bar, and call it... I don't know... The Ape's Banana, or something. It's demeaning."

"*Alright*, I *get* it," James said. "Look, it's not like I named the place."

Rook's wife turned to continue them on their way.

"What's a banana?" Opal whispered to Bullit.

He smiled. "Oh, don't worry. I'm sure James will try to show you later."

The overwhelming din of idling antigrav turbines, barking merchants, and carousing patrons was a maddening clatter all around them, yet was still insufficient to mask Belladonna's audible groan of disgust when she finally saw it. Tucked in a shaded corner where the towering vertical piers and their anchored vessels blocked the daylight, the landmark shone in neon outlines from the shadows, beckoning like a siren to all who passed. The offensive name of the establishment beamed above in colored lights, each letter a meter tall, and in a jaunty, backlit font. A giant holographic projection of an amorous seti woman seductively pawed and winked down at the passing throng, her features far more anime than actual, but nonetheless bearing a striking resemblance to Belladonna herself. Written in neon script between the cartoon's thighs was a dual promise—'Fully Nude, Free Lunch'.

Stansky looked up and cocked an eyebrow. "Bell, now don't take this the wrong way..." he began, staring at the hologram.

Belladonna interrupted. "James, before you utter another sound, let me educate you on something. The phrase 'don't take this the wrong way', has a *zero* percent success rate... *especially* with women."

The human's lips sealed up tight as they entered between the animated ankles.

Inside the nightclub was a pounding migraine of sound and color. A world awash with electric blue in the most unsettling of lusters, both too dark to clearly see, and yet too bright in which to hide. Here and there, waves of fuchsia backlit the mirrored bottle walls, highlighting the many bar areas, and providing welcome relief from the azure monochrome. Circular platforms with obligatory dance poles showcased exotic performers in mid revue, loosely undulating to a deafening techno beat whose baseline vibrated in the ribcage. A generic, monotonous noise, more repeating thump than melody, that could fit with any culture, yet clearly was from none of them. Illuminated white force spheres encircled each pedestal, protecting the dancers from unwanted fondling, while still allowing tossed credits to land inside. Each clink of fallen coinage garnered a moment of singular attention for the spender—attention that was brief, and fleeting, but which was lined up for, nonetheless.

Bullit and Stansky looked around with a growing sense of discomfort. Despite the name, and the feline theme, not all the dancers were of the seti race. Among the dozen or so on different stages, a chamai or two performed as well, and a metamorph on a central stage was changing form to suit every tipper. But that was not what surprised them. Their uneasiness stemmed from only half the nudity being female.

Bullit checked his six, assuring no dangling anatomy was violating his personal airspace. "I thought you said you'd been here before, recently," he said to Stansky. "You didn't mention it was... coed."

"Semi-recently... or so I thought. Maybe it's been longer than I remember." James stared straight ahead at Bullit. "But I'm telling you, it definitely was *not* coed when I was here last."

Bullit stared back at him, squinting. "Why are you looking at me like that?"

"Cuz," Stansky said, "I don't know where the hell else to put my eyes."

"Well not on me! Look at the floor or something, like a normal person."

Stansky's eyes darted down.

Belladonna's smile beamed. "Well, this place isn't so bad after all," she shouted above the noise. "Come on, James, don't be priggish. It's just a little harmless entertainment."

Stansky sneered.

"Where do we start?" Opal asked, directing them back to their urgent business. "I'm eager to find Denali's endgame."

Belladonna scanned the room, sizing up the crowd of men and women as if she was searching for someone specific. "I called in a favor before we came down, and got a little background on the owner," she said. "Rather than waste time going from dancer to dancer, I'll just get *him* to tell us if any of them can help us."

"How are you gonna do that?" Bullit asked.

"Starlaw has quite a file of secrets gathered on minor, foreign delinquents like him," she said. "I'll just drop a nugget or two of it. It'll convince him to be helpful." She located her quarry and pointed across the room.

An overweight chamai male with a wide, greasy smile toured the club pridefully, reveling in his tiny kingdom. A man of impressive girth, and equally unimpressive appeal, he nonetheless garnered a flirtatious touch from near every waitress who passed him—the ones who knew how to stay on the good side of their employer, anyway. His thinning hair was pulled up and over, from the very back of his head towards the front, and the wet stub of some burning weed was screwed tight into the corner of his mouth. He grinned at the money changing hands as he drifted up and down the rows, his grotesque potbelly thrust out before him, pulling him through the sea of patrons like a spinnaker filled with a vile wind.

Belladonna reached up to her shoulders, and again beneath each armpit, opening the clamps to release her thin armor's front breastplate. She pulled off the front panel, a piece that covered neck to navel, and handed it to Bullit. Then a tug on her inertia suit zipper loosed an impressive display of ample cleavage, a trapping to encourage the owner's interest in her conversation. She moved to intercept him.

The others watched without the benefit of being able to hear her, the driving music still resounding. But her lure worked, and the chamai leaned in as close as his projected belly would allow, leering downward, and chewing on clouds of pungent smoke as he spoke to her. She giggled like a bashful schoolgirl at what was surely some tiresome comment, but her theatrics were convincing, and he soon directed her to follow him. They walked away together to a quiet corner.

The direction of their conversation wasn't difficult to follow, even from a distance. He made some inappropriate sexual comment, with a seductive glare that could inspire nausea. She laughed again, then made a reply that seemed to confuse him. He reached out a hand, and took hold of her breast as if he owned it, a more demanding expression shown along with the accompanying comment. She didn't flinch or attempt to move it, but simply spoke to him flat and calmly. His hand dropped back away as quick as the blood drained from his face. He scanned around, wondering if anyone might have overheard what she had said to him, his expression teetering between nervousness and anger. She leaned in and whispered. His head nodded rapidly in response. Pointing to a distant alcove, he then turned and rushed back to his office. Belladonna looked over to her rapt audience, waving them to come over.

The small niche that the owner sent them to was a space reserved for private dances, and the four of them huddled inside it on a circular couch that ringed yet another pole, centered on a low platform. They closed the curtain, then sat in the flimsy illusion of privacy it provided.

"What did he say?" Bullit asked, handing Belladonna back her chest protection.

"He said military personnel are in all the time. Lately, to the point that it looked like a bootcamp in here. But that all stopped a week ago."

"Well, that timeline jives," Stansky said. "That's roughly when the mountain base was abandoned."

"He's sending one of the dancers over to talk with us, a favorite of some Oberonn officer that frequents the place."

As if on cue, the curtain parted, and long, unclad legs sashayed in. A thong of lace, in frilly white, the only cover on the seti's velveted skin—a scant pretense towards modesty that highlighted more than it hid. Bared fleece akin to spotted leopard, in hues of melted chocolate flecked on decadent butterscotch, led from slender ankle to graceful thigh, taut midriff to shapely chest. James and Bullit let their gaze follow the lure of that path, moving upwards, then shocked eyes quickly retreating back to the safety of the carpet.

She was a man.

"My name's Cheshire," he greeted warmly, his hands reaching back to draw the drapes closed behind him. An animatronic tail danced and wrapped around his chest, though exactly what it was attached was not entirely clear. "I'm told that you four are the most *V* of VIPs, and to give you my extra *special* treatment. Usually that wouldn't come until *after* you've bought me jewelry. But for you all, I'll make an exception!" He looked kittenishly at Stansky. "Goodness, aren't you a big one!" Directing himself back to the group, "Right, let's get the business out of the way, so we can get on with the pleasure. It's a hundred for a dance, or one fifty if you wanna touch. Or five hundred for a whole hour, but that includes a private bedroom out back... and whatever else your hearts desire." He turned to Opal and Belladonna. "Sorry... it's a little extra if you gals wanna join in. I usually cater to just the menfolk. But for the right amount of credits, I can be nothing if not flexible!" He turned to James and Bullit. "*Very* flexible."

James almost instinctively jerked for his sidearm, but quickly settled when Opal frowned at him. He was unarmed anyway, as their weapons were in the scramblers, and the scramblers had been mandatorily checked at the door.

"Cheshire, it's wonderful to meet you," Belladonna said, "and as lovely as that sounds, we won't be needing you for all of that. We'll happily pay you the full five hundred just the same, but all we need is some information."

Cheshire frowned and squinted at her, adjusting his sizable anatomy behind the entirely insufficient cover of the lace panty.

The men's eyes again sank deep into the carpet.

"What sort of information?" the dancer asked, sitting down on the edge of the platform, facing Belladonna.

His knees were spread uncomfortably apart from each other, and Belladonna reached out to gently close his thighs with two fingers atop each kneecap. "Information about some of your past customers. Specifically, anyone in the military. Regulars that come often, but have not shown up in the past week."

"Pfft. Well that's all of them, honey... or near enough, anyway. You'd think we'd gone to war the way they all up and disappeared." The dancer cocked his head, looking at her suspiciously again. "Wait, why? What about them?"

"Did anyone ever mention to you *where* they were going? *Why* they all disappeared this week?"

"Mmm... I'm not sure. How do I know I won't get in trouble talking to you? For all I know, you could be some kind of spy."

He had no idea how right he was.

"Make it eight hundred," she said.

Cheshire's objections all but disappeared, and he settled in like he was gossiping with his closest friends. "Well, there's this chamai praetor that comes in, always with a mercenary friend, some non-army type, at least twice a week. Oooh, the money he spends on me! He's got seti scratch fever, and I'm the only cure!" He leaned into Opal, loudly whispering, "Really it's the both of them. The praetor doesn't know his merc friend comes and sees me too, *without* him, if you know what I mean." He smiled at her, and gave a dramatic wink. Then he turned to Stansky, reaching over to boop his nose with a furred index finger. "A praetor is like a colonel, darling... in case you don't know your chamai rankings."

"I do," James answered, wincing.

"Ooh... smart and handsome! Where do I sign up!"

"Cheshire," Belladonna said, regaining his attention. "Please, did your praetor friend ever let slip *where* exactly they were going?"

"Let it slip? Hell no! He just came right out and said it! Couldn't stop talking about it, actually. Wanted to make sure I knew he was coming back." He leaned in again towards James and Bullit. "I think he's more than a little smitten with me. Well... why wouldn't he be? Just look at me!" He stared at one, and then the other, smiling wide at their blank expressions. "Are you two strapping men sure you don't want a little *bonus* for your money?" He began moving both his hands up and down in a suggestively rhythmic manner.

"Yes, quite sure," Bullit answered.

"No, thank you," Stansky added.

"Mmm, both so serious," he mocked through an exaggerated pout. "What a couple of party poopers."

"*Where*, Cheshire," Belladonna gently demanded. "Where did the officer tell you he was going?"

"Well, no place very special," the dancer answered, sitting forward towards the seti woman again. "The praetor is going to Ilshnar with his general, the metamorph homeworld. Then, after that, they're meeting the others somewhere."

"What others?"

"I don't know. The chamai fleet? The mercenaries? He didn't say. Just that he was going to Ilshnar briefly, then to meet the others at some base. But he would be back again to see me as soon as he could get free." He lifted his leg to show off a diamond anklet. "He gave me this before he left. Pfft, the cheap bastard. The gold's not even twenty-four karat."

"What base?" Belladonna insisted.

"They didn't say."

"But your friend, he's going with General Nylis to Ilshnar. You're sure."

"Oh yes, very sure. He promised to bring me back black orchids. Did you know all the plants on that world are completely black?"

Bullit interrupted. "What are they doing there, on Ilshnar?"

"Haven't the foggiest clue. I do know it won't take long. The general has some sort of meeting, and then they move on."

"To who knows where," Bullit said, frustrated.

"Well... I'm sure *they* know where, sweetie. But they sure as shit didn't tell me!"

Stansky turned to the other three. "The *P1* is smaller and faster than the *Okubi*. We can maybe still catch up with him, if we get moving right now... and hurry."

Bullit shook his head. "Why bother? What's the point? I mean that lead is pretty thin. Some secondhand drunken gossip, told to a... a..." he held a hand out toward Cheshire.

"*Watch* it..." the dancer said, his voice more baritone than before.

"Even if he *is* there," Bullit continued, "and we *did* catch up to him, which is doubtful, we don't know where on the planet he is. We don't know if Rook or Denali are with him. And if we miss him, we have no clue where to go next. I say we just continue on to Gel Gonahaar as we planned. I've seen evidence with my own eyes that Denali's got something going on there. We even have a street address to go to."

"What, a toy factory?" Stansky chuckled. "You think you're gonna find Rook or Denali making choo-choo trains?"

"Oh, my," the stripper gasped, "this all sounds so exciting!"

Bullit stood. "Thank you, Cheshire. We've wasted enough of your time... and ours. Let's get going, everybody. James, pay the man." He pulled the curtain and walked out.

"What?!" Stansky protested. "Why do I have to pay again?"

"I'm sorry," Belladonna claimed. "I didn't stop to bring physical currency with us in our rush from home."

The human sighed and began counting through his credits.

Belladonna leaned in to speak more privately with the seti dancer. "Cheshire, do you mind if I ask your *real* name?"

He looked at her in confusion, as if no one had ever even thought to ask before. "Well, my seti birth name is ⋔:ՈᐁՈ◯ю, but my common name is Kirin. It's a mythical Earth animal."

"Well, that name is beautiful! Why change it to Cheshire? You must realize that's a feline name from human literature. You're feeding into the stereotype that we are somehow related to cats."

"Yeah, honey, that's the point. Look around you. This whole joint depends on that stereotype."

"But doesn't that bother you? It's demeaning. It's demeaning to both of us. You don't mind being thought of as a dumb alien animal, just because your face has a similar shape?"

Cheshire held out his hand as Stansky dumped in his money. "Listen lady, I know," his deeper voice had returned again, "but I'm just trying to make a living here. I didn't create the situation, but I do have to live in it. It's not my fault if humans have some weird kink about fucking their pets."

James instinctively twitched again, but Opal's arm looping through his own steadied him.

"Thank you, Kirin," Lady Opal told Cheshire. "You've been a greater help than you can realize. And to be honest, I wish we had the time to stay and see your show." She winked at him.

"Let's go," Belladonna said, and moved to lead them out between the curtains. Then she stopped and staggered backward as Bullit reappeared and pushed her in.

"Change of plans," he announced, pulling closed the drapes behind him. "The club looks like a bootcamp again. It's packed with soldiers, looking for us."

"Oh God, what do we do?" Cheshire exclaimed, in genuine panic. "I knew I shouldn't have talked to you! I'm far too beautiful to go to prison!"

15.3

RELIC PUSHED THE REMAINING BITE of their shared dessert towards Bullseye, as she summed up her point to the enraptured seti across the table. "What I found, in rereading these myths and legends of our homeland," she said, "is that, as this nonliteral, imaginal, archetypal realm was opening up to me, I was finding myself discovering more and more ways in which those traditions and concepts could serve to advise me, in the reality of my everyday life."

Bullseye's eyes seemed to grin as wide as his smile. "This revelation gladdens me without end," he told her, nonchalantly pushing the dessert once again back toward her side. "I had an identical response to my deepening studies of the ancient stories. Although, to be fair, the response was driven into me through the hammer of many unyielding schoolmasters. You, whereas, seem to have found your way to this appreciation on your own."

She laughed. "Your compliments won't distract me from the fact that this last bite belongs to you," Relic told him. She carefully scooped the final morsel of oozing cake onto her spoon, then held the near dripping utensil out towards him, clearly intending him to eat from it.

It was a brief moment of physical connection that he could not resist, and he leaned forward, and allowed her to feed him the sweet confection. Did she linger with the spoon in his mouth as he did so? Did she linger with her eyes, locked on his, throughout the fleeting instant? It was hard for him to tell.

"Would you walk with me awhile," she asked, "so I can perhaps work off a calorie or two?"

"How could I refuse, after nearly forcing the indulgence upon you?" answered Bullseye.

The pair strolled along together, the longest way that they could, chatting themselves around the entire deck in a wide circle. He, in an ivory button-down achkan, dapper enough to show the possibility that he meant to impress her, but not so overly ornate to make it seem he was really trying. She, draped in a gauzy formal lehenga that shawled her shoulders in sheer fabric, yet was exposed to bare her midriff—because the invention of even the fanciest gown had been designed with one such as her in mind, and no one who laid eyes on her would ever dare question her in wearing it.

They stayed for some time staring through the windows of the port docking observatory, watching the purple and blue swirling storms on the giant world of indigo vapor Captain Lobo had selected to wait behind. As they continued walking, Relic shared tales of growing up in a house run by Rook and Belladonna—plenty of both sweet and embarrassing scenes that spoke to a side of his married friends that he had woefully chosen to miss out on. Bullseye repaid her with some embarrassing tales of his own, relating the story of their escape from the *Okubi*, and the chamai military base it led them to.

By the time he had finished describing to her captivated ears the strangely beautiful cavern city hidden beneath the blackened sands of Nol Qhan, the couple found themselves back up on C deck, in the quietly abandoned corridor, standing in front of her quarters, and thoroughly tired now of walking. The door slid wide to admit her, but Relic leaned back against the threshold instead. She looked with a playful, feigned sadness up at Bullseye, as if trying to say she didn't want the evening to yet end. "Would you… like to come in for a while?" she asked, clearly hopeful in her tone.

Bullseye peered seriously back and forth into the empty guest room from the doorway, as if he was certain some terrible danger lurked within, but could not tell where it might be hiding. "I do not know if… Perhaps it is not the very best of ideas."

"I'm not going to bite, you know," she said, sounding disappointed. "Are you afraid I might try to seduce you or something?"

He looked down into her eyes with the same serious expression. "No, not at all," he breathed out quietly to her. "I am, in fact, more in fear that you won't."

Relic looked struck for an instant, then her feigned frown curled its corners into a smile. She reached out her hand to him. "Well, come in for a little while," she said, "and I'll see if I can't put those fears to rest."

Bullseye took her delicate furred fingers in his own, and the two led one another into the room.

15.4

STANSKY PEERED THROUGH THE HEAVY curtains. "How do you know they're looking for us?"

"Cuz, I walked up right behind one of them. Almost bumped into him before I realized they were everywhere," Bullit told him. "I could see over his shoulder. Your face was on his multicomm screen."

"*My* face! Why not *your* face?"

"Well, I didn't almost topple a skyscraper."

Belladonna pulled Stansky back inside the private dance alcove. "I'm sure they have both your faces. They might even have mine, though probably not."

James looked toward Lady Opal, still veiled beneath the chamai flesh mask. "They don't have hers, we can be sure of that." Then he turned to Belladonna. "We've got to get her outta here, walk her out while we still can."

Belladonna thought for a moment, then took her turn to peek through the curtains. "Someone must have seen us come in here, they're stopping to check almost everybody," she said. "Everybody... except the people who work here." She pulled her head back in and turned to Cheshire. "Kirin," she said, taking hold of his bare shoulders as she used his real name, "I need you to believe me, that we're the good guys in this situation. We're working to save a lot of people from being hurt. Can you *please* help us?"

Cheshire stared back at her, a reluctant grimace drawing his face back.

"Another five hundred credits," Belladonna said.

"Of course I'll help! After all, we're like old friends now!"

"Good," Bullit murmured. "I thought I was gonna have to knock you out."

Cheshire scowled at him. "Don't be such a big bully! I told her I would help." He turned back to Belladonna. "What do you need from me, honey?"

"Well, we look to be the same size..." Belladonna started.

"Oh God, don't I wish!" Cheshire shouted. "I would *kill* for those hips!"

"I need you to trade outfits with me. My armor for your... undies."

"Whoa," Bullit said. "What good will that do?"

"This place is full of seti strippers, so I'm gonna become one. They'll leave me alone if they think I work here," she explained. "I'll walk Lady Opal right past those guards checking IDs, and into the private bedrooms, like she's paid for me."

"That still won't get you out of here," James said. "You can't leave in your underwear."

"Oh, sweetie, don't worry about that," Cheshire chimed in. "The closets in the bedrooms are simply *full* of costumes. Most are pretty outlandish. We get all types, after all. But there's a couple in there you can walk around in without drawing attention. There's a side exit at the end of the hall once you're down there."

"What about your armor?" Bullit asked.

"Kirin can keep it. I've got plenty more."

"Oh, my goodness, it's like my birthday!" Cheshire exclaimed. "I have a regular client who will simply just *die* for that cosplay!"

The two quickly disrobed, Cheshire in a mere second, and the dancer began putting on the seti's old Starlaw armor.

When Belladonna was down to just her jumpsuit, she looked back and forth at James and Bullit. "I'm not shy about going topless around this crowd of... blurry-eyed drunks," she said, "but there's no free show for you two. Turn your asses around and face the wall."

The pair dutifully spun on their heels, locking their gaze on a neon wall fixture, the sound of Rook's wife unzipping behind them.

"My lady," Stansky said, talking to Opal behind his back, "Don't worry, we'll catch up with you at the ship in no time. Belladonna will take good care of you."

The ashi'mar said nothing, but took a tight hold of his hand, squeezing it in a way that was every bit an embrace. Reluctantly, her fingers slipped away.

"They're gone," Cheshire told them, and the two turned back around. As stated, only the three of them remained behind now, Cheshire donning a fairly buxom set of female armor. "The guards are coming closer. What do you want me to do?"

James handed him a claim token. "Is there any way you can get our scramblers for us from the front desk?"

"Sure I can, sweetie. But I can't bring them back here without setting off the alarms. Best I could do would be to meet you out in front, if you can sneak your way around out the back."

"There's a back door?" Bullit asked. "What's out there?"

"A whole lot of nothing," Cheshire said. "Just a narrow catwalk that runs around the outside of the platform. I refuse to go out there. I can't stand the heights. But there's an alleyway between the club and the Earthan restaurant next door. It leads right out front."

"Perfect," James said. "Show us to your back door."

"Oh my God, I thought you'd never ask!" he joked.

They didn't laugh.

"Ugh! Fine! Follow me, poopers."

"Wait, do you have any kind of weapon?" Bullit asked. "Anything at all?"

"Of course I don't!" Cheshire said. "Where do you think I would have kept it?" He thought for a moment. "Just follow me to the door and wait. I'll see what I can find."

The three exited between the heavy curtains as nonchalantly as they were able, then walked calmly toward the rear of the club with Cheshire leading the way. In their periphery they could see Oberonnian soldiers in their green, gray, and silver armor, wandering deeper into the nightclub, examining the clientele. They stopped at each table, checking faces, and occasionally asking for identification. In the corner stood the owner, clearly furious at the interruption, yet unable to complain. He gnawed in anger on the smoldering stub, mumbling to himself, his face blooming red and swollen like a blister about to pop.

A cluttered back hall, full of stored lighting equipment and stacks of seating, led them to a heavy, metal door marked 'Emergency Exit Only', in both common and chamai lettering. Cheshire left them there and disappeared toward the kitchen, currently abuzz with the production of its promised free lunches. From the slightly rotten smell, the diners were getting what they paid for.

"You know," Bullit said, "Bullseye would probably say we shouldn't kill any guards if we don't have to. That the Oberonn army is not our enemy."

"Yeah, well... today they are," Stansky said. "And Bullseye isn't here."

"My thoughts exactly. Huh... looks like we agree for once," Bullit said. "I'm not sure that I like it."

"It is a little disturbing."

Cheshire reappeared, then handed a large foot-long chef's knife to James, and a short, slim, six-inch dagger to Bullit.

"What the hell is this?" Bullit complained, turning over the thin, fragile, curving blade.

"I don't know, it's the best I could do," Cheshire whispered loudly. "I think it's for fish."

"Great. Well, if I have to debone a salmon, I'm all set."

"Uhhh! Such a bully! It's all that I could find. And the human has been nicer to me!"

"It's fine, Cheshire," Stansky said. "Tell me, will an alarm go off when I open this door?"

"God, no. Crewmen use it all day when they see their officers come looking for them."

"Okay, thanks again. We'll meet you out front in a few."

Cheshire hurried off.

Bullit leaned against the doorway, opening it only the tiniest of slivers. The daylight outside shocked his eyes after so long in the darkened club, but a few moments of slowly relaxed squinting, and he could again manage the afternoon glare. It was just as Cheshire described it. The door opened to a short stairway leading to the right: five metal grated steps down to the catwalk below. The platform's perimeter walkway was a mere few feet wide, running between the back of the buildings and its parapet railing, overlooking the sea of warehouses some hundred feet below. Bullit suddenly let the door close again, and jumped back.

"What is it?" Stansky asked.

"Guard, coming this way."

"Fuck! We could really use a motion detector about now." James opened the door a hair's width to see for himself, then immediately had the same reaction. "Shit, he's coming up to this door. Alright, stand back. And be quiet so I can listen."

James squatted to a low crouch, like a sprinter awaiting a starting gun, and cocked his head slightly to listen for the footsteps. The guards' boots on the metal grating made an audible clanging sound, and the human counted them as he remained coiled, ready to spring. One—two—three—four—five—a slight pause on the landing, then the subtle movement of the door opening.

James burst into motion, his powerful leg muscles snapping straight, lowering his shoulder into the doorway, and flinging it open with a resounding bang. The guard outside was shoved back, slammed in the face with the heavy door, Stansky's bull strength behind it. The sentry flipped backward over the stairway banister to land face down on the catwalk below. Before he could struggle to rise, Stansky climbed to stand on the top rail of the stairway banister, and jumped straight down after him, driving his boots into the guards' back from a height of eight feet. Something cracked, loudly, and the guard bellowed in pain. James bent and roughly dragged the injured soldier to his feet. Then stealing the chamai's pistol from his holster, he flipped him over the railing. End over end, he tumbled towards the warehouses below. The soldier crashed hard onto a rooftop, but made no sign of moving again.

"Nice work," Bullit said, closing the door behind him as he came down the stairs. "Now give *me* the big knife, since you've got his gun."

"You have a knife already."

"No I don't, I have a toothpick. Gimme yours, you don't need it."

"I might," Stansky said. "I can't go shooting anyone unless there's no choice. It's too loud."

"Well then, give me the *gun!*"

"Pfft. Yeah right. Get your own."

Bullit cursed after him as Stansky left, crouching his way along the parapet, moving around the edge of the platform to the narrow alley up ahead. He peeked around the corner, then immediately pulled his head back. "Shit!"

"What is it?" Bullit asked.

"A whole crowd of them at the other end of the alleyway," Stansky told him. "And it looks like they're all over the platform in front, too. We'll have to figure another way."

A door opened just ahead of them, one atop a similar back staircase as that rear exit from the Cat's Meow. The sign above it read: 'Terra Firma — Earthan Cuisine'. An armored soldier stepped out, starting down the stairs before he stopped, and stared at the two.

Bullit immediately stood straight and walked toward the soldier, calling to him as he approached. "Excuse me, sir, I was just looking for you. I heard you were searching for some people, and I think maybe I saw them. I can tell you where they are."

The guard watched Bullit approach, curious, but without alarm. When the seti reached the base of the stairway, the slim fish knife came flashing, reaching around the soldiers' legs to sink deep behind both knees. The seti knew where the thinner flexible parts of the armor were, those joints of bendable rubber between the plating. The guard screamed out and fell forward, collapsing roughly down the staircase with a clatter. Bullit quickly lifted the heavily clad left arm of the struggling chamai, and shivved the blade repeatedly into the armpit, over and over in rapid succession. He sought out a narrow gap at the separation of the suit's collar ring, and slid the knife between, hammering it in with the flat of his palm against the ever-toughening skin of the chamai's natural defenses. Then he wiggled it back and forth violently, until the gurgling protests waned, and finally stopped altogether. The blade snapped off in the soldier's throat as Bullit tried to remove it, and he tossed the now useless handle over the side.

Bullit stood, breathing hard from his exertion, and splattered head to toe in blood. "Fuck you, and your stupid knife," he said to Stansky, retrieving the guard's sidearm from his holster. "Come on, get on over here, Mister Universe, and hump this heavy asshole up over the railing for me."

"Jesus. Why do you have to make such a goddamn mess?" James complained, dragging the seeping body and tossing it over the side.

"I had to do it quick, before his skin turned to stone, or whatever. If you had given me the gun, it would have been a lot cleaner."

"And louder," Stansky grunted, as the second corpse landed below with an echoed boom.

"*Wait* a minute... this pistol has a recognition grip!" Bullit said, realizing the handgun was useless, as it would only work for its original owner.

Stansky pulled out his own stolen sidearm and looked more closely at its grip. He pointed it skyward, yanking back the trigger a few times. Nothing. "For Christ's sake," he exclaimed, throwing the weapon over the side. "Doesn't anybody have any trust anymore?"

"Yeah, it's like they're afraid someone might steal their gun and use it against them," Bullit said sarcastically. "I mean, what are the odds of that?" He threw his overboard as well, spiraling it in a high arc. "Well... now I got nothing. Not even my little salmon scalpel." He looked up at the restaurant door. "Do you suppose it's safe to cut through the kitchen?" he asked.

"I don't see as we have any choice. Whether we get back our scramblers or not, the *Bugeye* is that way."

The hallway was filled with the fragrance of familiar cooking. Unlike the tangle of odors that twisted together on the expanse of the platforms, here they could individually recognize some of the unique flavors of their shared homeworld—though in uncommon combinations. Pizza was the predominant note in the air—the brick oven kind, with a bit of char on its edges. Beneath that was the tang of seafood, deep fried in old bay seasoning, and the salty aroma of Asian cuisine, with its signature hot oil, ginger, and soy. Up ahead was a hectic takeout window, the cook staff frantic behind it, and the crowded plaza of the platform beyond—ringed tight with armored uniforms. The two ducked into a large storeroom on the right.

Bullit braced the doorway with a mop handle while Stansky toured around the storage space. There was no other way out, except a ladder to a roof hatch. That wouldn't do them much good—they still needed to get across the plaza.

The two stared at each other.

"Well?" Bullit said. "You're supposed to be the demo guy. There's all kinds of shit around here. MacGyver something up!"

"Pfft. That shit isn't real. I can't make a bomb outta baking goods. What do you want me to do, stick some candy in a soda bottle and get everybody slightly damp?" Stansky started opening cabinets and cupboards, and flipped open the top of a freezer. "Look at this crap. I'd be more likely to bake a cake than build a bomb. And even if I could, it would be barely more than a distraction." He suddenly stopped then, returning to the freezer. "But maybe a distraction is all that we need."

"Uh-oh. You must have thought of *something*, I can see smoke coming outta your ears."

"I think I can cause a distraction that will get everybody running, *and* get them, and us, to cover our faces in the process. We can join in, cover our heads, and run away along with the rest of them." He reached into the freezer, and pulled out a twenty-gallon jug of liquid nitrogen.

"Alright, now you're talkin'," Bullit said. "What else do you need?"

"Some kind of pressure cooker. QEU powered, if they have one, so it can heat up without being plugged in," Stansky answered. "And pepper. *Lots* of pepper. Liquid, flake, powder... whatever you can find. The hotter, the better."

The well-stocked pantry was quite accommodating. In minutes, the pair were atop the roof and assembling their homemade tear gas, concealed behind a fog of greasy steam from the cookery's grill vents. An entire gallon of liquid cayenne, followed by powered dragon chili and red pepper flakes, all went into the three-gallon cooker. Then the remaining space was filled to the brim with the liquid nitrogen, already boiling away to gas in the heat of the afternoon sun.

Stansky paused for a moment before placing the lid. "How long do you think this thing takes to heat up?"

"What am I, your sous chef?" Bullit asked. "How should I know? I haven't the vaguest clue."

"Well, this liquid expands to almost two hundred times its volume when it turns to a gas. I don't wanna toss it too early, but I sure as shit don't wanna toss it too late."

"There's no pressure gauge on it?"

"Nuh-uh."

"Well, then... just make your best guess."

Stansky set the cooking temperature to maximum, snapped the pressure lid on tight, then held the cooker out behind him, wound up and ready to throw. He didn't know what he was waiting for, other than some sixth sense feeling that told him it was gonna blow. He waited, and waited, until he heard the telltale clicking of the container stretching, and a whistled groan of metal expanding. He swung the pot overhead, and let it fly spiraling through the air.

Somehow, despite the crowd, it managed to land without killing anyone, clanging down loudly in the center of the metal platform, and rolling around in small circles on its cylindrical sides. The two mercenaries ducked back as people looked upward, searching for where it had come from. Many ignored it, perhaps not even noticing in the rush and noise, but others were intrigued, even concerned and suspicious. An older chamai woman excitedly got the attention of one of the soldiers, and led him across the platform, pointing to the now motionless cookpot from a safe distance. He went right up to it, tapping it repeatedly with his foot, and looking straight up above, as if he thought it may have come from one of the docked ships overhead. Then he picked it up and started walking off with it.

Bullit raised an eyebrow. "Huh. Well, I guess that was a little too early then," he critiqued.

A thunderous blast tore through the platform with a cloud of white vapor and red mist, causing a stampede of terrified pedestrians running in every possible direction. The guard lay face down, his right arm vanished along with the pot, vaporized into a steam that was mixed with the aerosolized pepper. People below hacked and coughed, and covered their burning eyes from the stinging fog, which was dispersing with agonized slowness in the unstirring, humid air. The crowd scattered. Bullit and Stansky covered their faces with wet dish rags as they clambered down, dashing across the chaos of the platform back towards the Cat's Meow.

Their helpful stripper friend was easy to spot, being the only man standing around in breasted armor, and they rushed to his side to collect their belongings.

"My God, you people are terrifying!" Cheshire shouted. "Please, just take your things and go, before you put me back into therapy!"

"Ahh, thank you Cheshire!" Bullit praised him, happily taking his scrambler.

"What, no kiss of gratitude for a job well done?"

"As tempting as that is, I'm afraid I can't afford you."

"Oh, my goodness, a bully *and* a tease!" he shouted after them as they hurried off. "I would have given you a freebie!" He headed back into the club. "Be still my heart, how I do love a bad boy."

Bullit led their way across the platforms, heading one to the next back in the direction of the *Bugeye*, while still covering their faces and feigning distress from the pepper gas. But they couldn't carry on that ruse forever. Eventually, they made it far enough that they had to drop the act, as it now drew more attention than it averted, and they instead continued with the now calmer evacuating crowd, trying to keep their heads low. The seti looked up ahead, then suddenly stopped, pulling Stansky behind a supporting girder.

"What's the matter?" James asked.

"Look," Bullit said.

Stansky leaned his head out and peered the way they needed to go. A line of soldiers was stretched across the platform, nearly shoulder to shoulder, checking anyone who sought to pass. He pulled his head back. "Alright," James said, "it's your turn now. I got us outta the last jam, you get us outta this one."

Bullit sneered at him, then looked around. The base of one of the skyscraper docking piers was nearby, the closest of its three entranceways blocked off as 'under renovation'—or at least that's what Bullit assumed, being unable to read the chamai writing. "Come on, we'll duck in there until they pass by. It will give us a chance to descramble our gear."

The two angled their faces away from the advancing line of soldiers, and hurried toward Pier Seven: a narrow, white tower reaching a hundred stories in the air, with ten or more freight barges docked around its sides at various levels. Many other evacuees were heading the same way, seeking to return to the safety of their cargo ships, and Bullit and Stansky blended neatly into the crowd making for the door. As they got close, the pair veered off, heading for the barricaded entryway. Before they could reach it, a soldier stepped out of the main doorway, and very quickly noticed them stepping over the makeshift chain barrier. They both swore. The armored guard turned towards them and called out something in their direction. They ignored it. The second shout in common of "You there, stop!" was clearer, but they continued on as the sentry now hurried after them. The sliding door refused to admit them, but the two jammed their fingers in, ripping it open. They dashed inside.

The tower's interior was little more than multiple lobbies full of elevators, swift access up and down from the docked freighters up above. This particular lobby was empty, beyond a lone workwoman along the right-hand wall, firing a long stream from a plasma cutter to slice a steel panel she sought to access. The air was thick with the squelching sound of the blazing plasma beam, along with the accompanying pungent oxide of burning metal. Bullit marched right up to the unaware worker and shoved her aside, grabbing the tool from her hands. He rushed back to the forced open doorway, just as the Oberonnian soldier stepped through.

Bullit fired the scorching plasma beam directly into the guard's armored chest, then dragged the white-hot arc to trace a blackened line up his neck, straight into his face. The guard spun his arms wildly and tried to look away, staggering back as the blistering ray cut through plating, flesh, and bone. Any attempt to cry in out pain fell muted by his melted voice box. He finally toppled backward, slamming on the platform outside.

"There, how's that for no mess?" Bullit asked. "Didn't spill a single drop of blood."

"Oh yeah, that was spotless," Stansky answered. Then he turned around. "Fuck, where'd the lady go?"

The sliding doors on the opposite side of the lobby stood ajar, evidence that the worker had made a well-advised retreat.

"Shit, she's gonna snitch," Bullit said, peering outside at the closing blockade of soldiers still approaching. He pulled out his scrambler, and finally took the private moment to retrieve his gear. "Well, where do we go now? I'm open to suggestions."

Stansky felt some relief as his own helmet and armaments descrambled and materialized. "Well, we can't go out, so I guess the only way is... up. Did you happen to notice what level any of those ships were docked at?"

"*Nope,*" Bullit said, his voice now coming through the comlink as the pair pulled on their helmets. "*But, pretty high.*"

The two hustled aboard an awaiting elevator, Bullit slinging his AE rifle, and Stansky holstering his pistols. Then they selected an upper story at random by pressing a button near the top of the panel. Their protective force shields sprung to life with a reassuring hum around them as the doors slid closed.

"*You know,*" Bullit said, as they watched the digital readout track the passing floors, "*this situation... it might not turn out in our favor.*"

"*Yeah. It might not,*" Stansky admitted.

"*Well... I... I want you to know... just in case we don't make it... that, I've... well... I've always considered you a... a worthless piece of shit... and... just a terrible demo.*"

"*Ah, how touching. Don't worry, by the way. If I make it out, but you go to that giant litter box in the sky, I'll bury you in a shoebox in my garden. Right next to my childhood kitty, Mister Mittens.*"

"*You couldn't demo your way out of a wet diaper, which you're probably wearing.*"

"*Did you name yourself Bullit because of how many you waste?*"

The doors slid open, and they stepped off into a small foyer. The floor and dock number were painted in giant letters on a closed hatchway right in front of them, which neither of them could read. But the windows on either side made it clear they were high up, perhaps eighty stories. It was also quite clear there was no ship at this dock. There was one just below it, however, hovering at its mooring about forty feet down.

"Looks like we overshot," Bullit said. *"Let's go down one deck, and see if we can sneak on as stowaways."*

Stansky called for the lift door to reopen, but as he did so, the power flickered and died. The overhead light in the foyer went out, along with the elevator floor readings. One lift on the far left then powered back up, and began ascending towards them, rising up from the ground floor.

"Well, that can't be good," James said, stating the obvious. He turned around to the manual pump handle that would open the hatchway behind them. Bullit grabbed hold as well to help, and together they cranked back and forth until the door was forced wide.

The two gazed out the lofted opening onto the city of Krataar far below, a surprisingly refreshing breeze blowing through their armor's joint gaps way up here. In the near distance, at a height even with their own, the high-rises and superstructures of the business district loomed over the central plaza, as well as the residential suburbs further beyond. The vast east wall that hid Selene's workshop seemed a mere stepping stone to the lower tier of the jungle, and the sea of tents amid the grand bazaar was a patchwork afghan draping the valley. Far towards the distant horizon, beyond the river and high above the miles of tangled green, the daily assemblage of angry rain clouds were mustered in a tidy row, marching in lockstep as they began their journey toward the north.

The buzzing circulation of shipping drones was much more prevalent at this level, and they spun and whirled around the tower, pulling and stacking containers from the open barges. The areo-freighters were not much different from naval container ships of the seas—other than the fact they were made to sail above them—with wide flat decks that held stacked hexagonal containers in the open, held fast by magnetic fields. One such vessel sat directly below their now opened doorway to nowhere, its broad and level main surface nearly cleared of its cargo, and ready to accept a fresh reload from below.

Without speaking, the two simultaneously turned and deployed their tension reels into the back wall, and retreated towards the opening, prepared to rappel down.

Stansky paused and reached in his demo kit. *"Let me leave them a little welcome present."*

"Alright," Bullit said, *"but try and control yourself, please? We want to stop them from chasing us, not bring the whole tower down."*

Stansky slapped a wad of heurcanium to the door frame, and the pair zipped downward just as the lift doors began to open.

The soldiers must have caught on to their tension reels pretty quickly, as the micro-cables suddenly went slack when the two were still ten feet or so above the ship deck, sharply cut from above. They dropped abruptly downward, crashing hard onto the freighter's open barge level, tangling with each other as they swore and struggled to get upright.

There was shouting from above, mostly in chamai, though Bullit and Stansky got the sense the soldiers wanted them to halt. They chose not to, scrambling away from the tower instead. One of the guards fired a warning shot, or perhaps had his setting too low, and hit James in the back with a laser blast that was completely absorbed by his albedo shield.

"*Son of a...*" Stansky complained, and then turned and triggered his directional detonation. The three armored soldiers in the doorway were thrust back by a concussive blast of smoke and debris, but much to Bullit and James's satisfaction, the upper fifth of the tower remained standing. They turned and ran.

Traversing the open deck of the cargo ship was like running across an iron soccer field. Far towards the aft, behind the last remaining row of containers, the bridge tower stood overlooking their advance. Perhaps if they could make it inside, they could convince or cajole the captain into an early departure. To the left and the right, the dizzying height spiraled downward, funneling the two on ahead with no alternative of where else to go. Large drones buzzed about, one marked 'United Homesteads' descending right in front of them. Huge vise-like jaws under its belly clamped onto a set of four massive containers in one bite, the craft then hustling back off with them to the warehouses below. Thankfully they now had a more direct route to the bridge entrance.

A line of bullets struck the deck beside them, chasing them with a trail of angry ricochets and sparking. The pair ducked behind the last few containers for safety, peeking to look back the way they had just come. Three more soldiers now loomed in the open doorway above the one they had just destroyed, firing down on their position from near the very top of the pier tower. Stansky pulled his nine millimeters as he peeked out again to gauge the distance, then quickly ducked back from some resulting fire. Over three hundred feet away, and two hundred feet above—much too far for his handguns to have any sort of accuracy. He re-holstered them, then looked at Bullit.

"*Let me guess, too far for your pea shooters?*" Bullit asked. "*I suppose you want me to take care of it.*"

"*Well, that is your job, after all,*" Stansky said. "*Here, gimme your rifle. I'll do it.*"

Bullit yanked it away. *"Even if I'm shot stone dead today, you still do not touch my rifle,"* he said. Then he swung the barrel around the side of the container, and fired three quick blasts. He scored three quick hits. The two soldiers on each side flew back from helmet splitting headshots. The one in the center, caught in the waist, folded over to tumble out the doorway. He smacked hard on the edge of the ship deck below, then flipped over its side to continue the long, lonesome journey to the ground.

"Yeah, boy!" Bullit yelled, as he recoiled back behind the container.

"Easy shot," Stansky said. *"They were all lined up like sitting ducks."*

"What are you, nuts! Three kill shots in three seconds, from a hundred and ten meters out? That there is why they call me Bullit!"

"Yeah, but... you're shooting lasers," Stansky said. Then his head suddenly rang as if someone hauled off and cracked him with a bat, and he tumbled to the ground like a heap of armor dropped on the deck plates. He blinked hard and shook his head. *"Someone shot me,"* he said weakly.

The sound of Bullit's rifle erupted behind him, the crimson flash of laser all around, and he felt his hand pulled starboard as he was struggling to get up.

"It's the crew firing on us," Bullit told him, rushing them both behind the barrier of a half wall partition. *"Are you gonna live?"*

"Oh, man. Yeah, I think so. Might have cracked my skull on that one, though. Fuck! Where are they?" he asked, pulling his pistols and aiming toward the bridge tower.

"They're firing from up above. I think I killed a couple of crewmen on the deck though, so now I would definitely *like to avoid custody if possible."* Bullit popped up and fired a few shots to keep them at bay. *"What do you wanna do, try to get back down the tower?"*

A machine gun blast from behind put an end to that possibility, and the two huddled lower between the last shipping crates and the half wall.

"Goddammit, now what?!" Bullit shouted, popping his head around the huge container. A police aerocar was suspended there, hovering above the cargo deck. The officer opened fire from a mounted autocannon as soon as Bullit's upper body flashed into view. Rounds tore repeatedly into his left arm, the ammunition slowed by his shields and armor, but still sinking hard into his flesh, deep enough to tap the bone. He yelled out and pulled back.

"Now that is a bullet," Stansky said. He raised his pistols to fire on the crew above, the ship's company apparently growing brave enough to dare sticking their heads out, shooting down at them once more. They quickly ducked back away as the rounds peppered all around them.

The police vehicle began shouting in chamai over the loudspeaker, but neither of them had a clue as to what the officer was saying. They could guess easily enough, though. The amplified voice was noticeably changing position as the constable spoke, drifting slightly right to their exposed side, making it clear he was cautiously veering around in order to flank them. There was nowhere left for them to go.

"*I have levitation belts built into my larger armors,*" Stansky said. "*But I didn't have a loose one to wear with this light battle crap.*"

"*I huve one on,*" Bullit said, "*but it would never hold us both.*"

"*Yeah, I saw. And I know. It would barely lower just you alone safely from this height,*" Stansky admitted. "*But, if I hold these pricks off, even for a little bit... you can jump off the edge, and try and make a go of it.*"

Bullit turned to stare at him, incredulous. "*Pfft! Fat chance! As if I'd ever let your ass play the martyr for me. Wouldn't you just love that. I'd never fuckin' hear the end of it!*"

"*Well, it was worth a try. I just didn't want to go out still looking at your ugly face.*"

The police aerocar came into full view now beside them, hovering along the freighter's edge. The officer's tension-filled voice once again demanded—*something*—and the barrel of the mounted autocannon refined its focus on the injured mercenaries.

Stansky turned to Bullit. "*Well? How do you wanna play this? Hands up, or guns blazing?*"

"*Pssh. What the hell do you think? It's Butch and Sundance all the way.*" Bullit racked his weapon with a violent one-armed shake of his good hand.

"*Huh,*" James said, "*agreeing twice in one day. A new record.*" He cocked back the double pistols after slamming home a reload against his thighs, then prepared himself to pop to his feet. "*As long as you realize that you're Butch, and I'm Sundance.*"

Suddenly a shipping drone buzzed in low overhead, causing them to duck back beneath its whirlwind of exhaust plumes, seemingly having arrived to steal away the last of their covering containers. But it did not. It continued on across the freighter's deck and swung in above the hovering police car. Deploying its belly cargo-clamps, it grabbed the vehicle in its hanging jaws, and began crushing it slowly but firmly between them. The flashing strobe lights cracked and shattered, and the front windshield popped out—the pair of now-visible officers looking around in confusion as to what was happening. The drone now stopped and reversed its grip, the jaws opening wide again. The ruined car's grav-thrusters sputtered noisily as it slipped away, tumbling out of sight beyond the edge of the freighter's railing, and rolling slowly over itself as it plummeted toward the ground. The impact was too far down to hear the inevitable crash from up here.

The cargo mover was labeled with the name of a human distribution megacorp, their curved arrow logo below the front windows making it look like the vehicle was smiling at them. Drones were usually unmanned, though this one clearly had a pilot, and they swung the craft back above the freighter, gently lowering it onto the wide expanse of the open deck.

Bullit and Stansky exchanged glances, then stood and walked cautiously toward the cargo drone. The door opened as they approached, and a familiar face peered outside.

"Hey there Jimmy, you two boys need a ride?" Tàlto's voice came through their comlink.

The bounty hunter's bald head and purple eyes were a welcome sight, but not as welcome as Lady Opal and Belladonna seated casually behind him. Opal was still disguised beneath the mask of a chamai woman, and Belladonna was now draped in the cape and habit of a religious abbess.

"The ladies were having a bit of an issue getting back to your Bugeye," Tàlto said, *"so I thought I'd be neighborly, and give them a lift. For some reason, they insisted I pick you guys up too. Although you seemed to be doing just fine to me."*

"Yeah, well... I guess that's two *that I owe you,"* Stansky said as he clambered aboard. Then he turned to help Bullit hobble in after him.

"Oh, you don't have to keep count," Tàlto told him. *"I'll be sure to track it for you."*

The door closed tight behind them as the lyghtan swerved up and away from the freighter, diving down toward the warehouses, passing police and military craft hurrying their way upward. Tàlto ducked and weaved around the other shipping craft in those same robotic wide circles, his flight pattern appearing no different than the other hundred unmanned drones filling the sky. He swooped down below the platforms and headed towards the *Bugeye's* hideout.

James struggled off his helmet, rubbing the tender knot near his temple. Then the small cooling hands of Lady Opal slid in from behind him to do the same. He sat and enjoyed the tenderness of her touch for a moment, until a nagging sensation to his right forced him to turn and look at Bullit. The seti was staring at him.

"What is it?" Stansky said.

Bullit glared at him in disgust, slowly shaking his head. "You're Sundance, my ass," he said. "Let's make one thing clear, you old fart. *You* are Butch. *I'm* friggin' Sundance!"

15.5

THE LIGHTS WERE OFF IN Relic's quarters as she and Bullseye entered hand in hand, and both wordlessly made the decision to keep them that way. The sunken sitting room was nonetheless awash with the indigo palette of the planet below them, its storm-raged waxing crescent filling the wide windows that faced the endless vast. The starfield further beyond shone forever indifferent through the blackness, together a vista of such majesty as to make them feel at once privileged, yet insignificant. He gazed out upon its grandeur, a singular and unrepeatable glimpse into the beauty of all eternity, yet all he wanted to do was face away from it, and fill his eyes with the sight of her instead.

From behind him, he heard her ask the computer to play her favorite album, a recent release she told him, by the young Earth band Horse Mustaches. He turned to her at that and frowned disappointedly. She raised up a finger to plead for patience. His indulgence was well rewarded, by the tender strains and gentle bass line of a traditional seti ballad caressing his ears. He had to smile. She smiled back, then lowered the volume to a gentle lullaby.

The gossamer shawl slid free of her shoulders to be left behind her on the floor, and she watched the glint of wonder in his regard as she crossed the room to join him. There they stood by the high windows, their eyes deep within one another, as close as they could be without yet consenting to be touched. She raised a hand from her side and asked him if he would dance. He took her sweet, gentle grasp into his own, their fingers entwined, and drew her the remaining inches to rest her head against his collar. Together they swayed and held each other, much more so than truly dancing, but each with the same desperate rhythm inside of them.

He slid his hand along her silken dress to the open cutout at her midriff, and firmly curled his fingers against the inward slope of muscle at her backbone. She tilted her head slightly, the nose of her soft muzzle buried in his neck, and sent wondrous thrills across his body with each hot breath that she exhaled. The sensation awoke him below, a response her closeness was quick to feel, and she changed her swaying to be in opposition, their bodies no longer in unison, but rubbing in friction against each other. He was awoken further. She noticed that as well.

A delicate pace and tender touch as she moved with swift fingers to undress him, soon had him baring all before both her and the stars outside. She ran her caress across his rippled chest, years of hardened brawn beneath short raven fur, then stood back to let her own covering drop away along with his. They embraced again. She moved her mouth up towards his, then twitched to nip him lightly on the muzzle. He recoiled back, but she pulled him in harder, and beamed up a playful grin of pure delight. Now her eyes went more serious, her gaze somber and intense, and she pulled his mouth to hers, first lightly brushing, then fitting together, as if they were never meant to have been apart.

The warmth of her bosom against his body, the press of its arousal against his chest, combined to thrill him to a point that he could hear his blood rush between his ears. He grasped her behind the head to keep her close, as lips and tongues embraced their counterparts. His hand moved at a careful pace: from her neck, across her chest, towards her waist, around her bottom, delighting in every inch of her downy softness along the journey. His hand lingered at that final destination, finding a comfort in the feel of holding it, and he tightened his grip to pull her in even closer. His heart raced and his mind swam, his stomach clenching at her every touch. The taste of her mouth, the sense of her body, the curiosity of her hands all drove him to the edge of dizziness.

They stayed there to enjoy the closeness of each other for a long while, the most sensitive areas of each sliding against the warm, fleeced nakedness of the other. Finally he pulled back, and their gaze met one another's—golden eyes into green, in silent conversation. 'Perhaps somewhere more comfortable,' his look said to her. 'Come, follow me,' her eyes answered back.

They walked hand in hand into the adjacent bedroom, moving each other deliberately toward the mattress, made up tight and crisp with its fresh linens, snuggly tucked into sharpened corners. It wouldn't remain so for long. He sat her on the edge of the soft, pillowy bedspread, and slowly leaned her back against the cushion-fronted headboard. He moved downward with her, lips again entwined, each one exploring. Her tongue flowed as sweet as warm honey in his mouth, and it was a kind of agony for him to break from it, pulling away from its embrace. But his mouth had other places to be, and other work to do.

He started high up on her neck, tender kisses, delicately given. Behind her ears, across her throat, breathing her in as he moved along. The perfume of her flesh, the bouquet of her hair. He travelled down across the soft, yielding mound of her bosom, warm and flushed, and lingered there, giving attention where it was needed. The left side, then the right. She inhaled in tiny stutters, and sighed in pleased approval. Her belly twitched and her breath gasped as he continued the journey south across the smooth of her stomach, dancing his lips above, and then around her navel. Then below it.

Then even further.

The first taste of her excitement was like mulled wine upon his tongue, sweet and decadent, warm and welcoming, and he delighted in it with an enthusiasm that she appreciated with gasping whimpers, and trembling muscles. He was diligent, and attentive, and she appreciated it repeatedly. He remained there, relishing all he could of her, until she could take the delight of it no longer. Until she grasped quaking at his head, and led him back up to her. His mouth and tongue were weary, but fell back into the warmth of her lips with renewed energy.

She gently now moved downward, intent to return the favor, but he couldn't yet allow it—not this round, anyway. He delicately took her wrists and pinned them to the bed behind her, his weight upon her. He couldn't wait any longer, the time had come that he had to have her, and she acknowledged that in his eyes, and moved her legs apart to allow it. He positioned himself carefully above her, his eager anatomy aligned with hers, and slowly moved himself inside. He stared breathlessly watching her as he penetrated without haste. She stared breathlessly back as she drew him in deeper.

It was like sinking into a tub of steaming water on a chilly morning. Like cupping frigid fingers round a piping mug on a winter's day. A perfect warmth, a perfect fit, a perfect place for him to be. He didn't want to ever withdraw again, but retracted partially nonetheless, then moved forward again. Back, and then forward. Back—and then forward.

He knew almost immediately that this was not to be his finest showing. The feel of her around him was too wondrous, the sight of her beneath him too overwhelming, the friction between them too delightful to endure. His willpower to hold back was rapidly waning, but the quick and staggered rhythm of her panting as she gingerly bit his lower lip assured him that she was nearing the end as well.

The release nearly staggered them, muscles tightly tensed, then collapsing, breath held deep, then loud exhaling, minds swimming in that maelstrom of the sudden divine rush, then falling back into the calm euphoria of absolute exhaustion.

He slumped backward now into the largely disheveled bed, and pulled the crisp, clean sheet up over their rapidly cooling bodies. He drew her in tight to him—he could not seem to do so tight enough. She tucked in snugly to the crook of his arm, head on his chest, where she could hear his pounding heart race in rhythm with her own. His chin rested in the waterfall of her soft pomegranate hair, their legs intertwined and rubbing together, hers stacked on top of his. Suddenly, he began to hanker for that dessert he had so resisted earlier. The stomach butterflies finally flushed clean, along with other things, he found that he was rapidly becoming hungry. Starving, in fact. He told her so. She said that she was too.

A kitchen attendant arrived quickly, along with a growing dusk across the room: the world of color outside their window slipping from reflected daylight into night. Skimming the dark side of the giant world, her quarters now cast deep in shadow, the panorama of glittered stars seemed to double each passing moment. They sat with robes loosely tied at the intimate table near the window, trading spoonfuls, talking and laughing, as the turn of their orbit drew the fiery line of the galaxy's center into view. A distant, nebulous ghost, begetting life and death, fire and smoke. Endless patience over eternal time, yet its unrivaled pageantry and eternal wonder failing to temper the splendor of their own moment.

They went back to the bed after a time and sat up close to one another, snuggling tightly, and watching the parade of passing stars as they talked away the night. He asked about her recent schooling. She asked about his homeworld. He talked of lessons from his past adventures. She talked of plans for her future glory. He revealed his hopes and fears. She disclosed her wishes and dreams. They reminisced about times they knew together long ago. They fantasized about times together neither was sure could ever be. They avoided talking about the one thing they both knew—that their time like this was short. The simple fact of her parentage may forever after not allow it. Their time together like this was now—and perhaps, never again.

That didn't give them much.

But it gave them today.

As they talked, a light caress of her fingernails down his chest, then through the loose opening in his robe, stirred him again, evidenced by the rising fold of fabric below his waist. She took note of it immediately, and continued tracing her fingernails further down across his stomach, passing through and uncoiling the loosely drawn belt of his robe. She then took a gentle, but firm grip around what was supporting that newly-risen pleat of satin. He inhaled sharply and muscles twitched, as she leaned in to press her mouth to him. But she allowed only the briefest warmth of her kiss before pulling away, and letting her lips instead trace along the same path her hand had taken.

The shining lights of the endless night casting their glow through the windows beyond seemed somehow now *less* indifferent, as if perhaps they gleamed and sparkled just for them, each light-beam's journey of a million moments all undertaken in honor of this one. But time and the universe spiraled onward, despite every desire the two might have had to make them falter, and they sought to savor each passing instant, and stretch each heartbeat into a lifetime.

Chapter 16.1

PLANET EARTH HAD ENDURED CHANGE, both by time and by tide, but to no less a degree through the hands of its people. There was a time in centuries past when the population had foreseen a coming danger to their world, a change in its climate from the activity of those who lived there. There was a fear of drought, and of windstorms, and a rising of the sea. It took a great many decades, but the cooperation of industry did what cooperation of governments could not, and assuaged the growing threat, backpedaling the damage. The ice caps no longer at risk, the rising waters a fear of the past. But the human's fourth world war put an end to all that.

These were the early days of interstellar relations with other species, and not all Earthans welcomed this unknown community from beyond. Flags with the eban symbol began flying in front of some homes, then the windows of some businesses, and of course the inevitable graffiti. Soon enough, given legitimacy, it decorated the flagpoles of several governments. The United Humanist Front had been born.

Ironically, the eban symbol—which in West African culture represented a fence—was meant to signify love, safety, and security. But the people who rallied behind it were committing to a life of anything but. It was the Humanist Front, in trying to keep the Earth 'safe from alien infestation', which instead brought the planet to its knees. It was their weapons of war, and the ones used back against them, that brought the cities down. And the following long years of unregulated post war re-industrialization that raised the temperatures up.

The ice melted after all.

There was, at one time, a minor city known as Worcester, established high up in the foothills of a distant mountain range beyond it. It sat along the east edge of the North American continent, a mere fifty miles from the Atlantic coastline—and the same distance from its larger sister city of Boston. The thermobaric airstrikes, however, erased both these skylines from the map, and the rising oceans in the decades afterward turned those inland foothills into beachfront. But there's a New Boston on this new seashore, built where the ashes of old Worcester lay. A second shining city on a hill, that looks out proud onto its infant bay.

Meanwhile the bones of the old Boston still lay unburied, now some fifty miles out to sea, and it was here that Rook and Drake were headed, cruising in low above the towering skyscrapers of the New Boston, aimed for the crumbled, sunken ones of the old. Rook looked down from the small drop-pod that they had taken from the interceptor, the ship passing over what he falsely remembered as his onetime home. The place where Parliament first found each other through a serendipity of circumstance, one that still bound them together today. But this was not *his* home, but the other Rook before him, and he felt nothing but malice and loathing as he surveyed it from above. Denali's reinforced suggestions to him prior to his leaving gave no chance for his own true emotions to surface, though they may or may not have been very different.

"So, how do you want to handle this?" Rook grumbled to the other seti.

"Lord Denali has a preferred method he employs to persuade people he needs," Drake said, "whether it's a factory owner, or a planetary ruler."

"Which is?"

"He determines the person with the greatest influence and power, and promises them more of it. As an alternative, he also offers a horrific death as a second option, and will dependably supply a vivid example to assure them of it. And he makes sure, either way... power or pain... he *always* delivers on his promises."

"What do we intend to promise this Doctor Grivvux?"

"We have already made our promise to him, his predecessor's seat on the Khailian Council. A promise that was kept with Dr Cyyxill's early demise. But after fulfilling what he owed us, he abandoned his seat, and came to the Coalition to hide. Apparently, he was afraid we might ask him for something more."

"And he no longer wants to participate," Rook finished. "I guess that leaves only the pain, then."

"So it would seem," Drake agreed. "Though we need him in good shape. He'll be of no use to our master dead."

"Got it. Extreme pain, without permanent damage… for the moment."

The city of New Boston was now lost in the distance far behind them, and the small pod began to slow as it skimmed above the cold Atlantic waters. The ruins were all around them now, hidden beneath the surface, the jagged remains no longer visible projecting from the deep. The wind and waves had beaten down what scraps the bombings had left behind, and only a scarce few hints of the old city still remained to mark its grave. Up ahead, the blinking warning lights of the Tobin hazard beacons faded in and out on the horizon, warning seacraft to steer clear of the remnants of the upper scaffolding, the bridge's red, rusted skeleton still protruding from the water. Beyond that was one of several small islands, its surface choked with weedy vines. But in its center, at the very summit, the glitter of a felled golden dome peeked out between the tangled leaves. They cruised around it, then down they went, slipping through the wind-tossed waves, and lowering themselves in amongst the sunken streets of a toppled Boston.

The seas were dark here, the ruins old, and Rook could make out very little of the town's remains, beyond barnacle covered debris scattered between the waving fronds of seaweed. Drake seemed to know his way though, having studied the charts while en route, and navigated as confidently amongst the leaning wreckage as if he'd made the trip a dozen times. He slowed even further, then lowered the pod into a concrete canyon, towards a wide, looming abyss. The headlights of the craft cast themselves upon a corroded bronze plaque hung from the center pillar of the opening, and Rook leaned forward in his seat to try and read it.

It depicted a figure of a human viciously wielding back with a long club, as if about to strike someone in anger. Old English letters were written underneath. 'Ted Williams Tunnel' they declared, in a carved, blocky font.

Rook sat back again. "People live down here?" he asked in disbelief.

"I'm every bit as surprised as you," Drake told him. "But people who don't wish to be found can be quite innovative. I guess they've connected this particular tunnel to several more, all of which were already built beneath the sea floor. Once they were sealed off, it was a simple matter to pump them dry."

"Oh yeah, piece of cake."

"Well… for the Theseans, it was."

The tunnel continued some hundred meters, then ended at what was clearly a modern dike wall blocking the way. On both the left and right side were individual docking rings. Drake spun their small craft around, and backed their rear hatch into one. It connected with an echoed clang.

The tunnel that the hatchway led to was hardly a place anyone would care to live—a dank and musty roadway of filth, further coated with a dripping slime, and the smell of dead sea life. The scant overhead lighting flickered and hummed, and they used its unreliable illumination to follow a narrow path through piles of old garbage heaped on the wet and crumbled asphalt.

"You're sure about this?" Rook asked, even more unconvinced now.

"If the master says it, then it is so. He has eyes everywhere, and they assured him the khailian is here. The appearance of the entrance is merely a facade, meant to make intruders want to turn away."

"Yeah? Well, it's working."

They walked beneath a dangling road sign, rust encrusted where the green paint had chipped away. 'Logan Airport—Keep Right'. Drake reached a salt-corroded doorway between one side of the tunnel and the other, opened it wide, and led them through.

The ancient underpass on the southbound side was not much of an improvement: a mile-long row of piecemeal shelters in a line, one after another, crammed together in the left-hand lane. Some were built of iron panels or piled cretespray, while others were repurposed from old, rotted vehicles—a tour bus, a truck trailer, even some kind of taco canteen. Meanwhile, the right lane busied with a wide assortment of undesirable types, skulking to and fro, darting between the hovels like insects beneath a rotten log. The clean and well-armored pair drew much of their attention; conversations halted, crowds withdrew as they passed, and they carried along the uneasy stare of everyone they came across.

"So, what do you want to do?" Rook asked, fingering his pistol grip. "Split up and ask around? You talk to the riff, and I'll talk to the raff?"

"That won't be necessary. We've been given a quite specific location." Drake pulled out and double checked his multicomm, then beckoned for Rook to follow. "The woman that Grivvux paid to bring him here, she's the one who turned him in. She's keeping him on the comline right now, and I'm tracking the signal."

"Pssh. What happened to honor among thieves? You can't trust anyone anymore."

They continued onward beneath the off-putting orange hue of old suspended lighting, peering through the gaps and doorways in the varied array of shelters. Whatever transpired within these shanties, it hardly seemed on the up and up. There was a lot of whispering and sidelong glances. Packages plucked from secret places, then stealthily swapped for sweaty palmed fistfuls of gripped credits. All the while, the native population seemed torn between hiding from the pair, or following along behind as if to surround them. Rook noted that a little of both was rising in their wake.

Finally, they stopped in front of some sort of decrepit office trailer, a modular workplace in the shape of a shipping container, designed to be used at construction sites. It was rusted, and dirty, and the missing exterior door had been replaced with a flimsy curtain of fabric. But a gleam of lighting from inside showed through gaps in the boarded window, and backlit the threadbare curtain. A muffled voice from within rose and fell as if in an argument. Drake turned off the multicomm and nodded to Rook. He unholstered his laser pistol, and Rook did likewise with an acid sprayer. The trailing entourage of scurrying cockroaches behind them fell back at the sight of weapons, hurrying back into the shadows. The two pushed the curtain aside and walked in.

The khailian was large, as was typical of his kind, with long tendrils of braided hair in greasy, brown tangles down his back. He faced away from them as they entered, and spoke in loud, angry whispers to someone on his multicomm.

"Why you make I still wait? I wait long enough!" he growled hoarsely. "This place no good. I pay you much. You move me other place. Stay here no! I think better if stay home at Erie seven."

"Well, you should have thought of that before, Doctor," Drake announced from behind.

Grivvux dropped his device to the floor, and spun his ivory tusked muzzle around in surprise, raising his hands, while clearly confused as to who was holding him at gunpoint. Drake opened his mask, and the khailian's eyes went wide. "What you want of Grivvux? I did you asked. Deal over now."

"No, Doctor Grivvux, deal not over now," Drake explained. "We told you we may have need of you again, yet you went and made yourself very, very hard to get a hold of. Lord Denali takes that personally."

"What more you need. I not of council anymore. No can get more chemical for serum."

"Oh, don't you worry about that. We have someone else helping us on that end. What we need you for, is the expedited procedure for processing the serum you promised us."

"I no promise!" the khailian protested. "I say *maybe* can do, *maybe* I try."

"Well, I'm not quite sure Lord Denali recalls it that way. But fortunately for you, you've got another chance. We're gonna take you to our factory to work on it."

"No. I no can go. Not possible to do."

The two seti looked at one another, and Drake gave his partner a nod. Rook lifted his acid sprayer's muzzle to douse the khailian's leg.

"Whoa, whoa, whoa," Drake said, "we still need to take him with us. You make it so he can't walk, and we'll have to carry him out of here."

"You're right, my bad," Rook said apologetically. Then he lifted the muzzle higher, and shot Doctor Grivvux in his left hand.

The splash of gel-like liquid drenched his fingers and palm, and immediately began to smolder into heavy tendrils of white mist, which fell downward thickly towards the ground rather than floating up. The khailian let loose a scream that rocked the trailer. He grabbed his forearm with his other hand as he collapsed into a chair, staring at his skin and fur peeling back, and the blood beginning to ooze. His fingers melted like birthday candles, falling away in waxy drops, and he let loose another roaring wail of anguish as the bones in his palm became exposed.

Rook approached him. "You know, if you agree to help us, I can stop the damage from spreading any further. It's not even that bad. Nothing a good doctor couldn't fix right up." Rook squinted then and cocked his head. "Well... not one of your doctors, of course. I mean a real one. Look, I've got a fake hand too." Rook extended his tractor blades in front of him with a sliding click.

Doctor Grivvux bellowed at him in harsh khailian snarls. There was no need for it to be translated, his tone was more than enough to get the meaning.

Rook frowned. "Or... I go ahead and burn away the other one as well." He raised the muzzle.

"No! Stop! I give what Denali need!" Grivvux begged. "I have work already! In computer. Work ready for you! Take!"

Rook lowered the acid sprayer and holstered it at his side. "What computer? That one?" he asked, pointing to the dropped multicomm on the floor.

Grivvux nodded vigorously, watching the small remaining stub of his hand continue liquifying towards his wrist.

Rook lifted his left hand high, then brought the tractor blades down hard above the khailian's forearm, slicing the dissolved hand off completely, and leaving a fairly clean traumatic amputation at the wrist.

The scientist cried out again.

"I told you I'd stop the acid damage," Rook said, bending to retrieve the multicomm. "I'd get a tourniquet on that, though, if I was you."

The doctor struggled under Drake's watchful eye to wrap the bleeding stump of his severed hand. Beside him, Rook scrolled through the device, switching the system language to common, and searching the files. "Show me," he said to the khailian, holding the multicomm out in front of him.

Grivvux pointed with a thick, trembling, hairy finger, directing him to the proper folder.

Rook opened it and skimmed through the data, then took it over to show Drake. "I'm no chemical engineer, but this looks like it to me."

Drake looked up at the khailian who was back on his feet. "This is to make a larger batch?" he asked. "Faster processing?"

"Yes. Many larger," Grivvux said. "Many faster."

"And it works?"

"Yes, yes. Will work."

Drake stared at the khailian a long moment, as if trying to read him. "Okay, I guess we're good. Let's go, Doctor Grivvux."

Rook held up a hand and turned to Drake. "Hold up," he said. "If we have the multicomm, and he says that it works... do we really need to keep him around anymore?"

Drake scanned his eyes upward, looking left and then right, as if searching his mind for any possible reason. "Mmmm... not that I can think of."

Rook pulled an autopistol from his opposite holster, then leveled it between Doctor Grivvux's eyes.

"No!" the doctor shouted.

Rook fired once, and the large khailian fell dead, a trickle of blood upon his forehead, a gout of it on the wall behind him. "Sorry," he said to Drake. "I know that wasn't the usual drawn-out demonstration Lord Denali prefers to leave behind, but in the interest of time..."

"I think it will be fine, and I agree we should be leaving quickly," Drake said. "Let's get out of here, and back to the ship, before we further wear out our welcome."

16.2

DESPITE THE COMMINGLED PRAYERS OF the two lovers—*'oh, but if only the slowed hands of time might let us linger'*—the morning did what mornings do, and arrived on time nonetheless. Bullseye drew his eyelids ajar with apprehensive hesitation, like the tedious parting of weighty theater curtains, uneager to take note of the time on the clock. It was late. Late enough that the *Bugeye* could be arriving at any minute. Bullseye closed his eyes once again, and listened to the steady rhythm of Relic's breathing. It was music. He wanted to live on in this moment, the only pure and true joy he had felt in many years. But he knew this, as all things, must come to its end. He would seek to preserve it though—take a moment to gather the sense and feeling as he now lived it, and compress it like a jewel that he could lock away in his memory. Hoarded treasure. He touched her waist and pulled her tight, breathed in the scent of her, and caught the joy in her unconscious sigh. He savored with all his senses the passage of these final moments, then placed them within a diamond, and greedily locked it safe away. He could seldom recall his heart so heavy as when he pulled the tangled blankets back, and slung his legs to meet the floor.

The night was over.

Their night was over.

A frown crossed Relic's face as she reached out across the bed to feel him, and her hand found the space empty. She opened her eyes, and met them with his.

"Your mother and cousin soon shall mark their return," Bullseye told her.

She looked with sad longing up at him, then nodded her head in understanding, and sat up from the pillow.

The room was still bathed in partial dimness, save the lilac haze cast from the swirling giant out the window—an ambiance that was welcome, even instrumental to last night, but now merely a reminder that the stolen moment was truly over. Bullseye turned on the light—the mood was shattered. Relic walked around the bed and crossed the room to him, not the least bit bashful in her nakedness. She slid her arms around his back, and rocked her head against his chest—Bullseye liked to think she was creating a diamond of her very own. She kissed the center of his chest, then turned her face away. The two began getting dressed in silence.

After a few moments, Relic spoke soft and broke the quiet. "I would... like to see you again, very much," she said, adjusting an undergarment across her shoulders. Their backs were to each other as they sat on each bedside. "Like this, I mean. Like... last night. I know there might be some... resistance. But I'd like to see a way through it." She turned her head sharply around to look at him behind her. "That's if... of course, if... I mean... if you would?"

Bullseye sighed. "No greater reward could exist, that I might strive harder to achieve, than to spend such a night again in your company," he told her. He turned and met her gaze. "But I do not know that it can be, for reasons which you are aware."

"My family," Relic said.

"Your parents," he made more specific. "Your father is a friend, through great and many a course of years. He has witnessed facets to my nature that are valued when used in battle, but sour in flavor when thought of placed beside his daughter. Belladonna too... a vigilant guardian is your mother. Surely she would see better ahead for you than to pair with a broken man."

"What's broken about you, that I can't hope to fix?"

"Ah... if any could, 'tis surely you. But this should not be your lot, nary the three of us would opt it for you."

"I will choose my own lot, if you don't mind," she snapped. "I don't need the three of you making decisions for me."

"Fair and true, I entreat forgiveness. No person should yield to any resolution but their very own," he agreed. "I nonetheless must need their license and approval. I would not choose to buy my happiness at the cost of another's... least of all an ally and friend, such as my true companion who sired you."

"I understand," she said reluctantly. "Then... we'll just have to brave asking."

"Even if we were to dare, how then to approach it? And moreover, when? Certainly now is no ripe time, your father wayward, mother distraught. How could we, in good conscience, seek out a blessing for us now?"

She had no answer for that, and returned to her dressing. After a moment, she looked back. "But... you would..."

"My dear Relic, the past dozen hours have tested the finest of all my days," Bullseye told her. "If blessed again to relive them? Oh, to praise the luck that would see fit to make me worthy."

She beamed at him, and the two continued to prepare—she in a fresh floral wrap of blue and pink, he in the same formal wear of the evening gone past. He was gladdened to see that she had folded and smoothed it for him, retrieved at some point from the floor, and hung thoughtfully upon a chair. James would call his redressing in it for the return to his room 'the walk of shame'—but he felt none of that sentiment.

"I have something else to tell you, B," she said, returning to the usage of her pet name for him. "You're one of the only people I can mention it to. I was told never to speak of it, and so I've held my tongue for ten years or so now." She paused a moment, and took a breath before continuing. "But, I've overheard my cousin's comments. I can feel he has... concerns... over the loyalty of my father."

Bullseye could not deny it, and he would not shame himself to lie to her. He stood still, and said nothing.

"I... know about my father," she said.

"Of what precisely do you speak?"

"I mean, I know what he is... and I know who he isn't."

This conversation was treading near to topics Bullseye had pledged never to speak of. He held his tongue as he held her gaze.

Relic saw she would need to be far more specific in order to goad him to break his vow. "I know the father who birthed me, who brought me to this world, is gone," she said. "Killed, when I was perhaps ten. I know the father who raised me since is an exact replication made to substitute, but in my eyes, still my father just the same."

"Who has told you such things?" he asked, in that perfect median tone that neither confirmed nor denied.

"I've seen the evidence for myself, a long time ago now. I've always been my father's daughter after all, nosy by nature, just as he was before me. And at the risk of sounding immodest, nearly just as skilled at accessing information... as well as inclined to do so whenever temptation presents itself," she said. "My mother presented a temptation. Or her computer did anyway, while I was messing around with it as a child. Without permission, of course, trying to be like my dad. I found an encrypted folder, partitioned behind a hidden firewall. It was too tempting to not explore."

Bullseye still said nothing, but was slowly approaching her as she spoke.

She was nervous now that she shouldn't have said anything, but it was too late to turn back now. "It took me a few weeks. I had a lot to learn, and only limited time when I could sneak her multicomm from her. But in the end, I got in. I saw the messages between you and her, and she and the others. Mostly between Tachion and my Mom." Bullseye was right in front of her now, and for a moment she thought he might grab and shake her, or push her down.

He reached out his hands and gently took hold of hers, bringing them together between them. "I am ever remorseful that we dared not tell you. That you learned of it in such a way," he said. "Young and alone, left on your own to riddle your emotions."

"I was not on my own. I confronted my mother, right there and then," she told him. "She helped me understand both the tragedy, and the triumph of it. The crushing loss of one so loved, but the fortunate miracle that would return him."

"And Flashpoint?" Bullseye asked.

"He knows nothing. He couldn't have handled it," she said. "He's not even as mature now as I was way back then. He wouldn't understand. Nor would he keep it quiet, I'm afraid. I understand the need for my father to never know, for his own good."

"And you've held this all these years," Bullseye lamented.

"It was no great chore. The truth was easy to set aside. As I said, he's my daddy today, just as he was at my birth. There was no change in the man who raised me, from the one before, to the one after. The same love, the same humor... the same soul inside as far as I'm concerned," she explained. "This is how I know."

"Know what?"

"Know that your friend Rook would never betray you, teaming up with this Denali. Not of his own mind," she said. "It just isn't possible."

"Ah, but therein lies the rub, my dear Relic," Bullseye answered. "What we have learned of this Denali tells Rook may *not* be of his own mind. And your father, turned against us, would make a formidable foe."

"Just remember, please," she begged him, "if he *is* acting against us, that it could *not* be truly him. Give him a chance, before... before doing something rash."

"I... I do not know if I can promise..."

The ship-wide intercom rang a trilling whistle, interrupting him. Lieutenant Kinn-Ara's avian accent followed through the speaker. "*Bridge to Master Bullseye.*"

Bullseye released Relic's hands, and crossed to the wall intercom in the living room. "Bullseye here."

"*Oh, forgive me,*" she started, sounding confused. "*I had been trying to raise you in your own quarters, and your office. And your personal communicator is off.*"

Bullseye softly winced, realizing the possible scandal in answering from this station. He wondered as to the nature of bridge crew gossip, as he reached in his pocket, and reinitialized his multicomm. "You have found me now, Lieutenant. What is your message?"

"*The* Bugeye *is en route, now only minutes from the hangar bay.*"

"Understood. On my way," he told her, signing off. He looked down at his outfit. No time to change it now. He turned to Relic. "Will you join me to greet your mother?"

She looked at him almost sorrowfully. "No, I think not," she said.

He cocked his head at her and raised a brow.

"The moment we step through that doorway, we must go back to how we were before. I understand that, and accept it. But I'm not ready to turn my mind from you. Not just yet."

He smiled at her. "Then I shall go on ahead, and next we see each other..."

"I will behave," she told him.

"At least in public," he said, in a rare sly jest. Then he went to her, and took her face in his hands. "Before I go, I must impart my deepest thanks to you."

"For... what?" she whispered to him.

"For being... absolutely everything that I never knew I needed." He kissed her once, and walked away.

16.3

AS THE SWEAT OF DAY COOLED into the dewiness of night, the city of Krataar settled into a most uncommon quiet—The Cat's Meow and its neighboring ventures seeing their clientele dwindle with the passing hours, from some, to few, to none. The owner even had them turn the music down to barely audible, the deafening beat seeming awkward and silly with all the entertainers simply sitting around. Cheshire assumed the commotion of earlier was to blame. The death of eleven officers, and an improvised gas bomb detonating out front, were not the sort of publicity that made the patrons come running. But he had made a good day of it, the bonus credits from that strange foursome of probable terrorists helping greatly, and as his shift was nearly over anyway, he decided to break early, and head for home.

The hush of the nightclub was doubly magnified out on the platforms, with the bustling crowds and buzz of drone craft that usually rumbled unabated through the night, now somehow eerily gone silent. No ships filled the sky above. No cargo moved from the stores below. The raised walkways were barren enough that he could hear the clap of his designer heels against the metal paneling beneath him, and the nocturnal songs of the jungle echoed from all around. He had never been able to hear those things before walking home, at any time, day or night. High above him, among the stars, the lights of massive starships in low orbit traced their way across the night; far more than Cheshire had ever seen up there before. But then again, it wasn't his usual custom to look up and take notice.

He wasn't completely alone out on the platforms, however. Traversing the shipping district to make his way towards the central plaza, he passed several roving squads of soldiers along the route. No doubt extra security, he supposed, due to the dangerous excitement of the day. Still, the sidelong glances and suspicious stares he received as he made his way raised his hackles up. He pulled out his multicomm to summon a transport to meet him in the plaza, as he no longer felt like making the brief trek home on foot.

His device showed a good connection, both local and subspace, but for some reason he couldn't get the global data net to connect. Stupid service. It wasn't the first time he'd had problems. He would love to change carriers, if it wasn't for the fact there was only one corporate monopoly. Fine then, he was walking home as usual. He turned the collar of his cropped linen jacket against the dank warmth of the evening mist, wishing now the garment covered more of his midriff, and made a beeline through the city square.

The central plaza was similarly deserted, with seemingly only soldiers and police out on the town tonight—and there certainly were an awful lot of them. A bit overkill, in Cheshire's opinion. There were often firefights far worse than today's, after all. Almost weekly, it seemed. One of the perks of living in an intergalactic hub such as Krataar. He clutched against his chest the weighty bag of light battle armor that the dark-furred seti woman had left him today, and hurried onward.

As he entered the government district, the neighborhood he called home, he noticed a peculiar radiance of light up ahead of him, diffused by the dewy fog. A large building down the street was suspiciously illuminated, one that he was accustomed to seeing shrouded in darkness at this hour. The Magisterium for this prefecture, the seat of government for all this region's districts. The capitol building's windows were oddly aglow, a flurry of commotion obscured behind them.

The gated entrance to the complex seemed to have been knocked down somehow, and the driveway was choked with armored vehicles and police aerocars, the brilliance of their strobed warning lights blinding Cheshire's sensitive seti night vision. He looked away. Perhaps there was more to the violence than what occurred out on the platform today. Was there some sort of attack on the magistrate's complex, some threat to Krataar's prefect? Being in the windowless club all night could be like sealing yourself in a vacuum. No sense of day or night, or the passing of time, nor any insight into anything happening in the outside world. News programs were not welcome in that sort of atmosphere, and the workers didn't exactly have pockets to carry their multicomms. He tried again to connect to the network, to see if he could find out what had happened. Nothing. He would have to wait till he got home—or even ask his friendly neighbor in the morning. She was the communications magistrate for the prefect's office, so she would certainly have the inside scoop, if anybody did. He turned sharply down his street, under the watchful eye of a chamai trooper behind a vehicle mounted turret, and quickened his pace.

The life of an exotic dancer may not be an enviable one, but in Cheshire's case, at least, it certainly was lucrative. The seti's loft was a luxury listing, in one of the city's most exclusive districts—with a price tag to match. Not exactly the penthouse, perhaps, or even close for that matter, but even the worst apartment here was worth a small fortune. Yet despite paying exorbitant fees, the doorman who was usually out front was nowhere to be seen. Cheshire let himself in, breathing easier once he was safely home in his living room.

The holovision was of no more use than his multicomm was. Channel after channel simply displayed the message 'signal lost'. Great. Another example of the *excellent* service that the communications megacorp they all depended on consistently provided. He looked out his window at a corner of the prefecture capital building in the distance, still alight with its glowing windows and flashing strobes. Down below, his neighbor's apartment was pitch dark. Either she was already part of the commotion at her work, or she was sleeping through it. He pressed a button on the wall that turned his window glass from transparent to opaque. It looked like he would have to wait until tomorrow to find out what happened. He picked up a tawdry romance novel to take into bed with him, but exhaustion came over quickly, and he faded to sleep in the middle of the raunchy bathtub scene.

A loud crash of glass awoke him early, followed by a tirade of overlapped shouting. Authoritarian sounding chamai voices bellowing in their native language. Cheshire had lived on Oberonn for more than a few years now, but still had never managed to pick up much of the language. It just wasn't really necessary in the species-mingled district where he worked, where everyone just assumed to speak common from the get-go. He did know some dirty words though, and more than a few swears, solely for business purposes, of course. The shouting outside was laced with just about all of them. Some stupid workmen or something, berating one of their coworkers who broke an item of value. The seti rolled sideways, and pulled the sheet over his head to go back to sleep.

Another shocking sound jerked him upright, this one resounding sharply like a firecracker—or perhaps a gunshot. What were the odds of that, though, this early in the morning. And in this district? Nevertheless, he decided to get up and take a peek out the window. The holovision he had left on in the living room was finally working again, the fearsome face of some creepy, old, bald general jabbering away. Cheshire turned up the volume—he was jabbering in chamai. He clicked around the channels, but the old general was everywhere. He activated the translator to interpret the audio into common, but just as the general ranted something about Coalition interlopers, a piercing scream came from outside. The seti shut off the broadcast and rushed to the window. He activated the glass transparency and looked down.

Outside on the street was some sort of armored aerotransport vehicle. It was parked sideways across the road, like it had landed in a hurry. There was no marking on it that Cheshire could see, no police or military logo. From the building across the way, a pair of men in nonuniform fatigues emerged, dragging a chamai woman behind them—his friendly neighbor lady that worked for the prefect's office. She was putting up a struggle, but they were far too strong for her, and they slowly dragged her down the walkway towards the transport. What the hell was going on?! Was this some sort of kidnapping? Where were the police that had been all over the place last night? His neighbor fell over, and one of the men kicked her hard. Cheshire was going to have to do something—he couldn't just stand here watching. He could hold his own in a fight, after all. He had made it to third level in his martial arts class. In his line of work, you never know when someone might get too aggressive. It had been years since his instruction, but he thought he still remembered the basics, and from up here, at least, the kidnapers seemed to be unarmed. That's it—he was going. He rushed to the door, then suddenly stopped and looked at the bag on the floor. That nice set of armor might be enough to scare them off, even if it did have unnecessary breasts. In fact, maybe even more so because of them. He quickly slipped on just the torso plating and the gauntlets over his one-piece jumpsuit as he hurried down.

By the time he got to the street, the woman had already been roughly tossed aboard, and the two were locking the back of the transport behind her.

"Stop that, right now!" Cheshire yelled as he strode toward them across the roadway. He tried to channel some of the bravado of the mercenaries from the club yesterday. "What do you two think you're doing? Let her go this instant, or I'll report you to the police."

They looked him up and down, somewhat perplexed, then began to shout him down in chamai—with plenty of those dirty words he could recognize being tossed about. Cheshire saw he was wrong about them being unarmed, as both of the Oberonnians had energy-powered force maces swinging from their hips. Still, that's fairly poorly armed, even for low-level thugs. One of them shoved the seti, and Cheshire instinctively shoved back. The uniformed chamai landed hard on his ass.

A chuckle came from the building in front of him, and he saw three more emerge from his neighbor's apartment complex. They seemed quite amused with their friend's stumble and fall. Cheshire made note: they were all wearing the same sort of fatigues as the first two. Who the hell were these people? They were seeming less like hired thugs, and more like some sort of street militia. The one on the ground leaped back to his feet, and clearly needing to save face, pulled out his force mace. A hum of blue light came to life at the top of the handle, and Cheshire stuck defense pose 'pouncing ferox', as he had been taught in his self-defense class. The others laughed, circling around to watch.

A shout from behind them preempted the skirmish, much to the seti's relief, and he turned to see two armed and armored military soldiers crossing the street. They questioned the militiamen in the chamai language as they approached, but Cheshire interrupted, and stepped forward toward them. "Oh my, thank goodness. You two have fabulous timing," he said. "Another minute or so, and I would've had to teach this lot a painful lesson." He leaned in to the soldiers. "Probably more painful for me, unfortunately," he whispered loudly.

"What's going on here?" one of the soldiers asked him, carefully scrutinizing the seti.

"What's happening, honey, is that these men are kidnappers. They just *brutalized* my neighbor, and tossed her in this truck. I saw the whole thing myself, with these beautiful, brown peepers!" He batted his lashes at the pair of soldiers.

They spoke to the abductors for a moment, then turned back to address Cheshire. "Why are you interfering in official government security business, Coalition interloper?" he demanded harshly.

"*Interfering?...* in... You must be off your rocker, sweety. Wait a minute, what did you call me? Coalition inter-what's-it? I'm not Coalition *anything*, baby! I live right here, in Krataar. Shit, that's my damn house, right across the street!"

The other guard spoke now, a woman's voice beneath the armor. "You are seti, of the Coalition, here to interfere and subvert our society. You and the rest of your... secret spy police."

Cheshire laughed. "What are you, crazy? I'm no secret police. I'm an entertainer!" he said, ending with a flourish of jazz hands.

The trooper used the muzzle of her rifle to point to the seti's shoulder. Slightly obscured by a coat of thin coloring, but all the same completely readable, was the golden insignia of the Federated Planetary Coalition, S.S.S division—Starlaw Secret Service.

"Oh, well that," Cheshire started, awkwardly chuckling. "Well, it's... a long story, but see... it's not really my armor. It was a gift from..."

The blow from the rifle's shoulder stock cracked his skull with a blinding flash, and the seti dropped sagging and limp jointed to the pavement—a marionette with its strings cut. His face clapped against the roadway with a second bolt of sparks, and he laid there for a long while, trying to unblur his fuzzy vision, and unjumble what had happened. He heard laughing above him, and was rocked back and forth with kicks to the back and chest. They didn't seem to register with him though, thanks to the armor, until one of the boots drove into his uncovered stomach. The wind left him in a rush, some bile and blood along with it, and Cheshire lay doubled up on his side, straining to reclaim his breathing.

His vision was clearing now, and he saw a pool of blood in front of him on the pavement. He focused his eyes against the pain in his head and his jaw. Something white and gory was there as well, as he struggled to his hands and knees. He looked down at the mess—it was three of his teeth. He vomited onto the ground, which seemed to infuriate those around him. Another round of kicks to the stomach tumbled him back down into his own sickness, and an armored boot to the forehead completely turned out the light.

When he awoke, he was in shackles, his arms locked behind him in a painfully tight embrace, and affixed to the wall of the transport to keep him from moving about. Not that he could have, anyway. Not only did his head sing with the most excruciating of pain, making him spin with dizziness, but the aerotransport craft was aloft now, rolling the passengers dramatically back and forth against their restraints. An announcement was blaring through some sort of speaker, or perhaps a radio broadcast playing, more of that general's voice from this morning, droning on in chamai.

The back of the vessel was filled with far more than just his friendly neighbor. Cheshire could see through his one good eye that the rows were packed with other captives. Most of them were native on-worlders, but also a couple of seti and a human. He tried to open his other eye but it was puffed completely shut. He used the one that was still open to gaze up and down the transport, barely illuminated by the light piercing the high slit windows. Through his permanent wink, he saw his neighbor sitting across from him.

"I am so sorry," she said to him. "I could hear what happened. It's all my fault that you got involved. I know you were trying to help me, but I wish you had just stayed out of it."

"What the hell is going on?" Cheshire asked, lisping and whistling through his broken teeth and swollen tongue. "Who are these people? What did you do? What did *I* do?"

"Don't you know?" she answered. "Last night there was some kind of military coup."

The seti stared at her in surprise. "No, I had no idea. I couldn't get anything on my devices." He looked at the other twenty or so abductees. "Well, what do they want with us?"

"They're rounding up all the officials in the major city governments," she said. "The keystone cities anyway... prefecture capitals, hubs of administration, commerce, travel. All of us here, we all work together for the prefect in the magisterium."

"Do you know where they're taking us?" Cheshire asked.

"My guess? Some sort of reeducation camp. Maybe they want to make sure we're on the same page with the new regime, before putting us back in place."

Cheshire ran his tongue across the sharp remains of his shattered incisors. "Well, I hope they have a dental office there sweety, cuz those bullies sure didn't do my winning smile any favors." He tried to lift the corners of his mouth at her, along with the joke, to lighten the mood, but drawing his lips back into a grin was too painful—on many levels.

He felt the transport pitching forward now; hopefully, they were coming in for a landing. Cheshire was pretty sure his head needed medical attention, sooner rather than later. The looping speech playing over the loudspeaker rang in his brain like getting hit again. "Can you translate what this asshole is saying for me?" he asked his neighbor. Then he stretched up his long, graceful neck to peer through the slotted window above her.

"Coalition interlopers have kept Oberonn under the thumb of their political and economic might for too long," the woman interpreted. *"The dissolution of the Tristar Treaty was merely the first step in regaining our true sovereign independence..."*

Cheshire could see that they were descending into a heavy forest, somewhere up north by the looks of the trees and foliage—and somewhere mountainous. This was not the swampland jungles of Krataar. Suddenly the craft slowed significantly, then was plunged into darkness.

Her translation continued. *"...our Prime Minister has long been a mere puppet to the Coalition, trading favors with our financial oppressors for his own personal gain, and to the detriment of his own people. Therefore, as a loyal patriot, and with the sanction of the military behind me, I have taken the minister into custody, and assume control of the people's government, in their name, under an emergency powers act that my fellow officers drafted this morning..."*

Flood lights had come on along the exterior of the transport, shining bright against the walls of some decrepit, old concrete tunnel. They were moving underground, a passage beneath the mountains. Cheshire could see that the walls were crumbling with age—in some places damp with leaking water, in others decorated with painted graffiti. If this was to be their accommodations until he could convince them he was 'reeducated', it was bound to be a dismal stay.

"...this is a turbulent time, when we all must be vigilant. There will be traitors in our midst that seek to undermine these actions. To return our planet to a pawn of the Coalition. Therefore, to ensure peace and order among her citizens, I am hereby declaring that martial law is in effect. The constitution of Oberonn is officially suspended..."

The vehicle stopped.

"...this is effective immediately, and until further notice. These measures are for the safety and security of all chamai people. Additionally, all non chamai races must report for registration within..."

The engine shut off, and the broadcast went dead with it. His neighbors' translation followed suit. Cheshire leaned forward to whisper to her. "Maybe once they realize I'm not government, they'll just let me register and send me home," he said. "Whatever you do, honey, just agree with their silly reeducation. Do and say whatever they want to hear. Do what you can to get outta this place."

She nodded to him that she would follow that advice. The rear doors swung wide with a loud, echoing squeal.

After being led roughly down from the transport and forced to line up in a single file, Cheshire could see the reason for them getting out and walking. The long, gray tunnel they had traveled down ended in a pair of massive iron doors which the vehicle could not get around. At one time the gates could have swung closed, to seal the tunnel from the chamber beyond, but they were nearly rusted beyond recognition now, and had long ago fallen from their hinges—one resting against the wall, the other flat upon the floor. The line of marching prisoners snaked around them. On the other side, the space opened up to a huge subterranean garage, propped up by frequent pillars that were highlighted by makeshift floodlighting. But the parking lot was deserted. The seti dancer assumed because no vehicles could make it past.

They seemed to be heading to an entryway in the center of the long back wall, but as they approached, the line was stopped, and the abductees separated. An officer was barking orders that Cheshire couldn't translate, but whatever he was saying, his fellow prisoners didn't like it. One tried to struggle free, and more than a few began to weep openly. A soldier began going from hostage to hostage, slipping a thin, dark plastic bag over each one of their heads. Well, that wasn't gonna be comfortable. It would be difficult to breathe underneath that. Darkness fell over him as the loose sack veiled his eyes.

Cheshire was pushed, nearly tripping, shoved backward against the firmness of the cement wall behind him. He was glad to have the structure there for support, as the dizziness from his head wound was magnified in the blackness. His hands still bound behind him, he put the flat of his palms against the cool concrete, and leaned back, resting upright. The wall here was old as well, and he could feel the gritty dust of the ancient plaster chipping loose beneath his fingers. Longing for any form of sensation in the darkness, he slid them along the wall, picking at the crumbling cement with his furred fingers, until they came across a fractured indent—a pockmark in the wall. He slid his finger in. It was a chipped-out little cavity, with something cold and cylindrical lodged in the middle. He ran his fingertip round and round it, curious as to what it was, until his mind formed the image of a two-inch crater in the cement, the remains of the bullet that caused it wedged deeply in its center. Cheshire yanked his hand away, and thought to himself that he wanted his mother.

An order barked loud in chamai, the racking sound of a dozen rifles, then the echoed crack and muffled fall of history repeating.

16.4

THE *BUGEYE* HAD ALREADY SETTLED into the hangar bay's narrow resting spot as Bullseye arrived, the whir of her engines winding down like the descending groan of a hand-crank siren. True to his word, Chief Zvavi and his team were already scampering beneath the belly of the craft, even before her gangplank touched down. The chief was frowning with grieved concern as he probed the multitude of bullet holes with his finger, then shouted his crew into action.

From the rear of the craft emerged Bullseye's companions, though with one person more than he expected to see—a lyghtan male walking with Bullit and Belladonna. It was Tàlto. Then an unknown chamai woman at Stansky's side, engaged in conversation. He seemed almost to lean on her, as if he were having trouble keeping a straight line. Bullseye peered around, but there was no sign of the Lady Opal.

The chamai lady looked about in awe. "This entire starship is yours?" she asked in surprise.

"Well, it's all of ours, actually... the Parliament team members together, I mean," James said. He then lowered his voice, eyeballing Bullit's back. "But, I am the second highest ranking member... so technically, it belongs more to *me* than certain other people."

She laughed. "I think it's marvelous."

"I'm surprised you're so impressed. After all, you'll have an entire armada at your fingertips one day."

"Well, that has yet to be seen, depending on the success of our mission," she said. "How many in *your* armada?"

"How do you mean?"

"Well, you've christened her the *Parliament One*... so I presuppose that there are others. How many in your fleet?"

Stansky cleared his throat. "Well... we might have just been thinking positively when we decided to name her that," he confessed. "We have no other armada... beyond the few fighters in this hangar bay."

"Well then, I say you have a fleet of eight," she declared. "Small craft or not, it is still mightily impressive."

"There actually was a *Parliament Two* at one time, very briefly," James told her, loud enough for Bullit to overhear. "But that was just Bullit's little pleasure yacht, now resting comfortably at the bottom of Lake Winnipesaukee."

She glanced at the seti.

Bullit turned his head back to her. "It's a very long story," he said. "Very long, and very sad."

She laughed once again. Then she looked up, her eyes going wide.

Bullseye watched as the chamai woman rushed hurriedly right past him. He turned to see her clutch Tachion in a tight embrace as the android entered the chamber, the metallic medic uncomfortably freezing in place for fear of pinching her in his geared mechanisms.

"James has been hurt," she implored, gazing up at him, "shot in the head. Bullit too. Not in the head, but his arm is injured."

Tachion peered over her towards his teammates, giving them a quick cursory once over. They would live, for the moment. "Well, he certainly has a propensity for getting hit in the head. But don't worry, I'll be sure to take good care of both of them," he said. "I'm very pleased, however, to see that *you* are uninjured."

"Thanks to Miss Belladonna, and of course Tàlto once again."

Tachion turned and nodded to the lyghtan bounty hunter in thanks.

Tàlto nodded back.

Something occurred to Tachion then. "I just realized, you still haven't yet met our team leader," he told her. "Please allow me to introduce you." He turned her about, and they walked together back to Bullseye. "My ladyship, may I introduce to you Bullseye, senior member of the mercenary group Parliament. Bullseye, it's my honor to present Her Royal Highness, Lady Opal, First Ashi'Mar of Sovereign Capella, Most Eminent Heir to the Holy Temple Throne, Sacred Voice of the Holy Passel, and Chosen Guardian of the Divine Path."

Opal bowed ever so slightly, while Bullseye stared straight on, dumbfounded. "I would not ever have made the guess," he said, staring intently at her features. "This Guisemage you employed, Selene Maraspese... we must make good on our debt to her, pay her damages. A talent like this is not a bridge to be burnt." He suddenly caught himself awestruck, realizing he had ignored the introduction. "Forgive my manners, my lady, and my failure in etiquette. Though I was told you were incognito, I fear the extent caught me unawares." He bowed back to her. "My deepest regards, and divine blessings to you, Madam Ashi'Mar. I pray for you sweet water and shaded refuge. May the light of the path always lead your way."

"Flowing springs and safe haven, for both you and your clan. May the light that guides us both blaze the path to salvation," Opal responded. Then she straightened up. "There... now that we've gotten the formalities out of the way, let's not fuss over them again. All the pretense and protocol are not necessary here. Nor is the formal dress," she said, alluding to Bullseye's outfit. "You are now and forever *all* my friends, even those of you I've only just met. And my friends do not bow to me... except in the formality of throne room proceedings, perhaps."

"Your ladyship is too generous," Bullseye said.

"Not at all. In fact, it is I who should apologize, for introducing myself in costume. If you would pardon the vulgarity of it, I would just as soon remove it here, and greet you with my own face."

"As my lady wishes."

Opal unclasped her armor's collar plate, then lowered the zipper of the inertia suit beneath it to just past the top of her cleavage. The edge of the biomask was markedly visible here, the false ruddy flesh of the chamai disguise meeting her true ebony skin at the top of her bosom. At the border between the two, a fringe of sheer fabric laced with delicate circuitry and blinking microsensors protruded. She slid her fingers underneath, and peeled her entire face up and over with some effort, letting her natural features breathe for the first time in several days. She then reached toward her throat, pulling free the two small voice-modulating disks adhered there. Her face was damp and ooze covered, and marked with compression lines—but it was hers.

"The hair color and the eyes I will attend to in private," she said, the chamai accent now gone, her true voice softer and more demure. "I have certain chemicals and devices on hand to restore them... but for now, it is indeed a pleasure to finally meet you."

Bullseye maintained his bearings this time, despite the astonishment of the whole procedure. "The pleasure is all mine, My Lady."

"Opal," she corrected.

"*Lady* Opal," he compromised. "We have already prepared a room for you." He turned towards Tàlto. "And we will, of course, make one available for you as well."

Opal followed behind Bullseye's words, making a step or two toward the lyghtan bounty hunter. "Thank you, Tàlto, for risking yourself to rescue us... to rescue *me*. Honestly, it is more than I would have expected from you. I would have thought you'd just as soon collect the reward."

"Why would you think that?" he questioned her, in his gravel strewn voice.

"Well, when last we... went our separate ways," she reminded him, "you said some things to me that... well... that might be considered both heresy and treason, if the temple abbesses had overheard them."

"I must have still been upset at how things ended," he suggested. "I can't really remember, it was so many years ago."

She raised an eyebrow and looked insulted. "It was eleven months," she corrected.

"Oh... is that all? Huh. Well, you know what they say. Time flies..."

"When you're *what!*" she demanded angrily. "When you're not with *me?*"

Stansky approached, pulling free from Tachion beginning an inspection on his head wound. "Is everything all right?" he asked, eyeballing Tàlto.

"It's all good, Jimmy," Tàlto said, turning to walk off. "The lady was just expressing her appreciation."

"Yes, everything's fine, *James,*" she agreed with loosely veiled falsity. She touched his bruised head. "Let's just go and get you taken care of."

Tachion interceded. "I'll take it from here, Madam Ashi'Mar. I can manage to escort these two down to sick bay. I'll have them fixed right up and making themselves presentable in no time. Why don't you go settle in? I'm sure you'd like to get some of that unpleasant conductive gunk off your face. Perhaps Belladonna could show you to your quarters?"

Belladonna happily took the cue. "Of course, my lady. Please, won't you follow me," she chimed, walking the fuming ashi'mar off towards the rear hangar-bay elevator.

Tachion took the injured mercenaries in the opposite direction, toward the corridor.

Bullseye followed after Tàlto, who was wandering the hanger and admiring *The Dodger*. As the seti approached, the lyghtan said, "It is good of you to memorialize your comrades that have... gone before you like this. I am sorry for your..." he looked around at the various craft, "*many* losses."

"I am told we would have two more, if not for your timely intercessions."

"I'm pleased I could assist."

"If you feel so inclined to assist further, I would seek to formally commission your services from you," Bullseye offered. "'Tis sure a harsh road laid out ahead for us. A further experienced gun at our backs would certainly ease our travels."

Tàlto chuckled as he looked around. "Even with all this, I doubt your group could afford me."

"Our pockets run deep."

"Not nearly deep enough," he said. "You would not pay my price if I told it to you."

Bullseye scowled. "You think yourself so exceptional? I have never found any value in such conceit."

"It's not conceit if it's justified," Tàlto maintained. "I've never been cocky, where cockiness was not deserved."

Bullseye snapped his fingers at an avian crewman, who immediately headed to their side. "I will have you shown to your quarters, and we will seek to drop you along our way. You may choose any world you wish upon our path ahead, but I fear we may not stray from it."

"Hold on now," the lyghtan said. "All I said is you can't afford me. I didn't say I wouldn't help."

Bullseye raised an eyebrow.

"For the moment, it seems, our purposes align," Tàlto said. "The protection of the ashi'mar is my only concern."

"*Really*," Bullseye questioned skeptically, feeling there was something more the lyghtan was not saying. "Then please, make yourself our guest, and I will seek you out later... to discuss how we might further assist each other in our purposes." He turned to the crewman. "Show the gentleman to guest quarters fourteen." That would put him on deck D by himself, which ought to keep him out of trouble, and out of the way of all the others.

Tàlto walked off, following the crewman to the lift.

Bullseye turned and hurried after Tachion, James and Bullit, who were now far down the corridor, heading towards the medical suite. He jogged to catch up with them. "Before I lose you two to the Doctor's ministrations," he said, "what news have you? Did your inquisition on the surface glean insight of any worth?"

Bullit huffed. "No, not a thing. A total waste of time. And, one that nearly cost us our lives."

"Whoa, what are you talking about?" Stansky said in surprise. "That stripper told us *exactly* where to go next." James stopped walking, much to Tachion's irritation. "General Nylis is heading to Ilshnar. He has a meeting on the metamorph homeworld."

"Il...shnar?" Bullseye repeated slowly, seeming lost in thought at the answer.

"That information isn't reliable, just the ramblings of some man-whore," Bullit said.

"Told to him by a chamai praetor, from the general's own garrison. Were you not listening to the same conversation as the rest of us?"

"Oh, I was listening, and I heard nothing that would suggest we should change plans. Even if the hooker was correct, we would probably never catch up. And then even if we did, we don't have a clue where this meeting takes place."

"It wouldn't be hard to figure that out once we get there. Just track the..."

"*Or*," Bullit interrupted, "how long he's gonna be in it! He could be on his way elsewhere before we've even built up steam to full warp."

"Now you're just exaggerating," Stansky flatly accused him. "There's no reason to think we can't track him down in plenty of time."

"And no reason to think we can," Bullit countered. "The smart move is to continue as planned to Gel Gonahaar. Denali is moving *something* through that toy factory. We can find out what, where it's coming from, where it's going... and who knows, he might even be there."

"He *might* be there? That's pretty unlikely. But the general *will* be at Ilshnar."

Tachion interrupted, taking the two of them by their shoulders. "Alright, that's enough. Let's figure it out later. We can have a group meeting in a couple of hours, once you two are mended and rested." The android looked at Bullseye. "Both Gel Gonahaar and Ilshnar lie in the same general direction, toward the galaxy's center from here. So for now we can head that way, and decide on veering left or right once everyone's got their heads straight." He turned and dragged the pair off, like children being led to the principal.

Bullseye stood alone in the hall, still considering what was just told to him. Ilshnar? *Ilshnar?* He remembered that from somewhere; it was seeping up like an old dream. Yes—the general had said it to Admiral Yazir, when Bullseye was under the effects of the Zet A'zeta, cowering under the bar counter. What was it he had spoken of? The conversation returned to him in fractured slivers, like shattered glass, and he struggled to put them together again. Rook had been '*taken under their master's wing*', Nylis had said. Could that be true? The evidence so far seemed to support it. What else? The general himself may take Rook with him when he travels to— *Ilshnar!* What was the exact phrasing, though? What exactly did he say? Bullseye closed his eyes and tried to remember. *"He may even accompany me to the metamorph homeworld of Ilshnar,"* the general had said to Yazir, *"for my... renegotiation. Although Trojan needs that power boost quickly, so I may need to proceed ahead without him."*

What was he renegotiating? And what in the name of The Fallen was *Trojan?*

Bullseye spun on his heels, and hurried to his office.

16.5

DENALI WIPED HIS WANING ERECTION on the corner of the bedcover, then searched out a fresh spot of blanket to mop his chest of sweat, and wipe dry his brow. He crumpled the edge of the soiled linen, his panting breath recovering quickly, and discarded it with a toss back down onto the mattress. Striding nude across the stone-carved bedchamber, he looked out an open casement onto the Old City Temple below, and the historic district surrounding it. He would never get used to the lack of windowpanes in these archaic cavern cities—but with no wind, nor weather, and the consistency of temperature, the ancient builders apparently didn't think such trivialities were necessary. They failed to anticipate his enjoyment in making women scream and whimper so. A little forethought as to his need for privacy would have certainly been appreciated. Ah, well, it's of no matter. There wasn't a single abbess in the temple palace who would dare barge into Her Majesty's bedchamber, no matter what sounds they heard emanating from the yawning windows. Other things, however, he considered less appropriate for potential eavesdroppers, so he moved back towards the bed to speak with Queen Vasu in greater privacy.

The royal bedrooms, even the Holy Mother's, were not as ornate as the Old Temple's public areas, her room being a mere honed dugout near the top of the massive stalagnate pillar. The light of burning oil lamps cast a golden aura about the space, doubly intensified by the sandy-colored stone that surrounded them. The queen lay naked and recumbent on her side, an awkward sort of positioning likely meant to relieve the pains he left inside her. But her face betrayed none of that, her glowing eyes of solid blue being difficult to read, and she beamed up at him as he approached in a play of postcoital euphoria.

He sat on the edge of the bed. "I've been watching your weekly devotional broadcasts," he told her. "I'm glad to see your past many sermons have been laying the groundwork for the coming Foretold One."

"You honor me, my lord, with your attention to my words," Queen Vasu said.

"Don't take too much pride in it, Vasu. I endure your tedious homilies for *my* sake, not for yours. If I am to be this world's coming savior, I must keep tabs on what my apostles are saying about me." He stood and began gathering together his clothing. "Is the hierarchy of the temple prepared for the coming proclamation? It's almost time. Will they accept me as redeemer and guardian of the path, upon your say so?"

"Yes, my lord, and my love. I will merely be confirming suspicions I have shared with them for a year or so now... that you are the one whom we have waited for, the one foretold to us long ago. Rest assured, any of those who appeared... cynical... have already been dealt with." She rolled over and sat up. "I am more concerned with my subjects. The lyghtan populace in general will be far more skeptical. A notable percentage of my people no longer closely follow our religion."

"Your people do not concern me, only the few who wield power," Denali said. "If the leaders of your church and monarchy believe you, and those in charge of your armies continue to follow their orders, that is all that matters. Afterward, belief and subjugation of the people can be forced, if so required."

"As my lord wishes, so may it come to pass."

"The news has yet to leave Oberonn, but as we speak, the general's troops have usurped control of the chamai government. Nylis is in control now," he said, "even as he handles our affairs far away on Ilshnar. Admiral Yazir awaits Trojan at the predetermined rendezvous, with an even larger fleet than anticipated. I now control, through those proxies, an armada nearly large enough to rival the Coalition. Once I add Capella's to it, President Forestal will find himself evenly matched."

"Glory in the Path that is followed through you," she praised.

"Now is your time Vasu. I have shown you the Path, and you must lead your world to it. The one who will come from the stars to be a uniter of worlds is here. It is *me*. You must make your followers believe that. The lyghtan, chamai, and drak'min will become the basis of a *new* empire. One that has long been promised by prophecy, and one where you shall rule at my side... as long as you succeed for me tonight."

"Yes, holy master, all shall be as you say. I am, as ever, yours to command."

He looked down at himself as he finished smoothing a few wrinkles and adjusting his robe. Then satisfied, he looked at her silently for a moment—then drove a closed fist against the side of her face. Her neck spun with a crack, spattering droplets of blood across the limestone wall. Her nude form dropped heavily onto the rough stone floor. Instinctively the light in her bracelet sprang to life, her body seeking to heal her injuries, and defend itself. But she regained her composure quickly, knowing this to be unwise. The amber light went out, and she shuffled on the floor to face her master.

Denali sneered down at her. "Where is Opal, your ashi'mar, whom you let me believe had perished?!" he demanded. "What information does she have that she could be sharing with those who oppose me? Tell me the truth! Or I'll drag the information straight from your screaming brain."

Her Royal Majesty, the Queen of Capella, whimpered fearfully upon the ground, naked and trembling, and wiped the dripping blood from her swelling lip. "S-she... witnessed my conversation with Nylis," Vasu confessed through shallow sobs. "She overheard that... that you had designs on your old friend Rook. And that Nylis and I... planned to give our worlds to your empire."

"And?! Is that it? Nothing about Trojan, or the Drak'min involvement?"

"No, my lord, I swear it."

"What else?"

"She... stole one of the devices," Vasu admitted meekly. "One that was empty of serum. But I have teams of bounty hunters following her," she told him quickly with some pride. "They were last seen on Oberonn, in the city of Krataar."

"*They?*"

"She traveled through the grand bazaar a week ago, in the company of a human and an android. I do not yet know who they are."

"Oh, don't worry, *I* know who they are," he growled to himself. "This isn't the only trouble they've been causing me." He turned his attention back to the bleeding monarch. "And, so? Has she not been seen since?"

"No, my lord and master. And I have eyes all across the city."

Denali paced toward the window, and once more back again. "If they are still on Oberonn, they are no doubt trapped by the blockade of the coup. Of course, it's just as likely that they left there long ago." He turned back to look down at Vasu. "But you are certain she knows nothing of Trojan, or the rendezvous in the barren zone?"

"Not through me, she doesn't, my lord."

"Very well," Denali said. "We'll hope that if they got out, they'll continue their bumbling around until it's too late." He picked her royal robes off the bed and threw them down on top of her. "Get dressed then. I have temple members to charm before I lead your fleet on to Trojan. Go on, use the powers I've given you, and fix up your face. I want you to look your best when you introduce me. Not to mention you've got an important announcement tonight for your people."

16.6

THE WATER POUNDED HARD AND STEAMING, bringing a flush to the skin on Stansky's back, as the vibrorazor scraped clean the remaining scruff from his face. He loitered in the welcome stream, wasting much more water than his standard ration, it being the first shower and shave he had enjoyed since their little adventure started. Well, there was the swim in the pond of rainwater, he can't forget about that. But that was more a trudge through filthy runoff than any kind of a real bath. Stansky thought about that day, and his experience with the bracelet. Why hadn't he been honest with Tach, told him what was going through his mind? The power of the strange device had made him feel like he was invincible. Like he could conquer the world—and more terrifyingly, that he somehow *deserved* to conquer it. As if it was his for the taking. He liked the power it gave him, and had quickly become hungry for more. For that change in his mentality to overwhelm him so rapidly—the bracelets were clearly dangerous. He probably should come clean. The effects had worn off within hours, but he had still remained mute; perhaps more embarrassed for lying than still under any effects of the serum's spell. But maybe he would go and explain the whole thing to Tachion, before someone comes across another one, and makes the same mistake he had. He shut the water off, then wrapped his waist in a white towel.

Before he was even completely dry, someone entreating entrance rang his door chime. He finished scrubbing the moisture from his short hair as he went to answer the door, noting the rush of stars whizzing by through the living room windows. Captain Lobo had made way for whatever destination lay next. The door to his quarters slid open, to the surprised gawking of Lady Opal.

"I... I didn't... I hope I'm not disturbing you," she stammered, taken aback by his loosely covered nudity.

"No, not at all, my lady," James apologized. "Forgive me for answering the door this way, I didn't expect you to... Usually visitors can't access this deck, so I... I didn't think... I'm very sorry. Let me get some clothes on." He turned back toward the bedroom.

"No, don't," she called after him, sounding a little too insistent. She stepped inside, and the door closed tight behind her. "And, *please*... call me Opal. At least when we're alone together."

"Yes, of course. As you wish." He walked back to stand before her. "I have to say, it's a real pleasure to see your true face again... *Opal*," he said. "I found myself... missing it... even though I knew you were right there."

She smiled up at him, her green-eyed fire briefly flaring. "Thank you, James. It makes me happy to hear that."

"Is there... was there something you came to see me for?"

"Yes... I... wanted to make sure your head was okay."

"Oh yeah, no worries there. Tach got me patched up good as new." He rubbed the spot on his head where the bullet had dinged him. "Trust me, it's definitely not the worst bump I've ever gotten, but... thanks for checking on me."

"Also," she continued, "I... umm... How do I ask this?" She paused a moment. "My species lives a long life... but that doesn't mean I like to waste time. The opposite is true, in fact," she said to him. "So, in the interest of saving time... may I be perfectly blunt and honest with you?"

"I hope you'll never be otherwise," James assured her.

"Who... who is Tatiana?" Opal asked him.

James blinked in surprise at the question, but made the quick decision not to lie. "A woman back at home," he told her. "*Our* home, that is... hers and mine."

"And... are you in love with her? This Tatiana?"

He wavered a moment. "Sometimes I think so."

"And other times... you're more sure you're not?"

Stansky nodded reluctantly.

"You and I are much alike. We both suffer from hearts that feel the need to wander."

James' eyebrows went up.

"That was my problem with Tàlto... probably why he's now changed towards me so. I couldn't give him the devotion that he wanted, and he was... let's say... disappointed."

"I see," James said, still not sure where she was going.

She reached up a raven hand, and placed it on his massive chest. "You and I, you must realize... we could never be together," she mused to him.

"We... *what*?"

"I could never be paired to a human, when I one day sit upon the temple throne."

"I didn't... I never..."

She softly laughed. "Not to mention, you'd be long dead before I even hit my first century."

"I... *Hey!*"

"But I like you very much," she told him more seriously, turning her light touch into a gentle caress. "Not to mention, I find you attractive... *very*, as a matter of fact. I've grown more fond of you than I have of anyone in some time." She let the brush of her fingertips trace the deep grooves of his rippled abdomen. "But hearts such as yours and mine... we both know those sorts of fondnesses don't last forever."

He nodded dumbly.

"I'd like to collect this moment while I may, and not let such feelings go to waste."

He nodded again, but then slowly converted it to shaking no. "I'm sorry, Opal, I'm just not sure what you're trying to..."

"I'm saying I want to mate with you!" she declared, in no uncertain terms. "I want to take our fill of each other, and I wish to wait no more to do so."

"Well, geez," he told her. "You didn't have to take me through all *that* convincing." He reached down to touch her face, taking hold of it softly, letting his thumbs caress the length of her ears from their points downward. "With me, all you ever had to do was say so." He lowered his head, then carried her mouth to his own.

She stood on tiptoe to reach him, leaning her body hard against his, their lips dancing with each other while their tongues exchanged greetings. Her emerald gaze flared bright, till he could perceive it through closed eyelids, and he pulled back instinctively, smiling down at her.

"You're gonna blind me," he softly joked.

"I'm sorry," she laughed. "I'm honestly just a bit nervous. I've... I've never been with a human before."

"Well, we're both a first for each other, then," he said, much to her pleased surprise. He raised his arms. "Go ahead, if you want. Take a minute to explore. Cuz I'm telling you right now, *I* certainly intend to."

She beamed up at him, then ran her hands across his washboard stomach, enjoying the sensation of traversing the physique she'd so long admired. She moved her touch around his sides and felt the strength of his back. She put her lips to his chest and tasted his skin. Her fingers then slid beneath the tenuous curl of fabric holding the towel fast, and with a flick of one of them, released its grasp. His terry-cloth skirt tumbled free to the ground.

Opal took in his nakedness, scrutinizing upwards and then down, and lingering her gaze just below his waistline. She gave no inkling in her expression whether she was pleased with what she found there. James squinted at her. "It's not considered polite to stare."

She looked away. "I'm sorry. I guess I'm just... intrigued."

"Really?" he asked, glancing down. "Is it that different from lyghtan anatomy?"

"No. I mean... yes. Well... our men don't carry their reproductive organs in a little coin purse outside their body," she told him. "Isn't that just a tad... inconvenient?"

"Astoundingly so," he confessed. "And please, don't call it a coin purse. What else?"

"Well, lyghtan men are longer, certainly."

James frowned a bit at that.

"But significantly thinner as well."

And he flipped it back to a smile. "It does get bigger, you know."

"I look forward to seeing that."

She reached down and took hold of him, and his breath gasped in sharply. She rolled him over in her hands until, true to his word, he became larger. Her petite height made it convenient to bend and go down on him, and she did so with expertise that belied her earlier claim of naivety.

When he felt dangerously near climax, James stopped her and moved her away. He sat on the sofa, then gently guided Opal to stand in front of him. It was now his turn to gaze up expectantly, while she showed him all she could reveal. Her top slid away, freeing her dark, fleshy bosom from underneath—silken skin, soft as velvet, his fingers traced a line across her chest. Down her abdomen, around her waist, his touch followed close behind the lowering of her outfit. Finally, she stood fully exposed before him. He reached out and took one of her legs, spreading her stance wide as he placed her foot up on the couch beside him. James had glimpsed her like this once before, though only briefly, when she was skinny dipping. But now he relished in the lingering closeup, taking his time to locate all the places on her anatomy that needed heeding, his mouth learning the best way to pay tribute to each one of them. He was apparently an apt pupil, as was evidenced by her quickening breath, and growing readiness.

Opal pushed him back onto the couch, her arousal now nearing its apex, and clambered up on top of him. Sliding back and forth across his body, she spread repeated friction against his firmness. James lay on his back, staring upward at her slender frame, feeling her need in the rhythmic movements, and the warming glow that was radiating there. He felt the need in himself as well, and steadied her down against him to fulfill it. Entering slowly, cautiously, till he was sure he was fully in. He then pulled her up and away begrudgingly, and back down to fulfill it again.

Opal rose and fell with gentle grace, like a rider on a steed, each upward thrust from the mount below her rocking her hips forward in impassioned striding. Facing a wall hung with framed memories, she enjoyed her vague reflection in their protective glass: the echoed motion of her silhouette against the rush of stars from just behind her. She felt her pace quickening to keep up with them. The thrusting beneath now grew harder, fingers digging in his flesh, a cry beginning to escape her as her eyes rolled and scattered focus.

"Dear Mother of the Holy Passel," she yelled out in a breathy gasp. Opal reached down and clasped his shoulders, the harmony of her rhythm completely lost. "Wait, stop!"

"Don't worry, baby," he panted. "I'm almost there, but I'll pull out."

"No, it's not that," she insisted, his continued thrusts now awkwardly slapping. She shook him by the neck, "James, stop please! It's Lord Denali!"

"*What?!*" he shouted, rolling her off him in a panicked hurry. He scrambled clumsily to get his footing, then turned to face the door in a fighting stance.

But there was no one there.

The room was empty, the entrance still closed tight. James looked around in confusion, his equally confused erection fast receding from the sudden shock, and the comparative chilliness of the outside air. He stood up straight and stared at Opal, his arms raised at her in silent query.

She had shrunk backward on the couch, her discarded clothing now clutched before her, looking for all the world like she had been haunted by a phantom. She pointed to the wall, and Stansky's gaze followed her finger. Among the display of pictures, in a place of honor, proudly hung front and center, was an early photo of a young Parliament, at the dedication of a bronze statue in New Boston's public garden. Beneath lifelike castings of burnished metal stood their flesh and blood inspirations. '*Saviors of the City*', the plaque read, its date of dedication over two decades prior. Tachion was there, though slightly shinier than she now knew him. Stansky as well, a more youthful fullness to his cheeks. An unfamiliar human was to his right, although a name below was labeled Mishta. A somber Bullseye, glowering left of center, plus the seti Rook she had chanced to meet this past week beneath the mountains of Oberonn. There they stood, young and fresh, a journey of ages still before them—and huddled in their very center, another face she'd forever recognize. More youthful, yes, and longer hair— but the rewound years still failed to mask him.

James looked closely at the photo, then back at her accusing finger, certain he had somehow strayed from its line, and followed it incorrectly. But no, she pointed onward. He took an index of his own, and slowly traced her track to the photo, his finger finally resting on the other human in the middle. "*Him?*" he asked, incredulous. "That's not Denali. That's just Jim Dodger."

She shook her head as she looked at him, seeming confused and frightened at their association. "That man there... is Lord Denali."

James stared at her a minute, dropping his finger from the picture. "You must be confused, Opal," he said. "That's Jim Dodger, one of our founding members. Not to mention, he's been dead and buried for... Jesus, way over a decade."

"Where?" she asked him. "Where is he buried?"

"Well... he's not *really* buried. We never actually recovered him. See, it was kinda gruesome. His skinned body was trapped in some kind of big test tube, and..."

"By who?" she demanded.

"Huh?"

"Who trapped him? Who killed him?"

"Well, it was... the original Denali. The one we killed."

She stared at him.

"So... what? Our old dead teammate just somehow... took his place? Don't you see what you're suggesting? Don't you think it's pretty unlikely?"

"What so far about all this *has* been likely?" she asked.

"Well... not very much," he was forced to agree.

She leaned forward on the couch. "How certain are you, that it was him in that tube?"

"I... I don't know. *Very* certain, at the time." He shook his head. "But it was fourteen or fifteen years ago, and now you're making me doubt myself." He went and pulled the picture right from the wall, carrying it over to her, and laying the portrait down against the arm of the sofa. "*Him,*" he said firmly, pointing so hard at the image that his fingernail blushed red. "You're saying *him*... in the middle. *This* is the person you know as Denali?"

"Yes, that's him. I promise you."

"How certain are you?"

"Certain as the cleansing winds each night erase and redraw the dunes," she said.

He stood up straight and cocked his head at her. "*What?* What is that, a desert thing? I don't know what that means. Is that *very* certain, or just a little?"

"As certain as you are you, and I am me, *that* human there *is* Lord Denali," she assured him. "I swear it to you... on my honor, on my people, and on our friendship. He is Denali, and Denali is him. I've watched him too close, for too long, to be mistaken."

Stansky rehung the picture carefully in its place upon the wall, then turned back to her and took her hand. "Let's straighten ourselves up, and get dressed. We better go share this with the others, as soon as possible," he said. "This whole operation just got a little bit more complicated."

PART V

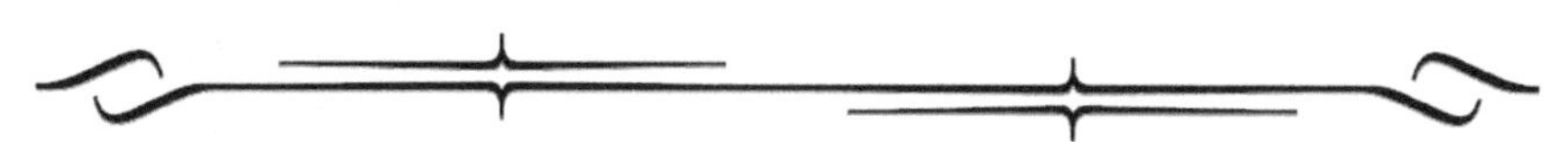

THE WASP
IN WINTER

Chapter 17.1

THE FOUR REMAINING MEMBERS OF Parliament gathered in the common lobby area of their private deck, opting for its more informal circular seating over the usual surroundings of the official conference room. James sat on a curved sofa with his feet resting on the central table, a polished, white disk that dimly mirrored the large, domed porthole just above it. The lighted points of a thousand star systems careened past in a flurry, like sparks of a bonfire lofting into the sky, as the vessel hurried in the direction of the galactic center at high warp. Stansky's three comrades stood about, still dumbfounded by his announcement.

"Perhaps I fail to understand," Bullseye said, questioning Stansky. "How is it the ashi'mar suggests such a prospect to be possible?"

Bullit interrupted, scoffing. "Pfft. I think we all know perfectly well how it's possible. Shit, we've done the same thing ourselves!" he reminded the group. "Clearly, someone didn't want Dodger dead... so they went and whipped up another one."

Tachion cocked his head, pondering. "It's a possibility," he suggested. "With the sort of equipment Denali had in that underwater lab, and with the right knowhow... he could have managed it."

"You see!" Bullit said. "And this fucked up Dodger clone now has his petri dish pal there to help him."

"Wait... *what?*" Stansky asked. "Are you talking about Rook?"

"Rook is dead," Bullit stated coldly. "I'm talking about his replica."

"Hold!" Bullseye cautioned. "We have seen no evidence to support such a supposition."

"Oh, really?" Bullit countered. "Go ahead, tell 'em Tach."

"Let's just put that aside for a minute," the doctor told him. "I want to know more about this alleged Dodger first. I admit the idea is possible, the original Denali's obsessions such as they were. And it certainly would explain a few things, like this common bond Opal said he talked about. And maybe even his seeming willingness to play games with us, infiltrate us, but not just outright kill us. Yet, anyway."

"But?" Stansky asked.

"*But,*" Tachion continued, "this clone's face would not be a new one. It has a history. It has a record. Did it not occur to the ashi'mar... nor any of the prior four of them before they died... when they were wondering who this strange, intrusive man was, just to simply run his likeness through facial recognition? We, as his past companions, might have been alerted earlier. Or, if they did so, why did nothing come back, if her speculation is correct?"

"I asked her that myself," Stansky told him. "She said they tried, but their access to Coalition databases from Capella was limited. Plus, it didn't occur to them to search through facial records of the long dead."

"It seems you ascribe to the lady's assertion," Bullseye suggested.

"Yeah, I do," Stansky answered. "I showed her a hundred holopics of Dodger, from every possible angle, and with each one, she just became more and more convinced."

Bullit nodded. "I believe her too. And to me, it makes *perfect* sense. That psycho Denali cooked himself up some kinda... Dodger pet. And after we put down his master, the pet moved in to take over."

"I believe her as well," a softer voice said behind them. They all turned to see Belladonna walking in.

Stansky flipped his palms upward in bafflement. "What the hell? I thought this deck was supposed to be private."

"My husband built your security," she told him. "You really think he didn't tell me how to bypass it?" She approached the circle, taking a seat on a sofa arm. "And there's no need to be rude. I just finished interviewing Opal, as you *asked* me to do."

"Good, then," Bullit declared. "What's your opinion?"

"I've questioned thousands of witnesses. I know how to reveal the faults in their stories, the cracks in their identifications. I know how to make them admit their uncertainties. I can tell you now... Opal doesn't have any."

"So that's it," Bullit said. "We have to proceed under the assumption this new Denali is a clone of Dodger. Which makes it all the more imperative that we find and get rid of him. He's much more formidable than we thought, much more of a danger to us all. The knowledge and skills of Jim Dodger, with the mentality of Denali? Plus this hocus pocus horseshit that's been built into him to boot."

"I agree," Bullseye nodded. "But we must do so sensibly. We shall trail Nylis to Ilshnar, and seek Denali's whereabouts in the general's wake."

"That's just stupid!" Bullit argued. "Sneaking around and following that old chamai isn't the answer! We have the location of Denali's factory, where he's probably making weapons, or those bracelets. We could shut down the operation, and maybe take care of both him and Rook in the process."

"I beg your pardon?!" Belladonna interjected angrily.

Bullit turned to Tachion. "Are you gonna tell them, or am I?"

The doctor looked up at the group, then at Belladonna.

"Well?" she prompted. "Please go right ahead."

"I... had been having trouble," the android started, "connecting to the Biological Society database from the *Bugeye*, trying to access it to aid my study of the bracelet ensensement device. I thought maybe it was a routing issue, trying to link through an unsecured chamai subspace connection. I don't know, computer networking isn't exactly my forte. All I knew was that my login was being rejected."

"So he asked me to look at it..." Bullit interrupted.

"*So...* I asked him to look at it, once we returned to the ship," Tach continued. "Turns out there was nothing wrong with the connection, it's just that my clearance has been rescinded."

James appeared puzzled. "How can they do that, when you're the director?"

"Well, I'm *not* anymore, or so it would seem. At least pending a further investigation. Doctor Eloff is now the current interim director."

"What justification could lie behind such an action?" Bullseye asked.

"Someone broke into my offices, got access to my lab computer... and leaked all my secret personal files to the Coalition Science Ministry."

"What?" asked Stansky. "Which files?"

"All of it. Everything. My notes on Rook's cloning, the doctored logs I've forged since. Even video recordings, a bird's-eye view of the whole thing." Tachion's voice, usually steady, wavered now between woe and fury. "My position as director has been revoked. My medical license has been suspended."

"Oh, Tachion," Belladonna gasped, a hand rising to cover her mouth.

"Not to mention, there's now a warrant for questioning out on me, from Starlaw Special Branch, and the Bureau for Civilian Rights."

"Jesus Christ," Stansky exhaled. "How did they even get all that, get past Rook's firewall?"

Tachion eyed Belladonna. "It's not hard to wiggle in for the man who originally built it."

She stared back at him, unbelieving. "What the hell are you saying?"

"I'm sorry, Bell. I didn't want to tell you this way... but it was Rook."

She shook her head, rejecting it. "How could you know that?" she demanded. "What makes you so sure?"

He crossed the room to her, circling the table beneath the window dome, and leading with an outstretched hand—a folded paper between his mighty digits. "He left me a message," Tachion told her. "And believe me, I got his meaning... loud and clear."

She unfolded the printed photo of two extended fingers in a vulgar gesture—her husband's hands. A pile of hacked evidence was laid out, a single black chess piece in the center. James snuck up behind her, peeking over her shoulder to get a gander.

Bullit approached, snatching the photo from her quivering fingers. He extended it in his other arm, passing the damning evidence on to Bullseye. "Our little science experiment has grown up," he said, "and has turned to bite at his handlers. He *knows* what he is now. He knows *everyone* here hid it from him. Now add the near-certain insanity of that realization, to whatever fuckery this Denali-Dodger is doing with him," he shook his head. "He's already proven to us now that he's looking for revenge. He has to be dealt with."

Belladonna interrupted. "This is your friend you're talking about, not to mention my husband!"

"My God, *wake up* cousin! Your fucking husband is dead and gone!" Bullit shouted. "And it's time for *all* of us to stop pretending that it's any different!"

Belladonna gasped.

He turned to their leader. "So what do you say Bullseye, can we head this boat to Gel Gonahaar, and find the two of them?"

Bullseye's gaze still searched the photo of his onetime friend's clear betrayal. "I... I am not certain."

"Well, you better get certain, and quick. And not only about that," Bullit advised him. "What are you gonna do once we find our lost partner? You once assured me you wouldn't shy away if the dirty deed needed doing. Well, it needs it. Sure as this bullshit Dodger has to go, so does our turncoat Rook."

"*No!*" a voice shouted, and they all spun around again to look. Relic was standing in the hallway that led to the elevator.

"What the fuck?" Stansky called out. "How do people keep getting in here?"

"I'm my father's daughter," Relic told him. "You think I can't bypass a simple thumb scan? Plus, put a locked door in front of me, I'm destined to try and pick it."

"Relic," Tachion said, "you'll have to excuse us, but we're discussing private matters that are best left..."

Belladonna shook her head. "Tach, don't worry about it. She already knows."

"She... already..." Tachion stuttered in surprise, "so, then... what about Flashpoint?"

"No, not yet. But I'll obviously have to tell him by day's end."

Bullit stepped to Relic. "Look, my little cousin, I'm glad you know the truth, but that only means you're one more person who's lied to him. One more enemy for his retribution."

"You can't be sure of that!" she berated him, "like it's automatically preordained!"

"He's a clone!" Bullit told her. "The record of people born into that is pretty clear. Suffice it to say that, once they know... they're never the same."

Relic ignored her cousin, and instead directed her plea towards Bullseye. "That isn't always true," she said. "And even when it is, not being the same isn't equal to being evil. Men don't just become someone they were '*born*' to be, good *or* bad. They don't become who they're forced to be... or who they're told they already are. At least not more than briefly. Ultimately, given a chance, they become only who they *choose* to be. Free men, anyway. Just like this Denali is doing to him now, you *thrust* a life onto him before. You tricked him, all of you. Programmed him to be the man who *you* wanted. To replace another man who once existed. But I know, I'm positive, that if we free him from this influence, whoever or whatever power is swaying him, and allow him to choose now, even knowing the ugly truth... the father I've known will still choose to be a good man. He will choose to be your friend, and choose to stay my dad. I know it in my heart. But you *must* let him live long enough to make that free choice."

Bullseye stared back at Relic with a corner of an upturned smile, a mix of pride and admiration conveyed in his eyes. And hidden somewhere behind that, a dropping sensation—like a lack of gravity lifting his innards as he even more quickly continued to fall for her. "I agree," was all he said.

Bullit was apoplectic. "What the hell are you talking about?! How can you listen to this fucking ignorant child?"

Bullseye rode a sudden swell of his species hereditary ancestral rage, defending his new paramour from Bullit's insult. He instinctively stepped forward in a menacing manner, not really sure if he actually meant to strike at him.

"B, no!" Relic cried, then clung tight at his elbow to stop him. Perhaps a little too tight, a little too close. Bullit shifted his gaze back and forth, from one face to the other, as the strange clinging went on too uncomfortably long to be platonic.

"Ho...ly... shit," Bullit puzzled out. "*You two* are..."

"Tread careful now," Bullseye cautioned.

Stansky's eyebrows rocketed upward. "Whoa, wait. You mean you guys are..."

A glare from Bullseye cut him off.

Bullit scoffed. "Pfft. And here I thought you couldn't fall any lower than on the *Okubi*... getting stoned out on a mission. But boy, I was dead wrong. Congratulations, I guess. Welcome to rock bottom." He slowly clapped his hands together in exaggerated applause. "So, what? You got smashed, and decided to bang Belladonna's daughter?"

"*What?*" Relic's mother balked, almost chucking at the idea. Then her eyes darted back and forth between the two. "What?" she repeated more seriously.

Tachion interrupted. "What's he talking about, Bullseye? Under the influence while on a mission?"

Relic stepped forward, standing between her new lover and her cousin. "I am *not* 'Belladonna's daughter'. I am Relic, my own woman, and I can be with whomever I want to be."

"Oh please, give me a break," Bullit murmured. "*Obviously,* it just so happens that he fits in with your... seti heritage obsession. But what's *his* excuse?"

Bullseye growled angrily at him. "You, my friend, are a betrayer," he said. "You swore it to me. My impropriety aboard the *Okubi* was *my* secret to reveal."

"Well, I guess it's your lucky day. Looks like I saved you the trouble."

Bullseye continued angrily. "You also made it known then of your intention to persevere in following me. If you be true to *that* sacred word, then your fealty must continue. How it is when we agree, must likewise endure when we differ. Following another's leadership is a pledge of faith, a covenant of trust upon which *both* must deliver. I to steer you rightly, and you to commit me your support. To buck and revolt upon disagreement is to reveal you no man of true loyalty, but merely a sycophant trailing along, making due whilst it remains convenient." He crumpled up the photo of

Rook and tossed it down onto the table. "The decision is mine to make, and I say Rook shall live and be recovered." He turned his back on the group and walked to the comm panel on the wall.

"You're a fucking fool!" Bullit snapped behind him.

"Insults are the last piece of luggage to be thrown overboard in a sinking argument." Bullseye said. "There is no merit in your speculation that the factory is suspect, nor any sound reasoning behind your theory that Denali is to be found there. Your argument is lost. The choice has been made." He pressed the comlink button. "Bullseye to the bridge."

"*Lobo here, go ahead.*"

"Captain, please make way for the planet Ilshnar. Best speed, if you would."

"*Understood, Master Bullseye. Changing course. Bridge out.*"

"Alright," Tachion said, "what's done is done, and there's no use shouting about it. Let's all just go take a couple of minutes to cool down." He went to Bullit, turning him from Bullseye by his shoulders. "Come on, let's get you back to your room. You still need to rest after your earlier injuries. We can come at this again later." The two crossed the common area towards the seti's quarters.

Stansky still sat with his mouth wide agape, staring at Bullseye and Relic. Belladonna stepped in front of him. "Close your mouth, will you, James? You're starting to draw flies," she said.

He took the hint, and hopped up from the sofa, heading to make himself scarce—one deck down in Lady Opal's quarters. He still had unfinished business with her weighing heavily on his mind—and elsewhere.

Belladonna turned to her daughter. "Give me and Bullseye a moment, would you, honey?"

Relic raised a suspicious brow, folding her arms in front of her in defiance.

"Everything's fine, darling. I promise. I just need to talk with him for a minute."

Her daughter acquiesced and wandered off, still looking curiously behind her.

Belladonna turned to Bullseye with a smiling face, but a menacing eye. "You and I, we *will* discuss this more later," she told him.

He nodded his head quietly in agreement.

"But for now... you do know what will happen if you hurt her, don't you?"

"My soul shudders to envision it."

She moved up close. "You're goddamn right it does," she whispered. "Now, if you'll excuse me... I have to go explain decades of lying to my son."

17.2

BULLIT WAS SEETHING IN ANGER as Tachion returned him to his room, grabbing a crystal ashtray from the sideboard, and tossing it hard across his quarters living space. The heavy centaurian quartz didn't shatter, but nicked the paint in a lower wall panel as it landed with a loud clang. "He must be out of his fucking mind, wasting our time on this ridiculous wild goose chase!" the seti shouted.

"I'm inclined to agree," Tachion told him. "I also think our best hope is the factory on Gel Gonahaar."

Bullit looked at him, stupefied. "Why the hell didn't you say anything? He would have listened to you over me!"

"Because, the way you approached it, you forced him into an adversarial position. Once you started chest thumping and insulting each other... nothing I said then would have changed his mind."

Bullit walked to the corner and retrieved the crystal bowl from the carpet. "What about the whole Rook situation? Where do you stand on what to do with him?"

"Well... I agree with you there also. In fact, perhaps even more so. His very existence was my doing, after all. It's therefore my duty to correct it." He saw Bullit staring at him, his look clearly questioning the android's earlier silence. "*But...* I'm not going to argue that fact right in front of his wife and children."

"Fucking hell, Doc! I really coulda used you in my corner," Bullit said.

"I'm in your corner, trust me. I just have to decide on how best for us to fight it." Tachion stepped down into the sunken seating area, then gazed out the wall of windows at the rush of starlight passing by. "Tell me what happened aboard the *Okubi*."

"I don't know. Bullseye was right about that one. I did promise he could share it in his own time."

"For better or worse, that promise is broken now," Tachion said. "The cat's out of the bag, so to speak, and I need more information before I decide how to move forward."

Bullit sighed aloud as he fell back, slumping into the sofa. He placed the ashtray on the side table. "We were trapped," he said, "under the sewer tanks. No idea where we were, or where we were going."

"So I read in your report."

"Well, what you didn't read is that when Bullseye went sneaking out to find us some food and water, he found a bottle of his favorite elixir there, Zet A'zeta, and decided to pour himself a little nightcap."

"But... that's... just so hard to believe," the doctor said.

"Well, to tell the truth, I'm *highly* understating it. He had a goddamn party there! A real raver. He came back *hours* late, leaving me alone and locked under the floorboards the whole time. Until he came staggering in, wasted. How he ever made it back without someone catching him is beyond me."

"Did he say why he did it?"

"Oh, he said much more than that," Bullit reported. "He's apparently had an addiction for a long while. He said it all started because of stupid nightmares, or some shit. Fuck, I have nightmares! Dreams about my brother Wyvern keep me tossing and turning to this day. But I don't use them as an excuse to become a hooch hound!"

"Zet A'zeta is a powerful dissociative somnific. Its psychogenic effects are much like Earth narcotics," Tachion told him. "What else?"

"He overheard a conversation, I'm sure you read that in the report too. But, he didn't have trouble hearing it, like he said in the debrief. He was right fucking there, barely inches away. He heard every word. He was just too damn wasted to remember." Bullit pulled a cigar from a small humidor on the coffee table, and lit it with a nearby micro-blowtorch. "If it wasn't for that, this whole incident might be long over."

"More so than that, it might never have started. I wonder if he would have taken General Nylis' commission if he had been of right mind. Rook might still be home safe. Dozens of officers and soldiers might not have needed to die."

"And your career wouldn't be circling the crapper, with a Coalition warrant out on your head," Bullit added. "Computer," he called out, "activate exhaust fan." The winding tendrils of cigar smoke sped towards narrow openings in the ceiling. "I will say, to his credit, he seemed to turn over a new leaf in the days after. We did have some long conversations while still stowaways on the *Okubi*, and during our visit to Nol Qhan. A lot about him letting his past stay in the past... mine too, for that matter... and not blaming himself for decisions that other people made… that kinda stuff. But he appeared to be taking to it. His mood was better… he was sleeping. He really seemed to make giant strides."

"Zet A'zeta is not physically addictive, per se," Tachion said. "But its mental fixation can be quite enslaving. That said, it's easier to break *any* addiction when not given another choice. When you're trapped in a desert, with nothing around you but a few waters to drink. I wonder now if he's remained so. Now that he's safe at home, with a possible supply of it nearby."

"He said he had one bottle onboard, but he poured it out."

"You saw him?"

"Well… no," Bullit said. "I was up here, greeting Bell and the kids." His eyes rolled thoughtfully upward for a moment. "But now that I remember it, when he showed up… he was acting a bit funny."

Tachion shook his chromed head in disappointment. "I fear Bullseye's sobriety is in serious question," he said. "Which means any of his recent decisions become suspect. I would have *no problem* following him to Ilshnar, even against my better judgement, since, as he rightly said, loyalty is loyalty, even when we may disagree."

"I feel like there's a 'but' coming."

"*But*, I don't know if we can trust him. His decisions might be made by the bottle, or his libido… or both, rather than him. And I don't see where there's enough time to figure out which of the three is in command."

"So, what then? Are you talking… mutiny?"

"No, of course not," Tachion said. "But perhaps… desertion instead. You and I can jump ship, make our way to Gel Gonahaar in the *Bugeye*. If we find Dodger and Rook, or perhaps just their whereabouts, we could always signal for the *P1* to join us."

"And in the meantime, leave Bullseye and Stansky to flounder around the metamorph homeworld," Bullit said. "Sneaking around after Nylis, and strutting for their ladies."

"Exactly. Or, well… I don't know about that last part. But something along those lines." Tachion looked at his multicomm. "We'll probably be at the closest passing distance to Gel Gonahaar in a few hours. I wasn't lying about you needing sleep, so get some rest while you can. I'll make sure Chief Zvavi has the *Bugeye* prepped and back together, and I'll stock our equipment."

"We won't be a tad shorthanded? Going in just the two of us?"

"If it seems too much when we get there, we could always call James and Bullseye for help. Provided we find something worthwhile to convince them."

"And if not?"

"Gel Gonahaar is a vile place," Tachion said, "full of desperate people willing to do anything for a few credits. Worse case, we commission some henchmen mercs. *If* we end up feeling the need for an extra gun or two."

"Sure, great idea. And hope they don't rob us on the way out." Bullit stood and laid his cigar in the recovered ashtray, then went to join Tachion at the window. "Honestly, I agree that this is the right choice," he said, "but I can't help but feel... guilty, for bailing on them."

"Don't think of it as bailing on them, think of it as... covering all our bases. More like 'divide and conquer'," Tachion said. "That must be a saying for a reason."

"Yeah, I'm sure it is," Bullit quietly answered. "But, so is 'divided we fall'."

17.3

THE BLADE FLASHED ANGRILY BENEATH the glare of reflected floodlights high above, piercing Bullseye's pupil with a glint of its mirrored brightness, and seeking to follow behind it with its steel. His hands strained and his muscles quaked, struggling to keep the knife from entering his eye socket. But the human sentry on top of him bore down with his full weight, driving the jagged point ever closer to its amber target. Bullseye was foolishly unarmored, but so was the guard above him, and in a desperate move, the seti's teeth sought purchase through the fabric of his assailant's uniform. He bit down on the young man's wrist, and bit hard. The pressure behind the knife wavered. The human cried out, and his weight shifted. Bullseye's loosened knee came up fast, making contact with the exposed groin.

Advantage shifted and the tables turned, the two rolling over each other in the wetness of the long grass, until Bullseye held the high position. The spotlight beaming from above now fully lit the former silhouette, and the seti could now see his human opponent was but a child. Eighteen at most, Bullseye figured, or whatever minimum age would be required. He wanted the boy to yield and accept his mercy. He would allow the young guard to live, if only he would surrender. But the blade still faced toward him, the push behind it unrelenting. The young human still sought to end the skirmish in a gout of blood.

So be it, then.

The boy was younger, but the seti stronger, and the set of hands upon the hilt soon faltered and wobbled backward. The shining tip swapped targets as it leaned back and away towards the human. The guard's eyes now resolved from furor into fear, as the rear of the knife neared the soft flesh of his neck. He whimpered and strained as the metal made contact, the cold tickle of the steel a harbinger of his own death. The dagger was inverted at this point, with its backside quite dull, and the human's skin resisted—furrowing back beneath the pressure, but refusing to yield. Bullseye pressed onward and pressed harder, the full weight of his chest now behind it. As their two faces brushed nearer, the boy breathed to Bullseye the first and only word of the whole skirmish—a gasping whisper beside his ear.

"*Wait...*" the human pleaded.

Then all at once, its threshold surpassed, the flesh gave way. It cleaved open wide along the blade's bitter edge, blooming forth in a bright spout— a grim and crimson bouquet. The seti stared down and watched close as the spark of life left the eyes—though the look of terror never did.

Bullseye struggled to get clear of it, though he knew it wasn't possible. This particular night terror always ended similarly, no matter how hard he fought to avoid it—a recurring memory in which he relived his first hand-to-hand kill. The fact he knew he was dreaming made no difference in the end. The vision always replayed itself exactly, and he was ever powerless to change it.

Pulling his awareness from the dream now that it was over, he strove to awaken, to climb out from his personal misery. As he labored towards alertness, a shadowy movement crossed the ruddy veil of his closed eyelids. Years of instinct and training drove his muscles without thinking, and his hand dove beneath the familiar feeling cushions beneath him, drawing out a small AE100. The weapon whistled in a brief crescendo as it charged itself for firing. He opened his blurry eyes.

Bullseye lay on the old, worn couch in his office, situated at the far opposite side of the room from his desk, and with the figure of Relic standing before him at the wrong end of his muzzle. She held a glass of water in her hand, but nearly let go at his sudden movement. Droplets sloshed over the edges to land on his hand-woven carpet.

"Good God," she exclaimed, with a hard, whispered breath.

Bullseye got his bearings, then quickly stowed the weapon away, somewhat embarrassed. "Relic, forgive me. You gave me a bit of a start."

"So I noticed," she said. "But it wasn't just that, was it? You were crying out. You were having a nightmare."

He rubbed his eyes and spoke through a yawn. "An unfortunate plague, with which I'm intimately familiar," he told her.

"It can't help that you're so tired, either. You fell off to sleep almost as soon as we came in here. Of course, it's to be expected. You and I did stay up awfully late last night." She winked at him cheekily, then leaned down to kiss his forehead. "I just wanted to bring you something, to help you rest more through the night." She held forward the glass of water, and an open palm with two white pills in its center. "I thought you may just want to stay in here, since you already seemed so comfortable."

"I... appreciate the concern and attention, but I prefer not to turn back to chemical substances to aid my sleeping."

"Oh, don't worry about that. It's just a simple herbal extract. It merely triggers your own melatonin to release, in case your sleep clock gets off schedule," she told him. "It's very mild."

Bullseye smiled up at her in gratitude, then took and swallowed the offered pills and water.

"I need to attend to my brother," she said, "when my mother is done explaining things to him, anyway. But I still have a little time to see you back to sleep." She sat herself down at the end of the leather couch, and pulled him to lay back on her, his head resting upon her lap. "Do you... want to tell me about this nightmare?" she asked with some concern.

"Merely a phantom from my past. A familiar friend who comes to visit."

"Oh? And why does he come to visit?"

"Ah... to ensure my perpetual guilt. A similar mission as all the others."

She passed her filed claws through the short fur near his ears, caressing his scalp in a rhythmic massage. "Our regret is the anchor that we each drag behind us," she said, quoting a seti proverb. "But if you are to make headway unhindered, you must haul it aboard... or cleave it free."

He smiled up at her, impressed. "A lesson I have long taught... though only *now*, am I myself learning."

She was quiet for a moment, then she asked, "Is it true? About the drinking with Bullit?"

"I did give you fair warning, I am a man who is broken."

"Nonsense," she said. "You simply lock too much inside. You need not do that anymore. You can share your anchor with me. I'll help you heave it aboard."

"I do not believe that I lock..."

"*Yes*, you do, B," she interrupted. "You have another face, one you always keep turned away. Like the dark side of the moon." She angled his head to look up at her. "Show it to me."

He found the young woman's plea irresistibly reassuring.

Bullseye began to talk, and Relic began to listen. He told her of his guilt after years of killing, of the founding of his school as an act of penance. He spoke of the betrayal of that contrition, when some few students then became his victims.

When he was done, Relic said to him, "But, these students of yours... they all knew what they were signing up for when they chose this life. They were aware of the risks, and made the decision themselves anyway. *You* did not make it for them. If anything, you were helping them. They chose you as their teacher, all of them chasing the same rare success that you managed to achieve. They wanted to be like you. Get close, and learn from you. You cannot blame the flame for the death of the moth."

"No, but perhaps the moth might."

"Hmm. So on the day you meet your maker, will you cry out with your last breath, cursing the man who schooled you in shooting?"

"I would surely not," he admitted. "Unless, perhaps, it was also he that had so rudely felled me."

Relic sighed. "Nothing I say today will change a mind so firmly settled. Your anchor is weightier than that, if I may belabor the metaphor. But with time, and patience, we might strain to haul it up together."

Bullseye realized something then, as he gazed upward into sanguine eyes. "Through this most recent chapter of my days, I have been impatiently awaiting my coming end time," he told her honestly. "Poised eagerly, in fact, for the cruel mistress to pounce, and finally catch me. In all truth, I oft thought to bait her. To turn and *rush* to embrace her." He reached up, and took her hand. "Yet... the prospect of our continued companionship has all but dissuaded that, and I suddenly find myself miserly for every moment I can hoard."

Relic beamed a smile down on him as he spoke.

"Alas, though I cannot coerce the rage of time to grind still, nor thwart being seized in her relentless jaws at the end, with you at my side, I will strive hard to make her chase me down. And, with some fair fortune, make her run like *hell* to do so."

17.4

THE VACANT CORRIDORS OF *PARLIAMENT ONE* seemed somehow more unnerving now to Tachion, though he was perhaps just a tad more apprehensive than usual. The third shift was well underway, with the majority of the crew sleeping, and illumination was dimmed throughout the hallways in a simulation of evening. He looked behind him nervously as he headed toward the galley. The doctor had every right to be here; no one would ever question him for roaming about. Yet each echoed pop and groan of the mighty vessel spun his head toward that direction, in a fear of being caught. Some of the guilt Bullit spoke of was starting to seep in. He couldn't let it.

Chief Zvavi had buttoned up the *Bugeye* to his usual high standards, the craft now able and ready—as soon as the two deserters were. The doctor had already restocked the shuttle's biobed, and stowed his and his coconspirator's gear, but in addition, now wore a small bag of extra ammo he had decided to bring with them. With it being just the two of them, he rightly figured he would be relied upon more than usual to engage in fighting. He was fine with that—the Android had been known to hold his own. He also brought a memory chip, his research into the bracelet and its serum. He could continue his analysis of the strange chemical compound on the way to Gel Gonahaar.

Tachion walked through the silent mess hall, then stepped into the galley. "Are you ready?" he asked to Bullit's turned back.

The seti jumped and slammed the fridge closed, spinning to face him with an armload of tidbits. "Goddammit! You scared the shit outta me," Bullit exclaimed.

"What are you doing?" Tachion asked. "We have the food replicator onboard."

"First of all, yuck! You don't have to eat it, so you don't know how bad it is. And second of all, I'm not getting caught in another starvation situation. So I'm bringing reinforcements."

"But we don't have enough refrigeration on board. You better bring something more... nonperishable."

"Ah," Bullit said. "Good idea." He turned and dumped the morsels back into the fridge, and instead immediately went about rummaging through cabinets.

"I... grabbed an array of armaments," Tachion told him. "I wasn't sure what would be best to... to try and quickly take down... our..."

"Our onetime friend?" Bullit asked him. The seti stopped snack hunting, and turned to lean against the counter. "Rook *will* be a tough one. He knows our style, and he knows our weaknesses. If we find him on Gel Gonahaar, it'd be best to get him in one shot."

"Yes," Tachion said thoughtfully, suddenly remembering something. "Actually, I need to run up to deck B for a moment, just to grab something real quick. Go ahead and load up. I'll meet you in just a minute."

"What? What do you... Oh, never mind. Just don't get caught."

Tachion hurried back along the corridor, then rode the lift to their private deck. The lights were lowered here as well, the area hushed in a similar eerie quiet, and the large android did his best to try to tiptoe around the circular lounge room. He passed Stansky's doorway, wondering if he was even in there; or perhaps with the ashi'mar in her guest quarters on the lower floor. He then continued down the side hallway towards the member's private offices. He passed his own, seldom used, being as he was far more comfortable in the sickbay than working up here. Then past several empty ones amongst the others, rooms unused since their owner's passing. He paused at Rook's office. He felt an urge to enter, but resisted. Somehow that made him feel even more resentful. He continued on to the last doorway.

Bullseye's study was darker than normal. The usual ever-present glow from his lighted memento wall was now reduced to a single nightlight, shining down to highlight an old leather-bound book. But that was all the light the android needed—he'd be in and out in a matter of seconds. He approached the dimly glowing shelf, and after a moment of peering around, took down the archaic volume to reveal the item behind it—the long, sleek barrel of the drak'min disintegration gun. If they had to put down Dodger, or even Rook, in one shot, this would certainly be the way to do it. He took the pistol from its place and set it on the desk behind him, then delicately moved to return the book exactly as it had been.

"Relic, have you returned?" a sleep crusted voice inquired behind him.

Tachion jerked, his large metallic frame knocking the desk, scattering some of Bullseye's items loudly across it. The drak'min gun teetered, then fell to the floor with a noisy clatter.

The overhead light came alive, revealing the resting seti now awakened. He rose from the couch sluggishly, then sat squinting at the android intruder. "Doctor?" he asked with confusion.

"Yes, I... I'm sorry," Tachion said, still clutching the leather book awkwardly. "Did... did you pass out in here?" he asked, looking around for a telltale open bottle.

"Did I... what?" Bullseye asked sleepily. He pushed himself up from the sofa to cross the room. "I don't follow your meaning? Were you seeking to speak to me?"

Tachion looked down at the fallen pistol through the transparency of the glass desktop. It lay plainly on the other side, between the workstation and Bullseye. The android took a small, casual sidestep to the left.

Bullseye followed the doctor's gaze, then stopped in his tracks when he saw the weapon. "What is your purpose here?" he almost demanded.

"I... I wanted to tell you," Tachion stammered, "I mean, I just came to let you know... I... I have decided that I agree with Bullit on where to proceed."

"The time for that decision is past," Bullseye said, the seti gesturing down toward the weapon, "and it seems you have come with far graver intentions in mind." He cocked his head slightly, his eyes narrowing in realization. "You did not presume to find me here, did you? You envisioned this room to most likely be unoccupied."

Tachion said nothing, but took another sidestep left.

"What then was your grand scheme? Abscond with the weapon? Escort Bullit on his... *absurd* vengeance quest?"

"Bullit's motives are not mine. I seek no vengeance," Tachion said. "Only to set right what I set wrong so long ago."

"This *wrong*, as you call him, is our ally, and friend. *Your* friend. I will not permit you to launch a crusade for his head, no more than I would allow he to come for yours."

"I'm sorry, Bullseye, but I believe you're no longer of sound mind to make that decision," the doctor told him. "You're under the influence of a chemical substance. One known to affect mood, and behavior. And now perhaps even more so by... the desire to please the whims of his daughter."

A curling of the upper lip betrayed Bullseye's outrage at that. "Neither of those malicious allegations hold true," he growled at him. "Furthermore, who are you to censure me? *You*, who come skulking about like a thief in the night?! *You*, who plan betrayal under the guise of something righteous?! Do not place us at cross purposes, Doctor. No good for either of us could come from such as that."

Tachion laid the book down on the edge of the table, then took a step forward. He was now nearly in front of the desk, the fallen drak'min pistol a mere step or two from his feet.

Bullseye's voice took on a different tone then, one with a loosely veiled suggestion of warning. "Life is a twisted braid of choice and circumstance, old friend, each bend and curve of one influencing the course of the other. Every decision we pursue results in a new circumstance. Each circumstance we're found in presents us a new choice. The choice I made to accept this mission has brought us to this *particular* circumstance, and I knowingly bear the weight of that. But it's *your* decision, *right now*, that will determine our next one."

"You forget, Bullseye, it was *my* choice that brought us here. One born of grief, fifteen years ago, bringing back Rook in the first place."

"Do not be selfish with that burden! The decision to resurrect him was on all of us, as should be the one to salvage him now."

"I'm sorry, but... I disagree."

Their eyes locked on each other for what seemed an eternity, each gauging the intentions of their longtime companion. Simultaneously, their glaring darted to the pistol on the floor between them, and quickly back to each other. It seemed an act of purest optimism for Tachion to even attempt to grab the weapon before his seti counterpart, as Bullseye leapt gracefully across the distance, retrieved and charged the weapon, and crouched to aim his eye down the sight line of the gleaming barrel, all before the android had barely taken a second step.

"Whoa, Bullseye, hold it," Tachion said, in a calming tone that did little to hide his nervousness. "I wasn't going to..."

"Silence!" Bullseye roared, his voice churned with rage and disappointment. "Tell me now Doctor, is this truly where you would have our diverging fates lead us?! We enduring comrades, now called on to wade deep through brother's blood!"

"I don't want to wade through *anyone's* blood, least of all yours," Tachion replied. "I made a terrible error in judgement all those years ago, and it is now my responsibility to do what I must to correct it. But that duty need not go through you, if you would only stand aside."

"And it is there where our sabers clash, for *my* duty lies in blocking you," Bullseye said. The seti then noticed, the doctor had used the distraction of going for the weapon to reach his hand inside his carried ammo bag. "Withdraw your hand for me now, old friend. But do so *very* slowly."

Tachion drew his hand back from the bag, while he held the other one high aloft, moving slowly as directed so as to not trigger any unfortunate accidents. When the synthetic black covering of his fingers finally appeared, they cradled in their grasp a small cylindrical device. A doze grenade, with its safety and trigger lever already popped. "I'm sorry," he all but whispered.

Bullseye collapsed to the woven carpet before he even had a chance to curse at him.

The doctor pulled the drak'min gun from his unconscious fingers, tucking it safely in his bag, then dragged his friend back to the couch to return him to his evening slumber. The unaffected android waited a few minutes for the clear and odorless gas to dissipate, while he re-dimmed the lighting, and placed the leather book back upon its shelf. He pulled the workstation right, and straightened its scattered desktop. Finally, he left a note, typed and floating on Bullseye's holoscreen—'Please forgive me' was all it said. He looked once more to his friend in contrition, then left the room.

When the doors opened to the elevator, Bullit was standing inside. "Where the hell have you been? What's taking so long?" he asked in quick succession.

"I'll... tell you when we're underway," Tachion answered. "Hangar bay," he commanded to the lift.

"Ah. Well... we need to make one more quick stop first," Bullit said.

"Where?"

As if in answer to his question, the lift came to rest on C deck. The doors opened up, and Flashpoint stepped aboard.

Tachion cocked his head down at Bullit.

"I ran into him in the hallway, and he sort of... got it out of me."

"I'm coming with you," Flashpoint told him.

"Flash, your mother would never forgive me," Tachion said. "And you know we're going... well... we're looking for your father, as well as Denali."

"He *isn't* my father, or so I found out just today. Though it certainly explains a lot," Flashpoint said. "And, I *know* you're heading to... that you're heading after him. I still want in."

"I tried to talk him out of it," Bullit said, "but we *could* use the backup."

Tachion glared down at him. "I have a feeling you didn't try very hard to be convincing," he said.

"To be fair," Flashpoint told the doctor, "I did threaten to rat you out before you even made it to the hangar bay. *If* he didn't agree to take me."

"Fine then, let's go. But you do whatever your cousin or I tell you to do, understood? You're not to make a *move* without our say so."

Flashpoint nodded. "You do realize," the boy said, "if we succeed... my mother will never forgive any of us anyway."

They did realize.

They said nothing.

The hangar bay was expected to be as deserted as the rest of the ship was, but much to their surprise, it was not. A lone figure stood leaning against the back of the *Bugeye*, suited in full armor, and ready to go.

It was Tàlto.

"You guys going cruisin'?" the lyghtan bounty hunter asked. "Mind if I tag along?"

Bullit answered. "We're just… going on a quick supply run. It'd be better if you stayed here."

"Oh… not still heading to Gel Gonahaar then? Looking for Denali and your friend, at the Great-1-Toys factory?"

The trio stared at him.

"Sorry for being nosy," Tàlto said, by way of explanation, "but gathering intel is kinda my thing. I was in the wings of your little pow-wow last night. I overheard that your buddy Rook has ruined the Doc here's reputation, and your zet-head leader Bullseye is givin' it to that young cute one."

"Watch it, dude. That's my sister," Flashpoint barked.

"No offense, kid. Just showin' I know what's goin' on. And I want in."

"Unbelievable," Bullit said. "Stansky's right. Our security on that floor is complete and utter garbage."

"Eh, it isn't that bad," the bounty hunter told him. "I'm just a lot better."

Tachion tilted his head in suspicion. "Why do you care about us finding our friend?" he asked.

"Your traitorous friend isn't my problem. I only care about Denali."

"I thought you only cared about protecting Lady Opal," Tachion replied.

"What better way to protect her, than to eliminate the threat completely?" Tàlto asked. "And I think Great-1-Toys is a better lead than going to Ilshnar."

"Oh? Why's that?"

"Do you know what the name Denali means?" Tàlto asked, looking back and forth between Tachion and Bullit. "Either of you? Well, I'll tell you. It's an old Koyukon Indian language, from the north side of a region that was once called Alaska, on Earth. It was their name for the North American continent's mightiest mountain, and it literally translates as… *'Great One'*."

"See, I told you!" Bullit exclaimed to Tachion. "I knew there was some connection."

"Alright, well... what do you wanna do with him?" Tachion asked Bullit in return.

"I suppose bringing him along is better than hiring some skell from the slumlands."

Tàlto laughed. "That's like saying finding a diamond on the ground is better than a kick in the nuts."

"Fine," Tachion said. "I'm not really fond of this sort of arrogance you've acquired, but seeing as we're shorthanded... you can take the ops station."

The makeshift crew boarded the *Bugeye*, and Tachion radioed to the bridge. Commander Abara answered.

"Bridge here, go ahead Master Tachion."

"Commander, we have a slight change in our plans. We would like you to drop out of warp so Master Bullit and I can take out the *Bugeye*. You may then continue on to Ilshnar."

"I... was not informed of this by Master Bullseye."

"It's a last-minute change. I apologize for the confusion."

"Understood," Abara said. *"But... you must realize, even at the* Bugeye's *top speed, you're still almost two days away from the closest system."*

"Thank you, Commander. We're aware of our location."

"Alright. Yes, sir. I'll have us drop out of warp immediately. Ready yourself for launch, and stand by to open bay doors."

Chapter 18.1

ILSHNAR WAS A PLANET OF ultimate extremes, a world with two faces—though neither of them appealing. The homeworld of the metamorph was snuggled tight to her mother's bosom, a red dwarf one tenth the size and brilliance of Earth's yellow sun. But the planet made the best of whatever energy its host would give her, circling so closely that she made her yearly orbit in just a week. A week, of course, based on other worlds. Here on Ilshnar, the word held no meaning. Nor did day or night, for that matter, as the fractured landscape experienced neither. Tucked in so close to its little sun, the planet had become tidally locked to her—one side facing in, forever bathed in solar fire, the other side knowing nothing but coldness and eternal starlight. Day and night did not exist here—only light and dark, sun and shadow—the side facing brightness, a vast wasteland of dust and sorrow, the other draped in blackness, a frozen expanse of bitter snows.

But there was a line in between the two, a band of gray between black and white—a swathe of temperance through the harshness, and it was here that life existed. A region from pole to pole, and running the edges in between, where heat and cold intermingled in an oasis of permanent evening. The melted ice formed a liquid seascape that traversed around the entire planet; a narrow ocean, dense with life, that teemed anxiously along its warmer shoreline. Lush woodlands huddled there, thriving on for many miles, until they cowered back and faded at the scorching desert's distal edge. The ruddy sun hung forever low in its eternal spot above the horizon, just visible above the treetops of the ebony forest spread beneath. The trees of this world bore foliage of inky black, a way to maximize their light absorption, and most animals had followed suit—a simple matter of effective camouflage.

The slightest wobble in Ilshnar's axis gave the only relief to this unchanging permanency, causing seasonal variations at the poles as the planet periodically leaned fore and aft. The northern pole had receded now, but was soon to tilt its way back forward, making it late winter in the area, the promise of spring on the near horizon. The forest here was long dormant, its dark leaves lost to the bitter winds, but eager buds were already forming, ready to burst forth with the coming season.

Soon, but not yet.

Spring was still perhaps a few weeks away, and winter clung desperately to hang on, hurling icy lances with every gust that stabbed surreptitiously through Bullseye's armor. They snaked through gaps between the plating, and narrow fissures in the joint hinges, causing him to stifle a jarring shiver as he stared onward down the sniper rifle. The woods surrounding the flat stone he lay upon were tossed in tempests of swirling snowdrift, knee high flurries of wind-whipped ice flakes that clattered noisily against his visor. With the snow being as dry as the scattered bones that adorn the sun-side desert miles beyond, the miniature blizzard could not stick, but spun and drifted, like windblown vapor off a tepid lake on a chilly morning. Gales washed in and then withdrew—like the ebb and flow of shoreline pounding—escorting in with it a clouded sphere of gray, a gift courtesy of the frigid dark-side. Out there, away from the sun, beyond woods and sea, a glacial barren lay beyond—the Valley of Glass—blustering and blowing to keep springtime at bay. Its breath swept in and out across the forest's empty branches, drawn back and forth like a well-rosined bow, the trees wailing their tragic music in harmony with the howling wind—a song of anguished lament for the woodland's lost vibrancy.

As different as this was from the scorching sands of Nol Qhan, Bullseye couldn't help but notice—this was the second time he found himself in a land near devoid of all color. The ground was white, the branches black, the sky above a frosted silver. Even the few conifers scattered about bore cones and needles of a sable hue, and the hardier weeds and brambles amongst the forest still held dry and shriveled leaves of onyx. Only the slightest blush of rose could be seen to tint the clouds above, a spot of warmth at vision's edge, where the flushing sun forever hovered.

He had awoken about an hour after Tachion and Bullit had forsaken them, taking with them Opal's protector Tàlto, and Relic's brother—not to mention the precious *Bugeye*. Despite his anger in the moment, Bullseye was now more disappointed than irate, placing half the blame on a lack of faith that his own actions had created. Still, to doze grenade him—that foul move was on the doctor, and at some point, the seti would seek his vengeance for that insult.

They were left to shuttle down in the *McKendrick* and the *Dodger*, dragging Chief Zvavi along with them as a pilot for the second craft. At least now it was easier to convince Lady Opal to stay behind, the lack of enough seating giving her no other recourse. Her protests were vocal, nonetheless. Zvavi remained in a nearby field with the two fighters, keeping them ready for a hasty retreat, while Relic was not far beside Bullseye in the frozen forest, watching his back. Belladonna was atop a tree some distance ahead, serving as his spotter, with Stansky beneath her, likewise watching hers.

They had found the *Okubi* still in orbit, and traced her shuttlecraft to a nearby complex—an unmarked facility of nondescript buildings, one fairly distant from the nearest civilization. Captain Lobo's crew were attempting to research the property owner through layers of corporate subsidiaries, while Bullseye's entire focus passed through the narrow scope of his ZajinBolt. He centered crosshairs on the structure's doorway that was closest to the landed shuttle, looking down from the gentle slope of their distant, woody hillside—uncertain of whose face he might see emerge, General Nylis, or his friend Rook. Perhaps both of them. Belladonna certainly hoped so. She had taken the news of her son and cousin's desertions quite badly, and hoped above anything, that she found her husband first. But Bullit and the doctor had made one fair point at least—there was no reason for them to follow the general about. If he was indeed here, Bullseye would use the opportunity to rid themselves of him, then follow his ship afterward. It will be more telling to see where the panicked body retreats to, after the head has been severed.

A pair of leathery flying creatures—like giant crows, but round as beach balls—scuttled across the snowy woodland at the periphery of Bullseye's vision. A brood of some thirty little ones huddled for warmth beneath their parent's wings, moving together in lockstep as they scratched and pecked at the forest floor. Occasionally, one would tumble out, then scamper hurriedly back to its roving shelter. One fell too far behind, overconfident in its lack of cover, and a dark, serpent-like appendage sprung forth from the snow behind it. It grabbed the squealing chick and yanked it back beneath the frost, like an arm of the undead reaching upward from its shallow grave. The two adults seemed not to notice—they continued onward, unimpressed.

Bullseye was distracted by none of it. He was in his other world now—a private domain, outside of this reality. A world of angles and wind speeds, of rhythmic breathing and ready fingers, of concentration, and finality. For every awkwardness he encountered outside in the real world, he found none of it in this one. Only confidence, clarity, and unwavering determination. Once he locked on, it became just him and the weapon. Very little could ever distract him, short of coming under enemy fire, or perhaps—

He looked to Relic.

A drab frozen forest wove around her, barren branches intertwined, a monotone existence as her backdrop, yet there she stood in defiance—bringing color, and life, to a land without any. Was it possible she was doing the same thing for him? He saw her there now—really saw her—as she paused typing on her mobile bypass, and innocently wiggled an armored finger to wave at him. He did something then he hadn't done spontaneously in several years. The corner of his mouth turned upward gently—and he smiled.

He was happy, *actually* happy, for the first time in—how long? But how was it possible to become this enamored so quickly? Because he was drunk on her, he realized—made giddy by her affections. He considered this. Was it possible he was just exchanging one addiction for another, trading his old elixir for a much headier brew?

Possibly.

Maybe probably.

But even then, so the hell what? Isn't this all that romance is? Altering one's mind with the addition of another? *While the delirium lasts, anyway*, his more pessimistic urges reminded him. Someday, their bliss would fade, like the warm vapor of his breath in this unforgiving winter air. Ultimately, given time, *all* romance must end in tragedy—either enmity, grief, or indifference—there can be no other outcomes. Though, can it not be said the same is true for life itself? He would never choose to forgo existence because a sorrowed end is predetermined. Perhaps then, it is only the experience of it that matters, for however long as it—or he—may survive.

How long would that be, he wondered?

He had not planned for it to be long. After all, being an enforcer is a job you quit early, or not at all. There are no *old* enforcers. And, as he had harbored no thoughts of retiring, this left only the more decisive ending he had so long pursued. But he did not wish that anymore. He did not wish to leave the possibilities of Relic prematurely. He did not wish to hold murder as his primary obligation. He did not wish to join The Fallen overhastily as a result of his profession. Was he too old to change now? He had a duty to lead his teammates for as long as they chose to follow him—and with this new Dodger threat, they may need to continue for quite a while yet. He looked around, noting the absence of his other teammates. Tachion would have been good for discussing matters such as this, but it seemed Bullseye was short a confidant, as well as their valued medic.

He thought about that a moment—could it be possible? A second corpsman would be invaluable, but—could he swap professions at this late stage?

Perhaps.

Perhaps his penance for so much bloodshed lay *not* in schooling others to do likewise—perhaps it lay in the healing of those who were affected! For the first time, Bullseye thought seriously of becoming a medic. He would talk to Tach about it as soon as he was able—providing they didn't resort to killing each other at first sight.

Bullseye tore his gaze from the allure of his young lover, and shook off whimsied thoughts of far-flung futures together. So she *was* a drug, after all—or at least equally distracting. He had never lost focus on a snipe like this before. He placed his visor to the eyepiece, and his finger aside the trigger, redoubling his efforts to burrow into the right headspace. The life of a medic may indeed one day lay ahead for him, but not this day. On this day, he was a hunter—and it was time to lure forth his prey.

Bullseye had provided Relic with the multicomm contact number General Nylis had first called him from. He hoped the novice at infiltration could hack the device, and force it to signal the old chamai—even if he preferred not to answer. It was time for a conversation. *"Relic, have you managed any headway on communication with the general?"* Bullseye asked over the comlink.

"Yes, I sub-jacked his satellite DMD tuner, so you can access him through his media display, and not his official military comms net-chip," she said. *"But the connection might be a little... iffy. The magnetic fields on Ilshnar are extremely strong. It makes this sort of low-band subspace carrier wave a bit... fickle."*

"Yeah," Stansky said, *"I'm having a similar issue with my optics. My visor keeps scrambling. I wish I knew earlier we would be so far near the pole. I would have recalibrated them."*

"I, too, experience the same," Bullseye said. *"But if it comes to it, I'll go without."* He focused in on the doorway again, the almost three-thousand-meter distance appearing more like thirty through his long scope. His ZajinBolt fires a beam of particles at nearly the speed of light, which would be affected by the pull of gravity, but by very little beyond that. Neither the long range, nor the gusting wind, would deter the heavy ions on their path. Bullseye need only factor the twenty centimeter per mile curvature of the planet, the molecular density of the atmosphere the rifle's discharge would

be passing through, and the Coriolis effect from the speed of the globe's rotation. Plus, of course, to somehow minimize his movements, despite the flurries and jarring windstorm. Through the scope at this range, every tiny vibration seemed an earthquake. "*Are you in position, Belladonna?*" he asked. "*No doubt I shall require target confirmation.*"

"*I'm set, with eyes on,*" Belladonna answered.

"*Alright then, proceed Relic. Connect the call, and we shall see if anyone is home.*"

There was a moment of hissing static, and a cacophony of juddered voices, followed by a prolonged whistled screech that had Bullseye nearly rip his helmet off. Then something more intelligible came through—a pair of voices, squabbling in chamai—one of them with a hoarseness that was undoubtedly familiar.

"*What's going on with this thing?*" the general demanded in his native language.

"*Someone is attempting access, your lordship,*" another said. "*You should turn it off, throw it away.*"

"*No, give it to me,*" Nylis answered. Then in common, he said, "*Whoever this is, your attempts to hack me are foolhardy. There is nothing of value to you on this device, and my ship will have you tracked and identified in a matter of seconds anyway.*"

Bullseye looked to Relic. She shook her head to deny the general's claim, then signed an alternative number with her fingers. He passed it on, "*One hundred fifty seconds, General. More than enough for a brief conversation.*"

General Nylis actually laughed, something he would have seemed incapable of—and from the sound of the dust clearing his vocal cords, something he hadn't practiced in some time. "*Ah... the petty mercenary leader. Perhaps you have not yet heard, Bullseye. My former Prime Minister has been deposed, the Oberonn government now bows to me. And though I have not yet decided on my official title, 'Your lordship', rather than 'General', is what I'm going by for now.*"

"*Alas, if considering names I would choose to call you, I must admit... that one fails to make the list.*"

"*Yes, as I can well imagine,*" the general grumbled. "*Though I'm inclined to forgive that, owing to the... favorable mood... I find myself in. I assume you are reaching out for some reason, if you care to share it. A desperate plea, I would guess.*"

"*No, nothing quite so dramatic. Just a simple matter of our invoice, General. You still owe a balance due upon the job originally commissioned.*"

"*Oh, don't you worry about that, my friend. Lord Denali will ensure you get everything that's coming to you.*"

"I must ask, why would you seek to align yourself with one such as him?" Bullseye inquired. *"Have you not seen the dangers in it? His unpredictable nature? 'Your lordship' or not, he disposes of his minions as easy as used tissue. It is a fool who fails to learn from the tragedies of those around him."*

"Your concern is touching," the general told him, *"though you have no need to worry. I have learned, trust me. I can ingratiate myself when needed, for the promise of power that he will bring."*

"You have such faith in him?"

"I do not think he's something holy, as the witch Vasu seems to believe. But I can say this, he has honored his promises, and is achieving his goals. He is... a great man."

"I know more truth of this villain than even you are aware," Bullseye told him. *"He is evil. He is then further twisted by that device which he wears. And, more than likely... he is quite insane."*

"The two are not mutually exclusive, Bullseye. It is a fallacy that a great man need necessarily be a good one. In fact, oftentimes, it merely gets in the way."

"And so you hope yourself someday also to be called great, on the back of this association?"

"History will refer to me however it chooses," Nylis said. *"My sole concern is my own today, not someone else's tomorrow."*

Bullseye looked to Relic for another time check. *"Then what be your plan now? Sit on your false throne? Play pretend that you're a ruler, while your master pulls your strings? Makes you dance as he pleases?"* the seti asked. *"Of course, there is the question of how you will return home for even that."*

"What do you mean?"

"I mean, General, that your ship has been spotted by some of our agents on Ilshnar, and I have a small fleet of mercenaries en route to intercept you. You are in Coalition territory now, without the benefit of your armada. We shall be there soon ourselves. Quite soon, in fact, seeking payback for that outstanding debt... as well as the return of our missing friend."

The general chuckled again—though this time, far less convincingly. *"Your information is flawed, I'm afraid. I am nowhere near Ilshnar. And your comrade, Rook, does not travel with me."* It was obvious he was telling lies about his location, but a subtle shift in his tone made the second claim ring truer.

"You are a proven deceiver, General Nylis. A swindler, and a fraud. And there is no believing a liar, even when he speaks the truth. We look forward to seeing you... soon." Bullseye signaled Relic to cut the transmission short.

Stansky's voice came over the comlink. *"Well... if he had been planning to hang here a while, that outta flush him out."*

"Let us hope so," Bullseye said.

"*Captain Lobo to Parliament,*" called the *P1*'s commander over the comm.

"*Go ahead Captain,*" Bullseye replied.

"*The* Okubi *is widening her orbit, and has raised her shields.*"

"*Keep yourself hidden, Captain. Stay across the globe from her at all times.*"

"*Understood,*" Lobo said. "*Also, Lieutenant Kinn-Ara has uncovered information on that property. It is listed as an equipment maintenance facility, owned by Notos Chemicals, a division of Aion Uniforms Service. Aion, however, is a subsidiary of PlayStar Amusements.*"

"*The vacation resort company?*" Stansky asked. "*What do they have to do with any of this?*"

"*Unknown,*" Lobo answered. "*However, the company president is a metamorph, and resides not far from your location.*"

"*Well done, Captain,*" Bullseye thanked her. "*Keep us apprised on any changes.*"

Belladonna cut in. "*Bullseye, I have movement,*" she reported.

"*Okay then. Everyone else, radio silence,*" Bullseye said. "*Belladonna, just you and I.*"

"*Roger. Two unknowns at the doorway,*" she relayed to him in a quieter voice. "*Correction, make that three.*"

"*Confirmed. I mark three warm bodies on infrared,*" Bullseye answered. "*Switching to enhanced zoom.*" His visor's display of heat signatures switched to a simple magnified view, with a data overlay. Through the blowing snow and the dreary light, the outlines of the figures were harder to make out this way. But three persons were coming out, making their way toward the waiting shuttlecraft. The figure in the center was clearly bald, and Bullseye focused the enhanced vision on him. A facial recognition prog began analyzing his features. "*I have confidence in target bravo, can you confirm?*"

"*Scanning,*" she whispered.

His own visor answered first. The name and photo of Nylis were overlaid across his vision—identification probability: ninety-four percent. He looked at the image. The picture of the general triggered another memory of that conversation—Nylis and Yazir, plotting in the captain's mess while Bullseye lay hidden. "*Trojan base is on its natural trajectory,*" the general had clearly said, "*and its orbit will enter the prohibited barren zone in just over a week from now. Three days after that, it returns to Coalition territory.*" What might he have been referring to, that roams in and out of the Barrens naturally? A satellite, or a comet? He re-engaged his IR and radioed to Belladonna. "*I have probable confirmation. Do you concur?*"

"*Affirmative,*" she said. "*Bravo target. In the middle.*"

"*Roger,*" he said quietly, placing his finger on the trigger. "*Clear me down range?*"

"*Downrange is clear, nothing significant behind the target.*"

He closed his lids for a long blink to rest his eye for a moment, then double checked his weapon's sight for scope shadow.

"*You better make it fast,*" she added. "*They're only thirty steps from the shuttle.*"

"*Roger,*" he repeated, even softer than before. "*Confirm distance?*"

"*Range... thirty-five hundred and sixty meters,*" she advised him. "*Coriolis effect... two mark one newtons, right hand deflection.*"

He made a minuscule adjustment. "*Roger,*" he barely whispered. The heat image in his visor began to jump and scramble, losing clarity. He paused a moment to wait it out, but the distortion wouldn't clear.

"*Fifteen steps,*" Belladonna called—quiet still, but with a note of urgency underneath.

Bullseye popped up his faulting visor, a rush of cold breaching his open helmet. He lay his own eyeball along the scope, blinking back against the wind and the pelt of ice crystals on his lashes. The visor's unreliable optics were more of a hindrance than a help right now, and he could—or should—be able to make this shot without them.

He was, after all, called Bullseye for a reason.

He breathed deep, and then held it, the cold air burning within his lungs. He re-aimed ever so slightly, up and to the left. Heads are small and move around a lot. They seldom make a reliable target. But he felt this shot demanded something a little bit more personal, and the gunsight wavered tremulously over the chamai's hairless scalp. His eye eased closer to the longscope, sheltering his vision from the icy wind, the drum of his own heartbeat playing calm and steady within his ears. Every muscle working together to keep the weapon's muzzle still and true, the crosshairs— slowly—settled right atop the general's temple.

"*Five steps left! you've gotta send it!*"

Bullseye drew the trigger back, and a thunderclap erupted. The scavenging birds and their flock of little ones burst upward from the snowy ground, scattering wildly, in a panic, across the gray and cheerless sky above them. The general's mind was scattered likewise, painting the hull plates of the *Okubi's* shuttle, his aids spun in confusion at the discharge—a full ten seconds before they ever heard it.

 18.2

IF THERE WAS A WRONG SIDE to the galactic tracks, Gel Gonahaar would be on it. Fairly lifeless when it was first colonized, beyond the very simplest of ocean algae, the early megacorps that were spreading out found it perfect for industrialization. A billion years of work by the planet's native pond scum left its air already oxygen rich—breathable and accommodating. There were no forests to clear, no indigenous species to try to tame, no environmental concerns—at least none that anyone cared about. And, as an unclaimed planet, all the land was completely free. All you had to do was be the first one to find a use for it.

The factories grew fast and grew thickly—corporations erecting buildings just to lay claim to the land beneath it. Within a matter of several decades, the virgin soil was barely visible; every usable inch constructed over, except where excess mining had torn it open. The surplus mills, plants and foundries built in those early days by the megacorps were sold off at huge profit to smaller corporations. Businesses without the capital, nor inclination, to maintain even their own industrial sectors, let alone the living conditions of their nearly enslaved generational workers.

Pollution grew.

Poverty as well.

With no governmental body to oversee it, the world descended into near chaos. Its general interests are represented by distant off-world councilmembers—faceless lackeys, owned by corporate lobbyists—and its streets are policed by Starlaw under the guise of being a federal district, but only in the barest sense. In truth, corporate barons now rule the factory districts and the workforce ghettos that surround them. Syndicates of gangsters run the city slums, and the commercial shop owners are forced to bow to them. It's a delicate ecosystem of violence and greed, of power and plight, of wickedness and despair. Yet, it's here that are made the multicomms you use daily, the furnishings you sit upon, the toys and games your children play. The tragedy of Gel Gonahaar is the Coalition's open secret—a crisis to be ignored, in the hallowed name of lower pricing.

One industrial metropolis here seemed fairly indistinguishable from any other, even the borders between the districts almost impossible to discern. Rook looked out across one of many of these nameless, stinking cities, from the catwalk above a factory floor, leaning against a door frame to a rotten balcony—one far too sketchy looking to step out upon. He wasn't sure which was noisier, the endless din of the machinery below, or the cries and caterwauls of the chaos surrounding. In either case, it made his head ache. Below him in the street, a monger of slum food hawked his wares—a ragged seti, covered in mange, desperate for anyone with actual coin to spend. A homeless human lay behind him, sleeping peaceful in the filthy street—if he was in fact even sleeping, it being just as likely he was discarded dead. A metamorph whore hawked her wares as well, changing appearance to suit any passerby who might afford it. There weren't many. In the end, she made a trade between herself and the mangy seti—a slice of tamis loaf for a blowjob. Neither one seemed particularly satisfied.

But Rook saw none of this distraction, his eyes set instead on a distant window. Through the blear of his troubled head, both throbbing and in confusion—and through a forest of chemical silos, all rusty and in disrepair—his gaze never wavered from the factory across the tainted river.

There it was.

It was there.

The stone terrace was long gone, yet the building itself still remained. Just within, behind that glass, was the office where he had killed Denali. Against that wall, where the balcony stood, his new master had silently crouched and watched him.

How did he feel about that?

Rook himself wasn't completely sure.

His mind had felt a jumble lately—not all the time, but at quiet moments. Random thoughts, abrupt and fleeting. One minute he'd be planning how to better bring Lord Denali's name to glory, the next instant he'd begin to wonder why he even followed him in the first place. It had been several days since he'd last seen his master, and the suggestions that had taken hold of him were wearing thin around their edges. Though, the seti didn't know this was the cause of his muddled distractions. He merely knew the comfort of his now familiar hate and anger were being interrupted by occasional thoughts of—

Oh, sweet Belladonna, how he longed once more to see her face. Black as the ocean on a moonless night, wondrous as the stars that sparkle above it. His lady— his life—his love. If he could only but—

His attention and his programming were pulled back by a sudden alarm, the doors and windows shuttering automatically, including the one that he had been musing out of. He turned back to the factory floor as the metal gate slammed behind him, the security far more advanced than the shambled building would have implied. He looked below, but saw no danger among the mass injection molding of children's sporting gear. His eyes darted up toward the distant payload docks, where his master's new devices were currently being loaded. He put on his helmet and radioed his partner. *"Rook to Drake, what the hell is going on?"*

"I don't know. We're showing intruder alerts all over the facility, but so far, we haven't seen anyone. Either there's a hundred invisible soldiers storming in..."

"Or someone set off every alarm, to cover the real one," Rook said. *"Goddamn motherfuckers. That's one of my plays!"*

"Get to the main security office. See if you can track them down on video or sensors. The interceptor's almost loaded. I'll guard the last of it getting boarded, and we can get the hell out of here in a few minutes."

"Understood!" Rook replied, already running for the sensor room.

The factory guards below the catwalk forced the laborers to the ground, clearing way for the line of fire should any invaders come their way. Rook sailed down a yellow painted metal stairway, and across the obstacle course of supine workers—men and women in filthy overalls, face down amongst rolling balls and dropped boxes. He burst into the security office and rudely pushed the attendant aside.

The screens flashed and danced, scouring through several dozen nooks and stairways, showing every corridor and cranny that the alleged threat could be coming from. But there was nothing there. Nothing visible on video. No heat detected on camera. No motion sensed on scanners. All empty. Rook's eyes narrowed suspiciously at the monitors for a moment, then rolled ever so slowly upward, squinting toward the ceiling. The unoriginal fuckin' bastards were doing a repeat of a raid from twenty-five years ago. They were on the roof.

"Get me a view of the outside," he sharply commanded to the security officer. "Tell me you've got some kinda eyeballs on the damn roof."

"Y-yes," he answered. "We have spy-eyes flying all the time." He leaned past Rook and tapped a few keys. The monitors changed in a flash to aerial views above the toy factory, each of the insect-sized drones zooming in on a pair of figures—just in time to see them zip down through an open skylight.

But it was too late. Rook had seen them and recognized their armor. Doctor Tachion Magna, and cousin-in-law Bullit—the top two names on his personal shit list. *"Drake, heads up,"* he reported. *"You've got two inbound from above. Old friends of mine, unlikely to be on their own."*

"Understood. Get down here as quick as you can. We'll leave security to deal with them. The ship's almost loaded. We've gotta go! ASAP!"

"Understood. On my way."

Just as soon as he made a quick little detour, that is. Bullit and Tachion would eat through these half-ass rent-a-cops like a spaghetti dinner before a marathon, and there was no way he was passing up a chance to see these lying shitheels laid out dead.

Plus, he wanted the pleasure of doing it himself.

He burst back out from the office as dramatically as he'd burst in, and began dashing through the factory, making his way toward the upper level. As he approached the general area where he'd seen the twosome drop in, he slowed, and moved more cautiously, heading down a maze of corridors—old, unused offices now employed for the purposes of mere storage. He drew his two acid sprayers and slunk forward on tiptoe. At an intersection of hallways, he paused, listening carefully, and checking his scanners for any movement. He saw a blip, then heard a scraping, like a small bag dragged across the floor.

Rook tuned the channel on his comlink. "*Tach old boy, is that you?*" he whispered into his helmet mic.

Nothing but silence in return. They'd been wise enough to swap their usual frequency and keep him from listening in. Another blip of movement, and a muffled clang from around the corner. Rook bent low, hugging the wall as he followed behind the sound. Looks like he'd just have to go see for himself.

He advanced to the spot where the motion pinged on his scanner, then stopped—a slightly ajar door leading into the power relay maintenance room. Did they plan to cut the power and stop the factory? Little good that would do them, the serum was already made and being loaded. And if that *was* their plan, they were certainly taking their time with it, not to mention sounding clumsy. Rook found it highly satisfying that they couldn't even turn out the lights without him. He aimed his sprayers toward the door, preparing to melt the faces he had fought beside for so long. The rusty portal swung wide, and out the figure stepped.

He recognized the armor all right. How could he not, when it was he himself who bought it? The one and only time he'd sought Stansky's insights into protection suits, and actually listened, and took notes, making sure he got the very best. If there was going to be a switch to demo, the very least he could do was keep his boy protected. It was *Flashpoint* in Rook's crosshairs, wearing his custom-made graduation present.

Rook turned to stone at the sight of him, as sure as if it were Medusa. His son did as well, the two visored faces staring at each other for what seemed like an eternity. Why was it Rook hesitated? This boy wasn't his child. Not really. His progenitor, the first Rook, was the one who conceived him. In fact, he now realized as a clone, it was probably impossible for him to have children at all—that fucking android just lying to his face when he'd gone to see him about it. But still, Rook felt something. A connection to this boy he'd tried so hard to bond with, who, despite all their conflict, he couldn't help but to—*love*.

He now wanted nothing so much as to see his child's face. Rook lowered his weapons, and raised the visor up on his helmet.

Three small marbles spat forth from a small opening on Flashpoint's headgear, the sonic beads blasting Rook with their stored micro-concussions. A resounding boom echoed out. He flew back against the wall and collapsed hard onto the dirty floor, clattering on the broken tiles, his brains rattling in his head. He lay there stunned for a long moment, his consciousness and vision spinning, but managing to snap his visor closed with a thought through the armor's brainlink. Too dazed and dizzy to get up, he clenched and waited for the final kill shot, staring blearily at his boy's boot as he braced for that fatal hit. But it didn't come. The boot just stood there, hovering over him for a minute. Then it turned and rushed away.

Rook lifted his head with some effort, thick red droplets coloring his inner visor. His ears were bleeding, running warm across his cheeks, and screaming like a flute blowing C-sharp against his eardrum. He looked around the hall, but the boy was gone—the goddamn fool. If he'd told him once, he'd told him a thousand times: never leave your opponent to rise again behind you. Just further proof this idiot child wasn't his son. He couldn't be. Rook would never have made the mistake of letting him live. Sure, he hesitated there—let Flashpoint get the best of him. But that was just because he was surprised, and it sure as *shit* wouldn't happen again. The boy would not get the same mercy his weakness had provided Rook. Next time they meet, there would be no hesitation.

Rook peered into the power relay room as he struggled to all fours, and saw what Flashpoint had been doing there—an LCD countdown was making its way toward zero. The little bastard armed the place to blow. The seti crawled his hands up the wall as he fought the dizziness to get upright, then radioed to Drake. No answer. With his helmet wide open, the sonic marbles had fried his comlink. Or maybe his eardrums. The doctor and Bell's cousin would have to wait for another day. Rook was in no shape to face them now, and according to Flashpoint's timer, there wasn't enough leisure for such fun anyway. He slid one shoulder against the wall, and began hustling for the payload bay.

By the time he arrived a minute later, he'd gotten his bearings enough to crookedly jog, and he hurried toward the idling interceptor as Drake waved him onward from the top of the cargo ramp. Rook stepped onto the gangplank just as the craft began to lift upward, grabbing a support beam to hold on to as they headed through the open ceiling. He turned and looked down into the bay just as his old friends appeared, seeing them dispose of the last line of security guards. A loud explosion rang out. Smoke and fire emerged from the far end of the facility, the lights in the factory flickering, and going out. Flashpoint wasn't down there with them—hopefully the idiot blew himself up. They gazed up at the seti as the ship exited to the sky, the two looking up at him, as he was looking back. Not a word nor signal passed from one onto the others, yet a compendium of understanding was in the resolve of their stares. They all knew where they stood now. No more secrets anymore.

Rook turned his back to them as the ship accelerated, his fist slamming the button to close the ramp.

18.3

PARLIAMENT ONE'S LACERTILIAN TACTICAL OFFICER silenced the audible alarm at his station, then double checked the readings. "Madam Captain," Lieutenant Kronn announced, "I'm detecting energy weapons' fire near our two returning crafts. Looks like they're being pursued by... a chamai 'B' class shuttlecraft. It's following them into orbit."

"Put it on screen," Captain Lobo told him.

"Sensors also detecting a squadron of fighters now, just launched from the *Okubi*," he continued. "Twelve Hellcats in route, four by four formation. Range, twenty thousand kilometers."

"En route towards us?" Lobo asked.

"Negative. Intercept course on the *Dodger* and *McKendrick*."

Lieutenant Kinn-Ara interrupted from her comms station. "Incoming transmission from Chief Zvavi, Ma'am."

"Put him on," Lobo told her. "Go ahead Chief, this is *P1*."

"*Apologies, my Captain,*" Zvavi's voice came through the comlink, the audible sound of shield impacts ringing in the background. "*It would seem Master Bullseye's interruption of the general's meeting was not appreciated in the least. We have lured an assailant to pursue us. A vengeful shuttle currently hunts, one most determined for its quarry.*"

"I'm afraid you have more of those hunters inbound, Chief. A dozen of them. Fifteen thousand kilometers, closing quickly. You're gonna need to rush back so we can cover you, and you'll probably end up landing those birds on the run."

"*Understood,*" Zvavi said. "*Perhaps you would do me the kindness of patching me through to my hangar crew.*"

Captain Lobo turned to Kinn-Ara. "Do it," she ordered.

"Bridge to hangar bay," the avian called into the comms.

"*Hangar bay, Ensign Rawlings.*"

"*Ensign, it's the chief,*" Zvavi's transmission broke in. "*Prepare the flight deck for emergency landing. Deploy the catcher's mitt, raise the aft wall inertia shield. Clear way in the landing zone, and all hands are to evacuate. I wish that hangar bay to stand empty, am I clear Ensign? We are coming in hot, as they say.*"

"*I... yes, of course, Chief. Emergency protocol underway!*"

"Fighters now at ten thousand kilometers," Lieutenant Kronn said.

"Zvavi," the captain called, "is there anything else we can do for you from here?"

"*Request permission to engage this shuttlecraft.*"

"Granted chief. You do what you must do to get home."

"*As you command.*"

Captain Lobo muted the comlink. "Alright everybody, looks like he's bringing the fight home to us. All hands to battle stations. Commander Abara, red alert please."

"Red Alert!" Abara barked over the wailing of the klaxon starting. The cooler hues of the *P1*'s bridge went angry red with emergency lighting. "Load torpedo bays! Charge munition banks! Tactical, get those shields up, full QEUs!"

"Helm, come about," commanded Lobo. "Bearing two two seven mark six. Let's line up our hangar bay, and give Chief Zvavi and Master Stansky a straight shot."

"Aye, Captain," the metamorph answered. "Two two seven mark six."

"Torpedo bays ready," Lieutenant Kronn advised. "Short-range missiles armed. Energy weapons at your command."

"Hangar bay doors open," Abara ordered. "Shut down all non-essential systems, divert power to the starboard field generators."

"Enemy fighters now at five thousand kilometers," Kronn said. "Assuming attack formation."

"And our ships?" Lobo asked.

"Only ten kilometers, but engaged in evasive action."

"Kinn-Ara, give me a split screen. Zvavi and the shuttle on the left, interior hangar bay cameras on the right. Helm, calculate your warp vector solution. Any heading, your discretion. I want us ready to jump out of here the *second* we see them onboard."

"*Zvavi to Master Stansky,*" the seti's voice came across the comlink, "*Master, if you draw them starboard, I will loop a negative Z axis beneath, and re-emerge abaft of her.*"

"*I don't think that big Ahab can make a sharp maneuver like that,*" Stansky said. "*You'll just end up exposing your belly, or coming up way back outta range.*"

"*Respectfully, sir, I am far more capable than that. I have Master Bullseye and Miss Relic in the gunnery positions, and I can put them right behind that shuttle's rear vent ports.*"

"*Okay then, you got it. Bell and I will let them catch up, then draw them starboard.*"

The bridge crew watched intently as the attacking shuttle drew closer to James and Belladonna in the *McKendrick*, nearly draining her aft shields with a constant stream of laser fire. The *Dodger*, just up ahead of her, suddenly banked downward impossibly sharply, cutting beneath both ships in a tight loop that made even the onlookers a bit dizzy. The Ahab popped back up behind the shuttle and opened fire, a supernova of beam weapons lighting up the sky. The shuttle was quite sturdy, but never meant to take that sort of barrage. A burst of light, a silent explosion, and the *Okubi* shuttlecraft flew no longer.

"Well done, Chief Zvavi!" Lobo exclaimed in relief. "Now get yourself on board, and step on it. Those fighters are already within weapons range."

"*Aye, Captain. Dodger and McKendrick incoming.*"

"Helm, be on the ready. Tactical, let's keep those birds occupied and off their backs. AE500s, fire at will."

The laser cannons of the *P1* lay down a spread of fire, one that the far more agile Hellcats were easily able to maneuver around. But it did serve to distract them, at least for a moment. The squad of twelve chamai fighters split into three groups of four, veering left, right and under, in order to divide the *P1*'s attention.

Commander Abara turned to Kronn. "Lieutenant, let's drop a frag charge aft, see if we can scuttle those bogies sneaking below us."

"Aye. Launching proximity mine... now."

"Can we target missiles on the four to our starboard?" Lobo asked.

"Negative captain, they're too close to our own vessels."

The ship lurched suddenly forward, jerking the crew in their seats, as the echo of an impact rattled through the hull plates.

"Damage report," demanded Abara.

"Minor Commander. The port side fighters are targeting our engines, but minimal damage. So far shields are holding," Kronn told him. "I have mine detonation, direct to the center of the four fighters. One ship destroyed, two are dead stick. The other is coming around to attack our rear with the port formation."

"*Stansky to P1, we're under heavy fire. Aft shields are failing.*"

"*Zvavi to Master Stansky, make quick for the hangar bay. We shall hold here and guard your stern. Keep your speed just shallow of fifty knots, and the catcher's mitt should slow you.*"

"*You want me to go tearing in there at fifty knots? I'll crush us against the back wall!*" A large explosion resounded in the background, and a whooping alarm began to sound. An automated warning voice began repeating 'fire' over and over. "*Oh shit, never mind. Tearing in there sounds just fine. Anybody in the shuttle bay, you best get up against the wall!*"

Through the split image on the bridge's viewscreen, they watched the *McKendrick* career into the hangar bay, a trail of fire and smoke belching from its port side engine. The craft slammed hard onto its belly, skidding sideways as it entered, and tearing through a textile web of inertia strapping that was laced across the entire landing area. A mere foot from the aft wall, the forcefield finally stopped them, and an avalanche of fire suppressant poured from outlets on the ceiling. The camera view of the hangar bay was clouded over by the whiteout.

"*This is Stansky. The* McKendrick *is down.*"

The *Parliament One* was rocked again, but this time the blast was harder.

"Okay, Chief Zvavi," Lobo said, "*it's your turn. Get aboard.*"

"*Ensign Rawlings to Chief Zvavi, I'm afraid the* McKendrick's *landing has taken out half of the catcher's mitt. And the craft itself is blocking the aft inertia shield. I... I don't think we can stop you if you come in that fast.*"

"*Understood Ensign. Just stay back, I'll take care of it.*"

On screen, the *Dodger* raced forward, even faster than the *McKendrick* had—far faster, in fact—bobbing and weaving a maze of weapons fire as they made a run for the hangar's safety. She lined herself up, then her engines flared hot and bright, a sudden last blast rocketing her homeward toward the *P1*. The thrusters fell silent. The Hellcats had a free shot as the craft drifted swiftly toward its target, zipping closer to the hangar at well over two hundred knots. Her dwindling aft shields were aglow from the fever of enemy fire.

"Chief Zvavi?" Lobo called, clearly nervous at the approaching collision.

She was met with empty silence.

"His aft shield is almost gone, Captain," Lieutenant Kronn reported."

The *Dodger*'s maneuvering thrusters fired then, spinning the craft on its axis, its inertia still carrying it on the hurried course toward the shuttle bay—but now streaking onward in reverse. Its forward shields took over, lighting up with deflected lasers, but only for a moment. Now that the ship's bow was facing its enemies, its beam turrets sprang to life. The vessel fired back relentlessly as it fell rearward at great speed.

"Ten seconds until he reaches us," the tactical officer advised.

"Helm, be on the ready. I want warp speed on my command," Captain Lobo said. She then tapped the ship-wide intercom. "All hands, brace for impact."

Eyes went glued to Zvavi's vessel as it flew back at them out of control. Fingers tightened against armrests, as each of their silent countdowns fell to zero.

Suddenly there was an explosion, a firestorm from the rear thrusters, her engines wide open in an attempt to finally slow her. The viewscreen of the hangar bay was ablaze with light, and the bridge crew averted their eyes against the brilliance. After a moment it dimmed again, just in time to see the *Dodger* alight softly to the deck plates, as if the first autumn leaf drifting down on a windless day.

The rest of the launch bay, however, had been fully ignited by the blaze.

The *P1* lurched hard again, and a rain of sparks spat from beneath Kinn-Ara's console.

"Engine room sector shields are down," reported tactical, "minor hull breach in the port service module."

"Helm, warp engines now!" Lobo commanded, and the *P1* vanished from its orbit of Ilshnar. The half of the viewscreen that had shown the planet below them was now the comforting dazzle of a starfield rushing past. The half monitoring the hangar bay, a holocaust of smoke and fire. The suppressors were spraying liberally, and the deck crew were all a panic. "Oh, mister Zvavi," she said to herself, "what have you done to your precious shuttle bay?"

Commander Abara turned to the captain. "I'm getting reports of a XM coolant leak in engineering. We're gonna have to drop out of warp before the manifolds overheat."

Captain Lobo shook her head as she stood from her chair. "Take her as far as we can go safely, but don't get out of long-distance scanning range of the *Okubi*. Our masters' plan is to follow them, so keep a sharp eye. I'm going down there. Commander, you have the bridge."

By the time she arrived, the fire was brought under control. Once the two fighters and the hangar bay were fully evacuated, it was a simple matter of purging the bay's air supply out into space. With the oxygen gone, so went the flame and smoke.

But not the smell—nor the wreckage.

"Chief Zvavi!" Lobo bellowed. "What's the meaning of this disaster?"

Zvavi spun in surprise, his large soot smeared form cowering before the little lacertilian. "My... gravest apologies, Madam Captain. I... uh..."

Lobo clapped him on the chest, and then twice lightly on his cheek. "We're all glad you made it back, Chief. *I'm* glad you made it back," she told him. "You did wonderful out there, as always." She turned to the window that looked through into the charred hangar bay. "But you're going to have your work cut out for you overseeing the refit. Assuming, of course, that our masters can afford to pay for it." She looked left and right to Stansky and Bullseye, both surveying the damage as they stood to either side of her.

James shook his head. "Maybe Opal will help, after what we've done for her."

"She is now a lady of scant resources," Bullseye reminded him. "At least until she sits restored to her rightful queenly station. But, should we succeed... such kind generosity would certainly be most welcome."

Zvavi joined them. "I would venture the destruction worse in appearance than in substance," he offered, "though it may be that the *McKendrick* is in truth unrecoverable. I shall call forth all duty shifts, and commence cleanup without delay."

"Belay that, Chief," Captain Lobo commanded. "You will do no such thing, but get your ass down to sickbay. I want you checked over thoroughly before returning to work. Those fumes in there were toxic... and I suggest the rest of you all join him," she added to Stansky, Bullseye, Relic and Belladonna.

The majority of them begrudgingly followed her advice, and exited to the hallway, passing a contingent of crewmen arriving to begin repairs. Bullseye, however, loitered behind for a moment.

Captain Lobo asked, "So your mission was a success, I would take it?"

"By whatever scales might weigh the success of carnage and fatality... aye, it was," Bullseye answered. "Though I admit, there now be one death I feel free from ever mourning."

"Nor should you," Lobo said. "In my opinion, you've done the galaxy a great favor. And likely, in the opinion of the people of Oberonn."

"The people of Oberonn are hardly free as yet, as some other pawn will surely fall quick to his place, succeeding the late general. Whether for better, or worse, is still left to discover. Tell me, Captain, what be the ship's status?"

"We incurred some damage in the engineering sector, a plasma coolant leak. We have a team working on it now. Meanwhile, we've shut down engines just at the edge of sensor range, and are keeping a close eye on the *Okubi*'s movements. Currently, they're in recovery efforts for the remains of their lost shuttle, but will certainly be looking to make way as soon as possible, before Coalition military comes to investigate our little skirmish. We're confident we'll be up and running in time to follow them."

"That is *most* imperative, else all hope might be lost," Bullseye warned. "Unless... Captain, if I may exploit your vast knowledge for a moment. Tell me, are you aware of a celestial body, whose routine tour of the universe draws it to and fro across the barren zone? Perhaps even so far as to approach Drak'min space, then return here to the Coalition?"

Lobo thought for a moment, brushing back her crown of plumage as she furrowed her scaly brow. "Nothing overly specific leaps to mind, I'm afraid."

"So, none, then, that you know."

"No, quite the opposite. Far too many to be counted. As you know, the boundary line of the Barrens is not some flat line. It's a wrinkled, twisting terrain of hills and valleys, an ever-shifting deformity. Projecting tendrils and deep depressions, and curling around landmarks that shift position, such as solar gravity wells, LaGrange points, and nebula clouds. There are hundreds of systems located along the border whose Oort clouds consist of circling ice asteroids or planetesimals, millions of which dip in and out of the amebic boundary line in their orbits. Not to mention roving comets, rogue planets, wandering black holes. Perhaps if I had more details to go on, I could..."

A sharp vibration shuddered through the vessel, causing the two of them to grab each other for balance. Once it dissipated, Lobo hit an intercom button along the wall with the side of her fist. "Lobo here. Report."

"*Captain, we've blown a conduit in the damaged engineering module.*"

"Any injuries?"

"*Ensign Leet-asa has minor burns. He's on his way to medical.*"

"Understood. How long is this gonna set us back, Commander?"

"*I'm being told at least a few hours. But, Captain... the Okubi has abandoned her recovery operation, and is leaving the system. She's headed for neutral space.*"

"We must pursue!" Bullseye blurted.

Captain Lobo held her hand up to him. "Keep me informed, Bronte. Lobo out." She ended the comlink.

"We must pursue," Bullseye repeated more calmly.

She shook her head. "We cannot, I'm sorry. Not until that cooling conduit is replaced."

"Then... give me Chief Zvavi. We shall take a fighter to follow."

"Firstly, the *Okubi* would have to stay sub-light just to give you the slightest chance of keeping up in a fighter. And secondly..." she pointed out the window into the adjacent hangar bay, blocked by smoldering debris and pieces of *McKendrick* wreckage. An overhead light fixture crashed down from the ceiling. "There is nothing we can do, Master Bullseye. We've no choice but to let them go. We can log their trajectory until they get out of sensor range, then follow when we're able, scanning for their Alcubierre field signature. Your ship here is a fast one. It's possible we'll catch up."

"Possible... but not likely."

She looked back at him seriously. "No... not likely, I'm afraid."

Bullseye turned and looked back out into the blackened hangar bay. "I find myself thwarted, once and again, like some brand of deliberate plot. But where to seek blame, beyond the visage of my own reflection. It seems perhaps I should have taken the council of Bullit and Tachion more dearly."

"Who's to say their luck's been any better? You can't blame yourself. It's not your choices that led to this."

"Oh, what truth you speak," Bullseye explained to her. "'Tis not choices I dared make that weigh down on me so heavily, but the burden of those I can only wish to have made."

18.4

BULLIT YANKED THE HELMET FROM his head and threw it angrily at his cousin Belladonna's son. "For fuck's sake, Flashpoint! What in God's name were you thinking?!" he shouted. "I mean, honestly. What the hell were you even trying to do back there?"

"You made an agreement," Tachion added in an accusatory tone. "You were not to make a *move* without our say so. Do you remember that? Because I don't recall asking *anything* like that of you."

"Nope, neither do I," Bullit agreed, eyeballing the boy as he waited for a response.

The three stood high atop a partially collapsed bridge to nowhere, a defunct construction project, clearly abandoned mid completion. It had instead now become a narrow hamlet of shanties for the downtrodden, rows of rickety seeming huts, made of corrugated sheathing and junked containers—though with a million-dollar view, overlooking the squalid city.

Back down the hill, toward the oily river and its putrid stench, a plume of smoke smudged the skyline—although a smudge that was hardly different from a dozen others which stained the sky. The bellowed exhaust of the district workshops already did its best to fill the heavens, the burning cinders of the Great-1-Toys factory just another defilement among the others. Flashpoint watched pensively at the flickering tongue of orange licked hungrily at the rooftops. He held Bullit's helmet out behind him, passing it back to the other seti. "I thought... I just thought..."

"Well, that's just it, isn't it," Bullit snapped at him, snatching his helmet, "you *didn't* think, did you?"

Tachion took a step closer, joining Flashpoint at the bridge's railing, and lowering his voice as he noticed a crowd of displaced vagabonds looking on. "We told you to wait, and secure the *Bugeye*," the android said.

Flashpoint turned to face them. "I didn't come all this way to stay behind, and guard the fucking ship!"

"Whoa, watch your tone, boy," Bullit warned the young seti.

"I thought I could help, shutting down that alarm."

Tachion shook his head. "We started those alarms on purpose. There was no reason to shut them down."

Flashpoint shifted his gaze from one to the other, somewhat confused. "I... I don't..."

"It was Tàlto's idea," Bullit explained to him. "That place might have looked like a rusted-out ruin, but its security was impeccable. Tàlto seems to have some fairly impressive infiltration skills, but this place... well, just a bit over his head. No matter where we entered, we were sure to set something off."

Tachion interjected. "Tàlto suggested we just set *all* of them off, to distract the guards. Scatter them, keep them guessing. It's actually a tactic your father used to use."

"All *you* managed to do," Bullit told him, "was quiet the confusion that was giving us an advantage, and nearly get us trapped inside when you cut all the power. *Plus,* draw extra attention that we now have to hide from."

Flashpoint's face turned defiant. "How much extra attention could I cause, with you two shooting up the place?"

"An internal corporate skirmish," Tachion explained, "is an everyday occurrence, and nowhere more so than here on Gel Gonahaar. Keep the citizenry out of it, and no Starlaw would have bothered us."

"But," Bullit finished, "when you burn down half a block, in a district that's made of rotted kindling... *that* draws attention. And I'm not talking about Starlaw, *those* dunces we can handle. I'm talking about the underworld baron of this sector, who's losing kickbacks from the factories that are now burnt to ashes. *That* sort of attention tends to follow you, and amass interest."

"I'm... I'm sorry, cousin Bullit. Uncle Tach," Flashpoint said. "I didn't... I'm sorry." He turned his back on the pair to gaze again at the dwindling fire.

Tachion reached out to lay a gauntlet-covered hand on the seti's armored shoulder. "It's all right, I know you didn't mean to... well... you were trying to help. These are things that only experience will teach you. But in the meantime, just listen to us. I know you were hoping to help us deal with your dad, but..."

"I saw him," the boy said.

"We did too," Bullit responded. "Just a little too late though, as he took off for... who knows where."

"No," Flashpoint said distantly. "I saw him up close... when I laid the charges."

"What?" the doctor asked.

"I... came out of the power relay room, and he was... right there. Right in front of me. He had me dead to rights, but he... he didn't fire."

"What happened?" Bullit asked. "How'd you get outta there?"

"He... lowered his weapons, and... opened his mask. I think he wanted to... surrender." Flashpoint speculated. "But I didn't believe it. All I could see was a... liar. I shot him. I fired three sonic marbles right in his face. He was down, injured... but I couldn't... I... I couldn't..."

"It's all right," Bullit said, putting an arm around his younger cousin. "Nobody would have expected you to... you know."

Tachion looked out at the diminishing blaze in the distant quarter of the cesspool city, while noting an increasing curiosity of the outcast refugees that surrounded them. "The commotion seems to be settling a bit," the android said, "and we seem to be stirring a second one up here. Perhaps we best make our way back to the *Bugeye*."

Bullit looked around behind them. "How is it that I keep ending up in cities built of rubbish?" he pondered.

"Hold up," Flashpoint said. "What about Tàlto? We're not gonna wait for him?"

"Pfft," Bullit scoffed. "He did the trick with the alarm, got us inside, and next thing you know, he's nowhere to be found."

"Perhaps he already made his way back to the ship," Tachion suggested.

"Yeah, well, if he isn't there waiting, as far as I'm concerned, he can stick out his thumb and start hitching."

They circled far around the still smoldering factory sector, opting instead to seek a more inconspicuous route through the quieter streets of the housing district. The foursome carefully picked their way through the shambled city, towards the far-too-expensive docking lot where they had left the *Bugeye*. The brief journey across the barrack wards was a lesson in humility, the sights and sounds of abject poverty a sobering vista to be recognized. Men and women draped in rags, little children gnawing scraps. But still, despite these trials, an aura of cheer and gaiety was prevailing. Smiles of welcome beamed on dirty faces, young ones playing in the filthy streets. The sound of laughter rising up, forcing those of tears to keep at bay. The golden sun was dipping low now, casting amber hues across the skyline, the towering apartments of rust and rubble almost beautiful in its warmth. Overhead and drifting low, makeshift junk barges slowly sailed, cobbled from odds and ends of every caliber, and powered onward by old, used hoverdollys.

"Where are we gonna go now?" Flashpoint asked of his two mentors, as the group paraded through lively neighborhood to much attention.

Tachion and Bullit looked unsure at each other, the large android's shoulders managing a clueless shrug. "Back to the *P1* I guess," the doctor finally decided, "with our tails between our legs. And that's if we can even catch her."

"Fuck that," Bullit countered. "Why should we turn up all apologetic? Rook *was* here, just as we said. We were right, but just too late to catch him. Thanks to wasting time in that pointless strip bar."

"True, Rook *was* here," Tachion agreed. "But Denali was not. If we had been on time to deal with that first issue, we'd still be here now, not knowing what to do next." The three of them turned a corner, making a shortcut through a wide alley. "Maybe Bullseye was right, taking the more careful approach of following the *Okubi* to their master. Who knows, that might be leading them right now to both Rook *and* Denali. But, without us."

"Uh... guys?" Flashpoint cautioned, directing their attention down the alley.

Just ahead of them, down the backstreet, a row of armored figures blocked their way. Not uniforms at all—not Starlaw, and not security. In fact, not uniform in the slightest, by any stretch of the imagination. The line of challengers were in gear that was piecemeal and purled together. A patchwork of disparate parts: pauldron, bracer and gauntlet from a set of crimson siege, cuirass and plackart off a chest of ebony heavy-battle. Suits of protection that were stitched together, like everything else in this quilted city—mismatched, but still functional.

Formidable as well.

Bullit immediately swung around, placing his back against his android teammate, guarding their rear against a similar threat currently surrounding them from behind. The seti charged his laser shotgun as Tachion drew two auto pistols, and Flashpoint toyed eagerly with a set of frag grenades, rolling the tiny canisters between his fingers.

The pieced-together platoon halted their approach, save for the one front and center, the only member whose full ensemble was of a single set, in forest green—excepting for the helmet, which was a shocking shade of canary yellow. A female sounding voice called out to them from beneath it, a slight Gel Gonahaarian perversion to her otherwise Earthan accent. "Greeting, off-worlder," she said, by way of introduction. "You visitor three, such trouble alsomore follow. Of manymuch workplace you bring hard destruction. *Manymuch* workplace, them workplace that tribute Ûmbara as protectorman."

Flashpoint whispered to Bullit and Tachion, "What is she saying? What the heck is *oom-bara*?"

"This planet's developed its own... dialect," Tachion explained. "One unique among those born here. Sort of a mishmash of coalition common, human, and metamorph. An ûmbara is what they call... the boss, of their local network of hoodlums."

"It's the gang leader in charge of the slum mafioso," Bullit clarified. "I told you burning that place down wouldn't go unnoticed."

"Alsomore, not unpaid for," the woman stated firmly. "Tributes that forgone now, off-worlder must make good of. On your ownsome."

"I'm certain we can come to some... fair arrangement," Tachion answered.

"*Alsomore*," she continued, "hard tribute price for rebuild. You must paysome manymuch. Bring all workplace up again."

Bullit looked up and down the crumbling walls of the decrepit alley. "I find it extremely unlikely you plan on rebuilding *anything* around here," he said.

Yellow helmet laughed. "Yah, maybe noway," she agreed, before her tone turned deadly serious. "But, offworlder newones... you make now big paysome anysame."

Flashpoint whispered again. "Why not just tell them who you are? Maybe they'll back down... or scare off."

"Uh uh," Bullit said. "Bad idea. I think you'll find announcing yourself to intimidate often has the opposite effect."

Tachion called back to the woman in the yellow helmet. "I'm afraid you've caught us unprepared. We're not carrying any credits on us to give for your Ûmbara's tribute."

"Mmm. Can paysome credits, or equipment. Both be tribute anysame. You make first paysome with pretty armor... and offworlder power sword."

"Ha!" Bullit cried. "Listen lady, whatever deal we come up with, none of that is gonna be part of it."

"Is okay," she declared, unphased. "You noway make paysome, we take all anysame."

Her rows of soldiers closed ranks as weapons were quickly drawn, the group's shields powering to life as they prepared to engage.

"Hold!" a shout came from somewhere up above. Drifting down on his levitation belt, Tàlto lowered himself slowly toward the ground. "For worthy protectorman tribute, I parlay."

Yellow helmet looked up at him, holding a hand aloft to halt her soldiers. "You council for offworlder, I for Ûmbara?"

"Aye," Tàlto said.

"Come then." She waved, and the bounty hunter landed beside her.

Tachion turned to Bullit. "Apparently, this popping in to help at literally the last minute is his signature entrance."

"Yeah, so I've seen. Look, I know this guy's got some skill, but... I gotta say, I'm not a fan."

They watched Tàlto with curiosity from their short distance back, the lyghtan removing his helmet, and explaining something in earnest to the leader of this gang of brigands. Explaining *what* exactly, they didn't know. After a minute of his gesticulating, she removed her headgear as well. There was some surprise to see a seti, not a human, emerging from beneath the protection of the yellow mask—one who now eyeballed both the trio and Tàlto with suspicion. Her hazel eyes were backed by a boldness of attitude, a fire of pretension that flashed in her gaze. Her stare was set amongst short fur of silky black, broken by a throat of brilliant porcelain extending up her chin and across her muzzle—then one final brush stroke painted between her eyes. Her mane was colored similarly, equal parts dark beside pale, the varied bandings drawn tight in a braid down her back. The woman was frankly beautiful, in the way some great dangers are. Like a supernova, or a lightning storm—wonders lovely from a distance, but certain doom to ever approach.

Exactly the sort of woman that Bullit found himself drawn to. "Ay, caramba. Well, hello there," he muttered.

Tachion looked down at him. "Alright, one Lothario on the team is more than enough. Don't you start now."

Before Bullit could respond, their attention was drawn back towards Tàlto. The bounty hunter whispered in the seti's ear, and she threw her head back to laugh. Then the pair clasped each other's forearms with one hand, and partially embraced with the other.

Bullit shook his head and pointed. "What the hell *is* this shit, Doc? Do they know each other? Are we being played?" the seti asked. "I'm starting to think this Tàlto is sketchier than DaVinci."

Tachion was beginning to agree. "I had made a case to Bullseye that we should invite him to join our crew. And James agreed, although reluctantly. But I'm starting to wonder if that opinion was a tad hasty. I don't understand the way he's been acting. I think he's hiding something, I feel sure of it."

"Well, you better vet this guy thoroughly before you make that kind of offer," Bullit told him. "Shhh, here he comes."

The mismatched militia turned their backs to walk away, and Tàlto approached, a cocky grin across his face. "Alright, we're free to pass," he told them, "but we definitely shouldn't linger. Let's get our asses back to the *Bugeye*."

"Who the hell was that?" Bullit asked, as they continued more quickly now down the alley.

"Well, it depends on who you ask, but here on Gel Gonahaar, she goes by Jaadoo. She's the right hand to the ûmbara of the Rumbl'garde Syndicate," he told them. "They're the racket who controls the ghettos in this district, and ten or twelve more surrounding it. Maybe not the biggest crime organization on this planet, but still... pretty big."

"And... you know her?" the doctor asked with curiosity.

"Don't be surprised, I know lots of people. In lots of places. Which is lucky for you guys, 'cause I got you a sweet deal."

"What deal?" Bullit asked.

"I told them you'd make good on one year of tribute," Tàlto said, "by the end of the month."

"Fine," Tachion said reluctantly.

"*And...* they also wanted ten percent towards construction costs of a new factory. Which, of course, will never be built."

"And you agreed?"

"Ehh, not exactly. I told them to make it twenty."

"What?!" Bullit growled.

"Twenty... as long as they pass half of it out to the now jobless displaced workers."

The destitute pedestrians they were passing made it hard to disagree.

"How do you know they won't just keep it for themselves?" the doctor asked him.

"That's just part of how it works here, winning the hearts and minds of the civilians. They may control the businesses through fear and violence... *lots* of violence... but the people they control through carefully measured acts of charity."

"Maybe we can renegotiate," Bullit said. "Or, for that matter, what if we don't pay?"

"The deal is done and done. And it's not a great idea to not pay. The Rumbl'garde will need to save face against disrespect like that. They'd send a team of Darkcloaks to come looking for their money."

"I can handle some bounty trackers."

"No, not for you. They'll send them after the boy."

Bullit turned to his young cousin, who was slinking along behind. "When we get finished with all this, you better find a team to work for and start making money quick. Cuz even if it takes you the next twenty years, I'm gonna watch you pay back every last nickel of this ticket."

Flashpoint looked up at him, but stayed silent.

They continued onward through the streets of hardship and destitution, the previous jovial attitude waning now that dinnertime was drawing near. The penniless paupers were now grouped in small clusters of immediate family, closely protective as they shared whatever meagerness had been rooted out. The earlier welcoming eyes of frolicking children had been replaced with the warning glares of their possessive parents—like vicious animals protecting a bone.

Tachion felt an extra pang of guilt upon seeing this, simply because none of the suffering passersby were members of his own species. Poverty such as this was inherently easier for the androids to escape from. The three basic necessities of food, clothing, and shelter helped to shackle the organic species, forcing them to spend most of their energy, and earnings, in pursuit of these basic requirements. Requirements that the androids simply had no cause to worry about. He had no need to eat, nor even breathe, and nothing less than the fiercest cold or cruelest heat could affect him. There were, of course, plenty of androids who struggled financially, but it's a basic truth that it was easier for the mechanical species to crawl out of that prison, simply because they could direct their sparse savings beyond just surviving.

The foursome finally reached the dockyard as the sun began to set, pinkening hues painting the smokestacks and the wispy clouds far above. They happily scrambled aboard the *Bugeye*, and closed the liftgate tight behind them.

As they stripped and stowed their equipment, Tachion confronted the bounty hunter. "Okay, Tàlto, now that we're out of the street's prying ears and eyes... what in the hell happened to you? Where did you disappear to at the factory?"

"As I told you in the beginning, Rook is your mission, not mine," Tàlto said. "I have no interest in finding your friend. I determined fairly quickly that Denali wasn't there. After that, I had no reason to participate, and went about my own business."

"No reason to participate?" Bullit snapped, incredulous. "How about the fact we were up to our asses in security?"

"You look to have managed all right," the lyghtan responded. "And so far, you've done fine without me all these years. Besides, I had other more important things to worry about."

"If we could have captured Rook," Tachion pointed out, "we might have gotten a lead on Denali. Thanks in part to your... *disinterest*... we now have *no* clue where to go."

Tàlto scoffed at that. "A very small part, I assure you. Also, I think you forget what it is I do for a living, why it is you wanted to commission me in the first place. While you three were keeping busy slaughtering working parents and burning down half the city, I was doing something actually helpful," he said. "I got out on top of that interceptor they were loading, and stuck a tracker on her fuselage."

Flashpoint got excited. "So, we can still catch her?" he inquired.

"Oh, God no," Tàlto laughed, looking around the old *Bugeye*. "This clumsy old bucket-of-bolts would *never* keep up with that interceptor. In fact, she's probably out of sensor range already. But my tracker is special, a design of my very own. It drops subspace microbeacons, every half light-year or so."

"Like a trail of breadcrumbs," Flashpoint said, "leading us right to them."

"Yeah, that's right. Smart kid," the tracker said to the young seti. "So we might never catch them, but we'll still get to where they're going."

Tachion and Bullit had trouble finding fault with that revelation. "Still," the android said, "let's communicate better in the future. I know you're used to working alone, but from now on, try and keep us in the loop of what you're planning."

"Sure Doc, you got it. I used to be on a team once," he said sarcastically. "I'm sure the gist of it will come back to me." He climbed into the cockpit next to Bullit as the seti was preparing to take off. "Oh, I almost forgot. While I was on the roof of that interceptor, I also took the opportunity to download the most recently used subspace frequency from the comm relay."

"What for?" Bullit asked.

"What for? I don't know. Monitor the frequency, maybe... if we can get close to them. Or just give the last contact code a hail, and see who answers. Might be interesting to see who your old buddy's been talking to." He turned back and looked over his shoulder. "Whaddaya say Tach. Interested?"

"Yes, sure," he admitted. "Send the frequency to my station."

The craft lifted and rocketed forward, a fuchsia thread across the sky, the city's wants and insufficiencies blurred invisible with the passing miles. Eventually, it was all the same—a world of gray, and slate, and pewter. A dusty globe in a distant corner, far too easy to disregard.

And, perhaps preferable.

They locked onto Tàlto's first microbeacon, and threw the ship into its highest warp.

"So," Bullit asked Tàlto, as Tachion tuned in the frequency he was given, "you *knew* that lady extortionist back there, but that's still the best deal you could get us?"

"Ehh. So I'm not a great negotiator, maybe. That's more your deal, isn't it? But still, I got you outta there."

"Who is she?"

"I told you, she goes by Jaadoo."

"No," Bullit insisted. "Who is she really?"

Tàlto turned and looked across the cockpit, eyeing the seti with a knowing smile. "She's a real viper, that girl. I'd be careful if I were you. One false move or wrong word, and you'll find a blade against a sensitive place."

"I'm just curious," Bullit lied.

"Alright. So Jaadoo is her current name, but her real one is Mystic. Or... at least that's what it was when I met her. For all I know, it's the other way around," he chuckled.

"What'd you whisper to her?" Bullit asked.

"If I wanted you to know that, then I wouldn't have whispered it."

Bullit was quiet for a minute. "So, she's a bad seed then," he determined.

"No, not at all. Well... not much, anyway. She's just doing like the rest of us, tryin' to make a life out of the cards that were dealt her. She was always just the littlest bit of a scoundrel, I guess. That's how we met, after all. But the organized crime, that's a new twist. Still not sure exactly what game she's playing there."

"She's running a con?"

"She's running something," Tàlto said. "I mean, she might have been down there long enough to have the accent of one now, but she's no true Gel. She's an off-worlder, like you and me. Hell, she went to ASU Tempe. That's where I first met her, over a decade ago. Running a short scam at a beach club on Arizona Bay."

Bullit stared at him, questioningly.

"What? I tend to get around."

Tachion at Bullseye's station finally finished patching into the stolen frequency. "Okay, I think I've got it. Let's just see who this call goes to."

The echoed chirping of the hailing signal pinged out over and over, without response. The doctor tried repeating it, boosting the gain of the wavelength, but if anyone received it, it appeared it would go ignored.

"We could still be out of range," Tàlto offered, "of... wherever they were calling."

"Or maybe it was just a one-time use frequency," Bullit suggested.

But then the comm monitor jumped, and an image flashed to life, resolving a staticky picture on the terminal in front of the doctor. The android stared. If Tachion's mouth was capable of opening in such a way, his jaw would have clanged against his metallic chest like a church bell. As it was, though, he didn't flinch, but sat and remained stoic, conveniently masking the emotions that were a whirlwind inside him.

"*Huh, so still flying around in the old* Bugeye, *I see,*" the unmistakable voice of Jim Dodger surmised, sparking a flood of old memories at the sound of its timbre. "*I feel I'd like to say I miss the smell of the old lady, but I think we both know... I've never really been inside it, have I?*"

Tàlto stood to hurry over, but Tachion put a hand up, warning the lyghtan to stay out of view. "Lord Denali, I presume," he spat with ample sarcasm, as if the very taste of saying it was bitter on the tongue. "So, at long last we meet... despite your efforts to keep us from doing so."

"*The efforts I devote towards your insignificant little group are negligible, at best. But I appreciate you using my rightfully earned name, and not Dodger.*"

"I wouldn't sully Jim's memory by using his name on you," Tachion said. "But Denali... well... that one fits you to a T."

"*Oh, don't get me wrong, I would never disrespect him either. After all, that's my progenitor we speak of. Without him, there'd be no me, and the galaxy would be a much more hopeless place.*"

"You think you bring hopefulness with what you do? I fail to understand that logic."

"Of course, I do, Doctor. What other explanation would the universe have had to make me? Jim and Denali both, just steppingstones on a long journey. It was destiny for Jim to die, to make me who I am. Just as it was destiny for you and Parliament to make Jim the man he was, and who still lives on, in part, within me. Each event and encounter is just a link in a long chain. A chain forged by the universe, to pull forth..."

"You!?" Tachion asked in a mocking tone. "The universe has forged this mighty chain, to bring forth *you* to rule us? I haven't seen a single thing to lead me to believe you're anyone special," the android told him. "I'd be very careful, *Lord Denali*, of mistaking coincidence for fate. That's a certain path to self-delusion. Although... it seems you've already been on that road for quite a while now."

Denali laughed. *"You see everything that I've done, all I've accomplished, as merely self-delusion?"*

"I'll tell you what I see," answered Tachion. "I see a man who was perhaps *engineered* to suffer these issues, at the genetic level. Further complicated by imprisonment, and knowing your jailer, I assume torture. I see a self-aware clone, presenting a textbook case of duplicant identity disturbance, who in order to define a purpose, took on not just the mantle, but the personality of his creator. I see a man who grew power hungry after years of feasting on nothing else, perverting his growing might into fantasies of grandeur, in order to find meaning. Fantasies reinforced by those abilities you were built with, culminating in a god complex to rival the worst ones in all humanity. And last, I see a man under the influence of an alien chemical. One that not only boosts those same unnatural abilities, but the grandiose delusions, and hunger for power as well. I see you can't possibly understand just how distorted your reality has become, and sadly, your success to have gotten this far only corroborates your false beliefs."

Denali shook his head. *"Whew, that's a mouthful. I'm sorry I even asked,"* he said. *"But while I appreciate the amateur armchair psychology, isn't it true that every great philosopher and revolutionary, at one point or another, is called power-hungry or insane? I'll take you lumping me in with those others as a distinguished badge of honor."*

Tachion studied the monitor as he listened, focused on strange markings in the background, and a curious, crystalline geometry inlaid into the surrounding walls behind Denali. The setting was unusual, yet somehow still familiar—something he had once seen before, but now couldn't quite decipher. "And was Rook as accepting of this vision of your destiny, or did you have to struggle to persuade him?"

"*Rook was no challenge for my persuasions. You made it extra easy, after all, with all the lies you fed him his whole life. He was hungry for the truth. Any truth. He was starving for it.*"

Did this mean Rook's turning was, in fact, mainly just Denali's influence? Perhaps there was yet hope after all that their friend could be recovered.

The human continued, "*And I've turned far more well-trained minds than Rook's just as easily,*" he couldn't help but brag.

"You mean the Starlaw metamorph, Esil Brin?"

"*Yes!*" Denali half laughed. "*You sure figured that one out quickly. Good for you. You always were a clever one.*"

"Well, I'd hate to take undue credit. To be fair, an injury from one of your own soldiers sort of gave it away. So not so much my cleverness, as your own ignorant stupidity."

Denali frowned. "*Now, now. We've had such a lovely conversation so far. Let's not resort to name calling, shall we? Oh... and speaking of polite conversation, I'd be remiss if I didn't thank you for your help on Gel Gonahaar. That factory was a money pit, and of no use to me anymore. Your kindness in getting rid of it, with any evidence still inside, as well as a healthy insurance payment to boot, all more than makes up for what you did to poor General Nylis.*"

Tachion stared, unsure of what he meant.

"*You don't know, do you? Are you and Bullseye not communicating? Do I sense trouble in Parliament paradise?*" Denali eyes roamed around, examining Tachion's background. "*The Bugeye does look a little emptier than usual.*"

"Yes, that's true. It's just me alone now, and a pilot from the *P1*. The others see things a little differently than I, so I thought I'd strike out on my own," Tachion lied. "Why don't you tell me where to meet you, and we can discuss this more in person."

"*As much as I would love that little reunion, I'm afraid I'm just too busy now to entertain guests at the moment. Besides, in only a few hours, I'll be out of range and out of reach. We'll just have to hold over our get-together for... another occasion.*"

"Are you sure? I mean, clearly we're still within live communications range, so we couldn't be more than a couple hours away," the android pointed out. "Or is it just that you know your mind control won't work on me?"

"*Well, the fact that androids can't be controlled, or ensensed, does limit their place in my future. It's unfortunate, but your species seems to have reached the extent of their evolution. I can't see a use for them in the new order, beyond perhaps servants, or workers. Although, probably best to just go ahead and eliminate them.*"

"You have that much fear for what you can't control with your... influence?"

"Oh, my powers of persuasion are a convenience, to be sure. But I have plenty of other ways to bend wills like yours if I so desire. But the thing is, I don't desire. You and your lifeless race are just not that important to me. I hope it doesn't hurt your feelings to hear me say that," Denali said. *"Anyway, Doctor Magna, it's been a pleasure catching up with you. Though if we get the chance to meet in person, I'm afraid I can assure you, it won't be nearly quite so pleasant."*

"Oh that, *Lord* Denali, you should have absolutely no doubt of."

The human sneered a contemptuous smile, then the monitor went black.

18.5

NOT UNTIL THE *PARLIAMENT ONE* was repaired, and well and truly underway, did Bullseye consent to reemerge from his office—it taking all of Relic's persuasion and appreciable feminine wiles to lure him forth. He had spent the last many hours poring over tedious star charts and solar system diagrams—all to no avail. Captain Lobo had been correct in her assessment. The number of individual objects which routinely violate the forbidden barren zone approached the uncountable, and stellar cartography not being his strong suit certainly didn't serve to aid him in his search. But dear Relic dragged him out, in hopes further research would not be necessary. The *P1* was at high warp now, hot on the trail of the *Okubi*, and she fed him every hope that the late general's ship would soon appear within sensor range.

Until the trail ran cold.

Its Alcubierre signature had long dissipated, giving ghost readings port and starboard, and it was decided the best course was to simply continue on straight ahead. But rather than grow in strength as they closed nearer to their quarry, the signal only faded further, until finally, it was gone. Their ship now sat drifting near the upper edges of Barnard's Loop, scanning desperately, and in vain, for any hint of a proper course bearing. Bullseye and Relic sat dejected on the circular sofas in the common area, the crimson brush strokes of the nebula shining through the dome above them like blazing neon.

Directly across the center table from the two, Belladonna sat looking at them thoughtfully. She leaned forward, "So... tell me once more, what *exactly* did Nylis say the plan was?"

Bullseye sighed. "He spoke unto Yazir, now an Admiralty of the Drak'min, of increasing energy requirements, and the need for more power. He was bound for the negotiations of this increase. 'Tis likely the same meeting which, just today, we so rudely interrupted."

"What else?"

"He spoke of the rigidity to their timetable, due the immutable orbit of their rendezvous point," he said.

"Because this supposed... 'Trojan base'... was on a trajectory that was due to bring it across the border? *Into* the Barrens?"

"Aye, you speak correctly. The plan seemed such that some armada, cobbled forth from mercenary, Capellan and Oberonnian fleets, would dock at this... base, riding its back safely through the forbidden territories. Then on approaching the far border, Yazir's caravan was to join him, adding Drak'min warships to this unseemly alliance."

"To what purpose?" Bell asked.

"What other purpose could be, then but clandestine attack upon the Coalition."

"And we have no idea where this alleged base is located?"

"Not one, I fear. I have studied the star charts to the very precipice of nauseum, but a thousand such objects breach the border every instant, none standing out to me as more viable than any other."

Relic put her hand on his. "How much time do you think we have?"

Bullseye searched his recollection, casting his gaze upward. "As best my memory can say, Nylis claimed but a week or more still remained. Which has nearly now elapsed since the fortune of overhearing him. Therefore, I would surmise that our timeline runs short." He stood and looked up through the domed porthole at the rosy nebula and the stars beyond. "Somewhere among this celestial tapestry flies a planetoid of sorts, one which will penetrate restricted space within the passing of meager hours. Then three days hence, emerge again, freighting villains into the Coalition."

James and Opal emerged from his quarters just as Bullseye finished speaking, and the human lingered for a moment, inspecting an array of fruits the chef had laid out on a side table. He grabbed an apple from a crystal bowl and tossed it in the air, bouncing it off the inside of his extending elbow, then catching it again in mid-flight. "Do I hear right?" he asked. "We're finally going someplace fun?" He slid himself rudely over the backrest of a sofa, flopping down heavily beside Belladonna. He took a loud, crunching bite.

Bullseye shook his head. "Nay. We discuss the likely harbor the *Okubi* travels to."

"Yeah, so I heard," James said, spinning the apple in his fingers, seeking to locate the perfect spot for a second bite. "A planet that enters the barrens later today, and comes back to Coalition space three days after that. You're talking about The Rock." Another crunch into the apple.

Belladonna swiped the fruit from him in utter annoyance. "What are you talking about? How do you know that?" she demanded.

"*Jesus,*" he said, glaring up at Belladonna. "What's the big deal? I know because I go to the casino there all the time."

"You do?"

"Sure. It just so happens they have an unbelievable massage parlor." He winked at her.

Belladonna's lip involuntarily curled in disgust.

He reached over, and stole back his apple.

Bullseye eyed him seriously, a glimmer of hope returning. "Are you quite certain of this? Mind you, no mistakes can be made."

"Oh yeah, I'm positive. All the regulars are aware of it. Shit, I even got a notification sent to my multicomm," James said. "I'm on their VIP contact list."

Opal looked confused. "What exactly is this... *Rock*?" she inquired.

Belladonna turned to answer. "The Rock is a rogue planet, roaming the galaxy without a sun to orbit. It became a bit of a boomtown after first being discovered. For a little while anyway. People rushed to it because it was covered with an ancient alien technology."

"Yeah, but that didn't last long," Stansky interrupted. "People went there to dig for whatever tech and gadgets they could sell, like some kind of... modern-day gold rush. But most of the stuff there, no one even knew what the hell it was. Or how any of it worked, even today. Strange facilities that don't seem to do anything. These gigantic, deep subterranean shafts of unknown purpose. Beyond a few small pieces, like Bullseye's teleportation triangles, most of it was just abandoned... left behind as useless garbage."

Bullseye nodded. "A curiosity to exo-archaeologists, but very few else," he said. "There was once a sort of... forge there. A molecular crucible of alien origin, which could blend disparate technologies to the formation of something new. But even that has been now destroyed, in a flawed attempt to steal it some years ago."

"It didn't work that often anyway," James said. "Half the time, it destroyed my stuff."

"So," Belladonna said, returning to Opal's question, "the single ancient city there was left standing empty. Until a wise investor came along, and bought it up to create a casino. One that doesn't bow to any regulations, or pay tax to any government. The Rock is its own island, with no one but its corporate investors to oversee it."

Relic realized something then. "This corporation that owns it, is it not... PlayStar Amusements?"

"That it is," Bullseye nodded. "One and the very same with whom Nylis met this day on Ilshnar. This possibility of James' grows more plausible by the minute."

Belladonna turned to the human. "James, what was in that notification the casino sent you?"

"Just a summary of regulations required by intergalactic treaty," Stansky said. "Anyone going to stay at the casino must arrive before it crosses the boundary. And, all ships must be landed. No craft are allowed to remain in orbit. Once on the surface, you are quarantined from leaving, until the planet reemerges in the Iota sector of the Coalition."

Opal wondered, "Are those giant alien shafts large enough to hide an entire fleet?"

"Yeah, easily," Relic answered. "We studied them in school. Some of those tunnels are over a mile across."

"James," Bullseye asked, "how close is the Rock's approach to Drak'min space?"

"I'm... not really sure. Pretty close, I think."

"It seems like the perfect plan," Belladonna said, "now knowing PlayStar's president is in league with them."

"Aye," Bullseye agreed. "So, Denali crowds the shafts full with the fleets of Nylis and Vasu, then onward they are carried through the banned region of the boundary zone. Upon approaching the other side, Yazir's drak'min will seek to join them. Strange bedfellows they will make in the lyghtan and the chamai," he said. "For a few days or more, they prepare, carried swiftly to their target. Hidden, until arrived at the very center of the Coalition. A surprise attack, swift and sure. As a troop of Athenians from a..."

"Trojan horse," Relic finished.

"Exactly."

James looked at his multicomm to check the time. "Well, if we're gonna catch them, we better tell Lobo to get a move on. We only have a few hours before the Rock crosses into the barrens."

"I will call to the bridge immediately," Bullseye told them. "James, you go get Chief Zvavi back on duty. Clearly the *P1* cannot land on the Rock, nor may she remain in orbit. Tell the Chief we need the hangar ready, though it need not be pristine. Merely clear enough of debris that we may take leave in the remaining fighters. Once on world, we shall track this surplus energy use Nylis spoke of, in hopes it will lead us to them," he said. "And, fates willing, Denali and Rook among the others."

Chapter 19.1

"PLEASE, THAT'S ALL I HAVE for now," the Coalition President explained sternly to the writhing, tumultuous crowd. "We won't be taking any further questions until we have more concrete information to share." The burning glare of lighting from the hovering holocameras left an afterimage in Harold's eyes, and he tried to rub away the ghostly spots as he ducked back from the hectic podium. The shouted questions and speculations still followed him out the doorway, the press ravenous for anything on the situation on Oberonn. Yet none quite so ravenous as President Forestal was himself.

His wife Deborah was waiting to meet him in the safety of the back hall, and marched by his side as they were escorted down the corridor. Harold signaled to Agent Adder to provide them a little space. The guard quickly acknowledged, holding the entourage of aides back a bit, allowing the president and first lady to move ahead out of earshot.

"I swear to God, Deborah, I told you this would happen," Harry said. "I knew there was something fishy with that general, way back after the TriStar summit."

"If you're trying to imply that this is somehow *my* fault," she answered, "as I recall, I told you to go ahead with checking up on your little theory. I just said to do it quietly. And what happened to all that?"

As if in response, General Isaiah appeared ahead, not so subtly signaling the president for a moment of his time. The threesome ducked into the Gold Room, Adder shutting the door behind them, then securing their privacy by standing just outside.

"General," the first lady snapped, "do you have any idea how this makes us look? A military dictator taking power the very moment our troops are pulled away? It looks like our supposedly mighty, and *definitely* expensive intelligence services are incompetent!"

"Deborah, please," her husband interrupted. "Let's hear what he has to say."

"Short of a resignation, I don't know I *want* to hear anything else from him."

"Well, I do!" Harold barked, uncharacteristically assertive.

His wife fell silent.

"Please Ephraim, what have you learned?"

General Isaiah glanced at the president's wife with trepidation. "Mr. President, I'm afraid that... this is your-ears-only information."

"Don't be ridiculous," Deborah scoffed. "Spill it."

The president eyed the general a long time, who remained silent looking back. "Deborah, would you please give us a minute?"

"*What*? Certainly not."

"Agent Adder!" Harold called, and his secret service guard quickly entered. "Would you please escort the first lady to our quarters?" he politely commanded.

"Yes, sir."

"Harold, you must be joking," Deborah cautioned. "You wouldn't."

"Agent Adder, you heard me."

"Right away, sir," the agent said. "Lady Forestal, if you'd come with me."

"Don't you lay a hand on me," the woman ordered, jerking her arm away from his guidance. "I'm perfectly capable of finding my own way." She turned to whisper to her husband as she headed toward the door. "We *will* discuss this later."

"Of that I have no doubt," he responded, once the door had been closed behind her. He sighed. "Alright Ephraim... let's hear it. The press are fucking killing me on this. One of our closest economic allies, taken over by a madman? How is it possible we didn't see this coming?"

"Well," the general said, "we're still backtracking all the moves. But... it seems very well orchestrated. It looks like he could have been planning this for years."

"Oh, please. That crotchety old bastard can barely plan to take a piss before he goes to bed. He might have once had a mind for military strategy...

once… but this kind of political gamesmanship is *way* out of his wheelhouse."

"Our analysts agree."

"It's that human, isn't it? The one you *still* have not identified. Is that who's supposed to lead this '*new empire*' Nylis was rambling on about?"

"It could be."

"Yes, General, of course it *could* be! I wanna know if it *is!*" the president shouted. "And what's this I hear of chamai vessels in Coalition space? Engaging civilian ships at Ilshnar?"

"That's why I'm here, sir. Those weren't just any chamai ships. That was the *Okubi* and her fighters. General Nylis' ship himself."

"What?" the president asked quietly, at once both confused and frustrated.

"And… the civilian ships…"

"Don't say it."

"Were… actually Parliament," Isaiah confessed.

"Jesus fuckin' Christ, Ephraim! What the hell is going on?! How were you not on this?"

"Well… space is large, Mister President. We can't monitor every place at once."

"Is that honestly the answer you're gonna give me right now?" the president asked, quietly seething. "Space is *large?* This didn't happen in some far-off rim quadrant! A military dictator was orbiting a Coalition planet! Directly above one of our bases!"

"Yes, sir, but he was only there less than half an hour."

"Where is he now?"

"Uhh… well… that's the other information I have to share," the general said. "According to reliable reports… we believe he's… been assassinated."

"What? Already? Jesus, Ephraim, you couldn't have led with that?"

"I'm sorry. I…"

"How?" the president asked.

"Right there on Ilshnar, sir. We believe Parliament to be responsible."

President Forestal stared at him, eyes burning with quiet rage. "Are you telling me, that the mercenary group whom I *specifically* tasked you with babysitting, assassinated a foreign dignitary? In Coalition space?"

"A criminal dictator foreign dignitary, sir. And, yes… so it would seem."

"I thought you were monitoring them. I told you to get closer."

"We are trying, Mr. President, but they've been jumping all over. Capella, to Oberonn… And now half of them went to Ilshnar while the others were on Gel Gonahaar. If we get too close, they might spot us. And it's hard to keep up while keeping our distance."

"Then close the distance, General! Something is coming to a head, and I mean real soon. Whatever it is, I don't wanna hear about it by reading it the paper the next day! Is that understood!?"

"Perfectly. Yes, sir!"

President Forestal took a breath as he paced a loop around the room. "Was anyone else hurt, in the incident at Ilshnar?"

"A chamai fighter was shot down, but the *Okubi* recovered all her wreckage. There was also a shuttle that was destroyed, which we believe carried General Nylis' body off the surface. But they also managed to collect most of that."

"Most of it?"

"Some scrap was left behind, nothing useful. And the remains of two bodies were discovered floating nearby. A known black-hat mercenary leader, and a chamai praetor, based out of the garrison at Krataar."

"Alright then. And what about Queen Vasu's part in all this?"

General Isaiah rolled his eyes. "I'm sure you've been briefed on her strange broadcast yesterday? Announcing the arrival of their long awaited... messiah?"

"Yes, I was. But I believe messiah's not the right term," the president said. Suddenly, his eyes widened. "Wait, don't tell me. The same human we've been chasing?"

"Unknown, sir. But that's the way our analysts are leaning. Anyway, she's disappeared from public view, ever since that announcement."

"Probably went into hiding when she heard about the general."

"Most likely, sir."

"Alright. I have to go over relocation plans for the Oberonnian refugees. The chamai are expelling all Coalition species from the planet," the president said. "Tell me, General, who is likely to take charge now that Nylis is out of the way?"

The general scrunched up his face.

"Let me guess. You don't know?"

"Well, we know who's next in the chain of command, but whether or not she's on board with the coup, or if she's the favored choice of the human running things... it's just not clear yet."

"Understood," Harold sighed, as he headed toward the door. "Oh," he said, stopping short. "Do you have any actual... evidence... that the assassination was done by Parliament?"

"Well, yes... some. But it's still inconclusive."

"Lose it," the president said.

"Sir?"

"You heard me. If Parliament is gonna be mixed up in all this, I want their brand name squeaky clean. You got that? Like… right-after-saving-New-Boston-twenty-something-years-ago squeaky clean."

"Understood, sir."

"Whatever comes up, within reason… you just bury it." He paused. "Or, better still," he tapped thoughtfully on his chin, "you keep it under wraps for later, in case we need it. A little leverage is always nice."

"Yes, sir, I'll make it happen," the general assured him. "Sir, are you sure you don't want to know about what happened on Gel Gonahaar?"

The president sighed. "Did they murder any politicians, or start an intergalactic incident?"

"Mmm, no sir. Not as such."

"In that case, Ephraim… absolutely fucking not."

19.2

INTERSTELLAR CELESTIAL OBJECT #RØ-KCC, known more commonly outside the official registry by its far simpler, and more appropriate name, *'The Rock'*, is but a lonely orphan, cold and lost, wandering the universe without its mother. Free floating and unbound from any star in which to orbit, it's a galactic nomad, traveling sunless, forever alone across the skies—or at least for the past few million years or so, maybe more. Likely thrown free due to some disaster from the solar system of its birth, it has looped instead for untold eons, on a path vague and indeterminate. Where it's come from, none could calculate—a gravitational relay among the stars. But where it's heading, the math grows simpler—lingering close by for the next millennium.

Many such objects traverse the skies, rogue planets being near as numerous as the very stars that surround them. Yet, The Rock remains unique, in both its makeup, and its manner. Comprised of mainly carbon, densely packed into the little world, it's now essentially a blackened diamond—its crystalline core, no doubt, a fitting jewel for any titan. Although it's a planetoid even smaller than Earth's distant dwarf cousin

Pluto, its density of mass allows a surface gravity far more accommodating to cultured living.

The Rock's fascinations, however, are twofold—the former natural, the latter not. At some point within her history, the lonesome planet had been occupied, the remains and ruins of a civilization still scattered across its ashy surface. Under and through it as well. A latitude line of crystal-walled boreholes—miles wide, and just as deep—blemish her equator, the purposes of which, if any, now being lost along with their builders. One lone city still survives, for countless eons utterly abandoned, yet its miraculous structures as strong and sturdy as if construction had just completed.

Shining out in the endless nighttime like a ship on a moonless ocean, the ancient city is now the home to PlayStar Amusements' Resort Casino. Like a flickering beacon in the darkness, the only spark upon the tarnished surface, it drew the *Bugeye* and its occupants onward like the proverbial moth towards its neon flaming.

Tachion looked down on the city from the monitor at his station, seeming unsure. "This is where the interceptor came? Are you certain?"

"Certain? No," Tàlto confessed, seated at Rook's old station at operations. "The last microbeacon was dropped over a half a light-year away. But this is the only place along their trajectory for a dozen light-years in any direction. Unless they continued straight on into the Barrens."

"Unlikely," the doctor said.

"I agree," Tàlto answered.

Flashpoint walked forward, leaning to look out the cockpit windscreen at the approaching planet. "Why would anyone want to vacation at a resort way out here? It's just a big, dead, black boulder."

"People don't come for the lovely views," Tàlto explained as he got up and headed forward. "They're not here for what they can see, but for what they can do. Which is just about anything. On the Rock, there are no rules. And if you prefer, no names." The lyghtan squeezed past the young seti, taking the copilot seat next to Bullit. "You better take us down somewhere out away from the city. The directive says we have to be landed on the surface before the planet passes into the barren zone."

"Hold up," Tachion said. "We have about twenty minutes still. Let's think about *why* exactly they would come here. Maybe we can figure a better place to put down. I mean... I doubt Rook and Denali are here for the pinochle tournament."

Bullit looked intently at the rows of ancient tunnels which pierced the world along her middle, visible already from their slowly lowering orbit. He pointed at them and shook his finger. "You know, Bullseye said something to me, about what he overheard on the *Okubi*," the seti told them, cautiously speculating. "Nylis and Yazir, they referred to their rendezvous base as... Trojan."

All four leaned forward, peering down at the lifeless-seeming shafts.

Flashpoint scratched his ear. "Do you think that they meant it literally? Like... an army hidden inside somewhere?"

Tàlto nodded slowly, the implication becoming clear. "This dirty old rock is due to approach Drak'min space pretty closely. Then in just a few days, reemerge in the Coalition. Wouldn't be the worst idea ever, to stash a fleet inside it. In fact," the tracker said, "it's probably exactly what I would do."

"But where?" Bullit asked. "Which one? There must be hundreds of them big enough. Between the dense carbon crust, and the shielding from the ancient walls of those tunnels... we'll never pick up anything if we try to scan down into them."

"And we certainly don't have time to fly over all of them and take a look," Tàlto added.

"No, we don't," Tachion said. "We have to be grounded in fifteen minutes. And even after that, flying around while in the Barrens is capped to a twenty-thousand-foot ceiling." The android stared silent for a moment, a sure sign that he was thinking. "Bullit, you said Bullseye claimed Yazir was going to meet at this Trojan base? With his own Drak'min fleet?"

"Allegedly, yes. If he wasn't hallucinating the whole thing."

"Well, we might not have much choice, other than simply wait for that to happen. After all, we can't scan the tunnels, but we can scan the skies. And, even cloaked, the wavelength displacement of a whole fleet of Drak'min vessels... That's bound to be detectable."

Tàlto turned to the doctor. "Yeah, that's good Doc. We just sit tight for a day or two, and when they show up, we follow them in."

Bullit shook his head. "But we can't monitor the whole equator, not from down there on the surface. Where the hell exactly are we supposed to land and still do this?"

Flashpoint spoke up quietly from the back of the vessel. "Well, the directive said no manned vessels can remain in orbit in the barren zone. But I didn't see it mention anything about satellites, or orbiting probes."

"Yeah. Good point cuz," Bullit said. "We can launch a Beagle probe and leave it in high polar orbit, and then pretty much just chill until it picks up the fleet. Maybe even get ourselves a nice relaxing suite at the casino."

Tachion shook his head. "I doubt it would be wise to show our fairly recognizable faces there," he said. "But, as to the rest of your plan... I can't think of any better."

Rook's son hopped up and got to work just behind them. "I'll take care of readying the probe," he called eagerly. "It won't take me but a minute."

"Excellent. Thank you, Flashpoint," Tachion commended him. "Bullit, why don't we begin our search for where we can land for a few days. Perhaps somewhe…"

The *Bugeye* suddenly lurched hard fore and starboard, tossing the passengers in their chairs. A deafening echo of shearing metal and popping explosions rumbled through the shuttle's hull. Flashpoint fell hard to the floor as a warning alarm began emphatically beeping. He quickly scampered back to his position to continue on his work.

"*Warning…*" the computer announced, in its unemotional tone, "*ionic pulse engines offline. Warning… auto-navigation has been disabled.*"

"Switching helm to manual!" Bullit shouted. "What in the fuck just happened?!"

"It sounded like a laser impact," Tàlto said, quickly toggling through a row of switches directly overhead.

"Checking sensors," called Tachion. "Shit, we have a ship on our tail. A big one. A 403-Ares, transponder registration out of Bruna Buru. It's taken out our sub-light engine, and main thrusters are failing. We're at twenty-five percent power."

"So I can tell!" Bullit cried, as he struggled against the yoke.

"Cloaking is offline," Tachion said, "but I've managed to get our shields up."

Tàlto checked his gauges. "We're losing altitude fast, one hundred twenty kilometers and falling."

"Yeah, thanks for the report," Bullit sniped, "but I can see that out the windscreen." Through the glass just in front of them, the dark planetoid was looming large—a sphere of blackened starlessness, with no real sense of the ground below them.

"Bullit, what's our status?" the android asked over the persistent beeping.

"We're just a minute or two from entering the atmosphere. I still have maneuvering thrusters working, and a little forward boost from the engine. But that's it."

"Can you keep us airborne?"

"For the moment, just barely," he said, wrestling with the controls. "But that's only if they let me. Another hit like that, the ground's gonna rise to meet us pretty quick!"

"I'm trying to hail them," the android said. He looked back over his massive shoulder. "Flashpoint, are you all right?"

"Yeah, I'm good," the seti chimed. "The Beagle probe is ready and activated."

"Well done. Tàlto, let's get that launched now, before we lose our chance to do so."

"Probe launching!" the lyghtan answered.

Finally, the other craft responded to the *Bugeye*'s hail. "*Unmarked vessel, this is Deldri Enzix, of the Darkcloak Bounty League,*" said a metamorph accent.

"What?! Are they here for me?" Flashpoint asked. "That lady Jaadoo, she said we had a month to pay!"

"*We have a guild sanctioned commission of apprehension against a member of your party. Land your vessel immediately, and surrender the Capellan ashi'mar, Lady Opal.*"

Flashpoint sat back in his father's seat, more than somewhat relieved.

Tachion responded. "Enzix, cease your fire! We have no such person in our company!"

"*Persons known to have apprehended her were seen boarding that vessel, in Krataar City, Oberonn.*"

"Fucking Stansky," Bullit mumbled, knowing just as easily it might have been him.

"*Your ship stands out quite a bit. An antique BG/i90, with no registry? No transponder? You know you'd be less inconspicuous with a fake one, than going around with none at all.*"

"He's right," added Tàlto.

"We appreciate the advice," the doctor responded, "but, as I told you, this Lady Opal is not with us. Many persons share use of this vessel. And we are on route here from Gel Gonahaar, not Oberonn."

"*I will give an opportunity to prove it. Land immediately to be searched. If the ashi'mar is not with you, you'll be free to go... with our apologies.*"

Tàlto shook his head. "Not likely. Trust me, I know these guys. I've worked with them. They'll interrogate us. Thoroughly. Until they get what they want. And then you and me, Doc, we'll no doubt have to pay for their losses in that rainstorm. I'm telling you now, there's no way in *hell* they're gonna let us go."

"Bullit," Tachion asked, "do you have enough control for evasive maneuvers?"

Bullit looked back, scrunching his face while still struggling with the yoke. "What are you, kidding me? I'm barely keeping us outta the dirt."

"Can we take them on the ground?" Flashpoint offered.

Tachion shook his head. "It's a scout class vessel," he told him, "more than three times the size as ours, and probably a minimum crew of twelve. Possibly many more.

A volley of autocannon fire lit up the night around them, racing past like a meteor storm, clearly intended as a final warning shot.

"Why have you never installed rear-facing guns on this thing?" Tàlto questioned.

"Have you seen all the nonsense on the top of this fuselage?" Bullit asked. "Where the hell would we even fit them? If only we had some sort of charge we could drop behind us."

Tachion's head popped up at that. "Ah! Perhaps we do," he said, standing to march toward the row of storage lockers. "Bullit, make more quickly toward the surface, as if we're going to land. Flashpoint, how was your instruction in more... improvised explosives?"

"I guess... alright. I think? What is it you want me to do?"

The android retrieved what he was looking for, then turned to pass it to Flashpoint. In his hands he held the portable nuclear powerpack he and James had taken from the chimor bunker back on Oberonn. "Can you rig this to overload?"

"Um, yeah. Yes, I think so. Sure! It's got over a dozen redundant fail-safes, though, specifically to keep that from happening. I'll need a minute or two to disable them. Or... fuck it, I'll just bypass them all, and cycle the power into a rapid feedback loop."

"Let me talk to the bounty hunters," Tàlto said. "I can try and stall them for a few."

Tachion looked at Flashpoint. "Do it," he said. Then he nodded to Tàlto.

"Deldri Enzix, this is Tàlto Lastnâm, independent tracker and duly registered member of the guild. As my associate already notified you, your prize is not aboard. But you must realize that, even if she was, I could claim my right of prior acquisition. By guild regulation, you are required to let us pass."

Bullit scowled at him. "Really? Finders keepers? You find that argument generally works for you?"

"I don't know," the lyghtan mumbled. "Figured it was worth a try."

"*Ah, a fellow guild member,*" the voice on the radio responded. "*Then as you're probably aware, the Darkcloaks have never been overly fond of that particular regulation.*"

Tàlto shrugged an '*oh well*' at Bullit. "Or any regulation," he answered into the radio.

"True enough," Deldri said. *"Tàlto, you say. I see your name listed here, as a recognized abettor of the ashi'mar's captors. You were one of those who helped her kidnappers escape from Krataar... despite your commission to the contrary. You know, the brother of my wife was killed in that skirmish on Oberonn. And unfortunately for you, still needs avenging."*

"Ugh, come on. Does he really?" Tàlto brazenly asked. "Be honest, Deldri, you probably want to thank me. I mean... nobody cares that much for their in-laws, do they?"

There was laughter over the comlink. *"Very true, fellow Lastnâm. My brother-in-law was a real jasiri's backside. But... I would never suffer another moment's peace, if my wife ever heard that I had somehow let you live."*

"Well, I won't tell her if you won't."

"Mmm. I appreciate the offer, but probably best if I simply carry your severed head home to her by the hair."

Tàlto rubbed his hand across his shimmering black baldness. "Yeah, good luck with that."

"I got it!" Flashpoint yelled, returning the generator to Doctor Magna. "But once I engage the overload, there won't be much time. Maybe only twenty seconds."

Bullit overheard that, and double checked his sensors. "He's only a hundred meters off our stern. I know that generator's small, but... if you throw that out the back, we might still be caught in the blast wave at that range."

"You'll just have to punch it," Tachion told him. "Use whatever boost we have left, and take advantage of the planet's gravity, maybe. Just... dive-bomb towards the surface, get us farther away from it."

"Oh, is that all? just *dive-bomb* toward the surface?"

Tachion and Flashpoint went quickly to the airlock and opened the inner door. The young seti laid the thrumming generator on the floor of the small alcove, and hovered his finger over a blinking button, preparing to bypass the unit's energy back into itself. "Ready?" he asked, looking up at Tachion.

"Ready, Bullit?" the doctor called.

"Sure," Bullit answered. "Why the hell not."

Flashpoint jabbed the button, and the device's warnings began to flash. Tachion pulled the seti away as he slid closed the inner door, counting down in his head with digital precision. When the passing seconds hit fifteen, he decided that was enough, and slammed his metal fist on the release switch for the outer hatch to open. "Go!" he shouted to Bullit, as the power case was sucked out.

The *Bugeye* then veered steeply downward as the remaining thrusters launched her forward, hurrying them toward the surface in a panic to get away. From behind came a flash of light, a bright but silent supernova, bathing the terrain they were descending toward in a brief moment of glaring sunlight—a splendor the dusty landscape had not felt in well over a thousand millennia. The brilliance faded once again as quickly as it had arisen, and for several long moments, the foursome sat in silence, simply waiting, watching through the cockpit as the *Bugeye* swiftly descended.

The impact from behind was like a wave tossing them in the sea, washing over them, and forcing them forward, as it rolled them in its wake. The field generator that usually kept occupants in their places cut out, and loose contents of the craft began tumbling around the cabin, as the passengers gripping tight to hold themselves in their seats.

"*Warning... inertial dampeners offline,*" the computer announced over a new array of beeping alarms.

"Status!" Tachion shouted.

"The Ares is going down!" Tàlto responded.

"Yeah, but we've got a new problem!" Bullit yelled above the beeping. "The electromagnetic pulse from that blast just took out our shield generators! All of them, including our thermal barrier!"

"Well, that's not good," Tàlto told him, checking the instrument readings. "Current velocity... mach twenty-five. Altitude... sixty kilometers, and..."

"Don't you dare say 'and descending'!" Bullit snapped at him. "Why don't you stop with the pointless play-by-play, and help me pull this bird up? Transfer power from the main engines to the maneuvering thrusters. See if we can get the nose of this old bitch up a little bit, flatten her belly against the atmosphere to slow our descent."

The darkened skies outside the windows began to glow bright with red-hot plasma, as the speed of their descent compressed and superheated the air before them.

Yet another alarm joined the chorus. "*Warning... exterior hull temperature exceeding recommended threshold.*"

"The atmosphere on this boulder is fairly thin!" Bullit shouted. "The hull on its own should still hopefully take the heat!"

There was an ear-splitting squeal of tearing metal and banging steel. "*Warning... communications array offline.*"

"The hull might take it!" Tachion responded. "But all our sensors and antennas surely won't!"

The craft shimmied and vibrated as it became fully engulfed in fire.

"Twenty kilometers!" Tàlto called out. "Current hull temperature, fifteen hundred degrees kelvin!"

They sat in silence for a tense while, watching the ferocious blaze outside the window. Finally, after several moments that seemed an eternity, the flames started to abate, just as the turbulence that shook them kicked itself into high gear. Bullit and Tàlto struggled hard together, trying to keep her flying level as she rattled like a jackhammer. The window on the co-pilot side suddenly cracked through the midline, the thick pane threatening to shatter and come crashing in on the lyghtan's face. Bullit immediately lowered the outer metal shielding on that side. "The last thing we need is that breaking. The air here isn't breathable."

"Nor particularly warm," Tàlto added. Another shearing crunch of metal vibrated through the hull. "Alright, so there goes the long-range sensor array!"

"That's okay!" Tachion assured them. "We can still get data from the probe!"

"Not that it's going to matter much," Tàlto said, "if this bird isn't still flyable!"

"Don't jinx me!" Bullit told him.

"Two kilometers!" Tàlto shouted.

Bullit poured all the ship's power into the front maneuvering thrusters—a final attempt to keep the nose up. "Okay! You guys better buckle up! This is probably not going to be one of my signature graceful landings! Doc, no offense, but you might want to secure yourself somewhere in the back! Last thing we need is your heavy ass flying across the fuselage!"

Tachion hopped up and struggled to his biostation, quickly retracting the bed into the wall. Then he activated the interior forcefield, trapping himself inside the area. The large android slouched down to sit on the floor, bracing his legs against one of the *Bugeye*'s support beams.

The dark, dusty terrain of the planet's featureless landscape made it difficult to visually estimate the speed or distance of their descent. There seemed to be no true frame of reference—nothing to indicate if that shadowy plateau up ahead was a mile across, or in fact twenty. But the latest emphatic warning from the computer let them know they were, in fact, quite hurriedly approaching it. *"Terrain, pull up... Terrain, pull up,"* it repeated.

Bullit hit a switch to shutter closed his windshield as well. "Okay everybody! Hold on to your asses!"

"Brace... Brace... Brace... Brace..."

The sturdy little ship came down hard with a bang, sliding through kicked up clouds of black carbon as the *Bugeye* scratched its way violently sideways across the landscape. Flashpoint flew forward across the deck plates, still strapped in his father's chair, as Tàlto rapped the side of his head violently on the row of toggle switches just above him. Tachion's leg bracing wasn't helpful with the constant impacts from the side, and he was flung repeatedly against the force screen, like a bug into a windshield. But the field held and he fell back, a sizable dent in his bicep plating. The ship continued its loud scraping as it slid across the surface, seemingly just waiting for something to dare to stop it—until it crunched its port stabilizer wing against a dark crystalline outcropping. The sound of the impact was deafening. Finally, the *Bugeye* came to rest, all its alarms suddenly falling silent, just the sound of the damaged hull creaking and popping, and an unhealthy stutter in the familiar wail of the engines winding down.

They sat there breathing, quiet in the darkness, until Tàlto broke the silence. "Well, I have to say... that was not too shabby overall. You should pat yourself on the back, Bullit. Although, I would have tried not to rip the wing off like that, if I were you. It's going to make it extra hard for us to ever get the hell out of here."

"I'll be sure to remember that for next time," Bullit remarked sarcastically.

Tachion clambered up to his station, looking at his remaining sensor readings. The Beagle's data was still displayed. "Well, planetoid #RØ-KCC has now officially entered The Barrens," he told them. "Welcome to that part of space where usually *no one* is allowed to be." He looked around at the scattered interior. "Flashpoint, are you okay? Tàlto? It looks like you're bleeding."

"Don't worry about me, it's just a scratch," said Tàlto. "Give me a wad of gauze to hold against it, and take care of the kid instead. Besides, a couple of extra scars aids my menacing appearance."

"I'm good... I think," said Flashpoint, struggling to his feet. "So... what are we going to do now? Call for help, and just wait for rescue?"

"No," the doctor told him, "all communications were lost when we burnt off our antennas. We'll have to evaluate the damage, and see if we can rig something."

"What about just calling on our multicomms?"

"The Rock doesn't have any comm relay satellites, so we'd be lucky to get a signal this far from the casino."

"Ah yes," Bullit said, crawling out from the jumbled cockpit, "the casino. Do you remember when I suggested we should just go wait there?

We could be all eating bottomless shrimp cocktails and relaxing at the bar right now."

"Believe it or not," Tàlto told him, "we're probably better off here. Checking out those ancient equatorial boreholes is only a guess. For all we know, Denali's actually back at the city right now, watching every camera for a glimpse of your familiar faces. Honestly... I can't think of anything *stupider* we could be doing right now, beyond casually walking in through the front door of that casino."

19.3

JAMES STANSKY, AND HIS COMRADE BULLSEYE, casually walked in through the front door of the casino. On the distinguished seti's left, clinging daintily with both hands to the crook of his angled elbow, hung his lovely escort, Relic, draped in her usual elegant attire. On Stansky's right, a chamai woman—one far closer to plain than she was pretty, despite the flash of her trendy costume—accompanied the dapper human with a similar attentive style. Behind them came Belladonna, the epitome of grace and glamour, marshalling the group forward toward the center of the massive lobby. Bringing up the rear, and some steps behind, a large white seti entered, walking backward—Chief Zvavi, still in dirty work clothes, and scanning around himself in amazement.

"Chief," Bullseye said, as their pilot nearly backed into him, "I heartily apologize for our need to wrench you from your duties, but with the *Bugeye*... otherwise occupied... we simply lack the requisite pilots among us for the multiple vessels that were required."

"Not at all. Think nothing of it, Master Bullseye," Zvavi reassured him. "No mortal soul was ever worsened by opening eyes to such new wonders. In truth, 'tis a pleasure to take in sights beyond what tool lay in my hand. And *here...* my goodness. What a beauty, and yet a tragedy, both at once to behold it is."

The alien city, from afar, was simply wonderous to be sure—a literal, polished gemstone upon a world of darkened ash. Built of the only abundant material widely available on the small planet, the tight grove of skyscrapers had been fashioned from compressed carbon, forming a crystalline skyline—towering spires of pure diamond, iridescent in the night sky. But even the marvel of that vista paled to the spectacle revealed inside it. The lavish, multicolored lights, which illuminated each and every crystal monolith, were cast through, then reflected off a million sparkling little facets. The walls themselves were a twinkling rainbow, countless pinpoints of mirrored colors, the cathedral ceilings as fluorescent as an aurora shining bright.

Those same lofted ceilings soared a staggering two hundred feet above them—though no exohistorian had ever reasoned why the builders wished them quite so high. Placed floor to ceiling, every few dozen meters throughout the expansive, vaulted space, towering angular columns of metal machinery seemed to help support the gemstone structure. The dark mechanical monoliths were illuminated with a myriad of shimmery lighting, but any intended purposes beyond that were but another mystery lost to the ages. The undulations of their persistent twinkling, in hues of white, and teal, and blue, cast ghostly patterns upon the patrons, like ripples of sunlight beneath the water.

The clientele themselves were, without question, the very crustiest of the upper crust; walking embodiments of class and culture, of elegance and stature, of stylishness and taste. The elite and powerful from every administration and every industry, yet that sophistication quickly devolved the very moment they were welcomed in.

All around the massive lobby, avarice and debauchery were on display. To the left, in a large forcefield-covered pit, several of the green, hairless rodents James had seen consuming corpses on the battlefield, now branded with numbers on their sides, snapped and grappled to the death over tiny scraps of offered sustenance. A circle of onlookers cheered and wagered. Around the more standard gaming tables wandered prostitutes of every manner—any shape, race, or preference of gender—unashamedly offering their labors, at what was almost certainly exorbitant pricing. Along with the servicebots offering spirits, were those as well dispensing chemicals— substances of a recreational nature—that were readily swallowed, snorted, or dripped into the eye, or under the tongue. For those without the good fortune to find their euphoria in the thrill of winning, one could always make do with a wide array of prescribed substitutes.

Opal gazed in disdain at the greed, gluttony and hedonism, the lip of her chamai facemask sneering upward at the corner. Directly above her was a holographic sign:

PlayStar's 'The Rock' Resort & Casino
Where There Isn't Any Daylight,
The Nightlife Never Ends!

She sighed. "And so it begins... the end of civilization," she mumbled sadly.

"Alas, dear Lady Opal," Bullseye interjected, "I fear the end of civilization, in fact, started at the very beginning of it."

The disguised ashi'mar nodded in somber agreement, then turned to look at James. "Does my face still look all right? I think it's a little bit more... wrinkled... than when the Guisemage, or rather Selene, put it on."

"It looks just fine," Stansky said, eagerly eyeing the casino floor rather than even facing her.

"*Fine?*"

"It looks fantastic, I mean," he told her, this time looking her in her chamai eyes.

"Mmm, I don't know. I wish Tachion had been there to help me."

James gazed down at his hands and silently wished the same. The last of the medication the doc had given him had been used up the day before. The tremors would likely return soon. He had become accustomed to the ease of a brief few days without them. But he shouldn't allow himself to forget, that beneath the relief of any medication, the disease grows on stronger nonetheless, indifferent to such temporary measures.

The congregation shuffled further across the crowded lobby. Belladonna glanced around, making note of the security system, pleased the great majority of the cameras were centered on the gaming floor. "Okay, James," she prompted, "you said you know someone here that can help?"

"Yeah, she's a... an old friend," the human explained, looking cautiously down at Opal. "Someone that I... used to know, but who still owes me a few favors."

"Remember," she reminded him, "we just need to know where the energy utilities control center is, and what rooms are nearest by. Those systems should be low enough priority that Relic can remotely gain at least 'read-only' access."

"All the systems of this planetoid," Bullseye explained further, "both those archaic and those modern, both found here and her equator, appease their ample lust for energy from the teat of a single bosom. A geothermal reactor, cloistered deep beneath the city. If Relic should be successful in determining the location of its utmost draw, we may well find ourselves a waypoint which conducts us toward Denali."

"And to my father," Relic added. "I only need to get within... oh... fifty feet or so of the computer. Just a room or two away. I'll download a snapshot of the entire power grid's current usage, and see if some excess need of energy can show us where Nylis' fleet is."

James rolled his eyes. "Yes, I get it! I'll find out where the utilities are!" he huffed. "I radioed to Shimara as soon as we touched down. She said she'd come find me near this lobby." He looked around the games again, clearly eager to go and play. "In the meantime, we shouldn't all stand clustered around, like we're waiting for the bus to Chinatown. We'd draw less attention if we mingle with the players a little bit."

"I don't know if that's a good idea," Belladonna cautioned, turning to point out the array of surveillance devices. "We don't want to get picked up by some security..."

But he was already gone, towing Lady Opal fast behind him.

The foursome of remaining seti headed to wait at the lobby bar, choosing a table near the gaming floor from where they could watch their impetuous friend. Bullseye instinctively took Relic's hand as they sat, but feeling the weight of her mother's gaze at the corner of his eye, he released it, and pulled away. Relic wouldn't have it. She reached out to retrieve it, and cradled it on her lap. Belladonna's stare abated.

Zvavi leaned in toward Bullseye, while a servicebot passed out cocktails that no one had asked for. "If I may inquire, Master Bullseye," the chief asked, "this Denali, is it truth he was once a member of your company?"

"Indeed," Bullseye answered. "Or, well... mayhap. It is yet uncertain. We believe him to be a human named James Dodger."

"*James* Dodger?"

"Aye."

"So then... there was, at one time, *two* humans... both by the name of James," Zvavi considered. "How were you able to discern the one from the other?"

Bullseye chuckled. "The similarity of human appearance tends to wane once you've come to know them, and been in their company for a while."

"Not to mention," Belladonna added, "they each have a unique... odor."

"Mmm. I did notice that," Zvavi was quick to agree.

"I grew up with them," Relic told him, "and it *still* gave me difficulty. But it's far easier than the metamorph. At least humans come in different colors."

Bullseye smiled at her joyfully. "Also," he said, turning his attention back to Zvavi, "our friend with us here, he now and always went by James. The other's preference was for Jim."

"What is Jim?" Zvavi asked.

"Simply... an abbreviation."

The chief nodded in understanding, then tilted his head in puzzlement. "Would the abbreviation for James, not in fact, become... Jam?"

"Ah. So one would think."

An uproar of applause drew their attention back to Stansky. He and Lady Opal stood at the far end of a large, rectangular table, playing a variation of a simple dice and domino game, made popular in the back alleys of Gel Gonahaar. The objective was quite straightforward—select from an array of marked dominos, with pips numbering from two to sixteen, and lay five of them on the table. Then roll a set of eight-sided dice, and try to match your bet; less than the lowest domino, or greater than the highest, or in between the two. The risk of the gamble entered in when forced to choose which bet you favored *before* each random selection, based upon your memory of what values still remain. It seemed that Stansky had, thus far, been making his choices correctly.

The crowd of gamblers fell to silence as he prepared once again to draw. He laid his entire credit stack with confidence on the line marked 'between', then reached a hand into the spinning drum to make his next selection. He placed the thick, ebony tiles one by one on the crimson velvet: six—six—seven—eight—eight. A most unfortunate draw. The throng of gamblers that had been cheering him quickly turned to hiss and boo, knowing now those who had bet along with him could only win if he rolled a seven. The casino dealer offered insurance, allowing him to push with a six or eight. But he declined. Taking such a deal to lessen the chance of losing would decrease his payout odds were he to win. Immediately the entire table took out insurance of their own against him.

James rattled the dice set in his hand, then blew on them within his fist. But just as he was about to roll, he stopped and turned to Opal. He handed the pair to her, bidding the ashi'mar to do the honors. She looked nervous, but so did he, holding crossed fingers out before him.

"What is the meaning of this gesture?" Zvavi asked. "The entwining of one's digits."

"An Earthan custom," Bullseye told him. "Humans seek to alter the winds of fate in their favor, by creating this symbol with their fingers."

"A prayer of religion?" The chief inquired.

"Not one that I've ever been able to ascertain."

"Hmm. Curious. And so then... does it work?"

Lady Opal shook her fist, then let the dice fly across the table, as a dozen and a half faces leaned in close to read the outcome. A cheer of triumph exploded up, and Stansky's coins were quickly quadrupled.

"Surprisingly often," Bullseye muttered.

A human woman approached the table, touching Stansky on the elbow—an Asian girl, with a freckled porcelain nose, and bright violet streaks through the bangs and ponytail of her raven hair. James collected his credits hastily, then awkwardly turned to embrace her, opting for the one-arm half hug rather than a full two-armed commitment. The lovely young human made a comment to Opal, who in turn made a face like she might haul off and smack her. Stansky quickly placed his large frame between them, and bending in order to whisper something to Lady Opal, he then sent her scurrying toward the table of watching seti. James and the strange woman sought out a private corner in which to speak.

"Are you all right, my lady?" Relic asked on her return.

"James' little... *friend* introduced herself by asking who the chamai hag was!"

Belladonna scoffed. "Well, our human cohort there... he isn't known for his taste in women." Then, suddenly realizing, offered, "I mean... present company excluded, Lady Opal."

"Don't worry. And *please*, just Opal. Especially around here."

James and the woman continued talking, it seeming more and more apparent that he was explaining himself out of something. Finally, she slapped his face—but then caressed it, and kissed his cheek. The ashi'mar's eyes were as deadly as freshly poisoned daggers. Eventually the pair came forward, the woman leading Stansky to the casino guide map. After pointing out several areas, she reached up once more to lightly touch him— then she was gone. The human watched her leave, then turned to wave his comrades over.

The large computer panel display was an entire map of the whole facility—this one local building of it, anyway. A blinking icon at the bottom declared in many languages that 'You Are Here'."

"Alrighty," Stansky said, directing their attention to the northeast corner. "Shimara says what we're looking for is in here, in this unlabeled back area. It's a power relay junction from the station below. We can't turn anything on or off from there, or affect the generator, or the power grid in any way. All that it does is reroute the juice from one capacitor to another. But, as such, it's low priority, and isn't encased in much security. Most importantly, it does have access to view the power grid dispersal."

"Perfection, it would seem," Bullseye asserted, "exactly fit to meet our needs." He pointed to the map. "This expansive chamber here, immediately adjacent. The Kohinoor Room. May we now journey our way there? Might it be unfettered for public access?"

"Well, no... not so much. That's where we have a problem," James said. "That room, unfortunately, *is* highly secure. It's for the high stakes tel'jagara tournaments. Just bigwigs and high rollers, and *strictly* invite only."

Opal scrunched up the nose on her wrinkled chamai face. "What, by the Originators, is a tel'jagara tournament?"

"A drak'min card game," Belladonna told her. "One recently trendy among the elite. I suppose for its perceived... exoticness? Or maybe forbidden nature?"

"So what can we do?" Relic asked. "I mean... I should only need about fifteen minutes or so, somewhere near that east wall."

James leaned in, speaking quietly. "Shimara is gonna enter us in the tournament," he explained. "Whichever one of us we choose. That person will have to go play, bringing you along as their guest. While the game is going on, you gain access to the utility servers. Unfortunately, the next opening at a table isn't for another thirty-two hours."

Relic's mother shook her head. "Thirty-two hours, or thirty-two weeks... it's not gonna work for us anyway. The group we have here? Any of us would be identified instantly when they run us through security. Except perhaps Opal in disguise. But by the looks of it, I'm not sure that mask can last another day and a half."

Opal hit Stansky on the chest. "See! I told you it was getting wrinkly."

Bullseye stoked at his beard hairs in thought. "We must need conjure forth an unknown. One whose foretime may be contrived to match that of a high-stakes gambler. Then dispatched as our champion, with Relic posed as paramour."

"That's not all we need," Stansky said. "They also have to learn to play championship level tel'jagara. In a *day*, no less. Or, at least play well enough that they can hold their seat for twenty minutes."

Zvavi chimed in from behind them. "The principles of the game are not overly perplexing," he told them. "'Tis rather akin to the seti pastime of 'omens and oracles', though bearing a far wider array of suits. And, of course, lacking the grim shadow of ominous portents."

Silence befell the group as they all looked knowingly at one another, then each of their heads swiveled to turn toward Chief Zvavi.

"Well, after all, I do abide upon a deep space vessel, mainly expatriates of the Drak'min Empire as my crewmates," he explained. "On idle weeks, betwixt charters, playing cards may grow quite loftier than some mere innocent pastime to ease the hours. It oft becomes a way of life," he chuckled.

The stares continued.

"I once claimed ultimate victory of the title match, no less, championing for the lower decks. And I... I... what? Wh-what is it?" Zvavi turned in confusion to look behind him, wondering what all the others might be gaping at. The large seti's snowy fur was marred with its usual spots of grease and oil, and his topknot of bundled mane was tangled in the straps of green-lensed welding goggles. The visor's shape had left a shadow of dusty filth against his forehead. The tan jumpsuit he wore today was less shocking than his usual orange, but still just as worn and dirty as every other in his daily wardrobe. He looked back at them. "Hold, but a moment. Master Stansky, Master Bullseye? You... surely cannot be of the mind of... commissioning *me* for this operation?"

Bullseye frowned. "What dare we think, masterful ladies? I fear an undertaking of such magnitude lies outside my expertise. Can in truth something be done with our loyal companion here? Can we fabricate his passing, for... a tycoon, of wealth and stature?"

Opal and Belladonna promptly began fussing with his hair.

"Let's get a room upstairs," Belladonna said, "and see what can be done with all this mess."

"Agreed," Bullseye said. "Several separate rooms might be wise, to concoct the illusion we travel not all bound together. James, you and I then, accompany me to the hotelier. And whilst we secure accommodations, Lady Opal, Belladonna, Relic... would you be so kind as to endeavor in chaperoning our friend Zvavi's shopping."

The ladies dragged the mechanic off, to much vigorous protesting.

19.4

"DOES ANYBODY HAVE THE SLIGHTEST clue what friggin' tool is meant to fit this part?" Bullit asked, clearly exasperated, and holding aloft a notched cylinder from beneath the *Bugeye*'s deck plates.

Tachion looked up from his own repair work to examine it. "Honestly? I don't even know what that thing is."

Bullit popped up his head and threw the canister in frustration. "Alright, we've been at this for a day and a half now, and we still haven't managed to repair a single system. We've got no Chief Zvavi, no Stansky. How did the other guys end up with all the mechanics on their side?"

"Perhaps we should have thought to recruit one before we went AWOL," Tachion snipped.

"I'm a bit of a mechanic," Tàlto told him, leaning back in Bullseye's chair. "Or... at least I know a thing or two."

"Fine. Then help me get this engine online, before we run down the battery and lose all our life support."

"I would," the lyghtan said. "But that's... not one of the two things I know."

Bullit furrowed his brow at him. "I'm not very fond of you," he growled, disappearing back below.

Tachion clattered a burned-out magnetic constrictor to the floor. "I don't know if it's a matter of tools or knowledge that's the problem," he said. "What we need are parts. If not for the engine, then at least for the comms relay."

Tàlto leaned forward. "Well... what about the downed Ares? I'm sure we could scavenge her for some junk."

The doctor cocked his head. "It's possible, I suppose. If we actually knew where she was. We lost sensor data before she impacted."

Bullit's head re-emerged. "The computer is still operational," he said, heaving himself up to sit on the edge of the deck plates, legs still dangling into the open floor. "Let's just ask it to extrapolate, based on the ship's last trajectory. I mean, she can't be more than three... maybe five miles behind us."

"Or maybe ten," Tachion told him.

"Still, that's totally doable. We could walk that in a few hours."

"*I* could walk it," the android reminded him. "You three would choke to death, if you didn't freeze first."

"We don't have any EV suits?" Flashpoint asked.

"Well, two of the last three environmental suits we had got left behind on the *Okubi*." Tachion told him, looking accusingly at Bullit. "But I suppose that means I could still take one of you."

"Not it!" Bullit called. "No chance. I promised myself after that last fiasco, no more heading out into the unknown without *proper* armor wrapped around me."

"As I recall," Tàlto suggested, "old Jimbo had an ample collection of PA armor he kept around. Is that still the case? I'm sure he wouldn't mind if we borrowed a suit... or three."

Within three quarters of an hour, they were exiting through the airlock, stepping out cautiously onto a convenient outcropping that was wedged against the ship. It would doubtless prove far less convenient later, when they tried to take off.

The endless starry depths of the void above were enough to shock one's breath away. Deep space itself was no unique sight; it persisted constantly out any porthole. But walking out here in the open, across the dark, dusty graphite surface, the galactic arm spiraled overhead, and a dozen light-years from any sunlight—without that familiar, comforting cocoon of a fuselage around them, it gave the unnerving impression of being adrift among the stars. The drastic curvature of the tiny planet was easily visible on the horizon, and the sensation they were merely clinging to an asteroid flung through space was palpable—almost nauseating. It could be enough to make those more faint of heart drop to the ground, and hold on for dear life.

They paraded off in the direction of what they decided to call east, the heading not really meaning anything on a world with no sunrise, nor magnetic poles, and a randomly chaotic rotation to its axis. They trudged onward across the eerie, black terrain, three in massive suits of powered armor—nicknamed Shimara, Valkyrie, and James' prized favorite suit Geeta—with Tachion leading the way, perfectly content in his regular battlegear. He had neither the need, nor ability, to fit in any of Stansky's larger sets.

The landscape here was truly alien—wide, desolate plains of utterly barren and unbroken darkness, followed by strange mountainous regions with the summits curiously inverted. The towering formations were widest at their peaks; jagged plateaus, tapering down toward a narrow base. To some they seemed akin to upside-down pyramids, somehow mushrooming from the ground. To others, the teeth of a cosmic dragon, broken off when it bit the world. It couldn't help but become foreboding, despite the common knowledge that the world around them was completely lifeless. At least, hopefully so. They carried on for several miles, a trail of imprints left behind them—heavy footprints through the dust where perhaps none before had ever trodden.

Close to three hours into their march, Flashpoint began to grow worried, and grow weary, despite the assistance of his armor's motors in his walking. He used the magnification mode on his visor to zoom in on the distance before them, but there was nothing. A far-off, black, tumbled escarpment beneath the same bright, uncaring stars. *"Maybe we've gone the wrong way,"* the young seti speculated through his helmet's comlink. *"We've come almost eight miles already, and I don't see any wreckage yet."*

Tachion checked the status of his companions' life support on his scanner. *"We might as well continue a bit further, until we get to maybe eighty percent of your oxygen's halfway point,"* Tachion told him. *"Don't forget, on this little dwarf world, the diameter is so small that the curve on the planet becomes a problem. Even on Earth, you can't really see more than three or four miles ahead at around sea level. Then things become hidden below the horizon. Here? We probably can't even see a full mile at the most. The Rock is so little, we might not get a glimpse of debris until we're on top of it."*

And then they were.

The smaller bits of wreckage were spread along a scar of about a quarter mile, although two huge pieces still remained largely intact, on either side of a triangular butte of diamond. The narrow and hardened cliff face had done a fine job of splitting the craft in two, leaving neither side seeming favorable for any unfortunate survivors. There didn't seem to be any. There were signs that fire had broken out, though the lack of oxygen had quickly extinguished it, but apparently not before it had seared a pair of crewmen along with the crumpled wreckage. They passed two broken bodies strewn here and there in the graphite powder, tossed amongst the flotsam. An icy coat of frost had accumulated atop the charred flesh—a fuzzy fluff of snow reminiscent of something long abandoned in a freezer.

The name on the torn Ares fuselage was inscribed as the *Sereya Mel*.

Tàlto surveyed the broken wreckage as he scanned with his sensors. He shook his head. *"The odds that we're gonna get anything useful out of this mess? Pretty slim, I'd say."*

"This was your idea," Bullit reminded him.

"Hey, it's not my fault their pilot steered into a giant rock. I mean... look at it! I don't even think we can get inside. Not through those jumbles of twisted steel."

"Maybe we don't have to," the doctor told them. *"Tàlto, why don't you and I go around towards the engine area, see if those 'one or two things' you know*

about mechanics can help us find a T-shunt to fit the plasma coupler. And hopefully a magnetic constrictor. Bullit, see if you can get atop her fuselage, salvage us a comms relay and an antenna dish, if you can find it. Flashpoint, take a tour around. See if you can find any access to the inside."

"Alright," Flashpoint agreed, heading to the forward part of the ship.

"We'll have to be quick about it," Bullit reminded them. *"We're almost at the halfway point of our oxygen."* He stomped off in the same direction.

Tachion and Tàlto made their way toward what appeared to be the engine wreckage, the way marked by a large, dissected thrust nozzle and manifold, perched precariously atop an angled, black rock like a tombstone. They journeyed quietly past it.

Tachion walked behind, moving to balance a hand atop his dangling sword hilt. *"Tàlto, I have to ask... what exactly you are doing here?"*

"Same as you, I suppose. I mean... I don't really understand the question."

"Well, you say you were hired by your queen to recover the ashi'mar. But you betrayed that royal command, opting to protect Lady Opal instead. Still, after all of that... a treachery which I'm sure won't make you a favorite in the eyes of the crown... you decide to abandon Opal after all, and travel here along with us. I guess I just don't get it. So it makes me ask again, what exactly are you really doing here?"

"I told you, better to nip the threat at the source, then to..."

"Yes, I know, I know," Tachion said. *"Take the fight to Denali, rather than wait for him to come to us. I just... I remember you as being far more... well... let's call it regimented, in your religious beliefs. And in your loyalty to the lyghtan throne. It seems surprising to me that you would have gone against Queen Vasu. But, assuming you realized just what she was up to, and that you intended to protect the integrity of the throne by turning to save Lady Opal... it then feels even less likely that you would later desert her. Clearly, you've changed. You're not exactly the man that I once knew, and that's fine. Even still, your choices make it seem like you're serving an agenda of your own. An agenda you have yet deigned to share with the rest of us."* The android tightened his grip on the EMD.

"You can trust me, Doctor Magna, when I tell you my agenda is the same as yours," Tàlto assured him. *"You have my word on that. My end goal is no different. As far as me seeming changed? Well, an awful lot of years have passed. There's been a lot of water under the bridge."*

"Has there."

Tàlto then pointed straight ahead. A large piece of tail section was still intact, with what looked like the central motivator of the ionic pulse unit still inside. *"Ah-ha, looky there! We might have some luck on our side after all,"* he said. *"Let's see if any of these Ares pieces will even fit into a Bugeye."*

Flashpoint called across the comm link. "*Hey, I found something. A hatchway maybe, or some kinda doorway. It's inside a sort of... tube... indent... chamber.*"

Tàlto squinted at Tachion. "*What the hell is a tube indent chamber?*"

Flashpoint called again. "*Oh! I think I know what it is. Actually, it looks like a...*"

He didn't finish.

"*It looks like a what, Flashpoint?*" Tachion asked him.

Only silence came over the radio.

"*Flashpoint?*" the android called, turning to look at the fuselage in the distance.

Still no answer.

"*Bullit, do you have eyes on Flashpoint?*"

"*Negative, I'm on the starboard side,*" he answered. "*Behind the cliff, up by the cockpit. I found an antenna. I'm just trying to detach it. Do you want me to go find him? He was going behind the port wreckage.*"

The doctor looked at his team's current O^2 levels. "*No, we're closer. Just keep going. We don't have much time.*"

They headed back past the engine tombstone, and around the carcass of the *Sereya Mel*, following the perimeter of her left side. Flashpoint's footprints led the way in the ankle-deep dust just ahead of them.

"*Flashpoint, do you read me?*" Tachion called as they traced his journey, slowing as they approached what appeared to be an alcove in the ship's hull. They each pulled an autopistol, then counting down together in handspeak, swung their weapons around the corner.

The alcove was just exactly as Flashpoint had described it, a sort of tubular indented chamber into the side of the vessel. A shallow, cylindrical shaft, with a hatchway at its terminal end. Tàlto and Tachion stood inside it, looking around.

Tachion asked, "*Does a 403-Ares spacecraft come equipped with... an escape pod?*"

"*Well, if it does,*" Tàlto answered, "*then this one's appears to be missing.*"

"*Oh, no,*" the android realized. "*So that means...*" The pair quickly turned around.

"*Weapons down please,*" an armored figure demanded, in a polite metamorph accent. His black cloak draped motionless in the absence of any wind. "*Fortunately, I'm still more interested in finding the ashi'mar, than in killing either of you.*"

"*Deldri Enzix, I presume,*" Tàlto greeted his fellow guild member. "*I thought you were interested in both. What happened to avenging your brother-in-law?*"

"Eh, what can I say. You were right. I never much cared for him, anyway. Under the circumstances, I'd just as soon quickly get a location from you and be on my way. This pursuit has already over-cost me."

"We did try to give you a chance to leave," Tàlto reminded him.

"Where's our companion," Tachion interjected. *"What did you do with him?"*

"Your young seti friend is just fine. For the moment, at least. My associate is... babysitting him."

"Wait, if you ejected in the pod," Tàlto asked, *"what are you doing back here? Looking for survivors?"*

"Actually, making sure there aren't any," Deldri laughed. *"You just increased my share of the bounty sixfold!"*

"Well, I'm glad we could be of service. Anything to help out a fellow tracker," Tàlto told him. *"So... there's just the two of you, then?"*

The shape-shifting bounty hunter retrained his AE rifle at the pair. *"Clever, trying to determine my numbers. But two, or two hundred, it doesn't matter much for you. Tell me where I can find the ashi'mar... exactly where... and who she is with, and how I can get to her. You do that, Fellow Lastnâm, and I'll consider setting you free."*

"Well, first of all, I haven't a clue. I know she was en route with the mercenary group Parliament, to your homeworld. But their intention was not to remain there. And I have no idea where they went next. Secondly, as far as trying to determine numbers, it's unfortunate that you didn't think to do the same with us."

"What?" Deldri asked, then turned around to look behind him.

"Hello," quipped Bullit, as he crossed the Darkcloak's helmet with a force mace.

The bounty hunter collapsed, his dropped rifle loudly skittering across a rock before it vanished beneath the deep ash. Tàlto produced an electrostunner from his side with the smoothness of a drawn saber, jabbing the arcing prod into the struggling tracker's side. He kept it there, Enzix convulsing wildly, until the lyghtan was sure the metamorph's consciousness was lost. *"Excellent timing,"* Tàlto announced afterward. *"A few seconds earlier, and I wouldn't have gotten my witty line out."*

"No, I would have waited," Bullit said. *"Nothing worse than someone jumping in before their cue."*

The three of them dragged the stunned body to the rear of the escape-pod launch tube, where Tàlto used a length of flexible trimithium zip cord to lash Deldri's wrists to the ship. Bullit cleared him of weapons, while Tachion snapped off the comms antenna from his dented helmet. *"He'll be asleep for several minutes,"* the doctor said. *"But, just in case, I don't want him reporting us to his friend."*

"Speaking of which," Bullit asked, *"any ideas of where he is? And my cousin with him?"*

"Shouldn't be hard to find," Tachion answered, pointing to blatant tracks Deldri had dragged through the graphite powder.

The trio moved to follow them.

The trail led around the broken remnants of the *Sereya Mel*, as well as the crystal bluff that had split her, then continued further west toward one of the smaller of the dragon's teeth. They approached the inverted hillside, cautious of eyes watching from above.

The cliff was relatively tiny—perhaps only forty feet high, while its largest neighbors seemed to reach for miles. The tower similarly seemed to be about forty feet across at the very top. But here, at the base, where its jagged point bit into the dusty soil, its width was slightly less than a single man laying prone. The trail ran cold here, the footprints ending just below it.

They gazed around, and then up. Bullit zoomed his visor in toward the top. *"Did that bounty hunter have a levitation belt on his armor?"*

"I didn't notice," Tachion answered.

Tàlto looked down at his own, circling the massive waist of Valkyrie. *"Well, fortunately, Stansky thought ahead, and put them on all his armor."*

"That's not gonna help me," the doctor said. *"They haven't made the belt yet that can manage to lift my weight."*

"Well, that's not exactly true. You can series a few together, get like four of them and..."

"Can you discuss that later?" Bullit interrupted. *"I'd like to try and find my cousin."*

Tàlto looked up. *"Well, I'm not fond of the idea of popping my head up just to get it shot off. If there's somebody up there, they must have seen us coming."*

Bullit thought for a moment. *"I'll go up from the side, you from the rear,"* he told him. *"That way, he can't get off a shot at both of us, and we won't be in each other's crossfire."*

"Ah, only a fifty-fifty chance of getting my head shot off," Tàlto said. *"That's much better. I'm in."*

Tachion waited helplessly behind as the two suits of armor took their places. Rising up from the powdery surface, the anti-grav belts hoisted their cargo, struggling somewhat against the mass of the mechanical armor. The doctor felt awkward and out of place as he stood idly by doing nothing, watching his two companions as they slowly neared the top. He wondered if it went bad up there, could his EMD sword cut through the crystal pedestal, toppling the plateau like a felled tree? Perhaps more importantly, could he move himself out of the way fast enough if he did? He'd have to be sure it was necessary before attempting it—both for his sake, and for theirs.

The pair of mercenaries reached the top, but to the doctor's surprise, there was no shooting. The android pulled his sword, and looked for the thinnest area he could slice through. "*Report?*" he requested.

He was greeted by a long silence.

"*Bullit, Tàlto, report please.*"

Finally, Bullit answered. "*We got him, Doc. Sorry, he had a comms jammer sitting next to him. We've disabled it.*"

"*He also had a tripwire strapped to his legs,*" Tàlto said, "*to keep him from moving.*"

"*I almost had it deactivated,*" Flashpoint told him.

"*You're lucky you didn't blow both your legs off,*" Bullit pointed out. "*Your mother would have had a hard time forgiving that.*"

"*Wait,*" Tachion called up. "*Where's his guard? Deldri's friend?*"

"*Well apparently,*" Tàlto said, "*he got his share of the bounty increased twelvefold instead of six. There is no guard. If there were any other survivors, Deldri used the excuse of the crash to make sure that they didn't stay that way.*"

Ten minutes later, they were back at the *Sereya Mel*. Bullit directed their attention to the cockpit section. "*If one of you gives me a hand, I can get that antenna dish off in half the time.*"

Tachion checked their life support readings, then gazed off westward from where they had come. He shook his head. "*Don't bother. There's no point now.*"

"*What do you mean?*" asked Flashpoint.

"*Even if we run at full sprint the whole way, we'll never get back to the Bugeye before you three run out of air. The Darkcloak's little delay has dragged us past the point of no return.*"

"*Great. Now what?*" Bullit asked.

Young Flashpoint looked around nervously. "*Maybe... well... what if we find an intact chamber inside the ship. Somewhere we can wait until you go back and get us more oxygen?*"

Bullit scanned the ship's interior. "*No good. I'm not picking up any area that isn't breached.*"

"*Not on this ship, there isn't,*" Tàlto said.

They all stared at him.

"*The Ares may be no good, but the escape pod is probably still intact. In fact, we might not need to return to the Bugeye at all. We just take that to get out of here.*"

"An escape pod?" Bullit asked. *"Basically a giant barrel stuffed with people, intended only to get you down alive."*

"Well, we don't have to fly back home with it. We just need to get off the ground. And maybe take her around the equator, once we know where that Drak'min fleet is gonna lead us."

"How are we gonna find it?" Flashpoint asked.

Tachion pointed to the ground. *"Same way we found you. Just follow the line in the sand."*

"We better get an idea of how far it is," Tàlto offered. *"I'll talk to Deldri, see what he has to say. Maybe you guys can scan the wreckage for spare O^2, or whatever else we might use. Just in case. And, of course, find the foot tracks of where he came from."*

Tàlto returned alone to the escape-pod alcove, while the other three headed off. Deldri was awake now, digging manically at the trimithium cord around his wrist, but fell back almost relieved when he saw the lyghtan return.

"Fellow Lastnâm!" he exclaimed. *"What a sight for sore eyes. I thought maybe you'd abandoned me here."*

"Your escape pod. How far is it?" Tàlto asked coldly.

"Ah, how the tables have turned. The quizzed is now the inquisitor," Deldri said. *"It's not far, perhaps a mile. Cut me loose and I can show you."*

"Just so you can lead me to some disabled wreck? Forget it."

"It's not disabled, it's in perfect shape. You can fly me back to the casino in it, no problem. Go ahead, I won't resist. You can turn me in for my multiple guild violations. That's, of course, if you're an honest man, and want a small reward. Or... you could just turn me loose there, if you're maybe somewhat less honest, and would prefer an awfully big one," Deldri offered. *"I have plenty of money to pay for my own personal safety."*

"Sorry, Fellow Enzix," Tàlto said sarcastically. *"I'm afraid I have duties elsewhere, and you've already delayed me enough. But thank you for the information. It's most kind of you to loan us your ship."* He turned to walk away.

"Wait!" Deldri cried. *"You owe me, you know. I didn't give away your secret. Professional courtesy, and all that."*

Tàlto turned back. *"What secret?"*

The chained Darkcloak cocked his head. *"Come now, I'm a metamorph. I might not be able to sense all your thoughts, but I can get the gist of them,"* he said. *"They don't know, do they... your two friends? They don't have a clue what's going on. I kept my mouth shut for you. You should do the decent thing of not killing me."*

Tàlto laughed. *"Oh, don't worry. That would violate guild rules. I have no intention of killing you. I'm just gonna walk away."*

"With me still strapped to this ship?" the tracker begged. *"What are you talking about? I have less than an hour's air left! Leaving me here is the same thing as killing me."*

"No, not exactly," Tàlto explained. *"This way, I save a bullet."* He turned and sauntered away from the diminishing cries of his fellow bounty hunter.

It turned out the Darkcloak had told the truth with his presumed last words upon listening ears. The escape pod was adeptly landed, slid through dusty carbon to ease the impact of her fall, and resting in a wide smooth plain beneath a cover of open airspace. There was, however, one small lie of omission in his report—he had failed to mention the ship's limited capacity.

Bullit opened the outer hatch and looked into the little capsule. *"This only has three seats, and each of those are pretty tight."*

Tachion peered inside. *"You'll... just have to go without me,"* he said. *"I'll walk back to the* Bugeye *and wait for rescue."*

"Ehh. I don't like that," Bullit said. *"I've had just about enough of getting separated."*

"I agree," Flashpoint told them. *"We can't leave you behind, Uncle Tach."*

Tàlto sighed. *"Well, this is all very sweet and selfless. Very 'no man left behind', and all that. But the doctor's right. He could easily walk back, and we could call to send him rescue."*

"Maybe it should be you who fuckin' walks!" Bullit snapped at the lyghtan bounty hunter. *"Or better yet, why don't you just keep on walking, right to the casino. It's only about five hundred miles that way."*

The argument was interrupted by an alarm from Tachion's scanner. He pulled out the device and studied the screen.

"What is it?" Flashpoint asked.

"The Beagle probe we left in orbit, it's picking up a massive distortion. Magnetic flux matching a cloaking field."

"Where?" Tàlto asked seriously.

"Entering equatorial orbit, and some already moving to descend. Somewhere between forty and fifty degrees longitude. It's huge, the distortion. Easily enough for a small fleet. But that general heading is all I can tell for now, until they land. We need to get closer."

"Alright," Tàlto said, *"so it seems the decision's been made for us. We're outta time, and we gotta go. All of us. But even if we yank out the stack of supplies behind those seats, there's only one way all four of us are gonna fit in this tiny, little ship."*

"Goddammit," Bullit moaned. *"You're gonna say we gotta leave the armor."*

"*It's the only way,*" the lyghtan said. "*We'll be all right. We've got our regular gear scrambled.*"

"*Yeah, as long as we put down somewhere pressurized, we'll be all right.*"

"*Well, if anyone's got a better idea...*"

They looked at each other.

No one did.

Tachion moved in front of them to command their attention. "*Okay then, listen up,*" he directed to them sternly. "*You'll need to move quickly. The air pressure here is about one hundred thirty millibars, about thirteen percent of Earth. But that's still below the Armstrong threshold, so you won't have to worry about your blood boiling.*"

"*Well that's a plus,*" Bullit muttered.

"*It's also about sixty-below-zero ambient air temperature. But with the thin, dry atmosphere and lack of wind, it'll take a longer time to draw out your heat. Plus, the air is fairly noxious, in addition to having no oxygen. But if you hold your breath and hurry up, you can pop out of those suits and jump into the capsule. I want you to aim for being armor off, and into the pod, with less than two minutes total exposure.*"

"*And, what?*" Flashpoint asked. "*Just leave James' armor here?*"

Tàlto shrugged. "*Well, I don't have room in my scrambler. Do any of you?*"

After a moment of silence, Flashpoint resigned to agree. "*Uncle James is gonna wanna kill us, just dumping his stuff in the dirt.*"

"*Actually,*" Bullit said, reaching down to loosen a boot clamp, "*that's the only part of this plan I like.*"

19.5

THE KOHINOOR ROOM OF THE ROCK Resort and Casino, which borrowed its name from a legendary crown jewel of Earthan culture, was as faceted and as crystalline as that moniker would imply. The vaulted hall itself took the shape of an Asscher cut stone, square with the corners clipped, making the space roughly octagonal. The thick, lucent walls continued the theme, with parallel bands of geometric gemstone— towering pillars of pure diamond, each locked tightly against the next, like hexagonal trunks of polished glass. They reached and refracted toward the soaring, tapered spire, curving to meet in a conical ceiling, dizzyingly high above the heads below. Inset panels of illumination stretched likewise just as high, adorning each wall, and casting subtle undulating hues of light salmon and dusty coral. The vaguely oranged tones shimmered and reflected through the crystal walls, filling the space with a warm luster, and gleaming off a steel catwalk, making it appear almost more like brass. The balustered walkway was similarly octagonal, following the perimeter of the room, providing a perch from where those VIPs and guests of players might eagerly observe the game below.

In the very center of their attention sat a wide, circular ring of a gaming table. Easily capable of seating twelve, even widely spaced apart, the play surface was backlit by an azure glow from underneath, highlighting marked regions for laying out game hands and discards. In the circle's center, a human tel'jagara dealer and her android supervisor now stood, each posing placidly, fingers folded, as they awaited the entrance of the tournament's initial players.

Through a tall, Gothic-arch entry that mirrored the peak of the Kohinoor room, strode an imposing seti of snowy white, with all the confidence as if he owned the place. His long, wintery mane was set in braids, tipped with aglets of gold, and the pointed tufts atop his ears were entwined with a gilded thread. His mismatched eyes of different hues were accentuated by colored jewelry. In his right ear, three hoops of crusted sapphire echoed the adjacent indigo iris. On the left, a single emerald-filled gauge mirrored the gleaming jade of the other. He wore a blue, tufted doublet with a high collar, woven of e'siagan silk, and draped with a long-tailed fleecy overjacket of gray, Peruvian vicuña wool. The lapelless hems were held loosely together across his ample chest with a set of brilliant byzantine silver chains. But perhaps his most dazzling decoration was the striking beauty on his arm, who clung to him fervently, as if he were her very world. A slender, calico seti woman, of black, white and fiery orange, whose backless, strapless, and waistless gown of lace seemed it could only continue covering her through the power of pure magic.

With his fur bright and shining as an ice-capped mountain in the sun, he slowed his entry at the doorway landing, and gazed pompously about the room. His uncommonly particular and persnickety regard made sure that all below met his approval. After a time, seemingly deciding it was at least sufficient, he continued down the stairway, his doting mistress at his side.

"Jesus Christ," sighed Stansky. "Isn't he overplaying it just a little bit?"

Bullseye shook his head in disagreement. "Chief Zvavi committed to our employ as flight deck master, and occasional pilot. Not for his proficiency as a gamester, nor capacity as a thespian. Under the circumstances, I find his confidence and commitment to be a fortune in our favor. Moreover, take careful note of his competition. His fictitious demeanor still as yet pales aside such consummate elitists. I, for one, find his performance to be outstanding."

The pair monitored Zvavi and Relic's entrance through the casino's internal closed-circuit broadcast, the tournament being aired live in every room with an interest to view it. Bullseye picked up his comlink. "Radio check, Relic, a mere signal if you can hear me."

The object of his affections lifted a hand to touch her nose, the prearranged signal for the affirmative until she could communicate more directly. Zvavi moved to approach the table, and Relic kissed him lovingly, and wished him luck, then went to join the VIP spectators atop the octagonal catwalk. She circled around slowly, as if she sought a better view of her lover's play. But in reality, she was simply centering herself in the perfect spot to hack the system in the adjacent space. Bullseye felt no jealousy at Relic's play of emotion toward the chief, only genuine pride in her, and heartfelt wonder. An increasingly more common smile of contentment crossed his lips.

"Alright," Stansky said. "If you can hold down the fort for a bit, and make sure those two don't get into any trouble, I have to go back and help Opal. Belladonna went to standby near the entrance of the tournament, so I guess that leaves just *lucky me* to help the lady get her face on. Boy, Maraspese wasn't kidding when she said we'd never do as good as she did."

"Should our endeavor today be so blessed," Bullseye reassured him, "within the hour we shall be gone. And such need for masquerades vanished along with us."

As James made his way out, Bullseye watched the holoprogram intently. The scene downstairs was cast across the suite's entire crystal-walled living space, as if it took place in this very room. Zvavi adjusted the cuffs of his doublet; the left one, then the right. Finally, he tugged his jacket straight, and settled into his seat with an air of aloof indifference toward his competitors. One after the next, the other players filtered into the room. Bullseye couldn't help but wonder if the chief knew exactly who he shared this venue with. Two seats to his left, the human CEO of the galaxy's second largest asteroid mining interest, whose questionable business practices in the area of worker civil rights had often found her face plastered across the news. It never seemed to stem the flow of her commodities, however. Directly across the table, the self-proclaimed lyghtan 'Governor' of the Citadel of Tartarus on Mulv'va Prime, a rim colony full of slave traders and their unfortunate living wares. Equally as unfortunate, located just outside the Coalition's purview.

The rest of the table filled slowly, with personas no doubt similarly infamous—though some Bullseye recognized and others he did not. And though all of them were quite wealthy, not a professional player sat among them—at least as far as the seti could tell. He would consider that good news. It should aid outcomes in their favor, as far as Zvavi not being ejected in the first minutes of the game.

The dealer began reviewing the house rules with the players, as a sonic and force shield enveloped the table, barring the contestants from hearing any outcries from the audience, or from being harassed, or helped, from outside of the game. Bullseye panned the holoprojection across to the viewing gallery. He watched as Relic continued moving to position herself, finally settling in at the back of the surrounding walkway, snug against the northeast wall. She pulled out her multicomm as if to make a call, and began scanning nonchalantly for any comms bugs within the room. He stared at her unabashedly as he thought about their last two days together.

He had, over the years, been to The Rock several times, for a mixture of varied purposes, some business and some pleasure—though perhaps mostly business. He had experienced the phenomenon of this novel outpost long ago, but was now seeing it all again for the first time, through *her* eyes. Her boundless energy renewed him, her enthusiasm was contagious, and he gained appreciation for little marvels he had missed here the first few times. Standing beside her, he felt more alive here and now than he had been in a long time—and even beyond that, glad to be that way. If all of it were somehow to end for him tomorrow, this brief time with Relic had at least made the chore of living now seem worth it.

He wondered then—could he possibly be giving back to her any of that which she provided him? He was older, and opinionated, and largely stuck in his familiar ways. Her younger eyes and open mind brought a freshness to his life he didn't realize was sorely lacking. But what did he bring to her—world-weariness and despondency? He had no desire to saddle her with that. Bullseye hoped he was beginning to step beyond those sorts of things.

Apparently finding the area clear to speak, Relic tapped the miniature transceiver within her ear. *"Chicken Little to Mother Goose, I have a wireless signal lock. Not a strong one, but best I can manage through these compressed carbon walls. It'll do though, just might take a little longer. I'm initiating the security bypass algorithm now."*

Bullseye shook his head. "Those are undeniably *not* the codenames we agreed upon," he told her sternly, though through an unseen grin. "Furthermore, I fail to comprehend the reference."

"Just a little joke, to let you know how protected I feel beneath your wing, knowing you're out there watching." She batted her eyelashes for him at the camera.

"It is truth that I watch closely. But what I can see, so may any other," he reminded her. "Prithee to be cautious, and mindful in your manner."

"Ah, you see? Just like an overprotective mother," she said teasingly. *"Don't worry, I'll just sink into the back. Make myself barely noticeable."*

"That would be the very definition of impossible," he noted, clearly admiring the scarcity of her evening gown.

"Ooh, what a lech. Now I don't know if I like you watching me after all," she softly joked. *"Heaven only knows what thoughts are going through that mind of yours."*

"Truth?" Bullseye asked, his voice taking on a note of seriousness. "My thoughts center on the consideration that... it is I who stand to reap the windfall of our continued interconnection."

"Interconnection?" she laughed. *"Is that what we're calling it now? And I don't know what you mean by saying that."*

"What I mean is, in short time, you have already altered me... for the better. Altered the very trajectory of my life. I gain new insight through your vision. I feel new excitement through your joy. You have reached out your slender hand, and... pulled me... from my very grave. Yet alas, in return, what can I hope to impart to you, beyond... stubborn temperament, and sore bones?"

She laughed. *"You are a cranky old warhorse. But then again, that's just one of the things that I... Well..."* She stopped herself and took a breath. *"You and I are two souls, lucky enough to find wonder in similar things. You say I bring you freshness, an amendment to your point of view? Well, you bring me wisdom. Knowledge, distilled by experience. You go right ahead and start a new life through me, and I'll take advantage of knowing a second one through you."* She beamed up at him through the holovision.

"Just a reminder, you two," Belladonna's exasperated voice broke in, *"this is, in fact, an open frequency... with your* actual *mother listening in. Let's try and stay professional, and save that talk for... oh God, I don't even wanna know when."*

"Mother!" Relic whispered harshly. But a moment later, her tone changed. *"Oh, wait. Okay... I'm through the password. We're in. I'll start searching for the system logs."*

A chorused groan of disappointment drew Bullseye's attention back to the center table. A slum baron, with ties to Gel Gonahaar's largest crime family, had apparently been eliminated, and was none too happy about the embarrassment. He scooped a fistful of the round, rigid playing cards from the table, and tossed the disks ferociously at the grinning vice president of WarTec Industries, who was seated directly across from him. A pair of armed representatives from security gently encouraged him to be on his way, the force screen snapping back up around the players as he was led from the room.

A robotic arm swept the table, clearing the discards from the last game, and drawing them beneath to be reshuffled. After a moment of waiting for the remaining players to pay their ante, a new array was dealt through hidden slots in the lighted tabletop. Bullseye watched as Zvavi collected his fresh hand: a parade of brightly colored images painted on small circular platters, each depicting drak'min digits from their base-eight counting system, and categorized within slews of aggressive sounding suits—the flame, the dagger, the fist, the lash—to name but a few. The first round of betting, Zvavi appeared quite assertive. But during the second round of retractions, he took back almost half of it. The other players were less than pleased with that maneuver. Zvavi peered disdainfully down his nose at them, uncaring at their bellyaching. Bullseye couldn't help but chuckle, despite having no idea what was transpiring.

Stansky returned then with Lady Opal, again disguised as a chamai, but perhaps a slightly less healthy one than they had only recently arrived with. "How goes it?" James inquired, as they seated themselves around the broadcast.

"The noble Chief, as of yet, has effected no forfeit of our mutual savings," Bullseye assured him. "Though whether by talent, or by happenstance, I am unable to ascertain."

"Well, either way is fine with me. Save my accountant from a heart attack."

"And yourself as well, I'd imagine."

Opal spun the view of the proceedings back to the spectators on the catwalk, where Relic was busily tapping away on her device. "And how does Relic's mission fare? Has she found us a trail to Denali?"

"Not as yet. She has most readily succeeded in her bid to breach security, and currently forages the intelligence from…"

"*I've got it!*" Relic loudly whispered then, as if in response to Opal's question. "*I've found the usage data logs. I'm downloading global consumption graphs for the past 30 days. That should show us where there's a spike in… Oh. Oh no.*"

"What is it?" Bullseye asked.

"There's somebody else in here, in the program. There's another hacker."

"Is it... your father?" The thought ran cold through Bullseye's blood like a gusting downdraft on the Valley of Glass. But why? Why such a sense of fear at the possibility of Rook's proximity? Was it merely the idea that their whole operation was being watched? Or was it perhaps, for him, a slightly more terrifying reminder; that the return of his old friend might spell the end of his new relationship.

"No, that's not possible," Relic answered. *"This one is far too clumsy. Too conspicuous."*

Bullseye sighed in relief.

"It seems like... they're looking for a way to cut power into this room."

Opal looked confused, then picked up the comlink. "Relic, I thought we were told the power can't be controlled from in there."

"It can't, but they don't seem to know that. They're going straight for an obvious honeypot."

"Honey... pot?" Opal asked.

"To the best of my understanding," Bullseye told her, "a virtual trap, for unwitting attackers. A lure of sorts, to tempt the quarry with something shiny. A false prize, behind false vulnerability." He tapped the comlink. "What may be a likely result, should your counterpart take such bait?" he asked.

"Well, these things are often intentionally designed just to study hackers, so they may just let them bounce around in there, and use what they learn from watching them to strengthen their systems."

"Or?"

"Or... they might decide it's just too risky, considering what's going on at this event. They might think it's part of a coordinated attack that they have to clamp down on, before it endangers any of the rich old muckety-mucks playing cards. Of course, if they do sound the alarm, it's going to cut off my download at the very least. I still need a few more minutes, just two or three. It's an awful lot of data, through a tenuous, remote connection."

"Is it, in fact, a coordinated attack?" Opal asked.

"I have no idea," Relic answered. *"But they want the power off in here for some reason."*

Bullseye looked at Stansky.

"I'll get our stuff," James said, hopping up and rushing out the door.

"Relic, honey, what do you suggest we do?" her mother interjected.

"I'm gonna try to stop them, or at least slow them down. I'll try and code barriers in front of them, until I can finish retrieving the data," she said.

Opal leaned in toward Bullseye. "If they are hacking the same system, they must also be in the same room," she said.

The seti nodded to her in agreement, then immediately panned the camera angle around the circumference of the gaming hall. He kept a sharp eye out for anyone likewise on a device, but there were too many. It seemed equally as likely, looking across the audience of onlookers, for any member of the crowd to be more absorbed by their multicomm screen than they were by the high stakes play they came to see. At least half of the spectators tapped away on little tablets, including the tel'jagara dealer's supervisor, and even one of the armed security guards. Bullseye stopped and zoomed in.

The guard on his device was a burly human, his partner a blueish-gray furred seti, and each stood across from each other at either end of the large, round game table. A prime position to snatch and grab the stacks of loot being exchanged before them, if only the force field were brought down, and perhaps a moment of darkness to add confusion. Bullseye zoomed in closer, filling the entire living room with the human's pockmarked face. His lip twitched and jerked in clear frustration, his eyes darting up and down across his multicomm screen. A single drop of flop sweat coursed its way down from his hairline, across his temple.

Bullseye clicked the comlink. "The security guards," he said confidently. "They hazard a play to purloin the table money."

"*What?*" Belladonna said. "*Are you sure?*"

"I read deviousness in the human's eyes, desperation in his manner. They alone are the privileged, allowed armaments within casino property. They aspire to sever the flow of power, drop the shields, and plunder the table at gunpoint."

"*That's a fairly lousy plan. They'll never get out of here alive. They'd have to run through the whole casino.*"

"Agreed, a masterstroke of cleverness it is not. Yet, I fear it is the one they harbor. Perhaps ingenious escape has been arranged, of which we are simply not privy," he suggested—though doubting his own words. "Relic, how goes your progress? It seems patience wanes with your meddling. They may choose to forgo their former plan, and forge ahead with the caper unscripted. You must need take your leave, quickly. Signal to Zvavi to forfeit his playing."

"*I'm almost done,*" Relic told them. "*Just another thirty seconds or so. But I don't think I can signal Zvavi. The sonic shield is blocking me from whistling to him or anything, and I don't think he can see me with the table lights blaring. Or, maybe that force screen is only see-through one way. He's not even looking this direction. He's just playing.*"

"You must then depart without him. Mayhap at some point when the shield drops, he will notice your absence, and move to conclude his game. But pray, be sure to..."

But he was interrupted. The human security guard had apparently had enough frustration with the power system, and he nodded to his seti counterpart, then threw the multicomm down. They each pulled their energy weapons, firing a volley of laser rifle shots into the floor beneath the catwalk. The crowd of onlookers screamed out in chaos and panic, first ducking for cover, then scrambling over each other to get away. But the gamblers beneath their shell of silence continued playing unabated, and unrealizing.

A line of crimson rifle blasts hit the ground in front of the retreating crowd, as the seti guard slammed closed the doors to the Kohinoor room. "All right everybody!" his voice boomed through the holobroadcast. "Hands up! Heads down! And those fucking devices on the floor! I see *anybody* on a multicomm, I'll smash it with your face, and take your fucking head off with the jagged pieces!"

Stansky reentered Bullseye's room, tossing a scrambler to the distraught seti, who quickly rematerialized his gear and armor in a pile behind the sofa. They both began hurriedly suiting up.

Belladonna's voice came across the comlink. "*Relic sweetheart, listen to me. If you see an opportunity open early, a chance to turn the tables... take it. Don't allow them to make it a controlled environment that they can handle. It'll be a lot harder to get you out once they completely own the room. But only if you see the opportunity! Don't take a chance that isn't there! Do you hear me? Do you understand? Don't take the chance if it doesn't present itself! Relic, do you hear me? Relic!*"

She didn't answer.

On the holoscreen, the scowling human was approaching Belladonna's daughter with a menacing glare. "What the fuck do you think you're doing, you stupid goddamn little bitch! What did my friend just tell you about that device? Drop it on the ground now, or I swear to god, I'll drop you."

Relic turned and knelt, placing it gingerly on the floor against the wall, then stood again to face him, her hands slightly raised in halfhearted surrender.

"You some kind of a smart ass? A tough girl? When I say drop it, I mean *fucking drop it!*" He grabbed her by the wrist and started dragging her from the catwalk. "Come on, little tough girl, get the fuck down here!"

Inside the force sphere, the game still continued on, Zvavi appearing to be doing remarkably well—at least based on the size of his coin stacks.

Another player was then eliminated: a lacertilian with a missing eye, and wearing a long, flowing, purple robe, as if he were dressed like ancient royalty. As he stood, he scattered his remaining coins across the table in frustration. The android supervisor lowered the surrounding shields in order for the ousted gambler to exit, and the seti guard leapt into action, quite literally. He sprung up and over the table, landing in the center circle in a single bound. He placed the muzzle of his pistol beneath what could be considered the android's neck, and fired without hesitation—quickly removing the pit boss's head, and sending its components clattering around the table. The remaining lifeless machinery collapsed heavily to the ground. The audience again screamed as the players jerked backward in surprise.

"Everyone's hands up on the goddamn table, or I'll blast 'em off like the android's head!" The seti shouted at the ring of card holders.

There was a moment of confusion around the table at the sudden twist of the room's mood. The players looked at one another, then the crowd, trying to absorb what was happening. But after seeing the corralled audience, one by one they followed the bandit's instructions.

Once he was sure they were all compliant, the seti slung his weapon, then began scooping the coined money into piles and dematerializing it into a pocket scrambler.

A thin-haired human male seated at the table leaned forward, the openly corrupt chairman of a galactic trimithium cartel. "Do you have *any* idea, who we are here?" the man asked. "Who these men and women are sitting at this table? Your life isn't going to be worth a single one of those credits once you leave here."

"That's still more than yours will be worth," the seti told him. He fired point blank at the man's face, instantly turning it into a hollowed crater of cracked char, and curdled fluids. Fresh redness rushed to seep out as his head drooped back, and his body slid lifelessly from the chair.

The other players went quiet, casting cold stares with hate-filled eyes, but expressing no further vocal protests.

Bullseye and Stansky were nearly suited up, but froze to watch the broadcast as the human pulled Relic up beside the table.

"This rich little whore has volunteered to walk us outta here," he told his partner, who was finishing his collection. "She wants to make sure we get out safe. Protect us with that little body."

The seti looked up as he stored the last of the money. "Mmm, you don't say. I can think of a few other things I can do with that body afterward."

Zvavi pushed back his chair and stood. "Hold," he said, approaching the human, with his hands up. "The security in this establishment will deem *no value* in her life. If you both, in truth, had been engaged as guards here, you would know this certainty as well as I. They will discharge a barrage cleaving through her to get to you. Your prize, and your lives, both will be forfeit. I offer myself. Secure me instead. I possess title to near *half* this facility," he lied. "It is, in part, my money which you steal. Those who labor in my employ would *never dare* train a weapon in my direction. I shall even supplement your reward on the way outward, such is my concern for these few most valued patrons. I shall thrust upon you as much coin as that scrambler may bear, if you simply let the woman be."

The human lowered his rifle a bit, and looked the wealthy-appearing seti up and down in consideration. "Mmm, you might just have something there, snowball. Get down here, hands up. Nice and slow." He then released his grip on Relic's arm.

With the speed of a striking cobra, Relic backhanded him in the throat. His eyes bulged and his mouth gaped as a fractured larynx blocked his airway. Within a half second of the first blow, she followed with a brutal kick to the human's groin, grabbing his rifle as his knees hit the ground, and spinning it in a flurry to crack his face open with the shoulder stock. She turned then toward the seti, but before she could raise the muzzle, the second guard drew, and fired at her.

The all-eclipsing form of Zvavi blocked her view as he jumped in the way, taking the blast full force to his lower chest. He crashed to the ground in front of her, face down and unmoving. The young seti woman deftly swung the gun around and fired. She caught the blue-gray seti in the head and he fell back, his weapon blazing toward the ceiling. The laser bolts refracted and ricocheted through the crystal mirrored surfaces like a blaze of fireworks.

The crowd of onlookers screamed and shrieked in renewed panic, and began rushing for the exit, just as security burst in, rushing the opposite way from outside.

Bullseye and Stansky charged toward the room's door, but Lady Opal darted quickly, determined to block their way. "Just where do you think *you two* are going?" she demanded of the armored giants, arms folded defiantly before her little form.

"Most Holy Ashi'Mar," Bullseye said, "please, stand aside. We must..."

"Must *what?* Go running through the casino as if you're dressed for Armageddon? Burst in, weapons swinging, just to supervise the cleanup? Relic and Belladonna are down there, and as you yourself have said, their faces have far less notoriety. There is nothing you can do now, your friends have handled the situation. You showing up afterward would only endanger the greater mission."

"But…" Bullseye protested weakly. "But, Relic…"

"*I* will go get Relic, *and* her mother, and bring them both back here. As well as make sure dear Zvavi is being properly cared for. Now get out of those ridiculous getups. Sit down, and leave it to us."

They stood staring after the priestess as she rushed out of the door.

James shook his head. "How did we end up on the sidelines, while a recent schoolgirl and our deck chief handle the mission for us?"

Bullseye threw his hands up, then again zoomed in on the broadcast.

Relic was sitting upon the lowest step to the catwalk, cradling Zvavi's head atop her lap, and smoothing his braided hair in worried reassurance. He was clearly struggling to catch his breath. His eyes occasionally darted wildly, like he wasn't certain where he was. Along his left chest and abdomen, the medium-gray wool of his now singed overjacket was slowly growing darker with a flush of spreading wetness. "Medic!" Relic cried out behind her as the casino security staff continued their stampede. She leaned down and kissed his forehead. "Oh, my foolish hero," they heard her say over the broadcast, rather than the comlink. "I think you took playing your part a little too seriously."

"I did only the least… that was required…" he assured her through shortened breaths. "What duty demanded… as a gentleman… and as your escort."

Her angelic chime of laughter burst forth from beneath her burgeoning tears. "And a finer date I've never had."

The large seti lifted his head a bit, surveying the damage to his side. "I fear I may have… somewhat marred the costume…" he worried aloud. "It seems improbable… to be refunded." He allowed his head to fall once more back to her, and again his blue and green eyes began to swim. "Confer my deepest apologies to… to…" He faded off.

Relic spun her face towards the doorway. "*Medic!*" she cried tearfully, even louder than before.

But security seemed content to continue ignoring her, as they funneled the panicked guests from the room into the outer lobby. Her shout jarred him back awake.

"Your… your device. You must secure it… quickly now, my lady… before it is mistakenly taken."

"I'm not leaving you. I'm not going anywhere."

"The advancement… of the mission… depends… It depends…"

"Chief, breathe slow. Take it easy. Stay with me now."

"Hard to breathe… becoming harder…" the seti confided as he closed his eyes. "Tell… tell Ensign Rawlings to… tell him to…"

Again he faded.

Finally, with the room near empty, Belladonna was allowed in, a wrinkled looking chamai woman running with her by her side. The two women charged forward, dragging a human medic behind them by his lapels, who in turn pulled a hover gurney loaded down with his equipment. He sank to his knees beside Zvavi, moving Relic out of the way, and looked closely at the burned chest wound. He ran him up and down with a medical scanner, then held it a long time over the injury. Turning to whistle sharply for security to come help, four men together struggled to heft the seti onto the levitating cot.

Relic touched him on the knee, and then took the opportunity to rush over and retrieve her multicomm from where she'd laid it on the catwalk. She checked it quickly and made a few keystrokes. Then looking up to notice Chief Zvavi watching her, gave him a smile and a thumbs up. He relaxed his head heavily back onto the gurney.

The medic placed an O^2 converter over the seti's face, and pulling out a laser scalpel, immediately cut through the expensive attire, and shaved away the ivory avalanche of fur hidden underneath.

Belladonna leaned into him. "Chief, I'm so sorry. I can't tell you what you've done for me. And... after the way that I treated you when you came to pick us up," she lamented. "I've lost so much already... a missing husband, a runaway son. If something had happened to my dear little Relic..." her voice caught in a subtle sob. "Today, you saved my life, just as surely as you did hers." She kissed his cheek.

"If I may, Miss Belladonna," Zvavi struggled to respond, "I will long make note of this day... to be shown such affection... not by one, but two beautiful... Ahhh!" His remark was cut short by a grimace of searing pain, the scalpel slicing an incision between his ribs that was hurriedly filled with a transparent chest tube. The catheter immediately charged with a gush of viscous, red fluid.

Zvavi gasped inward, long and deep, like a drowning man going under.

"What about me?" Opal questioned, doubtless hoping to distract him. "My horribly wrinkled face doesn't count as a beautiful lady? I think I might be personally offended."

"Yes, of course... you as well, my Holy..."

She placed a chamai finger to his lips.

"I mean, Miss Opal..." he spoke through it. Then another wince, and a grit of teeth, as the medic cut down the laser wound to look inside. The char on the surface of his skin looked as though it clearly extended deep beneath, and the human reached inward with a pair of clamps to attach a vein shunt to a deep, vigorous bleeder.

The seti cried out.

Opal put her lips by his tufted ear. "What you did here today... what you were willing to sacrifice, not only saved Relic and our mission... but possibly *all* the people of my world. We will know now how to stop Denali, and it's *you* who made that happen," she said. "When I one day retrieve my throne and position, you, Zvavi, shall be named as my knight-errant. Lord Paladin of The Originators, and cherished champion of the Holy Sovereigness."

James and Bullseye still stood watching, the scene zoomed in closely on the ashi'mar. "What the hell?" complained Stansky. "We've directly saved her life like a dozen times now. Why don't *we* get that?"

Bullseye sighed. "Moreover to the bestowing of titles, she has unintentionally conveyed her true identity to the viewership. We must need leave here, forthwith."

"Zvavi," Belladonna was calling, trying to arouse the now slackened seti. "Zvavi!"

But the chief was no longer responding.

The medic pulled her aside. "We have to go," he told her, and a team of many hands hovered the gurney up the stairs, and out the doorway.

Bullseye turned down the broadcast.

"I hate not having Tachion here," James said to him. "How did the other guys end up with the only medic on *their* side?"

Bullseye shook his head. "A question I have asked myself, yet have failed to give a suitable answer." Just then, an alert on his multicomm sounded off.

"What is it?" asked Stansky.

The dark-furred seti studied the screen for a moment. "It is Relic. She has dispatched the conclusions of her analyzed download. Seems there be, in truth, a massive power drain such as we seek. And from merely one, lone, ancient borehole. Located here, at the Rock's equator, where it intersects the forty-seventh longitude." He showed his companion the display.

James raised his eyebrows in pleasant surprise. "So, we were right then. Denali *is* holding up here, hiding a fleet in one of those tunnels. At least until we enter the Coalition."

"Aye, so he is indeed," Bullseye nearly growled. "Secreted safe within its depths, cowering. Like a wasp from the colder seasons. An insect, burrowed in his hive, awaiting only the first touch of summer's warmth, to fly forth once more... free to sting."

Chapter 20.1

THE TINY COCKPIT OF THE *Sereya Mel's* escape pod echoed with grievances from the center chair. "Holy hell," Bullit complained, "and here I thought the *Bugeye* was hard to maneuver."

Often, there was a zen-like, placid calm that could be found in circling a small moon like this: a colorless, cratered landscape, silent and unchanging for untold eons, rolling over for them far beneath—showing its secrets, and showing its scars—looking much as it always has, and in many cases, always will. But there was none of that here, sailing low above the Rock's surface. With no source of light to shine down and illuminate the terrain, the darkened dwarf became only darker, no hints given as to its contours, nor its content. In fact, the only way to be sure the little world still persisted beneath them, was that the eternity of stars above, was just a shadow of emptiness down below. The murky dimness all around extended as well into the pod's cabin, with the faces of Bullit, Flashpoint and Tàlto lit only by the flickering, violet haze of the little craft's monitors and control panel.

The muffled voice of their android surgeon arose from the darkness behind them. "I'm beginning to think that you complain about the performance of these vessels, only to seem more praiseworthy when we reach the ground alive."

"It has literally no aerodynamics," the seti explained.

"Which should hardly be an issue, considering there's barely any air," Tachion said. He spoke from a spot jammed tightly behind the crew seats, with only one of his massive arms visible, still dented from the *Bugeye*'s landing. It was extended forward between Bullit and Flashpoint, forcing the younger seti to lean awkwardly against his cousin as he tried to pilot. "I'd be happy to handle the chauffeur duties myself, if I hadn't been built so ridiculously large that I can't seem to squeeze into *any* cockpit."

With seating for only three—three *averaged* sized beings, that is—the doctor had no choice but to tuck himself into the area reserved for survival gear. Gear such as repair kits, medical supplies, inflatable structures, and food and water rations, not to mention the sizable scaffolding kit for the emergency long-range comms relay. Gear that would have been infinitely useful back at the old *Bugeye*, but which now lay strewn in the graphite dust, abandoned next to Stansky's armor. As the only one without muscles to cramp after hours in the uncomfortable position, there was no reasonable choice other than him to fill the back row—though personally, he would have preferred to see Tàlto stuffed back here.

Flashpoint had been keeping busy, and keeping calm, by playing navigator for the group. "Approaching the forty-seventh longitude," he informed them. "Almost coming up on Borehole Thirty-Two. The cloaking distortion is long gone now, so... they must all be docked inside."

"The question then," Tàlto wondered, "is whether or not they see us coming as well as we were able to see them. Personally, I'd like to make this a surprise visit."

Bullit adjusted the heading of the escape pod, bringing her closer to the unseen surface. "I'll get down low and skim the terrain. Hopefully, the same features of the shaft that keep us from scanning in, will keep them from scanning out," he said. "Still, it's probably a good idea that we're walking the last mile."

Though no xenoarchaeologist, nor exoengineer, had ever determined exactly what the ancient tunnels had been created for, expedition after expedition had fortunately mapped them thoroughly nonetheless—in exhausting detail. Multiple ancillary outposts fed subterranean hallways to the massive boreholes, their purposes and functions a similar enigma to the giant shafts they serviced. Whatever the web of corridors had originally been intended for, today they would serve as an opportune access point for the crew of the cramped pod. Bullit guided the capsule down, skidding its belly through the dusty carbon, deftly bringing it to rest beside the outbuilding poetically dubbed by its discoverers as 'Borehole Annex: Thirty-Two Omicron'. Tachion raised a thumb in approval on the arm extended into the cabin.

They were here, and it was time.

The weight of that reality silently crossed each and every mind—that only the four of them, alone, were left to somehow face Denali. And, his hired mercenary forces. And General Nylis' military armada. And Queen Vasu's army of lyghtan troops. And now Admiral Yazir, and his fleet of Drak'min. There was no reason to talk about it—there was nothing to be said. They were but a few, going against a great many—not an entirely new proposition. One they had faced many times before, even if perhaps not quite to this extreme. Tachion wiggled and clattered his way backward out of the craft, giving the others some room to stretch back and put environmental suits on. They dressed in silence.

What the *Sereya Mel*'s escape pod lacked in roominess, it more than made up for in equipment, and though most of it had been discarded, the three EV suits, one for each seat in the tiny little cockpit, had been a most fortunate surprise advantage, courtesy of the presumably-late Deldri Enzix. The foursome once again stood out in the open—three in their new space suits, Tachion in his regular armor—perched atop the black, powdery planetoid hurtling through space, and looked around, carefully scanning the terrain with helmet lamps, and weapon mounted floodlights. Beyond the craft they landed in, and the borehole entrance beside it, there was nothing to be seen. Absolutely nothing. The area was as flat and as smooth as a newly paved cretespray lot, not a single contour or crevice from one horizon to the other.

Bullit gazed around in a full circle. "Hopefully we'll remember where we parked," he jested.

Tàlto stuck out the toe of his boot and drew a pointing arrow in the deep graphite. "So we'll know which one is ours, in case another with the same paint job lands beside us."

No one was relaxed enough to enjoy the humor in either joke. They turned and headed for the entrance.

Despite the grandiose way the small world's structures generally appeared, the accessway they landed next to was distinctly unimpressive. A mere lumpy mound in the dusty soil, with a circular hatchway jammed in its side—like a cork plugging a bottle. This was certainly no ancient technology. This was a recent modification, likely intended to secure the site—though failing to lock it defeated the purpose. The rounded doorway swung open neatly for them, and they headed underground.

The drab indistinctiveness of the mundane outdoor entryway belied the fantastical wonderland hidden beneath. Leading away from the cylindrical portal, and descending steadily as it went, a narrow and unswerving pathway shot out straight ahead into the darkness. All around them, the hexagonal crystal columns that everywhere else came closely packed together, instead here were tumbled and fallen, like a massive game of pick-up-sticks. The randomness of the arrangement seemed almost *so* random, it must be organized, with white translucent pillars the size of tree trunks scattered about—left, right, and above—yet not a single one blocking the walkway. Their footsteps resounded and echoed back to them, boots clapping sharply on the overly-smooth pathway, the panning searchlights of their helmet lamps refracting brilliantly as they scanned in wonderment. They continued onward, delving deeper beneath The Rock.

It was difficult to determine whether the mass of elongated diamond pilings had always been this way, or if they perhaps had once formed a crystal colonnade for some now-fallen alien structure. Bullit surveyed a crisscross of four-foot-thick columns overhead as they passed beneath. "It kinda looks like... a collapsed Fortress of Solitude," he mused.

"What is that?" Tachion asked. "The name of your new boat?"

"What?" he asked in frustration. "And here I thought it was just Bullseye. How have I never realized before now how theatrically ignorant you all are?"

"I know what you're talking about," Tàlto told him. "Superman's hideout in the arctic. You know, the 2420 holofilm remake, they stole the design for the fortress from the 1978 film version."

"Yes, exactly! I *did* know that, thank you. Finally, someone with a little culture."

"Bullit?" Flashpoint asked quietly.

"Yeah?"

"What if I can't do it? What if... I choke again?" his cousin asked, clearly more worried about another topic.

"W-What?"

"What if I choke, when I... when I see him again?"

Bullit looked at Tachion, then back to the younger seti. "I don't want you to even think about that," Bullit told him. "No one expects you to be able to... to be able to do what you were originally planning. This clone, whatever he is, he's definitely not your true birth father. But, for better or worse, he *is* the one who actually raised you, since before you were even a teenager. That tie is going to bind you, whether you want it to or not. If the time comes... if we find him... you just leave everything to me."

Tachion shook his head. "I don't think either of you should bear the weight of that task," the android offered. "He's... rather, *it's*... my responsibility. Far more so than anyone else's."

Tàlto chuckled. "At least none of you three have to worry about *me* trying to steal your thunder. You guys can fight and scramble over who takes out Rook all you want. I couldn't give a shit. I'm here for one man and one man only... Denali. In fact, no offense Doc, I don't mean to disparage your small-arms weapons skills or anything, but... maybe you might want to pass that drak'min blaster off to someone a little more... specialized. I'll be more than happy to carry it. End this whole thing with one shot."

"Hmm. I appreciate the offer, but I'd just as soon keep that in house for now. Bullit or I are perfectly capable of using it."

"Okay, well, the offer stands. Remember they have a limited capacity. It might only have one or two shots left in it. Best to make it count."

The long, downward-plunging avenue suddenly led them to a massive doorway: tall and arched, and of a darkened metal, like the ones that might be seen in the casino city.

"What is this?" Bullit asked. "Are we there already? That didn't feel like a mile."

"It wasn't," Tàlto said. "We're only halfway there, at best."

Tachion pulled out his scanners and ran an analysis of the area beyond. "I'm picking up an atmosphere behind it, oxygen-nitrogen. Pressurized as well. And there's power in there."

"And movement," Bullit noted. "Two targets in motion, thirty meters. There, and there," he pointed a general direction through the closed doorway. "There could be more, though, just sitting still."

"Flashpoint?" Tachion asked.

The boy still seemed distracted. "Ah... Oh, yeah." He looked down at an archeological layout map on his multicomm display. "They call it the 'Naos Chamber'. Looks to be almost a hundred feet wide in both directions, and several columns and structures are spread all around. Plenty of places to hide behind, or get in your way... depending on your point of view," he told them. "The walkway continues out the other side."

"Alright," Tachion said. "Let's enter slow and careful, see what it is we're looking at."

They made their way through the outer entrance, and then an inner one that formed an airlock. A quick rush of wind pushed against them as they cracked the doorway open, the higher air pressure on the other side rushing to escape out to the crystal walkway. It was forceful, but fairly silent.

Perhaps more so here than anywhere else on the little planet, the chamber they peered down upon bore the aura of an ancient ruin. The striated walls and ceiling of tightly packed crystal battens were not clear and bright, like those of the outer walkway. They were dark and carbon filled, much more akin to those seen on the surface, with so many crags, chips and inclusions of the graphite powder, that their appearance was more reminiscent of the char of remnant firewood. Young Flashpoint had been correct. The room was roughly a hundred-foot square, and easily the same distance from the rubble-strewn floor to the distant, cracked ceiling. The doorway where they emerged was midway up the wall. Beneath them, the dusty ground was crowded with collapsed bits of crumbled ceiling: enormous trunks of black crystal shattered across the floor. Other wider columns had managed to stay intact, running floor to ceiling throughout the area, clearly helping to hold aloft the remains of the vaulted chamber. In the very center of the squared-off room, atop a mighty dais with sloping ramps, sat a towering, alien structure formed of the now familiar ebony metal.

With the shape of an enormous urn, or the curves of an Olpe vase, the fifty-foot-tall marvel commanded the attention of all who entered. Widest at its bottom, tapering at the waist, and then out again—like the contours of a Earthan cello, or the silhouette of a shapely woman. But the exterior of the structure was encased in extended barbs—pointed, metallic vines twisting upward from all directions, like the spikey flowerhead of a thistle. In the center of the view facing them, a circular medallion was proudly mounted; a gyre of hieroglyphics spiraling inward like a serpent. What the runes told of, no one could know. No equivalent to a Rosetta Stone had ever been found for The Rock's antiquities. The foursome looked at it with a mixture of awe and curiosity, unable to determine if the artifact might be monument, or machine.

But whether religious altar or engine, artistic sculpture or defensive instrument, it mattered not. No one was left behind to operate it, nor to pray to it—so like the rest of the tiny world, it sat abandoned, hoping to reclaim its lost purpose one day.

But not today.

They surveyed the rest of the room.

One of the movements their sensor detected was coming from an armored guard on the far-left wall, standing near an impromptu station of modern-day computers and portable lighting. The yellow cast of the flood lamp placed a golden glow across the darkened room, stretching shadows of the thorny statue across the wall on the other side.

"Where's the other one?" Tachion whispered to Bullit. "You said there were two motion targets."

"He left the room out the other side, where the tunnel to the borehole continues."

"Damn it," the android said, then thought for a moment. "Alright. Flashpoint, Tàlto, head to the right and stick to the shadows. Go and monitor the other walkway, in case the second guard decides to return. Bullit, you and I will take care of our friend there on the left."

The four of them separated, two heading one way and two the other, descending grandiose divergent stairways that had been hewn from the blackened diamond. It was a relatively simple matter for Bullit and the doctor to approach the guard. Obviously, the soldiers had been tasked with overseeing this ancient entrance, though they just as obviously never expected for anybody to actually enter through it. The sentry was lax and inattentive, more interested in staring at the computer screens than patrolling the area with any diligence. The two mercenaries crouched not far behind, and studied him.

His armor was something that they had never seen before—a horizontally segmented set of heavy battle, its charcoal coloring consistent with the ancient metal of the giant monument. A thigh-length overjacket was worn atop it, immense enough to fit around the armor, and made of thick, padded inertia fabric in banded quilting, with a satin sheen. The coat was of the same color and luminance as the plated armor it protected, creating the illusion of one piece: both a rigid and yet flexible alloy. The large, rounded helmet was smooth and reflective, and with a facemask that bore no visor. In place of any inset goggles with which to look through, three glowing red sensor lights adorned the front.

With no comlink in his borrowed EV suit, Bullit instead signaled to Tachion in handspeak. *"Gap under helmet... flexible covering... vibroknife,"* his fingers furiously signaled.

Tachion peered at the guard's neck, then cocked his head, unconvinced. *"Small gap... very small."*

"Big enough," Bullit signaled.

Tachion considered it a moment, then nodded reluctantly to the seti.

Bullit carefully studied the spaces between the fallen debris, planning his every footstep in advance. He arose on hushed haunches and slunk forward on tiptoe—or as close to his tiptoes as the inflexible EV boots would allow. He wished now he had removed them. Bullit continued forward slowly, and readied the vibrating blade, suddenly freezing like a statue as the helmeted head jerked unexpectedly left. There was nothing there of interest, and the guard turned his attention back to the computer screen. The mighty barbed urn in the room's center watched in uncaring silence as Bullit slid up within mere feet of him. Without warning, he made his leap.

Landing hard against the sentry's back, he staggered the soldier forward against a dark trunk of fallen crystal. Bullit wrapped his legs tight around the massive waist then pulled back hard on the helmet's lip, forcing the guard's face to crane upward. The tip of the vibroblade found the opportunity of the slender gap, and wedged inward as Bullit pushed, dragging its pulsing edge from one ear to the other. The rubberlike material beneath the collar cleaved freely, splitting open for the knife like a garment being unzipped. But Bullit could tell from the feel of it, he had not made purchase into flesh. He quickly did it again as the guard was recovering his posture, but it felt like he was attempting to slice through a trimithium column.

The soldier lifted his arms up before him, a strange yellow illumination glowing from each gauntlet, and with a quick snap of his fists closing, his body coursed with a bright clap of electricity. Bullit's body was thrown backward from the sharp blast of static, landing stunned amongst the rubble. He didn't move. The guard turned to approach him.

Tachion stood from his hiding place and quickly rushed forward, the blue plasma flame of his EMD bursting to life as he raised the saber. The guard merely flicked a finger, gauntlets ablaze in amber light. The sword went flying, ripped violently from the android's grasp by an unseen hand, nearly decapitating Bullit as it landed just beside his head. Tachion stopped in his tracks as the sentry stared back, defiant and unconcerned, with his trio of sensor eyes. The doctor drew his autopistols, this time more cognizant to hang on to them. But the push and pull of mental energy against the muzzles made it impossible for him to aim. The armored guardian pulled a Rageur M3 pistol, and fired it point blank at the center of the android's chest. Tachion stumbled backward, tripping to the ground over a block of diamond. The silhouette then hovered over him, raising the weapon again, pointing this time at his head.

A blade of azure fire suddenly projected forward through the helmet's three red eyes. The sentry's raised weapon arm fell limp, the light dimming in his gauntlets. The guard toppled forward to hit the ground right beside the reclining doctor, revealing Bullit standing behind him, wielding the EMD sword. He retracted the powered blade, then turned the hilt around to offer it to Tachion. "You all right?"

"Yeah, I think so. The grillweave suit under my armor absorbed most of the energy," the doctor said, scrambling to his feet. "So what happened to the gap being 'big enough'?"

"You're welcome, first of all. And second, it *was* big enough. But somehow his skin was impenetrable."

"A chamai maybe, with extra quick defenses?" The doctor removed the dead man's helmet. The charred face was horribly melted, but clearly human.

"I'm telling you, I couldn't cut him."

"Well, Opal said Denali could walk through walls with this device. If some of them can lower their density, who's to say they couldn't also raise it."

"And zap the shit out of me."

"And grab my weapons with telekinesis."

"*Hey.*" a shouted whisper came from the darkness across the room. It was Tàlto calling. "You guys made one hell of a racket. The other guard is coming back, in a hurry."

"You gotta take him in one shot," Bullit loudly whispered back. "Don't let it turn into a fight."

Tachion and the seti crouched back and waited, as a full thirty seconds of silence passed by.

A deafening explosion rocked the ancient chamber with a flash of light and rush of soot, shaking the timeworn tomb to drop a new layer of crumbled ceiling. A helmet clattered to the ground in front of Tachion and Bullit, as its corresponding body flipped through the air, landing to become impaled on the winding spikes of the center monument—perhaps a long overdue sacrifice for some archaic and sleeping God.

Bullit called out to Flashpoint and Tàlto as they headed over. "What in the hell was that?"

"You said make sure to drop him in one shot," Tàlto said. "Your young cousin slapped him on the back with a half-pound of heurcanium. Certainly did the job."

"Yeah, and almost brought the roof down. Don't tell me your gonna end up being another Stansky." The seti bent and picked up the helmet, the same tri-sensored charcoal model as the other had worn. "What are these, some kind of uniform?"

"Apparently," Tachion agreed. "The uniform of the *new* Denali's *new* world order."

"Yeah, well, if all his grunts are empowered with this ensensement device, we're gonna have an even tougher road ahead than we thought."

"So now we're not just fighting an army, but an army of magicians?" Flashpoint asked.

"There's nothing magical about it," the doctor explained, "just chemical manipulation of otherwise latent mental abilities."

Tàlto lifted the lifeless arm of the dead soldier, surveying his gauntlet. "Maybe we even the playing field, get a few of these devices for ourselves."

"No, we can't!" Tachion snapped, kicking the dead arm away. "Ever since we left the *Parliament One*, I've been using our flight time to make a thorough study of the devices, as well as the serum inside, using the scans I took from the one Opal gave us."

"And?"

"And… the compound does more to the brain than overcharge the areas responsible for ensensement," he explained. "It stimulates the midbrain as well, in the ventral tegmental region, amping typical motivations into abnormal ambition. It supercharges the amygdala and the hypothalamus, in the areas responsible for aggression. And it produces a dopamine surge in the nucleus accumbens, the pleasure-reward center."

Bullit shook his head. "Give it simpler, Doc, in the plain common tongue."

"Anyone who uses these long-term will not only become a violent megalomaniac, but enjoy being so. They'll become… another Denali."

"Why would he want a bunch of himself running around?" Flashpoint asked.

"Good question," the android wondered. "Perhaps he thinks he's powerful enough to control them. Or perhaps he doesn't realize. But the serum clearly wasn't meant for the chemistry of just any mind. Human, seti, chamai… it wasn't meant for any of these."

"Then who the hell was it meant for?" Tàlto demanded.

"I'm fairly certain… the khailian. It bears a lot of similarity to the serum once used to enslave them."

"The khailian?" Bullit asked. "What do they have to do with this?"

"Of that, I'm not sure," Tachion told him. "But if we get out of this place alive, maybe we should go ask them."

The breathable air and pressurized atmosphere continued into the next walkway, so the three EV suits were finally scrambled in exchange for their regular armor. Tachion had seldom seen Bullit looking so pleased. This tunnel was far less unsullied than the first half of their journey, with cases of random equipment being stored here, illuminated tripods set up for lighting, and a rope of entwined cables running the length from the Naos Chamber toward the borehole. The quartet now advanced forward much more cautiously, keeping the chit-chat to a minimum, and clearing every shadow as they descended even further. Finally, up ahead, a modern doorway blocked their path, complete with a security camera, and a standard access keypad.

They crouched from a distance while Flashpoint checked their location on the archaeological chart. "This is it," he told them, now able to communicate via comlink. "*It's labeled 'The Adytum Room'. This is the last junction of these corridors before entering the borehole.*"

"Why's it secured like that?" Tàlto asked. "What's behind it?"

Bullit scanned with his motion detector. "*There's people inside, but only a few,*" he said. "*I'm picking up three motion targets, but... they seem to be active, while staying in the same spot, all up against the walls.*"

"At desks maybe?" Tachion suggested. "Or working computer terminals?"

"*That would be my guess,*" Bullit agreed. "*We could probably take them easy by surprise, if we could get them to open the door for us.*"

"How do we do that?"

"*Well... I have one idea, if you're up for it. We could do like Princess Leia pretending Chewbacca was her prisoner, in order to get into Jabba's palace.*"

Tachion stared at him. "*I only understood half the words of that sentence.*"

"I know what you mean," Tàlto told him. "*You mean put on one of the helmets from the guards that we killed, and play like the doc is our prisoner. Get them to open the door.*"

"Yeah, that's right."

"Well, technically, that's more like the bunker on Endor, when Han called for reinforcements over the monitor."

Bullit slowly nodded. "*Hmm, you might be right. You know, you're not so bad after all. I might be changing my mind about you.*"

"I can't tell you how ecstatic that makes me," Tàlto said.

"*And... I've changed it back again.*"

A quick jog to retrieve the fallen helmet of Flashpoint's kill, and soon Bullit held a seemingly-shackled Tachion at gunpoint for the camera.

He tapped the comms button. "I've got an android intruder out here. Probably just an archeological tourist, but he's a big one. Pop the door for me. I need to find out what to do with him."

After a moment of deafening silence, the thick blast doors began to part. A crisscross of well-targeted fire from the mercenaries dropped the three unarmored soldiers before the portal was even fully open. They rushed inside and sealed the doorway behind them.

The crystal walled room, with several such doorways leading different directions, had been set up as some sort of makeshift workstation, with monitors and sensor banks controlling God-only-knows-what. God, and the three now dead.

"*Alright,*" Bullit said, replacing the borrowed helmet with his own, "*we made it this far. Now what the hell do we do?*"

"*Let's check out these computer systems, see if we can make anything out of it,*" Tachion instructed. "*We're looking for a main power source, or a way to remotely interfere with the fleet out in the borehole. Or, of course, anything that might lead us to Denali.*"

"*What's that noise?*" Flashpoint asked. "*It sounds like road construction going on.*"

He was right. In the background there was a steady hum, like dozens of diesel engines being moved around.

Tachion scanned it with his parabolic and seismic sensors. "*I don't know, it's too muffled by all this dense carbon. I can't find a match for the auditory signature,*" he said. "*Let's just look for info on that as well, somewhere in these systems.*"

Tàlto looked at a warning written in chamai, blinking on a display. "*We have a critical decompression venting atmosphere nearby. They might be thinking to remove the air and choke us out.*"

Bullit's scanner alarm began to beep and he quickly inspected the device. "*We've got motion incoming. Here, at this other door,*" he told them, pointing. "*Five targets inbound, and jogging fast. They must have heard us.*"

Tachion rushed to the doorway and slid closed the inner bulkhead. Then he pulled out an autopistol and fired a blast that destroyed the control wiring. "*That ought to hold them for a minute or two.*"

"*I'm not so sure,*" Flashpoint said. "*My demo sensor is picking up heurcanium. I think they're gonna try and blast it.*"

As the young seti finished his sentence, the steel door launched inward, torn from its tracks in a deafening explosion, and knocking both Tachion and Tàlto against the opposite wall with its sheer mass. As the metal bulkhead fell forward, the two toppled down along with it, unable to remain standing as a billow of smoke obscured the room.

20.2

A SHARED SILENCE ENVELOPED THE interior of the hastily chartered shuttlecraft, darkening the mood of its passengers, like the permanent shadow across the land below. They had arrived on The Rock in three separate fighter craft, ferrying two souls a piece, but now finding themselves absent Chief Zvavi to pilot at least one of them, it was determined that staying together, in a rented transport, was the safest option. The absence of their seti airman was a precursor to the quiet, none of them truly knowing if their deck chief, in fact, still lived. The unspoken worry over his wellbeing was a weight heavy on every mind, but not the only load they carried. The immensity of the task before them was just as palpable, just as pressing.

James, from the pilot seat, finally broke the silence, feeling he could almost literally hear the sound of Relic tearing her heart out in the chair behind him. "You know," he said matter-of-factly, "the hospital there is actually top notch. With all the important guests that dump their money there, and the lack of any nearby city, the casino spared no expense to make sure they were covered in case of emergency."

Belladonna smiled at him from the co-pilot's seat, grateful he was making an effort to reassure her daughter.

"But what will happen," Relic asked, "if he wakes up there all alone? He'll think we deserted him."

"He would never conjecture such a theory," Bullseye assured her. "The chief was distinctly mindful toward the gravity of our mission, as well as its urgency. He would harbor grander ill will at our loitering by his sickbed, than to arise and find us withdrawn. And, in the most unthinkable of situations, either for him, or for us, Captain Lobo will surely retrieve him. She stands awaiting our emergence on the Coalition side of the border."

"How much further?" Lady Opal asked then, hoping to redirect the conversation.

Stansky checked his readings. "This rental has an inhibitor on both its airspeed and altitude," he said. "I guess they didn't want some amateur treasure hunter taking it out, then deciding to run off to Kimiri or Liberty Station. So, it's slow going. But we'll get there, eventually. Just hope we don't have to get into a dogfight with this thing."

Belladonna turned her attention to a sudden blip on her navigation sensor. "I'm picking up wreckage on the surface. Recent wreckage. Within days, I'd say. Two separate craft, about eight miles apart."

"Might they bear the signature of lyghtan or chamai military?" Bullseye asked.

"No, neither. One is an Ares class, model 403. Registered as the *Sereya Mel*, a Darkcloak vessel out of Bruna Buru."

"Probably just here collecting a gambling debt for the casino," Stansky suggested. "What's the other one?"

"Unknown. I'm not getting any transponder signal. It must have been destroyed," she suggested. "I am picking up one weak life sign, though, outside the escape pod hatch at the Ares site. Oh, wait, make that... two."

Bullseye leaned back. "The sorted ventures of the bounty squads possess no bearing upon us," he said. "We continue onward."

Relic opened an archeological layout of the area on her multicomm, then leaned in comfortably against Bullseye, sharing it between them to show it to him. "Where do we intend to put down? There's lots of entry tunnels into Borehole Thirty-Two. We could land as far as a mile away, and *walk* in."

"I hazard such measures likely unnecessary," he told her. "Excepting an obvious installation constructed upon the surface, their scanners will not see past their own voluntary entombing. Nor should they have concern to. Denali is surely deluded in his safety, certain no craft is allowed in orbit, nor in fact anywhere within a hundred million miles. Yet we will see this overconfidence become his undoing."

"So then... where *do* you want to land? Certainly you don't intend for us to fly right down into the borehole?" she asked.

"Here, at this place," Bullseye said to her, pointing. "The Adytum flue, overheading the entry corridor from 'Annex: Thirty-Two Pi'. A natural chimney from the surface, conducting us nigh our destination."

Opal leaned forward, craning her head sideways to look at the layout. "But... that shaft is over a thousand feet deep," she pointed out. "How do you intend we make our way to the bottom?"

Bullseye looked confused at the question. "Well, within this very vessel, of course."

"Whoa, wait a minute," Stansky chimed in from the front. "Just how wide is this chimney of yours?"

Relic zoomed in close on the three-dimensional diagram. "Twenty feet across, at its most narrow," she told him.

"Uh... You realize this shuttle is at least fourteen."

"Providing an ample cushion of a full meter, fore and aft," Bullseye told him. "Unless you fear your aviation mastery not quite up to snuff with our comrade Bullit's."

"Oh, I'll get us down there. I just hope you took out collision on this rental, cuz I'm not paying for scraped paint."

The flight was long and monotonous, the scenery unchanging out the forward windscreen: the universe above, a void below. It was often difficult to tell if they were even moving. As they approached their target, James carried them forward even slower, dipping the shuttle down as low as he dared, skirting over the darkened landscape. But even from this shallow height, the edge of the mile-wide borehole could be seen in the distance, appearing like a sudden drop off marking the very edge of the little world. Even more interesting, with their eyes now long adjusted to the dimness of their surroundings, a pale, hazy glow could be discerned—a subtle incandescence from somewhere deep within the shaft. They were in the right place.

Stansky hovered over the opening of a deep channel in the ground, the Adytum flue, and scanned down into it. "We can't enter here. They're using it for something."

"Truly?" Bullseye asked. "How are you certain?"

"Because there's an atmospheric force screen half the way down, like on a hangar bay. The bottom of the shaft is pressurized. There's oxygen down there."

"And what else?" Bullseye pressed.

"What do you mean 'what else'?"

"What, in addition, does your scan divulge? Equipment? Machinery? Vehicles of any sort? What else may lay down there? Do you detect anyone living?"

"No, none of that. None of those things."

"Then I see no signs of occupancy that should deter our taking advantage of it," Bullseye said.

"But... why else would they pressurize it like that?" Stansky asked.

"Perhaps it was required, to ensure an atmosphere to a greater area. Regardless of the reason, it only increases its usefulness for us. So, downward ho."

James sighed, "Downward ho."

The insurance policy on the chartered craft would, in fact, not need to be utilized, as James lowered the shuttle with careful precision, over an excruciating expanse of many minutes. The jags and lances of a thousand fractured crystals pierced and projected from the carbon-coated walls, like the mouth of sharpened javelins lining a dug out ferox trap. He eased the vessel downward through the energized force screen—a barrier holding the breathable pressure in, and the toxic, frozen atmosphere of the surface at bay—and settled the ship down softly in a deep layer of graphite powder.

Bullseye, James, and Belladonna disembarked quickly, with long-practiced precision, sighting their weapons toward the ancient doorway, ready to engage whoever entered. No one did. Footsteps through the carbon revealed the room had definitely once been occupied, though apparently no longer, and when the sufficient passing of minutes made clear no welcome committee would come to call, the group lowered their guard, and began to suit into their armor.

"It smells like exhaust fumes in here," Relic reported, as she stepped out of the shuttle, and began stepping into a set of light-battle.

Belladonna nodded. "At least we know now what they're using this natural chimney for," she said. "They're venting some sort of engine emissions, trying to keep their air unpolluted."

"Emissions from what, I shall be eager to see," Bullseye added. "Rest assured, 'tis unlikely generators, as we have hitherto eyed proof of the origin of their energy."

James stopped in mid dress to look over at Lady Opal, the ashi'mar holding up the tasset of her battlegear, and trying to determine which end was up. He zipped his inertia jumpsuit, his massive set of PA known as Frösslind standing ready to climb into, and went to the little Capellan princess, gently taking her elbow to lead her a few steps away. "Listen. I know we couldn't leave you at the casino," he quietly told her, "but please, Opal... I need you to stay behind. I'm begging you, for me. My... desire to protect you might endanger the others, just by my distraction."

Her jade eyes flared, a shock of white eyebrow arching higher. "Leave me at the casino? Is that what you intended?"

"Well, originally. Until you..."

"Yes, I know. Until I gave myself away, not realizing my words were broadcast," she said. "But I *never* would have stayed behind."

"You don't understand. There's almost certainly fighting ahead for us, and you..."

"James, it is *you* who does not understand. I appreciate you wanting to care for me, and I comprehend your worry... oh, believe me, I do. I don't want to see you hurt either, and waiting behind... I know I would *obsess* on nothing else. But that's not why I insist on coming," she explained. "This Denali, or Dodger, he's perverted my onetime mentor, Vasu... a woman who raised me. He has either committed or commissioned the brutal murder of my queen, and two of my sistren ashi'mar as well. He intends to enslave my people, under a ruse of blasphemous lies and religious heresy. What kind of leader would I show myself to be, if I stood by to watch that happen? No... this travesty began with an assault on the lyghtan people. There shall be a lyghtan there to see it end."

The human had no response for her. He took the tasset from her hand and turned it the right way around, helping her to fasten it securely atop her hips. She stood on tiptoe and kissed him hard.

Bullseye's theory about the power source was fairly well proven near immediately. As they cautiously pulled open the massive arched doorway of ancient metal, just outside, humming away, stood a tall, semi-portable substation. The geothermal energy from the alien turbines under the casino was directed here, to be converted into a usable voltage, and distributed around the base. There were likely many such devices spread throughout. A very great many, based on the usage logs Relic had found.

Other than powering the atmospheric forcefield in the flue just behind them, this one also, at minimum, illuminated the rough-hewn corridor where they now found themselves. Only dimly illuminated, by weak, electric sconces, widely spaced—but illuminated, nonetheless. The harsh and jagged surface of the tunnel's edges made it clear that the pathway had been dug hurriedly, ripping through the dark rock and crystal—though not recently, of course, but untold eons ago. Distantly visible in both directions, a sort of aperture filled the hallways, like a shutter lens on an antique camera—both open now, but poised ready to slam shut. Heading right, toward the Adytum room and the borehole entrance just beyond, a different source of illumination cast a glow across the ceiling. A window, allowing harsh, white lighting from the other side to cast through, piercing the hallway, and painting the stone. But light wasn't the only thing coming through the viewport. The thrum of many engines, and the banging of steel, echoed through the hall.

"*What the hell is that noise?*" Relic asked over the comlink, looking up and down along the corridor. "*It sounds like they're repaving a highway.*"

Stansky lent an ear, then looked at Bullseye. "*Shit. I'm pretty sure I know what that is.*"

The five of them made their way furtively toward the window, a quintet of armored visors peering down into the room beyond.

It was just as James had feared.

A wide and well-lit loading bay was laid out before them far below, some hundred feet beneath the windows' vantage point, its dark, crystal walls doubly far apart as any hangar on the *Okubi*. A bustle of manpower and machinery fed a frenzy of rushed commotion. Waiting impatiently in single files, on the left, right, and center, in ponderously long lines that extended farther than their view revealed, was the source of the smelled exhaust, the engine droning, and the banging noise. Three slowly-moving rows of massive mechanical armor. Not suits of powered assault like the quaint dress Stansky was currently clad in, but marching heavy equipment: humanoid towers of walking steel, and each seven men high if they indeed measured a meter. Monstrous machines, squat down low on ready haunches, a startling array of deadly weaponry ringing the circumference of their gauntlets, and mounted squarely atop their chest and shoulders. A cavalry of mechanized nightmares, each operated by a pair of pilots, being herded one at a time aboard a lineup of waiting dropships. A twisted interpretation of Noah filling his ark.

"*Jesus…*" was all James could mutter.

"*Don't you start drooling now,*" Belladonna cautioned him. "*We don't have room for one of those in the shuttle, and your PA is plenty big enough.*"

"*What could they be planning with all that equipment?*" Relic asked in amazement.

Bullseye sighed. "*Clearly, they intend a ground invasion.*"

"*Of where?*" Opal wondered.

"*With that much equipment,*" Stansky answered, "*I'd say… everywhere.*"

"Hey! You there!" a voice shouted to them in common.

Five armored facemasks turned together, peering back down the hall from where they'd just come. Two soldiers approached, seeming unsure if they addressed friend or foe, in charcoal colored battlesuits covered with heavy, padded inertia jackets. Three glowing sensor eyes gleamed from each of them, bright red irises in the dim. The guard's hands moved tentatively, seeming to consider the unslinging of rifles.

James reacted first, lifting the barrel of his laser shotgun and launching a frag grenade from the undermount. The small explosive sailed true, careening toward the center of the two guardians. One of them lifted their hand, their gauntlets suddenly enveloped in a golden sheen of light, and seemed to stop the projectile in its tracks simply by bidding it to do so. The grenade spun and hurtled back at them, retracing its course straight toward Stansky. James had only a moment to instinctively react. He lifted the barrel of his long weapon, hauled back, and swung it—like Casey at the bat.

The frag sailed into the portable substation in a blinding blast of sparks and flame. With a stuttering flicker, the lights fell to darkness, only the glow through the nearby window left to partially illuminate a sliver of hallway. The two sentries raised their weapons, and the five mercenaries did the same. A grating squeal of shearing metal broke the moment before either fired, the massive set of alien doors suddenly torn free from their ancient hinges. They bent and crumpled, like reeds broken in the wind, ripping backward up the flue in a sudden flush of hurricane gusting. The loss of power had apparently cut the chimney's force screen, the base's higher-pressure atmosphere now rushing to escape—and taking with it what it could.

The two bewildered sentries went the same way as the doors, disappearing up the passage. Then the small shuttle they arrived in lifted slowly, and followed suit. The heavy coating of carbon powder became an opaque dust storm of inky black, the mercenaries struggling to hold their footing by taking advantage of the walls' sharp crags.

Stansky fired a tension reel through the aperture behind him. "*Come on!*" he yelled over the roaring of the furious wind. He scooped up Opal just in front of him and began retracting the microline into the reel. Bullseye followed suit, working with Belladonna to move Relic forward, the group pulling themselves along the cables like they were repelling up a wall. The grapple points of their mooring lines were drilled deep into crystal facades, but those anchors were beginning to tremble and loosen from the wind's vibrating judder. After a short, but difficult, horizontal climb, they pulled themselves through the open portal guarding the hallway, the gust seeming to double as it was forced through the narrow pass. A tangle of armor-clad appendages reached back, pulling Belladonna in lastly, ravenously feeding her through the hole to safety. They snapped the opening closed behind her.

In a blink, the wind was gone, like the turning of a mighty faucet. The exhausted companions sat slumped on hand and knee, breathing hard, and slowly being covered by a downy ashfall of drifting powder.

"*Well,*" Stansky huffed, "*there goes* that *fucking shuttle deposit.*"

The group took only a moment to gather their bearings, and their senses, now utilizing their helmet lamps to see through the ink-black darkness and blizzard of dust. The corridor was like walking on the very bottom of the sea, hidden from light of any kind, and awash with the falling detritus of every living thing above it.

Belladonna carefully inspected the condition of her daughter, dusting clean her visor. "*It's not gonna take them long to fix that, and repressurize,*" she cautioned. "*We need to keep moving.*"

"*Hopefully, they'll take it as an accident,*" James offered. "*I don't think those two had a chance to report us.*"

"*We dare not hazard such fate,*" Bullseye recommended. "*I advise we double-time toward the borehole, lest they set a battalion to blockade our way.*"

They jogged some distance through the dark, until they came to a modern, sliding doorway—one installed weeks or months ago, rather than in a previous millennium. They arrived just in time to hear the echoed coupling of the inner bulkhead, a second layer to bar their way. Someone was blocking them from the other side, but there was little choice of where else to go.

"*Four motion targets in there,*" Belladonna reported.

"*Relic,*" Bullseye asked, "*might you be able to open it?*"

The young seti infiltrationist accepted the duty that was once her father's. A microbore drill-head popped the cover plate clean in seconds, and she side-jacked the control wires with her security bypass mini-tab. She shook her head. There was no power. "*This panel is dead. Someone's killed the control wiring from the other side,*" she told them.

"*Then no choice is left to us. James, we need through this door.*"

"*Okay, stand back,*" Stansky warned. "*I have a pre-made directional ready to go, but it's a doozie.*"

Belladonna pointed. "*I show two targets right near the door.*"

"*Well, maybe we can take out two birds with one bulkhead,*" the human joked. He slapped a wad of heurcanium on the doorway, jogged backward, and pressed the trigger.

A blast of light and sound exploded forth, the ashy snowfall filling the air cleared aside from the sudden shock wave. The massive doorway launched itself inward, pinning the figures that lurked behind it hard against the wall. It then tipped to topple forward, the two unfortunates along with it.

Bullseye, James and Belladonna rushed into the smoke obscured computer room, peering through the shifting lighting of the swinging overheads, trying to get a lock on the enemy targets. They did—and then they froze. The dark-gray armor with red racing pinstripes was easy to identify, the gavel logo on the chest allaying any wavering doubts. It was Bullit. And Flashpoint just behind him. They spun their attention to the fallen bulkhead, as Tachion clambered dizzily back to his feet. Tàlto pulled off his helmet, rubbing his forehead of a sudden ache.

"Oh, my dear boy!" Belladonna ran to embrace Flashpoint, popping open her facemask as she rushed toward him. She hugged him tight, their armor clattering. "Oh my God. How are you? Are you all right?" She began patting him down, checking for injuries.

"I'm fine Mom, really. I'm not hurt."

She pushed him back and looked at him seriously. "And what about... what about your father?" she asked worriedly.

"I... I saw him, on Gel Gonahaar. We all did," he told her. "But... I couldn't. I mean, not at first. And then I did, but... I don't think I hurt him.

And I don't think I want to anymore. I think I was just mad. Or confused. I don't know. I think he let me go as well. I just don't..."

She grabbed him tight again and kissed his forehead. Relic came forward and hugged him as well.

Tachion looked at Bullseye. James looked at Bullit.

"Hey," muttered the human.

"Hey," Bullit gave back.

Opal pushed her way through the crowd and rushed over to hug Tachion—another awkward clanking of armor against armor. She glared at him, craning her neck nearly straight upward. "What foolish nonsense have you been up to, Doctor Magna? If we were on Capella, I'd have you incarcerated for making me worry!" She glanced down at Tàlto, finally struggling to his feet. "Both of you!" she announced.

Stansky approached Bullit. "How long have you been here? What frequency you guys on?"

"About an hour," Bullit told him. "We're on radio protocol six."

"We're on nine."

Bullit tapped his gauntlet and changed his comm channel.

Tachion took a quick visual survey, making sure no one was overly injured by the explosion. He turned to Tàlto. "Are you all right? Your head looks bad."

"No, I'm fine. Just got my bell rung a little bit. And my helmet's cracked."

"I don't mean from the explosion," the doctor said. "I mean that cut over your ear looks infected. The one from when we crashed the *Bugeye*."

The shocked voice of their leader came from behind them. "You... felled the *Bugeye*?" Bullseye inquired.

"Yeah, sorry. We sort of totaled it, I think."

"Pssh," Stansky chuckled. "We totaled the *McKendrick,* and maybe the *Dodger*. And made one hell of a shit mess of the hangar bay."

"Since we're getting things out in the open," Bullit offered tentatively, "we also burnt down half a city block on Gel Gonahaar. Or... *one* of us did."

James countered quickly. "Bullseye assassinated General Nylis."

"So we heard," Tachion told them, climbing over the fallen doorway to get closer. "We owe a couple of million credits to the Rumbl'garde Syndicate. Due within a month."

"And we could use some help paying it," Bullit added earnestly.

"We got Zvavi shot," Bullseye muttered, draining any humor from the conversation. "We know not if he lives or dies."

"What?" Tachion asked. "How?"

Flashpoint, trying to get into the spirit of the previous exchange, declared loudly, "We ditched half of Uncle James' PA armor in the middle of nowhere. Just left it in the dust. *Somewhere* on this barren moon."

"Wait, oh my God," James said. "No, you didn't. Did you?!"

Bullit scoffed. "Pfft. Of course, that's what sets him off." He turned then and went cautiously over to Bullseye, taking him aside a few steps by the elbow. "Listen. I'm sorry, about... you know... before."

"A sentiment we both share," his team leader answered back.

The group quickly debriefed each other, sharing information from which way they came. Opal sidled up to Tachion and clasped his forearm, begging his ear.

He bent down towards her.

"So, is that it? Is it over? Is this how menfolk make up after a fight?" she asked. "They just carry on? I've been in quarrels with my women friends for far longer, for infinitely less."

"Yes. I think male friends don't tend to stay visibly angry very long, over very much, beyond the two most major contentions... money, or women. We all have plenty of the first, and dissimilar interests in the second. For a simple difference of opinion... or perhaps not so simple... most likely we'll just carry our grudges silently till forgotten, and never mention them again."

Bullseye overheard as he approached the whispering pair. "I fear... not quite so easy as that, my old friend. There lie hard conversations ahead to be had, amongst us all, as one assembly. But now, without dispute, is certain no ripe time. Some outrageous fortune has seen fit to procure us here all together. Let us not test its sense of whimsy by ignoring such coincidence. We shall place bickering aside. Resolved as one we must be. Parliament... *all* of us... to the last."

Tachion nodded acknowledgement to him silently, pulling the drak'min pistol from his side, and handing it to him, grip first.

Bullseye nodded back, accepting it.

The group's attention was suddenly drawn to the sound of an opening doorway across the room. A single guard stood there, seeming surprised and more than alarmed, her three sensor eyes panning across the reunited party. She stood a moment, then moved to unsling her rifle.

Bullit drew a laser pistol from his hip, dropping the sentry with a single shot. It briefly backlit the settling smog in the crowded room, piercing her square between her sensor eyes, and knocking her back into the hall she came from. Almost immediately, a piercing alarm began to sound.

"Oh, great. Now look what you did," Stansky told him.

"Me?" Bullit asked. "You think shooting that one guard is what set the alarm off, but you explosively decompressing half the planet had nothing to do with it?"

Bullseye resecured his helmet, and rallied everyone over the comlink. *"The cause of the alert matters not. Urgency pushes us on, regardless. Come then, let us hurry. The press of destiny moves us forward. Let us now pierce the borehole's heart, and show what havoc we might cause."*

20.3

A WAR WAS BEING WAGED on the battlefield of Rook's mind. The uneasy confusion that had been seeping in since Gel Gonahaar, had now blossomed into something deeper. A tempest was tossing him back and forth between his loyalties, between his perceptions of reality, his very understanding of himself. The compulsions which controlled him were faltering and fading away, allowing him to spend fleeting moments in the company of his *true* thoughts. He wasn't fond of them. The certainty of implanted devotion at least gave him a sense of purpose, a larger meaning. But as he began to find doubt in those, he doubted the very reasons for his being. In those flashes of clarity, when he realized what was happening, his first instinct was rebellion, turning against Denali in favor of his family. *Both* of them. But then he remembered—they were actually no different. His wife and children. His friends and colleagues. The truth of the matter was, he'd been betrayed equally by all of them. He was utterly alone in the world. In the galaxy. In the *universe*. Then the clarity was gone, before he had time for any action. The emptiness of it all driving his mind back to Denali, and the comfort of his implanted reality.

But Rook kept this all hidden, the roiling turmoil in his mind. Or at least he tried. A persistent urge had been growing for days now—to see Lord Denali, to confide these thoughts to him. An urge that the human himself had seeded, knowing his suggestions would eventually need reinforcement. The seti was programmed to seek a booster when the prior effect began to fade—but he was being prevented. Denali had been delayed on business elsewhere, due to arrive soon with the Drak'min fleet, over a full day past due now. And Drake had grown suspicious, perhaps having caught a glare of contempt—or more than one—cast his way. Excuses had been made which kept Rook quarantined aboard the interceptor, but that lack of purposeful activity just allowed the disparate thoughts to echo louder.

And louder.

What would he do if he could see his wife again? And Flashpoint? Or little Relic? Would he be more inclined to run and hug them, or would he prefer to see them lying dead? At this point, he wasn't sure. And in fact, he began to wonder the exact same thing about Denali. His mind was so conflicted from one moment to another, he didn't trust himself to know just what he would do next.

His past three full days were spent sequestered in the cramped bunkroom of the interceptor; the seti's only view, a crystalline wall outside the window. He had spent hours staring at it: frosted translucence in hexagonal bands, a litany of runic hieroglyphs etched deep into the diamond. What did they say? He could only imagine. Was it an ancient prophetic text, extolling peaceful unity under Lord Denali? Or something more foreboding—a warning of devils to come. The more he came to fear the latter, the more his programming urged him back to family.

To this—his *new* family.

Finally, at long last, Drake came into his room. "Come on, get your armor on," he instructed him, dressed in his own—that same familiar mandibled helmet, giving him the look of a biting insect. "Lord Denali is ready to see you. Plus, we'll be in Coalition space within the hour."

"We're back to the Coalition already?" Rook asked, with equal parts relief and surprise. "You're kidding."

"What exactly about our time together has made you think of me as a kidder?" Drake asked. "This little rogue planet moves along at quite a clip. Thirty million miles an hour, five percent the speed of light."

"Shit, I wish you had told me we'd be emerging so soon," Rook complained, hopping up to put his light battle on. "If I knew we were so close to show time, I would have been preparing. Stretching out my hamstrings and warming up my vocal cords."

"Perhaps working on your witticisms," Drake huffed in irritation. "Don't worry, you'll have plenty of time to brush up your material. The attack is days away yet. But our master wants us prepared at all times, just in case of an eventuality."

"Oh, I'm prepared," Rook answered. "But don't leave me hanging. What *is* the attack plan?"

"We'll wait here in the borehole another six standard days, until we're well away from the border, and at our closest point to Tristar station. It will be easy to overtake them, and establish a beachhead using their base. A midway point between K'Tas T'Mir, Rhyana, and Earth, from which Lord Denali can deploy our ground forces. Once those three worlds have fallen, swift victory is assured."

"The seti, the android, and the humans all at once? That's a pretty big bite to chew."

"Our master has large teeth. Come outside, I'll show them to you."

The wall outside Rook's window had betrayed none of what Drake unveiled to him. Stepping out the airlock of the interceptor onto the wide catwalk ringing the borehole was more than a tad disorienting, like peering from the precipice of a towering skyscraper. Rook fought back a twist of vertigo as he made a quick survey of his surroundings. The balcony they perched upon was perhaps thirty foot wide from wall to banister, and made of the customary dark alloy found in all the ruins here on The Rock. It clung to the sheer cliff face that formed the walls of the enormous shaft: uniform columns of prismatic diamond which absorbed the running lights of the interceptor, and many other vessels that awaited here, breaking it, reflecting it back, in scattered shards of fractured rainbow. The seti peered out across the wide chasm. The farthest side of the crystalline channel was not difficult to discern, even a mile away through the dim, as vessels docked along its dizzying heights sparked a similar spectrum of refracted light.

Rook moved tentatively toward the insufficient looking railing, gripping tight with his armored gauntlets, and gaping at the armada stretching above him and below. Warships large and small—lyghtan, chamai, mercenary, and now Drak'min—encircled the walls of the ancient borehole, forming a metropolis more grand than any cavern city on Capella. Above him, the ring of massive starships spiraled upwards toward the surface, the star-filled heavens brightly visible beyond the canyon opening. The hazy glow of an atmospheric force screen shimmered across the entire width of the gap, securing their precious oxygen from the vacuum of open space. Below him, the amassed fleet continued downward—Nylis' *Okubi* waiting amongst them—the ships huddling against the walls, circling ever lower into the darkness, the wonder of the deepening channel seeming to have no visible end. The ghostly, ever-present echo of a hundred idling antigrav engines resonated, like the ocean roar in an Earthan conch shell.

"You look like you've never visited the boreholes before," Drake said, mildly amused at his comrade's astonishment.

"Yeah, well... I guess I missed that field trip in cub scouts. But you can give me the grand tour, den mother."

The other seti's amusement faded, and he turned to lead the way around the periphery of the ancient balcony.

The walkway they traveled on wasn't the only route around the borehole. Similar pathways were perched along the circumference of the walls, both up above and down below, connected by occasional ramps, and with shortcuts veering off, spanning out slightly over the open chasm. Drake led them down one of these, a bridge some distance away from the relative safety of the crystal wall, and Rook was forced to ignore a parade of dropships descending past, fearful a moment of turned attention might send him tripping over the edge. As they reached the other side, a figure in a hooded robe crossed the catwalk coming to meet them. Lord Denali, escorted by an entourage of armored soldiers, each with a burning trio of sensors glaring through the dim. Rook had never in his life felt at once so relieved, yet so afraid. His mind wavered between urges to bow and worship, or throw him over.

For the moment, he did neither.

"Drake, my old comrade," the human greeted the pair with uncustomary good spirits, "and Rook, my even older, and yet *newer* one as well. Have you seen?" He waved his arms around at it all. "The destiny I've long suffered for is finally coming to bear! Admiral Yazir's commanders needed a little more hand holding than anticipated. A little more *coaxing*, why don't we call it. Suffice it to say, they're all onboard now." He looked to his long-time deputy. "Drake, what's the status of the deployment?"

"As you've seen, my lord, the Mindgate armor has been distributed to our infantry. The mech cavalry are being loaded now aboard dropships, and dispersed among the lead attack vessels."

"Excellent," Denali said. "Proceed as you have been. Remember, I want it made clear to my new army their lord and emperor has no interest in taking prisoners. Our offensive must be ruthless. Merciless. Anything less than full submission must be met with agonized death." He turned his attention to focus on Rook as he finished. "Mercy of any kind can too easily be mistaken for weakness. Best to avoid any confusion, and demonstrate nothing of either."

"Understood, my lord," Drake replied. "I'll make your holy word known."

Denali still kept his eyes locked on Rook, evaluating him, scrutinizing his manner. "Say what you want about the old general," the man who looked like Dodger explained to him, "but he's laid out an extensive strategy for the first few months of our campaign that... well, we might not have resistance for much longer than that, if it goes to plan. They won't know what hit them."

"Where is the good General Nylis, by the way?" Rook inquired. "I still have yet to meet him."

"I'm afraid that distinct displeasure has been rudely stolen away from you. Turns out our old Parliament friends are a little more resourceful than I gave credit for. More resourceful than Nylis expected, at any rate. It seems they've exterminated him. Splattered his brains in dramatic fashion. Bullseye's doing, without a doubt."

"Hmm. Perhaps they've done you a favor. If he's already laid out the perfect strategy, what other usefulness did he serve?"

"What use indeed," Denali agreed. "It's true, I can't say I'm disappointed. Other than I won't get the joy of wringing the life out of him myself. I'll have to give a field promotion to one of his officer's, someone to take his place. I'll make that decision this afternoon," he told him. "In the meantime, you and I should have a more... private... conversation. But let's just see where we stand first."

Rook felt the human's mind searching his own—probing, prying—opening doors where he wasn't welcome; kicking them down, and barging in. Once again, the division of his mind overwhelmed him like a mania—his dread over the insanity of losing himself again, the yearning for the peace a lone, grim purpose seemed to bring.

"Yes..." Denali said. "I see we have *quite* a bit of work to do."

The tendrils retracted back from the seti's thoughts like the appendages of a startled sea creature, as one of the armored entourage interrupted them. "Lord Denali, Master Drake, we've had a decompression in one of the exhaust flues."

"Caused by what?" Denali asked, clearly irritated at being disturbed.

"We... aren't certain. Perhaps a power failure for some reason."

"What reason?" Drake demanded. "Check with the Adytum control chamber."

"We have, sir. Or... we've tried. We're not getting any answer."

"Here, give it to me," the seti barked, grabbing the multicomm from the sentry's hand. He made a few keystrokes on the touchscreen, and then silently gawked at it. After a few moments, he passed the device to Lord Denali.

Through a camera angle slightly hazed with slowly-settling smoke clouds, twelve figures could be seen—three of them his own soldiers, dead upon the ground, the remaining nine being members of Parliament and whatever friends they had brought along. A doorway behind the mercenaries opened. Bullit shot and killed the guard behind it.

"Sound the alarms, quickly!" Denali shouted, thrusting the multicomm back into Drake's chest. "Seal off all borehole entrances, if it isn't already too late!" He turned back to Rook. "Our old friends have come looking for us, and somehow, they've... You've served with them far more recently than I have. What will they do? What would their plan be?"

"I... I'm not sure. Planning ahead was never really our strong suit. We tended to work much more off the cuff, seat of our pants."

Denali gripped him by the chest plate and lifted him up hard against the precipice railing. "These insignificant insects are trying to derail my rightful destiny! What the Universe itself demands to be, they are seeking to prevent! Think, goddamn it! What would your tactic be if you were with them?!"

"I... I don't know, My Lord," Rook exclaimed, leaning back uncomfortably out over the edge. "Short of Stansky blowing up the whole planet, which I wouldn't put past them, I don't..." He looked upward at the dizzying height as Denali pushed him further rearward. "Wait! That!" He directed his finger straight upward.

Denali dropped him back to the catwalk, then looked up to where Rook had been pointing. "What? What is it? I don't... Oh, shit," Denali swore in realization. "Drake, Rook, you're with me. Let's get up there. Send a squadron up ahead of us. And I want every ready ship to launch. Get them into orbit. This borehole is a hazard until Parliament is taken care of."

"Yes, my lord, at once," Drake hurriedly acknowledged.

Denali pulled Rook in front of him, his eyes boring into his soul. "Now is your time. Show me whether you're part of this destiny we forge together, or if you're still living the lie your so-called *friends* created for you. *Now* is your chance to choose your *own* path!"

Yet the human's thoughts made the choice for him, crashing over him like a tidal wave. *"I want you to kill them all!"*

20.4

A WAFTING CURRENT OF DUSTY air was flowing steadily now through the ancient corridor—a subtle, steady breeze, which echoed around them in a low moan, vibrating against the crystal with its prolonged, sighing exhale. It was as if the giant chasm and its labyrinth of tunnels were all just the curving resonance of a massive musical instrument—one now playing a mournful dirge, composed of a single, ominous note. The party moved ahead with a hurried purpose, traveling steeply upward against the flurry of drifting soot, using the gentle draft of the borehole's breathing to find their way towards its heaving maw.

Bullit sighed hard with exertion. *"Phew. I don't remember another week where I've had to walk quite so much."*

"Yes," Bullseye mused. *"But in the apparent absence of any silver to be mined from this dark cloud's lining, at the very least, we might take comfort in the knowledge we have all achieved our weekly step count."*

Bullit chuckled, taken aback. *"Tssh. Wait a minute! Was that a* joke *that you just made? Did our illustrious and somber leader just actually make a jest?! I'm not sure if I like the idea. I think I prefer my Bullseye more somber and dignified."*

"What were you guys doing stomping around in my armor, anyway?" Stansky interrupted, clearly vexed, and ignoring the other comments.

Bullit shook his head at him as they trudged along through the drifting soot. *"Will you knock that off already! What the hell did you want us to do, suffocate out on the surface?"*

James said nothing, but tilted his head sideways.

"Well?"

"I'm thinking about it."

"There's really no need to worry," Flashpoint assured him. *"I can show you right where we left them."*

"I appreciate it," Stansky said, *"but actually that's not necessary. I have a hidden PPS beacon inside each of my PA sets."*

"Then what are you complaining about?" Bullit scoffed. *"You can track them even if someone snags them."*

"I'm not worried about them being stolen. I'm worried about them getting dirty."

"James," Opal said, *"don't you think you're being a little silly?"*

The human fell silent, and not another word was said about it. Bullit beamed a smile behind his helmet's facemask.

"The opening to the main shaft should be just ahead," Relic told them. But the growing rumble of thruster engines had already announced the fact ahead of her—their exhaust the likely cause of the rising breeze swirling around them.

The group slowed their advance, and proceeded with greater caution.

"*Relic, Flashpoint,*" their mother instructed sternly, "*it's probably best if you wait here, guard our six from...*"

"*Not a chance,*" Relic declared, equally sternly.

"*Really, Ma,*" Flashpoint echoed her. "*You want us to wait out in the hall like a couple of children? Besides, how do you know that's not more dangerous than out there?*"

Bullseye interjected on their behalf. "*Belladonna, your maternal apprehension is surely misplaced. An early Parliament, if you recall, realized a quarter score of missions by their age.*" The intensity of her scowl penetrated through her armor, and he sensed the gravity of his mistake. "*We shall keep a watchful eye, both of us,*" he promised her. "*You keep your boy close, and believe me when I say, I will allow* nothing *to hurt your daughter. Even upon my very life.*"

They reached the top of the ascending ramp, and stepped out through a narrow archway into the majesty of the giant borehole.

Though it was technically an ancient ruin, the term seemed hardly to apply. Not touched by weather, nor erosion, nor the inevitable vandalism of society's hand, the glassy walls and iron-like railing were still in astonishingly pristine condition. The dim backdrop of the massive chasm was illuminated by a parade of passing craft, shuttles and dropships descending down, frigates and star destroyers rising up. Relic and Opal moved forward, peering down over the balcony's ledge. The fleet of awaiting warships spiraled down into the bottomless distance, undocking from the edges each in turn, and making their way towards the surface. The nose of a massive battlecruiser pulled past the balcony, heading upwards, the vessel feeling nearly close enough to reach out and brush with fingertips. The group crouched back against the diamond walls, hoping their silhouettes weren't visible against the shimmer of the crystal behind them.

As the jet wash blew about, Tachion looked back and forth at the assembled group. "*Where the hell has Tàlto gone? Wasn't he with us when we left the Adytum?*"

Silent shrugs were his only answer.

"*Bullseye to Tàlto,*" their leader called him over the comlink. "*Tàlto, respond.*"

They were met with only silence.

"*I knew it,*" the doctor lamented. "*I knew we shouldn't trust that...*"

"*Asshole?*" Bullit offered.

"*His absence is of no matter,*" Bullseye stated flatly, "*providing he seeks not to betray evidence of our presence.*"

"He would never," Opal defended him.

"Besides," Stansky added, *"I'm pretty sure they're already aware."*

Tachion surveyed the shaft himself once the starship had rumbled past, a seemingly endless entwining maze of dangling balconies and crisscrossed bridges, along with an armada large enough to house many thousands of armored soldiers. *"I got to tell you Bullseye, I'm feeling a little bit lost here,"* the android admitted. *"We've got hundreds of ships, over miles of open shaft... I know we've got to do something, but... I mean..."*

"What the fuck are we supposed to do?" Bullit again finished his thought for him.

Bullseye shook his head. *"The very utmost that we might. Whatever we may achieve to frustrate their foul ambitions. In the very least, disrupt the comfort of this cozy hive. At most, if fortune favors, find its king and dethrone him violently."* He stood beside Tachion and gazed up and down the borehole as well. *"Though where to embark with either, I must open myself to suggestion."*

Belladonna was staring upward. *"Anything up there look familiar to you gentlemen?"*

The group followed her eyeline upward. Vessel after vessel was ascending the crystal canyon, passing through the force screen en route to the stars beyond. Already they could see the spot-lit outlines of several warships peering down from a low orbit.

"Yes," Bullseye said. *"The atmospheric shield generator, as the one in the Adytum chimney. Relic, would you wager you might deactivate it, if we were to escort you to a terminal?"*

"Why bother with all that?" James interceded. *"We can just take out the substations. I can see one there,"* he pointed at it high above them, *"and another one over there. If we take a couple of them down, that shit will collapse like the one in the flue."*

"Yeah, but with us here inside it," Bullit pointed out.

"No, of course not. We'll set it off by remote, with a timer backup just in case. We'll be long gone behind the tunnel bulkhead before we trigger it. That's if we can be quick and sneaky enough. We can drop Flashpoint at the first one, with half of us there to guard him, and I'll go on and take the other. I don't know how many of those power that field, but that should be enough to punch a big hole in it."

Tachion nodded thoughtfully. *"A decompression of that magnitude... it might yank many of these ships off their moorings. Perhaps even rattle a few into each other. That ought to cause a little damage."*

"And suck the breath out of any hostiles in these tunnels," Bullit added.

"It's agreed then. We drop the field," Bullseye declared, making it official. *"Though the question yet remains, how we intend to navigate our way up there."*

As if on cue, Tàlto emerged beyond the railing, his armored form slowly lifting into view, seeming to drift upward over the open chasm. *"Thought we all might need a ride,"* the lyghtan explained from the controls of a wide, flat hoverdolly. *"Honestly, I have no idea why you guys do so much walking."*

"Unbelievable," Bullit complained. *"I swear, this guy keeps doing this."*

"Well don't just stand there," Tàlto said. *"Your chariot awaits."*

The group climbed the ancient railing to clamber aboard the awaiting dolly, and huddled in a mass at its very center, the lack of any railing leaving the edges far less desirable. Tàlto pulled back from the wall, and began to deftly lift the party upward.

As the cargo mover slowly rose, James took Flashpoint aside. He pulled a blast remote from his demo kit: a small textured handle with the look of a dismantled pistol grip, a trigger at its front, and a red push button crowning the top. He handed it to the young seti, opening his facemask, and whispering without the comlink. "Here, use this. It's a remote with a dead man's switch. Just trigger the safety when you're ready to go set the charge. That way... you know... in case..."

"I know what it is," Flashpoint assured him, "and I understand. You mean in case I get killed while setting it, the charge will still go off."

"Not that that's gonna happen, but... yeah, you're right. Or, if you drop it, so... you know... *don't*." His helmet's mask slid back shut.

The ledge where the first of the portable substations was visible was not at all like the other balconies the group had drifted past. The hanging deck up here was instead a wide, stone veranda, which sat atop a lengthy stairway of broad, shallow treads made from the carved obsidian ore, and with a low, surrounding parapet. Inscriptions of unknown meaning decorated the edges of the heavy railing. The terrace extended back from the borehole into a large hollowed out gallery, with a similar cavernous height as the city's casino floor, and with the same staggered metallic towers helping to hold the roof aloft. Two of the catwalks from upper levels crisscrossed high above the cumbersome balcony, going so far as to run the circumference of the inner gallery. The floor of the vast chamber was stacked with boxes and crates, arranged in no discernable fashion, and tarp covered piles of stored supplies and provisions.

Tàlto tucked them in against the wall, aligning the dolly with the stone staircase.

Bullseye called out his orders over the roar of a star destroyer rising past. *"Flashpoint, Belladonna, Relic, myself, and Bullit. We disembark here, ensure the safety of our young demo expert. James, continue onward. Tachion, Tàlto, and Opal are with you."*

Just as he finished speaking, a barrage of gunfire rang out, both bullets and laser blasts, impacting randomly on the deck of the hoverdolly. Tàlto veered sharply forward, striking the shimmering wall of the borehole, and rudely dumping himself and his passengers at the base of the ancient stairs. The hoverdolly whined as it tipped back, spinning in circles down the chasm.

The party scattered in different directions, Belladonna and her daughter seeking cover behind the far support tower, while Bullseye, Tàlto and Flashpoint were equally sheltered by the closer one. Bullit and Stansky simply ducked behind the stone parapet, while Tachion rushed Opal to the safety of one of the supply stacks.

"Who has eyes?!" Tachion shouted. *"Where are those shots coming from?!"*

Bullit checked the motion sensor on his visor, then risked a visual peak to confirm. *"We have two catwalks above the balcony, a lower and an upper. There are sentries in that same uniform battlegear, all on the lower catwalk."* He raised his weapon at them, firing blindly.

"They benefit from a superior vantage point," Bullseye pointed out. *"A cleared shot is problematic, without hazarding exposure."*

"Maybe I can get them from back here," Tachion suggested. He descrambled his autocannon, and peering with it around the supply pile, let loose a rain of deafening lead.

Several of the guards raised their arms up, clad in brightly glowing gauntlets. Although many of the rounds hit true, only to be absorbed by inertia shields and armored padding, equally as many seemed to pass through, ricochet off, or even swerve around the line of soldiers.

Stansky scoffed. *"Looks like a superior vantage point isn't the only benefit they have."* He unscrambled a portable missile launcher, fitting it with an explosive warhead. *"Let's see if flying is in their little bag of tricks. Cover me. Keep 'em busy!"*

There came a barrage of blind fire from behind the supplies, towers, and parapet, as James slung the launcher atop the railing, and sighted down its target scope. The rocket launched, and hit. The alien catwalk disappeared behind a heated curtain of billowed fire, reappearing as the smoke cleared—sans a ten-foot section, and half the sentries along with it. The walkway buckled suddenly, tilting downward in a jerking motion, and depositing another two unlucky souls toward the distant bottom.

"*Hmm, how 'bout that?*" Stansky said, surveying the damage. "*Sturdier than I would've thought.*"

Bullit, Belladonna, and Bullseye opened fire on the remaining three, quickly burning through the guard's defenses as they held the railing for their dear lives. Lives that soon ended, nonetheless.

Tachion peered out as he kept Lady Opal safe behind the stack of boxes with a powerful extended arm. "*Is that it?*" he asked. "*Is that all of them?*"

"No, good Doctor!" an oddly recognizable voice called out, "not exactly *all* of them."

From a dark, arched doorway at the rear of the crystal-walled gallery, atop the higher of the two catwalks, a platoon of soldiers scurried out, dividing in each direction to surround the circumference of the space. Footsteps echoed as they clapped their heavy, armored boots atop the metal walkway. Behind them strode a familiar figure, swathed in robes of leather, and an aura of malice. Then came that spark of recollection, triggering memories, triggering moments. Opening floodgates of reminiscence—a younger life once lived, a lifetime ago.

"*Dodger*" Stansky muttered.

"*Jim,*" Bullseye breathed.

Then a second familiar figure followed on the coattails of the first, in a unique set of light battlegear—its hue a dark purpled-black like the stains of bone-deep bruising, the etched icon of a chess castle decorating the top of the left breast plate.

"Rook!" Belladonna shouted, imploring heartbreak in her voice.

Her husband instinctively drew an autopistol and fired on her position.

She ducked back, avoiding the ricochet.

"Dad, no!" Relic cried.

"The ghost of your dead husband now lives only to serve me!" Denali shouted, directing their onetime seti friend to join the soldiers on the far side. "I admit, not killing you years ago... *all* of you... is a mistake I won't repeat."

"Merely one in a long line of mistakes, it would seem!" Tachion shouted. "But don't worry! We'll make sure you don't make any more."

There was a flash of movement from near the balcony, behind the first dark tower of staggered ore. Tàlto leaped forward, moving quickly and without warning, pushing Flashpoint rudely aside as he snatched the drak'min weapon from Bullseye's holster. He dashed forward and rolled, training the elongated barrel of the disintegration pistol at Denali. He fired.

With the flick of a finger, Denali cast his nearest soldier out in front of him, the bewildered guard bearing the brunt of the weapon's terrible wrath. The fiery pulse of the beam hit him, immediately severing the atomic bonds of the sentry's molecular makeup, in an unstoppable chain reaction that was agonizingly thorough, and agonizingly slow. He cried out in high-pitched screaming, like a man overcome with fire, clawing at the air where his chest had been; until the sluggish disintegration ran its course, and the man was gone.

Denali was not pleased. With a wave of his hand, his cuffs aglow in amber fire, he tossed Tàlto hard against a covered pile of crates and boxes, smashing through them, and cracking them open. With a wave of the other hand, he threw Tachion through the air as well. The android sailed across the room like a nearly massless rag doll. But he wasn't in fact massless, and the immensity of his metallic frame came crashing down on top of Tàlto.

The two opposing forces opened fire on each other.

The doctor struggled to stand up, staggering away from where he was pinning the bounty hunter against a crystal column. He felt the lyghtan behind him slouch lifelessly down the chipped diamond, collapsing on the floor at the android's heels. The doctor stood and looked down. Tàlto's previously damaged helmet was now fully cracked wide open, his bald ebony head splayed just as rudely underneath it. A burst of laser fire hit Tachion's back, only to be absorbed by his albedo shield, but draining his QEU pack to nearly half. He spun from Tàlto's body, and ducked behind a wide trunk of crystal that was erupting from the stone floor. Looking back toward where Lady Opal still hid, he bade the ashi'mar to keep low, with exaggerated, emphatic hand signals.

Bullit and Stansky switched their position, from the parapet of heavy masonry that looked out over the chasm, to the one across the stairway rimming the wide aperture to the inner gallery. From here they were able to view the whole left side of the expansive space, while keeping a careful eye on the visor motion detectors guarding their backside. Yet another massive battleship was rising up behind them into orbit.

"*Over here, at ten o'clock,*" Bullit motioned. "*Those four are facing the side of their heads right at us.*"

James switched to his EM visor and took a look. "*They have albedo and sonic shields up. Shall we go with your namesake? Good old-fashioned bullets?*"

"*With pleasure,*" Bullit answered, slinging away his AE rifle and drawing out a set of rocket pistols.

James already carried his favored nine millimeters in hand. "*I'll start left, you go right?*"

Bullit nodded.

The pair rose from behind the barricade, firing at the foursome from the outsides working in. They targeted all their ammo on just the shiny, rounded helmets, watching them fall backwards like a row of carnival midway ducks. The two fist-bumped their armored gauntlets in rare mutual appreciation.

Meanwhile, Bullseye and Belladonna concentrated all their firepower around Denali, hoping to distract him from using his powers. The human was cowering back behind a hail of bullets and blaster shots, tucked in a shallow alcove along the catwalk, and protected by a soldier in a uniform different from the others—a dark-black suit of battle, with a mandibled helmet like an insect. The adversaries ducked in and out, exchanging volleys with each other.

"*We're never gonna get those substations blown now,*" Belladonna told him. "*What's the new plan?*"

"*We may still inflict some damage, scuttle a ship or two,*" Bullseye answered, "*even if we demolish merely this one lone transformer. James, might you manage it? Set your charge, then we retreat.*"

"*I'm closer! I can get it!*" Flashpoint claimed enthusiastically. He dashed from their veil of cover, and sprinted over toward the power cylinder.

"*Flash, no!*" his mother shouted.

But it was too late. He was already full-out running. He reached the substation and crouched at its side, engaging the remote as instructed before he began affixing a charge at its base. Belladonna, Relic, and even Opal from across the room, laid out a spray of cover fire in an effort to protect the boy.

From across the ancient gallery, and lofted high above, his father's eyes peered down upon him, swimming in the singular purpose that Denali had just compelled in him. He remembered his mistake in the toy factory on Gel Gonahaar, allowing a moment of foolish emotion to hesitate his trigger finger. That emotion was still there—Denali had not the chance yet to finally dispense with all of it. But now Rook was more aware, more determined, and more calloused, the feelings for his family buried deep beneath implanted will. He beat the screams and cries of his sentimentality down, and coldly pulled the trigger on the boy that he had raised.

Flashpoint buckled at the waist from the impact of his father's autopistols, lurching backward at the penetration, and collapsing on the stone floor. He dropped the demo charge from his left hand, and the dead man's switch from his right. The remote operated as intended, and set the blast off at Flashpoint's feet.

"*Nooo!*" Belladonna wailed, screaming over the echoed explosion. There was an ensuing rush of a sudden wind, drawing the smoke and debris up the borehole in a powerful gusting draft. Behind them, beyond the relative shelter of the stone balcony and its lofted gallery, the gale was a swirling tempest, tearing up and down the crystal borehole. The atmospheric force field had been breached. Nearly a mile away, on the distant far side of the chasm, a shuttle craft veered off course, and impacted against a passing frigate. Several explosions from far below told that the incident was perhaps not isolated. A descending drop vessel hurtling downward toward its mothership careened close to the cavernous gallery, nearly tearing through the massive blocks of the carved veranda. It missed it by mere feet.

With the smoke and soot cleared quickly by the rushing wind, the damage was plain to see. The substation was in shambles, its debris scattered across the balcony. Flashpoint, it seemed, had not fared any better—the upper half of his body lay unmoving on the ancient stone, the lower half as widely scattered as the shrapnel of the blasted cylinder. A single, broken, ivory femur, painted in gore and swaddled in tattered flesh, was all that remained of the young seti's former legs.

Rook looked down on the gruesome spectacle, anticipating a surge of pride. But rather than a fallen enemy laid out in defeat before him, all the seti could envision were reflections of his beloved child. A giggling infant boy held aloft in outstretched arms. An imitative youngster, hand in hand on their first hunting trip. His willful adolescent, choosing to follow his *own* path, unaware his loving father was secretly proud of him all the same.

But now all of this was washed away by the sickening vision of a spreading blood pool.

The emotions he was keeping down rebelled at the horrific sight, overpowering their oppressor, and usurping Denali's suggestion. It cleared his mind and set it free. He realized all at once just exactly what he had done, not only here and now, but everything he'd taken part in. His treachery in the doctor's laboratory. What he'd done to Dr Grivvux. And now, his own boy! The memories of his betrayal belched up acrid, like bile in his mouth, and Rook staggered back dizzily as the epiphany washed over him.

Bullit looked back at his young cousin's body as well, heartbroken and horrified, and he roared in anger through the comlink. His ancestral seti rage reverted from Lord Denali back to Rook, and he sought his former teammate through the scope of his weapon's sights. When Rook glanced down a second time, peering his head over the ledge of the balcony, it was the opportunity Bullit had been waiting for. He fired his AE200, the laser striking the other seti's chest, draining his remaining shields to nothing, and tossing him back against the crystal wall. His shoulder was visibly burnt. Rook didn't try to retaliate. He instead scurried to the right, to a point behind a metallic column that obstructed himself from Bullit, so that only Tachion was in view.

The seti began flailing wildly toward the android, in some unintelligibly rapid handspeak. The doctor fired a burst at him from his autopistols, sending Rook diving to the catwalk floor. But then he appeared again, this time struggling to raise his hands against the pain of his angry shoulder wound. Tachion paused and held his fire.

"*Help...*" Rook signaled, slowing his handspeak to be more readable, "*help Flashpoint... help my boy.*"

Tachion cocked his head at him, clearly dubious.

Rook released his collar clasp, pulling off his helmet and tossing it over the ledge to the ground below. His tangled, black mane whipped and spun in the eddied updraft, and he looked down on his android friend with pleading eyes, and a broken heart. "Please!" he mouthed at him, every ounce of him genuinely begging.

"*Yeah... that's good Doc,*" Bullit encouraged him, sneaking around for a clear shot amid the chaos of the distraction. "*You keep him right there. I'm gonna take the top of his head off.*"

"*No, wait! Hold your fire!*" Tachion called back.

"*But I've got the shot, T.*"

"*Hold a second! Do not fire!*"

Tachion leaned out to look at the distance between himself and Flashpoint, and was immediately hit in the side by an enemy bullet. He could register that his hip had been badly damaged, but as a benefit of being android, he didn't, in fact, feel any pain. Nonetheless, there was no way he could get to Flashpoint without being torn to ribbons from above.

He looked back up at Rook. "*Cease fire...*" he signed in handspeak.

Rook threw his autopistols over the balcony.

"*All of you... cease your fire... can't get to him...*"

Rook rushed over to the three soldiers closest to him, that were shooting down on Tachion's position. "Hold your fire!" he screamed at them.

They continued the fight, refusing to acknowledge him.

He grabbed the closest one by the shoulder, again ordering him to cease shooting.

The guard shook him off.

Denali's voice came to Rook now, echoing in his mind, demanding him to stop.

"Fuck you!" he sent the thought back. Then he pulled out his acid sprayers, and liberally doused the helmets of the three soldiers right in front of him.

As they dropped their weapons and screamed in agony, fingers melting in their gauntlets as they struggled to remove liquefying headgear, he helped them to their ends by flipping them over the railing one at a time.

"Goddammit!" shouted Bullit. He turned his attention back to Denali and his mandibled guard.

"Rook is with us again!" Tachion relayed, hobbling stiffly across the gallery. He reached Flashpoint's body with the help of covering fire from the boy's sister and mother, then dragged the upper half off the balcony, depositing it behind a tower where he might work on him less disturbed. He rolled him over. Even at first glance, he saw there wasn't much he could do.

Bullit carefully aimed at Denali's protector. He fired a blast from his laser rifle that struck the bodyguard in the head, splitting the insect-like helmet in two as it cracked back against the wall behind him. The target staggered, and pulled the damaged headgear free.

A incoming shuttle was struggling against the twisting wind, pulling along the wall of the massive borehole just adjacent to the stone terrace, near an offshoot of the crisscrossed walkways. Denali and Drake began to make their way towards it, keeping themselves behind additional soldiers that were filtering in.

"Do you see that?" Stansky shouted. *"They're trying to make a break for it!"*

"Might anyone have angle on that vessel's engines?!" Bullseye called.

Relic, enraged and distraught at her brother's grievous injury, dashed from her cover behind the metallic tower, and rolled to the parapet at the veranda's furthest edge. She aimed and fired a stream of protons at the shuttle's thruster ports, from her pair of Rageur M3s, an heirloom of her mother's Starlaw days. As another dropship was careening downward, an enormous starcruiser was heading up, its immense bulk unaffected by the massive rush of waning pressure.

It was the *Okubi.*

"Relic, I meant not you! Quickly, retreat back!"

The shuttle she fired upon began sputtering, losing antigrav power and drifting against the gusts, clapping loud against the wall and railing. Denali and the others lurched as the impact endangered the raised catwalk.

The human became furious. He raised his arms before him, glowing bracers on each wrist illuminating the upper gallery. He directed his will at the bulk of the downward approaching dropship, drawing it closer with his might, dragging the transport off course with the power and fury of his mind. The already askew vessel began descending toward the stone balcony, and lone Relic standing upon it.

Bullseye sprinted with all his seti might, legs dashing full speed toward the woman who had redeemed his life—the woman who unshackled him from a prison of his own making. The huge dropship was falling faster. He pulled a teleportation triangle from his chest, lofting it high in the air far behind him. But as fast as he was charging towards her, he clearly wasn't going to make it. She was a little too far, and the ship was falling too fast. He pulled the second magnetic triangle that was affixed to his chest, and diving towards her from meters away, cast it out expertly in front of him to land against Relic's back. The alien device clicked as it fastened to her securely, and blinked her away instantly to rejoin with its mate. Bullseye landed with a clattering roll to where she had been standing but a half-second ago, then turned just in time to see her reappear in safety. Relic spun in confusion to peer back at him, as he popped open his visor.

She would forever after always remember, for the remainder of her days, the look her lover gave her as the looming shadow expanded around him. The smile of unburdened calmness, the glint of heartfelt joy, the almost tearfully inexpressible gratitude within the shimmer of those amber eyes. He smiled at her—the corner of Bullseye's lip lifted with the pleasure of looking on her one last time.

"*Thank you...*" he mouthed silently.

He closed his eyes tight—then the dropship crushed him, and he was gone.

It tore through the stone terrace like a boulder tossed through a spider's web, vibrating the entire gallery with the force of its impact. For a moment, all was still—the firefight paused while both sides looked on aghast. As Bullseye himself had once expressed to Relic on the experience of witnessing the death of so many friends, 'a vision of horror the eye is loath to see, but from which it cannot be removed'.

Relic gasped in absolute devastation.

An explosion erupted from just below, the collapsing balcony and crumpled vessel tearing its way through an upward-bound frigate. The approaching supply ship impacted against the wall, then veered sharply backward as the gallery shook again. It plunged, burning—along with the dropship and their fallen leader—soon to be added to the expanding graveyard concealed somewhere far below, in the bottomless darkness of the crystal borehole.

Relic's mouth flew wide to cry out in desperate anguish, but her despair caught in her throat, unable to escape against a stuttering inhale of horrified sobbing, and gasping dizziness. Her eyes brimmed wet and red beneath the cover of her visor, the sorrow yanked forth rudely, along with all the possibilities of her future happiness. *Their* future happiness. Her frown of agonized sadness turned to gritted teeth, and a sneer of vengeance, as her seti blood rage began to boil, and her grip strained tighter against her weapon's pistol grips.

She turned her blazing proton pistols on anyone and everyone atop the catwalk, firing in wide sweeps, in unbridled, vengeful wrath. Rook joined in with his daughter, dropping to the gallery floor on a tension reel, and reemploying his retrieved autopistols on the remaining soldiers up above.

With the parapet having been torn away along with the stone terrace, James and Bullit now knelt for cover behind the steps of the remaining stairway. The pair still did their best to target Denali, but they were being blocked by the shields of the now unmasked seti bodyguard, the sentry protecting him with his body as they boarded the shuttle waiting to whisk them away.

"*Not so fast, motherfucker,*" Bullit swore under his breath. "*I'm gonna drop the asshole in front, you empty a clip in that fake-ass Dodger once he's clear.*"

"*Got it,*" Stansky answered.

Bullit retargeted his sights on the bare head of the other seti, the guard seemingly staring back at him through the magnification of the longscope—flashing orange eyes, amid fog-gray fur and darkened spotting. Bullit hesitated on the shot, his finger falling back from the eager trigger.

"*Do you have him?*" Stansky questioned.

Bullit stared onward and didn't answer.

"*Fuck! Never mind, I'll do it.*" James aimed his nine-millimeter and pulled the trigger.

Bullit lurched, knocking his teammate's arm, and shoving him backward as the gun went off. The round impacted the escaping gray seti's shoulder, clearly recoiling him in pain.

"*What the fuck are you doing!*" Stansky yelled, struggling to regain his crouched balance in the awkwardness of his heavy armor. "*They're getting away! Shoot him, now!*"

"*I can't!*"

"*What the hell's the matter with you? What are you switching sides now too?!*"

"No," Bullit explained. *"It's... I swear that seti..."* He placed his eye back along the scope and watched as they disappeared, the shuttle door closing behind them. *"I think that's... my brother, Wyvern."*

"What? You said he was dead."

"Yes, I'm aware of that!"

"So, then what are you talking about. It's impossible."

"Oh, is it?" Bullit asked sarcastically, turning his head to look down at him.

James didn't answer, knowing all they had been through proved maybe it wasn't.

As Denali's shuttle pulled away, darting behind a lyghtan troop transport, yet another squad of soldiers stormed into the upper gallery.

Belladonna had managed to scurry over to Tachion's side, watching helplessly as the android stemmed the bleeding of her precious boy— though in truth, the crimson flow was now slowing more due to waning volume, than the doctor's efforts. His hands were a blur, placing tools and instruments to hold the scraps together, the whole scene eerily unrealistic—the paradox of trying to equate a treasured loved one, with the meat and gristle that once contained them. He reached a blood-soaked hand for his scanner, and passed it once more over Flashpoint's body. His mechanized shoulders slouched in resignation. He reached into his kit, and pulled out a portable stasiscreen projector.

"You can't use that!" Belladonna sobbed behind him. *"It'll kill him!"*

"He is going to die, any moment now," Tachion told her. *"I'm sorry, but... there's nothing I can do to stop that now. At least not here, with this equipment. His only chance is if I suspend his tissues the very moment he passes away, and then... maybe... something could be done. If I get him back to a surgical suite, restart his heart, maybe revive him. If we can fill him with enough plasma, repair the damage. But even then, it's... only maybe."*

Rook's wife wept openly as the torrent of wind and gunfire raged around them. Just above Flashpoint's head, the holoprojection of his vital signs dipped lower, and finally flatlined; a single warning tone's cry struggling to be heard above the din. Tachion turned off the display, and began placing the corpse into protective stasis.

Then like the flicking of a switch, the wind whimpered, and fizzled out, the ongoing shootout seeming almost peaceful now in comparison.

James looked behind him up the shaft. *"I guess someone up there managed to bypass the dropped field section."*

"Probably for the best," Tachion said soberly, continuing his work. *"You and I could stay here all day, but the air was about to get pretty thin for the rest of them."*

Relic's weapons clicked. *"Shit, I'm out!"* she called. She ducked back behind the black tower, unable to fire back.

"I've been empty for a while!" Lady Opal admitted anxiously. *"And I don't even know if I've hit anyone."*

"I'm not far behind you," Bullit conceded, as another wave of soldiers crowded the catwalk from the back of the gallery. *"I'm afraid my energy clips aren't as endless as this stream of soldiers."* A bright flash from overhead shone off the walls of the chasm behind him, followed by a series of distant blasts. He leaned back and looked upward.

High above the fight, where the borehole opened out to starlight, a formation of fighter craft was strafing a battleship that was exiting. They circled back and forth, firing in unison, a row of explosions digging deep into the vessel's hull. From the bridge behind them, a multitude of warning motion signals drew Bullit and Stansky's attention. They turned to look quickly, squinting against an eruption of laser fire passing above them, raining down hard against Denali's sentries on the catwalk above the gallery. It was Coalition soldiers, dozens upon dozens of them, storming along every walkway, ancient balcony, and connecting ramp.

James used the opportunity to run and collect Lady Opal, wishing he was free of his bulky armor as he gathered her in his arms. He drew her from behind the supply pile, and escorted her quickly across the gallery. Bullit looked over to check on Relic, but saw her already safely sheltered behind one of the towers—and in the arms of her cloned father. He reluctantly turned away, instead joining Stansky, running with Lady Opal toward the doctor and Belladonna.

And, of course, Flashpoint.

The gruesome remains were now covered, and the ashi'mar put her slender arm around Belladonna.

A few meters away, as the onslaught continued above him, Stansky stared silently into the cavity where Bullseye had last stood. He could see the damage they had caused to a small percentage of the fleet, but there was no sign of his seti friend. He didn't really expect to see one. He lingered there a while to make his peace with it, and say goodbye.

"Doctor," Opal asked, *"what about... is Tàlto... I mean... is he..."* She looked back over to where his body lay—then unleashed a piercing scream.

The lyghtan bounty hunter was unsteadily approaching, with a shuffling and staggered gait, his gore painted face split rudely down the middle. As he moved closer, the flesh on one side sloughed off, and molted, sliding from his skull in a grotesque sheet atop his shoulder. Beneath the viscous oozing, a gossamer fabric was revealed—a mesh of silken gauze, embedded with microservos and blinking sensors. He reached up and slowly dragged the sheer hood from his face. The old flesh that was once Tàlto slumped wet upon the ground, the new flesh underneath a shocking visage they all recognized. He was paler and unshaven. Less sun-aged, and with longer hair. Not the same weary and worn patina, but still as recognizable as the one who just left.

It was Jim Dodger.

Again.

"You have no idea how good it feels to get that thing off," the human said, still with the graveled voice and lyghtan accent of the Capellan he had been portraying. He peeled free an adhesive disk from each side of his slime-coated throat. "Well then," he continued, the familiar voice of Dodger now returned, "I guess I probably have a little explaining that I should do."

The shoulder stock of Stansky's rifle struck the other human from behind, and he crumpled to the floor, slumping back into unconsciousness.

20.5

THE SHADOWY SILENCE OF THE borehole, a dim hush which had prevailed for eon upon eon, was now further shattered by the harsh, white floodlights and panning search beams of military shuttlecraft scouring the area. The shocking brilliance of one of these followed Tachion lifting Flashpoint's body, straining the eyes of the corpsman who moved beside him within its halo. A somber, slow parade, highlighted from above, that bore the boy's body onto a military evac shuttle. The doctor reluctantly turned him over, and stepped away.

Belladonna boarded as well, escorting her fallen son, and with Relic by her side—the young lady clearly torn between being there for them, or for her father. She paused atop the gangway, her gaze going instinctively to where she had seen Bullseye for the last time. Then she looked to her father before she stepped aboard, hoping for one last brush of eye contact before embarking.

She didn't get it.

Rook sat dejected, he and this new Dodger sitting handcuffed side by side, stripped of their armor, in the corner of the now crumbling gallery. He stared distantly down at the ancient stone, unwilling to lay his eyes upon her.

Upon them.

Belladonna looked back as well, but with an expression far less tender. Then the corpsman signaled for the ramp to close, and the seti's family was whisked away.

The flood lamp blinked out, returning Tachion to the shadows, and he stood there looking after them—then at his hands, crusted with blood.

"He'll get the very best of care, I can promise you that," a voice declared behind him. "And, of course, if all goes well, God willing... when your ship arrives, we'd be happy to transfer him back to the *Parliament One.*"

"Thank you, General Isaiah," the doctor said, turning around. "I admit, it's hard for me to turn him over to another physician. But, under the circumstances..."

The general held his hand out for the android's, with no concern or acknowledgment of the dried gore caked upon them. "Doctor Magna, it's a pleasure to meet you." Tachion gripped it and shook with him. "It's just unfortunate it couldn't be under less... chaotic circumstances."

"To be honest, I think I'm fine with meeting you when we did. We were getting in the weeds there a little bit. If you and your troops hadn't come along... I think maybe you and I met each other just in the nick of time."

"Don't sell yourself short, you were holding your own. This Lord Denali's fleet has scattered now, scampering back to Capellan and Oberonnian territory. But, best our analysts can surmise, you managed to destroy or disable maybe fifteen percent of it. Perhaps more. But even more importantly, you spoiled his plot, alerted us to the coming danger. Whatever he plans next, he's going to have to withdraw and regroup. In my book, you lot are heroes."

Tachion shook his head. "No, we're not. We were just lucky. Right place at the right time, if you can call this mess luck. We all *stumbled* our way here, each following our own agenda. The term hero implies a willingness to sacrifice for the sake of others. But more than one of us was here for just ourselves, myself included. No. *We* are not heroes, but we served in the company of one." He looked to the spot where the stone veranda once stood. The spot where Bullseye perished.

"I'm sorry for your loss. What I know of Bullseye and his history... he was a good man."

Tachion turned back to the general. "I have to ask, how did you..."

"We've been following you, covertly, on direct presidential order. Ever since one of you tried to hack the FPC databases."

"Ah, I see. I suppose we're probably in a bit of trouble for that."

General Isaiah laughed. "A little cyber trespassing is the *least* thing you're in trouble for. We've got violating weapons fire protocols while inside The Barrens treaty zone. Operating a starship without a transponder. The death of multiple peace officers and the destruction of property on Oberonn, one of our allies. Although admittedly, our status with them as allies is in serious question now. We've got arson of an industrial district of Gel Gonahaar. The assassination of a foreign dignitary on Ilshnar. Not to mention your personal troubles with the medical ethics board, among others." He looked at Rook and the other Dodger. "Cloning, huh? Looks like you've got two of them now."

"Yeah, well... I'm only responsible for one of them," Tachion told him. "And I have no intention of ever being responsible for another." He turned to look down at the general beside him. "Do you need us to turn ourselves in now, or... how will this work?"

"Ah, not so fast. I've been instructed to strike an arrangement with the lot of you."

"Instructed by who?"

The general's eyebrow went up. "There's only one soul with the power to instruct me on anything."

"I see. And what sort of arrangement are we talking about, then?"

Across the gallery, Lady Opal was interrogating the Lord Denali lookalike. "I can't believe the audacity! You made me worry about you. I mean him! What did you do with the real Tàlto? Did you kill him?!"

"What? No, of course not," the Dodger said. He was seated beside Rook on a fallen crystal column, Bullit close at hand, guarding the two of them. "Tàlto is a friend of mine. Or... well... a reluctant one, maybe. More of a business associate, I guess. We've helped each other out with a couple of things in the past, when our causes were in alignment. And he owed me a favor. Owes me a few of them, actually. And still does, for that matter. But that's a long story for another time."

"How were you able to fool the Capellan Royal Guard with that… getup?!" Opal demanded. "I can't believe they'd present you before the queen without scanning you first."

"I didn't go before the queen," the Dodger explained. "That was the real Tàlto. When Vasu assigned him to this bounty, he knew what was going on from his association with me. He gave *me* the gig, and I took his place. Thanks to the Guisemage."

Stansky interjected. "So, when he… I mean she… Selene… the Guisemage… When she said you were one of her best customers, that you had just been there days before… she wasn't talking about Tàlto. She meant *you*, underneath."

"Uhhh… yeah. I guess so. So, wait… the Guisemage is a woman?"

"*Oooh*. When I get my hands on Tàlto," the fuming ashi'mar threatened.

"Ah, don't blame him. Like I said, he owed me. I am sorry, princess, for pretending to be your ex. But I needed a face both you and them would trust. And besides, if you had gotten frisky, I promise I would have been a gentleman. After all, I didn't have enough time to cover up *every* inch of myself."

Stansky cocked his head at him, eyes wide in sudden anger, then charged a step toward the defenseless human. Bullit moved quick to stop him, but not as quick as a single frown from Opal.

She looked back to Dodger. "Just so you're aware, that is not the correct terminology. You will refer to me as ashi'mar, not princess."

"Ehh. Potāto potăto, right?"

"Wh-what? What does that mean?" she asked Stansky. "Did he just… swear at me?"

"No, Lady Opal," Tachion said from behind them, moving toward the group with the general at his side. "If I remember Jim Dodger, his being flippant like that only means that he's nervous."

"As he should be," Bullit added.

Dodger looked up at the Android. "I know that stoic, cast-iron face of yours doesn't usually register surprise, but I was hoping for *a little* reaction, Doc."

"I'm not surprised," Tachion said. "Or, I'm surprised that it's you, but I had become pretty sure you weren't the same Tàlto."

"How?" Bullit asked.

"A lot of little things. The way he spoke, the way he acted. Minor little discrepancies, like using the expression 'water under the bridge'. A lyghtan from a desert world would have no concept what that even meant."

"Yeah, wait a minute," James added, a realization dawning on him. "In the security footage of you guys running off with the *Bugeye*, you made a joke about getting kicked in the nuts. And *I* happen to know that the lyghtan don't have any."

"Oh my God," Bullit muttered. "Please nobody ask him *how* he knows that."

"Most Holy Ashi'Mar," the general bowed in greeting, interrupting them, "would you care to officially request asylum within the Federated Planetary Coalition?"

"My deepest gratitude, General, though I fear I must decline. I have no intention of sitting around in some stuffy embassy office, light-years away, while my planet, and my people, are embroiled in this coming war. I'd rather be on the front lines. I'd rather stay with Parliament."

"But... Madam Ashi'Mar, with all due respect... that is exactly what your position calls for. Exactly what your subjects expect. The days of rulers leading the charge with banners of royalty overhead are long past. It is the duty of those such as you, such as me... such as my president back on Earth, to keep ourselves sequestered. Protect the continuity of government, and the chain of command. Direct the course of those distant battles with a cooler heart, and strategic eye."

"He's right," James told her quietly. "You can't continue to fight with us. Your place is above, keeping an eye on the larger picture. And, keeping yourself safe. What would become of Capella if Vasu got ahold of you?"

She looked up at him, crestfallen, though clearly realizing they could be right. "I... don't know for certain what to do. The Path ahead for me is... unclear."

"The sign of a good leader," Bullit said to her. "Bullseye once told me, that one of the most assured paths to failure, is believing without question you know the path to success. Or... something like that. He would have said it better."

"Hmm. Even now his sage advice still rings true." She sighed and turned to the general. "I have no intention of living in your formal embassy. That is the first place Queen Vasu would look for me."

"You could... stay at my ski villa," James promised her. "I have a place in the mountains of T-1e. The Trappist-1 system. But I hardly use it, and..."

She was scowling at him. "Am I to be some kept woman, then? A scandal hidden in secret, roaming some bachelor apartment you keep on the side? Pacing my time away, while you spend your days with this Tatiana?"

"I... well, no. I mean... of course not. I just..."

"Relax," she said, smiling. "Don't worry, I'm fine with it. I just wanted to make sure we were clear on the arrangement."

Stansky looked embarrassed.

The general did as well. He cleared his throat. "I'll assign a detachment of SSS operatives for security." He turned to Stansky. "When you have a moment, my chief officers and I would love a debriefing as soon as possible. We'd like to know everything you can tell us about what's been going on."

"I'm sure that you would," James answered back. "We'd love a briefing as well, for that matter. Get all the details of what *you* know. But what are the odds of *that* happening?"

General Isaiah only stared at him.

"Yeah, that's what I thought."

Tachion took the general's shoulder, leading him a few steps aside. "Perhaps, just give them a minute. Or... a little longer."

The general looked back at the haggard, grieving party. "Right," he said. "Why don't we all just decompress for a little bit. Worry about swapping stories later."

"Good idea."

"Maybe you can find out from your new... *friend*... there, what he thinks this Denali will do next. He probably has a most... unique perspective... into his thought process."

"We'll see what we can do."

General Isaiah walked away, surveying the destruction and fallen bodies, and headed back across the gallery.

Tachion returned to the group.

Bullit looked at him questioningly. "So? What's up with us and him?"

Tachion glanced around at each of them. "Let's just say the government has us under their thumb, on more than a couple of issues. Issues they're willing to overlook, sweep some of our behavior under the rug. Even go so far as to restore my license and position, as long as we continue to... offer our assistance."

"Meaning?"

"We just continue doing what I'm sure we were going to do anyway. Look for Denali and his army of three-eyed, mentalist juicers. We just have to keep them in the loop, and *perhaps* take a few directions."

Rook muttered something then, breaking his catatonic silence.

Bullit leaned in. "What? What did you say?"

The handcuffed seti turned to peer at the Dodger seated next to him. "He told me you were dead," Rook muttered. "Lord Denali. He told me you were *all* dead. That he had killed every one of you."

"Every one of *who*?" Stansky asked, turning to look at the other human. "How friggin' many of you are there?"

The Dodger chuckled. "He *didn't* kill me, clearly. He didn't kill any of us. I guess he's not quite as smart as he looks. But then what does that say about me?" he laughed.

"Where'd Denali go!" Bullit suddenly barked at Rook, now seeming capable of answering. "And what's my brother doing with him?"

"Who?" Rook looked confused.

"My brother, Wyvern. The gray seti in the bug helmet."

"You mean Drake? I don't know. I don't know anything about him."

"You must know something!"

Rook ignored him and went silent again, falling back into his floor staring.

The Dodger watched him fade with curiosity, then turned back to the others. "His name is not Denali, by the way, as you obviously already know. It's Thirteen."

"Jesus. Fucking. Christ," Stansky said. "Thirteen? There's that many of you?"

"There was, once, and soon to be more. But as it worked out, Thirteen was the last of us." He lifted his head then and looked around. "Where the hell is Bullseye? He's missing my whole story."

No one spoke, but eyes fell tellingly to the ground in reverence.

"Ah, shit. I didn't realize. I guess I slept through that. And just when he had... him and Relic... Pssh. Even to the end, his life was a Shakespearian tragedy."

"So, thirteen of you," Bullit continued, egging him on impatiently. "And all of you... like *him*, I guess?"

"Oh, no," the Dodger laughed. "Thirteen is... one of a kind."

"What do you mean?" the doctor inquired.

"Well, let's just say they didn't get the recipe right straight away. Some were slightly deformed, others somewhat... mentally diminished."

James inspected the Dodger closely. "Well, I don't see any deformities, so I'm assuming that means you're of the *diminished* variety."

"Ah, how I've missed that Stansky wit," the Dodger said. "But no, I'm not actually even one of them."

"What does that mean?"

He reached up with shackled hands and tugged on the front of his inertia jumpsuit, pulling the collar downward as he craned his neck toward the ceiling. An angry looking numeral '1' was branded heavily upon his neck. "Not to sound callous or anything," he said, "I know Bullseye only just passed, God rest his soul. But technically... that does leave me the senior member now, so to speak. So, if someone can tell me where my flame pistols are at..." He looked around at the ring of disapproving faces. "Too soon?"

Opal stepped forward and slapped him hard across the face. "That is *incredibly* callous," she berated him.

Dodger wiggled his jaw around, making sure all the hinges still functioned. "Ouch. All right. Too soon, then, I guess."

Bullit approached and pulled down Dodger's collar to see the scar again. "So what, you're number one," he said. "The first reject, practice clone."

"No, I'm not 'one'. I'm *the* one. The one and only. The original recipe, Dodger classic."

"*Hmph.* How do we know that?" Stansky scoffed. "Or, for that matter, how would you?"

"I know it because I *choose* it. Because I feel it in my bones, and in my heart. And that's good enough for me. All these years, I've seen no proof to the contrary. I have no reason to believe I'm not the real Jim Dodger."

"Ha! I have no reason to believe I'm not the galaxy's greatest sharpshooter!" Bullit told him. "But that sure as shit don't make it so."

"It ain't so," Stansky said.

"So, wait a minute," Tachion asked him. "If Thirteen didn't kill any of you, then... where's the rest of them?"

"*I* took care of them. Every one of them. And it's kept me busy for *fifteen years.*" He looked up at lady Opal. "Tàlto might have helped a little with one or two of them, in exchange for times I helped him."

Her scowl at him deepened.

"I had no choice!" he asserted, defending himself against her disapproval. "Even if I could've somehow stomached the idea of their existence, they wouldn't have done the same. They would have come hunting for me in the end. Without question, it was me or them."

"Well," Tachion said, reaching for his medical kit, "it's a simple matter to find out, clone or not. I can determine it with a body scan..."

"No, don't!" Dodger shouted. "I don't wanna know! It doesn't matter to me!"

Tachion stopped and stared back at him.

"And if you ever find out, I don't wanna hear about it, understand? Either way, confirmed *or* denied. To me, I'm Jim Dodger, body *and* soul. I have no interest in hearing different. The last thing I want is to lose that truth, and end up all..." he cocked his head rapidly to the side, directing it towards Rook. "If you're not sure you can trust me, just look at what I've done for you. I've saved *all* your backsides at least once as Tàlto. Or if that's not enough, keep me like this for a little bit." He held up his restraints. "You'll see soon enough. I can be one of the boys again."

"Oh, don't worry about it," Stansky said. "You'll be that way for quite a while."

"Do you know where Denali is heading next?" Opal asked, in a voice reluctant to speak politely to him. "After all, you must plot along the same lines, like minds thinking alike."

"We've not thought alike for many years, and even then, only barely. That's why I spent my time hunting him for so long. He's been outfoxing me, without even knowing that I exist. Our minds have become quite distinct. It's a very long story, one that I can tell you later. But suffice it to say, I believe he represents only the worst parts of me. My basest urges. My most violent thoughts. I've spent years in that headspace, trying to think like him. But it's no good. We're too different now."

"Yeah, not that different, I think," Bullit said. "Your weapon of choice, after all, was a goddamn napalm pistol. I didn't say anything back then. I was young, and new to the team. But horribly burning people to death? I can still hear the friggin' screaming. I mean... just shoot them and be done with it."

"Ugh," Opal groaned. "Originators save me. Is that true?"

Dodger shrugged at her, guiltily.

Her permanent dislike of him was now visibly cemented.

Tachion knelt close to their recently recovered friend. "Rook?" he asked softly. "Do you have any idea where Denali was going?"

The seti looked up absently, and focused on him with tired eyes, but didn't answer.

"Alright then," the doctor said. "Maybe it's best we settle for a bit anyway. Figure out what to do with... whoever this is." He nodded toward Dodger. "Plus give me a chance to get our friend here some psychiatric care. Maybe we can get more out of him, once he's had a chance to..."

"We don't need to wait for that," Bullit protested. "We *have* a next stop we could make right away. You said the serum they use for ensensement is based on something khailian. So, we just pay a little visit to Erie VII, and blow away any remaining supply of the chemical. Before they can mix up another batch of it."

"Sounds like an idea to me." Stansky heartily agreed. "Taking away the magic tricks of Denali's special soldiers, that would be a step in the right direction."

"A big step."

Tachion was shaking his head through the whole conversation. "We can go talk to them at some point, definitely. But we can't just barrel in there, destroying all the serum. We don't know enough about it yet. There might be some positive benefit to it."

"What positive benefit?!" Bullit asked. "You said it was bad for the brain all around. That it would make more psycho Denalis."

"Yes, I did. But still..."

"Doesn't sound like a reasonable risk in my opinion," Dodger said.

"I agree with the clone," Stansky chimed. "Let's just go nuke it."

"Damn it," Tachion swore. "Look... James is dying."

"*What?*" Opal asked in shock, reaching up and turning the human's gaze to meet her own.

"What are you talking about?" Bullit pressed.

"Whoa, Doc," Stansky cried, pulling his face away from Opal's stare, "what about that doctor-patient privacy thing you're supposed to swear to?"

"James is dying," the android continued. "He has a degenerative brain disease, one that will kill him within the decade. Cripple him long before that. Thanks to his propensity for knocking himself in the head, I've had cause to do several brain scans this week, both before, and after, he *stupidly* tried to use the bracelet device. His cerebral damage... I'm not sure how... has been slightly reversed. It's like nothing I've ever seen. Or, can explain."

"Really?" Stansky asked hopefully, looking down at his hands. Now that he thought about it, the tremors *had* decreased in frequency. In fact, they had never returned after he had run out of medication.

"The lesions have shrunken back, markedly," the doctor told him. "So not just for your sake, but for millions of others it could be helpful for, we can't just destroy it all. We'll have to figure out something more..."

"Diplomatic?" Opal finished. "Maybe *I* can be helpful there, in some regard."

"Alright then," Bullit conceded. "We'll regroup for a bit. Take care of our wounded, and... grieve our dead. But, in the end, I think we *all* know what Bullseye would want us to do."

"Delete his search history?" someone joked in a quiet whisper, no sign joy in their voice. It was Rook.

Tachion felt joy though, knowing the dark humor meant his old friend was still somewhere in there.

"And, find Denali," Rook finished seriously, his eyes never leaving the floor.

"I agree with him," Dodger offered. "And I want in with you guys, if you'll have me. At least once we can agree to be more civil to each other." He held up his cuffed hands. "After all, hunting Denali... that's what I spent the last decade and a half doing. I have no intention of giving up on it now. Plus, as psychotic as Thirteen is, he's always been dead right about one thing."

"Oh yeah? What's that?" Tachion asked him.

"There can be only one."

POSTLUDE

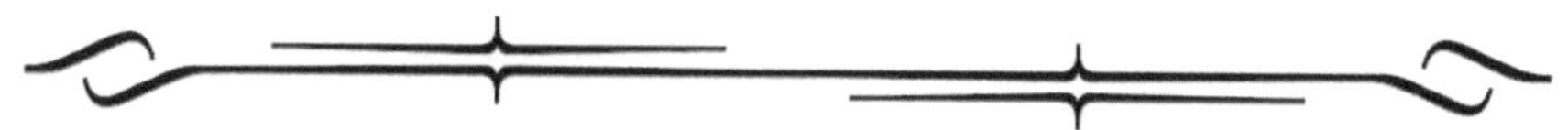

Epilogue 1

THE BALLAD OF NUMBER ELEVEN

THE DODGER CLONE KNOWN AS Eleven liked his name very much. It rolled off the tongue with lots of soft vowel sounds. Even when mean people said it.

Even when angry people said it.

Even when someone yelled his name at him—which Eleven thought was an awful lot of the time—it did not have any sharp T sounds, or hard clicking Ks, so it did not scare him so very much.

Eleven was very particular about sounds.

He knew which sounds he liked very much, and which made him most scared. He liked the deep, vibrating songs of the gigantic fish swimming outside. Some of them, he thought, might be bigger than an astrobus. He'd never seen an astrobus. Not for real.

But he very much did *not* like the loud, sharp tap-tap-tapping from the fancy machines in the big white sensor room. They *made* him listen to that, the guards, when getting his weekly thinking tests.

And he did not like hard, sharp sounds being yelled at him. K sounds he hated, but even more so T sounds. T sounds made him wince when they were yelled loud right near his ears, and sometimes T sounds that were very close also had spit with them that got his face wet.

He also very much did not like wet spit on his face.

He was very, very particular about that.

He often thought how lucky he was to be born in the right order— although Five always corrected him, saying he was not born, he was made.

Of all of his brothers, Eleven knew he himself had nearly the best name. The second-best name, in fact—which is almost the same as the best.

If he were born just one Dodger before or after, he would be called Ten or Twelve, two of the worst names you could have. Eleven disliked those names so much, he would have to whisper them when he tried to say them.

The only other name near as bad was Two, but Two was deaf, and Two was dead, so Eleven felt pretty lucky there was never a reason to ever say that name.

Four and Five were not very bad names. F sounds were usually not so loud, and didn't scare much. But Four and Five were both mean, so he did not say their names often anyway. They didn't like that he called the other Dodgers his "brothers", and also corrected him on this.

They were not born, they were made.

And they were not brothers, they were the same person.

This hurt Eleven's head to think about, so he still called them brothers—even though it sometimes meant being yelled at, with sharp, loud sounds. And sometimes, even getting his face wet with spit.

The only name better than his, was One. It was the only other name that started with a vowel. Well, other than Eight of course—but that ended with a T, and that made it much, much worse. 'One' was even softer on the tongue than the name Eleven, and it was shorter too, and easier for Eleven to say without stuttering. He only stuttered sometimes, not as bad as Nine did. But Nine was dead now also—Two stabbed him with a plastic fork, so maybe that made Eleven the worst stutterer now.

He didn't like that.

He sometimes wished that *he* had the name One, but was not too very mad about it, because Dodger One was nice to him. He was the only brother that was nice to him all of the time, so it was okay that he got the best name, and Eleven was mostly happy with having only the second best.

One was the only brother who protected Eleven against the other Dodgers, and sometimes even from the guards. Four and Five liked to team up, and tease Eleven until he got real scared. They would yell at him loud, or squish crunchy drinking cans against his face, until his head hurt, and his body shook, and sometimes he would go to the bathroom on himself. But One would see it, and make it stop.

It was extra good that One was nice, because he was the leader of all the Dodgers. He was here first, and everybody mostly did whatever One said to do.

Mostly.

When Thirteen came, he didn't like to do what One said. Thirteen wanted to be the new leader, but he was mean and nobody liked him. Even Four and Five, who were also mean. All the Dodger brothers still wanted One to be the leader.

One would also tell Eleven stories, which he liked very much. Not regular, out-loud stories, like the doctors would sometimes tell during the testing, when they wanted to ask questions afterwards. These were picture stories, that Eleven saw at night when he was sleeping.

Seven once tried to explain that these were not picture stories, and they were not told by One. These were dreams of memories, memories they all had. Memories from the first Dodger. The real Dodger. Eleven didn't understand what Seven meant by that. One *was* the first Dodger—that's why his name was One. And he was very real, because Eleven could touch him. Sometimes Eleven would see things that he couldn't touch, mostly when there were too many bad, loud sounds. He would get scared, and his head would start to hurt, and he knew that those things were not real because he could not touch them.

One had taught him that.

Also, Eleven knew the difference between stories and memories. He had lots of memories. He could remember that for lunch yesterday he had eel eggs and tamis loaf, which was special, because that was mostly for weekend breakfast only.

He could remember that last week, the Doctors tested if he could move things without touching them, which Eleven thought was very silly. But they got awfully angry when he couldn't, and they punished him with the pain chair.

But he could also remember things from a lot longer ago, like the time that Mr. Denali came in their rooms very angry, and choked number Two. Most of his brothers were scared when that happened, but Eleven remembered that he wasn't scared at all. There wasn't any noise. Mr. Denali squeezed Two's throat very, very hard, for very long, and Two punched and hit at Mr. Denali's arms. Mr. Denali's face was very red and shaky, and then Two's face got very red and shaky also, and then stopped. But there wasn't any bad noise. There wasn't any noise at all, except for Mr. Denali's hard breathing, and that sound didn't bother Eleven.

So he knew the picture stories he saw at nighttime were not memories. They didn't feel like they happened to him, like real memories would. The Dodger in the picture stories acted like only Dodger One did, that's how he knew the stories must come from him. None of the other brothers were as clever, or as tough, as the Dodger in the picture stories, except for One. Well, Thirteen was as clever and tough, but he was much too mean. The

Dodger in the picture stories wasn't mean at all. Also, Eleven had seen the picture stories long before Thirteen was born.

Or made.

There were lots of kinds of picture stories. Sometimes they were happy stories, about One when he was a child, and his parents, and his home, and his life when he was little. Sometimes they were sad, like when One's friend Phineas died. Eleven particularly liked the picture stories about Phineas. His name was long, and hard to say without a stutter, but it did not have any hard Ks or Ts, so that was still okay.

But mostly they were adventure stories. Lots of exciting adventures, with One's friends that wore armor. And One was very important, and people listened to what he said. And nobody teased, or yelled, or ever tried to scare him.

Eleven wished he could be like One in the stories.

One time he snuck a knife from the canteen, and took the stitches out of one of the numbers in the little '11' emblem on the chest of his uniform, and from the big '11' sewn on the back. The guards did not like it at all, and there was a lot of yelling, and Mr. Denali was there that day, and Eleven wondered if maybe he would be squeezed hard like Two was.

But he wasn't.

Instead, he was put in the bright, white room with the loud tapping machine, for a very long time. A very, very long time, and Eleven didn't like that at all. So even though he still sometimes wished he could be like number One, he did not change his uniform patches anymore.

One day there was a lot of noise and running around in the building.

Eleven didn't like that, it made him nervous. Everybody was being too fast, and too noisy. There were red flashing lights, and a loud horn noise from the hallway. He went to the common room, and stood in his safe corner behind the long couch, and crouched down there so people couldn't see him so well, and covered his ears with his hands.

He watched and waited for the noise and running to stop, but it got worse. Lots of guards were racing down the hall. They were putting on helmets, and carrying guns. Usually they didn't have their helmets on, and when they needed to punish one of the Dodgers, they used sticks that shocked you, and made you fall down. They usually didn't carry guns around his brothers. But today there were lots of guns, and lots of helmets, and lots of running.

And lots of noise.

After a long time, one of the guards came and talked to Thirteen. The Seti guard with the gray fur and spots. Eleven heard him tell Thirteen that Parliament had come. They had come to take them away.

Eleven knew who Parliament was. They were One's friends from the nighttime picture stories, and he thought it might be pretty okay with him if they came.

Thirteen told all the Dodgers to follow him quickly. But nobody listened to him, and Twelve started rocking in his seat, and yelling no, no, no over and over, and Five picked up a dining chair and threw it at him, and almost hit him. It hurts to get hit with a dining chair. Five threw them at Eleven all the time.

Then Thirteen talked to One, and One told everybody to follow him instead, and everybody did.

Eleven was very nervous to be taken away. He had never seen outside of the building in real life for himself, not other than on a computer screen during his thinking tests, and of course, One's picture stories. But he hoped that outside would maybe be quieter, and less running. So he kept his hands on his ears, and followed the gray guard and all the other Dodgers out into the hallway.

It was a very long walk.

Eleven never walked so far.

They stopped once in a dark room to look at a statue of Dodger One. Then later, they turned backwards, when there was shooting down the hall in front of them.

Finally, they went into a very big room, the biggest room Eleven had ever been in, and it had lots of small spaceships in it. They went inside one, closed the door, and it was finally quiet. Eleven could not hear the loud horn or the shooting from inside the ship, which made him very happy, and he took his hands off his ears.

They flew under the water, and up into the sky. Eleven thought it was very pretty. One and Thirteen were up in the front, driving, and Eleven felt sad they missed how pretty it all was. But then he forgot when he saw the clouds, and just looked out the windows with his other brothers.

Later, Thirteen came, and went into the back area. While he was in there with the door closed, One came out also, looking for Eleven. One told all the others to sit in the chairs and wait, except Eleven. He asked Eleven to come to the cockpit at the front of the ship, where all the controls were.

Eleven was happy about that, and very proud to be picked.

He followed One to the front, and smiled a wide smile, and squinted his eyes at his other brothers, and looked down his nose at them.

He entered the cockpit, and One closed the door behind them. He told Eleven he had a very important job for him to do. So very important, Eleven would have to be in charge now. He would have to be the new number One.

"Is it... because I have the second-best name?" Eleven asked.

"Because what? What are you talking about?"

"I-Is it because my name is second best? Is that why I'm in charge now?"

"I don't even… You know what? Sure, whatever. Yes, that's exactly why. Because you have the best name."

"Second best."

"Yes. The *second* best."

"Okay then."

"You have to give me your uniform, and I'm gonna wear yours."

One made him dress quickly, and then sit in the captain's chair. Eleven felt very important, and all the buttons were very pretty. One said his job was to touch nothing, and look out the front window. Eleven should look very hard, and try to see land, and if Thirteen comes in, just keep looking, and don't talk to him.

That part would be easy.

Eleven didn't want to talk to Thirteen.

Eleven tried hard after One left, he wanted very much to make him proud, and he looked far out the window. But there was only water, and no land. Eleven looked harder, and harder, until he started to get bored.

Then he heard Thirteen come back, and he smiled to himself, knowing he didn't have to talk to him. Knowing that One had told him not to.

Thirteen said nothing either, but walked up quiet behind the chair. He put his hand on Eleven's forehead and pulled on it. He pulled far. Something cold and stinging pinched him hard on Eleven's throat.

Eleven coughed, and it hurt him, and it was very, very hard to breathe. His coughing was also loud, and it made him wince. Thirteen spun the chair around, and pushed the stinging thing into Eleven's belly button.

It was a knife.

And it hurt.

Not like the white plastic knife that Two used to stab Nine with, but a big, metal knife—bigger even than the canteen uses.

Eleven's belly hurt badly, even more badly than his throat now. Almost as badly as the pain chair. Thirteen pulled him from the captain's seat, and was very mean and pushed him down.

Thirteen pushed him to the floor, and pulled the knife out, and that hurt badly also.

Now Eleven was bleeding.

He didn't like that. It was scary.

He heard Thirteen yelling at him inside his head. He did not even use his mouth to do it, and Eleven didn't understand. He didn't listen to what Thirteen was saying. He just wanted to be back in his safe place again. Back to the common room, and the special corner behind the couch. Thirteen gave a fat round bandage to Eleven, and told him to hold it on his neck.

He did.

It still hurt, though.

He still coughed, and it was hard to breathe.

Thirteen was talking an awful lot, but Eleven couldn't listen. It hurt so much that the pain felt loud. Thirteen used the same knife to break all wires in the control panel.

One was going to be mad at that.

But Eleven couldn't say anything.

Thirteen left then, and Eleven was alone, and he was glad. His stomach hurt, and he was dizzy, but he hoped that One would not be disappointed in him.

After a little while, One came back into the cockpit. He looked at Eleven for a long time, but didn't help him. He sat in the captain's seat, then got mad at the wrecked controls, just like Eleven knew he would. He could tell that One was angry from the bad words, and One tried to fix some wires, and flick some switches, and land the ship without crashing.

But Thirteen broke too much.

There was a loud bang, and a lot of shaking, and it made Eleven very scared. He shook too, like he did sometimes, and went to the bathroom on himself a bit. When he stopped and could look around again, he could see the front window had a big crack in it. There was some water outside the glass, and a little bit of it was dripping in.

Eleven could hear his brothers yelling in the room behind them, and then it was quiet.

One said bad words again.

He said an awful lot of them.

He said it wasn't good that Eleven's brothers were swimming away. Swimming far ahead of One, toward the raft city out the window.

Eleven wondered if One was going to make *him* go swimming. His belly ached, and he was getting dizzier. He was gasping hard, and he felt like maybe he might get sick.

One stood up quickly from the chair, then bent over low to talk softly to him. "I'm sorry, Eleven," One whispered. "You weren't supposed to die down here all alone. And what he did to you. That shouldn't have... well... I guess that was meant for me. But I never would have wanted you to suffer like this. You should have all gone down together, quick and quiet. But Thirteen, and the rest of them... well, he won't get away with it. I'll chase him down. I'll find all of them. Don't you worry about it."

But Eleven *was* worried.

He didn't want to die at all.

"You know, this *is* the way it has to be. I don't know if you feel that, or maybe you don't. That nagging, gnawing itch that the rest of us all have. That thing that reminds us always… there's only supposed to be one of us. I'm so very sorry, Eleven, but it's not gonna be you."

One stood up and left the cockpit then, leaving Eleven on the floor in the corner.

The light in the ship grew darker, and Eleven watched the water move up the glass. He was glad when it was so high that he could not see the sky anymore. Now it was like the common room, and his safe space behind the sofa.

But he did not like the sharp cracking noises that were coming from the dripping window. They got louder, and got faster, and the water dripped so much it made his feet wet. The sounds made him squint and shiver, with sharp, hard crunching, and loud, high squeaks. Then the whole ship got very noisy, like when Four would hold Eleven down and crush loud cans against his forehead, until the window burst, and the walls squished in, and the water hit him hard—like Five throwing a dining chair.

The last sounds Eleven listened to were the loudest and scariest he ever heard.

Epilogue 2

BLACK QUEEN'S GAMBIT

AN OIL LAMP WAS BURNING LOW, choking and sputtering as it flickered and fussed, belching tiny, blackened plumes that spat its coils against the wall, darkening the sandy limestone with its sooty, black, greasy tendrils. Sacred Queen Vasu of Capella, the promised Empress of the new regime, sat alone in her modest chambers, considering the viability of that alleged promise, her burning eyes lost deep in thought in the wavering lamplight of the faltering flame. Within the hour she was scheduled to broadcast her weekly sermon, extolling to her people the power and might of their new redeemer—the Shining Light upon their Path to glory—reporting that the day of Unification had finally come.

The crusade was underway.

But it had been over six days since Vasu had heard from Lord Denali, or heard any word of him, and news had already reached her ears, and was filtering out amongst her people, of the Prophesied One's failure at the Coalition border of the barren zone. A vocal minority she had effectively silenced had been opposed to such an invasion, and would surely use this misstep to rally rebellion, and become vocal again. Newer voices of dissidence had been blooming as well, the loudest being an upstart agitator from the North, calling himself some nonsense—the Phantom of Nol Qhan. Queen Vasu, however, had little concern for all their caterwauling. She had firm control over her field marshals, and they over their expansive armies, and Denali had been a fine example on just exactly how to flex that might. Her worry was more now on the best way to position *herself.* She had grown a lust for her *own* glory, a lust that demanded satisfaction.

She stood and crossed the carved-out bedchamber, stepping out through the open archway to the intimate balcony that hung outside, ornately chiseled into the stalagnate pillar. The queen looked down on the Holy Temple, the old quarter, and the metropolis beyond. The distant bustle of the planet's capital, where the more modern architecture of the downtown district climbed the cavern walls of Capella City, had gone very suddenly, eerily quiet. Far more so than a usual sermon day. The queen could feel in the vast silence the palpable unrest of her peasantry, the apprehensive uncertainty of the civilians, echoing a similar sentiment that was spreading planetwide. She could sense them huddled in their homes and businesses, anxiously surrounding their holovisions, awaiting word from their righteous leader, and wondering just where she would lead them next. Shall they further the path to all-out war, or would she turn them back before it was too late?

Vasu cared very little for what the people worried about. She had worries of her own to consider. The queen had come to realize that this new path she followed, the path the human had set her on, was her proper destiny all along. Empress she was promised, Empress she deserved, and Empress she would surely have—Lord Denali by her side, or no. But how would she move forward if Denali perished in the battle of Trojan? Without his power, or influence, how would she obtain what was rightfully hers? Her mind danced as fitfully as the wavering oil lamp in the inner room.

She realized then, laughing to herself, she had plenty of power and influence as well, did she not? Power from the bracelet, whose gifts of healing made her nigh invulnerable. Whose gifts of telekinesis made her fearsome to stand before. Power from her station, that gave her dictatorship over billions. Power from The Originators, as the chosen mouthpiece of their holy word.

Yes, it was true that she had already imparted to her temple, and to her subjects, the doctrine of Lord Denali—that *he* was the Divine Guide for whom they had long-awaited. A doctrine she no longer believed in. But Vasu could still exploit that, leverage his name to her advantage. She could simply concoct whatever sacred message served her purpose, and deliver it as Word on high from Lord Denali, or the Originators themselves! Uphold her holy edicts with the temple soldiers sworn to serve her, and bend the people to her will; if not through their faith, then through their fear of showing it flagging. The Heretic Courts would be empowered again, as they were in the days of old! She would praise Lord Denali and the Originators for decreeing it!

And who's to say they did not?

Oberonn, however, might make more of a challenge. But then again, perhaps not. With General Nylis thankfully gone, his ambitious underling would now take charge. And while Queen Vasu did not have the gift of persuasion that Lord Denali did, she did have her ways. The ways of privilege, the ways of politics—the ways of a woman, if it served her needs. And she had learned from Denali, the promise of power was a *mighty* thing. Dangle a title in front of the new general—Imperial Vizier of the Holy Infantry—dangle power, and dangle pride, and she would bring them to her heel. The more she considered it, the more she realized—she didn't need Denali.

The recognition of this was like a weight lifted off her shoulders. She had suspected for some time that she *alone* should be the true ruler. At one point or another, Lord Denali would only be in her way. She would have certainly needed to betray him, sooner or later—although he likely would have sensed it, making it difficult to achieve. But he was gone now—she could feel it. The galaxy was hers, and she would take it! She would go on to her weekly address, and begin laying the foundations for a new order— *her* new order, no longer his—and she would map out the path to ascend her throne above all the Universe!

The queen returned to her room, reinvigorated, eyeing the sleeping place she had shared with him, in disgust at her own prior weakness.

Her abbess chamberlain entered in, bent low in reverence, as was the custom, but visibly frightened, and with a noticeable limp.

"What is it, Prioress?" Vasu demanded. "I asked not to be disturbed before my broadcast."

"F-Forgive me, Most H-Holy Mother," the abbess spoke through gasping sobs. "I come bearing news t-that..." Her voice caught, and she began again. "I am sorry, Divine Eminence. It's just that h-he... he... the w-worshipers were at the temple, and h-he e-entered in such a *r-rage...*"

"What is it you're babbling about? What are you trying to say?"

The woman took a moment to catch her breath. "My apologies, Most V-Venerable Majesty, but The Foretold One, H-High Lord Denali, he is in your antechamber. He is h-here to see you."

Epilogue 3

IN MEMORIAM

HER BREATH SWEPT WARM AGAINST his neck, her contours pressed to his, bodies entwined.

The two were one.

Yet as she pulled away to look down at him, her welcome sultriness quickly evaporated. A sudden chill washed over his body, the cooling downdraft marking her absence—like the balm of a summer sun suddenly vanished beyond an errant rain cloud.

He looked up at her with a pouted mouth, the high arch across his eyebrows exaggerating a sullen expression.

She frowned at him. "I don't understand," Relic said. "You have the thing just sitting there, doing nothing. We know it could give you a possible advantage, so why not use it?"

It was their last night before leaving the *Parliament One* for The Rock casino.

"For one, we know not yet how it even operates," Bullseye reminded her, regretting he'd ever mentioned it, "and the doctor feels an abundance of caution mayhap be warranted, in light of th..."

"The doctor who betrayed you?" she interrupted. "Who ran off with my disloyal cousin, and turncoat brother?"

"'Betrayal' is perchance drastic. And 'disloyal'... well, that rings more true. Your brother, however, simply follows his passions. Same as you."

"So you still trust them, then?" Relic asked.

"The catalyst of our contention is a simple disagreement over course of action. There is no malice beyond that fact. Surely no intention to see us injured. I would wager my very life upon it."

"That may be exactly what you *are* doing," the impassioned young seti pointed out. "After all, James made use of it when he needed it, and he seems none the worse for wear. In fact, it saved his life! Why not use anything and everything available to protect your own?"

"Alas, 'tis not so simple," Bullseye told her. "And, in fact, it may fail to even function further."

"There's a human expression," Relic countered, snuggling back into her place tight beside him. "Start where you are. *Use* what you *have*. Do what you can. What could be more simple than that."

He recognized the quote, and this was not the situation it was referring to. It was meant as a motivational slogan, to take on challenges, waylay procrastination. But Bullseye saw no benefit in challenging her interpretation. Instead, he pulled her in close and felt the chill of her absence fading. The sun had emerged again. "I pledge to you," he said earnestly, "I shall give your argument consideration."

And he did.

Certainly the irony had not been lost on him that they were now headed for a dance with danger—and very likely, death—just when he had found the flavor of life truly appealing. He had a renewed palate for being present, one he would not have discovered without her companionship. He was not ready yet to join the Fallen, so why *not* take extreme measures?

Why *not* use what he can?

As he lay at the base of the jumbled pileup, he thought back on that exchange with Relic. Oh, what wouldn't he surrender, for the warmth of her sunlight now.

Instead, all he could feel was—absolutely nothing. No wounds. No contusions. No racks of pain where there surely ought to be. Was he paralyzed? He didn't think so. Though he couldn't move much, that was certain.

A ringing in his head placed a damper on the sounds around him, the echo of the sudden silence seeming as deafening as the collisions before it.

He looked over at his right arm, lifting his head ever so slightly to crane his eyes to their utmost limit. They seemed the only parts of his body he was capable of freely moving. But it was enough.

His armor was gone, perhaps unsurprisingly—punished into misshapen shards from the brutal violence of repeated impacts. The weight pinning his body down was immense, utterly incalculable, the burning debris of a dozen starships laying atop his fragile form.

Yet he did not feel injured. Not hurt at all. Not in the slightest.

An occasional flash of distant sparking, and a steady inferno burning nearer, both diffused their wavering brilliance through a haze of dust and escaping gas plumes. But neither lit the confines as brightly as the recovered jewelry around his wrist—a translucent, frosted bracelet shining heartily with an amber fire.

Bullseye had relented to Relic's advice after all.

And kudos for doing so, he thought—though he wondered what to do next. He lay his head back down to consider it with a growing understanding of what had happened now.

He had felt the power surge through him the moment he braced for the dropship's impact, closing his eyes tight, and clenching involuntarily. The device responded to that wishful demand by increasing his density a hundredfold. Or at least more than enough so that the impact did no damage.

Bullseye had been forced through the stone veranda like a stake pounded into dusty soil, spinning end-over-end, as repeated explosions and impacts rocked his body. Then for a while, only quiet—the surprising silence of the long fall. The seemingly *endless* fall. Wind whistling in his ears, his body chasing debris toward the inevitable bottom, as other debris chased after him. And finally, the insane calamity of that tumultuous collision, impossible to describe—an utter chaos of endless battering. Every sense driven to overload, as the weight of the world fell upon him.

But yet, he was still uninjured.

Near naked, and trapped, and in danger of being burned soon, but uninjured, nonetheless.

For the moment, anyway.

The illumination around him wavered as the bracelet flickered in its intensity. Not the best of signs, Bullseye assumed. He had no knowledge of how long these effects, nor the serum that sustained them, would last.

He wondered then if he might reverse it. If he was capable of increasing his molecular density, could he not perhaps do the opposite? Could he spread his atoms apart? Become a haze? Become ethereal? He had heard the report from Lady Opal that Denali allegedly moved through walls. Something like this could surely explain it.

Although even if that were possible, if he were to attempt it, and succeed, he could not go upwards. The fact that he would phase through anything he touched would deny him from climbing higher. He could not hold on to anything to pull himself forward. Perhaps if he had more time, could practice with the ability—but now the light of the bracelet fluttered like a dying campfire in a rising breeze. He was out of time. Only one choice remained.

He must go down.

Bullseye had no idea if it would work. And even if it did, he had no idea what lay below him, beyond solid bedrock, and miles of compressed diamond. Rematerializing in the middle of that would be undesirable in the extreme. But he had no other option. The area around this borehole was seemingly riddled with tunnels and chambers. He simply had to hope that the ancient designers placed one beneath him—one preferably supplied with a breathable atmosphere. He laughed to himself at the sheer absurdity of the situation. Perhaps he was better off to stay here, give his friends a chance to find his body, rather than be buried for all time in the core of a planetoid he despised. But the overwhelming desire to return to Relic called out to him—finding out if she survived the battle would become the beacon that would guide his way.

He steeled himself, and made preparations for his imminent death, sharing silent goodbyes amongst his friends and colleagues—kissing the air, and blowing it to *her*. He sent prayers high above to those he believed in—and even to a few he didn't. He placed an image in his mind—*light as air, thin as mist*—then took a page from his friend Stansky, and crossed his fingers—then wished it so.

The rubble above crushed downward eagerly, filling the void as he slipped below.

~ END OF MODULE ~

-Author's Note-

Reader reviews allow independent authors to continue
sharing their stories.

If you enjoyed this book, and would like to
help support more HiTec sequels, please consider
leaving a review on Amazon, Goodreads, or
other platform of your choice.

Thank you.

-Credits-

The following characters were my personal interpretation of ones
originally created and played by, and/or inspired by:

Bullseye – Edward Rios
James Stansky – Orest Luciw
Rook – Russell Theall
Bullit – Michael Curreri
Jim Dodger – Brendan Joyce
Dr. Tachion Magna 816 – John Grundy (myself)

Along with
Selene Maraspese – Patricia McNeil-Federico
Tàlto Lastnâm – also Russell Theall

And introducing as
Chief Zvavi – Andrew Hayes

Additional Thanks To:

Beta Reading – Developmental Editing
Jennifer Rubin
Alicia Fitzpatrick
Jonathon Hall
Jefferson Grundy

Literary Consultant
Michelle Bolser

Gamma Reading
Raul Walker
Amy Bailey
Erik Macs

Original Cover Artwork by
Alex Avduevsky
www.artstation.com/avduevsky

Published by
Paper Jam Publishing
www.PaperJamBooks.com

Contact the Author at
www.JohnWGrundy.com

or Follow at
wwwAmazon.com/author/JohnWGrundy
www.Goodreads.com/JohnWGrundy
www.Facebook.com/JohnWGrundy

For updates on future HiTec sequels, subscribe at:
www.ToCastleKingside.com

-About the Author-

JOHN W. GRUNDY IS A MASSACHUSETTS native who grew up in a suburb just outside of Boston, and over five decades later, he still calls the Bay State his home. Now nestled in a tranquil community far from the city, he resides there with his devoted wife, with whom he's shared more than two decades of unwavering love and support. Within this serene environment he finds inspiration, channeling the peaceful surroundings to craft his imaginative tales.

During his late teens, his passion for storytelling was ignited when he and his friends created an original sci-fi role-playing game. This early endeavor kindled his fascination with the art of narrative, particularly in the realms of science fiction and fantasy. While his career initially led him to serve as a paramedic in the city of Boston, he eventually transitioned into the world of business, where he and his wife partnered in co-founding a thriving small enterprise.

Amidst the demands of his professional life, he never lost sight of his lifelong passion for worldbuilding. With the release of this debut novel, he eagerly embraces the opportunity to put his storytelling to the test. This captivating tale marks just the beginning of his literary journey, as he envisions a future filled with enchanting narratives that will seize readers' imaginations, delving into the depths of human experiences, and exploring the boundless possibilities of science fiction storytelling.

He greatly enjoys hearing feedback from readers, as well as answering questions or comments from fans, and tries answer every inquiry he receives. You can communicate with the author via the contact section of his webpage, www.JohnWGrundy.com.

<u>Castling Kingside:</u>

A special move in chess that protects the king and activates its closest rook. The king retreats two squares toward its nearest castle piece, then the rook guards the king by moving around it, occupying the space that the king passed over. This is the only play where two pieces may be moved in the same turn.

9 798988 099314